D1104914

Shenandoah: An Anthology

Shenandoah:
An Anthology

James Boatwright, Editor

Library of Congress Catalog Card Number: 85-060719
ISBN : 0-916366-33-2

For information address
PUSHCART PRESS,
P.O. Box 380,
Wainscott, NY 11975

First Printing: August, 1985

Shenandoah is published quarterly at
Washington and Lee University
by *Shenandoah,*
Box 722, Lexington, Virginia 24450.

Manufactured in The United States of America
by RAY FREIMAN & Company,
Stamford, Connecticut 06903

. . . From the First 35 Years

ACKNOWLEDGMENTS

Shenandoah is pleased to present this collection of essays, fiction, and verse published originally in the magazine and is grateful to the authors, publishers, literary agents, and executors who gave their permission to reprint these works. The requested specific acknowledgments include:

"The Garrison" by W. H. Auden from *W. H. Auden: Collected Poems,* edited by Edward Mendelson, reprinted by permission of Random House.

"Revival," "Monkhood," "Friendless," "Drunks," and "One Answer to a Question" by John Berryman, ©by Kate Donahue Berryman, reprinted by permission of Kate Donahue Berryman, Executrix for The Estate of John Berryman.

John Betjeman's tribute to W. H. Auden reprinted by permission of The Estate of Sir John Betjeman.

"To Wystan Auden on His Birthday" by Louise Bogan and Edmund Wilson reprinted by permission of Farrar, Straus and Giroux, Inc.

"Showdown" by Michael Brondoli from *Showdown and Other Stories,* ©1984 by Michael Brondoli, reprinted by permission of North Point Press.

"*King Lear:* Its Form and Psychosis" by Kenneth Burke reprinted by permission of the author.

"April" by Alfred Corn from *A Call in the Midst of the Crowd* (Viking, 1978) reprinted by permission of the author.

"ev erythingex Cept:" by E. E. Cummings, ©1958 by E. E. Cummings, from *Complete Poems 1913-1962* and "what time is it? it is by every star" by E. E. Cummings, ©1962 by *Shenandoah,* from *Complete Poems 1913-1962* reprinted by permission of Harcourt Brace Jovanovich.

"The Problem of Form" by J. V. Cunningham from *The Collected Essays of J. V. Cunningham,* 1977, and "Epigrams" by J. V. Cunningham from *The Collected Poems and Epigrams of J. V. Cunningham,* 1971, reprinted by permission of Ohio University Press/Swallow Press.

"The Fountain" by Donald Davie reprinted by permission of the author with acknowledgments to Routledge, Kegan Paul, and to Oxford University Press, New York.

"Divorce" by Richard Eberhart from *The Quarry,* 1964, reprinted by permission of the author with acknowledgments to Oxford University Press, New York, and to Chatto & Windus, London.

William Faulkner's review of *The Old Man and the Sea* from *Essays, Speeches and Public Letters* by William Faulkner, edited by James B. Meriwether, reprinted by permission of Random House.

"Read to the Animals" by Irving Feldman from *Teach Me, Dear Sister,* ©1980, 1981, 1982, 1983 by Irving Feldman, reprinted by permission of Viking Penguin, Inc.

"Asiatic Day-Flower" by Donald Finkel reprinted by permission of the author.

"Observations on Technique" by Ford Madox Ford reprinted by permission of Robie Macauley, Executive Editor, Houghton Mifflin Co.

"The Dragon's Teeth" by Caroline Gordon later appeared in *Old Red and Other Stories* as "One against Thebes." Reprinted by permission of Farrar, Straus and Giroux.

"Graffiti from the Gare Saint-Manqué" by Marilyn Hacker from *Assumptions,* Knopf, 1985, reprinted by permission of the author.

"David Hume" by Donald Hall, ©by Donald Hall, reprinted by permission of the author.

"A Pre-Raphaelite Notebook" by Geoffrey Hill from *Tenebrae* reprinted by permission of Andre Deutsch Limited, London.

"Letter to Shadow" by Daryl Hine from *Resident Alien,* 1975 by Daryl Hine, reprinted by permission of Atheneum Publishers.

"Instructions to a Medium to Be Transmitted to the Shade of W. B. Yeats, the Latter Having Responded in a Seance Held on 13 June 1954, Its Hundredth Birthday" by Daniel Hoffman from *Striking the Stones* (New York; Oxford University Press, 1968), ©1965, 1968 by Daniel Hoffman, reprinted by permission of the author.

''On the Way to Summer'' by John Hollander, ©1983 by John Hollander, reprinted by permission of the author.

''Cattails'' by Richard Hugo from *Making Certain It Goes On, The Collected Poems of Richard Hugo,* ©1984 by The Estate of Richard Hugo, reprinted by permission of W. W. Norton & Co., Inc.

''Mao[4] or Presumption'' by Hugh Kenner from *The Pound Era* reprinted by permission of University of California Press.

''Office for the Dead'' by Thomas Kinsella from *Nightwalker and Other Poems,* Dublin, 1967, reprinted by permission of the author.

''Siegfriedslage'' by Lincoln Kirstein from *Rhymes of a Pfc.,* 1981, Godine, Boston, reprinted by permission of the author.

''Ford Madox Ford,'' ''Our Afterlife,'' and ''A Tribute to W. H. Auden'' by Robert Lowell reprinted by permission of Farrar, Straus and Giroux, Inc.

''The Dean in Exile'' by Robie Macauley reprinted by permission of the author.

''Francis Bacon, The Inventor of Spectacles Is the Ringmaster'' by Cynthia Macdonald from *(W)holes,* ©1978 by Cynthia Macdonald, reprinted by permission of Alfred A. Knopf, Inc.

''Country Music,'' ''The Romance Language,'' ''Nike,'' and ''The Help'' by James Merrill, ©by James Merrill.

''Bonnard'' by Christopher Middleton from *Our Flowers and Nice Bones* (Fulcrum Press, London 1969) and from *111 Poems* (Carcanet Press, Manchester and New York, 1983), reprinted by permission of the author.

''Bones and Jewels'' by Paul Monette, ©1976 by Paul Monette, reprinted by permission of the Julian Bach Literary Agency, Inc.

''Logic and 'The Magic Flute' '' by Marianne Moore from *The Complete Poems of Marianne Moore,* ©1956 by Marianne Moore, ©renewed 1984 by Lawrence E. Brinn and Louise Crane, executors of The Estate of Marianne Moore, reprinted by permission of Viking Penguin, Inc.

''Jean: Some Fragments'' by Howard Moss, ©1979 by Howard Moss, reprinted by permission of the author. ''Short Stories'' by Howard Moss from *A Swim off the Rocks,* ©1976 by Howard Moss, reprinted by permission of Atheneum Publishers.

''The Distances They Keep'' and ''Two Views of a Philosopher'' by Howard Nemerov from *The Collected Poems of Howard Nemerov,* University of Chicago Press, 1977, reprinted by permission of the author.

''Back Country'' by Joyce Carol Oates, ©1984 by Joyce Carol Oates, reprinted by permission of the author.

''A Stroke of Good Fortune'' by Flannery O'Connor from *A Good Man Is Hard to Find,* ©1953 by Flannery O'Connor, ©1981 by Mrs. Regina O'Connor, reprinted by permission of Harcourt Brace Jovanovich, Inc.

''Chinese Finches'' by Katha Pollitt from *Antarctic Traveller,* ©1980 by Katha Pollitt, reprinted by permission of Alfred A. Knopf.

''A Wreath for the Gamekeeper'' by Katherine Anne Porter from *Collected Essays and Occasional Writings of Katherine Anne Porter,* ©1970 by Katherine Anne Porter, reprinted by permission of Delacorte Press/Seymour Lawrence and of Isabel Bayley, Literary Trustee for Katherine Anne Porter.

''Notes for an Unpublished Canto'' by Ezra Pound, ©1971 by Ezra Pound, reprinted by permission of New Directions Publishing Corp.

''The Names and Faces of Heroes'' by Reynolds Price, ©1963 by Reynolds Price, reprinted by permission of Atheneum Publishers, Inc.

''Let There Be Translators!'' by Grace Schulman from *Hemispheres* (Sheep Meadow Press, 1984) reprinted by permission of the author.

''Woden's Day'' by Jean Stafford reprinted by permission of Farrar, Straus and Giroux.

''How Now, O, Brightener,'' by Wallace Stevens from *Opus Posthumous* edited by Samuel French Morse and ''Note on Moonlight'' by Wallace Stevens from *The Collected Poems of Wallace Stevens* reprinted by permission of Alfred A. Knopf.

''Variable Service'' by Dabney Stuart from *The Diving Bell,* ©1966 by Dabney Stuart, reprinted by permission of the author.

(Acknowledgments cont'd. on pg. 512)

CONTENTS

PREFACE

A year and a half ago, anticipating *Shenandoah's* thirty-fifth anniversary and wondering how to observe it, I was pleased when Bill Henderson of Pushcart Press suggested an anniversary anthology. Pushcart Press will be publishing this issue as a hardbound volume, to be distributed by W. W. Norton.

What I've had to leave out saddens me: so many other valuable stories, poems, essays, plays, interviews, reviews. Lord, the sweat that went into choosing everything over the years, and now, having to choose from the chosen. It's made me feel like Solomon and the baby. An added complication: making selections from the earlier volumes of the magazine, the first twelve years, before I became editor (for a partial history of those early years, see Andrew Kappel's essay "Ezra Pound, Thomas Carter, and the Making of an American Literary Magazine," in *Shenandoah,* XXXI, 3.) There was no way for me to be really just to the taste and judgment of the earlier editors, but I've done the best I could.

Early on, I decided to be arbitrary. The anthology wouldn't be "representative" or "balanced": it would be a purely personal selection of the best work *Shenandoah* has published over the years (actually, Richard Howard's hand hovers over the enterprise as well: I asked him to read through all the poems and make recommendations, which he did, with his usual generosity and skill. He recommended more than space would allow, so I must take responsibility for what is *not* here). I've also made certain arbitrary exclusions: no reviews (with one exception); no translations (with one exception); and no interviews.

The order is alphabetical, not chronological, although the date of publication is noted in brackets after each selection (exception to the alphabetical order: when a particular writer is being celebrated, the tributes are grouped after the writer's work).

My thanks to all the people who have worked with me over the years, particularly to Helen Schuyler, Dabney Stuart, Eleanor Ross Taylor, to Richard Howard, James Dickey, Stephen Goodwin, Reynolds Price, Peter Taylor, Robert Wilson, to all the student helpers—and to Sue Stewart, whose labor has been prodigious.

June 1985 James Boatwright

Alice Adams

ALASKA

Although Mrs. Lawson does not drink any more, not a drop since New Year's Day, 1961, in Juneau, Alaska, she sometimes feels a confusion in her mind about which husband she will meet, at the end of the day. She has been married five times, and she has lived, it seems to her, almost everywhere. Now she is a cleaning lady, in San Francisco, although some might say that she is too old for that kind of work. Her hair, for so many years dyed red, is now streaky gray, and her eyes are a paler blue than they once were. Her skin is a dark bronze color, but she thinks of herself as Negro—Black, these days. From New Orleans, originally.

If someone came up and asked her, Who are you married to now, Lucille Lawson? of course she would answer, Charles, and we live in the Western Addition in San Francisco, two busses to get there from here.

But, not asked, she feels the presences of those other husbands—nameless, shadowy, lurking near the edges of her mind. And menacing, most of them, especially the one who tromped her in Juneau, that New Year's Day. He was the worst, by far, but none of them was worth a whole lot, come to think of it. And she was always working at one place or another, and always tired, at the end of her days, and then there were those husbands to come home to, and more work to do for them. Some husbands come honking for you in their cars, she remembers, but usually you have to travel a long way, busses and street cars, to get to where they are, to where you and them live.

These days Mrs. Lawson just cleans for Miss Goldstein, a rich white lady older than Mrs. Lawson is, who lives alone in a big house on Divisadero Street, near Union. She has lots of visitors, some coming to stay, all funny looking folk. Many foreign, but not fancy. Miss Goldstein still travels a lot herself, to peculiar places like China and Cuba and Africa.

What Mrs. Lawson is best at is polishing silver, and that is what she mostly does, the tea service, coffee service, and all the flatware, although more than once Miss Goldstein has sighed and said that maybe it should all be put away, or melted down to help the poor people in some of the places she visits; all that silver around looks boastful, Miss Goldstein thinks. But it is something for Mrs. Lawson to do every day (Miss Goldstein does not come right out and say this; they both just know).

Along with the silver polishing she dusts, and sometimes she irons a little, some silk or linen shirts; Miss Goldstein does not get dressed up a lot, usually favoring sweaters and old pants. She gets the most dressed up when she is going off to march somewhere, which she does fairly often. Then she gets all gussied up in a black suit and her real pearls, and she has these posters to carry, NO NUKES IS GOOD NUKES, GRAY PANTHERS FOR PEACE. She would be a sight to behold, Mrs. Lawson thinks: she can hardly imagine Miss Goldstein with all the kinds of folks that are usually in those lines, the beards and raggedy blue jeans, the dirty old sweat shirts, big women wearing no bras. Thin, white-haired Miss Goldstein in her pearls.

To help with the heavy housework, the kitchen floor and the stove, bathtubs and all like that, Miss Goldstein has hired a young white girl, Gloria. At first Mrs. Lawson was mistrustful that a girl like that could clean anything, a blonde-haired small little girl with these doll blue eyes in some kind of a white pants work outfit, but Gloria moves through that big house like a little bolt of white lightning, and she leaves everything behind her *clean.* Even with her eyesight not as good as it was Mrs. Lawson can see how clean the kitchen floor and the stove are, and the bathtubs. And she has *looked.*

Gloria comes at eight every morning, and she does all that in just two hours. Mrs. Lawson usually gets in sometime after nine, depending on how the busses run. And so there is some time when they are both working along, Mrs. Lawson at the sink with the silver, probably, or dusting off Miss Goldstein's bureau, dusting her books—and Gloria down on her knees on the bathroom floor (Gloria is right; the only way to clean a floor is on your knees, although not too many folks seem to know that, these days). Of course they don't talk much, both working, but Gloria has about twenty minutes before her next job, in that same neighborhood.

Sometimes, then, Mrs. Lawson will take a break from her polishing, dusting, and heat up some coffee for the both of them, and they will talk a little. Gloria has a lot of worries, a lot on her mind, Mrs. Lawson can tell, although Gloria never actually says, beyond everyone's usual troubles, money and rent and groceries, and in Gloria's case car repairs, an old VW.

The two women are not friends, really, but all things considered they get along okay. Some days they don't either of them feel like talking, and they both just skim over sections of the newspaper, making comments on this and that, in the news. Other times they talk a little.

Gloria likes to hear about New Orleans, in the old days, when Mrs. Lawson's father had a drugstore and did a lot of doctoring there, and how later they all moved to Texas, and the Klan came after them, and they hid and moved again, to another town. And Gloria tells Mrs. Lawson how her sister is ashamed that she cleans houses for a living. The sister, Sharon, lives up in Alaska, but not in Juneau, where Mrs. Lawson lived. Gloria's sister lives in Fairbanks, where her husband is in forestry school.

However, despite her and Gloria getting along okay, in the late afternoons Mrs. Lawson begins to worry that Gloria will find something wrong there, when she comes first thing in the morning. Something that she, Mrs. Lawson, did wrong. She even imagines Gloria saying to Miss Goldstein, Honestly, how come you keep on that old Mrs. Lawson? She can't see to clean very good, she's too old to work.

She does not really think that Gloria would say a thing like that, and even if she did Miss Goldstein wouldn't listen, probably. Still, the idea is very worrying to her, and in an anxious way she sweeps up the kitchen floor, and dustmops the long front hall. And at the same time her mind is plagued with those images of husbands, dark ghosts, in Juneau and Oakland and Kansas City, husbands that she has to get home to, somehow. Long bus rides with cold winds at the places where you change, or else you have to wait a long time for the choked-up sound of them honking, until you get in their creaky old cars and drive, drive home, in the dark.

Mrs. Lawson is absolutely right about Gloria having serious troubles on her mind—more serious in fact than Mrs. Lawson could have thought of: Gloria's hideous, obsessive problem is a small lump on her leg, her right leg, mid-calf. A tiny knot. She keeps reaching to touch it, no matter what she is doing, and it is always there. She cannot make herself not touch it. She thinks constantly of that lump, its implications and probable consequences. Driving to work in her jumpy old VW, she reaches down to her leg, to check the lump. A couple of times she almost has accidents, as she concentrates on her fingers, reaching, what they feel as they touch her leg.

To make things even worse, the same week that she first noticed the lump Gloria met a really nice man, about her age: Dugald, neither married nor gay (a miracle, these days, in San Francisco). He is a bartender in a place where she sometimes goes with girlfriends, after a movie or something. In a way she has known Dugald for a long time, but in another way not—not known him until she happened to go into the place alone, thinking, Well, why not? I'm tired (it was late one afternoon), a beer would be nice. And there was Dugald, and they talked, and he asked her out, on his next night off. And the next day she discovered the lump.

She went with Dugald anyway, of course, and she almost had a very good time—except that whenever she thought about what was probably wrong with her she went cold and quiet. She thinks that Dugald may not ever ask her out again, and even if he did, she can't get at all involved with anyone, not now.

Also, Gloria's sister, Sharon, in Fairbanks, Alaska, has invited her to come up and stay for a week, while Sharon's forestry-student husband is back in Kansas, visiting his folks; Sharon does not much like her husband's family. Gloria thinks she will go for ten days in June, while Miss Goldstein is in China, again. Gloria is on the whole pleased at the prospect of this visit; as she Ajaxes and Lysols Miss Goldstein's upstairs bathroom, she thinks, *Alaska,* and she imagines gigantic glaciers, huge wild animals, fantastic snow-capped mountains. (She will send a friendly postcard to Dugald, she thinks, and maybe one to old Lawson). Smiling, for an instant she makes a small bet with herself, which is that at some point Sharon will ask her not to mention to anyone, *please,* what she, Gloria, does for a living. Well, Gloria doesn't care. Lord knows her work is not much to talk about; it is simply the most money she can get an hour, and not pay taxes (she is always afraid, when not preoccupied with her other, more terrible worries, that the IRS will somehow get to her). On the other hand, it is fun to embarrass Sharon.

At home though, lying awake at night, of course the lump is all that Gloria thinks about. And hospitals: when she was sixteen she had her tonsils out, and she decided then on no more operations, no matter what. If she ever has a baby she will do it at home. The hospital was so frightening, everyone was horrible to her, all the doctors and nurses (except for a couple of black aides who were sweet, really nice, she remembers). They all made her feel like something much less than a person. And a hospital would take all her money, and more, all her careful savings (someday she plans to buy a little cabin, up near Tahoe, and raise big dogs). She thinks about something being cut off. Her leg. Herself made so ugly, everyone trying not to look. No more men, no dates, not Dugald or anyone. No love or sex again, not ever.

In the daytime her terror is slightly more manageable, but it is still so powerful that the very idea of calling a doctor, showing him the lump, asking him what to do—chills her blood, almost stops her heart.

And she can feel the lump there, all the time. Probably growing.

Mrs. Lawson has told Gloria that she never goes to doctors; she can doctor herself, Mrs. Lawson says. She always has. Gloria has even thought of showing the lump to Mrs. Lawson.

But she tries to think in a positive way about Alaska. They have a cute little apartment right on the university campus, Sharon has written. Fairbanks is on a river; they will take an afternoon trip on a paddleboat. And they will spend one night at Mount McKinley, and go on a wild life tour.

"Fairbanks, now. I never did get up that way," says Mrs. Lawson, told of Sharon's invitation, Gloria's projected trip. "But I always heard it was real nice up there."

Actually she does not remember anything at all about Fairbanks, but for Gloria's sake she hopes that it is nice, and she reasons that any place would be better than Juneau, scrunched in between mountains so steep they look to fall down on you.

"I hope it's nice," says Gloria. "I just hope I don't get mauled by some bear, on that wild life tour."

Aside from not drinking and never going to doctors (she has read all her father's old doctor books, and remembers most of what she read) Mrs. Lawson believes that she gets her good health and her strength—considerable, for a person of her years—from her daily naps. Not a real sleep, just sitting down for a while in some place really comfortable, and closing her eyes.

She does that now, in a small room off Miss Goldstein's main library room (Miss Goldstein has already gone off to China, but even if she were home she wouldn't mind about a little nap). Mrs. Lawson settles back into a big old fat leather chair, and she slips her shoes off. And, very likely because of talking about Alaska that morning, Gloria's trip, her mind drifts off, in and out of Juneau. She remembers the bitter cold, cold rains of that winter up there, the winds, fogs thicker than cotton, and dark. Snow that sometimes kept them in the little hillside cabin for days, even weeks. Her and Charles: that husband had the same name as the one she now has, she just remembered—funny to forget a thing like that. They always used to drink a lot, her and the Charles in Alaska; you had to, to get through the winter. And pretty often they would fight, ugly drunk quarrels that she couldn't quite remember the words to, in the mornings. But that New Year's Eve they were having a real nice time; he was being real nice, laughing and all, and then all of a sudden it was like he turned into some other person, and he struck her. He grabbed up her hair, all of it red, at that time, and he called her a witch and he knocked her down to the floor, and he tromped her. Later of course he was sorry, and he said he had been feeling mean about not enough work, but still, he had tromped her.

Pulling herself out of that half dream, half terrible memory, Mrs. Lawson repeats, as though someone had asked her, that now she is married to Charles, in San Francisco. They live in the Western Addition; they don't drink, and this Charles is a nice man, most of the time.

She tries then to think about the other three husbands, one in Oakland, in Chicago, in Kansas City, but nothing much comes to mind, of them. No faces or words, just shadows, and no true pictures of any of those cities. The only thing she is perfectly clear about is that not one of those other men was named Charles.

On the airplane to Alaska, something terrible, horrible, entirely frightening happens to Gloria, which is: a girl comes and sits in the seat next to hers, and that girl has—the lower part of her right leg missing. Cut off. A pretty dark-haired girl, about the same size as

Gloria, wearing a nice blazer, and a kind of long skirt. One boot. Metal crutches.

Gloria is so frightened—she knows that this is an omen, a sign meant for her—that she is dizzy, sick; she leans back and closes her eyes, as the plane bumps upward, zooming through clouds, and she stays that way for the rest of the trip. She tries not to think; she repeats numbers and meaningless words to herself.

At some point she feels someone touching her arm. Flinching, she opens her eyes to see the next-seat girl, who is asking, "Are you okay? Can I get you anything?"

"I'm all right. Just getting the flu, I think." Gloria smiles in a deliberately non-friendly way. The last thing in the world that she wants is a conversation with that girl: the girl at last getting around to her leg, telling Gloria, "It started with this lump I had, right here."

Doctors don't usually feel your legs, during physical examinations, Gloria thinks; she is standing beside Sharon on the deck of the big paddleboat that is slowly ploughing up the Natoma River. It would be possible to hide a lump for a long time, unless it grew a lot, she thinks, as the boat's captain announces over the bullhorn that they are passing what was once an Indian settlement.

Alaska is much flatter than Gloria had imagined its being, at least around Fairbanks—and although she had of course heard the words, midnight sun, she had not known they were a literal description; waking at three or four in the morning from bad dreams, her nighttime panics (her legs drawn up under her, one hand touching her calf, the lump) she sees brilliant sunshine, coming in through the tattered aluminum foil that Sharon has messily pasted to the window. It is all wrong—unsettling. Much worse than the thick dark fogs that come into San Francisco in the summer; she is used to them.

In fact sleeplessness and panic (what she felt at the sight of that girl with the missing leg has persisted; she knows it was a sign) have combined to produce in Gloria an almost trancelike state. She is so quiet, so passive that she can feel Sharon wondering about her, what is wrong. Gloria does not, for a change, say anything critical of Sharon's housekeeping, which is as sloppy as usual. She does not tell anyone that she, Gloria, is a cleaning person.

A hot wind comes up off the water, and Gloria remembers that tomorrow they go to Mt. McKinley, and the wild life tour.

Somewhat to her disappointment, Mrs. Lawson does not get any postcards from Gloria in Alaska, although Gloria had mentioned that she would send one, with a picture.

What she does get is a strange phone call from Gloria on the day that she was supposed to come back. What is *strange* is that Gloria sounds like some entirely other person, someone younger even than Gloria actually is, younger and perfectly happy. It is Gloria's voice, all right, but lighter and quicker than it was, a voice without any shadows.

"I'm back!" Gloria bursts out, "but I just don't think I want to work today. I was out sort of late—" She laughs, in a bright new way, and then she asks, "She's not back yet, is she?"

Meaning Miss Goldstein. "No, not for another week," Mrs. Lawson tells her. "You had a good trip?"

"Fabulous! a miracle, really. I'll tell you all about it tomorrow."

Hanging up, Mrs. Lawson has an uneasy sense that some impersonator will come to work in Gloria's place.

But of course it is Gloria who is already down on her knees, cleaning the kitchen floor, when Mrs. Lawson gets there the following day.

And almost right away she begins to tell Mrs. Lawson about the wild life tour, from Mt. McKinley, seemingly the focal point of her trip.

"It was really weird," says Gloria. "It looked like the moon, in that funny light." She has a lot to say, and she is annoyed that Mrs. Lawson seems to be paying more attention to her newspaper—is barely listening. Also, Lawson seems to have aged, while Gloria was away, or maybe Gloria just forgot how old she looks, since in a way she doesn't act very old; she moves around and works a lot harder than Sharon ever does, for one example. But it seems to Gloria today that Mrs. Lawson's skin is grayer than it was, ashy looking, and her eyes, which are always strange, have got much paler.

Nevertheless, wanting more attention (her story has an important point to it) Gloria raises her voice, as she continues, "And every time someone spotted one of those animals he'd yell out, and the man would stop the bus. We saw caribou, and these funny white sheep, high up on the rocks, and a lot of moose, and some foxes. Not any bears. Anyway, every time we stopped I got real scared. We were on the side of a really steep mountain, part of Mt. McKinley, I think, and the bus was so wide, like a school bus." She does not tell Mrs. Lawson that in a weird way she liked being so scared. What she thought was, If I'm killed on this bus I'll never even get to a doctor. Which was sort of funny, really, now that she can see the humor in it—now that the lump is mysteriously, magically gone!

However, she has reached the dramatic disclosure toward which this story of her outing has been heading. "Anyway, we got back all right," she says, "and two days after that, back in Fairbanks, do you know what the headlines were, in the local paper?" She has asked this (of course rhetorical) question in a slow, deepened voice, and now she pauses, her china-blue eyes gazing into Mrs. Lawson's paler, stranger blue.

"Well, I don't know," Lawson obliges.

"They said, BUS TOPPLES FROM MOUNTAIN, EIGHT KILLED, 42 INJURED. Can you imagine? Our same bus, the very next day. What do you think that means?" This question too has been rhetorical; voicing it, Gloria smiles in a satisfied, knowing way.

A very polite woman, Mrs. Lawson smiles gently too. "It means you spared. You like to live fifty, sixty years more."

Eagerly Gloria bursts out, "Exactly! That's just the way I figured it, right away." She pauses, smiling widely, showing her little white teeth. "And then, that very same afternoon of the day we saw the paper," she goes on, "I was changing my clothes and I felt of the calf of my leg where there'd been this lump that I was sort of worried about—and the lump was gone. I couldn't believe it. So I guess it was just a muscle, not anything bad."

"Them leg muscles can knot up that way, could of told you that myself," Mrs. Lawson mutters. "Heavy housework can do that to a person." But Gloria looks so happy, so bright-faced and shiny-eyed, that Mrs. Lawson does not want to bring her down, in any way, and so she adds, "But you sure are right about that bus accident. It's a sure sign you been spared."

"Oh, that's what I think too! And later we saw these really neat big dogs, in Fairbanks. I'm really thinking about getting a dog. This man I know really likes dogs too, last night we were talking." Her voice trails off in a happy reminiscence.

Later in the day, though, thinking about Gloria and her story, what she and Gloria said to each other, Mrs. Lawson is not really convinced about anything. The truth is, Gloria could perfectly well get killed by a bus in San Francisco, this very afternoon, or shot by some sniper; it's been saying in the paper about snipers, all over town, shooting folks. Or Gloria could find another lump, some place else, somewhere dangerous. Missing one bus accident is no sure sign that a person's life will always come up rosy, because nobody's does, not for long. Even Miss Goldstein, in China, could fall off of some Chinese mountain.

In a weary, discouraged way Mrs. Lawson moved through the rest of her day. It is true; she is too old and tired for the work she does. Through the big street-floor windows she watches the cold June fog rolling in from the bay, and she thinks how the weather in California has never seemed right to her. She thinks about Charles, and it comes to her that one Charles could change into the other, the same way that first Charles in such a sudden way turned violent, and wild.

That thought is enough to make her dread the end of her work, and the day, when although it is summer she will walk out into streets that are as dark and cold as streets are in Alaska.

[1982]

A. R. Ammons

THE YUCCA MOTH

The yucca clump
is blooming,
tall sturdy spears
spangling into bells of light,
green
in the white blooms
faint as a memory of mint:

I raid
a bloom,
spread the hung petals out,
and, surprised he is not
a bloom-part, find
a moth inside, the exact color,
the bloom his daylight port or cove:

though time comes
and goes and troubles
are unlessened,
the yucca is lifting temples
of bloom: from the night
of our dark flights, can
we go in to heal, live
out in white-green shade
the radiant, white, hanging day?

[1964]

W. H. Auden

THE GARRISON

Martini-time: time to draw the curtains and
choose a composer we should like to hear from,
before coming to table for one of your
savoury messes.

Time crumbs all ramparts, brachypod Nemesis
overtakes sooner or later hare-swift
Achilles, but personal song and language
somehow mizzle them.

Thanks to which it's possible for the breathing
still to break bread with the dead, whose brotherhood
gives us confidence to wend the trivial
thrust of the Present,

so self-righteous in its assumptions and so
certain that none dare out-face it. We, Chester,
and the choir we sort with have been assigned to
garrison stations.

Whoever rules, our duty to the City
is loyal opposition, never greening
for the big money, never neighing after
a public image.

Let us leave rebellions to the choleric
who enjoy them: to serve as a paradigm
Now of what a plausible Future might be
is what we're here for.

[1970]

FIVE TRIBUTES TO W. H. AUDEN

John Betjeman

He is an old friend of mine from Oxford days and my regard for him is so great that I would not like to write what would seem an obituary when the subject is already alive, and this is what personal recollections would be. As for criticisms of his work others are better qualified to make these than I am. All I can recall of a critical nature emanating from him to me is this. He was always healthily intolerant of the pretentious. I was a pretentious undergraduate and I remember his coming into my rooms at Oxford and looking at my bookshelves and seeing there all the books that were fashionable at the time, but among them were several volumes of Edmund Blunden's poems. "These are what you really like" he said, and he was quite right and he still is. I remember, too, showing him some verse I had written whose meaning depended on its title. He said that a poem should not need a title to explain it. It should be its own title; he's quite right here, too. What I have always enjoyed about him is his splendid disregard for fashion. He reads poetry avidly, as I do, and takes it on its own merits and not because it is well known, or the thing to read. His recent anthology of nineteenth-century poetry is one more piece of evidence of this.

Leonard Bernstein

The least that can be said of the least good poem by Auden is that it is first-class. From that point judgment can only mount, as the poetry becomes playful, didactic, bitter, lyrical, or deeply touching. And all of it is informed with a virtuosity that, to my knowledge, has no equal in contemporary English poetry. One can only wish for many more birthdays, and many, many more poems.

Louise Bogan

Keeping his expression flexible, his enthusiasms (his deep interest in the relation of poetry to music is one) ardent, his attitude unfailingly humane, Auden has never failed the active idealism of his early years. His spiritual pattern has always been that of the Quest—one of the great mythic patterns of mankind. He stands today, more than a great many of his defeat-accepting contemporaries can realize, as a man of the future—for whom a passionate seeking out, an unflagging application of all that is lively in the modern mind and imagination has never ceased to count. He has not only read the books, but he has experienced the anguish and the bafflements of his time. The circular thinking, the vaporizing, the empty and vapid negation which have become part and parcel of the verse written in our day, have not touched him; he is still seeking out fresh diction, central emotion, sound assumptions. He is never idle; new ventures are continually under way: a libretto, a translation, a critique, a poem. Such a figure, we feel, can only be produced by rich and open societies, and in Auden we have the reassurance that our era, so terrifying in many respects, cannot be utterly poverty-stricken and closed.

M. F. K. Fisher

I have never met him face to face, although for many years (since the early Thirties) I have lived on the fringe . . . many mutual friends. This, and my steady enjoyment and excitement in reading whatever he has published, have made me feel a very respectful closeness to him. A few times when people have mentioned that he would be at somebody's house that night in London . . . Come along! . . . I have said that I was afraid to, and it was the truth, for my admiration of him remains as unreasoning as a schoolgirl's and I am basically shy, and unwilling to subject either of us to my blushes and murmurings.

It may be of some interest that I always feel very proud when I read something of Auden's whether new or long since printed. It is a personal reaction: here, in all the wasteful babbling, is a real user of the language, a poet who respects both sound and meaning, who will not utter one syllable because it is merely beautiful. It reassures me, in the morass of insultingly misused words I read and look at on television and listen to on radio. It is tonic.

What Auden says is exciting to me because it presents a constant challenge, behind and beyond the fascination of sound and rhythm, to my intelligence. Perhaps what I am saying in all this is that I "like" to read his poetry because it makes me feel more like a sensate human being than do most other forces now abroad.

I am sure from what friends have told me that I would like him in person. I always am pleased to find a picture published. But I am really in awe of him, and that is always a bore socially. I'd better stay on the fringe . . . .

Robert Lowell

Auden's work and career are like no one else's, and have helped us all. He has been very responsible and ambitious in his poetry and criticism, constantly writing deeply on the big subjects, and yet keeping something wayward, eccentric, idiosyncratic, charming, and his own. Much hard, ingenious, correct toil has gone into inconspicuous things: introductions, anthologies and translations. When one looks at them closely, one is astonished at how well they have been done. In his twenties, he was already one of our best and most original poets. For long years, he has lived with that genius, never betraying it, or exploiting it, but always adding and varying, a discoverer and a sustainer. His inspiration seems almost as versatile as his styles and his metrical forms, yet I am most grateful for three or four supreme things: the sad Anglo-Saxon alliteration of his beginnings, his prophecies that seemed the closest voice to our disaster, then the marvelous crackle of his light verse and broadside forms, small fires made into great in his hands, and finally for a kind of formal poem that combines a breezy baroque grandeur with a sophisticated Horatian simplicity. Last winter, John Crowe Ransom said to me that we had made an even exchange, when we lost Eliot to England, and later gained Auden. Both poets have been kind to the lands of their exile, and brought gifts the natives could never have conceived of.

[1967]

Edmund Wilson and Louise Bogan

TO WYSTAN AUDEN ON HIS BIRTHDAY

(Alternate lines by E. W. and L. B.—first line by E. W.)

Auden, that thou art living at this hour
  Delights us. How much duller wert thou not!
  And we have need of thee. A drear dry-rot
Spreads its dank mould throughout the Muses' bower;
The orc Tolkien usurps Aladdin's tower;
  The Groves of Academe are sold and bought;
  And countless other things have gone to pot.
O Wystan, hear us! Implement our power.

How like some Greenland grampus, dolphin-finned,
  Sporting with smaller fish of lesser price,
Shaking a spray that sparkles in the wind
  Or diving to depth-pressures in a trice
  —Unlike the tuna, never to be tinned—
  Thou hump'st a path through heavy seas of ice.
  Thou bear'st a banner with this strange device:
"Excelsior."

Composed in 1956

[1967]

Lincoln Kirstein

SIEGFRIEDSLAGE

Beyond the Isar,—*Reichsdrückmeisterei;*
Drück? Dreck. Vast warehouse bulked with Nazi fill
Of drug, gun, uniform,—feckless supply.
In leagues of corridor, abandoned room,
We've set High Headquarters, 'midst sloven chill,—
Our *ersatz* vict'ry and rankling gloom.

My bureau, a dust-sifted shoe-box cell
Usurps the top floor of which stair is shot.
I serve my Sergeant, Filthy Flaherty. He'll
Tell the World his canned Cagney Irishry;
Bathes once a month, need it or not;
Buzzed up at coffee-break and spat at me:

"Man. Get a load of this. Waiting below,
A wild man's parked, and he allows as he
Wants *you.* He must be nuts, but pronto:
Git. See for yourself. Gawd, it's just a farce,—
Some stimulated Major, V.I.P.
Who does not know his silly English arse
From one damned hole in our accurséd sod;
Hies here to Headquarters a lousy mess,—
In *carpet*-slippers, yet! Before Gawd,
He lacks his HELMET LINER, and is clad
In uniform which Patton must suppress."

Dunstan, driving from Kempten, else I'm mad,—
It's *you,* heaped high in Quixote jeep with loose
Bedding, valay-packs; manned by nordic cook,
Wehrmacht driver, yesterday's P.W.s,—
Enemy personnel, but how the hell,
Released to you? It beats for keeps, The Book.
Yet here you are, crummy and very well
To haul me off to supper, talk the night.

Sergeant is useless, never'd let me go;
I skip right o'er his head, which is not right,
Straight to my Captain, piteous pleading thus:
"Sir, an old friend awaits me here below:
May I go with him? Filthy'll make his fuss,
But I'll be back by dawn; inspection stand."

My Captain snickers: "Soldier, is this Ass?"
I play deep hurt: "Don't, sir, misunderstand.
It's (simulated) Major Morden, sir;
His invitation prompts a formal pass—
Of prose and verse th'ingenious author.
Here, his momentous present mission's for
Interrogating Pastor Wiemöller,—
Sage U-Boot Kapitän of the Erst Worldwar;
Whom Hitler jailed, or did he? It's obscure.
But Dunstan Morden will prompt, uncover."
"Permission granted. Back by dawn,—but sure."

His jeep was comfy, like a busted sack:
Pot, kettle, mattress, a fat case of books,
Floor-lamps, victrola, Wagner's profile plaque,
Discs, a crate of wine, God knows all what,—
Salvage or pillage. The teenage cook's
Worried about his steaks, a cute kid, but
The fierce chauffeur will kill us if he can,
Cuts every corner, never honks his horn
And barrels wrongside down the autobahn;
Finally achieves a silk Bavarian lake
For a four-color travel-poster born,
Schloss miniature, pasteboard cut-out fake
Domesticating Rheingold's local name,
Hight SIEGFRIEDSLAGE, mean memorial
To hero Siegfried of operatic fame,
Sieglinde's tenor, Mime's fosterson.

Upstairs, a dormitory; windows all;
Unrolled neat bedding for ten men, each one
An international-type specialist:
Dutch, English, Dane, plus two Americans,—
Morden, with chum Tim Burns, complete the list

Tho' Tim is Afro-Irish in addition,—
Intellectuals cosmopolitan
Sworn to high secrecy on topflight mission.
What they're now up to here, one may not say:
(Investigating the repentant kraut?
Did he mind bombing more by night or day?
From R.A.F. or from a U.S. plane?)
Has this some use? File and forget? No doubt
Archives are avid; still, it's to *my* gain,
For by this site I learned th'essential score,
Nervous prognosis of hist'ry ahead.

A poet sketched the full orchestral score,
Sight-read symphonic fate precipitate;
Defined some main determinings in man's
Hate which 'no man can ever estimate.'
Prussians have a sense of status only;
They must be over us all,—or under.
Equals are no compeers for these lonely
Infants who've one word: GROSS,—for great, big, grand,
Extraordinary, huge. Their blunder
Is semantic. "To rule" they understand
As enforced order by gross control.
They rest undefeated; this gimcrack peace
Is but a breather for us both, each soul
The same. Unwar, never a victory,
Bequeathed to all our epoch,—slight surcease:
"Organized hatred. *That* is unity."*

Twenty years on,—absolved, rich, competent
To kill again, but next time on 'our' side;
Russia an ally who shan't relent
Her quasi-oriental tricks of tension
So all the luck we wait on here,—denied
Or distilled to the dreariest dimension
Of mindless spirals in biomorphic daft
Jounce of organs' or organisms' junctures,
As free as pistons in a confined shaft;

*"Lines On the Death of Bismarck," by John Jay Chapman, l. 22.

Captious hide-and-seek of whimsical guns,
Cops and robbers whose gamesome punctures
Waste random blackmail on risky runs.

I get depressed. One often gets depressed
When pliant minds for whom the human aim
Spells complex logic logically expressed,
Are rendered sanguine by the basest acts,
Discounting tragic or ironic claim,
End up near truth with just the lyric facts,
Yet past complaint or wisecrack cynical
Reducing analysis to partial
Documents of the jejune clinical.
A poet made uncommon common-sense.

I change the subject. Aren't there some martial
Arts safe from ordinary murder? Hence
Asked the silly question,—as one must,
Concerning our 'war-writers': "What think you
Of Soanso?" whose combat verse was just
Out, Pulitzer-prized, compassionate, fine,
Deeply experienced, sincere; so true
It made me weep. I wished it had been mine.

"Thin stuff," he snapped. I knew it then: thin stuff.
"Poetry," he said, " 's not in the pity.
It's in the words. What words are wide enough?"
Yet if one's greedy in our craft or art,
Shrewd, apt, ambitious,—here's a recipe
To fix some blood-types for a wounded heart,
Resecting style, or better, grafting tones
Eavesdropped in anguish o'er field-telephones,
Wise walky-talking through our murky mess,
Rococo bingo, gangbang or deathdance,
A microscopic keyhole on distress,—
Merciless, wilful, exquisite, grim, frank,
As in some masterpiece ironwrought
By that tough butterfly, Ronald Firbank,
From whose "Flower Beneath the Foot" recall
The texts they taught: "What Every Soldier Ought
To Know"; the Hon. Mrs. Victor Smythe's "All

Men Are Animals"; field-manuals' skit.
No epics more. Grand style our wars are not.
Teasing is all. Let's skip the heartfelt bit.

He's restless now. Gossip is done tonight.
Kümmel. Then hit the sack, for *punkt* on 8
Morden rates Wiemöller in his light bite.

Near dawn I drag his driver deep from sleep
Too soon, but scared I'll make Inspection late;
In chill midsummer mist grope toward his jeep.
Coffeeless, furious, he whirls me fast
Towards Headquarters, through growing light, on time.
Dazed, do I meditate through forests passed:
History's long hurtle, my precious part
In decades left me and the health in rhyme;
How one believes, nay, *must* believe in ART.

Heavy the burden; indeed so onerous,
I needs must to my Sergeant spill it all.
Better: my Captain. He'll alert our Brass:
"Listen! d'you know what This is all About,
Really,—*about*?" Cassandra's howls apall:
OUR PRESENT VICTORY'S BUT OUR FUTURE
ROUT.

No dice. Who'd listen? No use, and, who cares?
With us, stout England, the' enfeebled French
Shall shrink our risks to what dubious shares
Of salvage as th'Imminent Will intends.
Stubborn enseamed inertia shall entrench
Its sturdy virus,—blind, complacent, send
Its livid chain through our complacency . . . .

Munich: 1945

[1967]

Stephen Spender

AUDEN AETAT XX, LX

YOU – the young bow-tyed near-albino undergraduate
With rooms on Peck Quad (blinds drawn down at midday
To shut the sun out) – read your poems aloud
In that voice that was so clinical
I thought it held each word brilliant in forceps
Up to your lamp. Images seemed segments
On slides seen through the iciest of microscopes
Which showed pale edges round dark blots
Of the West collapsing to a farce.
Yet not to be wept over, since the ruins
Offered the poet a bare-kneed engineer's
Chance of scrambling madly over scrap heaps
To fish out carburettors, sparking plugs,
A sculptured Hell from a cathedral porch,
Scenes from sagas, and a water-logged
Lost code. With nicotine-stained fingers
You rigged such junk into new strange machines.
Two met at dawn – boulders against the sky line –
A spy crouched on the floor of a parched cystern,
One with hands that clutched at the wet reeds
Was shot, escaping. (The joking word lobbed bombs
Into my dream that was the young Romantic's
Praying his wound would blossom to a rose
Of blood, bright under an ecstatic moon
Exclaiming "O"!)
Forty years later now, benevolent
In carpet slippers, you still make devices,
Sitting at table like one playing patience,
Grumpily fitting our lives to your game,
Whose rules are dogma of objective Love.

[1967]

J. R. R. Tolkien

FOR W. H. A.

Woruldbúendra sum bið wóðbora,
giedda giffæst; sum bið gearuwyrdig,
tyhtend getynge torhte mæðleð;
sum bið bóca gléaw, on bréosthorde
wísdóm haldeð, worn fela geman
ealdgesægena þæra þe úðwitan
fróde gefrugnon on fyrndagum;
sum bið wilgesíð, wǽrfæst hæle,
fréondrǽdenne fǽle gelǽsteð.
Sumne wát ic, secg héahmódne,
þe þissa gifena gehwane on geogoðféore
him ealdmetod éstum gesealde.
Wer wíde cuð Wíhstan hatte,
swilce wæs éac háten on eardgearde
Wǽgmundinga Wígláfes fæder
secga holdestan, and siððan eft
bearn Wíghelmes þe æt beaduwe gecrang
æt Mældúne be his mandryhtne
on gefrǽgan þam gefeohte. He nú forð tela
níwan stefne þæs naman brúceð
him to weorðmynde, Wíhstan úre.
Swa sceal he á mid mannum mǽre wunian,
þǽr sittað searoþancle sundor tó rúne,
snyttrum styriað sóðgied scopa.

Ic þis gied be þé to grétinge
awræc wintrum fród, Wíhstan léofa,
þeah ic þorfte hraðor þancword sprecan.
Rægnold Hrædmóding.

Among the people of earth one has poetry in him,
fashions verses with art; one is fluent in words,
has persuasive eloquence sound and lucid;
one is a reader of books and richly stores
his mind with memory of much wisdom
and legends of old that long ago
were learned and related by loremasters;
one is a mate to choose, a man to trust,
who friendship's call faithfully answers.
Another I know of noble-hearted,
to whom all these gifts in his early days
the favour of Fate freely granted.
Now wide is his renown. Wystan his name is,
as it once was also of the Wægmunding
in his far country, father of Wiglaf
most loyal of lieges, and in later time
of Wighelm's son who in war was slain
at Byrhtnoth's side by the Blackwater
in the famous defeat. He follows after,
and now anew that name uses
to his own honour. Auden some call him,
and so among men may he be remembered ever,
where as they sit by themselves for solace of heart
the word-lovers, wise and skilful,
revive the vanished voices of makers.

These lines about you I linked together,
though weighted by years, Wystan my friend:
a tardy tribute and token of thanks.
J.R.R.T.

[1967]

John Berryman

ONE ANSWER TO A QUESTION

This slight exploration of some of my opinions about my work as a poet, you may wish to bear in mind, is the statement of a man nearing fifty, and I am less impressed than I used to be by the universal notion of a continuity of individual personality—which will bring me in a moment to the first and most interesting of the four questions proposed by the co-ordinator, Mr. Howard Nemerov. It's a queer assignment. Sometimes I've complied with similar requests before, but never without fundamental misgivings. For one thing, one forgets, one even deliberately forgets in order to get on with new work, and so may seriously misrepresent the artist-that-was twenty years ago. For another, there are trade secrets. At the same time that one works partly to open fresh avenues for other writers (though one would not dream of admitting it), one has secrets, like any craftsman, and I figure that anyone who deserves to know them deserves to find them out for himself. So I don't plan to give anything away.

The question was this: "Do you see your work as having essentially changed in character or style since you began?"

I would reply: *of course*. I began work in verse-making as a burning, trivial disciple of the great Irish poet William Butler Yeats, and I hope I have moved off from there. One is obsessed at different times by different things, and by different ways of putting them. Naturally there are catches in the question. What does 'essentially' mean? what is 'character'? what is 'style'? Still the question if semantically murky is practically clear, and I respond to it with some personal history.

When I said just now 'work in verse-making' I was leaving out some months of proto-apprenticeship during which I was so inexperienced that I didn't imitate *anybody*. Then came Yeats, whom I didn't so much wish to resemble as to *be*, and for several fumbling years I wrote in what it's convenient to call 'period style,' the Anglo-American style of the 1930s, with no voice of my own, learning chiefly from middle and later Yeats and from the brilliant young Englishman W. H. Auden. Yeats somehow saved me from the then crushing influences of Ezra Pound and T. S. Eliot—luckily, as I now feel—but he could not teach me to sound like myself (whatever that was) or tell me what to write about. The first poem, perhaps, where those dramatic-to-me things happened was (is) called "Winter Landscape." It's mounted in five five-line stanzas, unrhymed, all one sentence. I admit there's a colon near the middle of the third stanza.

Winter Landscape

The three men coming down the winter hill
In brown, with tall poles and a pack of hounds
At heel, through the arrangement of the trees
Past the five figures at the burning straw,
Returning cold and silent to their town,

Returning to the drifted snow, the rink

Lively with children, to the older men,
The long companions they can never reach,
The blue light, men with ladders, by the church
The sledge and shadow in the twilit street,

Are not aware that in the sandy time
To come, the evil waste of history
Outstretched, they will be seen upon the brow
Of that same hill: when all their company
Will have been irrecoverably lost,

These men, this particular three in brown
Witnessed by birds will keep the scene and say
By their configuration with the trees,
The small bridge, the red houses and the fire,
What place, what time, what morning occasion

Sent them into the wood, a pack of hounds
At heel and the tall poles upon their shoulders,
Thence to return as now we see them and
Ankle-deep in snow down the winter hill
Descend, while three birds watch and the fourth flies.

This does not sound, I would say, like either Yeats or Auden—or Rilke or Lorca or Corbière or any of my other passions of those remote days. It derives its individuality, if I am right, from a peculiar steadiness of sombre tone (of which I'll say more presently) and from its peculiar relation to its materials—drawn, of course, from Brueghel's famous painting. The poem is sometimes quoted, and readers seem to take it for either a verbal *equivalent* to the picture or (like Auden's fine Brueghel poem, "Musee des Beaux Arts," written later) an *interpretation* of it. Both views I would call wrong, though the first is that adopted in a comparative essay on picture and poem recently published by two aestheticians at the University of Notre Dame. (If anyone is *truly* curious this can be found in the University of Texas *Studies in Literature and Language*, V, 3, Autumn 1963.) After a competent study, buttressed by the relevant scholarship, of Brueghel's painting, they proceed to the poem—where, there being no relevant scholarship, they seem less at ease—and so to the relation between the two. Some of the points made are real, I believe: to quote the two with which they begin, they say the poem's 'elaborate sequence urged on by the sweeping carry-over lines' (they mean run-on) '—within the stanza or between stanzas—preserves the same order of presentation and the same groupings of elements as the Brueghel composition.... Purposefully restricting himself to a diction as sober, direct, and matter-of-fact as the painter's treatment of scene and objects, Berryman so composes with it that he achieves an insistent and animated pattern of strong poetic effect.' And so on, to the end of the article where the two works' 'disclosed affinities' are found testifying to the 'secret friendship' of the arts. Nowhere is anything said as to what the poem is *about*, nor is any interest expressed in that little topic; and the relation between the works is left obscure except for the investigation of affinities. An investigation of *differences* would have taken them farther.

Very briefly, the poem's extreme sobriety would seem to represent a reaction, first, against Yeats's gorgeous and seductive rhetoric, and, second, against the hysterical political atmosphere of the period. It dates from 1938-9 and was written in New York following two years' residence in England, during recurrent crises, with extended visits to France and Germany, especially one of the Nazi strongholds, Heidelberg. So far as I can make out, it is a war-poem, of an unusual negative kind. The common title of the picture is "Hunters in the Snow" and of course the poet knows this. But he pretends not to, and calls their spears (twice) 'poles,' the governing resultant emotion being a certain stubborn incredulity—as the hunters are loosed while the peaceful nations plunge again into war. This is not the subject of Brueghel's painting at all, and the interpretation of *the event of the poem* proves that the picture has merely provided necessary material, from a tranquil world, for what is necessary to be said—but which the poet refuses to say—about a violent world.

You may wonder whether I dislike aestheticians. I do.

Very different from the discovery made in "Winter Landscape" if the foregoing account seems acceptable,—namely, that a poem's force may be pivoted on a missing or misrepresented element in an agreed-on or imposed design,—was a discovery made in another short piece several years later. It is called "The Ball Poem" and goes as follows: (it also is twenty-five lines long, unrhymed, but I think you will find it much more fluid)—

The Ball Poem

What is the boy now, who has lost his ball,
What, what is he to do? I saw it go
Merrily bouncing, down the street, and then
Merrily over—there it is in the water!
No use to say 'O there are other balls':
An ultimate shaking grief fixes the boy
As he stands rigid, trembling, staring down
All his young days into the harbour where
His ball went. I would not intrude on him,
A dime, another ball, is worthless. Now
He senses first responsibility
In a world of possessions. People will take balls,
Balls will be lost always, little boy,
And no one buys a ball back. Money is external.
He is learning, well behind his desperate eyes,
The epistemology of loss, how to stand up
Knowing what every man must one day know
And most know many days, how to stand up.
And gradually light returns to the street,
A whistle blows, the ball is out of sight,
Soon part of me will explore the deep and dark
Floor of the harbour . . I am everywhere,
I suffer and move, my mind and my heart move
With all that move me, under the water
Or whistling, I am not a little boy.

The discovery here was that a commitment of identity can be 'reserved,' so to speak, with an ambiguous pronoun. The poet himself is both left out and put in; the boy does and does not become him, and we are confronted with a process which is at once a process of life and a process of art. A pronoun may seem a small matter, but she matters, he matters, it matters, they matter. Without this invention (if it is one—Rimbaud's 'Je est un autre' may have pointed my way, I have no idea now) I could not have written either of the two long poems that constitute the bulk of my work so far. If I were making a grandiose claim, I might pretend to know more about the administration of pronouns than any other living poet writing in English or American. You will have noticed that I have said nothing about my agonies and joys, my wives and children, my liking for my country, my dislike of Communist theory and practice, etc., but have been technical. Art is technical, too. I feel myself to be addressing primarily professional writers or will be writers and teachers in the countries which may be reached by the Voice of America.

So far I have been speaking of short poems, and youth, when enthusiasms and hostilities, of an artistic kind I mean, play a bigger role in inspiration than maybe they do later. I don't know, because I see neither enthusiasm nor hostility behind "The Ball Poem." But I was nearly thirty then. I do know that much later, when I finally woke up to the fact that I was involved in a long poem, one of my first thoughts was: Narrative! let's have narrative, and at least one dominant personality, and no fragmentation!—in short, let us have something spectacularly NOT *The Waste Land,* the best long poem of the age. So maybe hostility keeps on going.

What had happened was that I had made up the first stanza of a poem to be called *Homage to Mistress Bradstreet,* and the first three lines of the second stanza, and there, for almost five years, I stuck. Here's the passage.

> The Governor your husband lived so long
> moved you not, restless, waiting for him? Still,
> you were a patient woman—
> I seem to see you pause here still:
> Sylvester, Quarles, in moments odd you pored
> before a fire at, bright eyes on the Lord,
> all the children still.
> 'Simon . . : Simon will listen while you read a Song.
>
> Outside the New World winters in grand dark
> white air lashing thro' the virgin stands
> foxes down foxholes sigh . . .

The dramatic mode, hovering behind the two meditative lyrics I've quoted, has here surely come more into the open; and also here I had overcome at once two of the paralyzing obstacles that haunt the path of the very few modern poets in English who have attempted ambitious sizable poems: what form to use, and what to write about. The eight-line stanza I invented here after a lifetime's study, especially of Yeats' and in particular the one he adopted from Abraham Cowley for his elegy "In Memory of Major Robert Gregory". Mine breaks not at mid-point but after the short third line; a strange four-beat line leads to the balancing heroic couplet of lines five and six, after which seven is again short (3 feet, like line three) and then the stanza widens into an alexandrine riming all the way back to one. I wanted something at once flexible and grave, intense and quiet, able to deal with matter both high and low.

As for the subject: the question most put to me about the poem is why I chose to write about this boring high-minded Puritan woman who may have been our first American poet but is not a good one. I agree, naturally, and say that I did not choose her—somehow she chose me—one point of connection, at any rate, being the almost insuperable difficulty of writing high verse at all in a land that cared and cares so little for it. I was concerned with her, though, almost from the beginning, as a woman, not much as a poetess. For four and a half years then I accumulated materials, and sketched, fleshing out the target or vehicle, still under the impression that seven or eight stanzas would see it done. There are fifty-seven. My stupidity is traceable partly to an astuteness that made me afraid as the next man of the ferocious commitment involved in a long poem, partly to the fact that although I had my form and subject I did not have my theme yet. This emerged, and under the triple impetus of events I won't identify I got the poem off the ground and nearly died following it. The theme is hard to put shortly but I will try.

An American historian somewhere observes that all colonial settlements are intensely conservative, *except* in the initial break-off point (whether religious, political, legal or whatever). Trying to do justice to both parts of this obvious truth—which I came upon only after the poem was finished—I concentrated upon the second, and the poem laid itself out in a series of rebellions. I had her rebel first against the new environment and above all against her barrenness (which in fact lasted for years), then against her marriage (which in fact seems to have been brilliantly happy), and finally against her continuing life of illness, loss, and age. These are the three large sections of the poem; they are preceded and followed by an exordium and coda, of four stanzas each, spoken by the 'I' of the twentieth century poet, which modulates into her voice, who speaks most of the poem. Such is the plan. Each rebellion, of course, is succeeded by submission, though even in the moment of the poem's supreme triumph—the presentment, too long to quote now, of the birth of her first child—rebellion survives. I don't remember how conceptual all this was with me during the months of composition, but I think: in a high degree. Turbulence may take you far toward a good short poem but it's only the first quarter-mile in a long one.

Not that the going is ever exactly tranquil. I recall three times of special heat, the first being when I realized that the middle of the poem was going to have to be in *dialogue,* a dialogue between the seventeenth century woman and the twentieth century poet—a sort of extended witch-seductress and demon-lover bit. The second was a tactical solution of a problem arising out of this, how to make them in some measure physically present to each other: I gave myself one line, when she says

A fading world I dust, with fingers new.

Later on it appears that they kiss, once, and then she says—as women will—'Talk to me.' So he does, in an only half-subdued aria-stanza:

It is Spring's New England. Pussy willows wedge
up in the wet. Milky crestings, fringed
yellow, in heaven, eyed
by the melting hand-in-hand, or mere
desirers, single, heavy-footed, rapt,
make surge poor human hearts. Venus is trapt—
the hefty pike shifts, sheer—
in Orion blazing. Warblings, odours, nudge to an edge—

Noting and overconsidering such matters, few critics have seen that it *is* an historical poem, and it was with interest that I found Mr. Robert Lowell pronouncing it lately, in *The New York Review,* 'the most resourceful historical poem in our literature.' The third pleasant moment I remember is when one night, hugging myself, I decided that her fierce dogmatic old father was going to die blaspheming, in delirium.

The *Bradstreet* poem was printed in 1953 (as a book here 1956, London 1959) and a year or so later, having again taken leave of my wits, or collected them, I began a second long poem. The first installment, called *77 Dream Songs,** came out in New York just one month ago, so it's early days to say much of it. Turbulence: the modern world, and memory, and wants. Form: 18-line sections, three six-line stanzas, each normally (for feet) 5-5-3-5-5-3, variously rhymed and not but mostly rhymed with great strictness. Subject: a character named Henry, who also has a Friend who calls him 'Mr. Bones.' Here's the first section, or Song, where the 'I' perhaps of the poet disappears into Henry's first and third persons (he talks to himself in the second person too) about himself.

Huffy Henry hid the day,
unappeasable Henry sulked.
I see his point,—a trying to put things over.
It was the thought that they thought
they could do it made Henry wicked & away.
But he should have come out and talked.

All the world like a woolen lover
once did seem to Henry's side.
Then came a departure.
Thereafter nothing fell out as it might or ought.
I don't see how Henry, pried
open for all the world to see, survived.

What he has now to say is a long
wonder the world can bear & be.
Once in a sycamore I was glad
all at the top, and I sang.
Hard on the land wears the strong sea
and empty grows every bed.

That's Number One of Book One (the first volume consists of the first three books) and editors and critics for years have been characterizing them as poems but I don't quite see them as that; I see them as parts, admittedly more independent than parts usually are. Once one has succeeded in any degree with a long poem (votes have been cast for as well as against *Homage to Mistress Bradstreet*) dread and fascination fight it out to exclude,

---

*The complete book of the same title has, of course, since been published by Farrar, Straus & Giroux. [Ed.]

on the whole, short poems thereafter, or so I found it. I won't try to explain what I mean by a long poem, but let's suppose (1) a high and prolonged riskiness, (2) the construction of a world rather than the reliance upon one existent which is available to a small poem, (3) problems of decorum most poets happily don't have to face. I can't discuss 'decorum' here either, but here's a case:

There sat down, once, a thing on Henry's heart
so heavy, if he had a hundred years
& more, & weeping, sleepless, in all them time
Henry could not make good.
Starts again always in Henry's ears
the little cough somewhere, an odour, a chime.

And there is another thing he has in mind
like a grave Sienese face a thousand years
would fail to blur the still profiled reproach of. Ghastly,
with open eyes, he attends, blind.
All the bells say: too late. This is not for tears;
thinking.

But never did Henry, as he thought he did,
end anyone and hacks her body up
and hide the pieces, where they may be found.
He knows: he went over everyone, & nobody's missing.
Often he reckons, in the dawn, them up.
Nobody is ever missing.

Whether the diction of that is consistent with blackface talk, heel-spinning puns, coarse jokes, whether the end of it is funny or frightening, or both, I put up to the listener. Neither of the American poets who as reviewers have quoted it admiringly has committed himself; so I won't.

[1965]

FOUR POEMS

REVIVAL

At seventeen (dear) I was strictly nowhere,
astray in sports & politics,
going through the motions of the Fifth Form
& editing *The Pigtail.*

I don't now know what brought me back to myself
& my five-year-old vocation.
A man I met long afterward in Manhattan
told me it was reading Gertrude Stein.

I never liked her maunderings at that time
it was only in a play about the *Maquis*
(I thought, dear)
that her unmistakable ability
found a human theme.

No, no: it was M. Pierre Clamens on *Phèdre*
that woke me back up.
And scribbling my own abominable poems
& listening in a classroom to Professor Van Doren.

I was an expert in *The Federalist* before I read Blake,
in Spinoza before I read *Othello.*
What an education.
I used to come on references to Iago

& I wondered *who* is *he*?
When I met him later, in my Junior year,
he seemed an old friend.
Of learned ignornance!—

O yes, Nicholaus Cusanus, that wise man
inspired me often, in my self-contempt
& despair, almost, of my odds & ends.
Jaspers has done him justice.

MONKHOOD

I don't show my work to anybody, I am quite alone.
The only souls I feel toward are Henry Vaughan & Wordsworth.
This guy Dylan Thomas though is hotter than anyone we have
in America
& hardly at all like Auden.

Pat's reading Conrad through for the second time
'to find out what I think', my new companion, without a penny
but 35/—a week from his solicitors.
I buy him *breakfast* at the Dorothy

& we dawdle over it discussing suicide.
He only has two things left (his wife *took* him),
a red sports car & a complete set of Conrad.
Maybe I ought to add

an all but preternatural ability at darts
which keeps him in drink.
He is sleeping with both his landlady & his landlady's daughter
one on the ground floor & one upstairs,

and he hates to go on across there back at night.
And I think in my unwilling monkhood *I* have problems!
He's studying with Wittgenstein & borrowing Kafka.
What a lovely though depressed talker.

* * * * *

I never went to see Wittgenstein or Broad,
I suffered a little from shyness, which was just arrogance
not even inverted.
I refused to meet Eliot, on two occasions,

I knew I wasn't with it yet
& would not meet my superiors. Screw them.
Along with my hero-worship & wish for comradeship
went my pride, my 'Satanic pride'

as Delmore later, when we were preaching at Harvard
together as kids, he far superior then to me,
put it to my *pleasure* one day
out of his gentle heart & high understanding

of both the strengths & cripplings of men.
Did even Eileen ever understand me sharper?
Many write of me these days & some with insight
but I think of Delmore's remark that afternoon.

Even Cervantes' judgment has not yet wholly overcome me.

Will I ever write properly, with passion & exactness,
of the damned strange demeanours of my flagrant heart?
& be by anyone anywhere undertaken?
One *more* unanswerable question.

FRIENDLESS

Friendless in Clare, except Brian Boydell
a Dubliner with no hair
an expressive tenor speaking voice
who introduced me to the music of Peter Warlock

who had just knocked himself off, fearing the return
of his other personality, Philip Heseltine.
Brian used to play *The Curlew* with the lights out,
voice of a lost soul moving.

These men don't know our poets.
I'm asked to read; I read Wallace Stevens & Hart Crane
in Sidney Sussex & Cat's.
The worthy young gentlemen are baffled.   I explain,

but the idiom is too much for them.
The Dilettante Society here in Clare
asked me to lecture to them on Yeats
& misspelt his name on the invitations.

Black hours over an unclean line.
Fear. Of failure, or worse, *insignificance.*
Solitudes, sometimes, of an alien country
no book after all will ever read me into.

I gorge on Peak Freans & brood.
I don't do a damned thing but read & write.
I wish I were back in New York!
I feel old, yet I don't understand.

DRUNKS

One night in Albany
on a geology field-trip, in a corridor
upstairs of our hotel
I found McGovern on his hands & knees

heading for his lost room after a drinking bet
which upright I had won.
I read everybody, borrowing their books from Mark.
It took me quite a while to get to Yeats.

I wondered every day about suicide.
Once at South Kent—maybe in the Third Form?—
I lay down on the tracks before a train
& had to be hauled off, the Headmaster was furious.

Once at a New Year's party at Mark Van Doren's
to which I took my Jane & Halliday
cautioning them to behave themselves
the place was crawling with celebrities

poor Halliday! got stuck in an upstairs bedroom
with the blonde young wife of a famous critic
a wheel at one of the Book Clubs
who turned out to have nothing on under her gown

sprawled out half-drunk across her hostess's bed
moaning 'Put it in! Put it in!'
Halliday was terrified
I passed out & was put in that same bed. [1970]

George Bradley

EXPECTING AN ANGEL

Not that the appearance would alter us,
That our anticipation was of any importance;
It seemed a recurrence, a matter of memory:
Infants had been named Angelo for generations,
And days already wore the colors of arrival.
Not that it would increase anyone's reputation;
We had long suspected the angel in ourselves,
Treated all strangers with a delicate surmise.
Nor would it in any way affect our self-esteem,
For angels were frequent, might light anywhere,
And this was not a thing of anyone's choosing.
But we were grateful for the prophecies nonetheless,
Rejoicing in their orotund interpretations--
Because our insignificant acts could take place
In high relief, in shadows cast by an event
Occurring minutely, continually, within us all.

[1977]

Michael Brondoli

SHOWDOWN

Nobody helped. The night Cammie Lewis quit the Only Bar not a soul helped. Her boyfriend who wasn't supposed to be there swaggered in at 9:30, a day early but they had their six hundred bags of scallops. He wanted her to kiss him, wanted to show her his hundred-dollar bills, wanted to show everybody what he'd come home to, what he'd been calling on the radio every night.

The pay phone rang but whoever called hung up—probably wanted to talk to Tish, who looked over from the other end of the bar, her face hot with expectation.

Ange Buthrell, Tish's husband, owner of the place, signalled for another round at the back table, where he and his friends were anteing for Nan Twiford to change blouses in front of them. She was prolonging negotiations.

Dressed to kill, Tish was drinking and talking up a storm. In the bar, and there alone, Ange let her go.

The Duke checked another half gallon of Beefeater's—this was North Carolina, you checked your liquor—for him and Dallas Alice, who was singing as loud as she could, which was loud. The Nunemaker brothers borrowed Cammie's screwdriver to crank up the jukebox. Already Conway Twitty sounded like soul music and the buzz of the bass notes made the wineglasses tremble foot to foot. Chas (the Razz) Rollins was weeping at the bar over getting in early to find his woman gone, down fucking that wop in Drum.

Then Tish left, answered the phone herself this time, told Cammie, "Take care of things a while," flashed a bright, tricky smile and left. Usually Cammie could handle a weeknight but the trawlboats were in and besides this was the dead of winter.

Nan changed, for fifty dollars, into an old blouse of Tish's from the office. Ange ordered a round for the house and asked her to travel to Bermuda with him, departure tonight. He asked Cammie to turn the rheostat to zero, leaving in all the bulbs in the place nineteen watts, and these negated by smoke. Nobody would have given Cammie trouble. Anybody would have killed for her or tried to. Still it would be a long night if Tish didn't return.

Cammie's boyfriend R. L. Fuquoy, half heifer, half Popeye—he needed his big shoulders to carry the chips—stood by the first booth checking things out, checking her out, trying to get easy with people. Cammie bore marks from his last trip in, a couple of which might scar, temporarily anyway. At least with R. L. there Chas quit asking her to wipe his tears with her lovely hands, gaze with her eyes of wisdom and so forth.

"Let's go back to the office, catch a buzz," R.L. said as she passed with two armloads.

"Yea, okay." She went to ask Ange to watch the bar, knowing full well he would not, would simply let people take what they needed. He justified his inability to accept money from people he knew as a form of public relations. Tish on the other hand refused the employee discount to her own sister.

"Shit, I missed you all the time," R.L. said in the office, a faint chunky rhythm going in his body. He removed his cap; the yoke of curly hair over his collar remained. "I almost caught my hand in the winch thinking about you." To his mind she was the prettiest woman on earth, the earth he'd seen, Water County, Cape May and Rhode Island. She might not have much of a figure but she carried herself with a nice cool style, good posture, knew how to dress—tonight she was wearing a corduroy skirt, a ruffly top, a thin silver necklace and dark stockings—and had these large eyes, the only part of her face she made up. And had this hair, so thick, so deep a red. When she tied it back for work it hung like grapes the size of eggs. Every time he saw her hair was as if somebody took a redwood log and split it open before his eyes.

"I really am getting varicose veins," she said, fingering a small bulge.

"That's not varicose veins, that's muscle from carrying beer. My mother, now she's got some varicose veins." On Cammie the veins had nowhere to lie except close to the surface and the skin was so tight even her breasts felt like muscle.

"I hope you're right."

"I'm right. I've been at sea two weeks."

"R.L.," she said: a warning. Although he couldn't help looking out of the sides of his eyes, it bothered her.

Sometimes, like now, she could look like an old maid on a farm. Other times she could look warm, she could look cold, she could look innocent, she could look hard, she could look like a little girl who loved her daddy. "You want me to come back at one, help you clean?"

"R.L. We've been through this a million times. I've got to go back out front."

"Serve me another Bud."

She raised her eyebrows to show it didn't matter to her, it was his business, and lit a Marlboro from the desk drawer.

Sitting at the bar was a newcomer, a stranger to Cammie and whom nobody was talking to. In her judgment he seemed a tad too handsome and hip, might even be a narc. Then she wondered if she hadn't been seeing nothing but crabbers and carpenters for way too long.

Ange was on the phone, hurting. Not everyone could have detected his mood, since he kept his face calm under any conditions, his voice low, but Cammie recognized trouble in him quicker than in herself. He never forgot his courtesies. Trouble in him rose like a hungry fish, never quite to the surface but causing a disturbance if you knew how to look. He dialed another number.

R.L. deck-walked out the door, pulling his cap down his nose, pulling his black coat around to hide the beer in his hand. He walked out thinking of her shoulders still dark with freckles from summer.

The regulars at the table with Nan called for beer but Ange wanted her to stay and talk first. He leaned against the backbar, thin and quiet, let his arms hang, looked at the floor, mumbled, "Cammie, I guess it comes to my having to ask you—I apologize, but I have to ask where she went, if you know."

"I have no idea, Ange. Don't go jumping to conclusions though."

"The situation is such—I mean what other damn conclusion can I jump to?"

The Duke ordered gin and tonics, two-thirds and one-third in twelve-ounce mugs for himself, Alice and her cousin Cecelia Curles at the middle booth, and a pack of Winstons.

"I don't know, Ange. She said something earlier about Cloth Barn Road." Without having to think she pulled out three Schlitzes, two Blues, a Bud, a Miller Lite and a red Malt Duck.

"Right, visiting my mother. Cammie, don't try to—" He didn't finish. He appreciated the difficulty of her position and never would have faulted her for anything anyway. "I'm riding up there, carrying Warren to his grandmomma's, then riding up to Norfolk and I guess taking my gun. Just, you know, close whenever your opinion—no more food starting now, no barbecue buns or nothing."

She delivered the drinks and went back to the office. Ange had put on his sportcoat, was mixing a thermos of Blue Hawaiis, using rum somebody had checked and forgotten the night before. "I know you're upset but really you could be wrong." She didn't think he was wrong.

"Who's that guy at the bar wearing a necklace?"

"I was wondering."

"He looks like a narc, do you reckon?"

"Maybe he's an A.B.C. officer."

"I don't believe so."

"Anyway you should sort of clean up a little."

This he was already doing, slipping baggies out of the adding machine, from behind the Busch Bavarian clock, from a case of Collins mix, from the spiral of the Only Bar Halloween photograph album. For all his skill at hiding his real self he was pathetically inept at keeping his other self under wraps. His debts, his schemes, his liking for a new drug became public overnight. A five-year-old could have walked in and uncovered every bit of stash in two minutes. He took a handful of ones from the cash box, put on his sunglasses, a sure sign he meant to go. Day or night he wore them whenever he left, sometimes in the bar, thinking they hid the redness.

"Don't take the gun at least."

"It's kept in the car."

"Don't *leave*." She ran to the front and pleaded with his closest friend Slue Swain to talk Ange out of this desperation.

"Shit," Slue said, his voicebox full of sand. He tipped his Blue Ribbon straight up. "Shit, he should have done this two years ago. But no, kept letting it slide and letting it slide, that's the way the man operates, tying himself in knots instead of hauling in the slack on anybody else."

One of the Nunemakers, Acey, came up from behind, rested his chin on Cammie's head. Booths and tables needed drinks. The jukebox stuck on the chorus of a Kenny Rodgers song. "Talk to him."

"Hell, I've tried to talk him into it for two years."

She waited.

"I'll talk."

He didn't have to leave the table. Ange was returning to make the rounds, shake his friends' hands, tell them he'd see them tomorrow and to give and take a look with each. "Riding up to

Norfolk to pick up our cruise boat tickets, first boat out," he said to Nan Twiford.

"You take care of yourself," she said.

"Slue," Cammie said.

Slue nodded and followed his friend out the door. When he came back he cried out, "Drinks for everybody and put it on my goddamn tab and I don't care if my engine stays laid up for a month!"

Cammie was out the door in time to see Ange's cream-color Lincoln pull onto the causeway road, which led across the bridge to the beach bypass to the upper bridge, which led back across the sound and north. He didn't peel out, he eased out, a worse sign, the tires not popping but squeezing gravel.

With close timing Police Chief Omie Marr rolled into the lot from the other direction and parked in Ange's space. Accompanied by a man whose suit and metal-rimmed glasses announced State A.B.C. Board, he ambled toward the entrance. "Got anybody watching the inside?" he asked Cammie.

"Me."

"Well now Ange has installed remote control. Is that in the manual, remote control?" he asked the A.B.C. man, who didn't respond.

The wind had shifted to south-southwest and blowing up the sound and across the marsh and the road smelled of oyster mud, bad fishing and false spring. For the how manyeth time, Cammie wondered, am I wishing I had a boat lying off the breakwater? She stayed at the Only Bar only because of Tish and Ange, who couldn't run the place without her and were her best friends.

Ange's Lincoln always gave Cammie the impression of riding in a space capsule. The quiet and casualness of handling, particularly in comparison with her Dodge van, approached no gravity. The radio tuned itself, its little eye bopping from station to station, its speakers turning guitars to harps. When she had her house, she wanted a livingroom as cozy as the Lincoln, as ideal for getting stoned in. Nearly every night Ange would say, "Let's go for a ride-around." They'd crawl up and down the beach road, pull off back of a dune, roll down the windows with the touch of a button, light up, listen to the waves. Ford Motor Company sold a line of automobiles whose purpose was to provide the rich with mobile livingrooms to get stoned in.

"Yea they're stoned all the time," Ange had agreed. He was. It suited his physiology, his gait and manner, his hospitableness, his chalky voice. On alcohol he used to wreck cars. On dope he glided, miles below the speed limit. They'd smoke, he'd talk about Tish and Del Benoit because if there was anybody he let inside anymore it was Cammie.

He wasn't rich, he just lived rich, in constant danger of being gill-netted by criss-crossing lines of credit in and out of town. The Only Bar—he despised the name, a result of his own neglect—was so in fact in winter aside from the Ramada Inn on the beach. The amount of cash spilling through screened him when he walked into a bank. People tended to believe in him, weak voice included. He'd taken a decomposing crabhouse, doubled the size, made tables and booths out of hatchcovers and sawed-up church pews, paneled it with barnwood, framed old pictures in rope—redneck, but tasteful redneck.

He didn't worry about money thus he was rich. He worried about Tish. Even at nineteen he'd known he'd never feel the same for anyone else. He'd tried stray but found it impossible to go more than once, once at night after which he pretended to pass out, once in the morning pretending she was Tish or nothing in the morning if he could sidestep. With her the thing seemed spring-loaded no matter how she treated him.

He wasn't redneck. Time and again he'd cut her slack. He'd kept his mind years ahead of the standards of Water County, educated it by dragging it to this and that cosmopolitan spot, ski resorts, San Francisco, Bermuda. People have to believe in each other's best interests, he liked to tell Cammie, who understood, act in good faith, help each other in trouble, talk and deal straight.

But with Del, Tish had fucked with him way beyond any maximum. He sat with his friends in his bar knowing, *knowing* that at that moment she was laying up with Del. Then he felt like a living fish on the gutting board.

On the mainland side of the upper bridge, turning up N.C. 158, he capped the thermos and lit a joint. Omie Marr himself back when they drank together gave him the gun he reached under the seat and slid into his pocket. Though he continued to drive languidly a determination set in, from button-down collar to Hush

Puppies, a cement that hardened from the inside out.

"Riding to Norfolk, riding to Norfolk."

"Now where do you suppose Ange's gotten to?" Omie Marr asked, directing his flashlight across the checked liquor bottles to make certain they were labeled with legal names, not Duke but Terrence H. Minton, not Chas or Razz but Charles O. Rollins.

"He went to buy plastic cups," Cammie said. She was keeping tabs on Timmy Spratt, a mean little scrapper whom Ange had barred a dozen times then put on probation a dozen. Omie and the A.B.C. man were going out of their way to avoid noticing the stranger. Normally Omie would have pumped the guy, offhand he thought, for some information about himself. Her worst nightmare was of having the bar closed down when she was on alone.

"Tell him I want to sit down with him," the Chief said.

"Oh, what for?" she asked, surprised at herself.

Omie appeared surprised too. It didn't take him long however to come up with, "Hallie across the road's complaining again about parking." Hallie Gaspar, who'd buried three full and several fractional husbands—among them Ange's daddy—had a fetish about parking, also about not using lights.

The A.B.C. man was fooling with a loose strip of paneling. Ange believed Omie, who held onto grudges tighter than the raffle tickets he preserved years past date of drawing, to be on a new tack. He'd never gotten an alcohol citation to stick, due to common sense and as everybody knew Del Benoit's political connections—no wonder Ange turned a blind eye, or put her up to her slutting. But there was no way a drug bust wouldn't stick.

Chas the Razz, having donned his Stetson and moved in on two women tellers from Planters Bank, was acting noticeably drunk, unusual for him, the noticeability. Omie cocked his head. "Girl, you know it's against the law to let anybody get drunk in a bar."

"I'll cut him off. Thanks. Did you gentlemen want anything to drink?"

"Yes m'am," the Chief said, "two waters."

For these the A.B.C. man dropped fifty cents on the bar and he and Omie proceeded to the door, slow.

Slue's wife called, he refused to talk. Cammie gave him the

message his dried-out chicken was going in the setter's bowl, a message intended to enrage him on the subject of a dog's esophagus and chicken bones. Cammie explained once again to Tobacco Ted how to spin quarters into the cigarette machine.

The Duke dragged Chas to the bar, told him to straighten out, right now and in general, ordered drinks and asked Chas if Cammie had ever described the special night they spent. "That was a real special night, wasn't it, darling? You never told Chas about that night, what went down, what kept on going down till the dawn's early light? Wasn't that one special night?"

"I guess it was."

"You know it was, darling, you know it was. Brother," he said to Chas, "brother, we got looned right on out, looned right on out to the *max.*" He brought his large, elegant, ruined head, loaded with energy, close to hers. Something about looking at the Duke resembled looking at the jukebox from too close up.

Chas ducked from under the Duke's arm and said, "I don't like you talking that way to my lady, she's too fine for that. She understands." He drew out *understands* to twice its length. "From the moment she stepped off the bus, even when she took up with my raggedy-ass brother, I saw she understood, understood everything, all the towns and the oceans and the winds of the soul, all the hopes and sorrows of the heart."

"Tell it, brother, tell it."

"You cocksucking liar."

"You blind son of a bitch."

"Cammie," Chas said, taking a breath, exhaling smoke, shaking his head as he lifted his eyes to hers and lifted his eyebrows like a hound's or a believer's in church. "Cammie," he said, and had to stop. He reached for her hand, shut his eyes as he pressed it to his lips.

"I wish I understood a few things."

"Don't give me that bullshit." A native of East Lake, Chas pronounced it boolshit. "Don't try and put that bullshit over on me. You're real. Cammie, you're real." Every time he said her name he shut his eyes.

Loaded with indecision, Budweiser and low-tar nicotine Tish Buthrell was zooming north on N.C. 158 towards Norfolk, empty bottles volleying beneath the pedals. The breeze boosted the horsepower of her 1968 Chevy, although with two warnings on her provisional license, good to and from work, she tried to watch the towns. She slowed to forty through the north end of Grandy, too many shadows under trees. Entering Barco she slammed on the brakes so hard the wheels almost locked—she'd remembered her cousin Nibbie's getting stopped there, past the Sunoco station. Outside town she tapped the brake pedal for stoplights.

She wasn't fooling herself. She knew what she was risking. People accused her of a self-destructive impulse; well now they'd have something to go on. At twenty-nine you are too young to spend your life dreading consequences. She wasn't cut out to be the devoted wife and mother three hundred and sixty-five days a year. Every now and then the human organism—she used Del's phrase—needed a little Mardi Gras like in New Orleans and those people are Catholics. She was risking the house, two years old, the longest brick house in Water County, everything in it, a good living, maybe even Warren though she doubted that. Warren could take care of himself but Ange couldn't take care of Warren.

But it was a damn good living, even if she had to kiss a few asses. She would kiss, she would slobber over Omie *Marr's* behind if that's what it took to make a living. And it was ever her, ever her lips sent on these missions, never Ange's lily-white kisser. He preserved his for preaching the brotherhood of the world. She had to fawn, she had to act gracious, my heavens. She supplied every other form of manpower too seven days a week, eleven a.m. to one a.m., ever there, ever hustling while Ange cut out with his buddies and stayed smoked up all his conscious moments. He supplied the ideas. Great, just great if there wasn't somebody to carry them out, talk to carpenters, talk to salesmen, mop, order, straighten the walk-in, hire and fire in summer, cook pizzas in the eight-thousand degree oven, collect tabs, return broken bottles for credit, feed a family on the quarters from the jukebox and cigarette machines. Right, they went skiing a couple weekends. What about the vacations he took by himself while she handled the bar, her and Cammie? He never finished a thing. Even the sign, the fifteen-hundred dollar sign saying Causeway Inn had remained in the crate so long the customers named the bar. In a week Ange spent at the outside ninety minutes in the place when he wasn't blowed out. She and Cammie carried the load.

Married at nineteen and seventeen they were supposed to settle each other down, a laugh. Ange hadn't settled, he'd merely gotten slower and stopped punching cops.

She realized she was putting her guilt onto him but he messed around, he took money from the register to gawk at Nan Twiford's puny tits, just because she didn't know jealousy didn't change that fact. She couldn't give up Del, didn't understand why she had to. Ange complained Water was too small for *his* ideas. Every woman loved more than one man but didn't do anything about it or did once or twice on the sly. Why should she care what people who'd bad-mouthed her all her life said? Why should he? They'd bad-mouthed him. Ange the sick drunk, Ange the dopehead, Tish the wildwoman. They couldn't live to please those blowfish.

She was no good at giving up. She'd tried with cigarettes, with beer, Lord knows with Del, sometimes going for weeks. Lucky nobody ever gave her heroin.

Ange would go crazy, break furniture and china, bash in the color set, lock her out of the house forever, rip her clothes and throw the shreds out the window, which is why she kept her best things, including her new dress for the Shrine Club dance, in the trunk. But he'd never find strength to give her up. Your nipples are like stethoscopes reading my heart, he'd croaked to her once.

How many more opportunities would Water County present her with? Her body was filling out, catching up with her frame. Her complexion aged two years for every one in the cigarette smoke of the bar, that tannery.

She figured she'd stop at a filling station before Norfolk to comb her hair, as she drove with the windows wide open.

"Riding to Norfolk." Ange couldn't decide if he wanted to overtake her or not, a far-fetched notion to begin with considering the rate she drove unless she broke down, a more likely notion, a habit. He didn't know if he could trust his hands once he snatched her out. She'd be cussing, hitting at him, as a damn joke, squealing like he'd nabbed her in nothing more than hide-and-seek. I knew you'd chase after me, she'd say, I wanted you to, she'd say, and try to thrust her pelvis against his. I'm coming home, I was planning to turn around come home if you didn't catch up. She'd tilt her head, relax her mouth for him.

Staying laid on back was definitely the right idea. The little eye on the fuel gauge started blinking and while there was plenty to reach Norfolk he turned in at a Sav-Mor self-service filling station, one pump under one light in the middle of nowhere. Fallow tobacco fields all around, a creek to the west flagged by trees. The breeze rustled his flat hair, which hung in front of his face as he fed bills. Looking toward the creek he thought he saw flashlights moving between trees, coon hunters. He'd taken Warren duckhunting, he and Del had a couple years back, but never to Stumpy Point after animal.

Steering with a wrist he passed the stores and early-to-bedder houses of Succutuck County. Reflecting his headlights in stale flashes they put him in mind of plywood tombstones.

His heart became a drum, a tub bass, a whole rhythm band of injury. For long stretches he set his vision on automatic pilot, went blind to everything but his own separate life, him, alone, in a space capsule—as Cammie called it—free, white and thirty-one, money in his pocket, credit cards, dope under the dash, full tank of gas and no reason to stop short in Norfolk, no reason not to go on to D.C., N.Y.C., Montreal.

An old pickup passing him brought his attention back to the road. He was entering Grandy. He entered Grandy as a gentleman but free. No reason was the best reason with a gun.

Coasting out of the north end of town he saw a phone booth, one phone with one light in the middle of nowhere.

Cindy Spruill flew off the barstool.

"Chas!" Cammie said.

Chas threw his hands up like a basketball player showing he didn't foul. "I brushed her by accident, I swear. Cammie, you know I couldn't hurt her back, even a heartsick old man like me"—he was forty-two—"couldn't injure a little girl"—she twenty—"who doesn't even comprehend the damage she does laying up with another man while I'm out on the goddamn, god-fucking sea working to where my arms grip the air in *sleep,* who doesn't even know I can see right through her pretty eyes, right into her soul when she walks in tells me she's been faithful to me."

The phone rang, wouldn't stop ringing. The Duke, everywhere at once, picked it up and nodded the receiver towards Cammie.

"I've got news for you," Tobacco Ted was saying, wiping foam out of his beard at the same time he missed the ashtray. "Damn you're a fine-looking thing, aren't you? What was your name?"

"Ted, how many times have you been in here? Cammie."

"Cammie, I've got news for you."

"How could I be blaming a little girl for failure to comprehend the passion of a man?" Chas asked.

Cindy, accustomed to hearing herself discussed, settled back next to him, straightened the collar of her blouse. "I'd lost my balance."

Cammie took the receiver. "Cammie, this is Ange." He always identified himself over the phone. "I don't suppose—Tish hasn't shown up or anything, has she?"

She considered lying but he'd be able to tell and anyway she couldn't face him were he to return and no Tish. He wouldn't get angry with her, she just couldn't bear the thought. "Not yet but really you know she could be anywhere."

"That's exactly my assumption I'm operating on. I meant what I said about closing, you know, if it gets too busy, or hell if it doesn't."

"It's already kind of busy. I wish you were here."

"I have to stick to priorities, for once. I guess I'll be seeing you."

"Well all right, Ange."

"You can search the whole world over," Tobacco Ted, retired from the Merchant Marine, was saying. "You can search the whole world over, and you will never find, a man, as sorry, as old Tobacco Ted. I'm telling you truth, you can search the whole world over."

"Aw, you're not so bad."

"I don't blame nobody for not liking old Ted," said Ted. "I hate him myself. But you can search the whole world over, but I've got news for you."

Thirty seconds later Ange called again. "Cammie, this is Ange. I forgot to tell you she's fired. I've fired her. Cross her name off the schedule, you hear me?"

"All right, Ange."

"Hard night, huh?" commented the narc, who insisted on coming on despite her obvious indifference, and nervousness now that R.L. was back, leaning, cap tight, into a group of mates at the middle table, making gestures that fell short.

"Normal," she said. She didn't let him light her cigarette, lit it from a bar candle.

The Duke cleared mugs out of the way and lay across to whisper at the level a bear might whisper, "I've got a little something for you, sugar darling, help you through the evening, little bit of fisherman's friend." He and Ange had gone partners on a few buys.

"Just shut up, okay?" She backed off, because of R.L. and because the Duke was liable to just stuff it in her hand.

"Check it out, check it right on out," he urged. He caught up with her emptying ashtrays and no longer pretending to whisper said, "It's some fine toot. My teeth are buzzed."

"The guy at the bar's a narc. Now you take anything you've got out to your truck and you leave it."

"The day anybody gets the balls to bust me is the day the damn geese grow balls."

"I'm not worried about you, I'm worried about the bar."

"Let me know when you can slip out and join me over my picture of Jesus."

At the table with Slue, Cal Quinley—once one of Ange's close friends now his blood enemy over rental of the Tourist Office—started chuckling, wheezing through his teeth rather. All Ange's enemies drank at his bar; he wouldn't stand for their not. When Del Benoit came in, Ange paid for his soda mixes, sat down with him, took him back to the office to indulge in the main thing they shared besides Tish, love of bullshit.

Cal grabbed Cammie around the butt. "One's a cocksucker, the other one's a whore and you love them both, don't you, girl?"

"I just want to keep the place open."

Del Benoit was sitting by the window on the fourteenth floor of the Holiday Inn, formerly the Triangle Hotel, his feet up on the air conditioning unit, a bottle of J&B in his crotch, a bucket of reamed ice cubes at hand. He looked down over the parking lots and church converted to a memorial for Douglas MacArthur and philosophized, which meant think about women—Woman, to be precise.

He maintained an apartment on the beach which nobody knew the whereabouts of, not his wife, not his men friends, not Tish. No telephone, only a CB transceiver. Two days a week in the off-season, or three, he holed up there, with a picture window out to sea, classical records, cases of J&B, two silk robes. Once he sent off for the complete Great Books for his hideaway. Twelve hours after their arrival, however, in the dead of night he'd packed the set in liquor boxes and dropped it at the county library without identification. "Bequest of the Delbert R. Benoit Memorial," read the endpapers, which pleased him, the librarian's knowing both his brand and his liver.

At age fifty he prided himself on having finished with the sex of life, the ins and outs of making money. He'd sweated blood to turn his brine-eaten frame inn into the landmark of what passed for hospitality. The middle class checked into the new brick places, eating fried oysters. The rich stayed in wood, dining on them raw. He'd knocked down walls, torn up floors, poured cement—him and the Duke—laid tile, added two wings in the old style. For fifteen years he'd given up liquor, gone stone dry from Memorial to Labor Days inclusive. This season he could afford to stand pat, didn't need to sacrifice a thing, except Tish, and she was merely the goad of all philosophy, the illumination of all liquor, the harmony of the sex not of life but of sex.

The Norfolk Holiday was the hotel, this the room that had worked the cure for alcohol fifteen years straight.

His wife couldn't have cared about his philandering nor he about hers. She saw some guy from Elizabeth City, some travel agent or arts director—whatever, he always had a mouthful of Lifesavers, and a pocketful of Del's money, which also he could have cared about. Maybe if he concentrated on his waitress from Greensboro College, made a fool of himself, he could transfer his feelings for Tish, not to the girl but to the making a fool of himself.

Granted he and Tish burned coal in bed. Granted she loved him for the unpredictability, the risk while loving Ange for real. In the beginning this had been his comfort. He'd preferred second fiddle, confirming as it did his theory that Woman is not basically polygamous but a fine tuner of monogamy.

Yet now. Yet now, occasionally, he and Tish would be ambushed in an embrace that sailed and sailed beyond every attempt at philosophy and he wondered if his life hadn't been a lie and if there had not been some moment when he didn't notice a face he was meant to stay very near the rest of his days.

Once or twice he'd tipped his hand, exposed his bleary dreams to the laser gun of hers. And she hadn't fired, she'd cried. Then fired.

He considered calling room service to remove his telephone but decided if he could keep liquor around to serve guests when he was on the wagon he could keep a damn phone in his room.

"Cammie, this is Ange."

"Where are you?"

"Coinjock. Sounds busy in there."

"Well I could use some help."

"What that means is she hasn't shown."

By now Cammie thought she could lie once, but never twice—when he asked to speak with Tish she'd have to tell him she was out buying ice at the Fishing Center or something, the ice maker had broken down again: making three lies. "Haven't seen her but I was hoping you'd take the hint. Everybody's in a hassling mood tonight, the Chief's on the prowl, Hallie's hot, Pook and Eljay waded in and I don't know about this narc."

"Seems to be a long way to Norfolk."

"Are you buzzed?"

"Like a bitch."

"You think you know what you're doing. I hope you don't end hating yourself."

"I'm neutral about myself."

"You're assuming."

"How about it."

Eljay raised two fingers, two three-quarter-inch dowels, for him and his partner Pook, captains out of Wanchese, huge, gray, gabardined men who when drunk lost consciousness wide awake without dropping any of their guard. Loose, they became less than animal but more than ordinarily dangerous to other animals. They didn't stagger or slur; they rarely talked. In slow motion they raised Luckies to their lips and barely seemed to drag although the ash burned with amazing evenness. They were like juniper trunks washed up on the shore, with depth charges inside.

"We ain't looking for no trouble," Eljay said when Cammie set the Blue Ribbons down.

"Of course you aren't, Eljay." He hadn't been home as his crew for the most part had, still smelled.

His cigarette took a good ten seconds to describe a perfect arc to the ashtray. "We come in to have a good time."

"That's right, I know you did."

"No trouble."

"Why would there be any trouble?"

"You can search the whole world over, but I've got news for you. Nobody likes old Ted, and I don't blame them. He'll do anything in the world for you but nobody likes him. They know he's no damn good on the inside."

"Shut him up," Eljay said. "We don't want to."

"Ted," Cammie said, wiping around his ashtray, "could you cool it a little while? You're sort of getting on people's nerves."

"See what I tell you. Nobody likes Ted."

"Getting on somebody's nerves doesn't mean they don't like you. People in love get on each other's nerves."

"You can search the whole world over, and you will never find, a person, in love."

"Possibility of getting another Heineken down here?" called the narc.

"Slim."

In the darkness Cammie relied on a sort of radar to track troublespots, an installation in the back of her mind that was constantly scanning, lighting up corners and groupings of bad energy. Tonight the screen had been busy but the blips hadn't come with the timing and density that signalled alarm. With Pook and Eljay there they brightened, quickened. Ange's departure had left an uneasiness in the back. The first night ashore drew the worst out of fishermen. The Chief, the narc and R.L. added to the strain, hers anyhow, as did the Duke, who never looked for trouble but was careless. Sides wouldn't prove that important, simply the existence of an excuse.

"There's them in here don't like us," Eljay said, or Pook—she couldn't tell which—causing Ted to turn his head with interest. Eljay or Pook was referring to Slue and his crew. Pook had pistol-whipped Slue's fifteen-year-old son off Cape May, left him in such shape the mate had radioed a helicopter to carry the boy to the hospital. Cammie didn't think Slue, hot-headed as he was, would give Pook the chance to settle the matter outright—he'd bided his time for months—but tonight she couldn't tell.

"Everybody's got people who don't like them."

"Ain't looking to start no trouble. You keep trouble clear of us, hear?" She not only couldn't see a mouth move, she couldn't see eyes under the brims of their caps.

The runners on the righthand cooler were getting stickier and stickier. She reached under the register for Crisco.

"That your boyfriend just left?" the narc wanted to know.

"Sort of." She knew exactly why he'd left, so he could sneak back and catch her leaning on the bar talking to the narc or letting the Duke hang on her while he whispered in her ear.

"You ever go out with anybody else?"

She narrowed her suspicion to the guy's fastidiousness, his pressed workshirt with the cuffs rolled back twice, his gold watch, his long hair hanging just so, the way he wiped the condensation off the bar with his napkin. Then she knew his background. It was that air that stayed with a guy forever, that scent he can never bathe, drink or smoke off, the Lysol of the service. She figured Army intelligence. "I try not to go out with anybody."

"You know, that's a crushing damn disappointment. Literally. I was developing this crush on *you*."

"Anybody develops interest in me's asking for trouble."

"Do you mean you're a heartbreaker or do you mean your boyfriend's a hard customer?"

"I mean I'm fucked up from head to toe."

Startled he spread his arms, smiled, causing a pendant to swing into view on his chest, a little gold cross.

"Shouldn't you be wearing a pair of those?" Cammie asked. Most nights she possessed stamina to burn but R.L. sucked it out of her. She took a bottle of Visine from her pocketbook. On the job she chain-smoked herself but by eleven the smoke, combined with the effort of keeping her radar focused, put embers in her eyes.

The phone—Del's disguised voice, which he disguised by talking timidly and accenting the wrong syllables or words. "May I please speak to Tish Buthrell?"

"Del, look—" She was sniffling with the Visine.

"Cammie? Cammie, tell Tish I want to speak to her but tell her don't say a word, I can't take the sound of her voice."

"She's not here, she—"

Before she could explain he hung up actually moaning.

Taking off from a crossroads where all four directions looked identical, scruffy trees, bumpy pavement, everything a dead shade of blue-gray, Ange was pitying her for her limitations. Every direction was a reflection in the rear-view mirror until the one in front backed down, resumed three dimensions. He hadn't turned, he swore he hadn't. She didn't know how to insert a split-second of thought between the information and the response. Because she lacked concentration she worked five times as hard as necessary. She had two phases, laziness and craziness, nothing in between, the one as full of deceit as the other.

He pictured her lying across the bar exposing the tops of her squashed breasts, dying for customers, talking to some old drunk like Tobacco Ted, rambling as if falling asleep word by drowsy word. Then in a heartbeat up strongarming some two hundred and fifty pound sea captain out the door.

Through the years the thing he'd longed for was stretches of plain and lingering tenderness. The minute you believed you had one, were safe, it dawned on you she was laughing up her sleeve.

Was that what that lard-ass drunk was able to draw from her, patient attention?

He assumed she'd reached Norfolk by now, was rapping on the door, making some teasing remark. Del might put on a show of turning her away but he enjoyed his weaknesses too much to hold out, especially if he was drinking. No if about it. He'd see her face lit up with beer, he'd see that shiny dress, the highheels she changed into in the parking lot—she wore deck shoes to drive—he'd see those eyes making fun of the situation. They were laughing, guzzling booze, going to it. He didn't delude himself they were laughing specifically at him but they were letting out some kind of giggle that shriveled his balls.

Try a little tenderness—that's what he'd say as he popped them.

He lit another joint to maintain the cool the job required, the feeling of being just another part of the Lincoln, an interior power accessory registering neither wind nor road. He took an uphill curve, flew across a little bridge. The headlights picked out a pinto pony, a beautiful thing, standing against its shed by the fence. Goddamn, he thought, goddamn beautiful peaceful animal, full of wisdom. It doesn't matter to him, my popping them.

The trees thickened up, met over the road. Branches whipped closer and closer in the slipstream. Maybe he did turn wrong. This wasn't far from skiing, nearly out of control toward the top of one range then sort of waxing into the next speed, the higher the speed the truer the aim. He knew damn well the road lay level here but it seemed to be falling away. He was through the next crossroads before he saw it come, before the flash that lasted in the car for miles like red perfume. The tons of vehicle rode on a single blade, perfectly balanced.

He'd better slow down, he was thinking when he crested a hill and five full pints of blood shunted to his head.

R.L. loved to see her wash mugs, for although not a native or sturdy looking she knew how to work as well as anybody. He wanted to press his face to that spot on her shoulder, get a faceful of both shoulder and hair, the one spot of her she couldn't drain of heat no matter how she tried. "I mean, couldn't we get together after closing and sit down and talk? Here, even, here's fine."

"It would be the same conversation. It's not what we say to each other, it's the sameness that drives me up the wall."

One in each hand, onto the brushes, right, left, she could wash those mugs. "I did wrong last time, but when a man finds his woman—" With her wrist she brushed back a couple reddish-copper hairs.

"We were *talking*. Damn it, this is what I mean. Never anything different, never the slightest thing changed. That's what'll drive me away from here, not what people do, the sameness of the doing."

"I bought some Thai sticks off Bud Loring. We could sit at the bar after we close."

"No!" She looked around the corner to the front, squinting out of the light over the sink. "You'll drive me right out of Water County."

"Cammie, I'm making a shitload of money. I'm saving three-fourths. I'll have enough for a downpayment, you know? Bud told me about this house on the soundside, you know, we might run by check out some time." His hands had caves in them where her hips were supposed to fit.

"I've got to get change."

Warren was lying on the office floor with sticks of wood, Eveready batteries, strips of bellwire around him, his head on a stack of placemats. He had Ange's straight black hair, Tish's wide mouth and eyes.

"Damn I thought I had a hard road," R.L. said. He spread his coat over him. Cammie admitted there was a sweetness to R.L.'s voice at times, to him, misplaced in this case.

When she shut the door to block out the jukebox, the high notes, Warren woke.

"What are you doing, boy?" R.L. asked.

"R.L., you like World War II?" He copied Ange's muffled tone.

"Yea."

"Look what Hammerhead gave me." He took a khaki tin of C-rations out of his jacket; he'd been sleeping on the thing. "Check this out."

"That's all right."

"Did you read it?"

"Yea, U.S. Army."

"I mean all of it."

"It says what's in it," Cammie put in.

"There's a chicken in here."

"Well not a whole chicken," R.L. said.

"There is."

"They took the bones out."

"Yea of course they took the *bones* out. Hell."

"That's really an all right thing to have."

"How much you give me? It's quite valuable, genuine World War II."

"A thirty-year-old chicken," Cammie said. "Thirty-one."

"It's still good."

"How much you asking?" R.L. said.

"Five dollars."

"Holy shit."

"Think how much a museum like in Norfolk'd give me."

"I think Hammerhead meant you to keep it for yourself," Cammie said. "He'd be upset if you sold it."

"I can do anything I want with it."

"He'd be upset."

"If he cared he wouldn't give it to me."

"Warren, I'm calling your grandmomma, see if she's home. R.L.'ll run you over there, all right?" She was asking R.L.

"I don't give a shit. I just hitchhiked from there."

"You got some mouth on you," R.L. said.

Warren cocked his head, bobbed it. "You got a ugly fucked-up mouth on you. Your mouth makes me sick to my stomach."

"Warren," Cammie said, "you ready to go back to your grandmomma's?"

"Yea, I'll sleep on the beach. I always sleep on the beach."

"You don't watch your mouth, boy, you'll be sleeping on the bottom of the sound. I'll pitch you out crossing the bridge."

"R.L., for God's sake."

"I like to see you pitch me out, you candyass, you old nerd."

"I better not see that new guy when I get back," R.L. told Cammie, his muscles betraying bad wiring. "I see him, his face is his ass."

"I've got to get back out front. I'll call from there."

At the bar she lit a Marlboro and pretended she didn't catch anybody gesturing or hear anybody call her name. She took partial consolation from Timmy Spratt's having left, unless he was in the john. Running out from the back, arms full, Warren asked, "You see any extra batteries around here?"

"Nope."

At the door R.L. transmitted a final message to assure her she wasn't putting anything over. At first she thought he was going to give her the finger; then she realized what dredged up wasn't anger but pain, so pure it shone.

Her mother had tried to help her father. A total drunk—Chas the Razz given ten years—visibly yellow, he used to grab her, and Cammie if handy, around the legs like timber after a shipwreck, convincing her mother he would kill himself if she divorced him.

At nineteen Cammie drove trucks for a construction company in Hampton Roads. The practical fact was R.L. didn't do it for her anymore and knew this but couldn't understand the last remedy in the world was harder.

Tish, southbound on N.C. 158, experienced a close call passing a groggy farmer up a hill. It reminded her of the beach when all the waves stop at once and silence falls heavier than lying underneath surf. She skinned by, thanks to the farmer's diddling, her reflexes and the big-ass Lincoln's lurch at the last moment but the incident persuaded her virtue didn't pay either. It was over too fast to fix the color of the Lincoln, yellow, maybe cream. If Ange *had* pursued her, he wouldn't have gotten this far at his usual fifty.

She had turned around. She'd stopped at a closed filling station, combed her hair in pump chrome and without fully deciding when she pulled out, pulled out south. She couldn't give up the work she'd plowed into the bar, not for one night when Del might spring something like not let her in or let her in to see some naked prostitute with scotch dribbling off her tits.

From now on she'll be goody-goody for the most part. Three beers per night, no speed—it wasn't beer, it was those little doozies when they overshot. Once in a blue moon she'll see Del. He'll never quit. "Don't talk, just listen," he'd said this afternoon. "I'm not telling you where I am (as if everybody didn't know). I'm telling you it's got to be over. Next time we're friends, mutual friends of Ange. We're on his side. I don't mean to deny nothing, try to prove nothing. We're historical friends, a couple of damn philosophers." She'd taken a breath. "Don't be heartless, breathing."

Coming to the bridge north of Grandy her headlights scared piss out of a pony by the side of the road, made him toss and paw.

The spies will carry no tales. She'll keep her legs ever crossed, her laughter ever low, perch on her twenty-nine-year-old hips like they are forty-nine, finish cleaning rooms, serve meals of something other than pizzas heated over. With the customers she'll let loose but stay this side of the line. No tight clothing. More time with Warren to prevent him from turning into another mumbling conniver. If only their skulls didn't have the same peanut shape.

She'll phone Cammie from the next booth. What would she do without that girl? She loved to see her driving her van, with not an expression on her face, not seeing anybody, not acknowledging a honk or wave, just sitting up there horsing the wheel, shifting gears, cutting corners, eyes miles down the road, just flying in that big blue van.

Omie Marr stalked minors, making sure nobody had gone to the bar, ordered mixed drinks and carried them to a table where a minor, just off a boat, sat with a warm beer sneaking hard liquor. Chas had sent Cindy home, sobbing, wailing out the door, which Cammie knew led to reconciliation, hopefully before the wop made the mistake of wandering in. Teresa Sawyer was waiting for her ex-husband to wander in with his girl from College Park, meanwhile staying near enough a man, any man, to cuddle and lick when he did. Slue, Quinley, the Nunemakers, Carl Peasley (County Dogcatcher, a political job thanks to Del) waited. Pook and Eljay, on their eighteenth Blue Ribbons—they raised their bottles slow but had to raise each only once or twice—were waiting and not waiting.

Even the Duke seemed to have entered anticipation, letting his women talk to each other.

Deucey Nunemaker dragged a plastic trash bag of scallops to the bar; in his best ladies' man style, blond, woozy, and sharp-eyed, asked Cammie to cook.

"Everything's off," she said. She couldn't deny he made her think how pretty his arms must be, the armpits too, full of cords and knots. He could dance.

"I want to give some to everybody."

"I can set them in the walk-in till tomorrow."

"I give that little girl, my little neice, two thousand dollars for a car for school and she never come back. I don't blame her for not liking old Ted."

Cammie didn't have to make up her mind about trying to call Del. He called; starting off sounding like a sick old chinaman, one of those you saw coming downstairs to Granby Street in Norfolk whom R.L. always wanted to ask for opium.

"God, Cammie." A native of Hatteras, he pronounced it Gawd. "You're good people, Cammie. Someday you'll turn into the lovely, heartful woman you're meant to be, I have faith you will. Just talk with me and don't put your bosslady on the line."

"Isn't she with you?"

"God no, our race is run. I've wanted to tell you how much I valued your putting up with us so long."

"She left here two hours ago."

"Don't tell me that. Don't tell me the black widow's still on the feed. Do you know why I call her the black widow?"

Her hearing went not long after her sight. She knelt behind the cooler, put a hand to her open ear. "You've told me." A thousand times.

"She doesn't know my room."

"Del, I want to tell you something but you have to give me a double promise. I mean promise for now and for when you're sober."

"I wish I could get drunk."

"You'll never say where you heard."

"If I wasn't true to anybody I'd be true to you. I don't need to promise to promise to you."

"Ange is on his way to the Holiday with his gun."

"Don't tell me that."

Cammie's radar picked up flashes so vivid she stood to look: Thad Scarborough strolling in with his new wife, a woman Slue Swain ran with prior to the marriage and Thad, the major buyer at the docks, was an associate of Pook and Eljay's—they and his daddy until his death last year welding high tackle made a trio—and why was Slue hanging around, why hadn't he gone home at his usual hour? Was all he was waiting for news of Ange?

"He's got his .32."

"Well that changes the lineup."

She knelt, caught a whiff of the sour beer that collected under the coolers, the marsh mice's swimming pool, the roaches' watering hole. She expected crabs to crawl out. "Del, get to another hotel. Now."

"I don't run scared."

"It's not scared," she began, then cussed herself for repeating that word with a drunk.

"In my life I've run blind, I've run ragged, I've run one-legged but I've never run scared. Does the mate of the black widow spider turn tail? He waits, fucking waits—excuse my French. That is his grace, and honor."

"I want to see you walking in here again."

"I carry a gun."

"Lord."

"I'd best get it out of my Dopp kit. You're good people, Cammie, damn solid people."

She went to wait on Thad and Ruelle although Thad, the perfect gentleman—to a point—when out with his wife, his prize, a woman his daddy would have taken to, always came to the bar to save her. She determined his and Slue's tables were ignoring each other, presenting backs and no glances. The Nunemakers showed the extra voltage more than anyone else. "When you going to cook scallops? We got butter," Slue said. "We want to share with our neighbors yonder."

"Call for you, sweetheart," the narc said at the bar.

"So how you doing," stated Tish over an excellent connection.

"Where are you, lady?"

"Oh I come over to see this girl who babysits, ask her to sit for Shriners."

"Warren needs a babysitter now?"

"Well I was sort of on the road to Norfolk. Damn it's dark outside this booth."

"Ange is driving up with his gun, Del's waiting with his."

"You're kidding me!" She attempted to drop to a somberer note. "When did he leave?"

"Half hour after you did."

"I'd better turn around."

"You'd better get here as fast as you can. If you show at the Holiday, Ange'll never believe why. Besides I can use some help."

"You don't imagine those two nerds'll do anything!"

"Hurry. Don't stop for beer."

"Where's a place *open*?"

"We'll call from here."

Two fingers from Eljay, one stub—the rest lost to a weeded screw—from Ted. The narc, pouring his third Heineken in two hours, was saying, "You know there's one thing I like as much as I like an attractive woman. You know what that is?"

"I don't care to."

"You'd never guess."

"I hope that's right."

He checked around. "Cocaine," he said. "Co, caine. And when I look at you I understand every toot I've taken had you in it. You know, I seem to come across a few passes on the old railroad."

"In your line of work you mean."

That gave him pause. "I've got a lot of lines of work."

The Duke, in full sail after a trip to the john, cut in and swung her away from the bar. "Won't you slip out with me for a minute, sugar darling? It breaks Jesus's heart not to share. Here, just to see you through the next couple hours, turn these ugly faces to angels, turn this bullshit into something you can listen to. Sneak on back to the office, sneak right on back, sugar. I'll handle all aspects out here."

She jammed it back in his pocket, which wasn't easy to locate under his Mexican shirt, his new and only style, comfortable on the belly. The narc was watching and R.L. was watching.

I suppose I've always been an extravagant man, Del Benoit thought, listening for her or his footsteps in the hall, fishing the last cubes from the water. He blamed alcohol, which as scientists claimed and he could substantiate destroyed braincells. What they hadn't discovered was alcohol didn't kill the sex cells of the brain but tumorized them, swelled them, pushed them out of every orifice.

Any one of those cars . . . footsteps; too far apart to be hers, with her center of gravity, too distinct for Ange. Intent on murder Ange would still shuffle.

He appreciated the effect of suspense on philosophy.

The candle on the back table melted a hole in Deucey's scallop bag and what seemed like gallons of milky juice ran on the floor, mixing with spilled beer, slippery as snot. Mop in hand, Cammie answered the pay phone.

"God, Cammie, how badly of me do you think for this?"

"If you're still at the Holiday not very highly."

"This is my bed and I'm laying in it, next to it to be precise, slipping shells in my little pistol, ready to frap if Ange noses in the door."

"Catching some long *dis*tance shit tonight, aren't you, darling?" the Duke wanted to know.

"Are you clean? I mean it, are you?"

"Everything but my head, and that's where it's all happening."

"I wish."

Slue rushed past, meaning to plug in the deep fat for scallops, unaware Cammie had thrown the circuit breaker.

"You heard us, did you?" Eljay said.

"Riding *in*to Norfolk, *in*to Norfolk"—by Ange's calculation the trip had lasted a half hour over. The drizzle continued as the Holiday Inn hove into sight. If there was any flaw to the Lincoln it was that the wipers had picked up a hum, which didn't disturb them in their sweeping, their near vacuuming of droplets but nettled him. In the way he sometimes became paralyzed on a vacation, he worried over action outside of Water County, where the checks and balances of private violence protected you. City laws, with ethnics to control, overlooked human rage and error, washed these into the gutters to keep the streets passable. His friend from boyhood Malcolm Sedgwick was the best lawyer in Water but what if he clutched in a city courtroom? Ange was looking at seven years before parole, seven years without so much as touching a woman.

There was only one woman for him anyway, and no reason to predict his lying down and dying after the act, not with D.C., N.Y.C. and Montreal calling his name, or alias.

He parked on yellow lines by the entrance. He took three or four tokes to clear the brain. With a hundred-dollar bill he took a toot of cocaine up each nostril to clear the muscles. A sort of electrical current dropped down his spine, electrical but liquid in that it pooled in his balls and sloshed as he got out and swung the door. In case he exited in a hurry he didn't lock. He didn't need to cut off the lights, which extinguished themselves after a passage of time. The night air, amazingly thin despite the rain, revealed seaweed and motor oil both in one sharp scent.

Across acres of thin carpet he approached and approached the desk, thinking midway that it stood too high, only his head would clear. He was aware he trailed disturbance. Suddenly he had to raise his hands to brake the forward motion. The desk hit belt level, covered the gun pocket. The dropped ceiling and angled wood converged on the blotchy, clever face of the night clerk, like faces Ange recalled from Las Vegas.

"How you doing this evening," Ange said. "Could you please— I'm here to see Del Benoit, friend of mine. What room's he in anyway?" He fingered the rolled-up bill while with his deportment dismissing any difference between monied caller and graveyard shift employee. They were twins, equal princes of night.

"Sir, I'm not permitted to give out the information."

"Shit I forgot to write it down, my own damn fault, as usual."

"We have instructions from the party."

He watched the clerk's hands as he notated cards and the clerk noticed he was watching his hands. They breathed each other, Ange through his iced nose breathing hairspray and a touch of Columbian, thinking the clerk breathed Lincoln heat and the same.

"You know who I'm talking about? Damn, I tell you, do they have freon running in this ceiling? I feel a draft."

"Sir, I understand this interior was stripped from an old wrecked rocketship discovered on Loft Mountain, in the Blue Ridge."

"I believe it. To tell you the truth I decorate with junk myself." He unrolled the bill.

"Please don't try that."

A few white flakes hit the blotter. "Squirrelly little sucker, legs like toothpicks, thick glasses, likes to mess with other men's wives."

The clerk twisted a turquoise ring on his fourth finger. "As I say, I can't give out the information. Obviously he forgot he asked a friend to call. You're free to look around, of course. Perhaps he'll be coming out of his room to go to an ice machine. There's one on the fourteenth floor for example. Perhaps luck will bring you together."

Ange understood he was to take his money back. He headed for the elevators, a lineup of the straightest faces he'd ever seen. Yessir, one said. "With you in a second," Ange said, having spotted the phone booths. Five times he got a busy signal before giving up on Cammie.

At the western end of the upper bridge, twenty miles shy of the Only Bar, Tish vowed never take their records off. Ange hadn't changed records in so long anyway the new were sliding all over the office, cracking underfoot. Once in a blue moon Del'll mosey over and punch "Try As I Might" or "Leaving You's the Easiest Thing (Since Leaving Town)." She'll mosey back and select "Crazy" or "Torn Between Two Lovers" or "Let's Just Kiss and Say Goodbye." He'll drink another scotch, tell the crew he has business at the courthouse, wander down to the dock phone, which lacks a booth. She'll answer in the office—not the first couple calls, Cammie can take those. She'll answer, speaking to the Sandler Foods man, asking time of delivery. She won't show. Next morning flowers will appear on the backbar. Next afternoon Del'll disappear to catch football practice at the school. She'll answer, whispering, hearing mostly wind from his end. These conversations amounted to reading lips over salty telephone wires.

Ange was locating the door by intuition, strolling up and down the hall waiting for one to communicate. From sitting in blinds together he knew the man's life, breath and sweat (part Ivory soap, part J&B). He'd eliminated two legs of the triangle and the inner wall by assuming Del would choose a view but not the sea—he had one of those from his secret pad up the beach. A view of melancholy, the parking lots, the church. He played the kids' game, You're getting hotter, You're burning up. Sooner or later a door would change from wood to skin to oilskin.

It was probably, but didn't matter, Acey Nunemaker who started chucking scallops. It might have been Slue, but all in all he'd been sitting pretty quiet for him. Whoever, they aimed at selected targets at first, Tobacco Ted, the Duke, R.L. at the middle table, all of whom took it all right, even R.L. It was definitely Acey who dumped the bag, got everybody chucking, aiming they claimed for bottles, candles, caps, apologizing for misses. The radar lit up like Christmas. Still, tempers stayed unnaturally cool unnaturally long. The hit threw back, Acey and Slue back and forthed, people threw scallops, ate scallops raw, slipped and fell on scallops until the pile was exhausted and they had to pick them off the floor, which worsened by the second—juice, drinks, boot mud, rain under the door, the leak from the men's urinal—floated cigarette butts.

"You sorry sucker!" Chas yelled at nobody in particular. "I'll whip all your asses!"

It didn't matter who yelled. People heard what they wanted to from the mouth they wanted to.

"Shut your jellyfish, toadfish, all-mouth mouth!" the Duke yelled.

"Shut it, candy-ass!" Somebody else.

"Goddamn right, I'll shut it tighter than your asshole!" Somebody.

"Come get old Ted! Put Ted out of his misery!"

Cammie wasted no time turning the lights up and getting to the back before scallops hit Thad Scarborough's table and he and Slue were on their feet and primed.

"I've wanted a piece of your ass so long I can taste it." Thad's hair flung in fishbooks across his forehead.

"Just because you can't satisfy her after a real man, that's a hard road, ain't it boy?"

"Thad, please," Ruelle pleaded, cracking her rosy makeup with the effort.

"Ready to take this outside, you all?" Cammie said.

Sides chose up. Pook and Eljay, who'd taken time to finish their twenty-first beers, were moving.

"Watch yourself, Cam, watch yourself," R.L. kept saying. He tried to stand in front of her but she wouldn't let him. She thought her two scraps of authority—that she was a woman and had the power to bar a person from the only actual bar in the county—might save things yet. Too, she counted on Slue to ease back finally, since against these odds to do so would count more as judgment than cowardice among the opinions that mattered. Not a man in the bar could be provoked to go against a black man, for example.

"She made her choice."

"And been regretting it ever since ain't you, Ru? Ain't you, baby?"

The screen blipped the Duke slipping out the back. Teresa hung on Chas; he shook her off. R.L. shed his coat, rolled his sleeves.

Pook and Eljay moved with the force, the listlessness of naval cruisers on the sound. They flipped the tables, kicked the chairs to either side without fury, rather as a service, as if clearing for a dance.

Slue climbed up on his chair, Thad up on his upholstered pew, and the air between them transformed into hull steel.

"You been begging to have yourself mangled."

"Damn if that ain't so," said Eljay, whose statement carried as easily as over diesel engines.

Cammie put her left hand to Slue's beltbuckle, her right to Thad's. "Outside," she said. "Omie Marr's shut down every other, you want this bar shut too?"

"I reckon I had her more ways than you ever will," Slue said. Next his chair sloshed out from under, he collapsed, and although the motion was the reverse of attack it was motion itself that triggered Thad. The table see-sawed. Pitchers shattered into icicles. The jukebox swung out from the wall like a toy, smashed into something, a second later sprayed colored glass and choked dead on the music. Suddenly you could hear the women around the edges cuss. Cammie crawled from under R.L., who'd thrown himself on top her, and wedged between Thad and Slue. Neither one hit her—they froze at sight of her—but she went down, from a combination of Pook and Eljay's vanguard and the footing.

When she came up she stopped everything.

Blood ran from her nose and from a gash in her hand—pulsed, didn't gush. She knew she was fine. Her nose bled all the time; the cut was clean, maybe off a wineglass. But working at speed her mind told her she ought to play this up. She rocked her head back so the blood spread over the lower half of her face; she raised her drenched hand in the pose of a prophet or Indian. "I don't mean the damn parking lot neither! I mean off this property completely!"

"Look at her—shame!"

"I don't care who I start on," R.L. gave notice.

Cammie shoved Slue to the door, slapping his chest, printing her cut hand, knowing he couldn't honorably resist.

"Outside'll go," Eljay said.

"I'm *turning* you inside out." Thad reached over Cammie to swing. She turned and beat on *his* chest.

"I'm waiting on you all parakeet dicks!" Slue said. "I guess me and Ange both settle tonight."

"Other side of the bridge!" Cammie yelled. "Beach Police!"

This surprised her: that Slue, dragging one moment the next was hopping out the door, with Acey, Deucey, Peasley, Chas and them bulling their way after him.

"Run, diarrhea, I'm on your tail!"

"Shut up, take care of this girl you injured," Ruelle said.

A ring of black smoke two feet in diameter wobbled in the door, firecrackers went off, and suddenly everybody inside knew what was happening. The Duke had backed his pickup to the door, was peeling out with Slue and the crew aboard.

"God*damn*!"

"This here's a island," Eljay said. He and his partners were the only ones not to take off running for the fastest cars in the lot, Quinley's stoked-out Ranchero, Merle Leekins's Bonneville.

Cecelia, Teresa and Alice clustered Ruelle, her hair sobbing around her head on the table, her orlon sweater sobbing on her back.

"You all too," Cammie said. She didn't mind showing no mercy. "Party's done."

"You're lightheaded," Alice said.

"I'm riding her over to the clinic," R.L. said, with the same frustration at missing the scuffle as missing a fuck. The clinic, the only doctor, was in Grandy.

"You aren't riding me. Go to my house and wait."

"Cammie, damn, you are lightheaded with loss of blood."

"The blood's nearly clotted. I'll be at my house in fifteen minutes. Don't let the cat out. If you don't listen I'll be so long gone you won't ever see, you won't dream of me again."

"Your blouse is soaked red."

"I promise you I won't."

She just wanted to get the door locked and herself out of there before the Chief returned and before she discovered what had happened to the narc. She remembered to cut off the hot dog steamer. Adrenalin ceased filling in for the missing blood. Threading her way out in the dark, slop coming over the tops of her sneakers, she noticed a wooziness, which explained her feeling sorry for Tobacco Ted pissing at the edge of the road, raising steam.

"Come on in, Ange, door's unlocked."

"Evening, Del. Wait, I'm—" Positive before, when the door seemed to go concave at his touch, Ange now thought he'd entered the wrong room. The face kept eluding him, kept twisting out of perspective. The details were right, chinese brocade robe, hairless chest, grinning bifocals, the target pistol in the hand. But the man was too small and flat and distant. Ange pivoted, thinking what he was facing was a mirror but pivoted to a reproduction of boys driving geese through woods and stream. He turned back, his eyes undeceived him. They deceived him, he saw this salesman in town to work a stall at a bathroom fixtures show, hardly somebody who could threaten his very being, hardly somebody who bore the prick that gave a woman whatever he could not. "Who warned you, Cammie? Hell I don't blame her." He stood at a multiple angle to Del, the bed and the vanity mirror.

"You tell *me,*" Del said.

He meant, You tell me if she's been here. If she'd been there Ange could have smelled her, sensed her the way when you're swimming a pocket of warmth will well up around your legs and chest. "She's in another room. I'll find her."

"Stop playing and give us the chance to prove ourselves."

If she'd set foot in that room the light from the polelamp would have changed. Ange gripped his gun so tight it turned waxy. He could scrape curls of metal off it with his thumbnail. "It don't make much difference she doesn't happen to be in here at the moment, or yet."

"You know what I'm thinking about with you ready to blow my head off? The riddle of the sphinx. What has four legs in the morning, two at noon, three in the evening."

"I've made up my mind, my mind's on ice. It's your prerogative to bullshit a while but why don't you work on what's real? You can goddamn empty that little twenty-two and not affect my aim."

Del placed the pistol on the air conditioning unit. "Would you take a drink with me?"

"I guess that's your prerogative. Glad to." He sat on the end of the bed, lifted the gun out and balanced it on his knee, accepted the bottle.

"Simplicity, that's what the goddamn riddle is about, the goddamn heartbreaking simplicity of the human organism. Did you ever have a dog that didn't want to romp and misbehave and eat and sleep and chase bitches? I ain't nothing but a hound dog. We ain't nothing but hound dogs."

"I never had a dog that married, raised a kid for ten years and built things. You never had a dog that bullshat."

"You never had a dog that didn't spend one night a week *howling* bullshit."

"You know what I'm thinking about after popping you? Riding to a brand new town, changing name and everything, finding people who deal straight and don't deceive and help each other live." He stood the bottle on the mattress in perfect balance.

"I appreciate your allowing me time."

"I'm waiting for a backfire."

After Cammie locked up, and loosened her hair, she headed straight for her van. When she was two strides from the door the narc, as she'd anticipated, walked out of the shed where they stored beer boxes.

"I've got a confession," he said, zipped up in his leather jacket.

"Make it to the seagulls. I don't enjoy standing in the rain."

"Two confessions. First, I'm a narcotics agent."

"Big surprise."

"Second confession, I want to spend some time with you, ride over to the beach, do a little coke, talk. Just talk. I won't try a single move."

"Let me pass." By the road Ted was warming his hands in his steam.

"Look, I can be heavy but I've got another side. Did you see the papers, five guys shot dead in Raleigh? That was my work in back of it. I'm out here mostly on a little r & r. The job doesn't have to be that important. We'll talk and I'll leave in the morning for Atlanta and that's it."

"Forget it."

"You sure you understand me? You're in the hotbox, baby."

She brushed past him, climbed in and pulled out of there. The narc, who was the one parked in front of Hallie's, pulled out behind her in his plain Plymouth without cutting his lights on.

She pushed to eighty, he stuck as if she was towing him across the bridge. Strut-strut-strut and boo-hoo-hoo, that was all for men, never a glimpse of middle ground and anytime you got beneath their talk all that really mattered was whether their woman fucked anybody else and would you fuck them. She mashed the accelerator, lit a Marlboro, planning her move a mile ahead. Her cut hand glued to the wheel.

The narc fell for it, drawing alongside and gesturing to the shoulder. Side by side they came up on Cuttlebone Junction, where the road split three ways, the bypass and beach road north, the cape road south, and there was a cement divider. She floored the gas then just as the divider appeared hit the brake. The narc peeled left but snaked past safely. At one second he was beside her, at two seconds he'd vanished, at three seconds he was in front jamming *his* brakes; his brake lights lit. But now she had steam and cut by him. He drew alongside, started tapping. She jockeyed from gas to brakes but he stuck, tapping, keeping the metal of the van in a shiver. Further up the bypass he began to bang, cinderblocks hitting, booming in the interior. Sand streamed across the road in a low fog, hissed underneath. Then a thunderclap—her right wheel jogged off the pavement and once into sand burrowed. The van knotted around the right front wheel.

She tossed her cigarette into the boxelders and stepped down, bringing the length of radiator hose R.L.'d intended to install. "You're really sick, man." She glanced back to appraise what damage she could in the backglow of the high-beams—some paint, a few dents, not too bad.

"You can't afford to stay nasty. We know the whole thing, the whirlybirds flying in from the trawlboats, landing in Ange's daddy's marshland."

"You're sick. That man can't organize the walk-in cooler. He can't decide where to stack Budweiser. You're out of your tree listening to Omie Marr. Ange dumped paint on his face on Water Street, that's the story if you're interested."

"We're doing us a job on Ange and Tish both if you don't reconsider. Come on, let's whiff a little, forget this."

"*Screw* yourself in the nose! You can all screw yourself in the noses!" Her hair, which sponged up the rain, puffed out as she whipped the big wire-wrapped hose so fast even he, with his experience, couldn't catch hold. He didn't lose his cool; he protected his face, stayed cool. "Baby, you just screwed your friends."

"I don't have friends."

Also, assuming the van started, she didn't have anywhere to run next—she'd rather face the narc than R.L.—except back to the Only Bar.

Ange told him, "Your bullshit comes out of your mouth like nickels and dimes out of a coin changer. Your mouth keeps shifting from here to here to here. You can't hit ducks, you sorry fool, you can't hit when you talk. They slither out and plop." He pictured him chucking himself all over her, tonguing the sweat she produced in pints. The room felt like a mausoleum already when the bathroom door yawned behind him, not a cop, not to release a cop but to give him space to move and fire in.

That the door was unlocked made Cammie wonder but she'd come to no conclusion by the time she was deep in the bar going for the phone, to call Del's room or the State Police, she didn't know anymore. She avoided overturned tables and chairs, she avoided bottles and pitchers, in the pitch blackness she avoided all obstacles until she ran full tilt into something: someone, flesh and arms so familiar yet scary she backed up her mind, retraced the last steps before deciding it was real and ought to be screamed at. Sweat, beer and perfume; rain, blood and shampoo—she and Tish collided, recoiled, collided and held on.

"Lord scare me to death," Tish said. Tugging Cammie's hair she clamped her closer.

"Don't."

"Where are you going? What happened? Why didn't you clean? What's all over this floor?"

"We have to call the Holiday Inn."

Bright blue bats winged one after another through the porthole in the door, followed by hammering.

"Open the damn door!" Omie Marr called.

"Fuck you it's open," Tish said. She cut the lights on.

Omie and the narc strode in like real jackboots, slack-jowled and oiled, wearing muscles off all the cops in the world, mouths stuffed with phrases of all the cops in the world. The narc carried an ax.

With them came Hallie Gaspar in her bathrobe, which her cats slept in. She looked her usual hurricane survivor warmed over, not that they'd yanked her from bed. She did two things in life and they were both walk, by day, by night, barefoot, August sun or winter moon. "That's the sleazy bitch right yonder!" she said, Tish.

"I reckon you won't be opening tomorrow," Omie said.

"I reckon I will. Show me a warrant."

He handed it over, a document whose creases perforated. "This lady has reason to believe your husband stole twenty-eight antique telephone insulators from her front room. We're going to have to tear the place apart unless you lead us to them. Or is our report true Ange's on his way to Norfolk to a collector?"

"Shall I start with the office?" the narc asked; asked Cammie.

"Who cares?"

"I care, so do you," Tish said. "You're not doing nothing till I get Malcolm Sedgwick on the phone."

"Don't listen to that whore!"

"Dry up! More! The wind tips your damn barricades, Hallie!"

"You can leave now, Hallie, we're grateful to you," Omie said.

"I'm not occupied." She regarded Cammie with a kind of sympathy, conveying she held no brief against the simply young or drunk but against those who failed to perceive terrors.

"This lady could've saved you trouble," the narc said, and headed back.

"What does he mean? What did you do?" Tish asked.

"I didn't do anything." Instead of taking her slicker off she buttoned it to the neck, and stuck her hand in her pocket.

"I'll follow this prick, you call Malcolm."

"Yea, right." She sat down at a booth where somehow a smudgy glass of chablis stood upright among spillage, breakage and napkin wads, tried not to let the words bother her. *What did you do?*

"You're staying patient," Omie instructed Tish. With two hundred pounds of body he blocked the way around the bar, with five pounds of right hand pinned the phone receiver.

"At eight in the morning you're out of a job. You'll go to California and not find a job, not security guard in K-Mart."

"I believe your influential boyfriend'll be hog-tied on this rig."

"Your name'll be shit."

"Better than being," Hallie said.

Tish's temper was nothing but bare brain on the fly, Cammie knew better than anyone. Yet when she tried to nudge the tonearm over it weighed too many tons. *What did you do? Why didn't you clean?* What had Tish and Ange done except for one thing let her paychecks fall five weeks in arrears through last Friday, less than they blew at Wintergreen, Virginia, on a weekend, not to mention bills out of her pocket like a hundred and forty dollars to the Miller man.

Furniture scuffed and screeched; drawers bounced on the floor; blows, chops reverbrated through the walls; wood splintered.

"He's wild in there. Your last fucking chance, Omie."

"Tell me about it."

"Cammie, will you run call *Malcolm*! Go to the dock phone, run call!"

More wood cracking—cedar shingles by the front as an automobile jumped the railroad-tie chock and hit the building, roared, died. R.L. walked in to the sight of Omie Marr and Tish Buthrell spitting at each other, smelly old Hallie twisting her toes in the muck, housewreckers ripping through the backbar and Cammie at a booth facing the door shaking in her coat.

Tish whirled. "R.L., praise Lord, run call Malcolm. We're staying all night, Cammie and I are staying in here all night."

Cammie reclined slightly, opened her eyes full, fluttered her lashes, shrugged, and sipped some wine.

Five times Del had tried to call Cammie without getting through. A quarter hour later he was dialing again when footsteps told him too late, partner, too damn late, the watch's done changed.

The room contracted. He felt something in his gullet or maybe solar plexus spring towards this man who entered hesitantly in shades and a stylish sportjacket that listed. He tasted situations in the back of his throat and this one tasted ripe and strange to think intellectual, intellectual in that it was scaly, clean and rang all the tastebuds at one lick.

He struggled to tell the truth but Ange, percolating like a porpoise, kept calling him down, forcing him to approach from every conceivable angle until he was picking through things he had no right to say to Tish's husband and any one of which might prove the triphammer. On the plane underneath this philosophy flew to pieces.

The creases in Ange's cheeks plumbed to the vertical. Del sensed the rise in velocity in the room. Mentally he strapped himself to his chair.

"She devours her mate after fucking," he said. "Were you aware of that? She fucks him, she eats him, every bristle of the poor bastard. He's had what he wanted, life goes on. She chomps him down, not giving a goddamn, stopping to test the web, test the breeze, make a few repairs. Climbs back finishes another leg—leaves one for him to hang with. Climbs back eats his ass. Doesn't occur to her, or him."

"You're telling me about disillusionment?"

"I'm telling you how simple life is."

Not solely as a result of the particular night, though it followed a long dry season, Cammie's reservoir had hit bottom. Tish and Ange irritated her sometimes but not being romantic she wasn't vengeful and would have given anything for it not to have run out tonight. At two a.m., at the instant R.L. appeared, she'd simply gurgled dry. The pouring rain outside turned into a sandstorm. The wine turned to dust on reaching her stomach. She regretted its happening tonight but there was nothing left to tap. Her hand hurt and she might as well leave.

She got up, told R.L., "I said I'd meet you at the house."

For the second time in their lives Tish put her hands on her. "You'll stay with me, won't you?"

"Tish, I don't know, it wouldn't do any good."

"Listen to the child!" Hallie said.

"You can't leave me in this mess."

"Well I sort of have to. R.L. and I are getting up early to househunt."

She avoided whatever expression R.L. flashed, probably one so direct it hurt him. "Yea, we got to get some rest. I haven't slept in two weeks," he said.

"R.L., let her stay tonight."

The narc presented Omie with a roach of marijuana out of the ladies' room and a small crumpled square of plastic.

"I'll come by in the morning, see how you're making out, okay?"

"God, you can't. I pledge we'll run this place really straight from here out."

"I know. I'll see you in the morning."

Outside, Cammie reiterated her demand that they meet at home but added he could wait in bed.

Ange wanted to parachute, horizontally, use the lobes of his brain in jellyfish propulsion over the lights of the city and on into the black across the sea and jet on.

"We have to learn from her," Del was saying.

Ange realized he'd let his attention wander plenty long enough for Del to have gone for his pistol. "Who do you mean," he asked, "Cammie?"

"Ange, I tell you."

It was the simplest thing, floats. Captain Del used cork or styrofoam floats or old Clorox containers that bobbed, dipped, generally rode high, painted black or orange or in the case of Clorox containers left white. Captain Ange favored glass like those Tish always looked for on the beach and which when Warren took swimming sank more than floated, rolled more than bobbed, swam, barely, in a saltwater the consistency of oil. Ange's lacked any excuse for visibility except what remained from reflecting the fast dead stars all night. He considered this room in the Holiday Inn to be the Atlantic, saw blown away floats running down waves in darkness, grouping, knocking, scattering when the next crest rose.

Paying attention wave by wave he saw them knocking each other to less and less distance—somebody had put magnets in them, obvious in styrofoam, trickier in glass—the pause between knocks growing shorter, the rebounds closing to a matter of inches then fractions of an inch, the knocks becoming taps the speed of a telegraph key then quicker until they were no more than molecular palpitations. A last wave cleared, the magnets homed to each other, the floats galvanized into a clump, a litter.

The racheting of a heavy-gauge door stories below vibrated the entire building. A delivery van backfired. Del could have buried him.

At Cuttlebone Junction Cammie turned south on the cape road, drove the seven miles to the inlet, crossed the bridge and drove nine miles south of there despite the front end jittering and complaining. She eased onto a turnoff of hard sand which she'd tested before, back to a spot where scrub hid her from the road. She couldn't see the ocean, certainly didn't step out to. All she'd find at night was ghost crabs, fish heads and wind; all she found in the day was seaweed, fish heads and wind.

She cracked the window on the side away from the rain, took off her shoes, peeled off her blouse and put on a sweatshirt and after sliding into the sleeping bag in back undid her skirt. The rain hit in tacks. The breeze shook her, fell to a lipless whistle, like beer bottles with bad caps. For some reason she thought of Tish at the beach, never willing to lie flat, ready to leave as soon as they arrived—then wondering why she didn't tan—every minute looking around, peering over her shoulder into the dunes.

More often than in her bed Cammie slept at turnoffs. She did fine in the cold, didn't mind waking up to sleet on the windshield. Some nights she even had the thought it would be all right to marry R.L. if they slept in here. Not R.L., not breath in winter, nothing filled the van. Lying in the van made her feel suited to lying in herself, for this was what her heart was like, a metal box forty times the size of a human being and there was no one to help.

[1979]

Kenneth Burke

KING LEAR: ITS FORM AND PSYCHOSIS

Prefatory Note: I view this essay as a kind of sequel to "Coriolanus—*and the Delights of Faction," republished in my collection,* Language As Symbolic Action. *And sometimes, in lectures, I have used bits of that essay as an introduction to this one. The first two pages of it indicate the ways in which practical social tensions or distresses* outside *the play can be used as a source of aesthetic pleasure within the play. At the close of the essay I give a definition designed to accentuate in general terms the play's dramatic functions. And on pp. 84-85 I illustrate how the "paradox of substance" (which I shall here make much of) operates. There I deal with the fact that the whole cast of characters is needed, if Coriolanus is to "be himself." But it is my claim that, whereas the paradox of substance applies to some extent in all works, in* King Lear *it is given maximum poignancy.*

The present essay involves a turn at the end of Part II. After we come to a kind of "dropping-off place," outside the realm of the dramatic, there is a reversal of direction—and we systematically ask what functions are "perfectly" ("entelechially") adapted to dramatic ends, in helping individuate and accentuate the "paradox of substance," itself not essentially dramatic, but philosophical.

K. B.

Mr. Burke's essay was delivered at Washington and Lee as a lecture, sponsored by the Glasgow Endowment Committee, Winter 1968. The other participants in the symposium "Approaches to Shakespeare" were C. L. Barber, Stanley Edgar Hyman and L. C. Knights. Mr. Knights' lecture appeared in the Spring 1968 issue of *Shenandoah*.

I

Some years ago, when I was taking notes on *King Lear,* my basic approach was as obvious as could be. I had in mind a well-recognized state of affairs that people commonly experience, in the mere process of growing older. As one sees one's descendants developing purposes and relationships of their own, quite outside the domain of their elders' particular inclinations or aptitudes, even though such new motives are not necessarily antagonistic to the older scheme of things, at best they differ sufficiently to be on the *slope* of conflict, and must be inchoately felt as such whether one exerts authority or yields. Even someone in the position to be an arrant will-shaker would often prefer to stand aside, neither claiming the right nor accepting the duty to settle every matter of dispute between the generations or among the young with regard to one another. And even if he were so minded, he would hardly be foolish enough to think that authority carried to such lengths is possible.

So my preparatory notes were taken on the assumption that, in its essence, the play appealed radically to this extra-literary pattern of experience. For I proceeded on the assumption that, whatever may be the virtues of a work considered internally (purely as an artistic structure enjoyed for itself alone), it must ultimately contain reference (explicitly or implicitly) to some profound area of motivation affecting us in our practical or ethical world outside the realm of art. And I wasn't too disturbed by the thought that such speculations might entangle me in a platitude—for all experience approaches platitude when reduced to so broad a level of generalization.

Next, it seemed to me obvious that, although the play is about a foolish old king who turned his kingdom over to his daughters, it certainly couldn't have been written for an audience of foolish old kings who abdicate their thrones. For what dramatist would write for so limited a public?

But where should we stop, when speculating about the play's proper public? For instance, is it essentially about the experience of aging? What then of the fact that this tragedy is also a favorite with many young people today? The underlying "psychosis" (or psychic bias) would not fit *their* experience.

Or should we say that, for the young, it would be a totally different play? Such a likelihood is not to be ruled out categorically. For the same work can mean different things to different people, or even to the same person at different stages in his life. And what is there for the young might happen to be quite different from what is there for oldsters. I see no binding reason why a critic might not build his study of the play around precisely such a dualistic version of its appeal, noting how and why it contains two quite different messages, one for youth, the other for age.

As a matter of fact, when I first saw it, and was shaken to my roots by the quality of what Aristotle would call its "tragic pleasure," I was several decades younger than I am now. And I had not then thought of the hypothesis on the basis of which I had begun my later tentative note-taking.

But even if, for the sake of argument, we grant the possibility that *Lear* is two plays, one for the younger and one for the older, there would still remain the possibility that both of these appeals, however different from each other, could be attributes of the same underlying substance, if I may adapt a Spinozistic way of stating the case. Clearly, for instance, there are certain aspects of the play's *structure* that appeal to audiences in general. The most direct example of this is to be found in the saliency of the diction, its pathos and its wildness. And I'd like to propose another possible general source of appeal.

For this purpose, I would begin with Tertullian's fertile formula, "I believe because it is incredible: *credo quia absurdum.*" Critics have written at great length, to detail the many absurdities of this play. How could any father with a grain of sense, for instance, have failed to learn the difference between Cordelia and her sisters? Or how could Gloucester be so gullible, in falling so promptly, for the deceptions of his bastard son, Edmund? And how could self-incriminating letters be so available at just the right time, and so on, as though people deliberately went out of their road to get caught? Or is it not too pat an arranging of the plot, when the King of France obligingly leaves the battleground in England, so that Cordelia can more readily fall victim to the machinations of her wicked sisters? And so on.

With some misgivings, I would try to argue for the notion that those very ways of imposing upon our credulity, of taxing our willingness to go along with the play's development, are a *positive* factor in the play's success, *When it is a success*. When we believe in something purely because it is rational, and thus seems to "make perfect sense," we are not wholly subject. The record of contemporary fanaticisms indicates that persons most ardently devoted to a cause will persist in repeating statements violently at odds with one another. And it is precisely in their refusal to be moved by rational argument that the intensity of their surrender lies. It is the sort of "loyalty" one confronts today among persons who, if a fantastically equipped army is sent to invade a tiny, technologically backward country thousands of miles away, feel nothing but righteous indignation when the victims of such intervention find ways of striking back.

Experimentally attempting, along such lines, to translate a theological proposition (Tertullian's *credo quia absurdum*) into terms of an aesthetic analogue, I'd propose that a corresponding motivational tangle of this sort may operate in the appeal of *King Lear*. That is: In the religious realm (as conceived after Tertullian's fashion) one truly surrenders only if one's faith is based upon a mystery (a doctrine, or nexus of doctrines not capable of rational explanation). And similarly, I submit, it is *precisely by straining our credulity to the limits* that this tragedy can produce in us an attitude of complete surrender. And I take it for granted that, the more nearly complete our surrender to its unfoldings may be, the more profound will be its effects upon us.

Perhaps you will decide that I have but belatedly found a way of repeating all over again what is meant by the "Theatre of the absurd." In any case, formally the willingness to silence our incredulity is reinforced (or more accurately, made possible) in *King Lear* by the speed with which the play's developments take place. Even at the original moment, when we might tend to reject the situation as preposterous, we are being driven headlong into further consequences of Lear's first mistaken judgment. That is to say: Even as we are first learning just what the *situation* is, it has already become transformed into a rapidly unfolding *plot*. And by the time the first act is over, all these major consequences of the situation have piled up, in quick succession:

(1) Lear has surrendered his kingdom to two hypocrites and disinherited a loyal daughter, who leaves for France.

(2) He has exiled a manifestly loyal follower, Kent.

(3) Another loyal follower, Gloucester, and his legitimate son, Edgar, have become dupes of the bastard son, Edmund.

(4) Kent has returned in disguise, has been accepted in Lear's service, without Lear's suspecting his identity, and has gratified us by his outraged treatment of Oswald.

(5) Lear's retinue of a hundred men is already being reduced by Goneril (with indications that Regan will treat Lear similarly). And this ingenious bit of bookkeeping (a marvellously effective way of inducing the audience to feel the pattern of development that will provoke Lear's impotent rage), culminates in the sinister foreshadowing of

(6) Lear's helpless apostrophe, after tauntings by his Fool:
O! let me not be mad, not mad, sweet heaven;
Keep me in temper; I would not be mad!

I happen to have read an article ("Cordelia and the Fool," by H. L. Anschutz, Research Studies, September 1964) upholding the notion that, after Cordelia's supposed departure for France, the Fool is really Cordelia in disguise. Though the thesis seems to me wholly unfeasible, it can be usefully transformed for different ends. I would apply it thus: The dramatic reason why Cordelia and the Fool never appear on the scene together is that each of these roles serves the same function; namely: as a device to make the audience realize to the fullest the foolishness and pathos of Lear's predicament. And to have them on the stage at once would involve a duplication of function that would be uneconomical, and thus poor workmanship.

I pass over the fact that, given the nature of Shakespeare's theatre, if Cordelia were intended to be seen by the audience as the Fool in disguise, in this play of many near-incredulous disguises, the situation would have been driven home with the bluntness of a meat-axe. Shakespeare's subtleties are of a quite different order. As with the Duke's disguise in *Measure for Measure,* Shakespeare's brand of dramatic irony is always designed to let the *audience* recognize unmistakably when characters on the *stage* are being deceived, for instance, as with the roles of Kent and Edgar in this play. But I do feel that Professor Anschutz's thesis helps us all the more to realize how basically aggressive the functions of Cordelia and the Fool are, in helping to motivate and accentuate for the audience the foolish and pathetic nature of Lear's condition. I shall return to the point later, in another connection.

Incidentally, before moving on, as regards Shakespeare's methods in general I might add: Note the distinction between this kind of form, which proceeds by unfolding a sequence of developments or consequences that were implicit in the situation,—and the kind of form one gets in a play, by, say, Pirandello, where the progress resides in the gradual releasing of more and more information about the situation itself. This latter kind of form is also characteristic of Faulkner's novels. But my main point, for present purposes, is to observe that, be the play's audience old or young, here would be a mode of appeal to which all might be susceptible.

Or if, as regards my basic claim that an essential ingredient in the play's appeal involves the audience's underlying surrender to credulity (a surrender in this case far more radical than Coleridge's "willing suspension of disbelief," but surely on the same slope), we might settle for less along these lines: The work implicitly draws upon such formal attitudes as an audience might bring to allegory or the morality play. For all their reality as "people," the characters are functional *types,* as though they were called Aged Father, Good Daughter, Bad Daughters, Good Son, Bad Son, Loyal Follower, Loyal Servant, etc., the "Fool" being the only one thus explicitly labelled. And once one sees a plot in such terms, the rules of consistency and verisimilitude are far from the sort that apply as we approach, say, the theatre of Ibsen in his most realistic period (though he also, in his way, began with somewhat allegorical figures, as in *Peer Gynt,* and ended with another kind of such, as in *When We Dead Awaken*). But ironically enough, the field in which contemporary audiences most readily accept the incredulous today is in farce or slapstick comedy, or the usual fare of TV skits. Shakespeare's play, we might say, asks us to accept the sublime much as we "normally" accept the ridiculous.

II

Now we're ready for a next step. It involves speculations of this sort: Let's modify our title somewhat. Instead of "*King Lear*: Its Form and Psychosis," let's now try: "*King Lear*, What is it *About?*" In effect, this way of transforming our title puts the two ("form" and "psychosis") together. For, as approached from this point of view, the play would not only be "about" a foolish old king whose bad judgment got him into fatal difficulties. Also we must characterize the plot in ways whereby it can be shown to involve an underlying extra-literary "psychosis," if there is such a thing as an underlying psychosis.

In the fifteenth chapter of the *Poetics,* Aristotle makes a suggestion which I have found perennially useful. He there proposes (for purposes not quite our present ones) that plots be summed up in *generalized* form. For instance, the *Odyssey* is summed up thus:

> A certain man has been abroad for many years; Poseidon is ever on the watch for him, and he is all alone. Matters at home too have come to such a state that his substance is being wasted, and his son's death is being plotted by suitors to his wife. He returns home after much suffering, reveals himself, and falls on his enemies. At the end, he is saved, and they are killed.

When plots are given in such generalized form, the terministic situation sets up conditions whereby the particulars of a narrative can be seen as embodying a "principle of individuation," behind which there lurk the kinds of universals proper to non-narrative nomenclatures.

This is not the place for me to attempt restating at any length my theoretic involvements in the vexing or wondrous vacillations between temporal and logical sequence that seem to me at the roots of human discourse. To sum up the matter as briefly as possible, I have in mind the difference between such a temporal series as yesterday-today-tomorrow and a logical series such as first premise, second premise, conclusion.

In contrast with a strictly *temporal* sequence the logical series is all there at once. As regards a narrative, on the other hand, the beginning comes first in a time sequence, the middle next, and the ending next. Yet it's not so simple as that. For instance, so far as the *text* of a drama or narrative is concerned, the beginning, middle, and end are all there at once, even before we undergo the succession of "revelations" whereby each page prepares us for the next (somewhat as theologians say that, whereas God is a nontemporal being, he is differently revealed in successive stages of history). A work as read or performed manifests itself in an irreversible sequence; but the relationships among its parts, such as would necessarily prevail were we to fill out the set of interrelations that are briefly indicated in the cast of characters (or were we to ask exactly how the first act is set up, with relation to the last, etc.) are nontemporal.

But what's the point? It all comes down to a consideration of this sort:

Suppose I begin by summarizing the tragedy in terms of purely narrative sequence, as befits the account of its plot. Here, obviously, I should say that the play is about an old king who abdicates his throne. Furthermore, he is made to abdicate foolishly, under conditions that, far from easing his burdens, involve him ever more deeply in misfortunes resulting in his death, and in the death and suffering of others, some of whom were profoundly loyal to him, and some fiendishly disloyal. Also, I might try to check off the series of steps that mark the play's unfolding, though possibly Aristotle would have wanted to consider those simply as "episodes" rather than intrinsic to the over-all outline. And perhaps I'd find it most convenient merely to tack on, as an addendum, a reference to the subplot involving what Francis Fergusson would doubtless want to treat in terms of "analogy" (namely: the respects in which Gloucester's relations to his bastard son and his legitimate son served as variations on the theme of Lear's relations to his loyal daughter and his two disloyal daughters). More on this point later.

So much for now, as regards a view of the play in terms of narrative/sequence (events in their *temporal* order). As regards strictly logical priority, however, have we as yet sufficiently generalized, in our quest for a universal "psychosis" that might underlie the play's appeal (some kind of ethical quandary not reducible to the comparatively particularized terms of an old king who voluntarily gave up his crown in a foolish way, and thereby let loose much suffering)?

Moving now to almost the highest level of generality conceivable, I'd propose to postulate, at least tentatively, this proposition: The play is about *abdication.* It is not about "abdication" in the sense that it is designed to tell us *why* men abdicate. It is about abdication in the sense that the theme of abdication presents rich dramatic possibilities.

If any other examples than the play itself are needed, recall the great public engrossment when the King of England renounced his throne, to marry a commoner. The then royal figure, now in his new identity renamed the Duke of Windsor, still avows that his decision was a wise one (nor should we forget that in our times the royal family is pretty much a captive of the bourgeois government). Yet think of how many persons at the time, branded the act as foolish.

But in any case, we have good reasons to realize: The idea of abdication touches upon a quite basic cluster or cycle of motives that are by no means confined to the theme of an old king foolishly giving up his throne. Might not the theme, for instance, overlap upon such relinquishing of authority as goes with *retirement* of any sort? And, a fortiori, might it not overlap upon such relinquishing of authority as has nothing directly to do with old age as such, but ultimately involves the psychosis of *authority pure and simple*?

In this respect, might not the appeal of the work even overlap upon such motivational quandaries as are implicit in thoughts of retreat or surrender, with no reference whatever to parents and their offspring? For instance, any threat to one's self-esteem might find sympathetic response in the tragedy of a man whose mistakes had strongly forced upon him the fear of impotence, with a corresponding sense that many of his utterances might prove as powerless as the rage of senility or infancy. I mean: Might not the appeal of *King Lear,* so far as an extra-literary "psychosis" is concerned, begin in such feelings as many people have at the thought, far afield, that our nation must not give, like a weak old man, but should go on expending its treasure until, still young and vigorously assertive, we shall have torn apart any enemy, even if it be but a distant victim of our own choosing?

Maybe yes, maybe no. In any case, for a time I would advance towards one further stage of generalization that is technically "higher" or "prior." Here, for the moment, going beyond even such generalized but still plot-like terms as "abdication," "retirement," "relinquishing of authority," "retreat," or "surrender," I would propose a sheerly "logological" term. It involves us in a step quite outside the realm of drama proper. Or, at best, it is a step from drama to "Dramatism." But I hasten to promise: Once we have gone thus far afield, from then we shall be able to swing back, and to recover lost ground quickly.

For this farthest step, I have proposed the label, "paradox of substance." By the "paradox of substance" I refer to the quandaries whereby one's personal identity becomes indistinguishably woven into the things, situations, relationships with which one happens to be identified. Philosophically, many abstruse and perhaps insoluble problems are involved here. But the issue can be made clear enough for our purposes. And it gets down to this: What is a king without a kingdom, a sea captain without a ship, a general without an army, a politician out of office, a job-holder without his job? Insofar as a man's person gains substance from social powers which are not intrinsic to him yet with which, by reason of his vocation or role in life, he becomes associated, what can he essentially be, once these extrinsic underpinnings are removed? As regards the present play, for instance, the whole cast of characters is needed, in their many interwoven relationships, if the ex-king is to have for us the kind of attributes that are intrinsic to his role.

To say as much is to realize that, with regard to the abrogating of a role in life itself, many makeshifts are available, and are resorted to. Florida, for instance, is aswarm with oldsters who have willy-nilly abdicated from some office or other and who though no longer employed by private or public agencies, concoct purposes for themselves by tirelessly seeking to pursue and slaughter as many poor little bits of sea-life as, in the attempt to make an humble, honest living, fall victim to such arbitrary extensions of human acquisitiveness. And there are various ways of puttering around in less predatory fashion, as with gardening, bird-watching, collecting fossils, photographing places one has visited, and so on. The ideal here, I guess, is a kind of Horatian *otium cum dignitate*.

The paradox of substance, as embodied in any mode of separation from some activity or status with which one had been radically identified, can be treated from many points of view. I think of a somewhat bitingly comic treatment, for instance, in Ring Lardner's story, "The Golden Honeymoon," which deals with oldsters hilariously and belatedly involved in a situation exploiting the theme of jealousy, yet not at all in the furiously tragic mode of *Othello*.

And now, having arrived at the dead center of our dialectic, let us reverse things. Let us assume that a certain playwright decides, of all things, to write not ultimately about an abdication, but about something so essentially extra-dramatic or non-dramatic as the "paradox of substance." Clearly, though such a concept as "paradox of substance" is not essentially dramatic at all (we might call it "philosophic"), once it is individuated in terms of *abdication* it immedately suggests typically dramatic possibilities of action and passion. Let us further decide that the playwright decides to deal with his theme not comically or idyllically or after the Horatian manner of gentlemanly dignified retirement, or such, but in the accents of *tragedy*. And with the play to help guide, or channelize our speculations, let's ask how the playwright might proceed to best effect. And so, to the next step in our discussion.

III

One point we have touched upon already. In order that his audience might confront the paradox of substance with maximum responsiveness, the dramatist should employ a kind of plot and treatment that adds a touch of allegory, or morality play (where the criteria of verisimilitude are not like those of a strictly realistic literary mode). For thereby, from the start, an added strain will be placed upon their credulousness. However, by the same token, they must be crowded a bit, so that things start happening precipitously, before the audience has time to ponder too exactingly about the situation itself. And I assume that the complaints of the critics arise, not from being hurried forward by the speed of an actual performance, but through a slow, line-for-line scrutinizing of the text, a process quite outside the temptations to surrender which all dramatic performance necessarily imposes upon an audience, by the sheer nature of the inexorably advancing form. (It's a point stressed by Mallarmé, in drawing a contrast between opera and his kind of lyric.)

How start the action as quickly as possible? Cordelia's two hopeless, helpless asides, when Goneril and Regan spout their nauseously fulsome protestations of filial love, are clear signs of how things are shaping up. And immediately after the old fool has spoken of disinheriting his heretofore favorite daughter, up speaks the obviously loyal Kent, to get unjustly banished.

Where are we, then? We are involved in a motive that is immediately activating; namely: loyalty, loyalty misjudged, and under conditions that already suggest a pattern of loyalty vs. disloyalty. Even before all this had happened there was the analogous scene in which Gloucester refers somewhat outrageously to his bastard son, in the son's presence. And it was a convention that from a bastard the audience might expect bastardy.

But though an alignment such as loyalty vs. disloyalty is clearly enough a promise of dramatic conflict, why precisely *this* duality of motives rather than some other? It fits particularly well, I submit, with the theme of lost identity that is intrinsic to the paradox of substance (which I have systematically postulated as extra-dramatic ground of the play's dramatic theme). For if certain central expectations as regards one's personal identity are dependent upon the powers of whatever office or role one happened to be identified with, to what might one appeal for loyalty, once these substantiating props were removed? Here I incidentally have in mind Locke's observation that, etymologically, the very word *substantia* means not the intrinsic, the within, but the "standing beneath," as when we call a well-to-do citizen a "man of substance." (See also, on the "paradox of substance," my *Grammar of Motives*, pp. 21-23)

Obviously, under such circumstances, one's best claim to loyalty would be by possessing an essentially appealing personality, whereby one might be "loved for oneself alone." But by making Lear initially so unjust to Kent and Cordelia, Shakespeare accentuates the nature of the problem (thereby also, of course, preparing the way for turns in the plot when Lear, like Gloucester, comes to realize his tragic mistakes). Thus, along with the fact that the theme of loyalty vs. disloyalty is so readily activating under *any* circumstances, there is also the fact that it fits in *particularly well* with any plan to treat the paradox of substance (or, if you will, the problem of personal identity, the question, "Now that

I have given up my office, who am I?") and in keeping specifically with the modes of tragic pleasure.

So, all told, we have a protagonist who will impersonate the paradox of substance as *perfectly* as possible. To this end, he should be an abdicator, either by choice or by necessity or both. It would seem to me that Shakespeare gives us a nearly ideal solution here, since Lear is abdicating of his own free will; yet within this freedom there are the necessities imposed upon him by the limitations of his character. If there is to be a bewilderment implicit in any loss of prior, well-substantiated identity, to that extent the victim is as someone fooled—and there's no fool like an old fool. So, to that extent, an old fool could well be endowed with the central tragic burden. And, by the same token, a professional Fool could be introduced to help point up the situation; and all the more so insofar as, once the dramatist has decided to individuate this issue in terms of an early King's voluntary abdication under foolish conditions, the sheer choice of a king allows readily for the introduction of a King's Fool.

The choice of an aging king has other considerations to recommend it. If, in a given social structure, there is a king, then the figure of a king is "perfectly" designed to impersonate any widespread motive intrinsic to that way of life, be the motive derivable from the given social order alone or from a wider-ranging realm of man's incentives. And as for his being an *old* king: Old age is as near as one can get biologically this side of death, to a state of "completion" without disappearing from the scene completely. Lear's senile rage also has the advantage that the underlying extra-dramatic realm of experience appealed to needs not be confined to the experiences of age. Even as infants, before our identities were shaped, all of us had in some form the experience of impotent rage, since our "claims to authority" were so absurdly at odds with our actual powers. And even with persons at the height of maturity and office, there is the sense that rage too spontaneously expressed can usually but lead to powerlessness.

In making the old king foolish, the dramatist confronts a further "natural" possibility as regards what, in keeping with Aristotle (and whether loyally or disloyally I must leave it for you to decide), I would want to label the "entelechial principle." By the "entelechial principle" I refer to the goad (in any given symbol-system) to work out or embody, as thoroughly as possible, the implications intrinsic to the given system. In this case, the entelechial "perfecting" of Lear's *foolishness* culminates in his moments of sheer *insanity*. And under this head, certainly, we should also most decidedly class the famous scene on the heath, with the madman, the professional fool, and the fugitive son of Gloucester simulating madness, while the heavens rage, to round out scenically what Lear calls "the tempest in my mind." This is rightly prized as among the greatest examples of dramatic amplification.

For the moment dismissing the paradox of substance that lurks ultimately and non-dramatically behind or beyond the strictly dramatic involvements as such, we could readily "generate" our *dramatis personae* in the secondary terms of loyalty and disloyalty alone. Lear is cast as the kind of character whose foolish way of abdicating is *ideally designed to set the conditions for such an alignment*. And all the primary members of the cast take their positions (and derive their identities) accordingly.

The motive of loyalty is most perfectly manifested in the fact that both Cordelia's devotion to her father and Kent's devotion to his sovereign prevail despite the old fool's unjust treatment of them. Thus, the very thoroughness of his mistake helps accentuate the purity of their motive. Another variant is Edgar's pitying concern for his victimized father, whose insight came only after being blinded. There is the supernumerary loyalty of the servant who lost his life when indignantly taking the life of Cornwall, Gloucester's torturer. But surely the most subtle loyalty of all is exemplified in the Steward, Oswald, whom we despise (feeling especially gratified when Kent lets loose at him), yet whose sins reside in his unquestioning loyalty to his evil mistress, Goneril. He impersonates the kind of loyalty exemplified by some angels in Milton's heaven, who revolted not directly against God, but through obedience to their immediate superiors. And desperate loyalties of this sort can even entail the tragic sacrifice of whole armies.

Goneril, of course, is on the other slope, of the fiendishly, monstrously disloyal, with Regan. And speaking of perfection here, we should note how the pattern gets rounded out when the corruptors (scheming against each other in rivalry for the hand of the equally scheming, disloyal bastard Edmund) end by one poisoning the other and then killing herself. Since such a pattern is "entelechially" completed when corruption becomes its own undoing, corrupting even its own corrupt intentions, one may in passing think of possibly corrupt governmental organizations that, in being designed for the dismal task of subversion throughout the world, and with literally billions of dollars to dispose of, lie quite outside the normal controls of public accountants' watchdog inspection.

The only other major character to be accounted for, or "generated," is the Duke of Albany, who fits the pattern by providing a good transitional function (as he only gradually comes to realize the full scope of Goneril's treachery, and having turned against her, lives to deliver the play's last words).

IV

I have said that the play is about abdication, not about why people abdicate. Thus, for its purposes, all that is needed, so far as motivation on this level is concerned, is Lear's remark as regards his "darker purpose";

> 'tis our fast intent
> To shake all cares and business from our age,
> Conferring them on younger strengths, while we
> Unburden'd crawl toward death.

I have suggested that, behind all this, there is the paradox of substance. But there is also another source of motivation. For we may ask: Precisely what is the underlying motive for choosing *tragedy* as the mode in terms of which to dramatize such a motive, or terministic situation, itself not intrinsically dramatic, but philosophic?

In my *Rhetoric of Religion,* I have attempted to show how and why the incentives to modes of expression embodying the "tragic pleasure" center in the nature of Order, implicit in which is a *sacrificial* principle. And tragedy involves a solemn way of utilizing this sacrificial principle to dramatic ends. This is no place to reconsider the full "Cycle of Terms Implicit in the Idea of 'Order,'" or to ask just how the terministic resources of *substitution* figure in the imagining of an ideal tragic victim, such as devoted Cordelia is in one sense, and poor foolish Lear is in another.

Some discussions of my paper have brought out the objection that I should have played up Lear's desire to be loved. The point is well taken. But should we stop there? Doesn't a foolish old man's desire to be loved, for himself alone, involve at every point precisely the paradox of substance we have been building on? And doesn't the issue take us to the next stop, the fact that Kent's loyalty to him as his sovereign and Cordelia's loyalty to him as her father are "perfected" by both his impotence and his unreasonableness?

A related consideration turned up. As for the sub-plot, I had assumed that Francis Fergusson's notions about "analogy" would be sufficient, to bring the two strands together. And such is indeed the case. But the analogy digs just as deep into the "paradox of substance." Consider, for instance, concepts of "familial" substance discussed in my *Grammar*. These figure in the confusions that cause Edgar to be deprived of the substance proper to him as legitimate heir, during the grim interregnum of the illegitimate son, Edmund's, triumph.

[1969]

Alfred Corn

APRIL

Awakened before I meant
By soft shocks outside, white wet
Light streaming in at eight or so.
That I carry my daze intact
To the window, where at a remove
Unfocused patches of color float—
Taxis, trucks, early risers—
Things that move and beep and talk,
Each on its comic errand, proves
This a day set apart. But how so?
White petals fallen on the floor.
Time to throw out the dogwood branch.
Think of all the flowers that suffered
And died for me, not deserving it.

Bits of the dream come back:
The Elysian Fields. Yes. Which looked
Like a boulevard, not a meadow.
Theaters. Cafes. Great has-beens
In the fancy dress strained out
From three thousand years of Western Civ.
Silent they stood in poses grave.
It seemed a certain stiffness
Was de rigueur among the dead;
Or they distrusted a body
Who hadn't yet arrived.
"Ages since any of us lived;
Not done now, flesh so outmoded,
Inelegant, opaque." Togaed
In vapor, a gray mirage at last
Spoke four oracular commands:
Travel. Love. Suffer. Work.
"You mean experience, knowledge?"
Know no more than you can do. Though
Knowledge is power, absolute knowledge. . . .
The rest was lost under drumrolls,

A procession headed toward the arch
And flame votive to the Unknown.

Good speech-making; but, as advice,
It's superfluous, no more than
What I've always done by instinct.
In time you come to balance the more
With the less remote. And compose
A life out of to you plausible
Nouns and verbs; convincing others
As well. Today will make a kind
Of pure, arbitrary sense, then—
Like that blurred array of colored
Patches down there, conjugating
In bright steam, rapidly changing
As thoughts, plans, thoughts about plans.
Occurs to you the city is
A printout of habit; and small wonder
I belong here with difficulty,
Restless, feverish with those four
Imperatives, navigating
With few instruments, my own
Method none but a mad desire
That everything be near at hand
In a world's monumental fluidity.

Even now five years drop aside
Like scattered documents: the day
Of the solar eclipse, and I
The last through a gate of the park
Where others wait quietly.
At the vacant top of a low
Rise I settle myself on dead
Brown grass for the viewing. The air
Goes yellow-gray, a color western
Say twenty years ago. Silence. Little
Breezy cyclones. The day reduced
To poor facsimile. Three figures
Below, aiming a pinholed card
To spotlight crescents on paper—

Something like a burning glass,
But cool, precise, droll.
All of them stand motionless,
In contrapposto, elbows crooked,
Casting ghostly shadows on the earth.
A boy gazes up through a shard
Of smoked glass, (dangerous, I've heard),
And the river stumbles southward
In unwonted twilight.
The scared stillness doesn't break.
And notice the grass by magic has
Communicated a wet coolness
To the seat of my pants. Then
It's over. The world wakes up.

A trapezoid of light has shrunk
Toward the window. Without moving.
Things dreamed and done and known:
The record is there that others read,
Notations strewn in my wake,
A language of roadside flowers,
Mostly illegible now to me.
The wasted passion stuns, as a cloud
Might pass across the mind's eye,
The dream of life opaque to life.

[1977]

Harry Crews

ONE MORNING IN FEBRUARY

It was a bright cold day in February, so cold the ground was still frozen at ten o'clock in the morning. The air was full of the steaming smell of hogshit, and the oily flatulant odor of intestines, and the heavy sweetness of blood, in every way a perfect day to slaughter animals for the smokehouse in Bacon County, Ga. I was five years old and that morning I had watched the hogs called to the feeding trough just as they were every morning, except this morning it was to receive the hammer instead of slop.

A little slop *was* poured into their long community trough, enough to make them stand still while one of my uncles or sometimes an older cousin went quietly among them with the axe, using the flat end like a sledge hammer. He would approach the hog from the rear while it slopped at the trough and then straddle it, one leg on each side. The uncle would wait patiently for the hog to raise its snout from the slop to take a breath, showing as it did the wide bristled bone between its ears to the hammer.

It never took but one blow, delivered expertly and with consummate skill, and the hog was dead. He then moved with his hammer to the next hog and straddled it. None of the hogs ever seemed to mind that their companions were dropping dead all around them but continued in a single-minded passion to eat. They didn't even mind when another of my uncles or cousins (this could be a boy of only eight or nine because it took neither strength nor skill) came right behind the hammer and drew a long razorhoned butcher knife across the throat of the fallen hog. Blood spurted in gouts with the still beating heart and a live hog would sometimes turn to one that was lying beside it at the trough and stick its snout into the spurting blood and drink a bit just seconds before it had its own head crushed.

It was a time of great joy and celebration for the children. We played games and ran and screamed and brought wood for the boiler and thought of that night when we would have fresh fried pork and stew made from lungs (called *lights* by farmers) and liver and heart.

The air was charged with the smell of fat being rendered in

the pots and the sharp squeals of the pigs at the troughs. Animals were killed but seldom hurt. Farmers take tremendous precautions about pain at slaughter. It is, whether they ever talk about it or not, a ritual. As brutal as they sometimes are with farm animals and with themselves, no farmer would ever eat an animal he had willingly made suffer.

The heelstrings, the Achilles tendon, was cut on each of the hog's back legs and a stick inserted into the cut behind the tendons and the hog dragged to the huge castiron boiler which sat in a depression dug in the ground so the hog could be slid in and pulled out easily. A fire snapped and roared in the depression under the boiler. The fire had to be tended carefully because the water could never quite come to a boil. If the hog was dipped in boiling water, the hair would set and become impossible to take off. Unlike cows which are skinned, a hog is scraped. After the hog is pulled from the water a blunt knife is drawn over the animal and if the water has not been too hot the hair slips off smooth as butter, leaving a white, naked, utterly beautiful pig.

To the great glee of the watching children, when the hog is slipped into the water, it shits. The children squeal and clap their hands and make their delightfully obscene children's jokes as the lovely turd slides into the steamy water. It smells a little like roasting chestnuts, not really unpleasant at all.

On that morning when I was five years old, my mother was around in the back of the house where the hogs were hanging in the air from their heelstrings being disemboweled. Along with the other ladies, she was washing hog guts, cleaning all the shit out good, so that the gut could then be stuffed with sausage meat.

Out in front of the house where the boiler was I was playing pop-the-whip with my brother and seven of my cousins. Pop-the-whip is a game in which everyone holds hands and runs fast and then the leader of the line turns sharply and because he is turning through a tighter arch than the other children the line acts like a whip with each child farther down the line having to travel through a greater space and consequently having to go faster in order to keep up. The last child in the line literally gets *popped* loose and sent flying from his companions.

I was popped loose and sent flying into the steaming boiler of water beside a hog that had just been dipped.

I remember everything about it as clearly as I remember anything that ever happened to me. Except the screaming. Curiously, I cannot remember the screaming. They say I screamed all the way to town, but I can't remember it.

What I remember is John C. Pace, a black man whose daddy was also named John C. Pace, reached right into the water and pulled me out and set me on my feet and stood back from me. I did not fall but stood looking at John and seeing in his face I was dead. The children's faces behind him showed I was dead, too. And I knew it must be so because I knew where I had fallen and I felt no pain—not in that moment—and I knew with the bone-chilling certainty most people are spared that, yes, death does come and mine had just touched me.

John ran screaming and the other children ran screaming and left me standing there by the boiler, my hair and skin and clothes steaming in the bright cold February air.

(Once I was in the woods with one of my uncles and several other men cutting pulp wood among pine trees. The wood was being cut with a chain-saw. One man felled the trees with the saw and the other men chopped the limbs off with axes and then the man with the chain-saw doubled back and cut up the trunks and the cutup sections were loaded on a truck. One day the man running the chain-saw went into a big head-high patch of gall berries and the entire patch simply exploded. Leaves flew, pine straw shot straight into the air, bits of sticks and limbs whistled about our heads and during it all the man inside the exploding gall berry patch was screaming. Then there was silence. And out of the weeds walked a naked man. He was cut from hairline to boots, which were still partially on his feet. In that stunned silence the bleeding man held out his hands toward us all and his mouth moved, trembled, but no sound came. We—all of us—had known him all his life but as if on a signal everybody turned and ran, ran as fast as we could, leaving him standing there red in his own blood, his hands out for help.

It was nearly ten minutes before one of the men could bring himself to go back and find out what had happened, which was this: there had once been a fence that went through that gall berry patch but had been allowed to fall when the posts rotted and the rusting wire had been lying just below the pine straw for the chainsaw to catch and whip around and around through the air flailing the man's clothes and finally his skin to ribbons.)

In my memory I stand there alone with the knowledge of death upon me watching steam rising from my hands and clothes while everybody runs and after everybody has gone, standing there for minutes while nobody comes. That is only memory. It may have been but seconds before my mother and uncle came to me. Ma tells me she heard me scream and started running toward the boiler, knowing already what had happened. She has also told me that once she saw me she did not want to touch me, could not bring herself to try to do anything with that smoking, ghostlike thing standing by the boiler. But she did. They all did. They did what they could.

But in that interminable time between John pulling me out and my mother arriving in front of me, I remember first the pain. It didn't begin as a bad pain, but rather like maybe sandspurs under your clothes. I reached over and touched my right hand with my left hand and the whole thing came off like a glove. I mean the skin on the top of the wrist and the back of my hand and the fingernails all just turned loose and slid off onto the ground. I could see my fingernails lying in the little puddle of flesh on the ground in front of me.

Then hands were on me, taking off my clothes, and the pain turned into something words can't touch, or at least *my* words can't touch it. There is no way for me to talk about it because when my shirt was taken off, my back came off. When my pants were pulled down, the bright skin covering my ass and thighs came down.

I still had not fallen, and I stood there participating in my own butchering. When they got the clothes off me, they did the worst thing they could have done, they wrapped me in a sheet. They did it out of panic and terror and ignorance and love.

There happened to be a car at the farm that day. I can't remember who it belonged to, but I was taken into the backseat into my mother's lap—God love the lady, out of her head, pressing her boiled son to her breast—and we started for Alma, Ga., a distance of about sixteen miles. The only thing that I remember about the trip was that I started telling my mother that I did not want to die. I started saying it and I never stopped.

And I remember that the car was very very slow. An old car and very slow and every once in a while my uncle Aulton, who was like a daddy to me, would jump out of the car and run along side it and scream for it to go faster and then he would jump back on the running board and ride until he couldn't stand it any longer and then he would jump off again.

But like bad beginnings everywhere, they sometimes end well. When we got to Doctor Sharp's office in Alma, and he finally managed to get me out of the sheet, he found that I was scalded over two-thirds of my body but my head had not gone under the water (he said that would have killed me) and for some strange reason I have never understood the burns were not deep. He said I would probably even outgrow the scars, which I have. Until I was about fifteen years old the scars were very pronounced on my buttocks and back and right arm and legs but now their outlines are barely visible.

The only hospital at that time was thirty miles away and he said I'd do just as well at home if they built a frame over the bed to keep the covers off me and also kept a light burning over me. So they took me back home and put a buggy frame over my bed to make it resemble, when the sheet was put on, a covered wagon and ran a line in from the Rural Electrical Association so I could have a light continually burning just above me. Dr. Sharp gave them some medicine that was sprayed on out of an atomizer and turned black and raised to form a protective scab when it dried.

It wasn't a bad life under that buggy frame. It was a time for fantasy and magic because I lived in a playhouse, a kingdom that was all mine. And like every child who owns anything, I ruled it like a tyrant. There is something very special and beautiful about being the youngest member of a family and being badly, nearly mortally, hurt.

I spent alot of time with the Sears catalog, started writing and nearly finished a detective novel, although at that time I had never seen a novel, detective or otherwise. I printed it with a soft lead pencil on lined paper and it was about a boy who for his protection carried not a pistol but firecrackers. He solved crimes, gave things to poor people, and was fearless.

I was given a great deal of ginger ale to drink because the doctor or my mother or somebody thought that where burns were concerned it had miraculous therapeutic value. This was the store-bought variety, too, not some homemade concoction but wonderfully fizzy and capped in real glass bottles. Since my brother and I almost never saw anything from a store, I drank as much ginger ale as they brought me, and they brought me alot. I never learned to like it, but I could never get over my fascination with the bubbles that rose in the ginger ale under the yellow light hanging from the buggy frame.

A goat grew up with me under that buggy frame. His name was Old Black Bill, and he was called Old Black Bill from the moment he was born until his untimely death. No animal is allowed in a farmhouse in Bacon County, Georgia, or at least to my knowledge. Dogs stay in the yard. Cats usually live in the barns. And goats, well, goats only get in the house if they have first been butchered for the table. But I had been scalded, and I was special. I was in fact, as I mentioned, a tyrant. So since we had almost a hundred head of goats, and since I had been used to playing with them everyday before my accident, I insisted a goat be brought to my bed. At that time I was about three weeks into my convalescence, but still a long ways from recovery. Still, I was well enough to assert myself, and I thought a goat would be good company.

They brought in the youngest, smallest one they could find which turned out to be Old Black Bill, who was a billy, solid black, and born only three days previous to my unseemly demand. I fed him bits of hay and shelled corn under my buggy frame. We had long conversations. Or rather I had long monologues and he, patiently chewing, listened. That was about all he did except to stink alot.

At first he was only brought in for an hour or two, then longer, then finally he more or less stayed in the house with the exception of those times he was taken out to run. He spent the night in the barn with the other goats, but there toward the end, say the last month, he stayed in my bed more than a few nights. He was—all in all—the most agreeable companion I ever had.

I was in the bed with my burn for nearly five months, and like a dog a goat is pretty much grown or at least has, say, two thirds of his growth at the age of five months. It was decided that I would be allowed to leave my bed on my birthday, the seventh of June. I was healed nicely and my mother, with the doctor's consent, said we ought to make a celebration of my leaving the sick bed. Ma said she'd bake me a cake, we'd have fresh things from the field, and within her means she would cook whatever meat I'd like. After all, it *was* my birthday and I should have something I'd enjoy.

Like any good tyrant anywhere, I told her to cook Old Black Bill. My favorite was goat. It still is.

[1974]

E. E. Cummings

TWO POEMS

POEM

what time is it?it is by every star
a different time,and each most falsely true;
or so subhuman superminds declare

—nor all their times encompass me and you:

when are we never,but forever now
(hosts of eternity;not guests of seem)
believe me,dear,clocks have enough to do

without confusing timelessness and time.

Time cannot children,poets,lovers tell—
measure imagine,mystery,a kiss
—not though mankind would rather know than feel;

mistrusting utterly that timelessness

whose absence would make your whole life and my
(and infinite our)merely to undie

[1962]

POEM

ev erythingex Cept:

that
's what she's
got

—ex

cept what?
why
, what it

Takes. now

you know (just as
well as i
do) what

it takes;& i don't mean It—

&
i don't
mean any

thing real

Ly what
; or ev
erythi

ng which. but,

som
e
th

ing: Who

[1951]

J. V. Cunningham

THE PROBLEM OF FORM

I shall stipulate that there is a problem of form in the poetry of our day, but I shall treat *form,* for the moment, as an undefined term, and I shall not until later specify the nature of some of the problems. I am, at the outset, interested in pointing to certain generalities, and to certain broad, simple-minded, pervasive attitudes and dualisms, of which the problem in poetry is to a large extent only a localization. These will give in outline the larger context of the problem.

To begin with, it is apparent that in our society we have too many choices. When we ask the young what they are going to do when they grow up, we should not be surprised or amused that the answers are whimsical and bewildered. The young poet today has a large and not too discriminated anthology of forms to realise; only illiterate ignorance or having made the pilgrimage to Gambier or to Los Altos will reduce the scope of options to manageable size—and even then there will be a hankering for further options. On the other hand, the young poet 250 years ago had it easy in this respect. He wrote octosyllabic or decasyllabic couplets, and the rhetoric and areas of experience of each were fairly delimited. For recreation he wrote a song in quatrains, and once or twice in a lifetime a Pindaric ode.

We come now to those attitudes and dualisms that make the problem of particular forms peculiarly our problem. We are a democratic society and give a positive value to informality, though some of the ladies still like to dress up. We will have nothing to do with the formal language and figured rhetoric of the *Arcadia,* for that is the language and rhetoric of a hierarchical and authoritarian society in which ceremony and formality were demanded by and accorded to the governing class. Instead, we praise, especially in poetry, what we call the accents of real speech—that is, of uncalculated and casual utterance, and sometimes even of

---

Read at the National Poetry Festival, Library of Congress, October 24, 1962.

vulgar impropriety. Now, if this attitude is a concomitant of the Democratic Revolution, the value we give to anti-formality, to the deliberate violation of forms and decorum, is a concomitant of its sibling, the Romantic Revolution. The measured, the formal, the contrived, the artificial are, we feel, insincere; they are perversions of the central value of our life, genuineness of feeling. "At least I was honest," we say with moral benediction as we leave wife and child for the sentimental empyrean.

If informality and anti-formality are positive values, then the problem of form is how to get rid of it. But to get rid of it we must keep it; we must have something to get rid of. To do this we need a method, and we have found it in our dualisms of science and art, of intellectual and emotional, of regularity and irregularity, of norm and variation. We have been convinced, without inquiry or indeed adequate knowledge, that the regularities of ancient scientific law, of Newton's laws of motion, are regularities of matter, not of spirit, and hence are inimical to human significance. And so we embrace the broad, pervasive, simple-minded, and scarcely scrutinized proposition that regularity is meaningless and irregularity is meaningful—to the subversion of Form. For one needs only so much regularity as will validate irregularity. But Form is regularity.

So we come to definition. The customary distinctions of form and matter, or form and content, are in the discussion of writing at least only usable on the most rudimentary level. For it is apparent to any poet who sets out to write a sonnet that the form of the sonnet is the content, and its content the form. This is not a profundity, but the end of the discussion. I shall define form, then, without a contrasting term. It is that which remains the same when everything else is changed. This is not at all, I may say, a Platonic position. It is rather a mathematical and, as it should be, linguistic notion. $a^2 - b^2 = (a+b)(a - b)$ through all the potentialities of a and b. The form of the simple declarative sentence in English is in each of its realisations.

It follows, then, that form is discoverable by the act of substitution. It is what has alternative realisations. And the generality or particularity of a form lies in the range or restriction of alternatives. It follows, also, that the form precedes its realisation, even in the first instance, and that unique form, or organic form in the sense of unique form, is a contradiction in terms. For it is the essence of form to be repetitive, and the repetitive is form. It follows, further, that there may be in a given utterance simultaneously a number of forms, so that the common literary question, What is the form of this work?, can only be answered by a tacit disregard of all the forms other than the one we are momently concerned with.

It is time for illustration. Donne has a little epigram on Hero and Leander:

> Both robbed of air, we both lie in one ground,
> Both whom one fire had burnt, one water drowned.

What are the forms of this poem? First, both lines are decasyllabic in normal iambic pattern. Second, they rhyme. Third, it is phrased in units of four and six syllables in chiasmic order. Fourth, there are three *both's* and three *one's* in overlapping order. Fifth, the whole story of the lovers is apprehended, summarised, and enclosed in the simple scheme or form of the four elements. Finally, it is recognizably an epigram. Now Sir Philip Sidney, a few years earlier, in one of the *Arcadia* poems has the following lines:

> Man oft is plagued with air, is burnt with fire,
> In water drowned, in earth his burial is . . .

The lines are decasyllabic in normal iambic pattern. The adjacent lines do not rhyme, for the form of the poem is terza rima, an alternative form. It is phrased in units of six and four in chiasmic order. The first line repeats *with,* the second *in.* Man, not Hero, and Leander, is apprehended in the scheme of the four elements, and in both cases the order of the elements is not formally predetermined. Finally, it is not an epigram, but part of an eclogue.

I have illustrated in these examples and in this analysis something of the variety of what may be distinguished as form: literary kind, conceptual distinctions, and all the rhetorical figures of like ending, equal members, chiasmus, and the various modes of verbal repetition. That some of the forms of Sidney's lines are repeated in Donne's, with the substitution of Hero and Leander for man, shows they have alternative realisations, and that so many operate simultaneously shows, not that a literary work has form, but that it is a convergence of forms, and forms of disparate orders. It is the coincidence of forms that locks in the poem.

Indeed, it is the inherent coincidence of forms in poetry, in metrical writing, that gives it its place and its power—a claim for poetry perhaps more accurate and certainly more modest than is customary. For this is the poet's *Poetics*: prose is written in sentences; poetry in sentences and lines. It is encoded not only in grammar, but also simultaneously in meter, for meter is the principle or set of principles, whatever they may be, that determine the line. And as we perceive of each sentence that it is grammatical or not, so the repetitive perception that this line is metrical or that it is not, that it exemplifies the rules or that it does not, is the metrical experience. It is the ground bass of all poetry.

And here in naked reduction is the problem of form in the poetry of our day. It is before all a problem of meter. We have lost the repetitive harmony of the old tradition, and we have not established a new. We have written to vary or violate the old line, for regularity we feel is meaningless and irregularity meaningful. But a generation of poets, acting on the principles and practice of significant variation, have at last nothing to vary from. The last variation is regularity.

[1963]

EPIGRAMS

A periphrastic insult, not a banal:
You are not a loud-mouthed and half-assed worm;
You are, sir, magni-oral, semi-anal,
A model for a prophylactic firm.

* * *

Cocktails at six, suburban revelry:
He in one corner with the Chest Convex,
She in another with Virility.
So they went home, had dinner, and had sex.

* * *

Some twenty years of marital agreement
Ended without crisis in disagreement.
What was the problem? Nothing of importance,
Nothing but money, sex, and self-importance.

[1970]

Donald Davie

THREE POEMS

THE FOUNTAIN

Feathers up fast, steeples, and then in clods
Thuds into its first basin; thence as surf
Smokes up and hangs; irregularly slops
Into its second, tattered like a shawl;
There, chill as rain, stipples a danker green,
Where urgent tritons lob their heavy jets.

For Berkeley this was human thought, that mounts
From bland assumptions to inquiring skies,
There glints with wit, fumes into fancies, plays
With its negations, and at last descends
As by a law of nature to its bowl
Of thus enlightened but still common sense.

We who have no such confidence must gaze
With all the more affection on these forms,
These spires, these plumes, these calm reflections, these
Similitudes of surf and turf and shawl,
Graceful returns upon acceptances.
We ask of fountains only that they play,

Though that was not what Berkeley meant at all.

GOING TO ITALY

Though painters say Italian light does well
By natural features and by monuments,
Our eyes may not be fine enough to tell
Effects compounded of such elements.

And yet we trust our judgment, as to fires
In their effects more subtle still, like love,
Which is a light that dwells upon its squires
To tell the world what they are thinking of.

That fortunate climate is so apt for this,
As some aver, that not a thought can pass
Through spiritual natures but it is
Seen in the light like glitter in a glass.

If Rome should see us wrapped in such a flue,
And all our even inward motions edged
Thus with the crispness of their follow through,
I'd think not we but Rome was privileged.

CHRYSANTHEMUMS

Chrysanthemums become a cult because
No Japanese interior is snug,
For even Fuji can be brought indoors
As lamps turn amber in an opal fog.

Here in the thick of opals, where the horn
Blurts from the seaward mountain through the pall,
Now fires are lit and the snug curtains drawn,
Shock-headed clusters warm the dripping wall.

A brazier or the perforated tin
Of watchmen huddled at a dockyard gate
Glows with such amber as the night draws in,
As these bronze flowers, blossoming so late.

Chrysanthemum, cult of the Japanese,
You teach me no Penates can be lost
While men can draw together as they freeze
And make a domesticity of frost.

Yet bivouacs of revolution throw
Threatening shadows and scorching heat;
And embers of unequal summer glow
A hearth indeed, but in a looted street.

[1955]

James Dickey

PAESTUM

One cloud in the sky comes from Greece
The sun, set at noon, moves toward it
And is ready to change into rain.

Around a lemon tree throwing
A still shadow easily drawn
From the depths of Italian rock,
All things drop off their names
And softly stand in the warm
Speechless ruin of their being, and pride.
A wave falls, back of some trees.
Sound blooms as from a seed;
The human face wears for an instant
A white flash, vital and mortal,

Like the star on a horse's brow.
A man puts cautiously down
The useless, blue-eyed floating of his soul
Over the ruins, around
The eternal youth of well-water.
Down a road a thousand years old
Growing dazedly through the oats,
Awe comes into the city
As into a dead artist's home,
Where the stone and the unpicked lemon

Give the same hand-burning power
As to the curved palm
Of a genius sculpting.
Brightness goes under the fields
Travelling like shadow

Through the well-stones and brier-roots;
Dead crickets come back to life;
Snakes under the cloud live more
In their curves to move. Rain falls
With the instant, conclusive chill

Of a gnat flying into the eye.
Crows fall to the temple roof;
An American feels with his shoulders
Their new flightless weight be born
And the joy of the architect
Increase, as more birds land.
He remembers standing in briers
Ten minutes ago, in the sun,
As cast among tiny star-points
That cramped and created his body

By their sail-shapes' sensitive clinging,
Making him stand like a statue
With its face coming out of the stone
From the thousand shrewd, perilous scars
Left by the artist on marble.
The chipped columns brace in the rain-rays
For the crucial first instant of shining.
At the far edge of cloud, the sun
Arrives at its first thread of light.
Unpacking them slowly, it lays

Itself at the door of the temple.
Shining comes in from the woods,
Down the road at a walking pace
Like a thing that he owns and gets back.
Crows open their wings and rise
Without wind, by the force of new light.
Every woman alive in the ruins
Becomes a virgin again.
His nose, broken badly in childhood,
And the brier's coiled scratch on his wrist

Begin to hurt like each other.
A wave of water breaks inward
And a wave of grain lifts it up
And bears it toward him,
A crest he must catch like a swimmer,
Just as it breaks, to rise
Up the stairs of the temple.

The image of a knife bronze-glitters
With the primal, unshielded light
Of a bald man's brain

As he climbs to the place of sacrifice
Where the animals died for the gods
And cried through the human singing.
Crows set their wings to glide
In with him through the portals
But rise without will to the roof.
The shimmering skin of his head
Sheds a hero's blond shade on the ground.
He stares at the drops on his wrist
As at animal blood

That has power over Apollo.
His smile is brought slowly out
Of his unchanging skull by the sun;
He feels its doomed fixity turn
Uncertain and strange in the space
Where a wave shall break into light,
A crow feather whirl upon stone
And the brow-stars of horses shall flicker,
Gone bodiless, in the dark green
Middle limbs of the pine wood

Seeking human and stone broken faces:
Where a wave shall catch the noon sun
In a low, falling window and break it
And a statue shall break its nose off
Revealing a genius's smile

And the great fleet of thorns in the weeds
Shall sail for Piraeus
Bearing a man shaped by nettles
Like a masterpiece made by a bush
In the sculptor's absence:

Where the sails shall set course
By the star on a stallion's brow

And bear him, upright, in a track
Like the ram's horn etched on his wrist,
Inward, all night in an aching
Impossibly creative position
With a crow on his shoulder,
With his arms and his nose breaking off,
Till he wakes at the heart of Greece,
Steps down, is whole there, and stands.

[1963]

Richard Eberhart

DIVORCE

The rock that withstands man's arrogance
Is nature's own rock high above the land;
Lofty in the fogs; pure height on walking days,
Something to look at with an aspiring eye.
Yet never its greatness and true strength
Appear until new divorce breaks old forms.
We do not possess it any more,
Not at all, the forms are ruined by arrogance,
Parents and children are sundered by separation.
Life sprawls in unkempt acres.
It is then the rock stands triumphant, beyond man's
Pride that kept him from a noble union.
But divorce separates us also from the rock.

[1961]

William Faulkner

A REVIEW

THE OLD MAN AND THE SEA. By *Ernest Hemingway*. Scribner's. $3.00. (1952) Prior publication: LIFE Magazine, 1 September, 1952.

His best. Time may show it to be the best single piece of any of us, I mean his and my contemporaries. This time, he discovered God, a Creator. Until now, his men and women had made themselves, shaped themselves out of their own clay; their victories and defeats were at the hands of each other, just to prove to themselves or one another how tough they could be. But this time, he wrote about pity: about something somewhere that made them all: the old man who had to catch the fish and then lose it, the fish that had to be caught and then lost, the sharks which had to rob the old man of his fish; made them all and loved them all and pitied them all. It's all right. Praise God that whatever made and loves and pities Hemingway and me kept him from touching it any further.

[1952]

Irving Feldman

READ TO THE ANIMALS, OR ORPHEUS AT THE SPCA

A woman called and offered me a hundred dollars to read in San Francisco. I said, "Okay, but only for dogs and cats." "What?" she said. I said, "I charge five hundred dollars to read for people, but I'm interested in how pets respond to poetry. They hear humans speaking all the time, and I'm curious if they can tell the difference between ordinary speech and poetry." "Can't a few people be there too?" "No," I said, "five hundred dollars for people, one hundred dollars for household pets. I can only give so many readings a year, and I want to earn the most from them." So she said, "I don't see the difference. You're reading anyway, whether to dogs and cats or to people." She's dead serious about this. I said, "Well, the dogs and cats don't tell anyone how long you read or how much you gave it."

. . . . .

The last time I called [Adrienne Rich] I did so because a mutual friend said she was depressed and I might cheer her up. So I phoned her and got through her bodyguards, and she said, "Yes?" And I said, "Hello, Adrienne, this is Phil." She said, "Phil?" "Yeah, Phil Levine." "What do you want?" I should have said, "I want some pussy," because she was using a voice Mussolini would have used to a street cleaner. Instead I think I said, "Nice to talk to you."

Philip Levine, interviewed in Antaeus, *Summer 1980.*

Dear Mr. Levine,
You can call me Rex.
I am a two-year-old male dog—big, short-haired,
mostly shepherd—living the last six months
in a shelter for wayward animals.

I read in a magazine how you looking
to adopt a cat. Me too. Even if
I am canine, living with them day in
day out, I can say they totally cute.
Which probably is why they never seem
enough to go around. So flash on this:
our bitches really been getting the job done
—so maybe you adopt "some *puppy*" instead?

I also seen how you looking to read
your poetry to us. We all were jumping.
We don't have budget for poetry reading,
so all us guys been saving up for you.
Cool you cutting your fee. I pretty sure
we be able to hack the hundred bucks.
Supervisor say she be writing to you
on official paper, she say anyhow
after you seen our facility, you want
to turn it all back to our building fund.
But I say, Tell her to go stuff, yeah! I say,
Keep it—cost of cat *always* going up!

Lot of poets starting to come around.
We animals got to be *in* thing now.
Bet you surprised how much poetry we dig.
Dickey, he read here couple a three times.
Ginsberg too. They charge humans thousands a pop,
but they wouldn't even take nothing from us.
I really dug Ginsberg's show—he got us
to sing along with him. *Om, om, om, om.*
Oh wow, us canines really turned on to that.

Hey, they both great kids. And both of them say
they will come to live here when they retire.
I can dig. How often they meet up with
a group that groove on their stuff—and show it?
Fame have got to be a mean trip: get yourself
disappointed, misunderstood—a touch too much
idolizing here, a touch too little there.
Got to be why big shots get down on mankind.
Then mankind turn around, give them the bum rap,
yeah, mankind say they stuck up on theirself.
I say they got to lick theirself front and back
—in the right doses, at the right times and places.
Hell, they never brag, if we gots art to praise them right!

Hey, bet you don't believe all the fans you got.
Every time *New Yorker* hit the catbox,
cats and dogs be fighting to read your poetry.
They really dig your deep humanity,
they dig your compassion for the underdogs.

They *know* you give them respect, feed them good,
never polish up your boot-tips on their bellies.
And be others here that get off on misery.
Pure breeds. Always be slumming. They kinky. They go,
"Oh, daddy, tell us what it was like to be poor!"
They *rub* their furs all *over* those fat pages.
Make me *sick* when they do that to your poetry.

Mr. Levine,
I was born in the streets.
Never knew my dad.
Never seen the inside of a house.
Never ate from a dish.
Never got to go on paper.
Yeah, I sniffed on the sidewalks,
I licked in the gutters
—I ain't shamed of that.
But now I want to make it to the top,
get to get 500 bucks a shot,
get to say anything I want to,
get to *go* on paper.
Get to beat the canine rap
—I be up there walking on two legs,
I be human, like god.

Mr. Levine, you got to help me bad.
Hey, you adopt *me,* teach me to write poetry.
If they tell you no, then you sneak me out
after you read. Just wait till things quiet down,
then I tip you the high sign and we split.
But you watch out for Supervisor. Her bad.
Her Lady Cerberus. Her the Bitch Goddess.
Her never miss a trick. They's a whole bunch here
she caught already. Scottie and Ernest,
Dylan, Delmore, Berries, Cal. She tell them,
You got to kiss my butt, 'cause this here the Hell of Fame.

Mr. Levine, you lucky, you not famous,
but her *make* us famous, her make us household *pets.*
Give us fame-rabies just like them other cats.
I *seen* them on fire, raging and thrashing
to get theirself comfortable and couldn't
—their bodies all red with burning rashes,

like ten thousand hot tongues of wildfire rumor
was kissing them all over with their names,
telling them *who* they is. Pitiful how
they howl in pain, awful how they beg for more.
That fame, it's junk, and junk make you tame.
Best minds of my time foaming at the dentures!

Got to cut out now. You remember what I wrote.
One way or other, I be busting this joint.
Hope this note don't smell too bad. Destroy it,
if you got to. Keep my secret. Rex.

7/20/81.

[1982]

Donald Finkel

ASIATIC DAY-FLOWER

One blue eye beside the path
Peers up the secret thighs
Of girls and winks in the wind. Not
Of course lewdly. However, imagine
Roots digging their nails into
The sod, and imagine also one
Eye on frail neck straining
To see what it may not touch.
(Nor I, Mister.) Under the fabric
Swiftly the thighs caress each other.
(But not I, mister, not I.
The eye inside my mind peers
And strains.)

And at my feet, heeding
Transience of flesh in his blue stare,
Beside the path the calm pornographer
Waits out the finite season of desire. [1957]

Ford Madox Ford

OBSERVATIONS ON TECHNIQUE*

Conversation is the best means by which a "character" in a piece of fiction may be indicated. This is the only purpose for which direct quotation should be used. Conversation should never be employed to carry the story along, develop the plot, or to indicate action. If the author uses his characters' speech to develop his story, the reader will wonder whether or not the character who speaks is being allowed to tell the truth. Therefore, the author should never let this doubt enter.

All the narration of the story should be done by the author himself.

The first speech of a character is important in as much as it serves to "fix" or typify or indicate the kind of character we may expect.

Never let characters remain static throughout the course of the story—each important character *must* be altered by the circumstances touching him and surrounding him or the story may easily fail.

My method to make conversation seem more natural and to imitate the continual breaks, unfinished sentences and undeveloped thoughts of ordinary converse is to use the pause.... before the speech. The reader loves what he takes to be "real" conversation—not "speech" and not some artificial exchange of neat sentences that has been concocted by the author.

Usually in a conversation neither speaker cares very much what the other is talking about. Each will go along following his own theme of thought and quite oblivious to the interruptions of the other.

Conversation must be realistic, not "real." There must be just enough normal-sounding breaks, pauses, catch-phrases and well-worn expressions in a long speech to make it convincingly human and not literary.

---

*Some notes on a lecture given by FMF at Olivet College in June, 1938.

Example of Projection: "The glass had bubbles." Example of Narration: "He looked and he saw that the glass had bubbles." Projection: the author telling the story and moving the character about with his hands. Narration: a character moving through the action of the story and the author simply on hand to record what happens, what is thought or felt.

In narration the author may conceal his literary idiosyncrasies. In first-person narration, by filtering the story through a carefully-conceived set of prejudices, ideas, habits of thinking and observation owned by his chief character, the author may avoid the difficulty of too personal and too autobiographical style. De Maupassant never bothered to conceal his method in this way. (Reference: "The Field of Olives.")

[1953]

Robie Macauley

THE DEAN IN EXILE: NOTES ON FORD MADOX FORD AS TEACHER

Ford used to have tea served in his office once a week. It was a small shadowy room in the basement of the library at Olivet College and I think he was aware of the number of ironies in the portrait he sat for every seven days. "The Dean of English Letters," as he rather wryly thought of himself now and then, ought to end up in a library room of his own, prosperous and respected. He ought to be surrounded by all the mementos of his long career—Christina Rosetti's writing desk in the corner, the death mask of Oliver Cromwell on the wall, a gallery of pictures from Ford Madox Brown through Wyndham Lewis and Juan Gris, on the shelves all the autographed and inscribed Victorian first editions along with the letters from Conrad, the books of all the writers he had helped to launch—and his own.

These would be the solid evidences he might reassure himself with in the last year of his life; but he had none of them. The books on the shelves were leftovers from the stacks upstairs—books of theology that all seemed to have been published in Chicago around 1901, a few tracts against the tobacco habit and a scattering of novels, the most distinguished of which were those of Robert Herrick. On his desk was a pile of manuscripts sent him by young writers, the pages of the book he was now working on *(The March of Literature)* and a few packs of his corrosive French cigarettes ("Dust and dung," he said). All he had left was the tremendous reference file of his memory and his imagination had tampered a good deal with that.

It was, nevertheless, still the most extraordinary memory I have ever encountered. In a way, I suppose, it had rewritten a good deal of the world's literature. Ford could talk a good book out of anything he happened to like and I remember once when he was discussing *The Anabasis,* he gave a remarkable picture of the lost army, suddenly discovering itself in a bleak, unknown land, returning, making the long slow march across dreary plains, through icy rivers and mountains, held together only by the will of a steely puritan who commanded it. It was a great epic, as he told it, though you mustn't call it Xenophon—as I later discovered. Yet it was distilled out of Xenophon and it created an action and a picture in my mind that even the grim plodding in Greek I. could never kill.

Ford had none of that sense of time and death that turns books into mere middens or archaeological finds for critics and scholars. He was the least academic man who ever taught and for him all books, in themselves, were contemporaneous. *Don Quixote* or *The History of the Peloponnesian War* were as fresh subjects of conversation as was *Nightwood.* He could talk equally imaginatively on any of the three. He succeeded in giving the impression for instance that, though he had just missed meeting Marlowe in London, he knew all about him and was very much excited by the young man's work. To Ford, no good book was ever entombed in the Dewey Decimal System; it had always just been published and most of its career was before it.

This might sound like a romantic and fanciful denial of the

long process of literature. Actually, he was very much aware of it—it appeared to him as a kind of family tree. One writer "descended" from another in that the accumulated knowledge of the older passed on to the younger. By this figure, he would have most likely chosen James as his father and Flaubert as his grandfather and traced himself back to Horace, at least. He liked to talk about one writer's apprenticeship to another and often took as his instance Maupassant learning from Flaubert, drawing a picture of Flaubert angrily throwing Maupassant's early stories into the fire, one by one, until at last they began to fit his exacting ideas.

Ford despised dilettantes and this was one of his ways of getting at a hard fact—that a writer committed himself at the beginning and had to remain committed through all the mischances of life. Though he encouraged a great many people, essentially Ford had little respect for the part-time author. It was a single profession and it had to be followed always, even if it ended you finally without reward or possessions in a little Michigan college several thousand miles from Provençe, which was the heart of the civilized world and the only place to die in. I think many people teach writing capably without ever giving their students the idea of what *being* a writer means. Ford never actually taught writing (though he discussed manuscripts) but nobody who listened to him carefully could miss the meaning of that essential and difficult lesson. If you accepted it, you could be only part-time and unimportantly a newspaperman, a teacher or an office-worker. They were odd jobs you took along the way and might easily give up. But this was only the beginning—there was much more to it. Ford once became angry with me when I said that I didn't know whether I had enough talent to become a writer. "You've *got* to know," he wheezed. "Right now. Otherwise you'd better get out." He thought of it as something like a priest's vocation.

This is a very subversive idea and, if it were taught clearly enough, it would probably be the end of all summer "writing conferences" and would reduce all the "creative writing" classes in colleges and universities to a couple of students here and there.

Ford's method of teaching was narrative and anecdotal. Almost any question could be answered or any idea presented in the form of a story and he was ill at ease in any more abstract conversation.

I think that every subject he knew or cared anything about—and they were a great many, from garden farming to world politics—he conceived in terms of character and action, finally working into a plot. Usually his stories were not simple illustrations of the point; they contained a great many relative and tangential things. Thus, a student asking a question about drama, might get as an answer a quite involved and probably half-imaginary story about Goethe that seemed to end up a considerable distance from the original question. If he thought about it, however, he would realize that along the way Ford had introduced a dozen relevant ideas and, though he had never given a direct answer, he had given an extraordinarily complete one. After listening to Ford, I always found other teachers something like a human true-and-false test. There is a little book called *The Legend of the Master* in which the editor discounts most of Ford's stories about Henry James as fabrications. However the point—which the editor grudgingly half-admits—is that Ford's brilliant little fictions about James are altogether more lifelike, more full of insight, more characteristic and idiosyncratic and, in the end, "truer" than any mere factual accounts.

To people involved in more rigid kinds of logic, fiction always seems like a very disorderly way of getting at any kind of truth. Similarly, Ford's last book, *The March of Literature,* must seem to critics more like a series of raids than any progressive advance. (The London *Times,* with great innocence, called it a kind of crib-book for students in literary courses. Any student who depended on it for a crib would undoubtedly be sternly flunked.) The book is more or less an expanded and polished version of the lectures he gave at Olivet and his way of teaching can be seen in it. To anyone who wants a thorough survey, it is an exasperating book. It is full of Ford's prejudices and personality and it slights or ignores everything he considers dull. Both the lectures and the book were strangely disproportionate—thus, for instance, Ford could overpraise Turgenev and rather underestimate Dostoievski and, on the whole, come off with a queerly impressionistic view of Russian writing. Finally, the critical standard was personal taste carried to an extreme but within the borders of what Ford liked the criticism was carried on with such selectivity and enthusiasm that one forgave him his arbitrary general method. If the march was somewhat haphazard, the raids were always brilliant. If Ford recognized Dostoievski rather blankly, he pointed out the virtues of Turgenev with great discrimination and pleasure.

In a time when criticism tends to be sound, dull, abstract and official, Ford is much out of fashion. Critics speak to other critics and to professors of literature; Ford always spoke to writers and readers.

At Olivet Ford lived in a miniature house not much bigger than a hen coop. He was a large stout man and I was always surprised to see that he actually fitted inside. My impression was that the place was in complete chaos and that Ford was the center of disorder. Some operation was always ponderously, with many interruptions, under way, whether it was cooking *coq au vin* (Ford was a magnificent chef) or marking the proofs of a book. In the midst of all this mobilization, Janice Biala, Ford's wife, was always perpectly composed and efficient. Quite different in temperament, she was a good balance. She was (and is) an excellent painter, witty in conversation, attractive, and as direct and informal as Ford sometimes was overawing and roundabout.

Quite a few people who have written about Ford (especially Douglas Goldring and other English writers) have seemed a little puzzled over his connection with such an obscure small college as Olivet. Not many of them realize that, for one brief period under the presidency of Joseph Brewer, Olivet College had an extraordinary life as a center of education in the arts. It has since declined back into dullness, but at one time such people as Ford and Sherwood Anderson taught writing there. Allen Tate, Caroline Gordon, Katherine Anne Porter, William Troy and others taught in the summer sessions. Count Korzybski, the semanticist, gave a series of lectures one year. Among the occasional speakers were Gertrude Stein, Carl Sandburg and Carl VanVechten. The work in music and art was likewise good. The trouble, as usual, was lack of money and after President Brewer left, a new reactionary regime triumphantly returned the college to its former level of mediocrity.

All through his life Ford was engaged in the promotion of talent in writing. He often neglected his own interests and his own work in efforts to bring young writers to the attention of publishers and readers. The list of their names is too long and too well-known to repeat here; however, it is still a little surprising to remember, as John Hutchens said to me recently, that Ford's literary promoting began with Joseph Conrad and extended through half a century to Eudora Welty. Ford's *English Review* and *transatlantic review* were the results of this wish. Near the end of his life, he was planning still another literary magazine for the same purpose.

Nevertheless, I think that Ford's greatest accomplishment as a teacher and mentor was that indefinable sense of stimulation he passed on to younger writers. To write honestly and well was the most important thing in the world.

[1953]

Robert Lowell

FORD MADOX FORD

1873-1938

The lobbed ball plops, then dribbles to the cup.
A birdie, Fordie! But it nearly killed
The ministers. Lloyd George is holding up
The flag. He gabbles, "Hop-toad, hop-toad, hop-toad!
Hueffer has used a mashie on the green!
It's a filthy art, sir, a filthy art!"
You answered, "What is art to me and thee?
Will a blacksmith teach a midwife how to bear?"
Bulldog of the King' English, what is art?
New thresholds, new anatomies? Or was
It war, the sport of kings, that your *Good Soldier,*
The first French novel in the language, taught
Those Georgian Whig magnificoes at Oxford,
At Oxford decimated on the Somme?
Ford, mustard-gassed and buried seven miles
Behind the lines at Nancy or Belleau Wood,
And five times blackballed for promotion, you
Emerged, a Jonah—O divorced, divorced
From the whale-fat of post-war London. Boomed,
Cut, plucked and booted! You had learned your art.
Sandman! Your face, a girlish O. The sun
Is pernod-yellow, and it gilds the heirs
Of all the ages there on Washington
And Stuyvesant, your Lilliputian squares—
Here writing turned your pockets inside out.
But master, mammoth mumbler, tell me why
The bales of your left-over novels buy
Less than a bandage for your gouty foot.
Wheel-horse, O unforgetting elephant,
I hear you huffing at your old Brevoort,
Timon and Falstaff, while you heap the board
For publishers. Fiction! I'm selling short
Your lies that made the great your equals. Ford,
You were a kind man and you died in want.

[1955]

Eugene K. Garber

THE LOVER

I

Here is a beginning. I am a tow-headed boy in the depression South, walking a dusty road by a creek. I am with two other boys, brothers. The older and taller is Abner Ellis, Junior. The one my age and height is Frank. Abner is seventeen. Frank and I are fifteen. Their mother is thousand-eyed. In my dreams I see her beautiful ocellated face fan out and cover the stars. She knows me, knows that I desire Frank. Abner has no inkling. Frank himself does not understand it. But she knows.

If she had been of a higher caste she undoubtedly would have had a significant history. Maybe she forfeited celebrity when she married Dr. Ellis upon his graduation from Tulane medical school, but I don't think so. Marie Crevet. There are no socially prominent Crevets in New Orleans, not even a marginal family who might marry an extraordinarily beautiful daughter upward into the ruling classes.

Anyway, she came as a bride to Laurelie in south Alabama, melon capital of the world, a patchwork of loamy fields and red clay hillocks, rank with the sweat of blacks and raucous with the hymns of Baptist farmers. No apparent destiny here for her beauty. The doctor liked seclusion. Probably he didn't trust the gentlemen of larger towns. Who could blame him? He was an unlikely husband for such a bride—gangly, big-eared, deformed by an Adam's apple that rode under his collar like a thieved melon in the toils of a creek, and crack-voiced as though his glottis were arrested in perpetual adolescence. Everyone knows the type, "raw-boned, Lincolnesque." Everyone has read dozens of such biographical sketches. He made the archetypal sacrifices of the poor country boy to secure his degree in medicine: scrimped to save his tuition while still helping to support a widowed mother, studied bleary-eyed by midnight oil for his entrance examinations, et cetera. By the time I knew him he'd already had one heart attack. There was good reason for it, other than his youthful sacrifices—an exhausting practice among blacks bloated by fat-back and cornmeal, among gnarled fundamentalist dirt farmers too guilt and God-ridden to come in time with their ripe tumors. So I despised him from the first for the constant outpouring of his charity, which left us in his home only the rind of his love.

I was his nephew, sent down in the summers from a motherless home in the great city of steel, Birmingham, by a sodden coal-blackened father. And it was I finally who provided the occasion for the heroism which such beauty as my aunt's inevitably has exacted of it.

Marie Crevet Ellis bore to her husband two sons, Abner and Frank. Abner was his father's son—blue-eyed, willowy, an effortless charmer of girls. Frank was his mother's son, dark and beautiful. He was marvelously hirsute, his nostrils dark and densely ten-driled, his face shadowed below high cheek bones. His chest and limbs and even his back bristled with hairs that made beautiful black rivulets when he rose like a young sea god from our creek. But such dark beauty was uncouth in those parts, and so he was lonely.

So was my aunt lonely, in constancy to her faith. She attended Mass every Sunday afternoon. It was celebrated for her and two old women by a circuiting priest at a side altar of the Episcopal church, rented no doubt for the occasion through an uneasy alli-ance of prelacies in that benighted stronghold of fundamentalism. In the dead heat of July and August she still put on her black dress, covered her head with a black mantilla, and walked through the downtown streets to her devotions. The ice-cream eaters in front of the drugstore and the old men on the hotel verandah star-ed, but they said nothing. I myself would have liked to ask: why this penitential black in the seasonless summer, Lent past and Advent yet to come? What was she guilty of? Failing to rear her sons as Catholics? Later she had more to confess.

I began to succeed in my advances toward Frank. But I can say this for myself: as unthinkable as were my desires in that time and place, I always kept in view his good. When his gentle loneliness began to unfold to me, I touched it always with delicate love. If he wanted to tell me that I was beginning to trespass on his feel-ings, he only had to speak my name with a hint of admonition and I would stop. Still, I confess, my yearning outstripped the slow melting of his reserve. I found it more and more difficult to guard my feelings, even in the presence of others. Once at supper my uncle, noting our silence, suddenly said, "All right, Frank and Joe, what's the big secret?" Caught completely off guard, I blushed hotly. "What are they up to, Marie?"

My aunt's dark eyes looked straight into mine. "Oh, I think they've found something at the creek."

"They spend enough time down there," said Abner. "It must be a mermaid." His own wit surprised him and he guffawed.

"We don't have any secret, Father," said Frank with a voice as clear as a bell.

"Good. Then let's talk to each other instead of acting like we're at a wake."

I don't know where the conversation went from there, but I do remember that when my frightening embarrassment had passed, I was suddenly suffused with great pity—for the man with the youthfully cracked voice and the dying body; for my beautiful aunt, whose dark eyes pleaded with me to spare her son; for Frank, who was forced now for the first time to lie to his father; and even for Abner in his innocent ignorance. I should have leaped up and cried that I was the serpent in their bosom, that they must scotch me or be ruined. Instead, I excused myself on pretense of nausea. And after that I made ready a face to meet any comment that might touch my relationship with Frank.

For a while I kept my distance from Frank, sensing his revulsion toward the lie he had told his father, though it was not a deep lie. After all, we had only feasted eyes, touched hesitatingly. So, a few days later I resumed my courtship, and I was overjoyed to discover that the lie had left no taint, that the warm promise of his slow yielding was still there. One day when we had swum a while nude in the Blue Hole, we lay together on a flat rock at the lip of the deep pool. We embraced. I felt the hairs of his back, exposed to the motley sun in the trees, dry and grow erect. But after a few moments he disengaged himself and rolled over on his back. I leaned beside him, my body intensely hot. He looked up through half-closed eyes. "What is this thing, Joe?"

Then I knew that he felt, as I did, a palpable presence embracing us. I might have called it the god of love. I actually thought of that, but I only said, "I don't know. I don't have to know." I leaned forward and kissed his teat in its nest of black hair and it hardened against my lips.

"I do need to know," Frank said.

"Tell me when you find out."

Do I make it sound as though there were only these episodes of pursuit? Not at all. We played American Legion baseball. Abner was a star pitcher. We flew model airplanes. Frank's, the most delicately balanced, stayed up longest. My aunt caught us and made us mow, weed, shell peas. My forte was frogging. Many nights we waded the creek. Frank carried the gunny sack. Abner hypnotized the frogs with the flashlight, and I snared them in the long net that I myself had woven, hooped, and secured to an oak sapling. My uncle loved the legs breaded and fried, but he had to cook them himself because my aunt could not bear to watch the final contractions in the pan. Of course, we boys one night saved out a hapless creature for the classic experiment. When it was newly dead, we passed through it a small battery current. The twitching of legs bewitched us. We tumbled over each other and gyrated splay-legged about our bunk room—three adolescents having a saurian orgy. But even in that crude prank, as in the chores and play of every day, the current of my love for Frank never for one moment ceased to galvanize my heart.

Besides my aunt's vigilance, there was one other threat to my love for Frank—a series of monologues that Abner delivered in the bunk room when he got home from dates. He would lie on his back in his bunk and light up cigarettes that he had stolen at the drugstore. In the morning the room would have a dreadful smell, but Abner's nicotine crimes were never detected because my aunt was forbidden by my uncle ever to set foot in the bunk room. His motives were two-fold, he explained. No lady should have the offensive job of cleaning up after boys. Conversely, boys must have their sanctuary. Every Saturday afternoon my uncle himself inspected our quarters. For this we carefully spruced up, or titivated, as the doctor was fond of saying. Otherwise, the room remained a congeries of clothes, balls, bats, string, balsam scraps, etc. So Abner would light up one cigarette after another. He didn't inhale and probably didn't even like the taste. But he obviously liked the big white plumes of smoke that rose up into the moonlight at the window bequeathing his words a ghostly presence and wreathing about them the wraith of eroticism and nocturnal mystery. Here was the essence of his story repeated over and over with little variation. He had two girl friends, Betty and Harriet. Betty, the hotel manager's daughter, was only a decoy, Abner said. Harriet, a rich farmer's daughter, was his true love. Frank and I had seen them often, of course, and they were true in appearance to the character that Abner assigned them in his midnight monologues. Betty was a saucy little thing with black hair and dark eyes. Harriet, on the other hand, was blond, the perfect Aryan match for Abner. Betty must have absorbed what little there was to learn of vice in Laurelie, living in a hotel suite and helping with the travelers, because a great number of Abner's narratives dealt with her innovations in kissing—frenching, the love-bite, the lobelolly, etc.

I found all this repulsive, but I wondered what Frank thought. He made no signs in the dark, no response until one night he pressed Abner for details of a rare kiss from Harriet. "It was a soul kiss, Frank. Our tongues never touched, but it was a soul kiss, better than all of Betty's kisses put together."

"What do you mean, a soul kiss?"

"I mean the kind of kiss that makes you feel like you aren't there any more. You feel like you left your old self behind, like snake slough."

"Where did you go, into Harriet?" A dense fountain of smoke shot up toward the ceiling. "It's hard to tell, Frank. I did sort of feel like I was dropping down into her mouth if you can think of a mouth as big as night. But I wasn't thinking *this is Harriet.* I was just . . . going out of myself."

The halting of Abner's ending was more eloquent than his words. Silence descended on us. But I lay awake thinking: what has Frank learned from this? That one kiss from a true love is infinitely better than all the inventions of promiscuity? That the only true love for a man is a woman? But I found that I could not imagine for myself Frank's thoughts or desires, probably because my own were so simple: I wanted him.

That night's exchange with Abner had a profound effect on Frank. The next afternoon, when we were alone at the Blue Hole lying in shoaling water on the lip of the pool, I caressed his thigh, but he set my hand aside. "Don't touch me, Joe, and don't talk to me about it for a while." I feared he meant forever. I feared it with a wintry contraction of the heart that numbed all my senses.

And I felt helpless, forbidden to plead my case with the one I loved. He was determined to work things out alone. My uncle noticed Frank's abstraction and joshed him. "Any chance of you getting out of the dog days of August, boy?" Yes, the summer was almost over, and I knew in my bones that it was this summer or never. I knew that if I could possess Frank even once, I could go back to my smoky city and my sodden father and sing in my heart despite their sooty faces. But if I went back with my desire all locked up, I could not live until another summer.

My aunt watched. One night I overheard her say, "I know what it is, my Frank. I know you will choose the good way." They were in her sewing room. I couldn't see them, but I imagined her taking his hand, stroking his hair, speaking dark eyes to dark eyes, excluding me forever. My heart raged against her. But I made no sign. I knew that if anything caused Frank to suspect I did not love her he would shut me out of his heart forever. So I was the serpent under the flower, waiting for something to come my way. And just when my patience was wearing dangerously thin, I was rewarded. The one who had almost ruined me gave me new hope —dear crude Abner.

My good fortune came on a Tuesday night. Abner was eating with Betty at the hotel and then they were going to the movie. Later, Frank and I learned that her parents were out of town for the night. From Abner's excitement I might have guessed as much, but there was something else on my mind. At supper my uncle had revealed that a much loved fellow doctor over in Minnville was hopelessly ill.

"Physician, heal thyself," I said. The moment the words were out I was horrified. It was as though a demon had spoken through my mouth. My uncle lay down his knife and fork. "The reason he is dying, Joe, is that he has worked himself to the bone for the people of Minnville. He couldn't turn away a sick nigger on Christmas morning." He spoke sharply.

"That's what I meant, Uncle Ab, about small-town doctors. Their patients take everything."

"Joe's right, Abner. You all work too hard." Pity and love streamed out of my aunt's eyes: for the husband with the slightly ashen face whose death would not lag far behind his friend's, for the son in whose dark eyes toiled warring images of awakening sex, and, yes, even for the perverse nephew whose thwarted love tipped his tongue with involuntary malice. She was our mater dolorosa. But I couldn't love her, not even for redeeming in Frank's eyes my wayward remark.

After supper the house seemed full of gloom. Half-heartedly I suggested frogging. To my surprise Frank agreed: Down at the creek we waited for the deepening dark to bring the sound of the big croakers. I had one of Abner's cigarettes, which I lit as soon as we had settled ourselves on a rock. Frank must have been surprised because I had never smoked before, but he said nothing. The smoke made a pale image against the moonless sheen of the creek. "Want a drag?" Maybe I hoped that mixing spit on the cigarette paper would seal our lips.

"No."

A moment later I threw the cigarette into the creek and spat after it. "I don't know what Abner sees in those things."

We waded into the creek. Frank went ahead with the flashlight. I followed him closely with my net. The croaker sack was tied over my shoulder. One by one I dropped the big frogs into it. But when we had maybe a half dozen, I began to be invaded by a curious feeling of deep kinship with the frogs—slimy singers of unmelodious love songs flung into a hairy darkness to writhe hopelessly until a hammer delivered them from confusion. So strong became this projection that it grew almost hallucinatory. The flashlight beam did not hypnotize them more than their glistening eyes fixated me.

"Are you going to get this one or not, Joe?"

"No. It's a mama full of eggs. We got enough. Let's quit."

Back at the house I pretended to knot the neck of the sack before I dropped it outside the bunk-room door. But I didn't. I knew the frogs would wriggle free. But could they find the creek a half mile away? Could they follow its sound or smell? Or would the sun catch them struggling lost in the crab grass and thickets? It was do or die for them once more, just as it had been the moment before I netted them, when they made that last jump. Some had cleared the hoop and won freedom, but these had landed in my net. That's what I determined to do now, make my leap. In just a moment, when we were both naked, I would take Frank into my arms as gently but as strongly as I could—my fatal leap of love.

Abner saved me at the last possible moment bursting in on our nakedness. We had been undressing in the near dark, by the small night light—like white-bellied frogs, I was thinking, when the edge of the flashlight beam first touches them. Abner's bunk was closest to the door. He went straight to his bed light, turned it on, and looked at us with an expression of wild triumph. I shook fearfully. Somehow, I thought, his dull eye had spied me out, detected the truth in our surprised nakedness. But it was quickly obvious that I had misunderstood. The wild triumph was something he brought from the hotel, where he had been in Betty's bed. He quickly flung off his clothes and stood before our tall mirror inspecting himself minutely.

"What's going on?" said Frank, his voice already touched with disapproval.

"I was in her, in her." I looked at Frank. Disgust narrowed his eyes and turned down the corners of his mouth. So I pressed Abner with pretended innocence.

"Who?"

"Betty." He was still admiring himself in the mirror.

"In the car?"

"In her room at the hotel." He turned around suddenly and threw himself with a groan face down on his bed as though onto some palpable afterimage of Betty's body. Frank turned away. I followed his lead. A moment later we sat simultaneously on our beds.

"You won't believe it when you finally get some," he said. A tone of coarse tutelage crept into his voice, but when he turned and looked at us, that changed radically. "What the hell's the matter with you two?" Neither of us answered. "You, Frank," he said, "what are you looking like that for?"

"Why don't you go take a shower?" I had never heard Frank's voice so hard.

"Take a shower!" He sat up suddenly. "Take a shower when I saved the perfume for you boys?" I would not have guessed that Abner could be so sardonic. But he had obviously seen the utter disgust in Frank's face, and it infuriated him. He leaped from his bed and threw himself on Frank. I saw the naked limbs of the two brothers writhing together strenuously as Abner deliberately smeared on his brother the secretions of love. Then there was suddenly a cry. Frank had driven his knee into Abner's groin. Abner fell to the floor with a groan and lay there doubled up. Frank hurried into the bathroom. I heard the instant hiss of the shower. After a while he came back and put on his pajamas. Abner was now lying supine on his bunk with the back of his hand over his eyes. "Don't touch me," he said. I had been wondering which of them would say it first.

The next afternoon, as the two of us lay naked in the shallows of the edge of the Blue Hole, Frank allowed me to lave him with cool water. I touched him everywhere, chastely. I was consoling him, of course, and washing away Abner's bestiality. But I was also making him ready for my embrace. All my intuition assured me that on the next afternoon would come the full consummation of our love. Yet it was not to be. When we returned to the house we found my aunt and uncle making arrangements necessitated by the death of the doctor's colleague in Minnville. My aunt, who lay in bed, was saying, "I don't feel well enough to go, but you go, and take the boys. They ought to be there. Jep has been like an uncle to them."

"I can't leave you alone, Marie," said the doctor.

"It's nothing serious, Abner, and besides, I've got Joe."

I had even then an inkling of the truth about my aunt's illness, but I did not reflect on it because I was so upset by the prospect of being separated from Frank.

At last, at my aunt's insistence, my uncle agreed. They would have to spend one night away, no more. And before they drove off, my uncle laid upon me the usual charge: I was the man of the house in his place and must see that nothing happened to my aunt. I promised and then watched them leave. Abner assumed the older brother's prerogative and sat in the front seat beside his father. Frank sat alone in the back, keeping his eyes constantly on me as a kind of promise until the car turned out of the driveway.

II

I sat in the living room that afternoon as my uncle had instructed me. I was also to sleep in the guest room that night with the door open so that I would never be out of earshot of my aunt's voice. About three, an old black woman came to the kitchen door. A half dozen sacks hung from her shoulders. "Field peas, crowders, black-eyed peas, snaps, butter beans," she sang through the screen.

I hurried out to the kitchen. "Be quiet," I said. "Mrs. Ellis is sick."

"Lemme see her then."

I had run into this old black before and she had always looked at me curiously out of her rheumy brown eyes. She was either addled or preternaturally wise. She made me nervous. "Didn't you hear what I said? Go away. If you wake her up, I'll tell the doctor when he gets back." Too late. I heard my aunt's bare feet on the floor behind me. "It's all right, Joe. I'll speak to her." I went off into the dining room but I hid behind the door and listened.

"Hello Granny. What do you have today?"

"That one say you sick." Why did she say *that one?* It gave me a start. Was she pointing at the dining room doorway, knowing I was there? Or did she say *that one* because she considered me a creature unnameable? I listened.

"You want me to send Seth with some of the black pot?"

I almost burst out laughing. Obviously the hag regularly sent this concoction to my aunt, a doctor's wife and a Catholic still clinging to some old creole superstition. But if I had known then what I know now, I would not have been tempted to laugh. I listened. My aunt said something in a hushed voice. All I caught was the insistent concluding phrase, "You remember."

"I remember, Miss Marie, if you sho' that's what you want." My aunt apparently was sure, because the old woman left. I retreated quickly to the living room, where my aunt now came instead of returning directly to her room. "I'm sorry," I said. "I tried to keep her from waking you up."

"I wasn't asleep. It's too hot." Her cheeks had a hectic flush, and pin-points of perspiration moistened her upper lip. She stood before me as if dazed. The light from the window shone through her sheer nightgown except where the cloth folded upon itself, so that I saw the outline of her body broken only here and there by thin streaks of shadow. It was beautiful in silhouette. In the flesh it would have the same delicate ivory as the skin of her arms. But I didn't go far with this imagining. Something in her manner put me on guard. For the first time I got a definite intimation that she had contrived for the two of us to be alone so she could separate me from Frank permanently. She must have guessed the day after Abner's midnight abominations that our relationship had resumed with a passion. After a few moments, saying nothing further, she walked slowly and not quite steadily down the hall to her room.

Now my mind began to work with a fierce heat, assembling a jumble of possibilities. Yet even in those first stages of thought, chaotic as they were, I had no doubt that I could pierce my aunt's intentions. If that seems too precociously self-confident for a boy of fifteen, remember: I had a mother who had been beaten to death by poverty and abuse, a father who was a villainous drunk with the strength of an ox, and wretched schoolmates who watched for every opportunity to humiliate me because I learned fast and whetted my tongue on their stupidity. It was only quick perceptions that enabled me to escape the fate of my mother, the sister whom the doctor had not saved. So I sat in the chair in my uncle's living room with an unread book in my lap. Here is what I had to think about. What was it that my aunt had ordered from the old black? Was it more of the same potion that already was causing her to change—some vial of it left from a much earlier episode which the old black had to fetch up from memory? I thought it must be. But why? Why make herself woozy and strange? It must relate to Frank and me, but how?

I let the questions tumble about in my head. Meanwhile I listened carefully for any noise which would signal a secret delivery by Granny's Seth. I asked myself more questions. If behind the potion and the mysterious behavior was the intention of separating Frank and me, why hadn't she gone about it more directly? Why not plead with my uncle to send me home? He wouldn't refuse her. Or why not call Frank in and tell him that he must break off from me? There was such a strong bond between them that she would inevitably be persuasive. But even as I considered these possibilities, I understood why she wouldn't accept either. The separation must come from us somehow. Otherwise, Frank would be left with crudely detached emotions which later might attach themselves, even more tenaciously, to a similar partner. Perhaps she was also concerned in this way for me. That settled that. But if severance was her goal, how did the potion-induced change fit? Was she going to tell me that my perverse love of Frank was driving her to addiction? That would explain why she ordered from the hag not curative black pot but some potion of different effect. On the other hand, she would know that it would be very difficult to convince me that she was so suddenly and deeply stricken. And even if she could convince me, was that likely to separate me from Frank? She must have known that my passion was strong beyond virtually any compunction. Here I came to the end of my thinking. I was confronted by possibilities none of which seemed quite right. So there was nothing to do now but listen and watch. I would find the answer. I was confident.

For supper, at her request, I brought my aunt a dish of chilled consommé and a glass of iced tea. I tasted both before taking them to her. The dark consommé surprised my tongue. I had never tasted it before. Its rich saltiness suffused my mouth, startling me, bringing back a dim memory of the taste of blood.

"What are you having, Joe?" my aunt said, sitting up, setting the tray carefully on her lap. She seemed more alert, more herself except that her solicitude for once sounded a false note.

"I already had a double-decker sandwich."

"Then you can sit with me."

I took a chair by the window. The sun was down, but the yard was still full of the gentle gray light of the long August dusk. I looked at my aunt, lovely in the failing light, her thin blue nightgown darker now against the white sheet and the pale ivory of her throat. But it was her eating that arrested me. She spooned up the consommé very slowly, allowing each globule to melt on her tongue before she took the next, hand and mouth moving as if in the slow rhythm of a trance. But the uncanny thing was that my own mouth began to salivate, to fill up with salty flavor. So powerful was the taste that I feared I was being hypnotized. All my other senses were dimmed by the rich sensation in my mouth. Then a bizarre thought came to me: the consommé contained the potion. Seth had somehow slipped it by me.

"I'm not much company, am I Joe?" She smiled. "But the consommé was so good." She put the glass of iced tea on the table by the bed. "You can take the tray now please."

When I approached the bed, she sat forward. "Here. Give me a kiss, poor boy, left to take care of an ailing aunt." I bent down and took the tray, offering her my cheek. But she turned my chin gently with her fingers and kissed me lightly on the lips. I went away to the kitchen careful not to lick the trace of salty saliva her kiss had left on my lips. At the sink I washed my mouth out and scrubbed my lips roughly with the back of my hand. Then I went to the back door and breathed deeply, but the air was not cool yet though dark was descending rapidly.

I was just beginning to work again at unravelling my aunt's intentions, which were growing clearer now, when Seth suddenly appeared around the corner of the house and stopped at the foot of the steps. I looked down at him. "What took you so long? Mrs. Ellis needs the medicine." I held out my hand.

Seth shuffled. "My granny say give it to Miss Marie herself."

"All right then. You'll have to come back to her bedroom." Seth shook his head. "One way or the other," I insisted, continuing to hold out my hand but at the same time making room for him on the steps if he chose to enter the house. After a long pause he finally handed me the potion. It was a small glass vial about as big as my thumb. "I'll see that she gets it," I said. But he just stood there. "I said I'll see that she gets it." He left then. The fast falling dark swallowed him up—head, torso, and limbs first, then the colorless cotton of his short pants.

By the kitchen light I examined the potion. It was about the color and consistency of molasses. In fact I suspected that it really was mostly molasses. I unscrewed the cap and smelled it—saccharine and bitter at the same time. I smiled—ground bone of bird's leg, frog's eye, drop of woman's blood. You don't catch me, aunt. I hurried to her bedroom, anxious to see her reaction to my knowledge of this folly.

"What is it, Joe?"

"Seth brought you something." I walked to the side of the bed and handed the vial to her. Then I stepped to the window and called, "You can go now, Seth. She has it." I had heard him rustle in the bushes. Now he burst out with a great thrashing and raced across the yard. I laughed and turned back to my aunt. She was smiling. I could barely see her face now. "You won't tell on me, will you, Joe?"

"What is it?"

She made a high girlish laugh that I had never heard from her before. She was holding the vial in both hands next to her bosom as though it were some tiny creature, a bird or a mouse. "It's a magic potion."

"What's it supposed to do?" I spoke harshly, feeling that I had a definite advantage now.

"It's dream medicine. It makes me dream wonderful dreams and wake up all new."

"Let's turn the light on and look at it," I said, dropping my words as heavily as I could on the song-like lilt of her voice. If the bed lamp were on, the light would reveal the lines in her face, the neck and arms beginning to go sinewy. It would show those simple hands with the unpainted nails foolishly clutching the old black's worthless concoction. It would be the end of her plot against Frank and me.

"No. The light would hurt my eyes." She spoke absently as though she had to fetch her mind back from distant imaginings. Then she sat forward a little on the bed, held the vial out and unscrewed the cap.

"Molasses," I said disdainfully.

She put a little of the viscid fluid on her finger and touched it to her tongue. "Yes," she said. "Yes." Not, of course, assenting to me but affirming that the formula was correct according to taste. She took several more drops from finger to mouth.

"Molasses," I said.

"Take some, Joe. Taste it."

"Why? I'm not sick."

"It doesn't hurt anybody to dream, especially if things are out of tune."

"Nothing is out of tune with me."

"Yes there is, Joe. We know that, don't we?"

"No."

"What a bad trait in one so young." She tossed herself back and made a little bumping noise on the headboard.

"What?"

"Holding on to something you ought to let go of, especially when there's so much else."

"I never had much, Aunt Marie. So I hold on to anything I get."

"And being foolishly afraid of something nice, something different from anything you've ever had."

"I'm not afraid."

"Yes you are. You're afraid of me. You're afraid of my dream medicine. You say it's molasses, but you think it's a love potion."

That made me swallow hard because it showed that she already knew what I was thinking. So she was ahead of me. She had the advantage. "I'm not afraid,"I repeated doggedly.

"Here then." She sat forward and streaked the end of a finger thickly with the black liquid. I hesitated. She licked it off herself, but quickly made a new smear. "If you're going to take him away from me, Joe—in a room that I can't even enter—don't be a common thief in the night, a low miner's son. You're better than that. Win your love. Have courage. Here." I stepped over, took her wrist and licked the viscid fluid off her finger. It tasted like molasses. "Am I supposed to take more?" She shook her head, sadly I thought. I didn't feel any effect. Of course. It was just an old hag's silly concoction. I began to be a little sorry for my aunt, having to put on this stupid act with dim lights and a sheer nightgown. And suddenly the wrist I held felt as brittle as a bird's wing. I dropped it.

"Kiss me good-night, Joe." I bent and kissed her lightly on the lips. "Now go to sleep. You will dream of me and I will dream of you. In our dreams we will settle with each other."

"I always dream of Frank," I said.

"If you dream of him tonight, then you have won, Joe." She spoke very simply.

I left then. I went straight to the back steps and sat down. This was my fixed resolve: if the potion did begin to work on me, I would run to the creek and throw myself in. But nothing happened. A high breeze in the moonless sky stirred the tops of the pines. The crickets made great bursts of chirruping and then sank into silence, on and off as they sometimes will, I don't know why. When I was sure that the potion was a fake, I went in to the guest room. I undressed and put on my pajamas and then opened the door as my uncle had instructed. Down the hall my aunt's door was closed and no light shone underneath. I lay in bed listening to the crickets and the passing of an occasional car along the road at the end of the long front walk. For a while I was too uneasy to sleep. But it was not fear. It was this—my aunt, self-hypnotized by her own curious behavior and by her irrational belief in the potion, might do something horribly embarrassing for us both. But the house remained quiet, and after a while I fell into a light and dreamless sleep.

Sometime much later I awoke to the sound of my aunt's crooning. It was like nothing I had ever heard before—high, piercing, unearthly, coming from no particular direction, and burring my head as though a fatal earwig were boring into my brain. It unnerved me badly. I got out of bed and stepped into the hall. My aunt's door was still shut and dark. The crooning was almost constant, but in the short silences I heard the stillness of the night. The crickets were quiet. I went out into the kitchen and shut the door behind me. There was a moment during which I heard the comfortable low rattle of the refrigerator. But the crooning quickly resumed. I went out on the landing of the back steps and shut the kitchen door behind me. At last I heard only the mild susurrus of the pines. She wouldn't follow me there and I could doze until morning leaning safely against the door. As I grew drowsy, I began to fill my mind with sweet images of Frank lying naked in the creek, his penis wavering under the light current and the hair of his body slanting downstream like deep green water grasses. But soon I went into a black sleep where even my unconscious marked no time so that when I awoke, or thought I awoke, it was into the body of a borderless night. I was lying on my back looking up. The wind in the pines had become water among dark tresses. Frank was gone. My aunt was bending over me. Her mouth, even in the black night, was red. It came down on my lips hot and salty. I began to throb. I felt the creamy essence of my desire rise for her as she stroked me with hands as gentle as the water-winds of my dream. So she had been right. Why cling to Frank when there was this? I slipped out of my pajamas, entered the kitchen, crossed it, and opened the hall door. The house was full of warm breath. I felt my desire quicken as I stepped down the hall to the door of my aunt's room, where I did not pause but immediately turned the knob. She was waiting for me there in the dark, I was sure, because the moist heat of her breathing was suddenly denser. I started to make a sound, her name or merely a moan, to show that I had come from my dream to answer her call. But at that moment, I will never know exactly why, my mouth filled up. I do not say with saliva because the liquid was saltier and denser even than my aunt's consommé. And when I swallowed it down, it almost made me gag, for I suddenly knew what it was like—the terrifying richness of a tongue-bitten mouth full of blood. So the door I had just opened was not into my aunt's bedroom but into the heart of a night three years before. It was the summer after my mother's death, the eve of my first visit to my uncle's house, the only time my father had driven me down. That day he came home from work and drank nothing. He bathed himself violently, sputtering and fuming. Then he put on the suit he had not worn since my mother was buried. We left a little before dark. For a while he drove in silence, then he began to talk almost as furiously as when he was drunk, stitching his words together in angry patches. "They'll talk about me like I was coal dust. That's all right. They'll say I'm a God-forsaken drunk and a demon. That's all right too. But if they come down on you, boy, if they start to give you chicken gizzards and nigger's work, you write me. I'll visit them." He laughed wickedly. "I'll have a set with that saw-bones and his cajun beauty." He ranted on. "Glorified vets and bayou belles don't lord it over me or mine." I had heard all this before. I stopped listening and went to sleep.

I woke up to the sound of my father's curses. At first I thought he must have had some whiskey in the glove compartment and had drunk himself into a black fury. Even in the pale dash light I could see the sweat standing on his forehead and the jaws tight around his clenched teeth. "Goddamned son-of-a-bitching suck-egg frogs," he hissed.

"What is it?" I cried out in alarm.

"Sucking frogs."

I sat up and looked out over the hood of the car. Frogs by the hundreds were making white arches in the headlights, thumping against the car and bursting under the tires. In the glare above the highway I saw their mad glazed eyes, saw the flat bodies and pallorous under-bellies gliding toward death. "Stop!" I cried.

"Shut up! These suckers have been crossing ever since we left Harlow County." He beat on the horn. "No end to the sons-of-bitches, goddam 'em."

"Stop!" I hollered again.

"Shut up, you little peckerhead. I'll mash you same as I mash these sucking frogs." He stepped on the accelerator and howled out his execrations. The tempo of the thumping and popping of the frogs rose until I couldn't bear it. "Stop! Stop!" He hit me with the back of his hand and made me bite my tongue. My mouth filled with blood. I swallowed it. A moment later I threw up. "Stick your head out of the window, goddamit!"

When we got to my uncle's house, I was white and rank with the smell of vomit. "We passed through a frog migration twenty mile long," my father said grinning. "He'll live, though he is of the delicate kind."

Standing there in the door of my aunt's room, I saw again the doomed white frogs, heard the drum and hiss of their innumerable deaths, felt the weight of my father's blows, and smelled the acid odor of my own vomit. My aunt stirred. "Joe? Joe, is that you?" I ran. Wriggled out of the sack. Ran through the grass toward the creek. Ran for my life from the angry glaring light that raced across the gray morning toward the horizon.

I thought I would not make it. In my frenzy I missed the path. Blackberries snared me and bled me pitilessly. And soon the sun would blaze forth and cook me down to a dry parchment of brittle bones. I could feel its great heat poised behind the pines, ready to beat me down. But when I had fallen a dozen times and a dozen times been turned back by thickets, I at last heard the murmur of the creek. That gave me courage. I burst through the last barrier of underbrush and plunged into the shallow water. I cried out because the cold water at first burned my wounds. Even the creek, I thought, had betrayed me. But after a while the current became more soothing. So, sunrise did not catch me in the open after all. Even so, moved by a lingering fear of the heat, I made my way downstream to the Blue Hole. There I dove down into the dark water and for a while hung by roots in the shadow of the high cut bank. Underneath me wavered the image of my splayed, foreshortened body, the little frog that had miraculously made it across the sun's wide way.

After a time I paddled over to the lip of the Blue Hole and lay in the shoals looking at my body, which was lengthened and human again, though badly scratched. As I lay there, hope and fear divided my heart, but neither finally imaged itself beside me in the water—the black-haired body of Frank or the ivory body of his mother. I tried to think about that, but I couldn't just then.

I got up and walked around to the sand bar and looked down at my image in the quiet backwater. My face was so scratched and puffy that it hardly seemed me. I'll tell you what it did look like though. It looked like the face of my father the morning after a particularly bad night, one in which he'd lost a fight. The thought made me smile. The smile was crooked like his because my bottom lip was torn. "Well, father," I said to the image, "you were almost right. They didn't give me gizzards and nigger's work, but the cajun beauty gave me nigger's medicine and it almost made me crazy and killed me." Then I spat on the image.

About that time Seth came down to the creek calling out my name in a quavering voice as if it were the name of a demon that might start up after him at any moment. "Here I am, Seth."

"Miss Marie say come back to the house." He kept his distance.

"Go get me some clothes."

When he came back with them, I put them on and went up to the bunk room and began to pack. My aunt came and stood in the door in her housecoat. "What are you doing, Joe?" I looked at her carefully. She seemed entirely herself. "I'm going now, Aunt Marie. The medicine worked."

"That's backwards, Joe. It means it's safe for you to stay here now, as long as you want to."

"Yes, it's safe," I said. I kept packing.

"Come in the house and let me put some salve on those cuts."

"No. I don't need any, Aunt Marie. But I'll tell you what I could use is some money, for bus fare."

"Your uncle Ab would never forgive me if I let you go this way."

"You couldn't explain to Uncle Ab what way I went if you wanted to, Aunt Marie. So just tell him I ran off. I'll never tell him different. In fact, it's the truth. I am running off."

"Where are you going?" That surprised me a little, how obviously she knew I was not going home. When I didn't answer, she shook her head. "They'll take you back to him."

"Maybe once or twice, Aunt Marie. But I'm a smart boy. Everybody says so. I'll learn pretty quick how to get away for good."

"From us, too, Joe?" I nodded. "I never wanted that, Joe."

"I believe you, Aunt Marie, but you knew it had to be, even if you didn't want it."

She went off and got some money and brought it back to me, almost a hundred dollars. I gave half of it back to her. "It's too much, Aunt Marie. I have to start learning right away how to get it myself."

My aunt looked at me with a face so drawn in upon itself that I thought she would begin to weep. But all I wanted then was to get away from her. Before many years, though, I would pity her. This is how it must have been with her. There I stood destitute, having lost mother and cousin lover, having renounced father, uncle, and aunt. All I had was an old grip, forty-odd dollars, and a scarred face and body. But I was free. And there she was, twenty-five years older, with a dying husband, one son no more like her than day is to night, and another son separated from her by the perpetual secret of what she had just done for him. All she had left was her God. Or had she even traded God for son that night?

"Tell Frank I said good-bye."

III

My aunt Marie was wrong. They never did take me back to my father even once. I went straight from Laurelie to New Orleans I changed buses three times, traveled mostly at night, and never talked to anybody.

My aunt laid upon me either a great blessing or a terrible curse. Here is how it has been with me. For over thirty years I have been absolutely free of desire. Remember? At the lip of the Blue Hole that last day no image appeared, neither Frank's nor hers. None has appeared since. Of all the beds I have slept in, I have shared not one—all as clear as the limpid water of the imageless creek. From what I have seen I would count this a blessing. But I don't press the point. Each must be his own judge.

[1976]

Caroline Gordon

THE DRAGON'S TEETH

That way you shall forever hold this city,
Safe from the men of Thebes, the dragon's sons.

Oedipus at Colonus,
translated by Robert Fitzgerald

A child is walking along a road, a dusty road which runs from one end of a farm to the other. It is an afternoon in mid-summer. The dust is hot and lies so thick on the road that each time she puts her bare foot down it sinks out of sight in the soft, fine dust. From time to time she glances to the other side of the road where a Negro girl, a little older than she is, walks, so briskly that the dust stirred by her feet rises in a cloud as high as her head. In front of them a Negro woman strides, a basket over her arm. A Negro boy, older than either of the girls, runs behind the woman. He lurches from side to side as he runs and occasionally looks down over his shoulder to smile at the trail his own feet have left in the dust. The child gazes at it, too, and thinks how it might have been made by a great snake, a serpent as large as any one of them, hurling itself now to one side of the road, now to the other, and thinks, too, how she and the other girl and the boy and even the old woman seem to move in its coils.

There is a row of peach trees on one side of the road, a pasture filled with grazing cattle on the other. A moment ago the Negro boy, who is called "Son," stopped and picked a yellow cling stone peach up from where it lay in the grass and handed it to her. The child had been about to bite into it when she saw by his face that it had a worm in it and threw it down to hurry after the others.

A cow that has been grazing near the road suddenly lifts her head and stares at the little girl out of great, luminous dark eyes. Her body is greyish white but her face is almost black. The tip of her nose is black, too, and would feel wet if you touched it.... An old woman in a fairy story she had been reading that morning lived alone in a deep forest in a hut made all of peach stones. She had a cow that would come and stand before her when she sat in the doorway of her hut, but that cow was no colour; you could see through her body to the black trunks of the trees that grew about the hut. Why were the tree trunks black and the cow no colour?

They have come to a house. It is old and grey, because it has never been painted and trees grow thick about it. Their trunks are stout and twisted, as if, the child thinks, a giant passing through the grove had bent them carelessly to his pleasure. She knows that the bark of the tree trunks is white but it is so deeply pitted that from where she stands it looks black.

A gate bars the entrance to the yard. Aunt Maria has lifted the chain and the gate swings open. Aunt Maria takes little shinting buckets out of her basket and gives one to each child, then walks over to the corner of the yard where the peach trees grow. Olivia and Son move after her. Olivia stoops to pick up some of the peaches that have fallen on the ground. Son has climbed up into one of the trees.

The child nodded docilely when she was handed one of the buckets but she has not moved to join the others. She is staring up into the boughs of the silver poplar trees that rise high above the house. Their leaves are a glossy green on top but the child knows that if you tear a leaf in two it will show white—as if the leaf were made of cotton. She has been told that she, herself, was born in this house but she has no memory of ever having lived here. All her memories cluster around the tall, ugly grey house at the other end of the farm. That house stands in a grove, too. Sugar maples, planted by her grandfather, "after he got back from the War," have grown so thick about it that now all the rooms are dark. When they set out from that house a little while ago a woman was standing on the porch. Her grandmother, whose name she bears, had come out to give the old Negro woman some directions. They were about the people who lived in this grey house. (You called them "croppers"—but not to their faces.) The child had listened at first, and, then, wearying of the sound of the rapid impatient voice, sank down on the grass to think about something else.

She takes a slow step forward now and halts. A woman has come out of this house, too, and is standing on the edge of the porch. A thin woman, wearing a faded sun-bonnet, whose greyish dress is almost the same colour as her face. She has just said something to Aunt Marie who smiles and points to her basket. The sallow woman says that they cannot have the peaches, that they are her peaches. Aunt Maria smiles again and says that the peaches belong to the child's grandmother and uncle. The child will always remember how the woman on the ramshakle porch turned her face away for a second to look at the peaches hanging heavy on the brittle boughs, saying, as if to herself: *"I wisht I'd picked 'em yesterday . . . I wisht I had! . . . I was just letting them sun one more day. . . ."* and turns and walks into the dark hall then pauses on the threshold to put her hand up to her writhing lips but spread fingers cannot keep back the anguished shrieks and the names, names the woman is calling her grandmother and uncle, whereupon the old Negro woman smiles and says that they may be what the white woman has called them but they like peaches and gives one of the trees a light shake and bends over and begins filling her basket with the rosy fruit that now lies scattered all over the ground.

The child bends, too, and, trailing her hand among the grasses, pretends to be gathering the fruit which she now has no heart to touch. The Negro woman and her two children move swiftly and silently from tree to tree. When their basket and buckets are full they leave the yard and walk along the dusty road and out on to another larger road and down into the hollow where it is always cool because the branch runs through there under a little wooden bridge and then up the rise along the big road whose dust is dry again and hot until they come to a house larger than the other houses, built of brick, and set far back on a lawn that has tall oak trees growing on it.

There is a double row of cedar trees on one side of the lane where buggies and carriages go on the way to the stable. But people who are not going to stay long hitch their horses to the long rack in front. Aunt Maria and Son and Olivia have already started down the cedar drive but the child lingers, looking back over her shoulder at the hitching rack. She knows every horse that is hitched there. Susy is the old pony. Susy's coat is red and shines in the sun but her mane and foretop and tail are yellowish-white. Lather is dried white on her rump and there is a dark, wet place under her mane; Tom and Wallace Brewer had trotted her every step of the way over here. In August, too, when you are not supposed to lather horses.... Wallace Brewer had been at Merry Point two weeks and he was going to stay another week. That was because his father and mother lived in town. He was two years older than Tom and every day he thought of something to do that nobody had ever thought of before—like stringing telephone wires from the big sugar tree they climbed in to that old gum tree over by the fence. He made the receivers out of tin cans and he asked her to go and sit on the limb of the gum tree while he talked the first message and last night when she was sitting on the steps after supper, watching the lightning bugs, he came and sat down beside her on the steps and asked her if she ever caught lightning bugs and put them in a bottle and she said, No, because she wouldn't want anybody to put her in a bottle and he said he wouldn't, either, and he didn't say anything for a while and then he asked, *"What you like to do better than anything?"* and she thought how she liked to wade in the branch and then she thought of how in the spring she and one of the white girls on the place, Ada, used to take along a wooden spoon apiece and go to the woods, hunting guinea nests and she was about to tell him how guinea eggs were different from hen or turkey eggs, smaller and covered all over with tiny brown spots and how you had to lift each one out with a spoon and not touch the nest or the guinea would never come there again when Marjorie called from the bay window and asked Wallace if he didn't want to play "Seven Up"—she was fourteen years old and already wore a Ferris waist. Wallace said he did and he got up and went in the house and the child sat on the steps and watched the lightning bugs till somebody came along and told her it was time for her to go to bed and to be sure and wash her feet.... She could have driven over here with them in the pony cart today if she had had had her slippers on when Tom got ready to go. She was about to go upstairs and see if she couldn't find her black slippers when

Tom looked at a little bit of blood she had on her foot and said that if she would look where she was going on she wouldn't stub her toe so much and she thought how just last summer he always had a bloody rag on *his* big toe and before she thought she said, "*What?*" and he said "What? Riggety Rut! . . . *I'M* going to a birthday party. That's what!" and he knew and she knew that the party is for Alice who is the same age she is and she said, "You old fool!" and he said, "She who calleth her brother a fool is in danger of hell fire" and she said, "I never called you a fool. I called you a crool" and he started towards her and said, "What's a crool? Whoever heard of a crool?" and she shut her eyes and when he got close to her she opened them and said, "There are more things in Heaven and earth, Horatio, than are dreamt of in thy philosophy" and he knew that if he came any closer she would tell her father so he backed off and Wallace laughed and said, "She always talk like that?" and Tom said, "She don't know what she's saying half the time" and they got in the pony cart and drove off and she wouldn't have driven with them to save either of their necks or a single bone in their bodies. . . .

There is a table made out of a mill-stone in the shade of a tall tree over at one side of the house and the children are all gathered around the table, laughing and talking. But this child cannot join them until she and Aunt Maria and Son and Olivia have gone up the steps of the big house. A woman is sitting in a rocking chair on the porch and she gets up when she sees them and comes and stands on the top steps and smiles as she takes the basket of peaches from Aunt Maria's hand, then smiles again and, descending a step, lays her hand lightly on the child's shoulder and makes a gesture towards the rear of the house, uttering the words the child has heard every time she has come to this house.

The child nods and goes down the steps and walks off alone. Aunt Maria and Son and Olivia are still standing there on the steps while Aunt Maria and the woman talk but there is no need for her to wait for them, for even if they were walking along beside her now it would be only for a little way; nobody ever goes with her all the way to the place she has to go before she can join the ones who are laughing and talking under the trees.

The cabins are in a row back of the big house. They are white-washed. The trees that grow around them are white-washed, too, and so are the stones that edge the flower-beds in front of each cabin. The cabin she is going to is the first one in the row. One time she came here and people were sitting on the porch, laughing and talking, but there is nobody on the porch now. The porch slants a little and is so narrow that she covers it in two steps and at once is plunged into the darkness, (which, when she tries to recall it always seems to be compacted more of fetid smells than the absence of light), and the expected sound comes and she walks towards it and it comes again in a rising note and she murmurs something and feels her own hand grasped by another hand which is hot and dry and somehow brittle but yet has strength enough to force her to her knees for a moment, a moment during which the voice creaks harshly, complainingly in her ears until she, murmuring back, finds strength from the all at once blessed darkness to rise to her feet, so suddenly that the dry, reptilian clasp is broken and she runs through the room which does not now seem so dark, across the threshold and out into the blinding light and is about to plunge towards the big house when a voice speaks from the next cabin:

"How Aunt Emily making out today?"

Aunt Maria is sitting in a split-bottomed chair on the porch. When the child does not answer she leans forward and calls her name. The child says, "All right," aware that Son and Olivia have come up behind her and are sitting down, side by side, on the edge of the porch.

Aunt Maria inclines her heavy body forward. "How her rheumatism?"

"She didn't say . . . I reckon it's all right."

The woman rocking beside Aunt Maria laughs. "She had a hollerin spell towards day-break. You'd a thought she was dying . . . Sometimes I think I ask Mister Richard to move me away from that old lady. . . ."

"You better not do that," Aunt Maria says sharply. "You better stay right where the Lord flung you."

The woman laughs again and calls the child's name. "You run on to the house . . . They got peach ice-cream."

The child says, "Yes ma'am . . ."

She has been looking from one woman to the other but all the time she can feel Son's and Olivia's eyes on her face. Son's skin is only a little darker than the dust of the road they have been walking on. That may be what makes his eyes seem so dark. They are larger than Olivia's or Aunt Maria's or her own, which, she heard some grown person say the other day, are too small and set too deep in her head. Son can look at you a long time and you will not know what he is thinking.... He is not looking at her now but before he looked away a change came over his eyes, as if something as bright and quick as a snake had flashed up from a deep pool, shimmered for a second over its surface, and then, before you could be certain of what you had seen, flashed back again into the depths.

She turns and runs towards the house and as she runs it seems to her that she can feel on her back the heavy-lidded, incurious gaze of the four who sit on the porch.

A mock orange bush grows at the corner of the house. She steps back into the shadow and stares through the green, pointed leaves at the row of white-washed cabins. Rebecca gets up from her chair and walks heavily across the porch. She is going to sit with Aunt Emily a while.... Aunt Emily is a hundred years old. Is it because she has lived such a long time that she always has to come first?... "Have you been to see Mammy yet?" Cousin Margaret will ask almost before she knows you are there.... Or is there another reason? *"Blood,"* Tom was saying the other night when he was sitting on the porch between Billy and Jimmy and it was so dark he didn't know who had come out of the house. *"She eats blood... She likes it fresh, too.... That's why they all time losing some of them little nigger babies...."* She shivered slightly as she stood in the cool shade, then deliberately steadied her nerves, as she often contrived to do, by reflecting on the inconsistencies, the illogicalities and the injustice which she found embodied in her older brother. If he heard *you* say "Nigger" he'd go and tell some grown person but *he* said it any time he got ready.

But that wasn't why Son had smiled—for that was what had flicked across his eyes: a smile. He was smiling because she had said, "Yes ma'am" to Rebecca. You didn't even say "Yes ma'am" to Aunt Maria all the time and she had gone and said "Yes ma'am" to Rebecca whom she had heard Aunt Maria call "a flightly chap"! . . . But Rebecca said "Yes ma'am" to Aunt Maria and *everybody* said "Yes ma'am to Aunt Emily. They were all alike, said one thing one time and one another. . . .

She stepped out from behind the mock orange bush and walked slowly across the lawn. They had finished the game and were sitting down around the table that had been a mill-stone once down at Barker's Mill. Alice saw her coming and tried to get Janie Ellis to move over but Janie wouldn't move till the grown person who was ladling out the ice cream called to her and she had to stand up and the child slipped in where Janie had been sitting and Janie turned around and made a face but she had to go and sit somewhere else after she got her ice cream. It was peach ice cream as Rebecca had said it would be. The child had three helpings. There was cake,too, and after that lemonade. She could have had as many glasses of lemonade as she wanted but they were choosing sides for "Stealing Sticks" and she and Alice wanted to be on the same side so she set her glass down before she had drunk it dry and ran over to where Wallace Brewer was choosing sides. They played "I Spy" after that. Tom was the first to hide his eyes: *"Honey, Honey, Bee Ball. . . . I can't see y'all. . . . All sheep scattooed? . . ."*

Alice and Ellen wanted to hide in the mock orange bush but she didn't want to go back on that side of the house where she knew Olivia and Son were still sitting on the porch—unless they had gone down to the sink-hole to chunk turtles—so she persuaded them to hide between two box bushes on the side walk and Alice tore her dress and while they were trying to see how bad it was Wallace Brewer came around the corner of a bush and tagged all three of them. She had to be "It" twice and was just shutting her eyes to be It again when she saw Aunt Maria and Son and Olivia standing under the cedar trees on the drive and she told Cousin Margaret and the others goodbye and was starting down the drive with them when Tom called to her: "What you come over here bare-foot for?" She didn't say anything but he kept on hollering. "Wait a minute and you can ride home with us." She turned around then and stuck her tongue out at him. He waited a second and then he hollered again: "All right. Go ahead! Burn your feet off . . . See if I care!"

They turn out of the cedar drive on to the big road. "He don't care for nothing or nobody but himself" the child mutters. The words are words she has heard on Aunt Maria's lips many times but Aunt Maria does not seem to like to hear them from other lips. She looks down at the child's stiffly starched white piqué skirt and says: "That dress do all right, but no use talking, you'd look a lot better if you'd put your slippers on."

"I don't care" the child mutters again. "It's summer time!"

Hoofs beat on the road behind them. Suddenly they are breathing acrid dust. The old woman makes a peremptory gesture and she and the three children step quickly to the side of the road and press their bodies back among the tall reeds as the pony cart whirls past. None of them move for several minutes, then Aunt Maria gives a short laugh as they step back on to the road where the dust is still settling slowly in little eddies. "It summer time, all right," she says.

They have come up out of the hollow and are turning into the road that runs through the place. Aunt Maria and Olivia and the child walk slowly. Son is so far on ahead that they can and the child walk slowly. Son is so far ahead that they can see only the cloud of dust his feet raise.

Son lives with his father and mother and brother and sisters in a cabin back of the tall, ugly grey house the child lives in during the summers. There are two rooms in the cabin and a little room they call "the lean-to" tucked on at the back. There is a window in each of the rooms but some of the panes of glass are broken and Aunt Maria has stuffed rags into them to keep the wind and the rain out in winter. The rags stay in the windows in the summer time, too, because, the child's grandmother says, Aunt Maria is too lazy to take them out. There are two beds in each room of the cabin. Son's father, Uncle Jim, sleeps in one bed, with two of the boys. The two girls sleep in the other bed. Son sleeps on a pallet on the floor. So does Aunt Maria. She says she is not going to sleep in the bed with any old man. The child did something once that she is ashamed to remember. She is not yet clear how it came about but one day she told her grandmother where each person slept in the cabin. Her grandmother laughed and said it was too bad Aunt Maria didn't practice what she preached.

Her grandmother calls Son "Sawney." She says she will not call any nigger "Son." . . . The house girl, Leota, has a baby that is exactly the kind of baby the child thinks she would like to have as her own as soon as she is old enough to do as she pleases. Her name is Ellabelle and she is one and a half years old. Leota dresses her in a clean white, starched dress every morning and brings her up to the house and she will let you hold her in your arms a long time if you are careful. Yesterday the child sat on the door step of the out-kitchen and held the baby in her arms till she went fast asleep. Son was over in the shade of the big sugar tree, turning the handle of the ice-cream freezer. He had on his white coat that he wore when he worked around the house. Her grandmother came out in the yard and said, "Sawney, you get through freezing that cream, you better bring up some ice."

The ice got low this time of the year and you had to go down a ladder to reach it. Son did not like to go down that far into the ice-house. He said snakes lived there. He said "Yes'm" to her grandmother but he did not look at the child, even after her grandmother had gone back into the house. Leota came out and when she saw that the baby was asleep she picked her up and took her into the kitchen to lay her down in the big split basket that had mosquito netting all over it so the flies couldn't get at her.

The child had been reading in her *Green Fairy Book* before Leota told her she could hold the baby. It was still lying there beside her on the door sill. She picked it up and went over and held it out to Son. He kept on turning the freezer and did not look up. She bent over and slipped the book down into the pocket of his jacket. When she thought of the book now she saw the green cover that had gold letters and a picture of a fairy on it in gold sliding down into the white pocket. She would not ever see it again. . . .

They were passing the Old Place. She left the road and going over the fence plucked a leaf from one of the sprouts that sprang up around the roots of all the trees and tore the leaf in two and held the broken parts in her hand a second, then let them drift down into the dust and walked on. Sometimes she and Alice and Ellen picked clover blossoms and tied them together to make wreaths to wear on their heads but the first wreath that anybody ever made was of silver poplar leaves. Heracles and Prometheus each made one and then each one gave his wreath to the other. Her father had told them that last night. When she asked why grown men were making wreaths to wear on their heads he said, "It was for a pact they made" and when she asked "What pact?" he said, "Oh, I forgot... Why'n't you read about it yourself?"

That was when they were all sitting on the porch after supper and Cousin Joseph had been talking for a long time. "You listen up to the Punic Wars," Auntie told Cousin Kate, "and I'll take over then. I swear I will," but Auntie didn't come out of the house and Cousin Joseph kept on talking. When he got to Hamilcar Barca and how he was probably related to the Barkers here in the neighborhood her father had started talking right over him, the way he did sometimes. He was whittling on a stick he kept over in the corner and whittled on when somebody else got to talking. He said that as soon as Heracles was grown he went out in the woods and got himself a stick, only he called it a club, and it was about the size of one of those silver poplars in the yard at the Old Place. Wallace wanted to know what kind of tree Heracles cut down to make his club. Her father said it was wild olive. "He didn't cut it down, either. Just broke it off. Might have trimmed it down a little, but it was a whole tree trunk. Carried it all his life. Must have had it with him when he climbed up on his pyre."

"What did he climb up on that prye for?" Jimmy asked.

"To get rid of that Nessus shirt, Boy. It was burning him to death. He couldn't stand it no longer. He preferred to be burnt up, himself."

Wallace said he didn't see why he put it on, anyway.

Her father said that Heracles put the shirt on because it was his Sunday shirt that his wife, Deineira, had made for him. "What made her put poison on it?" Wallace asked.

Her father said that Deineira didn't know it was poison. The centaur, Nessus, gave it to her after Hercales shot him with an arrow when he was carrying Deineira across the river and tried to run away with her.

Wallace wanted to know why Heracles didn't carry her across the river himself. Her father said that that was an error in judgment on Heracles' part. He thought that she would be safer riding on the centaur's back than for him to carry her in his arms, because horses can always swim.

"Was he a *horse?*" Jimmy asked.

"He was half horse and half man," her father said.

Tom said he didn't believe there ever was a man that was half horse. Sometimes her father's voice could cut like a knife and yet sound soft as silk. He said: "I suppose, Sir, that you don't believe in Scylla or Charybdis or Medusa or Lamia or the Sphinx that had the head and shoulders of a woman and the body of a lion? . . . Has it ever been called to your attention that Erechtheus, the ancestor of the Athenians, had legs that ended in coiled serpents . . . or that the Labdacidae were descended from the dragon's teeth that Cadmus sowed?"

Tom never gave up right away. He said: "I wouldn't want to be made out of no old snake's teeth . . . and I wouldn't want to be named Labdaky, either."

"It's none of your business, Sir, how you were made," her father said. "Snaps and snails and puppy dogs' tails I've been told. The origins of the House of Labdacus are none of your concern, either, but you will have to know who the Labdacidae are—and the Atreidae, too—unless you want to be branded as an ignoramus." He couldn't talk to children long at a time without getting tired, but then he couldn't talk to grown people long, either. . . .

Son still ran on ahead. He had stopped at the branch and had broken off one of the big cat tails that grew there. Sometimes he carried the stalk slung over his shoulder and sometimes he swung it from side to side as he ran. When he came to a place where the trail his feet had made earlier in the afternoon still showed he would whack the dust—as if he were trying to beat a snake to death. . . .

Aunt Maria always sat in the brick breeze-way to churn. Yesterday the child's grandmother had brought a chair out and sat there, too, stringing snaps. Aunt Maria said that when Son was a year old she put him under a tree on his pallet and the next time she looked out he was holding a black thing in his hands and whipping it up and down and when she got out there it was a black snake. Her grandmother said, "Humph! An infant Hercules!" and when Aunt Maria asked who that was she said that Hercules strangled two serpents in his cradle. "I never seen any serpents," Aunt Maria said, "but I sure don't like snakes. Son don't either. Looks like that experience turned him against them, though he too little to know what he doing warn't he?" "Dunno," her grandmother said, "My experience they never too young to do meanness."

She stepped to one side of the road to avoid the serpentine trail that Son's feet had left in the dust. . . . Her father said Heracles and her grandmother said Hercules but they were the same person . . . Aunt Maria didn't know that serpents were the same as snakes . . . Sometimes they were called monsters instead of serpents and sometimes they were called dragons and were big enough to cover a whole acre and when they threw their heads back fire came out instead of breath—enough to burn the whole countryside. But no matter how large they were or where they lived they always had tails like snakes. And their heads were snaky, too. Sometimes there would be seven or nine serpent heads on one body. Like the Lernean Hydra. That was the first monster that Heracles killed. . . .

She walked faster, fast enough to bring the dust up around her in a cloud, the way Olivia did, the way Son did. . . . She would never see *The Green Fairy Book* again but she remembered some of the words and said them to herself as she walked along in her cloud of dust: *But where will we go? asked the Little Princess. We will ride on this cloud, the Fairy Godmother said. To my crystal palace in the wood. There is a gold crown laid out on a bed for you there and silver slippers and a veil of silver tissue, embroidered with the sun and the moon and the stars . . . . the sun . . . . and the moon . . . . and the stars. . . .*

[1961]

Marilyn Hacker

GRAFFITI FROM THE GARE SAINT-MANQUÉ

—for Zed Bee

Outside the vineyard is a caravan
of Germans taking pictures in the rain.
The local cheese is Brillat-Savarin.
The best white wine is Savigny-les-Beaune.
We learn Burgundies while we have the chance
and lie down under cabbage-rose wallpaper.
It's too much wine and brandy, but I'll taper
off later. Who is watering my plants?
I may go home as wide as Gertrude Stein
—another Jewish Lesbian in France.

Around the sculptured Dukes of Burgundy,
androgynous monastics, faces cowled,
thrust bellies out in marble ecstasy
like child swimmers having their pigtails towelled.
Kids sang last night. A frieze of celebrants
circles the tomb, though students are in school,
while May rain drizzles on the beautiful
headlines confirming Francois Mitterrand's
election. We have Reagan. Why not be
another Jewish Lesbian in France?

Aspiring Heads of State are literate
here, have favorite poets, can explain
the way structuralists obliterate
a text. They read at night. They're still all men.
Now poppy-studded meadows of Provence
blazon beyond our red sardine-can car.
We hope chairpersons never ask: why are
unblushing deviants abroad on grants?
My project budget listed: Entertain
another Jewish Lesbian in France.

I meant my pithy British village neighbor
who misses old days when sorority
members could always know each other: they wore
short-back-and-sides and a collar and tie.
She did, too. Slavic eyes, all romance
beneath an Eton crop with brilliantined
finger-waves, photographed at seventeen
in a dark blazer and a four-in-hand:
a glimpse of salad days that made the day for
another Jewish Lesbian in France.

Then we went on to peanuts and Campari,
she and her friend, my friend and I, and then
somehow it was nine-thirty and a hurry
to car and *carte* and a carafe of wine,
Lapin Sauté or Truite Meuniere in Vence.
Convivial quartet of friends and lovers:
had anyone here dreaded any other's
tears, dawn recriminations and demands?
Emphatically not. That must have been
another Jewish Lesbian in France.

It's hard to be almost invisible.
You think you must be almost perfect too.
When your community's not sizeable,
it's often a community of two,
and a dissent between communicants
is a commuter pass to the abyss.
Authorities who claim you don't exist
would sometimes find you easy to convince.
(It helps if you can talk about it to
another Jewish Lesbian in France.)

A decorated she-Academician
opines we were thought up by horny males.
No woman of equivalent position
has yet taken the wind out of her sails.
(How would her "lifelong companion" have thanked her?)
Man loving Man's *her* subject, without mention
if what they do is due to her invention
—and if I'd been her mother, I'd have spanked her.
(Perhaps in a suppressed draft *Hadrian*'s
another Jewish Lesbian in France.)

Then the advocates of Feminitude
—with dashes as their only punctuation—
explain that Reason is to be eschewed:
In the Female Subconscious lies salvation.
Suspiciously like Girlish Ignorance,
it seems a rather watery solution.
If I can't dance, it's not my revolution.
If I can't think about it, I won't dance.
So let the ranks of *Psych et Po* include
another Jewish Lesbian in France.

I wish I had been packed off to the nuns
to learn good manners, Attic Greek, and Latin.
(No public Bronx Junior High School fit all that in.)
My angsts could have been casuistic ones.
It's not my feminist inheritance
to eat roots, drink leaf broth, live in a cave,
and not even know how to misbehave
with just one vowel and five consonants.
This patchwork autodidact Anglophone's
another Jewish Lesbian in France,

following Natalie Barney, Alice B.
Toklas, Djuna Barnes, generous Bryher,
Romaine Brooks, Sylvia Beach, H.D.,
Tamara de Lempicka, Janet Flanner.
They made the best use of the circumstance
that blood and stockings often both were bluish;
(they all were white, and only Alice Jewish)
wicked sept/oct/nonagenarians.
Would it have saved Simone Weil's life to be
another Jewish Lesbian in France?

It isn't sex I mean. Sex doesn't save
anyone, except, sometimes, from boredom
(and the underpaid under-class of whoredom
is often bored at work.) I have a grave
suspicion ridicule of Continence
or Chastity is one way to disparage
a woman's choice of any job but marriage.
Most of us understand what we renounce.
(This was a lunchtime peptalk I once gave
another Jewish Lesbian in France

depressed by temporary solitude
but thinking coupled bliss was dubious.)
I mean: one way to love a body viewed
as soiled and soiling existential dross
is knowing through your own experience
a like body embodying a soul
to be admirable and loveable.
That is a source that merits nourishment.
Last night despair dressed as self-loathing wooed
another Jewish Lesbian in France.

The sheet was too soft. Unwashed for three weeks,
it smelled like both of us. The sin we are
beset by is despair. I rubbed my cheeks
against the cotton, thought, I wouldn't care
if it were just *my* funk. Despair expands
to fill . . . I willed my arm: extend; hand: stroke
that sullen shoulder. In the time it took
synapse to realize abstract commands,
the shoulder's owner fell asleep. Still there
another Jewish Lesbian in France

stared at the sickle moon above the skylight,
brooding, equally sullen, that alone
is better after all. As close as my right
foot, even my bed stops being my own.
Could I go downstairs quietly, make plans
for myself, not wake her? Who didn't undress,
slept on the couch bundled with loneliness
rather than brave that nuptial expanse
five weeks before. Another contradiction
another Jewish Lesbian in France

may reconcile more gracefully than I.
We're ill-equipped to be obliging wives.
The post office and travel agency
are significant others in our lives.
Last summer I left flowers at Saint Anne's
shrine. She had daughters. One who, legends tell,
adrift, woman-companioned, shored (is still
revered) in the Camargue, her holy band's
navigatrix, Mary, calming the sea
—another Jewish Lesbian in France?

It says they lived together forty years,
Mary and Mary and Sarah (who was Black.)
Unsaintly ordinary female queers,
we packed up and went separately back.
We'd shared the road with Gypsy sleeper vans
to join Sarah's procession to the shore.
Our own month-end anabasis was more
ambiguous. Among Americans
my polyglot persona disappears,
another Jewish Lesbian in France.

Coeur mis à nu in sunlight, khaki pants
I've rolled up in a beach towel so ants
and crickets from the leafage won't invade
their sweaty legs: in a loaned hermit-glade
pine-redolent of New Hampshire, not France,
I disentangle from the snares I laid.
Liver-lobed mushrooms thicken in the shade,
shrubs unwrap, pinelings thrust through mulch. Noon slants
across my book, my chest, its lemonade
rays sticky as a seven-year-old's hands.

[1982]

Donald Hall

DAVID HUME

"I dine, I play a game of backgammon,
I talk and I am merry with my friends.
Discourse of politics and art extends
To anecdote and mimicry and pun.
If later, when society is done,
I turn to work, where thought with thought contends,
Endeavor seems ridiculous, and sends
My body dumb to bed, the friend of none."
Who knows the sentence to unite the two?
Distinctions grow distincter. Now men drink
Most likely all night long to prove they think,
And in the morning write. What satisfies
A taste for nothingness will never do
To laugh at us when we are being wise. [1956]

Geoffrey Hill

A PRE-RAPHAELITE NOTEBOOK

Primroses; salutations; the miry skull
Of a half-eaten ram; viscous wounds in earth
Opening. What seraphs are afoot!

Gold seraph to gold worm in the pierced slime:
Greetings. Advent of power-in-grace. *The power*
Of flies distracts the working of our souls.[1]

Earth's abundance: the God-ejected Word
Resorts to flesh, procures carrion, satisfies
Its white hunger. Salvation's travesty

A deathless metaphor: the stale head
Sauced in original blood; the little feast
Foaming with cries of rapture and despair. [1962]

---

[1]Adapted from Pascal.

Daryl Hine

LETTER TO SHADOW

Bit by bit, as in a picture puzzle,
   The prospect of this present disappears
Into that panorama of the past.
   Dotted with illegible menhirs
The flat and sentimental landscape that
   You read as a romance, the prose plateau
Of fancy half-developed like a snapshot
   Lies printed with the alphabet of shadow.

From left to right, an amphisbaenic sense,
   Black on white, a sensuous photograph
Of a too formal period, life's sentence
   Closing death's emotional paragraph,
Tuneless, tasteless, without text or tincture,
   (N.B., hieroglyphics have no tenses)
Lucid and superficial cynosure,
   Literature is all a letter says.

What alternative to tell a vision?
   So doting on the idiotical light
Within's like staring at the sun: one
   Sees no more than if he looked at midnight . . .
Midday composes shortest, sharpest shade,
   Underlining objects in italics
On our universal page whose man-made
   Margins a little intuition fix

In the dictionary mirror.
   Seeing if you nab one you feel nothing,
Imitation, neither less nor more,
   Its shadow is the name of anything,
The mystery whereby sight were baffled,
   Sacrament and written character,
Labarum above the battlefield
   Of words, which always was a massacre.

[1974]

Daniel Hoffman

Instructions to a Medium To Be Transmitted to the Shade of W. B. Yeats, the Latter Having Responded in a Seance Held on 13 June 1965, Its Hundredth Birthday:

You were wrong about the way it happens,
You, unwinding your long hank of that old yarn
    Spun from our common dream since chaos first receded,
    As though a superannuated Druid were needed.

What looms now on that desert where the birds
Turn in their frenzy and scream uncomprehending?
    Not a cradled beast in whom divinity
    Could repossess the earth with fierce majesty;

We've seen the coming of a dispensation
Miniaturized in our set on the tabletop:
    Blazing from its pad, that rigid rocket
    No longer than the ballpoint pencil in my pocket

With its sophisticated systems for manoeuvre
And retrieval, the bloated astronauts within
    Plugged to cardiometers in weightless flight
    —Their radiant spirals crease our outer night.

Well, you were wrong about the way it happens.
Our radar scorns all horoscopes. Where Phaedrus
    Tumbling past perfection fell toward birth,
    Junked satellites in orbit ring the earth

And circuitry has made the Tetragrammaton
As obsolescent as a daft diviner's rod.
    Yet you, a boy, knelt under Knocknarea
    Where the cragged mountain buffeted the sea

And knew a cave beside that desolate shore
Had been the gate through which Christ harrowed Hell.
    But what can knowledge of that sort be worth?
    Imagination could not rest; from that day forth

God-driven, you strove through our long darkening age
To do the work the gods require. In love, in rage,
    You wrote no verse but glorifies the soul.
    What's history, that we should be imprisoned

By the contention of the passing minute,
No sooner won than lost by those who win it?
    All action's but a strut between the wings.
    Our part you knew we each must play by heart,

By heart-mysteries that no invention changes
Though knowledge further than our wisdom ranges.
    'What matter though numb nightmare ride on top?'
    You knew there'd be a perturbation in the skies,

You knew, whatever fearful turn would come
By our contrivance, or immortal from the womb,
    Violence must break old tables of the law
    And old solemnities to desecration draw,

But how conceive coherence with our power?
Old ghost, you seem to beckon from your tower
    As though moon-magic were but the grammar of your speech,
    A cast of thought to keep within our reach

The tragic gaiety of the hero's heart
That blazes where the soul consumes in art
    All reality as faggots for its fire,
    Revealing the desired in the desire.

Then man, though prisoned in his mortal day,
In imagination dominates all time,
    Creates that past and future between which his way
    Unwinds with the fated freedom of a rhyme.

[1965]

John Hollander

ON THE WAY TO SUMMER

1

May-day, the day of might, day of possibility
That became the name of cries reaching out for help from
General disaster: it has come and gone again
With all its shows of power—the phallic mayhem round
The village pole; the parading of the red banners;
The branches' payday after weeks of budding, silver
And gold of first blossom yet unspent in the heyday
Of later flowering. Then June will waste her substance
In riotous living, then that auxiliary
Verbiage with which the sociable seasons discourse
Of their own vainglory will parade itself and raise
Ruckus enough for millions of dancing villages,
Scarlet petals enough for all the new worlds in earth.

2

Patterns of light and flakes of dark breaking all across
The surface of the stream—rhyming words of wave, strophes
Of undulation, echoings of what just had been
Going on upstream a ways—we like to take all these
As matters of surface only, as part of the shaping
Or framing of the banks. But that would make the water
Stagnant and silent, whose face gives no interesting
Access to its depths. Yet when the brook gets to bubbling,
Really has something to say for itself, the surface
—Broken, flashing, loud—changes place with what depths
there are.
The what forms up on top will have been troped up from below,
And the otherwise still, soundless and motiveless bottom
Will be constantly noisy with the figures of light.

3

What there is to hear from the particular sea-mews
Homing in on our local point cuts through clarities
Of fair evening and the difficult radiance
Fog exhibits, high-noted observations whose tone—

High, personably middle, or far from simply low—
Is muted by the sheer pitch of the winged outcry.
What there is to see in the running out and back in
Of our local inlet sighs, through barriers of firs
Along the low intervening islands, with rumors of
The ocean's legerdemain, which by mere sleight of land
Keeps taking back what ground it appeared to have given.
What there is to know from the touch of the silent wind's
Hand gathers these raw reports and sifts them for the truth.

4

When to say something of what stretches out there toward one
—Greens, rock grays, colors of water making up spaces
That speak to what we dream up as distance and depth—seems
Uncalled for, one is almost made to reproach oneself,
Asking, *How can we sing a strange song in the Lord's land?*
Mouth evasive and emphatic scat-lyrics of all
The mess of exile, there at the heart of a place famed
As the terminus of the longest expedition?
And yet, what made one abandon each land was the
Blaring of some general canto, whose unisons
Comprised their own imperious mode of noisiness.
One rejoiced in an inward air as one underwent
Wandering: here still one must intone that undersong.

5

The shad and asparagus are over, the berries
And late bluefish still to come; and yet beyond these wait
The successive New Years at harvest, mid-darkness and
Arisen spring—three points each of which could be a pure
Spot of origin, or a clear moment of closure.
As it is, they whirl by as bits of what is being
Measured than as milestones, as parentheses
Which turn out to have been what was being put between
Brackets in the first place. Occasions usurp the false
Fronts of giddy centers on circumferences. How
The lazy susan of the seasons turns around! piled
Chock-a-block with delectables, eased about by Time,
Our most thoughtful and, ultimately, murderous host.

[1983]

Richard Howard

FRAGMENTS OF A "RODIN"

for Emma Joseph, who provided

In March, 1970, an act of violence and vandalism was committed in Cleveland, Ohio, its victim a cast of Rodin's statue known as *The Thinker*: dynamite had been wedged between the grasping bronze toes, and sometime after midnight the figure was blown off its pedestal, the lower portion suffering considerable damage. Though put back in place, the statue itself has not been restored, and it looks—legs torn open, buttocks fused, the wonderful patina even more spectacular where the metal is gashed and split, a slender steel palisade boxing in the unbalanced torso—it looks like a "modern" statement now, something closer to a Reg Butler hominoid impaled on its thorns or a realization in the seething bronze of one of Francis Bacon's horrors, neatly jailed, keeping or kept at its distance, than to the celebrated figure created in 1879 and crouching, as we all know, before so many museums, colleges and courthouses across the country.

Growing up in Cleveland, I had seen this particular *Thinker* at work in front of our art museum—had seen it every week, sometimes every day, and inside the museum I had seen other statues I was told Rodin had made, particularly a pair of creamy marble clumps, *The Kiss* and *The Hand of God* (modelled, Miss McFeeley said, after the sculptor's own hand!)—which appeared very different indeed, lapped so smooth the light found nowhere to go but inward, from the rugosities of the image we visiting schoolchildren entitled, with an allegorical impulse quite as merciless as the Master's, *The Toilet*. And when I read in the papers, even in the New York *Times,* about the explosion of this childhood icon (by now I had seen its consessioner before Philosophy Hall at Columbia University, and I had visited the Rodin Museum in Philadelphia and even the Musée Rodin in Paris), I realized as surely as if I had heard the nymphs crying "the great god Pan is dead" when Christ was born, that an era was over, that a hinge had folded, and that life, as Rilke said apropos of another broken statue, must be changed.

Why, I wondered, had "they", nameless and faceless agents of Darkness, done the deed at all? No slogans scrawled on the pedestal indicated the provenance of such destruction, yet the mischief was too intricate to be no more than some mid-west version of an *acte gratuit*—it lacked the adorable spontaneity of the Absurd. At first I inclined to believe *The Thinker* had been blasted because it was *thinking*. This was 1970, after all, and anti-intellectualism is scarcely a minor tributary to the stream of American life. But there was a ruinous paradox in my reasoning—indeed, had I not already noticed that the somewhat squashed effigy had a new pertinence, a deeper significance? The wounds merely enhanced the wonder of thinking. The only way to overcome a thought is by . . . another thought. And the only victory over *The Thinker* would be, say, disposable earthworks or primary sculpture, some emblem of unthought—not the vandalization of a received emblem of thought.

Then, recalling that the figure had been enthroned, originally, above the lintel of *The Gates of Hell* and that Rodin intended it to be called *The Poet,* for it was to represent Dante conceiving the tormented universe of forms which writhed beneath him, I presumed that the same negating hostility to association, to history and to the very presentiment of the past had functioned here as had dictated the cancellation of the program-cover of the Republican Presidential Convention in 1956, when Rodin's *Three Shades*—chosen by a committee to illustrate Peace, Progress and Prosperity—were discovered to be the guardians who point down into the same swirling inferno over which *The Thinker* so creatively broods. Yet most people have no notion that Rodin's most popular work is not seen by them as he intended it to be seen—as part of an encyclopedic, and unfinished, apocalypse; any more than they realize that Rodin never touched a chisel, never "carved" all those caramelized creations that came out of his *atelier* from the hands of Italian artisans busily producing sentimental marble facsimiles of what the master's hands had modelled in clay, plaster and wax.

No, *The Thinker* had not been blown up because it was thinking, or because it was thinking about Hell or history, or because it would be fun to blow it up; *The Thinker,* I was obliged to conclude, had been blown up because it was a special kind of art, because it was by Rodin. What, then, had that come to mean—"by Rodin"?

The answer might lie in a name-dropping still-life with a title lifted from Kipling, who certainly belongs in the picture: *A sonata is only a sonata, but a cigar is a good smoke.* Under a framed lithograph of Brahms playing the piano and puffing on a cheroot—a Brahms bearded like Whitman, like Ibsen, like God and like Rodin himself (whose hand, I knew, already partook of divinity)—there was a shelf of books in our house, and the biggest book, with the same luxuriant margins, the same gravure illustrations shielded by a wisp of tissue-paper, the same *propos* of the Master gathered as in a chalice of reverent inquirendo by Paul Gsell, was to be found in the houses of all my parents' friends, if not under Brahms then on top of the piano, among the folds of an art-scarf which might have been snatched from Isadora's chubby shoulders. This was the book republished now by Horizon Press, and on its spine were but two words, though they appeared in very large letters: ART, and beneath that, a trifle larger, RODIN.

For my family and their friends, for an aspiring middle-class America in the first four decades, say, of this century, the assumption was not that Rodin made art, but that Art was what Rodin made (as poetry, for the preceding generation, had been what Tennyson wrote). Objects which came, or were said to come, from Rodin's hands were art because they were made by an artist *(cherchez l'homme* is the motto of the middle class), and they were great because they were made by a Great Artist—not because of their intrinsic qualities, formal properties, but because of a justifying aura of comment supplied by the Master. That is how the middle class has always recognized art: by the directives of the artist and his ape the critic. Only an aristocracy, of course, can afford to respond to such objects *unmediated;* even triumphant, the bourgeoisie never asks "is that what I like?" but only, anxiously, "what is it supposed to mean?" Rodin, among others, told us, and we believed, we recognized. This book is one of the places and ways in which he told us. But to determine an analogous recognition in the history of sculpture, to affix a *cachet* with the same complacent unanimity, we should have to look back as far as Canova, perhaps as far as Bernini—and that far back, no such recognition could be made by the middle classes, which were merely rising; by the time I was poring over ART by RODIN—or was it RODIN by ART?—they had risen.

Other books, as I mentioned, shared with Rodin that shelf which showed forth, until it showed up, the last word in middle-class taste, and though it appears to be period taste now (which means taste, period), who can afford to condescend to such choices when we consider our own last words? There were the works of Maeterlinck and Rostand and d'Annunzio and Anatole France (a long red row, the latter, from which I would learn, as again from Schnitzler, that *libertine* was a diminutive of liberty); there were the scores, on the piano, of Puccini and Massenet (the "Meditation" from *Thais* was played at my mother's wedding!); and there were certain numinous figures, living persons whose appearances and performances (often, as in the case of the Divine Sarah, identical) had to be granted the same inviolable veneration with which certain books were to be read: Nijinsky, Caruso, Duse . . . Certainly, after the Great War there was a Great Snobbery about the other side of the Atlantic, a great craving for spoils. But more than any other creative figure —even more than Richard Strauss (music, after all, even music orchestrated by Strauss, could not be *owned* in the way marble and bronze and mere clay could be owned, as chthonic trophies) —Rodin satisfied that craving, fulfilled the needs of the class and circumstance in which I grew up — the class defined, abruptly, by the circumstance of having "been" by which was meant having been to Europe. A class which is, today, a has-been, for it has been had—by its own possessions, despoiled by its own spoils, among which few were so proudly carted home as the statues of Auguste Rodin.

There were, of course, several Rodins. There was the Rodin who did—if indeed he did them—marble busts of Mrs. Potter Palmer and her friends for colossal sums; there was the Rodin who scandalized the townspeople of Calais by insisting that civic virtue and patriotic sacrifice were not always noble and exalted, that heroism is a form of solitude—a suffering form; there was the Rodin who questioned the very pride of the body he glorified, who in *The Old Courtesan* articulated with unendurable persistence the miscarriage of life, the futility of effort, the impotence of the mind, the weakness of the flesh; and there was the Rodin who, taking a big mouthful of water and spitting it onto the clay to keep it constantly pliable, did not always aim well and soaked George Bernard Shaw:

> At the end of the first fifteen minutes, he produced by the action of his thumb a bust so living that I would have taken it away with me to relieve the sculptor of any further work . . . But this phase vanished; within a month my bust passed successively, under my eyes, through all the stages of art's evolution. The careful reproduction of my features in their

> exact dimensions of life . . . went back mysteriously to the cradle of Christian art, and at this moment I had the desire to say again, stop and give me that. It is truly a Byzantine masterpiece. Then, little by little it seemed that Bernini intermingled with the work. Then, to my great horror, the bust softened in order to become a commendable eighteenth-century *morceau,* elegant enough to make one believe that Houdon had retouched a head by Canova. . . . Once again, a century rolled by in a single night, and the bust became a bust by Rodin and it was the living reproduction of the head that reposes on my shoulders. It was a process that seemed to belong to the study of an embryologist and not to an artist.

With characteristic acuity Shaw hits on what appealed to Rodin's public—not only to his patrons who wanted to be flattered, consoled, immortalized, but to a vast audience which knew what art ought to be, though it may not have known what it liked: art was science ("the study of an embryologist"), not the genesis of a vision, not revelation, but realism, but the reproduction of what we see with our own eyes. By this dispensation, art need not—always—reassure, but it must tell the truth, and that was what Rodin the evolutionary biologist claimed to do: "I am not a dreamer," he said, "but a scientist . . . There is no need to create. Genius comes only to those who know how to use their eyes and their intelligence."

This, even more than the indulger of duchesses, was the Rodin that was detonated on the steps of the Cleveland Museum of Art—the mediator of an eternal human nature (that pretext of capitalism), the mouthpiece of the bourgeois aesthetic which makes art an art of detail. Based on a quantitative representation of the universe, this aesthetic demands that the truth of any whole be no more than the sum of the individual truths which constitute it—as Rodin used to say that a statue was the sum of all its profiles. In consequence, an emphatic significance is attributed to the greatest possible quantity of details, and the mimetic surface thus produced is one of literally sensational intensity. As Albert Elsen, Rodin's most scholarly critic, puts it:

> within an area confined to a few inches on the sculpture, each fingertip will encounter surface inflections of a different character; feeling one's own arm, one gains the impression that the surfaces conceived by Rodin are more richly complex.

It is an art which refuses to transform the world (choosing, as Elsen shrewdly suggests, to *enrich* it, to capitalize on our losses), which urges instead its obsessive record; indeed, an art which offers its hypertrophied mimetic surface not merely as an enrichment but as an homeopathy: to innoculate us with a contingent ill in order to forestall an essential one. This is what Roland Barthes calls the Essentialist Operation: to insinuate within an Order the complacent spectacle of its servitudes as a paradoxical but peremptory means of glorifying that Order. *The Age of Bronze, Eternal Spring, The Cathedral*—our middle-class *frisson* upon finding these "noble" titles affixed to works of a convulsive naturalism fades into acceptance, an acceptance of their ulterior and not their inherent function. To label *Dawn* (or *France* or even *Byzantine Princess*—it comes down, or climbs up, to the same) the semitransparent wax mask of Camille Claudel, the poet's sister and the sculptor's mistress, may rid us of a prejudice about the individual human countenance, but it is a prejudice which cost us dear, too dear, which cost us too many scruples, too many rebellions, and too many solitudes. To call an image of human flesh *The Thinker* is an allegorical holding-action, an alibi which manifests initially the tyranny and the injustice of that flesh, the torments it endures, the reproaches it incurs, only to rescue it at the last moment, *despite* or rather *with* the heavy fatality of its complaints, by calling it so. *Saving the appearances* by sovereign appellation, that is the Rodin who buttered up Puvis de Chavannes and his wan aristocratic allegories, that is the artist, and that the art, which passed—with its audience—from universal acclaim, from smug persuasion, in a flash of gunpowder. For it is written: I will show you fear in a handful of dust.

ii

In the Print Room of the British Museum, if you have managed to murmur the proper words in the proper quarters, an attendant will set on the table before you any number of green buckram boxes, each large enough to contain an overcoat. Inside them, however, are not overcoats but the majority of the watercolors of Joseph Mallord William Turner, mounted though unframed, many with Ruskin's characteristic annotations ("nonsense picture") on the reverse—thousands and thousands of works, constituting one of the greatest achievements in art, though only a few of these pictures have been reproduced and a few more exhibited.

Here or in another such room, a deplorable scene occurred soon after the painter's death, at the age of 76, in 1851—a scene which nothing but the profusion and perfection of what is in these boxes can keep us from mourning as more than an incidental loss: according to W. M. Rossetti, Ruskin (who was not yet 35 at the time) found among these works several indecent drawings "which from the nature of their subjects it seemed undesirable to preserve," and burned them "on the authority of the Trustees" of the National Gallery. Rossetti had been helping Ruskin to sort the Turner bequest, and neither he, Ruskin, nor the Trustees were swayed by the fact that Turner evidently considered the sketches *desirable to preserve*. Nevertheless, we find in these green boxes many rapid drawings and watercolors, executed after the artist's fiftieth year, of naked lovers copulating, of naked girls embracing. According to Turner's biographer, the genitals in many sketches are plainly shown, even enlarged. These erotic works illustrate what Turner himself, in a verse written much earlier, called "the critical moment no maid can withstand/when a bird in the bush is worth two in the hand." Apparently there were many more of these caprices than the ones which survived the Rossetti/Ruskin sifting, but as in the case of the great mass of the Turner watercolors, they were not executed for sale or for exhibition—they were executed for the artist's sole delectation. Turner was the first major artist to show this division between a public and a private art—between the astonishments of Varnishing Day and the unvarnished truth of the studio.

In the archives of the Musée Rodin, there are about seven thousand drawings and water-colors by the Master; no one may see them, for as anyone knows who has attempted to undertake research in that country, France is a bureaucracy tempered by spitefulness, and though the canonical 50 years since Rodin's death have passed, the work has not been made accessible to students. About 200 drawings and water-colors are exhibited in the museum, and there are perhaps as many in other collections. Nothing, apparently, has been destroyed, but we are in something of the same case as with Turner: the world lies all before us, where to choose?

Like most of Turner's water-colors, like all of his later ones, Rodin's were painted for himself; they are a private art. So often accused of melodrama, of oratory, of sensationalism, both men, we must remember, created an entire *oeuvre* apart in which nothing happens but in which nothing is kept from happening—the art of the late Turner, of the late Rodin (who first permitted a large group of his wash-drawings to be exhibited in 1907, when he was 67) is the greatest example with which I am familiar in the history of art of an art without history, an articulation of a life that can be lived without repression, without sublimation, in eternal delight, in endless play, in the undifferentiated beatitude of bodies and earth and water and light whose realm is eternity, not history. The eroticism, even, of Rodin's and of Turner's pictures has nothing to do with the drama of sex—it is the ecstatics of a condition, not of an action, and when we label it polymorphous-perverse we mean merely that it is playful, exuberant, gay.

In considering the pleasant symmetries of the two artists: that each of them ended and began a century of taste; that each of them lived over three-quarters of a century without ever marrying, though entertaining intractable relations with an "unsuitable" woman; that each of them conducted two opposing careers,—the first charged with virtuoso scandal—it was Hazlitt who as early as 1814 saw "a waste of morbid strength, visionary absurdities, affectation and refinement run mad" in Turner, and an organizer of the American National Sculpture Society (in 1925!) who saw in Rodin "a moral sot" and in his *Walking Man* "proof of the working of a mind tainted with sadism"—and the second entirely an interior rapture, no longer the assertion of selfhood but rather the collection of an identity (motionless or moving, rapt or reft, suggestive or stark) from the very lineaments of what is *other*: this private creation of Turner and Rodin is the highest expression Western art can show of an identification with what is not the self but seen, the making of an inwardness from what is outside—as I have said, an *ecstatics* of art . . . In considering then the remarkable analogies between Rodin and Turner, let us not forget that to each genius was attached a young and voluble literary man whose attentions were not so welcome to the artist as they are to us: Ruskin who by his late twenties was determined to dedicate his fortune and vocabulary (both enormous) to the exposition of his "earthly master"; Rilke who at the same age served as Rodin's secretary, and though ignominiously dismissed managed to patch up the misunderstanding by patience, admiration, servility even—and of course by one of the most beautiful essays in the entire range of art criticism, which Rodin may never have read. One sentence from each writer must suffice to manifest the degree of suffusion, the deep dye these passionate young men had taken:

> Rodin and Rodin only would follow and render that mystery of decided line, that distinct, sharp, visible but unintelligible and inextricable richness, which, examined part by part is to the eye nothing but confusion and defeat, which, taken as a whole, is all unity, symmetry and truth.
>
> Turner was a worker whose only desire was to penetrate with all his forces into the humble and difficult significance of his means; therein lay a certain renunciation of Life, but in just this renunciation lay his triumph, for Life entered into his work: his art was not built upon a great idea but upon a craft, in which the fundamental element was the surface, was what is seen.

Ah no, I have the names reversed: the first sentence is by Ruskin, the second by Rilke. There is always a confusion, is there not, when literary men meddle with art?

iii

Between the "wrong" Rodin mutilated on the steps of the Cleveland Museum and the undivulged Rodin I have suggested as an antidote, between the emblem of an abject ideology and the ecstatics of a released identity, it is good—it is corrective—to stand a moment before the masterpiece of Rodin's sculpture and the supreme sculptural expression of the nineteenth century, *The Gates of Hell,* begun in 1880, left unfinished (in plaster) and cast only a decade after his death. The first cast is in Philadelphia, the second in Paris, both gifts of the same American millionaire who created the Rodin Museum in the former city and who restored Rodin's villa outside the latter, housing hundreds of original plaster studies and drawings which had been inadequately protected—a gesture never acknowledged by the French authorities. Looking at the spectacular patina of the bronze, the terrific shadows which are Dantesque indeed, one is easily distracted from the Master's intention:

> My sole idea is simply one of *color* and *effect* . . . I have revived the means employed by Renaissance artists, for example, this mélange of figures, some in low relief, others in the round, in order to obtain those beautiful blond shadows which produce all the softness . . .

Rodin had hoped to make the individual figures in wax, attaching them to the plaster frame, which would have created even subtler "blond shadows", but the technique was impracticable, and year after year the portal remained in his studio, endlessly altered, figures added, removed, shifting in scale and inclusiveness, the only fixed point being the tombs near the base of the doors, which were the last major additions before Rodin's death. Almost all the images we associate most readily—and not always with relish—with the sculptor are here, frequently in a context which challenges the connotations they have come to have for us: *The Thinker, Adam, Eve, The Prodigal Son, Crouching Woman, The Three Shades, The Old Courtesan, The Kiss, Fugit Amor, Ugolino* . . . In particular Man as *The Thinker* replaces Christ in the judgment seat, and in general, chaos and flux supplant the hierarchies of doctrine. For Rodin himself, the work was as private as the swiftest of his drawings, the most summary of his clay sketches, and its inflection—though I have called it ecstatic, though I am certain it is exalted and even exultant—is catastrophic. Michelangelo called Ghiberti's doors *The Gates of Paradise,* and surely Rodin accepted the challenge in calling his own *The Gates of Hell.* They are the consummate expression of that encyclopedic impulse, that effort to gain access to prophecy by means of process, which we link to Courbet's *Atelier,* for example, and to the *Comédie Humaine* of Balzac—Balzac, of whom Rodin gives us the most *unwavering,* the most Promethean image—for their subject is not so much a version of Dante as an inversion: *La Tragédie Humaine.*

Corrective, then, to pre-empt this apocalyptic and yet intimate Rodin—apocalyptic in the sense that he creates a world of total metaphor, in which everything is potentially identical with everything else, as though it were all inside a single infinite and eternal body. The last great artist for whom art, nature and religion are identical, Rodin was faithful to what Pater calls the culture, the administration of the visible world, and he merited Revelation, which might solace his heart in the inevitable fading of that. His delights, as it says in Scripture, were with the sons of men, and in *The Gates of Hell* we read their fortune; it is ours.

[1970]

BEYOND WORDS

Song is miraculous because it masters what is otherwise a pure instrument of self-seeking, the human voice.
—Hugo von Hofmannsthal

He was a man whom words obeyed.
—Richard Strauss

His last month was July, the Summerland
he called it, when one son
(the older boy) had taken poison: then,
quite suddenly, he died too.

Look—through the crooked window
he could never open, between branches
of an old sour-cherry tree
bright with fruit—orderly there on the desk,

letters from his old ally and foe,
paperweighted in packets
by two Offenbach scores: *La Belle Hélène*
beside *Orpheus in Hell.*

'You know this inmost aim, this
arrogance of my nature,' he confessed,
'to produce out of myself
a whole theater, a repertory:

not works, but rather a literature.'
In a real sense the man died
of responsibility, the sustained
pressure of remembering

what had long been dismembered—
Europe, the wide land. Deep secrets hide
in surfaces, he knew, where else
could they go? and the spells we desecrate

run from mouth to mouth, unguessed, exhausted.
He fell, then, the Conjuror,
and all the puppets with him into whose
sawdust he poured so much blood.

Speechless they lay where he lay,
corpses who once had proved that what lovers
or friends mean to each other
is made clear by exchanging magic rings,

the presentation of a silver rose . . .
All gestures were ruined now:
the Madman's knee in Zerbinetta's eye,
Sophie with the awful nurse

hanging on her, Mandryka
sprawling, broken, obscene really, like them
all at this remove—merely
the others of *him*. That much of dying

could be rehearsed: for we are not ourselves
until we know how little
of our selves is truly our own. He knew,
now, how little and how much,

the Magician who leaped from
the father's into the son's body and
back, changing like clothes The Forms.
You can see the papers still, by this light,

though not the thread of script: it is too dark.
Branches move at the window
and bitter cherries like dead tanagers
brighten the grass where they lie,

shed the night before—droppings.
They sweeten, rot and dry. In an early
poem he said, "and yet, to say
'evening' is to say much." It is evening.

[1970]

Richard Hugo

CATTAILS

It's what I planned. The barber shop alone
at the edge of Gray Girl swamp, the town beyond
drowsing that battering raw afternoon,
the radio in the patrol car playing westerns,
the only cop on duty dreaming girls.
When I walked in, first customer, the barber
muttered 'murder' and put his paper down.
I hinted and hinted how sinister I am.
The barber said 'I'm sorry' when he cut my ear.

This is where I'd planned the end, in cattails
and cold water, my body riddled, face down
in the reeds, hound and siren howling red,
camera popping, the barber telling the reporter
what I'd said. And wind. Always wind that day,
bending the cattails over my body, bringing cloud
after cloud across the sun and in that shifting light
women whispering 'who was he?', and the cop
trying to place me, finding my credit cards,
each with a fictitious foreign name.

When my hair was cut, I walked along the bank
of Gray Girl swamp and watched the cattails rage.
When I drove out, my radio picked up the same lament
the cop had on. I tuned in on his dream.
They came to me, those flashing, amber girls,
came smiling in that wind, came teasing laughter
from my seed like I'd done nothing wrong.

[1973]

Hugh Kenner

MAO[4] OR PRESUMPTION

Notes, drafts, outlines for a course of lantern lectures on Chinese poetry cram page after page of notebooks Ernest Fenollosa kept during his period of American lecturing (1901-6). Certain themes recur: that language springs from creative metaphors in which "man and nature come to brotherhood," these intertwined with mythologies and primitive poetries; that all words act, enact, verbwise—the very prepositions channellers of force; that ideograms show forth this energy, which in our languages we must uncover by etymologizing; that (nature being in metamorphic process) the transitive sentence partakes of and imitates nature, and ideograms in successsion mime vital processes with "something like the vividness of a moving picture."

The Vitoscope, the first practical projector, dates only from 1901, so viewing moving pictures had just become possible. Can we recover the freshness of Fenollosa's pioneer analogy? In "things" he saw "cross-sections cut through actions, snap-shots;" likewise in single ideograms and single cinema frames. Both exist for the sake of their blended succession, the moving picture, the sentence, the poetic line.

When "The Sun Rises in the East,"

and we see the sun in each character, or when "Man Sees Horse"

and running legs carry each character, we should imagine them as if on the screen in visible metamorphosis (as nature works; as for instance trees grow and species evolve), the recurrent element like that constancy from frame to frame that confers on the projected happening an intelligible identity. To make happenings run through words, not to join static categories with copulae, the writer might, as "perhaps his finest training," "compose a page that contained no single use of the copula." (You have just read such a page.)

Metamorphosis—identity persisting through change—gives the rationale of "artistic unity:" in music, the key; in painting, the harmony within which "the farthest and faintest influence of each potent tint melts into the enormous sum of the influences of all," and "every color modifies every other;" in poetry, the control of metaphorical overtones, the "halos of secondary meaning" which vibrate "with physical wealth and the warm wealth of man's nature," and yet must "blend into a fabric as pure as crystal." Flagrant cases of failure, he says, we call "mixed metaphor," and (words being polyvalent) the best poet will find it almost impossible to avoid "the crossing and jarring of some of the vibrations." Shakespeare time and again does the impossible:

> . . . Death, that hath suck'd the honey of thy breath
> Hath had no power yet upon thy beauty.
> Thou art not conquer'd. Beauty's ensign yet
> Is crimson in thy lips and in thy cheeks,
> And death's pale flag is not advancèd there. . . .

We can imagine an ideographic script that might point up such coherences, and for the best Chinese poems Fenollosa claims simply that to their technique of sound (which his notes discuss at length) they add both visual grace and visual reinforcement of the metaphors everywhere flashing. "The elements of the overtones vibrate against the eye" (whereas in such a line from the 18th century as Thomson's torrent "springing through rocks abrupt," the overtones of *abrupt* [cf. *rupes,* rocks] come only to the etymologizing mind), and "the frequent return of the same element into new combinations makes possible a choice of words in which the same tone interpenetrates and colors every plane of meaning."

Hence as in the new century we "enter into [the] new conception of 'Comparative Literature'," we must understand oriental poems, commonly thought trivial, "as a true part of the world's poetry, but as a new species of it."

About 1904 (probably) he pulled everything into a draft for the first lecture: "The Chinese Written Character as a Medium for Poetry." It lay in his notebooks, presumably never delivered, until in the winter of 1914-15 Ezra Pound extracted, shortened, polished and typed it.

And where, in wartime London amid the Georgians, did one publish such a piece of exotica? "The adamantine stupidity of all magazine editors delays its appearance" (Pound, June 1915). In the same letter he calls it "a whole basis of aesthetic." And to a poetess who had used "become" where an active verb might have glistened, "You should have a chance to see Fenollosa's big essay on verbs, mostly on verbs. Heaven knows when I shall get it printed." (June 1916) He even tried *Seven Arts* in Greenwich Village. Hope dawned eventually still further west, where in La Salle, Illinois, a saturnine journal called *The Monist* had printed two philosophical essays of Eliot's. The typescript crossed the torpedo-infested Atlantic, got accepted in early 1917, and commenced a long sojourn in a "pending" basket in La Salle. Only Pound and an unknown number of editors had read it.

* * *

Meanwhile, in a crystal cloud above Brookline, Mass., far-darting Apollo was preparing to smite with an illumination Amy Lowell, the "hippopoetess," to argue with whom, Carl Sandburg once remarked, was "like arguing with a big blue wave." The lady in whose company she received the revelation was to undergo seven years' nagging rather than argue. Moreover illuminations ran in the family. Thus her brother Percy ("a fine chap," Pound once remarked, "and she is delightful") had suddenly grasped the rationale of the newly-discovered Martian "canals"—intelligent efforts to irrigate a dying planet—and founded an observatory to follow the matter up. Thus Amy, on 21 October 1902, had suddenly, aged 28, sat down and "with infinite agitation" written her first poem. "It loosed a bolt in my brain and I found out where my true function lay." In 1913, concurrent with the arrival of the January *Poetry*, another bolt was loosed: "Why, I too am an *Imagiste*." She hied her twice from Massachusetts to the Imagist headquarters in London, crossing like a big blue wave or like Daisy Miller, in '13 to join the movement and in '14 (with maroon-clad chauffeur and matching auto) to appropriate it since she had not been properly accepted. As against *Des Imagistes* which displayed only one of her poems, she proposed to sponsor a new book with equal space for each poet, selection of the poems by vote of all, and freedom from the decisions of a tiresome man who supposed that impersonal standards were accessible to his judgment. Democracy in the arts was her credo, with herself as chief democrat. The Aldingtons, Richard and H.D., were soon at her feet. By September Aldington had reported encouragingly that Ezra looked "terribly ill." It had been a model campaign. She had ended his reign, and neatly separated him, she thought, from everyone who mattered: Richard and H.D. and Flint and Lawrence and J.G. Fletcher. He was nothing, clearly, without this betyrannized crew; for (Amy wrote) "he does not work enough, and his work lacks the quality of soul, which, I am more and more fain to believe, no great work can ever be without." (Soul was a Lowell commodity.) She relayed hints that he was tuberculous, and that the bacilli had attacked his brain. "This is merely surmise. The fact remains"—she was tipping off Harriet Monroe, his one American editor—"that where his work is concerned he is failing every day." September 15, 1914; signed, Amy Lowell.

But in 1915 he had the impertinence to publish *Cathay,* in 1916 *Certain Noble Plays of Japan,* and in 1917 *Noh, or Accomplishment.*

Now the Orient was Amy's by right of Lowellship. Her brother Percy when Pound was in his cradle had travelled there and written four books, one of which lured Lafcadio Hearn to Nippon. Percy had sent back photos and copious curios, and once returned with a Mr. Miyaoka who talked to the pinafored Amy on his lap about fox-sprites and spider-demons. "From those days," recalled an admirer she had coached, "Japanese prints and wood-carvings became an intimate part of Amy Lowell's entourage, and books on Japan always lay upon her table." This heritage for some reason lay fallow until Macmillan published the Pound-Fenollosa *Noh;* whereafter, "becoming more and more absorbed in Japanese literature," Miss Lowell dashed off some "Lacquer Prints" and a long poem on the opening of Japan by Commodore Perry. Its account of hari-kiri has been called "blood-curdling in the white heat of its vigor and restraint." Still her daemon went unassuaged. "In this poetry business," she once avowed, "there are rings of intrigue." Might one not "knock a hole in Ezra Pound's translations"?

A hole seemed knockable; clearly his weak flank was Fenollosa, whose name Miss Lowell did not always manage to spell. For "he having got his things entirely from Professor Fenolosa, they were not Chinese in the first place, and Heaven knows how many hands they went through between the original Chinese and Professor Fenolosa's Japanese original." But being no more a sinologue than Pound, Miss Lowell was hardly in a position to assail what she took Fenollosa's ignorances to be. Then in the autumn of 1917 an old acquaintance, Florence Wheeler Ayscough, came to Brookline for a long visit. She brought some Chinese scrolls of which she had made rough versions to illustrate lectures. (One had culture? One spread it.) Moreover she had been born in Shanghai. "Miss Lowell was immensely interested." They began working up translations. And the lightning descended. Miss Lowell seized the bolt: it was just what could be hurled at E.P. Mrs. Ayscough recorded the Apollonian moment:

> We were at work upon a poem, and I read aloud the character *MO*: "It means 'sunset'," I said, and then added casually, "The character shows the sun disappearing in the long grass at the edge of the horizon."
>
> "How do you mean?" asked Miss Lowell.
>
> "Why, what I say," I replied, and forthwith showed her the character or pictogram in its ancient form. . . . She was more enthralled than ever.

"I have made a discovery," Amy later exulted. No one out of China had realized it before. *The key to Chinese poetry lay in the overtones imparted by the written character.*

Aha! And so much for dependence on Japanese intermediaries. This was just what Fenollosa could not have known: just what would knock that desirable hole in *Cathay* (where, it may be, she did not notice "flowers that cut the heart," nor guess that it was based on a notation of *knife* and *gizzard* components). And poetic justice should be administered in *Poetry*. The two of them set to work to vivify *vers libre* with "split-ups," Amy's nickname for dissociated roots. The catalytic sun-behind-grass proved intractable: only "sunset" would fit. Nevertheless they had made a great discovery. Florence was put to work etymologizing every character. In June eleven poems were in the hands of Harriet Monroe, whose first response, that the lines were rather cut up—

My son is ill and neglects to water
the flowers

—Miss Lowell deflected with some bluff about cadence. "You see I have made an awful study of cadence. . . . No such study has been made by any other of the *vers libristes* writing in English. Even Ezra has felt and announced his convictions, rather than tabulated, measured, and proved." ("I wrote back and sounded as learned as if I really knew something," she confided to Florence. "It is always well to take a high hand with Harriet.") But cadences were a side issue. More important, the expert hand was transforming poor Florence into what the age needed, the hyper-sinologue *de nos jours*. "I also gave her a great song and dance as to your qualifications as a translator. I told her you were born in China, and that it was, therefore, in some sense your native tongue (Heaven forgive me!) . . . I explained that in getting you she was getting the *ne plus ultra* of Chinese knowledge and understanding; it being assumed, of course (though not by me expressed), that in getting me she was finding the best Englisher there was going." One longs for the finesse with which Henry James would have here suffered to emerge a salient datum about Florence: that in China she spoke only "Shanghai pidgin to her servants."

And on, to the construction of the torpedo: a prose statement by Florence of "that root theory of ours." ("Oh, I am certain of it; it is a great discovery." It was also "ours" whenever Florence was to sign for it.) "It will make Ezra and the whole caboodle of them sit up, since it will prove that their translations are incorrect, inasmuch as they cannot read the language and are probably trusting to Japanese translators, who have not the feeling for Chinese that you have. I tell you we are a great team, Florence, and ought to do wonderful things." So Amy to Florence, June 28, 1918.

* * *

By now the Fenollosa typescript had gathered Illinois dust for more than a year. Since February demands for its dislodgment, on John Quinn's legal letterhead, had assailed Mr. Carus of *The Monist*. Space was waiting in the *Little Review*, with 64 pages per month and a guaranteed printing bill (guaranteed by Quinn). *The Monist* continued neither to print the manuscript nor to return it.

* * *

As words, T.S. Eliot had remarked, flew obediently from trope to trope at Amy Lowell's bidding, so persons were disposed in whatever postures of incompetence or expertise she required. Florence, greatness thrust upon her, had commenced struggling with a Chinese primer. ("I will only try to conceal the extreme shallowness of my knowledge.") Back in China she hunted out a teacher, a Mr. Nung who could barely understand what they were driving at, in part because he understood no English whatever. He bewildered her with explanations. For years, as Amy drove the mad enterprise through another ten dozen poems, Florence was to complain what a fool she felt, how stupid. "Oh, dear me, I wish I knew more!! I read *so* slowly, and the whole thing is so dreadfully difficult." She forwarded misinformation, found it was wrong, prostrated herself with apologies. Amy was unperturbed, except when Mr. Nung's dicta conflicted with her intuition ("perfectly foolish; it is what is known in literary technique as the 'pathetic fallacy' and is considered one of the very worst things to do in literature.") Her contempt for Mr. Nung, eventually for Waley and for all the sinologues, served to keep up to the end her assurance in what she had told Harriet Monroe about Florence.

Florence in the early months even doubted if it were wise to proclaim "our grand discovery" about roots. Nonsense, replied Amy, it must be divulged, and for a good reason: "it is simply and solely to knock a hole in Ezra Pound's translations." ("It would be most impolitic to come out and criticize Ezra in so many words; I do not think you had better mention him at all." Suffice it to mention the utter impossibility of getting "the real Chinese effect through a Japanese translation.") "Dearest Amy," Florence replied, "please don't think that I am shirking;" but "I feel utterly incapable of saying anything that would 'knock a hole' in Ezra Pound's translations. You know I am very diffident of my own powers, and I know that *you* could say something *so* apt." No, Amy wired, "it must be over your signature, not mine;" for "being a rival of Ezra's, and in some sense his enemy," words of mine would be put down for pique. "I obey," Florence replied, feeling, she said, like the ruler of the state of Shang who "with fear and trembling" knew he must save the country whose king was "a degenerate idiot." She prepared a draft. Amy wished it stronger. She strengthened it, though not with conviction.

* * *

It was now August 1918. At the *Little Review* Miss Anderson had Pound's instructions to notify him if by September 1 the Fenollosa essay had not arrived from La Salle. "I will in that case have the damn pencil scribble recopied and get it to you by Nov. 1st or thereabouts." By 20 August it had arrived ("Thank GOD"). There is no record of its exciting Miss Anderson. She announced it for the January 1919 issue, but then delayed.

* * *

So Fenollosa was nowhere in print to give anyone pause when the "Written Pictures" rendered by Florence and Amy, together with Florence's little essay, appeared in *Poetry* for February 1919. Cadenced according to Amy's "awful study," the verse was often preposterous:

> I am sick,
> Sick with all the illnesses there are,
> I can bear this cold no longer,
> And a great pity for my whole past life
> Fills my mind.
> The boat has started at last. . . .

Nor is the essay's hemoglobin conspicious. Florence wrote it, Florence's caution suffuses it. She did, under duress, mention the need for analysis of the ideographs, of which each element "plays its part in modifying either the sense or sound of the complex," and did also gently protest that Chinese poems "translated from Japanese transcriptions cannot fail to lose some of their native flavor and allusion." This was hardly the Big Bertha of Amy's desire, but a deed was nevertheless done: the disclosure of the great principle, and eleven poems. The acid could be imagined eating through Ezra, whose *Cathay* had been unadvantaged by any such insight. "Poor Ezra," Amy wrote Harriet Monroe in July, "he had a future once, but he has played his cards so badly that I think he has barely a past now."

* * *

In September "The Chinese Written Character as a Medium for Poetry," cut up into four installments, commenced running in small type at the back of the *Little Review*. Nowhere in Miss Lowell's correspondence with Mrs. Ayscough do we find any mention of it. Their discourse ran on about the "split-ups."

This great idea, on which they never ceased to congratulate one another, worried poor Florence all the years they worked on at *Fir-Flower Tablets,* in part because she was never sure how much Amy meant her to claim for it. Was it quite the omnipresent indispensable key it had seemed? Amy exacted analyses of every character out of simple lust for the blood of a rival poet whose mentors must not have known the characters mattered. Florence, in Shanghai, stuck with this appalling labor, needed support no one would give her. Were Chinese readers, for instance, aware of the character elements? Not at all, said whatever English sinologists she could get at; means "east," and never mind the sun in the tree. That generation's sinologues were in China for missionary and for consular purposes, with little more interest in etymological niceties than a ward boss in the connection between "candidate," "candor," and a toga's whiteness. One Britannic Commissioner "was very angry" after she had argued with him for two hours. Yet a poet was one day to write, in the way of poets,

> what whiteness will you add to this whiteness,
> what candor?

and a Chinese poet, Florence suspected, may on similar principles discriminate among synonyms. She had no poets to call on. One scholar did sound promising; he was interested in archaic forms of the characters, and had translated a 13th century treatise on their history. In 1921, just before their book appeared, she sounded him out. But his lack of interest was radical. He could not see why people ever wrote poetry. "It is the poorest way of saying things." His name was L. C. Hopkins. His late brother Gerard Manley (d. 1889) had been raised three years previously to some poetic notoriety by the editorial attention of the Laureate.

And Florence Ayscough's distress was all to no purpose. After those thousands of hours etymologizing, perhaps "a baker's dozen" of the etymologies ended up in Amy's text. Not a mistaken theory, nor a theory ridden too hard, nor even "inaccuracy," makes *Fir-Flower Tablets* unreadable today, but Amy Lowell's impregnable vulgarity: the bluntness of mind that decked a Li Po farewell with phonetic bellyaching—

. . . I bid good-bye to my devoted friend—Oh-h-h-h-h—now
he leaves me
When will he come again? Oh-h-h-h-h—When will he
return to me?
I hope for my dear friend the utmost peace. . . .

—and needed informing by Florence, in one of the last letters to pass between them, that when lecturing before huge audiences on one's new métier, Chinese poetry, one ought not to use the word "Chinamen" ("For some reason or other the Chinese resent this very much.")

Note on sources. The Fenollosa quotations are from an early draft of "The Chinese Written Character as a Medium for Poetry." I have them through the courtesy of Mrs. Dorothy Pound, Mr. Harry Meacham, and the University of Virginia Library. The correspondence of Ezra Pound with Harriet Anderson is in the library of the University of Wisconsin at Milwaukee. Amy and Florence published their *Fir-Flower Tablets* ("Poems translated from the Chinese by Florence Ayscough, English Versions by Amy Lowell") in 1921. The letters they exchanged, and Amy's letters to Harriet Monroe, were edited by H. F. MacNair (*Florence Ayscough and Amy Lowell—Correspondence of a Friendship,* Chicago, 1945). Biographical data from S. Foster Damon, *Amy Lowell, a Chronicle,* Boston, 1935, and Horace Gregory, *Amy Lowell, Portrait of the Poet in her Time,* N.Y. 1958. Mr. Wai-Lim Yip supplied me with the Chinese word in the title. It is No. 4373 in Mathews' Chinese-English Dictionary.

[1970]

Thomas Kinsella

OFFICE FOR THE DEAD

The grief-chewers enter, their shoes hard on the marble,
In white lace and black skirts, books held to their loins.
A silver pot tosses in its chains as they assemble
About the coffin, heavy under its cloth, and begin.

Back and forth, each side in nasal unison
Against the other, their voices grind across her body.
We watch, kneeling like children, and shrink as their Church
Latin chews our different losses into one.

All but certain images of her pain that will not,
In the coarse process, pass through the cloth and hidden boards
To their peace in the shroud; that delay, still real

—High thin shoulders—eyes boring out of the dusk—
Wistful misshapenness—a stripped, dazzling mouth—
Her frown as she takes the candle pushed into her hands,
Propped up, dying with worry, in the last crisis. *Sanctus.*

Sanctus. We listen with bowed heads to the thrash of chains
Measuring the silence; the pot gasps in its smoke.
An animal of metal, dragging itself and breathing.

[1965]

Carolyn Kizer

THREE POEMS

FOR JAN, IN BAR MARIA

After Po Chü-I

Though it's true we were young girls when we met,
We have been friends for twenty-five years.
But we still swim strongly, run up the hill from the beach
without getting too winded.
Here we idle in Ischia, a world away from our birthplace—
That colorless town!—drinking together, sisters of summer.
Now we like to have groups of young men gathered around us.
We are trivial-hearted. We don't want to die any more.

Remember, fifteen years ago, in our twin pinafores
We danced on the boards of the ferry-dock at Orcas Island
Mad as yearling mares in the full moon?
Here in the morning moonlight we climbed on a workman's cart
And three young men, shouting and laughing, dragged it up
through the streets of the village.
It is said we have shocked the people of Forio.
They call us Janna and Carolina, those two mad *stranieri*.

LINES TO ACCOMPANY FLOWERS FOR EVE

who took heroin, then sleeping pills
and who lies in a New York hospital

The florist was told, cyclamen or azalea;
White, in either case, for you are pale
As they are, "blooming early and profusely"
Though the azalea grows in sandier soil

Needing less care; while cyclamen's fleshy tubers
Are adored, yes, rooted out by some.
One flourishes in aridness, while the other
Feeds the love which devours.
But what has flung you here for salvaging
From a city's dereliction, this New York?
A world against whose finger-and-breath marked windows
These weak flares may be set.
Our only bulwark is the frailest cover:
Lovers touch from terror of being alone.
The urban surface: tough and granular,
Poor ground for the affections to take root.

Left to our own devices, we devise
Such curious deaths, comas or mutilations!
You may buy peace, white, in sugary tincture,
No way of knowing its strength, or your own,
Until you lie quite still, your perfect limbs
In meditation: the spirit rouses, flutters
Like a handkerchief at a cell window signalling
Self-amazed, its willingness to endure.

The thing to cling to is the sense of expectation.
Who knows what may occur in the next breath?
In the pallor of another morning we neither
Anticipated or wanted! Eve, waken to flowers
Unforseen, from someone you don't even know.
Azalea or cyclamen: we live in wonder,
Blaze in a cycle of passion and apprehension
Though once we lay and waited for a death.

ON A LINE FROM SOPHOCLES

I see you cruel, you find me less than fair.
Too kind to keep apart, we two brutes meet.
Time, time, my friend, makes havoc everywhere.

Our stammers left to hunger in the air
Like smoke or music, turn the weather sweet:
To seek us, cruel; to find us, less than fair.

Testing our own reflections unaware
Each caught an image that was once conceit.
Time, time, my friend, makes havoc everywhere.

Eyes lewd for spotting death in life declare
That fallen flesh reveals the skull: complete.
I see you. Cruel. You find me less than fair.

The sacking of the skin, the ashen hair—
But more than surfaces compound the cheat!
Time, time, my friend, makes havoc *everywhere.*

The years betray our vows to keep and care.
O traitors! ugly in this last defeat,
I find you cruel, you see me less than fair.
Time, time, my friend makes havoc everywhere.

[1964]

Cynthia Macdonald

FRANCIS BACON, THE INVENTOR OF SPECTACLES IS THE RINGMASTER

ALL MOUTH

1.

It was all mouth; only
The frill of flesh around the lips and
The rudimentary bag might have been considered
Differentiated tissue.

The mouth part was perfect
And was exhibited — the bag hidden beneath —
On a blue velvet cushion to emphasize
This was a patriotic display.
During sideshow hours it would play
Columbia, the Gem of the Ocean on its kazoo
And mouth slogans like,
"A slip of the lip may sink a ship."

There was a lot of argument about its sex.
Experts said, "female, that's obvious."
But when it stuck out its tongue to show what it thought
Of experts, some changed their minds and said, "androgynous."
All Mouth did not care what they said;
It would eat anything.

2.

All Mouth's pregnancy was difficult.
It did not like to sunbathe
Or swim at the pool or beach;
It was embarrassed about the bulge of its bag.
But it needed water all the time, needed immersion to
Cool. None of the circus administrators
Could understand why it shunned public swimming
When it took it the pillow each night without a murmur
And would gladly stick its tongue in ink to autograph
Photographs. But its kin knew that displaying
Your triple hump or the fountains in your aorta or
Your elephant skin or your star-spangled vulva in the sideshow
Did not mean you could bare it outside.

3.

All Mouth had given birth to part of what it lacked
And kept All Ear close night and day,
Rocking it on the rim of its cradle
Which all ears have built in, savoring its pet name,
Ma petite oreille, whispering secrets to it,
Caressing its intricate passages.

Sleep, little baby ear.
All Mouth will sing you to sleep
With Brahms and charms and
Edward Lear,
Blue Boy and Little Bo Peep.

ALL EAR, twenty years later

1.

It was off to the side, off center.
It tried to sing, All Mouth its model.
  Hear me, hear me;
  Take me inside you.
  I would make waves of sound rise and ebb in you
  Till your climax swamps you and you drown,
  Wagner green, Debussy yellow.
  Let me stuff your cunt with slick explosions,
  Let me enfold you in the circle of my flesh.
But All Ear, only receptive, made no more sound
Than a windless wind tunnel.

2.

All Ear willed its transformation.
It smelled a little, but it wouldn't
Give two cents to become a nose.
Such narrow circles, really ovals,
And pipes without tunes.

3.

Ear, hear, he, her, hearing,
Unheard. All Ear's frustration mounted,
Using its own stirrup.
It rode words like an empty boat,
Lashed itself with words of needs unmet,
Irritation and hate until
A drop of blood formed.
Blood tears circled its canals,
Circled red around its hole,
A whirlpool, an iris.
The ringmaster flicked his whip,
Honoring the ire of what once had been
The ear, and in the twinkling of one,
The eye, the new star, was spotlighted in *The Black Tent of Marvels,*
Mysteries and Wonders, an amazing Gallery of Actually
Forty, beautiful, living, blended supernatural Visions.

ALL EYE

1.

Hurry, hurry, hurry
To see the Italian,
The third in the Eye, Ear, Nose and Throat team.
See its spaghetti tears;
Listen when I pinch it, it will go ai, ai, ai.
("What do you mean, lady, didn't you ever hear of a Jewish Italian?)
And I'm going to ask you little girl, "What does
An *I*talian wear to a masked ball?"
"Mascara"

2.

All Eye, which had been staring at the sky, closed its lid
To close out the peripheral circus,
To follow the sun's blue afterlife
Diagonally up and across the red sky. Blue off the edge,
Trailing fainter suns as the lid sky deepens
To purple then black.

3.

The eye is the most courageous organ because, in a sense,
It must always face itself. It lies in its moist socket,
The pot of seeing and never says that what it sees in dream
Is less than what it sees. Image and imagination,
Those eyes indivisible.
In the deep of my eye I see to the edge of self (all
Those translucent pronouns)
And beyond into the dark quarter of the circle.

[1979]

J. D. McClatchy

THE APPROACH

Behind, a spectral wake of fume on foam,
Gasoline prism breaking up the weeks
    Of drift. To chance
    Upon a horizon

Rind studded with some solid evidence—
Vantages of rock, a shell-chalked harbor—
    First sets the course,
    Then calms the glaring swells

With reflections the ferry muses over.
On board, we stare ahead, at each other,
    As if alive
    To every aspect.

A livid cloud cap, drawn across the eye
Of a storm still hours off, seems the print
    Of negatives
    Developed in the sea's

Solution—sharp exposures, looming scapes
Of the island itself, floating in sleep.
    Anchored, awe-struck,
    The dreamer is held down

By scaly arms and links of fire, embraced
Above by panic coiled into the shapes
    Necessity
    Takes us by. Suddenly

He turns over, or the boat just lurches
To a landing. The arrival wakens
    My oldest fears
    Of staying on in time

That comes and goes, lapping the stony shores,
Eroding, grain by groan, the grounds I have
    To stand on here,
    And never can approach.

[1978]

William Meredith

AN OLD PHOTOGRAPH OF STRANGERS

On the big staircase in this picture
They are having a pageant.
The queen comes down between heralds whose trumpets are raised,
And a man, also in fancy dress, welcomes the queen,
And there is another woman in powdered hair
At the foot of the staircase, acting.
The rest of the people are guests
But caught up in the moment and serious,
In evening clothes of the nineties,
They look only slightly more real.
I suppose they are all dead now
But some of the faces are just like faces today.

It seems to be lighted electrically
Or by very bright gaslight, behind us.
They must have held still a long time.
A dark young man is holding a watch that opens.
The woman whose head is too near,
And that old man settling his glasses, would always have blurred.

On the landing a stained-glass goddess
In milky Tiffany glass
Is faint where her window is dark. She is faint, it seems,
With the darkness outside on this one particular night.

[1963]

James Merrill

FOUR POEMS

COUNTRY MUSIC

Catbirds have inherited the valley
With its nine graves and its burned-down distillery

Deep in Wedgwood black-on-yellow
Nowhere cracked, of bearded oak and willow.

Walls were rotogravure, roof was tin
Ridged like the frets on a mandolin.

The sherriff missed that brown glass demijohn.
Some nights it fills with genuine

No proof moonshine from before you were born.
This here was Sally Jay's toy horn.

A sound of galloping—Yes. No.
Just peaches wind shook from the bough

In the next valley. Care to taste one, friend?
A doorway yawns. A willow weeps. The end.

THE ROMANCE LANGUAGE

When first in love I breakfasted by water.
The chestnut trees were in full bloom, I fear.
A voice at my elbow breathed, "Monsieur désire?"
I understand perhaps, but could not utter.

Some stay years, and still are easy to lie to.
Frog and prince have been witty at my expense.
My answers when they come make less than sense
Although I tell the god's own truth, or try to.

NIKE

The lie shone in your face before you spoke it.
Moon-battered, cloud-torn peaks, mills, multitudes
Implied. A floating sphere
Your casuist had at most to suck his pen,
Write of *Unrivalled by truth's own*
For it to dawn upon me. Near the gate
A lone iris was panting, purple-tongued.
I thought of my village, of tonight's "Nabucco"
You would attend, according to the lie,
Bemedalled at the royal right elbow. High
Already on entr'acte kümmel, hearing as always
Through your ears the sad waltz of the slaves,
I held my breath in pity for the lie
Which nobody would believe unless I did.
Mines unexploded from an old one lent
Drama to its rainbow surface tension.
Noon struck. Far off, a cataract's white thread
Kept measuring the slow drop into the gorge.
I thought of her loom and crutch who hobbled
At your prayer earthward. What she touched bloomed.
Fire-golds, oil-blacks. The pond people
Seemed victims rather, bobbing belly-up,
Of constitutional vulnerability
Than dynamite colluding with a fast buck.
Everywhere soldiers were falling, reassembling,
As we unpacked our picnic, you and I.

[1968]

THE HELP

Louis Leroy, gentleman's gentleman
Among cashmeres and shantungs never quite
Caught smoking. Shiftless Beulah with her fan,
Easing her dream book out of sight.
Jules all morning sharpening the bright
Kitchen knives, his one dull eye on Grace . . .
The whole arranged so that *we* might,
Seeing nothing, say they Knew Their Place.

Gods they lived by, like the Numbers Man
Supremely dapper in the back porchlight,
Their very skins, cocoa and tan
Up the scale to glistening anthracite,
Challenged yet somehow smiled away the white
Small boy on Emma's lap: home base
Of common scents. Starch, sweat and snuff excite
Me still. Her arms round me, I knew my place.

James Madison, who chauffeured the sedan!
Shirt off in the garage after a fight
"At my friend's house," red streamers ran
Down his tall person, filling me with fright
—Or had I gained an abrupt, gasping height
Viewed from which pain shrugged and wore his face?
("We loved our darkies"—Cousin Dwight.)
I've since gone back up there. I knew the place.

Father and Mother, side by side tonight
Lax as dolls in your lit showcase,
Where are those souls? Did they at last see right
Into our helpless hearts, and know their place?

[1977]

Christopher Middleton

BONNARD

Does the body rest against his eye, the cool
changing its colors: rose, purple, silver
framed in a door, the enamel of a bath

their life the elements dream through
figures all facing at different angles
do not touch, they include one another—

dwelling on a thing, the eye feeds its boutons
energy sprayed from a few co-ordinates: loaf & horse
each its own dimension in the starred dream

shields the colors! blue skins
cocooned girl's crotch, or aloof apple
a buffoon child, flowers in a bowl

& her face everywhere, turning from a cup
to smile with a mouth like a slice
of baby watermelon, celestial clown girl

or bored, sprawling bare on a rumpled bed
brown arm thrown across her ribs
the left hand tilting a small breast—

but where the skin starts it is the idyll
playing out any boundary to scan
throbbing ascensions in the space around

streets dappled with skirts & metal
woodland blue with edible branches
crimson billow of a kitchen cloth

it is where the dogs do battle
canaries roast in evacuated rooms
the history-makers unload their dead

hack it to pieces. To pick it up again
restore it, whole, a lifetime on fingertips
grinding a rainbow from the ignorant dew.

[1966]

Josephine Miles

VIGILS

We are talking about metaphor.
The fog comes in as Sandburg says it does
Dark over our streetlights and our houses.
What Jim says of metaphor Fred cannot abide
And I cannot abide, but in more silence.
Look, we are getting nowhere, it is midnight,
Get home out of this warm firelight into the fog,
We will solve them yet, metaphors,
Their common properties.

Later from their lab the physicists
Come for their friends and hear a poem or two.
How they hear the wrong ones, the right go by them,
And folks go off to buy the daily bread, pale,
Not yet reinforced with wheat germ.
How do we survive? Do we survive?
The red shift startles us, the solid state,
That dialectic,
And such wonders as would drive us out
Into the attics of our driven friends,
Vigils of the academic dark.

[1983]

Paul Monette

BONES AND JEWELS

. . . though I was met by a man with a cart,
he did not, for some curmudgeonly Cape Cod
reason, drive me all the way to the house,
but dropped me some distance away from it,
so that I somehow got lost in a field and
dragged my suitcase through scrub-oak and
sweet-fern in the breathless hot August
night. At last I saw a gleam—a small house—
which I approached from the fields behind
it, and there I found the Millays . . .
—Edmund Wilson, THE SHORES OF LIGHT

What with the life I lead, the force I spend,
I'll be but bones and jewels on that day,
And leave thee hungry even in the end.
—Edna Millay, 'Thou Famished Grave"

Time has simply got to shut up. Or else
I'll beat him senseless, bind his hands, and saucer
his fat bachelor's face like a discus
on the wind. Then let him try to talk to me
as if I had manners and must make do.
Morbid broken boy, to favor those in pain,
turn me twenty-nine without a wrestle
if you can, so long accustomed to tired
women. I have decided to fight you
early—
because, one, I am on vacation.
Two, I can use my nails, not much given,
in war at least, to honor yet (and yet
I long for forms, for formulas, I mean—
I can't marry now, my darling x. Why,
I can't thread a needle, and my mother
signed me away at birth to z, who is
in oil. My promises, such as they are
are not my own.) And three, why I hate you,

you remind me of the men in Maine.
Of all
the coasts the sea is heir to, this, this tongue
of Massachusetts, will be taken first—
not, it seems, for several hundred years,
but soon enough. The locals, if they care,
lack the captain's impulse either to sink
with the ship or, like Noah, to pick and choose.
One day, I expect, they will notice how
the high tide seeps among the lilacs (When
did we lose the garden? Wasn't there once
a field as well? And further back, did we,
or am I dreaming, didn't we live high
in the dunes?), and then they will leave the table,
the lobsters cracked and hardly touched, out, down
to the bay to row to Boston.
Things to do.
Research before September first the death
of grasses. This far south, when does the brown
come in? Write to Bunny (oh, but lightly).
Ask the Sunday hunter on Ryder downs
why he won't wear red. What is he after?
Stop retrieving shells. The men with buckets,
the tide, the birds won't leave them be. All right,
you leave them be.
"Bunny dear, I know you
hate me for a fishwife. I've run away,
where you would lose your temper, have a gin
and lemons, then undertake to reassess
Melville and the whale. The Baptist minister
in town (call him Ishmael) says he won't
dispute the bits of seascape in the Bible.
If they swore that Jonah ate the whale whole,
it is all one to him. Come to Truro,
Bunny (or not! or not!). You are always
in the heart of
Edna (St. Vicious) Millay."
Fog again. And written down again. Why
bother? Clearly a writer keeps his sad
diary current on ghostly afternoons,

and only then to avert the dark fingers
from the throat. Meteorologically,
assume the worst unless otherwise stated,
as in passages given to paradox,
the notes for a life lived on the loose—
"Sunny.
From bed"—abrupt, in the New York style—"I watch
Achilles dress. I take my Baudelaire
from under the pillow, play at reading it,
and then write in the flyleaf how he is
something less than Achilles in a tie.
He watches me. He thinks I am doing
a poem, as one does, um, one's knitting
or one's horoscope. We'd kill each other
for a price. Unless we got paid, we wouldn't
trouble to pull a trigger and soil the rug—"

Long since, the bitch with the books and time to burn
has come to the end of America. The heat
she heaps on boys, on warriors and thugs,
belies who is it loves *her* least. She's not
a girl in a story, though the story goes
that she was once so pale, a candle passed
in front of her still lit the room beyond,
no matter how she held it, shook it, blew
and spit at it. Here, pen in hand, she walks
the brink, not in a shawl at the lip of a cliff,
but further than is safe. To tell the truth,
the seas with any drama are confined
to Maine—the undertow, the shoals the shape
of Lincoln's face, and grave after grave troughed
in the open water. Here is, if life is
a place, just the place to write, and no rage
at the edges, no liaisons where the rocks
and water go at it, wasting time.
Three
thirty. The last mail at five.
"Dear Wilson,
it has come to the attention of the Friends
of Better Books that poetry, mother

of culture, is practiced now (May I be
blunt?) by riffraff elements. The War has
shaken the temple. Ours is to rally
round the bardic mantle where it is worn
with *style.* Would you, to this end, please inquire
what tone Vincent Millay lately takes. Such
an ear! But there are rumors. Use a ruse.
Go disguised as a weekend guest—"

"Listen,
Bunny Wilson, listen good. The maiden
whore is sorry. Edner M'lay is stuck
for an obligatory scene to close
her broken-hearted book, *The Belle on Board:
A Vassar Girl at Sea.* What do you take
for writer's block? Bring me a fifth of it.
(No, wait. A pint is probably enough,
I have it all written in my head.) And ice.
I can't take medicine neat—"

"Who is the best?
Me? I am sick to death of burning bright.
Honestly, Bunny, do I have to be
so Godawfully young? The debutante
champagning in a hooped dress, her daybook
tucked in her reticule. I want to write
The Iliad (at least). And you know what's
funny? I'm old. (I know I don't *look* it.)
I need you here, and I will probably
drive you away. Risk it, rabbit.

Your bard."

August 5th. Fog.

6th (7th?). Bright out.
At last. Released from a blank tower, no
nearer the moon. Because a woman's body
is a man's clock (due to the tick of it),
she is the one who takes the time. Bathing
is her reward, a long afternoon's soak.
She is given a tub, a shelf of sponge
and unguents; and when she is not in the bath,
she rubs her wrists and temples with a lily
cologne kept cold in the kitchen by her maid.

She buys it by the case. Also bourbon.

Or so I think (I think too much) today,
swimming alone, afloat, tucked in a wave's
hollow jaw. I wish to be occupied
with just my skin. If anyone calls, I'm
being massaged. Unless it is the boy
Time, threatening a scene. It sets him off
to catch me making up and mirroring.
"Hurry," he says, "our car is here. I *won't*
walk in in the middle, like a tailor
given a pair of tickets by a count
who wants his suits perfect. Your gloves are here.
Your furs. Your fan." Oh, we are off, taking
the corners on two wheels. Nothing is said
about my hair.
Tuesday. Bunny accepts.
Jesus.
The beach. Mumbles and Norma waltz
the slopes, careering down the sand, and lean
shoulder to shoulder to hoot at me. Their hats
are whole umbrellas, and they carry striped
canvas sacks as big as awnings. "Tea time!"
Norma cries. At that, as if hurrahing,
Mumbles' hat takes off to sea, going end
over end, a balloon, a kite. Is it
that I can write it down that I will have
forever mother's face caught in the fast
photograph she makes at the loss of a hat?
Halfway down the dune, her hands on her head,
appalled at the wind's perversity. And glad,
because things have a way of staying on
too long. She huffs over "*Baggage*!" and draws
the line, has always drawn it there.
The tea
is tabled on a beached timber, inches
from the ocean. A tart and biscuits, three
painted cups, and wrinkled, mismatched linen.
Mumbles says that, as we're to have a guest
from The City, we must practice eating
normally, one with another again. We've come

to a pass where a bit of pear and crackers
and a book won't do. "Not for *dinner*. We must
be *rational,*" she says, slicing the air
with a spoon. Like old Canute, bellowing "Well?"
over the surf, "What is a little water
to a king?" Our Norma says: "Bunny will think
our meals are like the meals in *Alice,* Ma.
Besides, Bunny is not coming to eat."
We all three titter like spinsters as we pack
our dirftwood tea.
                                        Eleven thirty. Thump.
Someone is bringing a body up the steps
to the porch. The bell. And in comes Bunny, wet
with the night heat: "Christ, it's the lost continent."
He drops his steamer trunk and says, Cockney,
to Mumbles: "Mum, does Edna St. Louis
Missouri live hereabouts?" At midnight
mother produces fish, and now she is
Little Women, radiating gumption
and The Cape Cod Folks. Oh dear
                                                        I hound Bunny
with *my* thousand questions about Eng. Lit.
"Like the Eumenides," I tell him.
                                                        Frown:
"Well, I think you mean the *Sphinx,* don't you?"
                                                                        Hmm.
"Something hungry, then. Fanged. Inquisitive.
And it's got Man's number and eats its young."

One learns to write to write about the years,
one of the Truro sonnets starts. Look at
the second "write." It occupies a place
above the—what?—the fog of sentences
and meaning what is there (when what is there,
if it is true, is far too still to hear).
It doesn't mean, that second "write," *write.* What
am I trying to say? Ah, Bunny knows.
Sunday. Will I marry, he wants to know.
We are throwing shells off Provincetown pier.
I answer lightly, with a line of mine.

No, no, I haven't heard him right. Will I
marry *him?*
Oh.
"Oh I can't marry now,
my darling Bunny. Why, I can't thread a
needle, and my mother signed me away
at birth to a mogul. It's out of my hands."
Then, because we are sad, because it is
always better left for another day,
"Give me," I say, "some time, With *two* of us–"
I was going to say the girl's story
stops here, but I don't mean it. It goes on.

Captain Curmudgeon, the man with the cart, halloos,
calling us back, and cuts us short. He's done
the butter-and-egg provisioning for half
Truro, and is the best the village has
in taxicabs. All the way home, Bunny
and I are sailors, keeping the stuff and us
aboard. Some of the time, caught in the ruts
others have wheeled in the way, we click
like a trolley. For the rest, the skipper veers
and blazes a trail, we rattle overland
in fits and starts, and the eggs are on their own.
We disembark at Ryder's field and wait
to watch the captain out of sight, a cloud
of sea birds fanning him off like a sail.

"Would we be the Brownings, Bunny?"
Below,
the harbor cups its dream, the going in
and going out only what they are. We
are sea people who do not hold this hill,
this edge, this instant shaped in sand.
"You mean,
will I take care of you?"
"Oh no. You must
release me from my father's house."
"Your father?"
"He is mad. He tells me my paralysis
is fatal. I can do nothing but write."

"Your father's dead. And anyway, you are
a changeling."
"Literal Bunny. He's not
really my father. More of a boy, really,
but a tyrant. It's Oedipal as hell."

"Will you marry me?"
"Maybe." (*No* is what
I mean, but there you are.) "In the morning
you go back, and I will mull it over."

And that, as they say in the stories, is that.
Or *would* be, but for the moment on this height,
watching the sun go down. We are foolproof
for a little, though the land is running out
like an hour in a glass.
Nobody buys
the time in a nice way. It costs the earth.

[1976]

Marianne Moore

LOGIC AND "THE MAGIC FLUTE"[1]

(impressions of a première)

Up winding stair,
here, where, in what theatre lost?
was I seeing a ghost—
a reminder at least
of a sunbeam or moonbeam
that has not a waist?

[1]First telecolorcast by RCA, January 15, 1956.

By hasty hop
or accomplished mishap,
the magic flute and harp
somehow confused themselves
with China's precious wentletrap.[2]

Near Life and Time
in their peculiar catacomb,
abalonean gloom
and an intrusive hum
pervaded the mammoth cast's
small audience-room.
Then out of doors,
where interlacing pairs
of skaters raced from rink
to ramp, a demon roared
as if down flights of marble stairs:

"What is love and
shall I ever have it?"[3] The truth
is simple. Banish sloth,[4]
fetter-feigning uncouth
fraud. Trapper Love with noble
noise, the magic sleuth,
as bird-notes prove—
first telecolor-trove—
illogically wove
what logic can't unweave:
you need not shoulder, need not shove.

[1956]

[2]The precious wentletrap: a winding-staircase *(scalaria pretiosa):* one of any elegant usually white marine shells. (Webster)

[3]DEMON IN LOVE by Horatio Colony (Hampshire Press, Inc., Cambridge).

[4]Banish sloth; you have defeated Cupid's bow. (Ovid: *remedia amoris).*

Herbert Morris

DAGUERREOTYPIE DER NIAGARA FALLS (AUFGENOMMEN VON BABBITT 1852)

Seven figures positioned at the Falls,
positioned as they will not be positioned
unless the dream retrieves them, or the dance,
or the dream of the dance we call the past,
silhouetted against the blaze of summer,
against the haze mist of the Falls sends up,
no wind tugging long skirts, no perspiration
encroaching, darkly, slowly, on starched shirt-fronts,
the men in stovepipe hats, though one goes hatless,
the women parasoled against the sun,
except for one, who lets it come down on her
as it is bound, all afternoon, to come,
lets it come down with nothing to deflect it,
nothing, all day, between her and this weather,
Niagara, summer, 1852,
interventions neither given nor asked,
foliage leafing out richly before them,
darkening into foreground after foreground,
background obscure, neglected, muted, vague,
the past thin, but tomorrow limitless,
underbrush, from this distance, lavish, lush,
wholly impenetrable, one would guess,
weighing the green of breadth, the miles of depth,
not ready to be crossed, surveyed, pronounced,
American, it seems, and yet resisting
definitions too easily arrived at,
placements too definite, too pure, too fixed,
at our feet, or at theirs, a little clearing,
or at least what one thinks of as a clearing,
what the mind will insist must be a clearing
(holding to clarity with a foreboding
befitting such dark figures darkly fixed),
affording what, that year, the caption-writer

called a view of "the changing panorama"
downstream from two momentous cataracts
over which water tumbles at the spillway
in a haze of perpetual suspension
caught, it states, by "the magic of the camera,"
caught "forever", as though it knew what that was,
a beach, an overlook, a promontory
of coarse sand, stones, bleached grass, boulders to sit on,
where, for this moment of their lives, they come
together (though they come by inadvertence),
or where, with an intent you know eluded
the attention of each of them, attention
straying through the long, sultry afternoon,
someone has made it seem they come together,
group composition against sky and water,
Seven Figures Positioned at the Falls,
for what perhaps were deemed artistic reasons
by a figure we do not see whose camera
sees all that there will be to see, and more:

three men, three women, one boy in a hat,
flat crown, wide brim, which seems the very hat
a youth would travel in from somewhere downstate
on a summer day's outing to Niagara
(one almost dreams the train-stub in his pocket
which takes him back through endless summer darkness
later that night, after he eats cold chicken
from a wicker hamper under the stars,
has a name written on it like Elmira,
Elmira of church suppers, elms, white porches;
one almost glimpses ink smudged on the ticket,
one almost smells night-jasmine down the track).

The boy sits dreaming under vast, dark trees
as beautiful as our name for them, larches,
leaves and branches lowering on his head
shade for the length of this long afternoon,
shade at once both tumultuous and still
(shade which will prove impenetrable, too,
weighing its tone, its texture, from this distance),
even if, later, he should change positions,
lie on his back, study clouds in the shape of

Indian arrowheads, decide to doze,
begin, if one should look in their direction,
to wonder who the others are who come
by stage or train, like him, to view the Falls
on a day's outing, late in summer, wonder
what the weight of their lives is, what the weight
of his own life will be, far from here, far,
tomorrow, where the sight-lines, distant, blur,
foliage leafing out before him, darker
than one can weigh the length and breadth of, deeper
than one can cross, while there is light, white water
spilling, light coming down, heat building, clouds
changing to arrowheads, fragrance of jasmine
haunting us down the track on the way back,
on the way we insist is the way back,
all of it, spillway, cataract, mist, water,
impenetrable underbrush, converging
somewhere where seven figures loom transfixed
the moment someone peering through a camera
pronounces, in three syllables, convergence,
Niagara, summer, 1852,
light coming down, heat building, water spilling,
a ticket stamped Elmira, so the dream says,
put in his pocket, earlier that morning,
by a boy whose hat is the very hat
to travel to the Falls in late in summer,
fragrance of jasmine spilling to the track
when the dark, falling, complicates still further
what we think of when we say the way back.

All day he peers intently at white water,
water over the brink, water converging,
wearing the hat we know to be the hat
in which a boy will journey from Elmira,
just the hat, and for just this day in summer,
will journey just to peer and peer at water,
as though no peering here could be enough
for his purpose, whatever that might be,
as though it were his life at which he peered
(although he does not know that), and his life
were nothing more nor less than mist, than water,

all day light coming down, all day heat building,
all day the sun hammering on their backs
(though he sits in the shade, all day, of larches),
everything late in summer someone meant
from behind the view-finder of a camera
when whispering those syllables: convergence.
It is enough to sit here now, to peer.
Relentlessly white water spills, converges.

One of the women, parasol on shoulder,
has, though we cannot know how she arranged it,
managed to seat herself with an advantage
the rest quite clearly lack, or have no wish for,
with a view of both water and the others,
can study both their faces and the mist,
the clouds changing their features or the spillway,
depending on her mood, or on her need,
not yet ready, it seems, to choose between them
nor even to concede that she must choose;
so that, without having to crane her neck,
turn her head, shift the level of her gaze
(one almost wants, in this heat, not to move),
she can view the others, the Falls, or both,
can, it seems, have all of it, all at once,
or as much of it as she has a use for.

Then there is the one who has turned her back,
turned with a force too final, too symbolic,
the only woman of the women there
without a parasol against the sun,
turned with the full weight of late summer on her,
turned where the heat builds, where the light comes down,
turned as it seems she has not turned before
and, for all we know, will not turn again,
she who has cried out No to water, No
(though it is not just water she cries No to),
with an eloquence one can almost touch,
touch at her wrists, if she could bare her wrists,
touch at her ankles, could you find her ankles
somewhere adrift beneath layers of skirt,
beneath this heat which will not be deflected,
who, having traveled hours by stage to get there,

a long summer day's outing from a county
south of here, somewhere downstate, somewhere lost,
tired and thirsty, hems coated with dust,
corseted, laced, impeccably contained,
perspiring gently under bodice, flounces,
weary of looking, weary of not looking,
hears the Falls roar behind her but has turned back
all of it, cataract, spillway, the long drop,
turned where all day the sun hammers against her,
turned her back on the sight of it, refuses
to look at what she traveled miles to look at,
to see the thing she came this far to see,
has no use for the Falls, refuses even
a glance in the direction of the others,
those who have come, like her, to view the Falls
(six who are grouped together for convenience,
for reasons that must have to do with art,
who, it becomes apparent, are quite separate,
having arrived alone, who stand alone
because there seems no other way to stand,
who perhaps do not even see the Falls,
though it will be the Falls they came to see,
the Falls one thought committed them, the Falls),
fools that they are, content to look, and look,
to look and know no end to all that looking,
refuses to consider who they are,
what, elsewhere, in the dark, their lives must be,
why they are here, and why alone, refuses
to put her passion into speculation,
refuses all of it, cataract, spillway,
acquiescence of water meeting water,
refuses the long giving way, refuses
that slow, seductive ache of going under,
that feverish surrendering of borders,
heat yielding light, light yielding heat, refuses
all of it, contemplation of the drop,
light coming down, heat building, spume, haze, roar,
six seen through mist, that whole configuration
of figures against landscape, or of figures
somehow becoming landscape, turns her back

as we know she has never turned before
(and, for all we know, will not turn again),
sits all day with light coming down, refuses
in the heat of late summer at Niagara,
far from where she had started, south of here,
somewhere windless and downstate, somewhere lost,
anything that might comfort, intervene,
anything that might break the fall of light
coming down all day on her, coming down,
faces the camera squarely, almost dares it
to penetrate that stare, that stance, unravel
what one will call, or come to call, her reason,
refuses it an opening, refuses
to give even a clue of what she feels
except that, clue enough, she turns her back,
turns as you know she has not turned before,
turns as you know she will not turn again,
has cried out No, would cry out No again
if she could turn or cry again, refuses.

[1980]

John N. Morris

TWO POEMS

THE GIFTS

All year in the appropriate North his elves,
Working like Germans in our pretty tale,
Labor for nothing. Nothing is for sale.
A brilliant junk amasses on the shelves.

Each child is flat in his exhausted bed.
As a cold breath upon the million fires
Out of the year huge Santa Claus transpires
To leave each granted wish behind for dead.

They are the day when nothing is for sale
And at great cost. Though trivial defects
At once appear, at first no one suspects
Each lovely whole shebang's designed to fail.

[1975]

IN THE RESTAURANT POLAR

In Kyoto's rooftop
Restaurant Polar
My table's particular
Fifteen ice inches
Of carved polar bear
Diminish quietly.
He weeps all over
Into the radishes
The size of mice
(Said to be raised
From only the purest garbage)
That he is set to guard.

With what mysterious
Pointless care
This possibly comical
Creature has been made
To disappear!
It is 1955. Under miles
Of wet roofs in all directions
Japan is waiting, as if it were
The future. He is a thing of tears.

[1973]

Howard Moss

SHORT STORIES

"Lover, you are the child I will never
Have . . . *have* had . . . *will* have," she wrote.
That was in Denver. October or November.
Long before she married a lawyer.
They're living, now, unhappily forever.

He was writing in Greece, and from:
" 'In the time it took not to get to the castle,
Space developed its chronic asthma . . .'
I'm fleeing with the cat to Hydra.
Escapes and such have gorgeous results.
I'm giving it up. Can't write at all.
So long. And scratch one nightingale."

If you climb to the top of a bank building
In Denver, the highest one around,
All you can see for miles are mountains.
Banks and insurance companies have
The money to build and build and build.
"The *hell* with architecture," he said—
A trustee of The Wheat and Bread
Amalgamated Holding Co.—
"Get a contractor. And let's go."
His wife was home, drinking again.
She thought: I mustn't forget to eat.

"It is the dumb, intractable
Retarded who are sexual
And hold the mystery in their hands . . ."
A professor wrote, after his class.
Revised, rewritten, then recast
Into the form of a Gothic novel
About a nun who meets the devil,
Bewitches him—the usual *kitsch*—
Half put-on and half spiritual,
It sold over a million copies
And made the professor very rich.

Meanwhile, a thousand miles away,
On a bulletin board at IBM's
Six hundred thousandth factory,
The following message found its way:
"If anyone hears of a small, unfurnished
Air-conditioned person . . ."

"Children, you are the lovers I
Could never get," she almost said
Under her breath, which was just as well
Since it was nine-tenths alcohol.
"It's time for another drink, I guess.
Yes? . . . No . . . No? . . . Yes."

In Greece, he started to write again,
"The Underground Sonnets" in four-beat lines:
"And I would find it hard to say
Who went where and who which way,"
Interrupted by the arrival of
One of the Greek hoodlums of love . . .

The following month his editor wrote,
"*An*drew, *what* is *hap*pening to you?
You know the ms. is unpublishable . . ."

The professor, after his first success,
Went back to poetry. Which did not, alas,
Return the compliment. And so he wrote
A book of comic meditations
Filched from sources not hard to trace.
He was saved by tenure and an understanding
Dean, spent six weeks at a *place*,
Where everyone was nice but the nurses.
The doctor said, "It's no disgrace . . ."

In Denver, the hotel bar's discreet.
A layman (ha ha) would never know
What's going on, it looks so straight.
After it closes . . . *you* know . . .
A little car on a back street,
And so forth.

"People aren't really built to stand
The kind of tension you get these days;
Betrayal in personal relationships
Is the very worst, of course, because
The Oedipal syndrome is revived again . . .
I think that guilt, not fear's the thing
For which we pay the highest cost;
I, personally, find it hard to feel
Guilty—except at not feeling guilt . . ."

The professor listened but wasn't cured
And produced that long, astonishing book,
"Counting Sheep or The Shepherd's Crook:
Deviation on the Western Plains,"

Which has just come out as a paperback
With an introduction by a poet back
From Greece . . .

She read it in a nursing home,
Having arrived at the same place
The professor recently left. And soon
They dried her out and sent her home.
She's fine in public now "but not
So hot in bed," the trustee said—
The trustee of the Wheat and Bread.

"One more poem, one more try,"
The prof to the poet said, whose sly
Rejoinder was, "With me, it's vi-
ce versa . . ."

One night, back on the sauce, she said,
Looking the trustee straight in the eye,
"*You* are the death I would never have,
I *thought* . . ."

The message on the bulletin board
Has had several replies, but none
Satisfactory. And yesterday
It disappeared. Or was thrown away.

[1976]

Howard Nemerov

TWO POEMS

THE DISTANCES THEY KEEP

They are with us always, but they have the wit
To stay away. We are walking through the woods,
A sudden bush explodes into sparrows, they
Show no desire to become our friends;
So also with the pheasant underfoot
In the stubble field; and lazy lapwings rise
Giving their slow, unanimous consent
They want no part of us, who will not say,
Considering the feathers in our caps,
They are mistaken by the distances they keep.

And still the heart goes out to them. Goes out,
But maybe it's better this way. Let them stay
Pieces of world we're not responsible for,
Who can be killed by a clever cruelty
But, being shy enough, may yet survive our love. [1963]

TWO VIEWS OF A PHILOSOPHER

painted in oils at eighteen, he survived
into the age of photography, which took him

Behold the genial boy who promised much,
And made the Will beget upon the Mind
A dark incredible scheme in double Dutch
That told of happiness for humankind

Against the odds (which were the odds he set)
That dumb would be our best intelligence
Against the dreaming fury driving it
To make its mind up never to make sense.

Behold the lapsing embers of that spark
Out at the limit of his latest year,
The curls all vanished from his shiny sconce,
His painted smile shrunk to a sepia sneer.
He lifts the last light of his learned glance
And sees it swallowed in a box of dark. [1970]

Joyce Carol Oates

BACK COUNTRY

It was a night of patchy dreams, strangers' voices, rain hammering on the tar-paper roof close overhead. Before Marya was awake she could see through her trembling eyelids her mother's swaying figure in the doorway; she could hear a hoarse level murmuring—not words, not recognizable words, only sounds. Her mother's angry breath catching in her throat. Half-sobbing. Coughing. Earlier, through much of the long night, Marya had been hearing voices and footsteps outside the house; the noise of car motors, car doors slamming shut, the churning of tires in gravel. She waited for her father's raised voice—he often shouted if somebody was backing out of their driveway crooked, headed for the deep ditch by the road: but she hadn't heard him. She had heard her mother instead.

Several times during the past summer Marya had wakened frightened from sleep—there were often men in the house, her father's friends, co-workers, union organizers—and she'd run out of the house to hide in the cab of a derelict pickup truck in the field next door. She was safe there in the truck: she could sleep on the seat until morning, nobody would know she was gone. Once, when she'd been particularly frightened at the loud drunken talk and laughter, she had taken her brother Davy with her—but he cried too much, he wet his pajamas like a baby, she hated him sucking his thumb the way he did and nudging his head up against her. She wasn't sure if she cared what happened to him: him or the new baby either.

You! You and you and *you*! I don't give a shit about you, I wish you were all dead, Marya's mother once screamed at them, but right away afterward she said she was sorry. She hugged them, kissed them all over like crazy, you know I didn't mean it, she said, and Marya believed her.

Once when Marya slept out in the truck her father had found her. It was freezing cold: her teeth chattered and her fingers and toes were turning blue. Her father hadn't been angry, in fact he had laughed, poking his head and shoulders through the rust-rimmed window of the truck to peer at her upside down. Hey, what's this? What the hell kind of a hiding place is this? Marya was his favorite, he liked to run his fingers through her curly hair, playing a little rough, teasing: but he never meant to make her cry when he was teasing. Another time, though, Marya's mother was the one to find her in the truck and she hadn't thought it was funny at all. It was a new trick of Marya's. Something Marya did to spite her, to shame her. Another thing that required punishment—a succession of hard quick slaps, a blow to the buttocks with her fist. We're not animals, Marya's mother said, her face flushed dark with blood,—we don't sleep out in the fields like animals!

In Shaheen Falls they talked, they stared, and Marya's mother knew though she couldn't always hear. Such people, they said, hill people, they shouldn't be allowed to have children, aren't there foster homes . . . ? Why doesn't the county . . . ? The state . . . ? Like animals, they said, whispering, staring. Marya was lost in Woolworth's, separated from her mother and Davy, so she ran up and down the aisles, wild, panting, half-sobbing, bumping into people, pushing her way through a knot of women shoppers, using her fists, even butting with her head. Isn't she a little savage, someone said in disgust, just *look* at her, those *eyes* . . . .

Marya clapped her hands over her eyes and disappeared: she couldn't see anybody then and they couldn't see her. She just disappeared—the way dreams do when a light is switched on.

Wake up, Marya's mother was saying.

Wake up, she said, her voice rising impatiently,—we're going out.

Marya heard the rain still hammering on the roof, dripping from the eaves. At the corner of the house the rain barrel would be overflowing . . . . The smells were of tar paper, asbestos siding, kerosene, rain-rotted wood . . . .

Marya was watching her father back out the driveway, one arm on the back of the seat, the other snaked around the steering wheel. He gunned the motor so hard that the Chevy's chassis rocked and the rear bumper struck the gravel. She and Davy were playing in the rain, trying to jump over the longest puddle without getting their feet wet; but they were already wet. When the mud dried on Marya's legs she picked it off like scabs, which was maybe why her mother was so angry. Stop touching yourself, stop picking at yourself, you kids are driving me crazy—

Marya's mother was hunched over the bed, shaking her by the shoulders. The overhead light that Marya hated had been switched on, a single naked bulb that made everyone's eyes ache.

Marya, God damn it, her mother said, panting, get up, I know you been awake all along and I know you been listening, get up and get Davy dressed.

Marya's mother was wearing the black cotton slacks that were too tight at the waist, and one of Marya's father's flannel shirts, only half buttoned. Marya could see her heavy breasts swinging loose inside the shirt. Her hair was matted and wild, her eyes looked wild too, you could see that most of her lipstick had been worn off, or caked in queer little cracks on her lower lip.

Davy was already awake, whimpering, frightened. When Marya tried to haul him out of bed he kicked at her: so she pummelled him and said, God damn it, don't you try none of those tricks on *me.* Her mother had already gone back into the kitchen.

Davy was three years old, small for his age, always whining, crying, wiping his nose on his sleeves. When he groped at Marya, blinking like a kitten only a few days old, saying, Mamma, Mamma, she slapped his hands away. Damn baby, Marya whispered, you hadn't better of wet the bed.

Where are we going? Marya asked, trying not to cry. The kitchen smelled of kerosene, wood smoke, spilled scorched food from the night before. Are we going to town?

Never mind, her mother said. She wasn't looking at Marya: she was stooped over the baby in his high chair, spooning cold baby food into his mouth.

Where's Daddy? Marya asked. She knew the driveway was empty but she looked out the window anyway. Where's the car?

Make sure Davy eats something, her mother said. Her voice was low, flat, quick. It was a voice Marya hadn't heard very often. And don't you spit that stuff out when I'm not looking—that's all the breakfast you're going to get.

Marya was supposed to be feeding Davy while her mother fed the baby in his wobbly high chair, but it was too early to eat. The clock on the window sill had stopped at three-twenty-five. The sun wasn't up, the rain still pounded hard on the roof and against the windows,

Marya could hear a drip, a rapid dripping, in one of the corners, her eyelids closed and when she opened them she became confused and couldn't think what to do. The yellow plastic cereal bowls, the spoons, the box of Wheatchex with the monkey on the side, the milk she'd brought from the refrigerator that had gone slightly sour . . . . Davy gagged; or pretended to; and Marya didn't want any cereal herself, her stomach was too excited . . . .

Marya's mother must have scrubbed her face hard with a wash rag, her skin shone like dull metal; like the spoons. Her eyes were threaded with blood and moved about the kitchen without coming to rest on anything, like fish darting.

Is Daddy in town? Marya asked. Her voice always came out louder than she meant. She was afraid her mother would suddenly turn to her, and see something she was doing wrong, but at the same time she wanted her mother to look: she hated it when adults didn't take notice of her: when they looked right through her.

But her mother was wiping the baby's messy face with a paper napkin and didn't seem to hear.

Marya didn't think she was in any danger of falling asleep at the table if she was aware of herself sitting there, the bowl of cereal in front of her. But people were talking nearby—people she didn't know. In another room. Inside the rain. Men's voices, a woman's raised voice, the slamming of car doors, car motors starting.

She woke and her heart fluttered because her mother hadn't seen her: because now there was a stink in the kitchen and her mother had to change the baby's diaper.

There was sugar on Davy's cereal but he wanted more, so Marya let him have more, then she poked her finger in the sugar bowl herself and sucked it. She had on two sweaters but she couldn't stop shivering. It was too early, it was still night, where was her father, why wasn't the car in the driveway if they were going out . . . ? They would have to get a ride with old Kurelik, or maybe with his son. Marya's father got very angry when her mother asked the Kureliks for a ride, or if she could use their telephone . . . . I don't want anybody knowing my business, Marya's father said, and Marya's mother said, fast and mocking: Nobody gives a damn about knowing your business, don't flatter yourself.

But it wasn't true. Even Marya knew that people talked.

Don't you start crying, Marya's mother warned her. Once you get started you won't be able to stop.

She wasn't drunk because she didn't smell of drinking but she swayed and lurched on her feet, and when she zipped up her jacket a strand of hair caught in the zipper and she didn't notice—just left the zipper partway up. When she lifted the baby she grunted and staggered backward, as if his weight surprised her, and Marya thought—She's going to drop him and I will be blamed.

They left the house without locking anything up and hiked over to the Kureliks' farm through the rain, Marya and Davy running ahead, pushing at each other, squealing, as if nothing were wrong. Even out here the air seemed to smell of kerosene and rotting tar paper. The sky was lightening minute by minute from all sides, a cold glowering look to it, not exactly morning. Marya couldn't remember what time it was. She splashed through a mud puddle, flailing her arms: but she was thinking of the secret tunnel she sometimes made in her bed, in the bedclothes, burrowing down to the foot of the bed like a mole and lying there without moving. She could hide there forever, she thought, not even breathing.

They followed the old saw mill lane, which was partly grown over with scrub willow and cottonwood. The roof of the mill had nearly rotted through, there were open spaces in the shingles, and patches of green moss: bright green patches that leapt at the eye. Marya thought it was funny that trees—small trees—baby willows a few feet high—had begun to grow in the drainpipes. How tall could they get, she wondered, before their weight broke everything down: then the building would collapse. Marya's father had worked in the mill until the mill shut down and then he started work with the Shaheen Mining Company until there was trouble *there*—but Marya didn't know what kind of trouble except he was "dropped from the payroll," that was how he phrased it, but he was expecting to go back, he was waiting to go back any day. Marya didn't even know where the Shaheen mine was except somewhere in the foothills north of where they lived, six or seven miles away.

Marya's father told them not to play around the saw mill because it could fall in at any time and kill them. And not to run barefoot in the grass because of nails—there were rusty nails and spikes dumped everywhere, and pieces of broken glass. His youngest brother had died of blood poisoning, he said, from a rusty nail that went halfway through his foot when he was nine years old; he didn't want his kids ending up like that. Marya pretended to listen because her father would have been angry if she hadn't but really she was thinking her own thoughts: she wasn't going to die of anything so silly.

(Then it happened, not long afterward, Marya, running around barefoot in the weedy grass behind their house, stepped down hard on something sharp, and cut her foot; but she hadn't told anybody about it. And though her foot bled for five or ten minutes, and throbbed with pain, she didn't cry—just sat hunched in the drainage ditch, where no one could find her, waiting for the bleeding to stop.)

Marya's mother, carrying the baby on her hip, managed to catch up with Marya and give her a cuff, a light blow on the shoulder. Come on, she said, get going, the two of you—I don't have any time for smart-assing around. So Marya and Davy followed along behind her, where the path was wide enough for only one person, a fisherman's path along the creek. Marya's head felt strange, her eyes too—she kept blinking to get her vision clear. Her throat tightened up—the muscles of her face tightened too—as if she was about to cry: but there was no reason for crying.

Once you get started, Marya's mother always said, you can't stop. So you kids don't start—hear me?

Sometimes, when Marya's father was away for a few days, her mother would lie in bed all morning, even into the afternoon, not bothering to dress. Maybe she'd have Marya bring her a sweater. She wasn't drunk, she said—just didn't feel like getting up—she had a touch of the flu, maybe—her head ached like hell—she had to take medicine straight out of the bottle—had to get back her strength. If the baby cried and cried it was up to Marya to take care of him, she just wasn't strong enough to climb out of bed. Get out of here and let me alone, she told Marya and Davy and they obeyed.

Other times, sprawled lazy and smiling in the bedclothes, propped up on pillows twisted any which way, she wanted Marya to nap with her, just the two of them; she hugged Marya close, and held her tight as if she thought someone might snatch her away; her breath was hot and smelly in Marya's ear—*You* know what's going on, you're just the same as me, you and me, we know it ahead of time, don't we? Marya had to hold herself very still or her mother would get angry, and hug her harder, or push her away with a slap. Don't you love me? Why don't you love me? her mother would ask, staring her direct in the eye, shaking her. You *do* love me—you're just the same as me—*I* know you!

Marya was embarrassed that her mother refused to come inside the Kureliks' house when Mrs. Kurelik invited her. Wouldn't they like to dry off a little, wouldn't they like to get warm, Mrs. Kurelik asked nervously, staring all the while at Marya's mother, who never seemed to exactly hear what was being said, and wouldn't look her in the face—just stood at the edge of the veranda with her shoulders hunched in the soiled wool jacket, the baby sleeping and twitching in the crook of her arm, her gaze sullen and hooded, looking over toward one of the barns where Mrs. Kurelik's son was loading up. Mrs. Kurelik was saying that she'd made sweet rolls the day before, maybe the children would like some, but Marya's mother didn't reply and Marya and Davy knew better than to answer on their own. Away from home, when people talked to Marya's mother, or asked her questions, she never replied right away, always a minute or two later, when you thought she wasn't going to reply at all.

Suddenly she said in a flat hard angry voice: They already had their breakfast. They do their eating at home.

Marya remembered, a long time ago, her and her mother walking along the road toward town. There'd been a quarrel at home and Marya's mother dragged her out, she hadn't brought Davy, the baby wasn't born yet, just the two of them, Marya and her mother, walking toward town. Marya's mother was saying things but not for Marya to hear. She had broken a willow branch off a tree and was slashing at weeds alongside the road, at the Queen Anne's lace in particular because it was growing all over and it had a tiny black dot at the center, she told Marya never to look because it was nasty, the tiny black dot at the center, you'd think it was an insect or something, a surprise, not a nice surprise—this pretty flower that looks all white but has a tiny black thing in it, hidden unless you got close. She told Marya not to look but of course Marya did, when her mother wasn't around.

They'd been walking perhaps half an hour when a car braked to a stop, raising dust. A man asked out the window would they like a ride, were they going to town?—a man Marya hadn't ever seen before, not one of her father's friends who came by the house. But Marya's mother kept on walking as if she didn't hear, as if she hadn't noticed the car. She was still switching the willow branch about; her long black hair was all windblown and snarled down her back. Marya wouldn't look at the man but she knew he was staring at them both.

I asked you—you two want a ride?—you going to town?

Marya's mother ignored him and kept walking, and he drove alongside them for a while, watching out the window, saying things Marya knew she wasn't supposed to hear, saying them over and over again in a mocking low voice, certain words, certain combinations of words, Marya knew she wasn't supposed to hear but sometimes repeated to herself when no one was around. Only when he asked Marya's mother if she had Indian blood, was she part Mohawk, maybe, did she turn to him and say: I'm Joe Knauer's wife and he'll kill you, he lays hands on you, you bastard fucker, you better get out of here.

The drive to Shaheen Falls took about twenty minutes; once they turned off the highway Jerry Kurelik drove fifty, fifty-five, sixty miles an hour, as fast as his father's old truck could go. In the rear the tall milk cans rattled and vibrated against one another, a noise that lulled Marya into sleep, then startled her awake again. It was confusing—the raw glaring sky, all massive clouds that looked like outcroppings of rock, had something to do with the fragment of a dream, or with the sore insides of her eyelids: but when she blinked hard, and stared, it drew away again and was nothing that could touch her.

Even in the cab of the truck, where they were jammed together—the baby on Marya's lap, Davy on her mother's, Kurelik big and fleshy behind the wheel—Marya could see her breath steam. She hated the smells—exhaust and gasoline and Kurelik's manure-splattered overalls and the sweetish mixture of milk and urine that shook loose from the baby's blanket; and the strong rank smell of Marya's mother's hair which hadn't been washed for a while. Marya told herself she wouldn't have to breathe until it was safe but she always gave in and sucked at the air like a fish.

The rain lightened. Kurelik turned on the windshield wipers, then turned them off again, then turned them on again, until the windshield was smeared and Marya hated to look through it. There were parts of insects mashed against the glass; near-invisible rainbows shone from all sides. For a while, headed down the curving Yew Road, Kurelik didn't say anything except to Marya and Davy, then on the highway, when he was driving faster and maybe his words didn't count for as much, he asked Marya's mother a few questions in a low guarded voice as if he thought Marya and Davy might not hear: was anybody going to do anything about it, where had the sheriff been, did she need any money?—but Marya's mother was staring out the window at the cars they were passing and didn't seem to hear. Marya could feel the muscles of her mother's body stiffen as they did sometimes when she was holding Marya close and Marya wanted to squirm away; she knew her face was tight and closed as a fist.

Kurelik shifted behind the wheel, embarrassed, or maybe angry—you couldn't tell with men like him or Marya's father.

Finally he said in a different voice—I got some left-over cherry cough drops in the glove compartment there, you kids want to reach in and help yourself—and Marya didn't wait for her mother to say anything, she scrambled around and got the box out and shook three of the candies into the palm of her hand, her mouth already watering. Davy took two: he loved anything sweet. Marya let the candies melt on her tongue, sucking slowly at them. The faint medicinal fumes made her eyes water.

Keep the box, take it with you, Kurelik said, and Marya murmured okay, without thanking him. She shoved it into her jacket pocket.

As soon as they came to town Marya's mother told Kurelik to let them out. He stopped the truck and said irritably, You're going to need a ride back, aren't you?—when are you going back? Marya's mother swung the truck door open and climbed down with Davy in her arms, then leaned back to take the baby from Marya. Marya saw that her face was hard and tight and closed but her eyes were red-rimmed, the whites tinged with yellow, threaded with blood. When she spoke her voice was hoarse as if she hadn't used it for a long time. I got my own plans, she said.

You're not going to take those children in there, a woman was saying. She was as tall and as big-boned as Marya's mother: but her face was neatly caked with powder, her eyebrows had been pencilled in, her wide fleshy mouth was bright with red lipstick. You're not going to take those children in there, she said, her voice rising in a way Marya would remember thirty years later,—you can leave them out here with me.

Marya's mother wiped her nose roughly with the side of her hand. She was facing the woman, standing with one shoulder slightly higher than the other, smiling a queer gloating smile Marya hadn't seen before. It's my fucking business what I do, she said.

In the end they talked her into leaving the baby behind; and Davy too—he started crying and couldn't be quieted.

What about the girl? a man was asking Marya's mother. He worked a burnt-out cigar around in his mouth, shifting it nervously from side to side. He wore soiled clothes, a kind of uniform—a short-sleeved white smock over dark trousers. You could maybe leave your little girl outside, Mrs. Knauer, he said.

She goes with me, Marya's mother said in her flat hard satisfied voice.

Marya was sucking on another of the cherry cough drops. Her mouth flooded hungrily with saliva. She knew better than to try to twist away—her mother's fingers were closed tight on her wrist.

The man with the cigar hesitated; he ran a hand through his thinning hair. He began to speak but Marya's mother cut him off. She goes with me, she said. Her name is Marya but she's the same as me—she knows everything I know.

Mrs. Knauer—

Fuck Mrs. Knauer, Marya's mother said.

She wasn't angry; she didn't even raise her voice. Her words were short, flat, calm, hard with satisfaction.

They really worked him over, didn't they, Marya's mother said afterward, to anyone who would listen: the woman with the bright lipstick, clerks in the sheriff's office, people outside on the street who had never seen her before and didn't know what she was talking about. They really worked him over, didn't they? Marya's mother said, marvelling. Shit, I wouldn't even know who it was.

She wiped at her nose, her eyes. When her big-knuckled hand came away from her face you could see she was smiling—one side of her mouth twisted up.

While she was in the sheriff's office Marya and Davy ate chocolate peanut sticks from a vending machine in the foyer. A woman came over to Marya and gave her two dimes—Marya hadn't glanced up to see who it was, her fist had simply closed on the coins—and now she and Davy had a treat, and it was still morning, not even ten o'clock. Marya was so hungry her hand trembled holding the peanut stick; she felt a tiny trickle of saliva run down the side of her chin.

Davy didn't ask about anything and Marya didn't tell him: there was nothing to tell. She'd seen a man lying stretched out on a table—a table that was also a kind of sink, but tilted, and badly stained—she'd seen a man who must have been naked, covered with a coarse white cloth that hung down unevenly—but she hadn't had time to see his face because her eyes had filmed over: or maybe because he hadn't had any face that you could recognize. The skin was swollen and discolored, the left eye wasn't right, something had sliced and sheared into the cheek, the jaw must have been out of line because the mouth couldn't close . . . . Marya thought of a skinned rabbit her father had dropped into the sink at home, she thought of squirming rock bass the boys caught in the creek and tossed onto the hard-packed ground, stunning them with the heels of their boots. Once, her cousin Lee Knauer, who was maybe four, five, years older than Marya, slammed a carp—a garbage fish—against a rock, again and again, until most of its head was gone: Lee was madder than hell, he'd wasted a worm on a fish he didn't want.

Why hadn't there been any blood on that table, Marya wondered, licking chocolate off her fingers. And there hadn't been any smell except a faint trace of lye soap—maybe because the room was so cold, like the inside of a refrigerator.

So *that's* it, Marya's mother had said, her hands on her hips, rocking slightly from side to side,—so *that's* it.

She didn't say anything else. There wasn't anything to say. Her voice was hard, jeering, but not very loud.

So *that's* it . . . .

Marya had slipped her wrist free of her mother's fingers but she hadn't run away. And her mother hadn't noticed in any case.

Now Davy stretched out sideways on the orange plastic chairs and fell asleep, sucking his thumb. His pale blue watery eyes weren't quite closed. His mouth was smeared with chocolate and the front of his canvas jacket was dribbled with snot but Marya didn't give a damn: if anybody asked she'd say she didn't know who that kid was.

She got restless waiting. She tore little strips of a magazine cover, one after another, as narrow as she could get them, then she put the magazine back; nobody was watching. She went across the foyer and asked one of the clerks for a dime—just stood there until a woman noticed her, a woman with fluted pink glasses and tiny creases beside her mouth—maybe the same woman who had given her the dimes before. Marya didn't smile, she didn't wheedle or even complain that she was hungry, she just asked for a dime, and she was given it, as easy as that, so she treated herself this time to an ice cream bar from the vending machine. Though the chocolate wafers were stale the bar tasted even better than the peanut stick: she devoured it in five or six bites.

She left the building when nobody was watching and stood on the steps, not minding the rain. Traffic circling the square, a Greyhound bus with its headlights on, a farmer's pickup truck that looked like the one her father had junked in the field . . . . She stood watching, staring, seeing no one she knew, expecting nothing. Gusts of wind blew the rain slantwise across the pavement. Then it lifted and the rain seemed to disappear. Then it came back again, stronger. Marya shivered in the cold but she didn't think it was because of the cold, she was really trembling with hunger.

The secret thing was, she still had Kurelik's box of cherry cough drops. There must have been four or five candies left, wadded up in the waxed paper, and all for Marya, only for Marya.

[1984]

Flannery O'Connor

A STROKE OF GOOD FORTUNE

Ruby came in the front door of the apartment building and rested the sack on the hall table. It had two cans of number three beans in it and was too heavy for her to be toting around. The collard greens were sticking out the top and had kept brushing in her face on the way home. She and Bill hadn't eaten collard greens for five years and she wasn't going to start cooking them regular now; but looked like Rufus wanted them so bad. Lord, she hadn't thought he'd be the way he was.

Rufus was her baby brother who had just come back from the European Theater of War. He had come to live with her because Eastrod where they were raised was not there any more. All the people who had lived there had left it, either had died or had gone to the city. She had married Bill B. Hill—he sold Miracle Products—and had come to the city. If Eastrod had still been there, Rufus would have been in Eastrod; if one chicken had been left to walk across the road there, Rufus would have been there too. She didn't like to admit it about her own kin, least about her own brother, but there he was—no count. She seen it after fifteen minutes of him. She reckoned there wasn't much help for it. He was like the others. She was the only one in her family who had been different, had any gumption. She got out a pencil from her pocket book and wrote on the sack: "Bill—you bring this upstairs." Then she braced herself at the bottom of the steps for the climb to the fourth floor.

She was an urn-shaped woman with red hair stacked in sausages around her head, and one dark tooth in the front of her mouth. Her expression soured when she looked at the steps. They were a thin black rent in the middle of the house, covered with a mole-colored carpet that looked as if it were growing from the floor. They stuck straight up like steeple steps, it seemed to her. They reared up. The minute she stood at the bottom of them, they reared up and got steeper for her benefit. She was in no condition to go up anything. She was sick. Madam Zoleeda had told her, but not before she knew it herself.

Madam Zoleeda was the palmist on Highway 87. She had said, "A long illness," but she had added, "it will bring you a stroke of good fortune!" Ruby had already figured out the good fortune—moving. Bill Hill couldn't hold off much longer. He couldn't kill her. Where she wanted to be was in a subdivision—she started up the steps—where you had your drugstores and groceries and a picture show right in your own neighborhood. As it was now, living downtown, she had to walk eight blocks to the main business streets and farther than that to get to a supermarket. She hadn't made any complaints for five years much but now with her health at stake as young as she was what did he think she was going to do kill herself? She had her eye on a place in Rosedale Heights, a duplex bungalow with yellow awnings. She stopped on the fifth step to blow. As young as she was—twenty-nine—you wouldn't think five steps would stew her You better take it easy, baby, she told herself, you're too young to rip your gears.

Twenty-nine wasn't old; wasn't nothing. She remembered her mother at twenty-nine—she had looked like a puckered-up old yellow apple, sour, she had always looked sour, she had always looked like she wasn't satisfied with anything. She compared herself at twenty-nine with her mother at that age. Her mother's hair had been gray—hers wouldn't be gray now even if she hadn't hennaed it, wouldn't be any gray in it at all. It was all those children done her mother in— eight of them: one born dead, two died the first year, one run under a mowing machine. He mother had got deader with every one of them. And all of it for what? Because she hadn't known any better. And there her two sisters were, both married four years with four children apiece. She didn't see how they stood it, always going to the doctor to be jabbed at with instruments. She remembered when her ma had had Rufus. She had been old enough to know who was screaming and for what. All that for Rufus. And him without any more get-up than a floor mop. There he was. She saw him waiting out nowhere before he was born, just waiting, waiting to make his ma that much deader. Lord, she was disappointed in him. You would have thought that when the army got through with him, he'd come back with some spine, but after she had told all her friends her brother was back from the European Theater of War, here he comes, sounding like he'd never been out of a hog lot. It beat her.

He looked old too. He looked older than she did and he was seven years younger. She was remarkable young-looking for her age. Not that twenty-nine is any age and anyway she was married. She had to smile, thinking about that, because she had done so much better than her sisters—they had married from around. "This breathlessness," she muttered, stopping again. She reckoned she would sit down on the step.

There were twenty-eight steps in each flight—twenty-eight.

She sat down and jumped quickly, feeling something under her. She caught her breath and then pulled the thing out: it was Hartly Gilfeet's pistol. He was a six-year-old boy that lived on the fifth floor. If he was hers she'd have wore him out so long ago so hard so many times he wouldn't know how to leave his mess on a public stair. She could have fallen down those stairs as easy as not when she felt that thing. But his ma wasn't going to do anything to him even if she told her. All she did was scream at him and tell people how smart he was. "Little Mister Good Fortune," she called him, "all his poor daddy left me." His daddy said on his death bed, "There's nothing but him I give you," and she said, "You give me a fortune!" and so she called him Little Mister Good Fortune. "I'd wear the seat of his good fortune out," Ruby muttered.

The steps were going up and down like a seesaw with her in the middle of it. She did not want to get nauseated. Not that again. Now no. No. She was not. She sat tightly to the steps with her eyes squinched shut until the dizziness faded a little and the nausea went down. No, I'm not going to no doctor, she said. No. No. She was not. They would have to carry her there knocked out before she'd go. She had done all right doctoring herself all these years, no bad sick spells, no teeth out, no children—all that by herself. She would have had five children right now if she hadn't been careful.

She had wondered more than once could this breathlessness be heart trouble. Once in a while, going up the steps, there'd be a pain in her chest along with it. That's what she wanted it to be—heart trouble. They couldn't operate on you for that. They'd have to knock her on the head before they'd get her near a cutting table, they'd have to—suppose she would die if they didn't?

She wouldn't.

Suppose she would?

What'd she want to think about that for? She was only twenty-nine. There was nothing permanent wrong with her. She was fat and her color was good. She thought of herself again in comparison with her mother at twenty-nine, and she pinched her arm and smiled. Seeing that her mother or father neither had been beauties, she had done right well. They had been dried up. Dried up and Eastrod dried into them, them and Eastrod shrunk down into something all puckered up. And she had come out of that. Something as alive as her. She got up, smiling to herself. She was warm and fat and beautiful and not too fat because Bill Hill liked her that way. She had gained some but he hadn't noticed except that he was maybe more happy and didn't know why. She felt the wholeness of herself, a whole thing climbing the stairs. She was up the first flight now and she looked back, pleased. As soon as Bill Hill fell down those steps once, maybe they would move. But they would move before that! She laughed aloud and moved on down the hall. Mr. Jerger's door grated and startled her. Oh Lord, she thought, *him*.

He peered at her coming down the hall. "Good morning," he said, bowing the upper part of his body out the door. "Good morning to you!" He looked like a goat. He had little raisin eyes and a string beard and his jacket was a green that was almost black or a black that was almost green.

"Morning," she said, "hower you?"

"Well!" he screamed. "Well indeed on this glorious day!" He was seventy-eight years old and his face looked as if it had mold on it. In the afternoons he walked up and down the sidewalks, stopping children and asking them questions. Whenever he heard anyone in the hall, he opened his door and looked out.

"Yeah, it's a nice day," she said languidly.

"Do you know what great birthday this is?" he asked.

"Uh-uh," Ruby said. He always had a question like that. A history question that nobody knew; he would ask it and then make a speech on it. He used to teach in a high school.

"Guess," he urged her.

"Abraham Lincoln," she muttered.

"Hah! You are not trying," he said. "Try."

"George Washington," she said, starting up the stairs.

"Shame on you!" he cried; "and your husband from there! Florida! Florida! Florida's birthday," he shouted. "Come in here." He disappeared into his room.

She came down the two steps and said, "I gotta be going," and stuck her head inside the door. The room was dark except for one yellow bulb burning down on Mr. Jerger and a table.

"Now examine this," he said. He was bending over a small book, running his finger under the lines: " 'On Easter Sunday, April 3, 1516, he arrived on the tip of this continent.' Do you know who this 'he' was?" he demanded.

"Yeah, Christopher Columbus," Ruby said.

"Ponce de Leon!" he screamed. "Ponce de Leon! You should know something about Florida," he said. "Your husband is from Florida."

"Yeah, he was born in Miami," Ruby said. "He's not from Tennessee."

"Florida is not a noble state," Mr. Jerger said, "but it is an important one."

"It's important alrighto," Ruby said.

"Do you know who Ponce de Leon was?"

"He was the founder of Florida," Ruby said brightly.

"He was a Spaniard," Mr. Jerger said. "Do you know what he was looking for?"

"Florida," Ruby said.

"Ponce de Leon was looking for the fountain of youth," Mr. Jerger said, closing his eyes.

"Oh," Ruby muttered.

"A certain spring," Mr. Jerger went on, "whose water gave perpetual youth to those who drank it. In other words," he said, "he was trying to be young always."

"Did he find it?" Ruby asked.

Mr. Jerger paused with his eyes still closed. After a minute he said, "Do you think he found it? Do you think he found it? Do you think nobody else would have got to it if he had found it? Do you think there would be any person living on this earth who hadn't drunk it?"

"I hadn't thought," Ruby said.

"Nobody thinks any more," Mr. Jerger complained.

"I got to be going."

"Yes, it's been found," Mr. Jerger said.

"Where at?" Ruby asked.

"I have drunk of it."

"Where'd you have to go?" she asked. She leaned a little closer and got a whiff of him that was like putting her nose under a buzzard's wing.

"Into my heart," he said, placing his hand over it.

"Oh." Ruby moved back. "I gotta be going. I think my brother's home." She got over the door sill.

"Ask your husband if he knows what birthday this is," Mr. Jerger said, opening his eyes and looking at her coyly.

"Yeah, I will." She turned and waited until she heard his door click. She looked back to see that it was shut and then she blew out her breath and stood facing the dark remaining steep of steps. "God Almighty," she commented. They got darker and steeper as you went up.

By the time she had climbed five steps her breath was gone. She continued up a few more, blowing. Then she stopped. A pain was in her stomach. It was a pain like a piece of something pushing something else. She had felt it before, a few days ago. It was the one that scared her. She had thought the word, cancer, once and dropped it instantly because no horror like that was coming to her because it couldn't. The word came to her with the pain that was in her stomach but she slashed it in two with Madam Zoleeda. It will end in good fortune. She slashed it twice through and then again until there were only little pieces of it that you couldn't recognize, wiggling slightly. She was going to stop on the next floor—God, if she ever got up there— and talk to Laverne Watts. Laverne Watts always cheered her up.

She got up there, gasping and feeling as if her knees were full of fizz, and knocked on Laverne's door with the butt of Hartly's gun which she found still in her hand. She leaned on the door frame to rest and all of a sudden something happened: the floor around her dropped on all sides and the walls darkened and she was reeling without breath in the middle of the air, terrified at the drop that was coming. She saw the door open a great distance away.

Laverne doubled over. She had a laugh like a hog being butchered. "That gun!" she yelled. "That gun! That look!" She staggered back to the sofa and fell on it, shaking and pointing and doubling over.

The floor came up to where Ruby could see it and remained, dipping a little. She stepped down to get on it. She concentrated on a chair and headed for it, putting her feet carefully one before the other. "You should be in a wild-west show!" Laverne Watts said. "You're a howl!"

Ruby ran into the chair and then edged herself onto it. "Get me some water," she said hoarsely.

Laverne sat up and then fell back on the sofa and shook again.

"Quit that!" Ruby yelled. "Quit that!"

Laverne sat up and looked at her. She was a big blonde with a wise cat face and eyes that seemed to know for themselves without asking her brain. "Are you really sick?"

"I'm damn sick," Ruby glowered.

"Well, what do you come in here with that gun for then? Where'd you get it?"

"Sat on it," Ruby muttered.

Laverne turned quickly and went off to the kitchen. Ruby sat sprawled out in the chair, glaring at her ankles. The room got still and she raised her head cautiously and looked around. Everything was still. I'm not going to no doctor, she started, I'm not going to one. I'm not going. "Not going," she began to mumble, "not going, not . . ." She realized, staring at them, that her ankles were swollen. Her heart began to pump in her neck. Laverne came back with a glass of water and handed it to her.

"Are my ankles swollen?" Ruby asked.

"They look like they've always looked to me," Laverne said, throwing herself down on the sofa again. "Kind of fat." She lifted her own ankles up on the end pillow and turned them slightly. "How do you like these shoes?" she asked. They were new grass-green sandals.

"I think they're swollen," Ruby said. "When I was coming up that last flight of stairs I had the awfulest feeling, all over me like . . ."

"You ought to go to the doctor."

"I don't need to go to any doctor," Ruby muttered. "I can take care of myself. I haven't done bad at it all this time."

"Is Rufus at home?"

"I don't know. I kept myself away from doctors all my life. I kept—why?"

"Why what?"

"Why, is Rufus at home?"

"I thought I'd show him these shoes. I like new shoes," Laverne said. "I like to lie up and look at my feet in them."

"Why Rufus?" Ruby said. Laverne was thirty years old. She was a year older than Ruby even.

"Can't he look at shoes?" Laverne asked, sitting up to adjust the strap to one.

"Rufus ain't but twenty-two years old," Ruby said. And doing nothing. No count. She saw him again waiting out nowhere before he was born, waiting to make his ma that much deader. "He don't have no time to be looking at women's shoes," she said. "He ain't got that kind of time."

"You don't say," Laverne said. She swung her feet down on the floor and sat up and took off one of her shoes. "I believe your ankles are swollen," she said.

"Yeah," Ruby said, twisting them. "Yeah. They feel tight sort of. I had the awfulest feeling when I got up those steps, like sort of out of breath all over, sort of tight all over, sort of—awful."

"You ought to go to a doctor."

"No."

"You ever been to one?"

"Once."

"What'd he do to you?"

"Nothing," Ruby said. "He didn't get the chance. Three of them holding me didn't do no good."

"What was it?"

"What you looking at me that way for?" Ruby muttered.

"What way?"

"That way," Ruby said, "like you are, like you know something I don't."

"I just asked you what it was."

"It was a boil," Ruby said sullenly. "A nigger told me what to do and I did it and it went off. I'd do that for whatever I got now only this town is too big; you can't get the things."

"What things?"

"Just things. What do you think you know? What do you . . ."

Laverne got up and began walking around Ruby, bending her knees and holding her hands behind her, like Sherlock Holmes. Ruby revolved in the chair, glaring up at her. "What do you think you know?" she growled.

"Put them all together they spell MOTHER," Laverne sang and rolled her eyes.

"Not me!" Ruby shouted, jumping up. "Not me! I take care of that. I been taking care of that for five years. That ain't going to happen to me. That ain't going to happen to me!"

"Well you just slipped up once," Laverne said. "About four months ago you just slipped up once."

"I don't reckon you know anything about it," Ruby said fiercely. "You aint' even married, you ain't even . . ."

"I bet it's not one, I bet it's two," Laverne said.

"It is not!" Ruby shrilled. She thought she was so smart. She didn't know a sick woman when she saw one, all she could do was look at her shoes; shoe em to Rufus hah. Twenty-two years old shoe em to him. She was thirty, a year older, and thought she was such a chicken, well, "Rufus is only twenty-two years of age," she said.

"You told me that," Laverne said. She lay down on the sofa again and started shaking, holding her hand over her mouth.

"You quit that!" Ruby yelled. "I ain't going to have any baby!"

"Ha ha," Laverne said.

"I don't know how you think you know so much," Ruby said, "single as you are. If I was so single, I wouldn't go around telling married people . . ."

"Not just your ankles," Laverne said, "you're swollen all over."

"I ain't gonna stay here and be insulted," Ruby said.

"I'm not insulting you. I'm congratulating you. Why don't you celebrate and get yourself a pair of shoes like these?" She stuck her ankles off the sofa.

"I don't like them," Ruby said with dignity. "I'd like something a little more stylish. I gotta go." She got up and felt the floor steady under her and went to the door, keeping herself erect and not looking down at her stomach the way she wanted to.

"Well, I hope you both feel better tomorrow," Laverne said, pulling the ends of her mouth straight.

"I think my heart will be better tomorrow," Ruby said. "But I hope we will be moving soon. I can't climb these steps with this heart trouble, and," she added, "Rufus don't care nothing about women's shoes, not them green things anyhow."

"You better put that gun down," Laverne said, "before you shoot somebody."

Ruby jerked the door shut and looked down at herself. She was big there but she had always had a kind of big stomach. She did not stick out there different from the way she did any place else. It was natural when you took on some weight to take it on in the middle. She felt the tightness of her skirt but hadn't she felt that before? She had. It was the skirt; she had on the tight one that she didn't wear often, she had . . .

she didn't have on the tight skirt

she had on the loose one

but it wasn't very loose. But that didn't make any difference, she was just fat.

She put her fingers on her stomach and pushed down a little; and then took them off quickly. She began walking toward the stairs, slowly, as if the floor were going to move under her. She began the steps. The pain came back right away. It came back with the first step. "No," she whimpered, "no." It was just a little feeling, just a little feeling like a piece of her inside rolling over; but it made her breath very tight in her throat. Nothing in her was supposed to roll over. "Just one step," she whispered, "just one step and it did it." It couldn't be cancer. Madam Zoleeda said it would end in good fortune. She began crying and saying, "Just one step and it did it," and going up them absently as if she thought she were standing still. On the sixth one, she sat down suddenly, holding on to the banister.

"No," she said, her face crinkling all over. She looked between the banister poles and into the stairwell and gave a long hollow wail that widened and echoed as it went down. The stair cavern was dark green and mole-colored and the wail sounded at the very bottom like a voice answering her. She squinched her eyes shut. No. No. It couldn't be no baby. She was not going to have something waiting in her to make her deader, she was not, she was not. She couldn't have slipped up, the man said she couldn't. It was guaranteed and worked all that time and it could not be that, it could not. She caught her breath and held her hand tightly over her mouth. She felt her face drawn puckered: one born dead two died the first year and one run under like a dried yellow apple no she was only twenty-nine years old she was old. Madam Zoleeda said it would end in no drying up. Madam Zoleeda said oh but it will end in a stroke of moving, she had said it would end in good fortune. Moving. She had said, of course. She felt herself calming, getting almost calm, and thought she got upset too easy, heck, it was gas. Madam Zoleeda hadn't been wrong about anything yet, she knew more than . . .

Ruby jumped: there was a bang at the bottom of the stairwell and a rumble rattling up the steps, shaking them even up where she was. She looked through the banister poles and saw Hartly Gilfeet, with two pistols leveled, galloping up the stairs, and heard a voice pierce down from the floor over her, "You Hartly, shut up that racket. You're shaking the house!" But he came on, thundering louder as he rounded the bend on the first floor and streaked up the hall. She saw Mr. Jerger's door fly open and him spring with clawed fingers and grasp a flying piece of shirt that whirled and shot off again with a high-pitched, "Leggo, you ol' blind mole!" and came on nearer until the stairs rumbled directly under her and a charging chipmunk face crashed into her and rocketed through her head, smaller and smaller into a whirl of dark.

She sat on the step, clutching the banister pole while the breath came back into her a thimbleful at a time, and the stairs stopped seesawing. She opened her eyes and gazed down into the dark hole, down to the very bottom where she had started up so long ago. "Good Fortune," she said in a hollow voice that echoed along all the levels of the cavern, "baby."

"Good fortune, baby," the three echoes leered.

Then she recognized the feeling again, a little roll. It was as if it were not in her stomach. It was as if it were out nowhere in nothing, out nowhere resting, and waiting.

[1953]

Robert Pinsky

DAUGHTER

i

She thinks about skeletons,
Admires their symmetry,
Responding with fear
To the implied movement
And the near-absence of expression.
In the museum
Of natural history
She pressed up close
To the smaller ones;
But shook, studying the tall
Scaffolding of dinosaurs
From the next room.
Back home, sitting in the john
With the door open
She claims to see, in a mirror
Down the dark hall, her own.

ii

At certain times, midway
In a meal, or feeling
The dried mucus of her nose,
She stares nowhere like a cat.
It is not quite the same
As the damp sensual trance
Of her thumb. It does not
Seem to be thought, nor
The deep stare of a cat
Concentrating on a noise
Or a smell. It is like a cat
Staring nowhere. When she comes
Out of it or is interrupted
A great emptiness flares,
Of profound privacy,
Like a good Christian's death.

iii

With people, she deals oddly.
Normally too savage for bribes,
She attaches herself
In the way of a feudal tenant
To a grandma, overweight,
Spendthrift. The vassal
Declares prices,
Then haggles for a while.
She watches the two
Parents as they watch her
Pleasing herself with cheap
Toys and half-eaten sweets.
Chattering as two equals,
Nicole who calls herself "Mary"
And the woman nobody loves enough
Trot downtown for their perms.

iv

Like most children
She paints firmly and well,
Somewhat like Henri Rousseau.
She and her friends paint
With a mild firmness
Of attention. Their great
Interest when they discuss
Paintings they have made
Seems partly affected:
A habit, maybe, grown
From the ineluctable
Deal that their kind make.
Is the painting also
Part of the deal? Often, she
Smears over her work, thick
Strokes, as for painting a wall.

v

She chats quietly
With a few cronies
On the subject of death.
They all have something to say,
Her contribution being
To list her close family
In correct order of age,
Declaring that we will die
In the same order. Nobody
Disagrees. *I know it,*
They say, *I know it.* One
Tells about graves. And then
They drift off the subject
Like that many businesslike
Starlings, flying away
From one tree among trees.

[1974]

Katha Pollitt

CHINESE FINCHES

Their housewarming present to themselves
hung in a bamboo cage between
the aspidistra and Boston fern
and hid a sort of cabbagy ooze
from somebody's drain. That was the year
he papered the wall with Roland Barthes
and shrieked when he'd had a Scotch or four,
"I *am* contemporary literature!"
Her mother called each night at one.

She dreamed of blood. *And in Shanghai*
the young bride tucks her tiny feet
under her luck-embroidered gown
and thinks of dynasties of rice
plump, immaculate, bagged tight
in gleaming jars on the storeroom shelves
and wonders why she feels so sad.
Her horoscope says: sons. So these
coy darters chittered on their perch

deaf as golden lotuses
or carp in an ornamental pond
to tears or slamming doors or shouts
as winter dawn crept back again
to blanch the gay Design Research
pillows to ash on the borrowed couch.
Let love go down to disarray,
they sipped their water peaceably
and nibbled the seed in their spoonsize manger

for all the world small citizens
still of that practical, prosperous land
where the towns sleep safe in the Emperor's hand
and fields yield fruit and women sons
and red means wealth and never danger
and even the thief hung up by his thumbs
bares black snaggle teeth with a sort of pride
to demonstrate for the watching crowd
to what swift grief all folly comes. [1980]

Katherine Anne Porter

A WREATH FOR THE GAMEKEEPER

The dubious crusade is over; anybody can buy the book now, in hardback or paper cover, expurgated or unexpurgated, in drugstores and railway stations, and 'twas a famous victory for something or other; let's wait and see. In passing let us remark that we may hope this episode in the history of our system of literary censorship will mark the end of one of our curious native customs: calling upon the police and Post Office officials to act as literary critics in addition to all their other heavy duties. It is not right nor humane and I hope this is the end of it; it is enough to drive good men out of those services.

When I first read *Lady Chatterley's Lover,* thirty years ago, I thought it a dreary, sad performance with some passages of unintentional low comedy, one at least simply beyond belief in a book written with such inflamed apostolic solemnity. (I shall return to this later.) And I wondered at all the huzza and hullabaloo about suppressing it. I realize now there were at least two reasons for it—one, Lawrence himself, who possessed to the last degree the quality of high visibility, and two, the rise to power of a demagoguery of censorship by unparalleled ignoramuses, not only in the arts but in all society. There were organizations and leagues for the suppression of vice, and for the promotion of virtue, and some of these took some very weird and dangerous forms. Prohibition was their major triumph, with its main result of helping organized crime to become big business; but the arts, especially literature, became the object of a morbid interest to these strange beings who knew nothing about any art, but knew well what they hated.

Being a child of my time, naturally I was to be found protesting. I was all for freedom of speech, of action, of belief, of choice, and all this was to be comprehended in the single perfect right of authors to write anything they chose, with publishers to publish it and booksellers to sell it, and the vast public gloriously at liberty to buy and read it by the tens of thousands.

It was a noble experiment, perhaps, a root idea of freedom of mind and spirit, but in practice it soon showed serious defects

Katherine Anne Porter, as Glasgow Visiting Professor at Washington and Lee University in Spring, 1959, inaugurated there an endowed program "to promote the art of expression by pen and tongue."

and abuses, for the same reason that prohibition of alcohol could not be made to work: gangsters and crooks took over the business of supplying the human demand for intoxication and obscenity—a market that never fails no matter who runs it. It did not take certain publishers long to discover that the one best way to sell a book with "daring" passages in it was to get it banned in Boston, or excluded from the United States mails. Certain authors, not far behind the publishers, discovered that if they could write a book the publisher could advertise as in peril from the censor, all the better. Sure enough, the censor would rise to the bait, crack down, and the alarm would go out to all fellow writers and assorted lovers of liberty that one of the guild was being abused in his basic human rights by those hyenas in Boston or the Post Office, and the wave of publicity was on; and the sales went up. Those were the days when people really turned out and paraded with flags and placards, provocative songs and slogans, inviting arrest and quite often being hauled off to the police station, in triumph, perfectly certain that somebody was going to show up and bail them out before night. Writers—I was always one of them—would sometimes find themselves in the oddest sort of company, people they wouldn't have let in their houses for anything, defending the strangest things and points of view, being champion for the most awful, wormy little books they would not have given shelf room; and I suppose for a lot of us, this must just be chalked up to Experience. After a good while, I found myself asking, "Why should I defend a worthless book just because it has a few dirty words in it? Let it disappear of itself, and the sooner the better." No one comes to that state of mind quickly, because it is dangerous ground, but one comes at last. My change of view came with the first publication in 1928 of *Lady Chatterley's Lover.*

He has become, this lover of Lady Chatterley's, as sinister in his effect on the minds of critics as has Quint himself on the children and the governess, in Henry James' "The Turn of the Screw." I do not know quite what role Lady Chatterley should play to Quint-Mellors; she is not wicked, as Miss Jessel is, she is merely a moral imbecile; she is not intense and imaginative like the governess, she is stupid; and it is useless to go on with the comparison except for this one thing—the air of evil which shrouds both of these books, the sense of a dreary, hopeless situation to which there can be no possible outcome except despair; only the Lawrence book is sadder, because Lawrence was a badly flawed, lesser artist than James, and did not really know what he was doing, or if he did, pretended to be doing something else; and the blood-chilling effect of this anatomy of the activities of the rutting season between two rather dull people comes with all the more force because the relations are not between the vengeful dead and living beings, but between the living themselves, who seem to me deader than any ghost.

Yet for the past several months there has been a steady flood of very well-managed publicity in defense of Lawrence's motives and the purity of his novel; and censorship, I am not sorry to say, was loudly defeated at least for the present; and though there were this time no parades, I believe, we have seen such unanimity and solidarity of opinion among American critics as I do not remember to have seen before. And what are we to think of them, falling in with this fraudulent crusade of raising an old tired Cause out of its tomb? For this is no longer just a book, and it never was a work of literature worth all this attention. There is something touching, if misguided, in this fine-spirited, manly chorus in defense of Lawrence's nasty vocabulary and the nobility of his intentions. I do not question either; I only wish to say I think from start to finish he was about as wrong as wrong can be on the whole subject of sex, and that he has written a very laboriously bad book to prove it. The critics who have been carried away by a generous desire to promote freedom of speech and give a black eye to prudes and nannies overlook, sometimes—and in a work of literature this should not be overlooked, at least not by men whose businesss it is to write criticism—the fact that purity, nobility of intention, and apostolic fervor are good in themselves at times, but in this case they are simply not enough. Whoever says they are, and tries to settle for them, and to persuade the public to do so, is making a grave mistake, if he means to go on being a critic.

Lawrence began the uproar himself, loudly and bitterly on the defensive as always, throwing out nearly everything he did as if he were an early Christian throwing himself to the lions: "Anybody who calls my novel a dirty, sexual novel is a liar." And further: "It'll infuriate *mean* people; but it will surely soothe decent ones."

The Readers' Subscription, in its brochure offering the book, sets the tone boldly: "Now, at long last, a courageous American publisher is making available the unexpurgated version of *Lady Chatterley's Lover*—exactly as the author meant it to be seen by the intelligent, sensitive reader." No, this won't quite do. I happen for one to have known quite a number of decent readers, not too unintelligent or insensitive, who have been revolted by it, and I do not propose to sit down under this kind of bullying.

Archibald MacLeish regards the book as "pure" and a work of high literary merit. He has a few reservations as to the whole, with which I heartily agree so far as they go. Yet even Mr. MacLeish begins trailing his coat, daring us at our own risk to deny that the book is "one of the most important works of the century," or "to express an opinion about the literature of the time or about the spiritual history that literature expresses without making his peace one way or another with D. H. Lawrence and with this work."

Without in the least making my peace with D. H. Lawrence or with this work, I wish to say why I disagree profoundly with the above judgments, and also with the following:

Harvey Breit:

> The language and the incidents or scenes in question are deeply moving and very beautiful—Lawrence was concerned to reveal how love, how a relationship between a man and a woman, can be most touching and beautiful, but only if it is uninhibited and total.

This is wildly romantic and does credit to Mr. Breit's feelings, but there can be no such thing as a total relationship between any two human beings, and from some things he wrote and said on the subject, I think Lawrence would have been the first to object even to an attempt at it. He demanded the right to invade anybody, but he was noticeably queasy if anyone took a similar liberty with him.

Edmund Wilson:

> The most inspiriting book I have seen in a long time . . . one of his best written . . . one of his most vigorous and brilliant . . . .

This reminds me that I helped parade with banners in defense of Mr. Wilson's *Memoirs of Hecate County,* a misguided act of guild loyalty and personal admiration I cannot really regret. But I still prefer *To the Finland Station* and any of Mr. Wilson's criticism and essays on public or literary affairs.

Jacques Barzun:

> I have no hesitation in saying that I do not consider Lawrence's novel pornographic.

I agree with this admirably prudent remark, and again when Mr. Barzun notes Lawrence's ruling passion for atempting to reform everything and everybody in sight. My quarrel with the book is that it really is not pornographic—the great wild free-wheeling Spirit of Pornography has here been hitched to a rumbling little domestic cart and trundled off to chapel, its ears pinned back and its mouth washed out with soap.

Mr. Mark Schorer, who contributes the preface, even brings Yeats in to defend this tiresome book—Yeats, bless his memory, who, when he talked bawdy, knew what he was saying and why. He enjoyed the flavor of gamey words on his tongue, he loved good smut in sex, and never deceived himself for one moment as to the true nature of that enjoyment; he never got really interestingly dirty until age had somewhat cooled the ardors of his flesh, thus doubling his pleasure in the thought of it, in the most profane sense. Mr. Schorer reprints part of a letter from Yeats to Mrs. Shakespear:

> These two lovers the gamekeeper and his employer's wife each separated from their class by their love and by fate are poignant in their loneliness; the coarse language of the one accepted by both becomes a forlorn poetry, uniting their solitudes, something ancient humble and terrible.

This is a breath of fresh air upon this fetid topic. Mr. Yeats reaches in to the muddlement and brings up the simple facts: the real disaster for the Lady and the Gamekeeper is that they face perpetual exile from their own proper backgrounds. Stale and pointless and unhappy as both of their lives were before, yet now they face, once the sexual furor is past, an utter aimlessness in life it is shocking to think about.

And further, Yeats notes that only one of the lovers uses the coarse language, the other merely accepts it—"a forlorn poetry." The Gamekeeper talks his dirt, and the Lady listens, but never once answers in kind—and if she had, the Gamekeeper would have been scandalized.

Yet the English language needs those words, and they have a definite use and value, and they should not be used carelessly or imprecisely. My contention is that obscenity is real, is necessary as an expression, a safety valve against the almost intolerable pressures and strains of relationship between men and women, and not only between men and women but between any human being and his unmanageable world. If we distort, warp, abuse this language which is the seamy side of the noble language of religion and love, indeed the necessary expression of insult and revenge towards the insoluble mystery of life, which causes us such cureless suffering, what have we left for words to express the luxury of obscenity which, for an enormous majority of men, is one of the pleasures of the sexual act.

I do not object, then, to D. H. Lawrence's obscenity, but to his misuse and perversion of it, his wrongheaded denial of its true nature and meaning. Instead of writing straight healthy obscenity, he makes it sickly sentimental, embarrassingly so, and I find that obscene sentimentality is as hard to bear as any other kind. I object to this sickly attempt to purify and canonize obscenity, to castrate the roaring boy Ribaldry, to take the low comedy out of sex. We cannot and should not try to hallow these words because they are not hallowed and were not meant to be. The attempt to make pure, tender, sensitive washed-in-the-blood-of-the-lamb words out of words whose whole purpose, function, meaning in our language is meant to be exactly the opposite, is sentimentality and of a very low order. Our language is rich and full, and I daresay there is a word to express every shade of meaning and feeling a human being is capable of, if we are not too lazy to look for it, or try to substitute one word for another, such as calling a nasty word—meant to be nasty, we need it that way—"pure," and a pure word "nasty." This is an unpardonable tampering with meanings, and I think it comes of a very deepgrained fear of sex itself in Lawrence; he was never easy on that subject, could not come to terms with it for anything. Perhaps it was a long hangover from his childish Chapel piety, a violent revulsion from the inane gibberish of some of the hymns. He wrote once with deep tenderness about his early Chapel memories, and said that the word "Galilee" had magic for him, and his favorite hymn was this:

> Each little dove, and sighing bough,
> That makes the eve so dear to me
> Has something far diviner now,
> That takes me back to Galilee.

> Oh Galilee, sweet Galilee,
> Where Jesus loved so well to be
> Oh Galilee, Sweet Galilee,
> Come sing again thy songs to me.

His first encounter with dirty words must have brought a shocking sense of guilt, especially as they no doubt gave him great pleasure; and to the end of his life he was engaged in the hopeless attempt to wash away that sense of guilt by denying the reality of its cause. He never arrived at the sunny truth so fearlessly acknowledged by Yeats, that "Love has pitched his mansion in the place of excrement," but Yeats had already learned long before that Love has many mansions, and only one of them is pitched there; a very important one that should be lived in very boldly and in hot blood in its right seasons; but to deny its nature is to vulgarize it indeed. My own position is this, that anything at all a man and woman wish to do or say in their sexual relations, in love-making, or call it what you please, is exactly their own business and nobody else's. But let them keep it to themselves unless they wish to appear ridiculous. If they need the violent stimulation of nasty acts, vile words, pornographic pictures or even low music—there is a Negro trumpeter who blows, it is said, a famous aphrodisiac noise—I think it is a pity that their nervous systems are so blunted they have to be jolted into pleasure like that. Sex shouldn't be such hard work, nor, as this book promises, lead to such a dull future. For nowhere in the sad history can you see anything but a long dull grey monotonous chain of days, lighted now and then by a sexual bout. I can't hear any music, or the voices of friends; there is no wine or food, no sleep or refreshment, no rest and no quiet—no love. I remember then that all this is the fevered day dream of a dying man sitting under his umbrella pines in Italy. As for his sexual fantasies—for Lawrence is a Romantic turned wrong side out, and like Swift's recently flayed woman, it does alter his appearance for the worse—they are all easy and dreamlike, not subject to interruptions and interferences, a mixture of morning dew and mingled body-secretions, a boy imagining a female partner who is nothing but one yielding, faceless, voiceless organ of consent.

An organ, and he finally bestows on those quarters his accolade of approval in the language and tone of one praising a specially succulent scrap of glandular meat fresh from the butcher's. "Tha's a tasty bit of tripe, th'art," he says in effect, if not in just those words. And adds (these are his real words), "Tha'rt real, even a bit of a bitch." Climbing onto his lap, she confirms his diagnosis by whispering, "Kiss me!"

Mr. Schorer in his preface hails the work as "a great hymn to true marriage." That it is not, above all. No matter what the protagonists think they are up to, this is the story of an affair, and a thoroughly disreputable one, based on the treachery of a woman to her husband who has been made impotent by wounds received in the war; and by the mean trickery of a man of low origins trying to prove he is as good as the next man. Mr. Shorer also accepts and elucidates for us Lawrence's favorite, most pathetic fallacy. He writes:

> The pathos of Lawrence's novel arises from the tragedy of modern society. What is tragic is that we cannot feel our tragedy. We have grown slowly into a confusion of these terms, these two forms of power, and in confusing them we have left almost no room for the free creative functions of the man or woman who, lucky soul, possesses "integrity of self." The force of this novel probably lies in the degree of intensity with which his indictment of the world and the consequent solitude of his lovers suggest such larger meanings.

If Mr. Schorer means to say—he sometimes expresses himself a little cloudily—that the modern industrial world, Lawrence's pet nightmare, has destroyed, among a number of other things, some ancient harmony once existing between the sexes, which Lawrence proposes to restore by using short words during the sexual act, I must simply remind him that all history is against this theory. The world itself, as well as the relationship between men and women, has not "grown into confusion." We have never had anything else, or anything much better; all human life since recorded time has been a terrible struggle from confusion to confusion to more confusion, and Lawrence, aided by his small but vociferous congregation—for there remains in his doctrine and manner the style of the parochial messiah, the chapel-preacher's threats and cajolements—has done nothing but add his own particular mystification to the subject.

One trouble with him, always, and it shows more plainly than ever in this book, is that he wanted to play all the roles, be everybody and everywhere at once. He wishes to be the godhead in his dreary rigmaroles of primitive religion, but to be the passive female, too. Until he tires of it. Mr. Schorer quotes a passage from a letter Lawrence wrote to some one when his feelings were changing. "The leader-cum-follower relationship is a bore," he decided, "and the new relationship will be some sort of tenderness, sensitive, between men and men, and between men and women." He gets a good deal of himself into these few words. First, when he is tired of the game he has invented and taught as a religion, everybody must drop it. Second, he seems not to have observed that tenderness is not a new relationship between persons who love one another. Third, he said between men and men, and men and women, but he did not say between women and women, for his view of women is utterly baleful—he has expressed it ferociously over and over; women must be kept apart, for they contaminate each other. They are to be redeemed one at a time through the sexual offices of a man, who seems to have no other function in their lives, nor they in his. One of the great enlightenments of Lady Chatterley, after her experiences of the sentimental obscenities of her Gamekeeper, is to see other women clearly, women sexually less lucky than she, and to realize that they are horrible! She can't get away from them fast enough, and back to the embraces of her fancy man, who, to give him his due, runs through quite a varied repertory of styles and moods in his love-making; and yet—and yet—

True marriage? Love, even? It seems a very sad, shabby sort of thing to have to settle for, poor woman. She deserves anything she gets, really, but her just deserts are none of our affair. Her fate interests us as a kind of curiosity. It is true that her youth was robbed by her husband's being wounded in the war; I think he was pretty badly robbed too, but no one seems to feel sorry for him. He is shown up as having very dull ideas with conversation to match, but he is not any duller than the Gamekeeper, who forgets that the Lady's aristocratic husband wasn't born impotent, as Lawrence insists (through his dubious hero) that all upper-class men were. At about this point the confusion of ideas and feelings becomes nearly complete. It would take another book to thread out and analyze the contradictions and blind alleys into which the reader is led.

Huizinga, in his book, *The Waning of the Middle Ages,* tells of the erotic religious visions of a late medieval monk and adds: "The description of his numerous visions is characterized at the same time by an excess of sexual imagination and by the absence of all genuine emotion." Lawrence used to preach frantically that people must get sex out of their heads and back where it belonged; and never learned that sex has many mansions in every part of the body and must be given freedom to run easily in the blood and the nerves and the cells, adding its glow of life to everything it touches. And the solemn God's-earnestness of these awful little love scenes seems suddenly heart-breaking—that a man of such gifts could live so long and learn no more about love than that!

[1959]

Ezra Pound

NOTES FOR AN UNPUBLISHED CANTO

1935

La carence or damn slimness
des affaires caracteristiques, this week of La Bourse
Le Journal 25 Juin mil neuf cent trente cinque
1935
or any time in the past 20 years
at any time during
Informations little encouraging from N. York
Whereas the rents London and Paris
and a heavy tendency *au debut de la huitaine*
but on the other hand coal mines in Silesia
the lady pianist is playing even scales
de fine amor vient science et beauté WITH expression
The sun, as Guinicelli says, beats on the mud all day
and the mud stays vile
Birds to the wood, as of sleep in sapphire inherence
as the sun to the mortal eye or as Zeus remarked of OU TIS
the fellow is one of us.
A man with a mind like that
the fellow is one of us
Shines in the mind of heaven, as I quoted in
Canto LI
God who made it, more than the sun in our eye.
As says Pliny the younger
That one man help another. God is that
one man help another. In the time of the Emperor Titus,
or Guinicelli about 1274
encircling all movement stillness
and the glaze of its own made light
as time scuttles under the door jamb
or they say 'Omeros was lacking in purpose

because he had no need to dispute with the reader
'ERI MEN AI TE
as Ibycus in the spring time, or Roland
by god I have broken the olifans I have broke that damn
elephant horn fine
and scattered all its encrustment
"Bigod," he said, "that pagan is done for,"
Bigod Barney is finished, he is indeed,
and the fighters were Gesell and Douglas and Fack
and Odon with diabetes, and Jeff Mark against usury
all very prosaic and Orage and Benton and Woodward
not to say Kitson and old T.C. back in the seventies
and said Mr. Bryan to Kitson
"of course Bimetalism isn't IT"
IT is the national credit
control of the national credit
there was and is not rest in this war
His phiz like an honest man's
and his tail over hell pit
"Bigod I have broke the encrustment,
that was the best horn in this army"
Tin leaves on an unnamed grave
anonymous
in fact un amico has written
"barbed wire wiz tin crosses"
without seeking the cause in money
without interesting himself in such causes
Gestalt an interest grief
Said John Adams "I pity the pore bastids in winter"
as for pattern they see stewed oatmeal in a bowl
dissociation of ideas seems inhuman
their world a sub-species of porridge bowl
is
an imminent conscience to be managed by levers?
an imminent consciousness working the levers,
being a spoiled priest from his infancy
or says Leibnitz and so forth
God is that one man helps another.

[1971]

Reynolds Price

THE NAMES AND FACES OF HEROES

After an hour I believe it and think, "We are people in love. We flee through hard winter night. What our enemies want is to separate us. Will we end together? Will we end alive?" And my lips part to ask him, but seeing his face in dashboard light (his gray eyes set on the road and the dark), I muffle my question and know the reason—"We have not broke silence for an hour by the clock. We must flee on silent. Maybe if we speak even close as we are, we will speak separate tongues after so long a time." I shut my eyes, press hard with the lids till my mind's eye opens, then balloon it light through roof through steel, set it high and cold in January night, staring down to see us whole. First we are one black car on a slim strip of road laid white through pines, drawn slowly west by the hoop of light we cast ahead—the one light burning for fifty miles, it being past eleven, all farms and houses crouched into sleep, all riders but us. Then my eye falls downward, hovers on the roof in the wind we make, pierces steel, sees us close—huddled on the worn mohair of a 1939 Pontiac, he slumped huge at the wheel, I the thin fork of flesh thrust out of his groin on the seat beside him, my dark head the burden in his lap his only hollow that flushes beneath me with rhythm I predict to force blood against my weight through nodes of tissue, squabs of muscle that made me ten years ago, made half anyhow, he being my father and I being nine, we heading towards home not fleeing, silent as I say, my real eyes shut, his eyes on nothing but road. So we are not lovers nor spies nor thieves and speaking for me, my foes are inward not there in the night. My mind's eye enters me calm again, and I brace to look, to say "How much further?" but he drops a hand which stalls me, testing my flannel pajamas for warmth, ringing my ankle and shin and ticklish knee (in earnest, tight not gentle), slipping between two buttons of the coat to brush one breast then out again and down to rest on my hip. His thumb and fingers ride the high saddle bone, the fat of his hand in the hollow *I* have, heavy but still on the dry knots of boyish equipment waiting for life to start. I roll back on my head to see him again, to meet his eyes. He looks on forward so I go back blind and slide my right hand to his, probing with a finger till I find his only wound—a round yellow socket beneath his thumb where he shot himself when he was eight, by surprise, showing off his father's pistol to friends (the one fool thing I know he has done). My finger rests there and we last that way maybe two or three miles while the road is straight. Then a curve begins. He says "Excuse me, Preacher" in his natural voice and takes his hand. My eyes stay blind and I think what I know, "I love you tonight more than all my life before"—think it in *my* natural voice. But I do not say it, and I do not say I excuse him though I do. I open my eyes on his face in dashboard light.

I search it for a hero. For the first time. I have searched nearly every other face since last July, the final Sunday at camp when a minister told us, "The short cut to being a man is finding your hero, somebody who is what you are not but need to be. What I mean is this. Examine yourself. When you find what your main lack is, seek that in some great man. Say your trouble is fear—you are scared of the dark, scared of that bully in your grade at school, scared of striking out when you come up to bat. Take some great brave, some warrior—Douglas MacArthur, Enos Slaughter. Say your trouble is worse. Say it's telling lies. Take George Washington—personal heroes don't need to be living just so they lived once. Read a book about him. Study his picture. (You may think he looks a little stiff. That is because his teeth were carved out of cypress. A man makes his face and making a good one is as hard a job as laying road through solid rock, and Washington made himself as fine a face as any man since Jesus—and He was not a man.) Then imitate him. Chin yourself on his example and you will be a man before you need a razor." I need to be a man hard as anybody so riding home from camp and that sermon, I sat among lanyards I plaited and whistles I carved and searched my life for the one great lack my foe. He had mentioned lacking courage—that minister. I lack it. I will not try to do what I think I cannot do well such as make friends or play games where somebody hands you a ball and bat and asks the world of you, asks you to launch without thinking some act on the air with natural grace easy as laughing. He had mentioned lying. I lie every day—telling my mother for instance that the weeks at camp were happy when what I did was by day whittle all that trashy equipment, climb through snakes in July sun with brogans grating my heels, swim in ice water with boys that would just as soon drown you as smile and by night pray for three large things—that I not wet the bed, that I choke the homesickness one more day, that these five weeks vanish and leave no sign no memory. But they were only two on a string of lacks which unreeled behind me that Sunday riding home from camp (unseen beyond glass the hateful tan rock turning to round pine hills where Randolph is and home), and on the string were selfishness to Marcia my cousin who is my main friend and gives me whatever she has, envy of my brother who is one year old and whose arms I purposely threw out of joint three months ago, envy of people my age who do so easily things I will not and thus lock together in tangles of friendship, pride in the things I can do which they cannot (but half pride at worst as the things I can do, they do not want to do—drawing, carving, solo singing. I am Randolph's leading boy soprano and was ashamed to be till a Saturday night last August when I sang to a room of sweating soldiers at the U.S.O. I was asked by the hostess for something patriotic, but I thought they would not need that on their week-end off any more than they needed me in Buster Brown collar and white short pants so I sang Brahms' *Lullaby* which you can hum if you forget, and if it was a mistake, they never let on. I do not mean anybody cried. They kept on swallowing Coca-Colas and their boots kept smelling, but they shut up talking and clapped at the end, and as I left the platform and aimed for the door blistered with shame, one long soldier gave me the blue and gold enamel shield off his cap, saying "Here you are"), and far graver things—wishing death nightly on two boys I know, breaking God's law about honoring parents by failing to do simple things they ask such as look at people when I talk, by doubting they can care for me daily (when my mother thinks of little else and Father would no more sleep without kissing me goodnight than he would strike me), sometimes doubting I am theirs at all but just some orphan they took in kindness. I made that list without trying seven months ago, and it has grown since then. Whenever I speak or move these days new faults stare out of my heart. The trouble though is I still do not know my greatest lack, my *mortal* foe. Any one if I stare back long enough seems bound to sink me. So I seek a hero grand enough to take on all my lacks, but for seven months now I have looked—looked hard—and am nowhere near him. Who *is* there these days, who has there ever been broad enough, grand enough to stand day and night and ward off all my foes? Nobody, I begin to think. I have looked everywhere I know to look, first in books I had or bought for the purpose—*Little People Who Became Great* (Abraham Lincoln, Helen Keller, Andrew Carnegie), *Minute Lives of Great Men and Women* (a page and a picture for everybody including Stephen Foster) and a set called *Living Biographies of Great Composers, Philosophers, Prophets, Poets and Statesmen.* I have not read books that do not show faces because I study a man's face first. Then if that calls me on, I read his deeds. I read for three months and taking deeds and faces together, I settled on Caesar Augustus and Alexander the Great as final candidates. They were already great when they were young, and they both wore faces like hard silver medals awarded for lasting—I got that much from *Minute Lives*—so I thought they were safe and that I would read further and then choose one. But as I read they fell in before me—Alexander crushing that boy's head who brought bad news and when they were lost in a desert and famished and his men found one drink of water and gladly brought it to him in a helmet, him pouring it out in the sand to waste, and Augustus leading the wives of his friends into private rooms during public banquets, making them do what they could not refuse. All the dead have failed me. That is why I study my father tonight. He is the last living man I know or can think of that I have not considered, which is no slight to him—you do not seek heroes at home. No, when the dead played out, I turned to my autographs and started there. I have written to famous men for over a year since the war began. I write on Boy Scout stationery (I am not a Scout), give my age and ask for their names in ink. I have got answers from several generals on the battlefield (MacArthur who sent good luck from the Philippines, Mark Clark who typed a note from secret headquarters, Eisenhower who said in his wide leaning hand, "I do not think it would be possible for me to refuse a nine-year-old American anything I could do for him"), from most of Roosevelt's cabinet (but not from him though I have three notes from Miss Grace Tully to say he does not have time and neither does his wife), from Toscanini and a picture of Johnny Weissmuller on a limb crouched with his bare knife to leap, saying "Hello from Tarzan your friend." But studying them I saw I could not know enough to decide. They are surely famous but I cannot see or watch them move, and until they die and their secrets appear, how can I know they are genuine heroes?—that they do not have yawning holes of their own which they hide? So from them I have turned to men I can watch and hear, and since I seldom travel this means the men I am kin to. I will not think against my blood, but of all my uncles and cousins (my grandfathers died before I was born), the two I love and that seem to love me—that listen when I speak—and that have dark happy faces are the ones who are liable at any time to start drinking and disappear, spending money hand over fist in Richmond or Washington until they are broke and wire for my father who drives up and finds them in a bar with a new suit on and a rosebud and some temporary friends and brings them home to their wives. My father has one brother who fought in France in the First World War and was playing cards in a hole one night when a bomb landed, and when he came to, he picked up his best friend who was quiet at his side and crawled with him half a mile before he saw that the friend lacked a head, but later he was gassed and retired from battle so that now, sitting or standing, he slumps round a hole in his chest and scrapes up blood every hour or two even summer nights visiting on our porch from Tennessee his home. My other male kin live even farther away or do not notice me or are fat which is why as I say I have come to my father tonight—my head rolled back on his lap, my ears sunk in his shifting kernels so I cannot hear only see, my eyes strained up through his arms to his face.

It is round as a watch when he does not smile which he does not now, and even in warm yellow light of speedometer-amp meter-oil pressure gauges, it is red as if he was cold, as if there was no plate glass to hold off the wind we make rushing home. It is always red and reddest I know, though I cannot see, under his collar on the back of his neck where the hair leaves off. There is not much hair anywhere on his head. It has vanished two inches back on his forehead, and where it starts it is dark but seems no color or the color of shadows in old photographs. Above his ears it is already white (he is forty-two and the white is real, but five years ago when it was not, I was singing in bed one night "When I Grow Too Old To Dream," and he heard me and went to the toilet and powdered his hair and came and stood in the door ghostly, old with the hall light behind him and said, "I am too old to dream, Preacher." I sang on a minute, looking, and then cried "Stop. Stop" and wept which of course he did not intend), and each morning he wets it and brushes every strand at least five minutes till it lies on his skull like paint and stays all day. It is one of his things you cannot touch. His glasses are another. He treats them kindly as if they were delicate people—unrimmed octagons hooked to gold wires that ride the start of his firm long nose and loop back over his large flat ears—and in return they do not hide his eyes which are gray and wide and which even in the dark draw light to them so he generally seems to be thinking of fun when he may be thinking we have lost our house (we have just done that) or his heart is failing (he thinks his heart stood still last Christmas when he was on a ladder swapping lights in our tree, and whenever I look he is taking his pulse). And with all his worries it mostly *is* fun he thinks because when he opens his mouth, if people are there they generally laugh—with him or at him, he does not mind which. I know a string of his jokes as long as the string of my personal lacks, and he adds on new ones most days he feels well enough. A lot of his jokes of course I do not understand but I no longer ask. I used to ask and he would say, "Wait a little, Preacher. Your day will come" so I hold them mysterious in my skull till the day they burst into meaning. But most of his fun is open to view, to anybody's eyes that will look because what he mainly loves is turning himself into other people before your eyes. Whenever in the evenings we visit our friends, everybody will talk a while including my father, and then he may go silent and stare into space, pecking his teeth with a fingernail till his eyes come back from where they have been and his long lips stretch straight which is how he smiles, and then whoever we are visiting—if he has been watching my father—will know to say, "Mock somebody for us, Jeff." ("Mocking" is what most people call it. My father calls it "taking people off.") He will look sheepish a minute, then lean forward in his chair—and I sitting on the rug, my heart will rise for I know he has something to give us now—and looking at the floor say, "Remember how Dr. Tucker pulled teeth?" Everybody will grin Yes but somebody (sometimes me) will say "How?" and he will start becoming Dr. Tucker, not lying, just seriously turning himself into that old dentist—greeting his patient at the door, bowing him over to the chair (this is when he shrinks eight inches, dries, goes balder still, hikes his voice up half a scale), talking every step to soothe the patient, sneaking behind him, rinsing his rusty pullers at the tap, cooing "Open your mouth, sweet *thing*," leaping on the mouth like a boa constrictor, holding up the tooth victorious, smiling "*There* he is and you didn't even feel it, did you, darling?" Then he will be Jeff McCraw again, hitching up his trousers with the sides of his wrists, leading us into the laughter. When it starts to die somebody will say, "Jeff, you beat all. You missed your calling. You ought to be in the movies," and if he is not worried that night he may move on through one or two more transformations—Miss Georgie Ballard singing in church with her head like an owl swivelling, Mrs. V. L. Womble on her velvet pillow, President Roosevelt in a "My friends" speech, or on request little pieces of people—Mr. Jim Bender's walk, Miss Amma Godwin's hand on her stomach. But it suits me more when he stops after one. That way I can laugh and take pride in his gifts, but if he continues I may take fright at him spinning on through crowds of old people, dead people, people I do not know as if his own life—his life with us—is not enough. One such night when he was happy and everybody was egging him on I cried to him "Stop" before it was too late and ran from the room. I am not known as a problem so people notice when I cry. My mother came behind me at once and sitting in a cold stairwell, calmed me while I made up a reason for what I had done. She said, "Let your father have a little fun. He does not have much." I remembered how she often warned me against crossing my eyes at school to make children laugh, saying they might get stuck, so I told her he might stick and then we would carry him home as Dr. Tucker or Mrs. Womble or Miss Lula Fleming at the Baptist organ. That was a lie but it was all I knew, all I could offer on such short notice to justify terror, and telling it made us laugh, calmed me, stopped me thinking of reasons. And I did not worry or think of my terror again till several months later when he came in disguise. It was not the first time he had worn disguise (half the stories about him are about his disguises), but he did not wear it often, and though I was seven I had never seen him that way before. Maybe it is why he came that night, thinking I was old enough and would like the joke since I loved his other fun. Anyhow the joke was not for me but for Uncle Hawk, an old colored man who lived with us. I was just the one who answered the door. It was night of course. I had finished my supper and leaving the others, had gone to the living room and was on the floor by the radio. After a while there came a knock on the panes of the door. I said, "I will get it" to the empty room, thinking they were all in the kitchen, turned on the porch light and opened the door on a tall man heavy-set with white hair, a black derby hat, a black overcoat to his ankles, gray kid gloves, a briefcase, a long white face coiled back under pinch-nose glasses looking down. It was nobody I knew, nobody I had seen and what could he sell at this time of night? My heart seized like a fist and I thought, "He has come for me" (as I say, it is my darkest fear that I am not the blood child of Jeff and Rhew McCraw, that I was adopted at birth, that someday a strange man will come and rightfully claim me). But still looking down he said, "Does an old colored man named Hawk work here?" and I tore to the kitchen for Uncle Hawk who was scraping dishes while my mother cleared table. They were silent a moment. Then my mother said, "Who in the world could it be, Uncle Hawk?" and he said "I wonder myself." I said, "Well, hurry. It is a stranger and the screen door is not even locked." He did not hurry. My mother and I stood and watched him get ready—washing with the Castile soap he keeps for his fine long hands tough as shark hide, adjusting suspenders, the garters on his sleeves, inspecting his shoes. Towards the end I looked at my mother in anxiety. She winked at me and said, "Go on, Uucle Hawk. It certainly is not Jesus *yet*." Not smiling he said, "I wish it was" and went. Again I looked to my mother and again she winked and beckoned me behind her into the hall where we could watch the door and the meeting. Uncle Hawk said "Good evening" but did not bow, and the man said, "Are you Hawk Reid?" Then he mumbled something about life insurance—did Uncle Hawk have enough life, fire, burial insurance? Uncle Hawk said, "My life is not worth paying on every week. I do not have nothing to insure for fire but a pocket knife and it is iron, and Mr. Jeff McCraw is burying me." The man mumbled some more. Uncle Hawk said "No" and the man reached for the handle to the screen that separated them. Uncle Hawk reached to lock the screen but too slow, and there was the man on us, two feet from Hawk, fifteen from my mother and me. Hawk said, "Nobody asked you to come in here" and drew back his arm (nearly eighty years old) to strike. My mother and I had not made a sound, and I had mostly watched her not the door as she was grinning but then she laughed. Uncle Hawk turned on her, his arm still coiled, then back to the man who was looking up now not moving, and then Hawk laughed, doubled over and helpless. The man walked in right past him slowly and stopped six feet from me, holding out his hand to take—he and I the two in the room not laughing. So I knew he had come for me, that I was his and would have to go. His hand stayed out in the glove towards me. There were three lines of careful black stitching down the back of the pale gray leather, the kind of gloves I wanted that are not made for boys. Still I could not take his hand just then, and not for terror. I was really not afraid but suddenly sorry to leave people who had been good to me, the house which I knew. That was what locked me there. I must have stood half a minute that way, and I must have looked worse and worse because my mother said, "Look at his eyes" and pointed me towards the man's face. I looked and at once they were what they had been all along—Jeff McCraw's eyes, the size and color of used nickels; gentle beyond disguising. I said to him then fast and high, "I thought you were my real father and had come to get me." He took off his derby and the old glasses and said, "I *am*, Preacher. I *have*, Preacher," and I ran to circle his thighs with my arms, to hide my tears in the hollow beneath the black overcoat. And I did hide them. When I looked up, everybody thought I had loved the joke like them. But I had not. I had loved my father found at the end with his hand stretched out. But I hoped not to find him again that way under glasses and powder, mumbling, so when he came into my bedroom to kiss me that night, I asked would he do me a favor. He said "What?" and I said, "Please warn me before you dress up ever again." He said he would and then my mother walked in and hearing us said, "You will not need warning. Just stare at his eyes first thing. He cannot hide those." But he always warns me as he promised he would—except at Christmas when he comes in a cheap flannel suit and rayon beard that any baby could see is false—and even though in advance that on a certain evening he will arrive as a tramp to scare my Aunt Lola or as a tax collector or a man from the farm office to tell my Uncle Paul he has planted illegal tobacco and must plow it under or suffer, still I fasten on his eyes and hold to them till somebody laughs and he finds time to wink at me.

As I fasten on them now heading home. He travels of course as himself tonight in a brown vested suit and a solid green tie so I see him plain—what is clear in dashboard light—and though I love him, though I rest in his hollow lap now happier than any other place, I know he cannot be my hero. And I list the reasons to myself. Heroes are generally made by war. My father was born in 1900 so the nearest he got to First World War was the National Guard and in October 1918 an Army camp near Morehead City, N. C. where he spent six weeks in a very wrinkled uniform (my mother has his picture) till peace arrived, so desperately homesick that he saved through the whole six weeks the bones of a chicken lunch his mother gave him on leaving home. And when I woke him a year ago from his Sunday nap to ask what was Pearl Harbor that the radio was suddenly full of, he was well and young enough to sign for the Draft and be nervous but too old to serve. He does own two guns—for protection an Army .45 that his brother brought him from France, never wanting to see it again, and for hunting a double-barrelled shotgun with cracked stock—but far as I know he has never shot anything but himself (that time he was a boy) and two or three dozen wharf rats, rabbits, and squirrels. Nor is he even in his quiet life what heroes generally must be—physically brave. Not that chances often arise for that class of bravery. I had not seen him face any ordeals worse than a flat tire till a while ago when we had our first mock air raid in Randolph. He took an armband, helmet, blackjack and me, and we drove slowly to the power station which was his post and sat in the cold car thinking it would end soon, but it did not and I began to wonder was it real, were the Germans just beyond hearing, heading towards us? Then he opened his door and we slid out and stood on the hill with great power batteries singing behind us and looked down at the smothered town. I said, "What will we do if the Germans really come?" Not waiting he pointed towards what I guessed was Sunset Avenue (his sense of direction being good) and said, "We would high-tail it there to where your mother is liable to burn down the house any minute with all those candles." He did not laugh but the siren went and lights began and we headed home—the house stinking tallow on through the night and I awake in bed wondering should I tell him, "If you feel that way you ought to resign as warden"? deciding "No, if Hitler comes let him have the power. What could we do anyway, Father with a blackjack and me with nothing?—hold off steel with our pitiful hands?" (the hand he touches me with again now, his wounded hand but the wrist so whole so full, under its curls so ropey I cannot ring it, trying now I cannot capture it in my hand so I trace one finger through its curls, tracing my name into him as older boys gouge names, gouge love into trees, into posts—gouge proudly. But with all the love I mentioned before, I do not trace proudly. I know him too well, know too many lacks, and my finger stops in the rut where his pulse would be if I could ever find it (I have tried, I cannot find it, maybe could not stand it if I did). I shut my eyes not to see his face for fear he will smile, and continue to name his lacks to myself. He makes people wait—meaning me and my mother. He is a salesman and travels, and sometimes when school is out, I travel with him, hoping each time things will go differently. They start well always (riding and looking though never much talking) till we come to the house where he hopes to sell a stove or refrigerator. We will stop in the yard. He will sit a minute, looking for dangerous dogs, then reach for his briefcase, open his door and say, "Wait here, Preacher. I will be straight back." I will say "All right" and he will turn back to me, "You do not mind that, do you, darling?"—"Not if you remember I am out here and do not spend the day." He of course says he will remember and goes but before he has gone ten yards I can see that memory rise through his straw hat like steam, and by the time a woman says, "Step in the house," I am out of his mind as if I was part of the car that welcomed this chance to cool and rest. Nothing cool about it (being always summer when I travel with him), and I sit and sweat, shooting out flies and freezing if a yellowjacket comes, and when twenty minutes has gone by the clock, I begin to think, "If this was all the time he meant to give me, why did he bring me along?" And that rushes on into, "Why did he get me, why did he want me at all if he meant to treat me the way he does, giving me as much time each day as it takes to kiss me goodbye when I go to school and again at night in case we die in each other's absence?" And soon I am rushing through ways he neglects me daily. He will not for instance *teach* me. Last fall I ordered an axe from Sears Roebuck with my own money, asking nobody's permission, and when it came—so beautiful—he acted as if I had ordered mustard gas and finally said I could keep it if I promised not to use it till he showed me the right way. I promised—and kept my promise—and until this day that axe has done nothing but wait on my wall, being taken down every night, having its lovely handle stroked, its dulling edge felt fearfully. And baseball. He has told me how he played baseball when he was my age, making it sound the happiest he ever was, but he cannot make me catch a fly-ball. I have asked him for help, and he went so far as to buy me a glove and spend half an hour in the yard throwing at me, saying "Like this, Preacher" when I threw at him, but when I failed to stop ball after ball, he finally stopped trying and went in the house, not angry or even impatient but never again offering to teach me what he loved when he was my age, what had won him friends. Maybe he thought he was being kind. Maybe he thought he had shamed me, letting me show him my failure. He had, he had. But if he knew how furious I pray when I am the outfield at school recess (pray that flies go any way but mine), how struck, how shrunk, how abandoned I feel when prayer fails and a ball splits hot through my hopeless hand to lie daring me to take it up and throw it right while some loud boy no bigger than I, no better made, trots a free homerun—he would try again, do nothing but try. Or maybe there just come stretches when he does not care, when he does not love me or want me in his mind much less his sight—scrambling on the ground like a hungry fice for a white leather ball any third-grade girl could catch, sucking his life, his time, his fun for the food I need, the silly clothes, sucking the joy out of what few hopes he may have seen when his eyes were shut ten years ago, when he and my mother made me late in the night. —That is the stuff he makes me think when he goes and leaves me stuck in the car, stuck for an hour many times so that finally sunk in desperation I begin to know he is sick in there—that his heart has seized as he knows it will or that strange woman is wild and has killed him silent with a knife, with poison or that he has sold his stove and said goodbye and gone out the back in secret across a field into pines to leave us forever, to change his life. And I will say to myself, "You have got to move—run to the road and flag a car and go for the sheriff," but the house door will open and he will be there alive still grinning, then calming his face in the walk through the yard, wiping his forehead, smiling when he sees me again, when he recollects he has a son and I am it (am one anyhow, the one old enough to follow him places and wait). Before

I can swallow what has jammed my throat, my heart in the previous hour, he will have us rolling—the cool breeze started and shortly his amends, my reward for waiting. It is always the same, his amends. It is stories about him being my age, especially about his father—Charles McCraw, "Cupe" McCraw who was clerk to the Copeland Register of Deeds, raised six children which were what he left (and a house, a wife, several dozen jokes) when he died sometimes before I was born—and he needs no crutch to enter his stories such as "Have I told you this?" He knows he has told me, knows I want it again every time he can spare. He will light a cigarette with a safety match (he threw away the car's lighter long ago out the window down an embankment, thinking *it* was a match) and then say, "No sir. If I live to be ninety, I never want to swallow another cigarette." That is the first of the story about him at my age being sent outdoors by his father to shut off the water when a hard freeze threatened. The valve was sunk in the ground behind the house, and he was squatting over it cursing because it was stiff and pulling on the cigarette he had lit to warm him—when he looked in the frozen grass by his hand and there were black shoes and the ends of trousers. He did not need to look further. It was his father so while he gave one last great turn to the valve, he flipped his lower lip out and up (and here at age forty-two he imitates the flip, swift but credible) and swallowed the cigarette, fire included. Then he may say, "How is your bladder holding out, Preacher? Do you want to run yonder into those bushes?" I will say No since I cannot leak in open air, and he will say, "Father had a colored boy named Peter who worked around the house. *Peee-ter,* Peter called it. The first day we had a telephone connected, Father called home from the courthouse to test it. I was home from school—supposed to be sick—and I answered. He did not catch my voice so he said 'Who is this?' I said *'Peee-ter,'* and he thought he would joke a little. He said 'Peter *who?*' I said 'Mr. *McCraw's* Peee-ter,' and he said, 'Hang up, fool, and don't ever answer that thing again!' I waited for him to come home that evening, and he finally came with a box of Grapenuts for me, but he did not mention Peter or the telephone so I didn't either, never mentioned it till the day he died. He died at night . . ."

But *tonight.* This hard winter night in 1942 and he is silent—my father—his eyes on darkness and road to get me safely home as if I was cherished, while I rush on behind shut eyes through all that last—his size, his lacks, his distances—still threading my finger through curls of his wrist, a grander wrist than he needs or deserves. I find his pulse. It rises sudden to my winnowing finger, waylays, appalls, *traps* it. I ride his life with the pad of flesh on my middle finger, and it heaves against me steady and calm as if it did not know I ruled its flow, that poor as I am at games and play, I could press in now, press lightly first so he would not notice, then in and in till his foot would slack on the gas, his head sink heavy to his chest, his eyes shut on me (on what I cause), the car roll still and I be left with what I have made—his permanent death. Towards that picture, that chance, my own pulse rises untouched, unwanted—grunting aloud in the damp stripes under my groins, the tender sides of my windpipe, sides of my heels, the pad of my sinking finger. My finger coils to my side, my whole hand clenches, my eyes clamp tighter, but—innocent surely—he speaks for the first time since begging my pardon. "Am I dying, Preacher?"

I look up at him. "No sir. What do you mean?"

"I mean you left my pulse like a bat out of Hell. I wondered did you feel bad news?"

"No sir, it is going fine. I just never felt it before, and it gave me chills." He smiles at the road and we slide on a mile or more till I say, "Are you *scared* of dying?"

He keeps me waiting so I look past him through glass to the sky for a distant point to anchor on—the moon, a planet, Betelgeuse. Nothing is there. All is drowned under cloud but I narrow my eyes and strain to pierce the screen. Then when I am no longer waiting, he says, "It is the main thing I am scared of."

I come back to him. "Everybody is going to die."

"So they tell me. So they tell me. But that is one crowd I would miss if I could. Gladly."

I am not really thinking. "What do people mean when they say somebody is their personal hero?"

It comes sooner than I expect. "Your hero is what you need to to be."

"Then is Jesus your hero?"

"Why do you think that?"

"You say you are scared of dying. Jesus is the one that did not die."

He does not take it as funny which is right, and being no Bible scholar he does not name me the others that live on—Enoch, Elijah. I name them to myself but not to him. I have seen my chance. I am aiming now at discovery, and I strike inwards like Balboa mean and brave, not knowing where I go or will end or if I can live with what I find. But the next move is his. He must see me off. And he does. He tells me, "I think your hero has to be a man. Was Jesus a man?"

"No sir. He was God disguised."

"Well, that is it, you see. You would not stand a chance of being God—need to or not—so you pick somebody you have got half a chance of measuring up to."

In all my seeking I have not asked him. I ask him now. "Have you got a hero?"

Again he makes me wait and I *wait*. I look nowhere but at him. I do not think. Then he says, "Yes, I guess I do. But I never called it that to myself."

"What did you call it?"

"I didn't call it nothing. I was too busy trying to get through alive."

"Sir?"

"—Get through some trouble I had. I *had* some troubles and when I did there was generally a person I could visit and talk to till I eased. Then when I left him and the trouble came back, I would press down on *him* in my mind—something he told me or how he shook my hand goodbye. Sometimes that tided me over. Sometimes."

He has still not offered a name. To help him I hold out the first one at hand. "Is it Dr. Truett?" (That is where we are coming from now tonight—a sermon in Raleigh by George W. Truett from Texas.)

The offer is good enough to make him think. (I know how much he admires Dr. Truett. He has one of his books and a sermon on records—"The Need for Encouragement"—that he plays two or three nights a year, standing in the midst of the room, giving what wide curved gestures seem right when Dr. Truett says for instance, " 'Yet now be strong, O Zerubbabel, saith the Lord; and be strong O Joshua, son of Josedech, the high priest; and be strong, all ye people of the land, saith the Lord, and work; for I am with you, saith the Lord of hosts: according to the word that I covenanted with you when ye came out of Egypt, so my spirit remaineth among you: fear ye not.' " And here we have come this long way to see him in January with snow due to fall by morning.) But he says—my father, "No, not really. Still you are close." Then a wait—"You are warm."

"Does that mean it is a preacher?"

"Yes."

"Mr. Barden?"

"I guess he is it."

I knew he was—or would have known if I had thought—but I do not know why. He is nothing but the Baptist minister in Copeland, my father's home—half a head shorter than Father, twenty years older, light and dry as kindling with flat bands of gray hair, white skin the day shines through if he stands by windows, Chinese eyes, bird ankles, a long voice for saying things such as "Jeff, I am happy to slide my legs under the same table with yours" and poor digestion (he said that last the one day he ate with us; my mother had cooked all morning, and he ate a cup of warm milk)—but he is one of the people my father loves, one my mother is jealous of, and whenever we visit Copeland (we left there when I was two), there will come a point after dinner on Sunday when my father will stand and without speaking start for the car. If it is winter he may get away unseen, but in summer everybody will be on the porch and Junie will say, "Jeff is headed to save Brother Barden's soul." My mother will laugh. My father will smile and nod but go and be gone till evening and feel no need to explain when he returns, only grin and agree to people's jokes.

But *tonight*, has he not just offered to explain? and to me who have never asked? So I ask, "Mr. Barden is so skinny. What has he got that you need to be?"

"Before you were born he used to be a lot of things. Still is."

All this time he has not needed his hand on the wheel. It has stayed heavy on me. I slip my hand towards it. I test with my finger, tapping. He turns his palm and takes me, gives me the right to say "Name some things." I fear if he looks at me, we will go back silent (he has not looked down since we started with his pulse), and I roll my face deep into his side, not to take his eyes. But they do not come. He does not look. He does not press my hand in his, and the load of his wrist even lightens. I think it will leave but it lifts a little and settles further on like a folded shield over where I am warmest, takes up guard, and then he is talking the way he must, the best he can, to everything but me—the glass, the hood, the hoop of light we push towards home.

"I have done things you would not believe—and will not believe when you get old enough to do them yourself. I have come home at night where your mother was waiting and said things to her that were worse than a beating, then gone again and left her still waiting till morning, till sometimes night again. And did them knowing I would not do them to a dog. Did them drunk and wild, knowing she loved me and would not leave me even though her sisters said, 'Leave him. He won't change now,' would not even raise her voice. O Preacher, it was Hell. We were both in Hell with the lid screwed down, not a dollar between us except what I borrowed—from Negroes sometimes when friends ran out—to buy my liquor to keep me wild. You were not born yet, were not thought of, God knows not wanted the way I was going. It was 1930. I was thirty years old and my life looked over, and I didn't know why or whether I wanted it different, but here came Mr. Barden skinny as you say, just sitting by me when I could sit still, talking when I could listen, saying 'Hold up, Jeff. Promise God something before you *die*.' But Preacher, I didn't. I drank up two more years, driving thousands of miles on mirey roads in a model-A Ford to sell little scraps of life insurance to wiped-out farmers that did not have a pot to pee in, giving your mother a dollar or so to buy liver with on a Saturday or a pound of hominy I could not swallow. And then that spring when the bottom looked close, I slipped and started you on the way. When I knew you were coming—Preacher, for days I was out of what mind I had left myself. I do not know what I did but I *did* things, and finally when I had run some sort of course, your mother sent for Mr. Barden and they got me still. He said, 'Jeff, I cherish you, mean as you are. But what can I do if you go on murdering yourself, tormenting your wife?' I told him, 'You can ask the Lord to stop that baby.' I told him that. But you came on every day *every day* like a tumor till late January and she hollered to me you were nearly here. But you were not. You held back twenty-four hours as if you knew who was waiting outside, and Dr. Haskins told me—after he had struggled with your mother all day, all night—'Jeff, one of your family is going to die but I don't know which.' I said,

'Let it be me' and he said he wished he could. I went outdoors to Paul's woodshed and told Jesus, 'If You take Rhew or take that baby, then take me too. But it You can, save her and save that baby, and I make You this promise—I will change my life.' I asked Him, 'Change my life.' So He saved you two and I started to change my life, am trying right now God knows. Well, Mr. Barden has helped me out every once in a while—talking to me or just sitting calm, showing me his good heart. Which, Preacher, I need."

I can tell by his voice he is not through, but he stops, leaving raw quiet like a hole beneath us. I feel that because I have stayed awake, and my finger slips to the trough of his wrist where the pulse was before. It is there again awful. I take it, count it long as I can and say, "It feels all right to me, sir" (not knowing of course how right would feel). He says he is glad which frees me to see Mr. Barden again. I call up his face and pick it for anything new. At first it is very much the same—bloodless, old—but I settle on the faded stripes of his lips and strain to picture them years ago saying the things that were just now reported. They move, speak and for a moment I manage to see his face as a wedge—but aimed elsewhere, making no offer to split me clean from my lacks, *my* foes. So I let it die and I say to my father, "I still think Jesus is your real hero."

Glad for his rest, he is ready again. "Maybe so. Maybe so. But Mr. Barden was what I could *see*."

"Who has seen Jesus?"

"Since He died, you mean?"

"Yes sir."

"Several, I guess. Dr. Truett for one."

I know the story—it is why I have come this far to hear an old man tremble for an hour—but I request it again.

"Well, as I understand it, years ago when he was young, he asked a friend to come hunting with him. He came and they went in the woods together, and after a while he shot his friend. By accident but that didn't make him feel any better. He knew some people would always say he killed the man on purpose."

"Maybe he did."

"No he didn't. Hold on."

"How do you know?"

"The same way *he* knew—because after he sweated drops of blood in misery, Jesus came to him one evening in a dream and said not to grieve any more but to live his life and do what he could."

"Does that mean he really saw Jesus?—seeing Him in his sleep?"

"How else could you see Him since He is dead so long?"

I tell him the chance that is one of my hopes, my terrors—"He could walk in your house in daylight. Then you could step around Him. You could put out your hand and He would be there. But in just a dream how would you know? What would keep Him from being a trick?"

"The way He would look. His face, His hands."

"The scars, you mean?"

"They would help. But no—" This is hard for him. He stops and thinks for fully a mile. "I mean whether or not He had the face to say things such as 'Be ye perfect as God is perfect'—not even say '*try* to be,' just '*be*'—a face that could change people's lives."

"People do not *know* what He looks like, Father. That is half the trouble." (We are now on one of our oldest subjects. We started three years ago when I first went to vacation Bible school. At the end of that two weeks after we had made our flour-paste model of a Hebrew water hole, they gave us diplomas that were folded leaflets with our name inside and a golden star but on the cover their idea of Jesus—set by a palm under light such as comes after storms (blurred, with piece of a rainbow) and huddled around Him, one each of the earth's children in native dress, two or three inside His arms but all aiming smiles at His face (jellied eyes, tan silk beard, clean silk hair, pink lips that could not call a dog to heel much less children or say to His mother, "Who is my mother?" and call her "Woman" from the bitter cross). I took the picture but at home that night I handed it to my father and asked if he thought that face was possible? He looked and said it was one man's guess, not to worry about it, but I did and later after I had studied picture Bibles and *Christ and the Fine Arts* by Cynthia Pearl Maus full of hairy Jesuses by Germans mostly—Clementz, Dietrich, Hofman, Lang, Plockhorst, Von Uhde, Wehle—I asked him if in all the guessers, there was one who knew? any Jesus to count on? He said he thought there was but in Student's Bibles, the ones they give to boys studying ministry. I said had he seen one? He had not and I asked if he could buy me one or borrow Mr. Barden's for me to trace? He said he did not think so, that Student's Bibles were confidential, secrets for good men.

So tonight I ask him, "Then how did He look in your mind when I was being born and Mother was dying?"

"He didn't look nohow *that* day. I was not seeing faces. I was doing business. If I saw anything it was rocks underfoot, those smooth little rocks Paul hauled from the creek to spread in his yard."

"I think it is awful."

"What?"

"Him not appearing. Why did Dr. Truett see him and you could not?"

"Maybe he needed to worse than me. He had killed a man. killed somebody else. I was just killing me, making others watch me do it."

"That is no reason."

"Preacher, if I was as good a man as George W. Truett—half the man—I would be seeing Jesus every day or so, be *fishing* with Him."

"I am not joking, Father. It is awful, I think—Him not helping you better than that."

"Preacher, I didn't mind"—which even with this night's new information is more or less where we always end. It does not worry my father that he is not privileged to see the secret. But it scalds, torments any day of mine in which I think that the face with power to change my life is hid from me and reserved for men who have won their fight (when He Himself claimed He sought the lost), will always be hid, leaving me to work dark. As my father has done, does, must do—not minding, just turning on himself his foe with nothing for hero but Mr. Barden when it could have been Jesus if He had appeared, His gouged hands, His real face, the one He deserved that changes men.

We are quiet again, so quiet I notice the sound of the engine. I have not heard it tonight before. It bores through the floor, crowds my ears, and turning my eyes I take the mileage—sixty-three thousand to round it off. My father travels in his work as I say, and this Pontiac has borne him three times around the earth—the equal of that nearly. It will get us home together, alive, and since in a heavy rush I am tired, I sleep where I am, in his heat, in his hollow. Of course I do not think I am sleeping. I dream I am awake, that I stand on the near side of sleep and yearn, but it *is* a dream and as sudden again I wake—my head laid flat on the mohair seat, blood gathered hot in my eyes that stare up at nothing. My head lifts a little (stiff on my neck), my eyes jerk round collecting terror—the motor runs gentle, the knob of the heater burns red, burns warm, but the car is still and my father is gone. Where he was the dashboard light strikes empty nothing. My head falls back and still half dreaming I think, "They have won at last. They have caught us, come between us. We have ended apart." I say that last aloud and it wakes me fully so I lie on (my head where his loaded lap should be) and think what seems nearer the truth—"He has left as I always knew he would to take up his life in secret." Then I plunge towards the heart of my fear—"He knew just now what I thought when I pressed his pulse, and he could not bear my sight any more." Then deeper towards the heart—"God has taken him from me as punishment for causing his death just now in my mind. But why did He not take me?" Still He did not. I am left. So I rise and strain to see out the glass, to know my purpose for being here, what trails lie between me and morning, what vengeance. The first is snow. The headlights shine and in their outward upward hoop there is only flat gobs of snow that saunter into frozen grass and survive. The grass of the shoulder is all but smothered, the weeds of the bank already bent, meaning I have slept long enough for my life to wreck beyond hope—my father vanished and I sealed in a black Pontiac with stiff death held back only long as the draining battery lasts and now too late, no hero to turn to. My forehead presses into the dark windshield. For all the heater's work, the cold crawls in through glass, through flesh, through skull to my blood, my brain.

So I pray. My eyes clamped now, still pressed to the glass, knowing I have not prayed for many weeks past (with things going well), I swallow my shame and naked in fear ask, "Send me my father. Send me help. If you help me now, if you save my life, I will change—be brave, be free with my gifts. Send somebody good." My eyes click open on answered prayer—coming slow from the far edge of light a tall man hunched, his face to the ground hid, head wrapped in black, a black robe bound close about him, his arms inside, bearing towards me borne on the snow as if on water leaving no tracks, his shadow crouched on the snow like a following bird, giant, black (killing? kind?). I stay at the glass, my further prayer locked in my throat, waiting only for the sign of my fate. Then the robe spreads open. The man's broad hands are clasped on his heart, turned inward, dark. It is Jesus I see, Jesus I shall touch moments from now—shall lift His face, probe His wounds, kiss His eyes. He is five steps away. I slip from the glass, fall back on my haunches, turn to the driver's door where He already stands, say silent, "If Father could not see Your face, why must I?"—say to the opening door "Thank you, Sir," close my lips to take His unknown kiss.

He says, "Excuse me leaving you asleep," and it is my father come back disguised. "I had to go pee—down that hill in the snow." (He points down the road as if he had covered miles not feet.) "I thought you were dead to the world."

I say, "I *was*"—I laugh—"and I thought you were Jesus, that you had been taken and I was left and Jesus was coming to claim me. I was about to *see* Him."

Standing outside, the warm air rushing towards him, he shrugs the coat from his shoulders, lifts the scarf from his head, lays them in back, slides onto the seat. Shrinking from cold I have crawled almost to the opposite door, but kneeling towards him. He faces me and says, "I am sorry to disappoint you, Preacher."

I say "Yes sir" and notice he smiles very slow, very deep from his eyes—but ahead at the road. Then he says I had better lie down. I crawl the two steps and lie as before, and we move on so I have no chance to return his smile, to show I share his pleasure. Still I root my head deep in his lap and hope for a chance before sleep returns. The chance never comes. Snow occupies his eyes, his hands. He cannot face me again or test for warmth. Even his mind is surely on nothing but safety. Yet his face is new. Some scraps of the beauty I planned for Jesus hang there—on the corners of his mouth serious now, beneath his glasses in eyes that are no longer simply kind and gray but have darkened and burn new power far back and steady (the power to stop in his tracks and *turn*), on his ears still purple with cold but flared against danger like perfect ugly shells of blind sea life, on his wrists I cannot ring with my hand, stretched from white cuffs at peace on the wheel but shifting with strength beyond soldier's, beyond slave's—and I think "I will look till I know my father, till all this new disguise falls away leaving him clear as before." I look but his face shows no sign of retreat, and still as he is and distant, it is hard to stare, painful then numbing. I feel sleep rise from my feet like blood. When it reaches my head I shut my eyes to flush it back, but it surges again, and I know I have lost. My own hands are free—he has not touched me, cannot—so my right hand slips to the gap in my pants, cups itself warm on warmer trinkets long since asleep, soft with blood like new birds nested drowsy. I follow them into darkness, thinking on the threshold, "Now I have lost all hope of knowing my father's life," cupping closer, warmer this hand as I sink.

First in my dreams I am only this hand yet have eyes to see—but only this hand and a circle of light around it. It is larger by half than tonight, and black stubble has sprung to shade its back, its new thick veins, its gristly cords showing plain because this hand is cupped too, round like a mold, hiding what it makes. It lifts. What it has molded are the kernels, the knobs of a man still twice the size of mine I held before I slept, but cold, shrunk and shrinking as my hand lifts—their little life pouring out blue through veins gorged like sewers that tunnel and vanish under short lank hairs, grizzled. Then I have ears. I hear the blood rustle like silk as it leaves, retreats, *abandons,* and my hand shuts down, clamps on the blood to turn its race, to warm again, fill again what I hold. But the rustle continues not muffled, and my hand presses harder, squeezes the kernels. Through my fingers green piss streams cold, corrosive. But my hand is locked. It cannot move. I am bound to what I have made, have caused, and seeing only this terror, I find a voice to say, "If I cannot leave may I see what I do?" The light swells in a hoop from my hand filling dimly a room and in that room my whole body standing by a bed—the body I will have as a man—my hand at the core of a man's stripped body laid yellow on the narrow bed. Yet with this new light my original eyes have stayed where they started—on my crushing hand and beneath it. I tear them left to see the rest. So I start at his feet raised parallel now but the soles pressed flat by years of weight, the rims of the heels and the crowded toes guarded by clear callus, the veins of the instep branching towards shins like blades of antique war polished deadly, marred by sparse hair, the knees like grips to the blades, the thighs ditched inward to what I crush—his hollow, his core that streams on thin with no native force but sure as if drained by magnets in the earth. Then his hands at his sides clenched but the little fingers separate, crouched, gathering ridges in the sheet. Then his firm belly drilled deep by the navel, his chest like the hull of a stranded boat, shaved raw, violet paps sunk and from under his left armpit a line traced carefully down his side, curved under his ribs, climbing to the midst of his breast—the letter J perfect, black, cut into him hopeless to dredge out a lung, laced with gut as stiff as wire. Then under a tent of soft wrinkled glass his face which of course is my father's—the face he will have when I am this man—turned from me, eyes shut, lips shut, locked in the monstrous stillness of his rest. So he does not watch me, shows no sign of the pain I must cause. Yet I try again to lift my fingers, to set him free, but rocking the heel of my hand, I see our skin has joined maybe past parting. I struggle though—gentle to spare his rest. I step back slowly, hoping this natural movement will peel us clean, but what I have pressed comes with me as if I had given love not pain. I speak again silent to whoever gave me light just now, say, "Set him free. Let me leave him whole in peace." But that prayer fails and turning my eyes I pull against him ready to wound us both if I must. Our joint holds fast but the rustle beneath my hand swells to scraping, to high short grunts. "Jesus," I say—I speak aloud—"Come again. Come now. I do not ask to see Your face but come in *some* shape now." A shudder begins beneath my hand in his core, our core that floods through his belly, his breast to his throat, bearing with it the noise that dims as it enters the tent. I stare through the glass. His head rolls toward me, his yellow lips split to release the noise, his eyes slide open on a quarter-inch of white. The noise scrapes on but behind the tent it is not words—is it rage or pain or wish, is it meant for me? With my free left hand I reach for the tent to throw it back, saying, "Stop. Stop," but I cannot reach so "Father," I say, "I beg your pardon. Pardon me this, I will change my life—will turn in my tracks on myself my foe with you as shield." But he yields no signal. The eyes shut again, the lips shut down on the noise, the shudder runs out as it came, to our core. What my free hand can reach it touches—his wrist. What pulse was there is stopped, and cold succeeds it till with both hands I press hard ice, final as any trapped in the Pole. I can see clearer now, my terror calmed by his grander terror, the peace of his wounds, and facing his abandoned face I say again (to the place, the dream), "Pardon me this, I will change my life. I make this . . ." But pardon comes to stop my speech. My cold hands lift from his hollow, his wrist. My own hot life pours back to claim them. Then those hands fail, those eyes, my dream. A shift of my headrest lifts me from sleep.

I face my live father's present body—my present eyes on his belly but *him, tonight,* above me, around me, shifting beneath me. My lips are still open, a trail of spit snails down my cheek, my throat still holds the end of my dream, "I make this promise." So my first thought is fear. Have I spoken aloud what I watched in my dream? Have I warned my father of his waiting death? offered my promise, my life too early? I roll away from his belt to see—and see I am safe. He is what he has been before tonight, been all my life, unchanged by my awful news, my knowledge, undisguised—his ears, his cheeks flushed with healthy blood that also throbs in the broad undersides of his wrists on the wheel, in the wounded fat of his hand, his hollow, even in his eyes which are still ahead on the road for safety, able, unblinking but calm and light as it through snow he watched boys playing skillful games with natural grace.

His legs shift often under me now—braking, turning, accelerating—and we move forward slowly past regular street lamps that soar through the rim of my sight, gold at the ends of green arms. We are in some town. From its lamps, its wires, its hidden sky, I cannot say which—but not home yet I trust, I hope. I am not prepared for home and my mother, the rooms that surround my swelling lacks, direct sight of my doomed father. I need silent time to hoard my secret out of my face deep into my mind, granting my father twelve years fearless to work at his promise, freeing myself to gather in private the strength I will need for my own promise the night he dies, my own first turn on what giant foes I will have as a man. And clamping my eyes I seize my dream and thrust it inward, watching it suck down a blackening funnel, longing to follow it. But his legs shift again, his arms swing left, our wheels strike gravel, stop. Beyond the glass in our stationary light are bare maple limbs accepting snow, limbs of the one tree I climb with ease. Too sudden we are home and my father expels in a seamless shudder the care, the attention that bound him these last three hours. His legs tense once, gather to spring from beneath my weight, then subside, soften. I ride that final surge, then face him—smiling as if just startled from sleep.

He takes my smile, stores it as a gift. "Did you sleep well, Preacher?"

I hunch my shoulders, say "Thank you, sir," and behind my lie floods sudden need—to rise, board him, cherish with my hands, my arms while there still is time this huge gentle body I know like my own, which made my own (made half anyhow) and has hurt nobody since the day I was born.

But he says, "Lift up. Look yonder at the door."

I roll to my knees. Through glass and snow, behind small panes, white curtains, in the center of the house no longer ours stands my mother in a flannel robe, hand raised in welcome the shape of fire. "She waited," I say.

"She waited," he says and reaches for his scarf, his coat, beckons me to him, drapes them around me, steps to the white ground and turning offers me open arms. Kneeling I ask him, "What do you mean?"

"I mean to save your life, to carry you over this snow."

"Heavy as *I* am?—you and *your* heart?"

But he says no more. His mind is made, his trip is ended. He is nearly home, facing rest, accepting snow like the trees while I stall. Then he claps his palms one time, and I go on my knees out of dry car heat through momentary snow into arms that circle, enfold me, lift me, bear me these last steps home over ice—my legs hung bare down his cooling side, face to his heart, eyes blind again, mind folding in me for years to come his literal death and my own swelling foes, lips against rough brown wool saying to myself as we rise to the porch, to my waiting mother (silent, in the voice I will have as a man), "They did not separate us tonight. We finished alive, together, whole. This one more time."

[1963]

Liam Rector

THE EVENTUAL MUSIC

for David St. John

Eventually someone knocks at your door eventually
just as the moon is eventual & just
as you were thinking that the only trust
is the trust of meat, the shift of need,
& eventually someone knocks & you stand
at your own door   & you know then
that you are the door-opener & that someone
will enter, & someone does   & you tell someone
that you have been holding the world in its place,
in its place without music   you tell her
that fashion goes deep, fear goes deeper,
that you are intrigued by the chemistry
of what comes next   & someone eventually announces
that she is actually here & has arrived with music boxes,
tiny porcelain objects that never leave,
always stay & always music she apologizes
for having come so late to your door   you speak to her
of the bones that deny the music, of the arteries
& their race towards the skin, of the blood
that hears music always & eventually
runs away from home

& you lie down, with someone, in your opened door
& you hear all that music that was not there before.

[1979]

Jean Ross

UNFINISHED BUSINESS

The last year of their marriage, Ann and Walker Lashley sometimes spent the evening in different rooms of the house, writing to each other. Ann sat at the dining room table writing rapid longhand full of dark underlinings and exclamation points; Walker sat in his study, typing in a fierce rat-a-tat-tat. Josh, who couldn't read yet, drifted uneasily back and forth between them, making up messages for the grandmothers to whom they pretended to be writing. Some nights they hired a sitter so as to carry on the quarrel away from Josh; they drove around, they parked on deserted streets in front of closed business establishments. It would grow late; other people, happier people, would come out of movie theaters, get into cars, and drive away; and Ann and Walker still would not have had it out. They saw, that year, that they never would.

After the divorce, Ann believed she'd come through it creditably. She'd settled business matters with Walker as quickly and agreeably as she could; she'd explained everything to Josh patiently, over and over; she'd been close-mouthed with curious friends. When Walker and one of his students came in a U-Haul truck to get his things, she put on a good show of cordiality, partly for Josh's sake; she gave them coffee and maneuvered them into taking Josh for a ride in the truck. When they left, and the high-backed truck moved clumsily off down the street, she thought with relief that it was over and that she'd behaved quite decently.

It was when she thought of Irene, Walker's mother, that it would occur to her that there might be unfinished business. She and Irene had got along well enough—not too well, not too badly; now she wished that she had been a little nicer and Irene a little less so, so that she could write Irene off along with Walker. But why should she hesitate to do so? She'd been nice enough—nicer than a lot of daughters-in-law. Wasn't Irene herself full of stories of selfish girls who dragged their husbands all the way across the country to some God-forsaken state where the girl's family happened to live, or who quarreled with their mothers-in-law and then tried to keep the husband and his mother apart? In one of these stories, the mother met her son on the sly, waiting in his car in the parking lot behind his office; she would crouch low or lie down in the back seat so as not to be seen by anyone who might report it to his wife. Whenever she told this story, Irene would begin to sob. Walker, of course, would have drifted out of the room, leaving Ann *stuck* with Irene—the two of them at opposite ends of Irene's gold-threaded brown sofa, faced off like the pair of jewel-eyed seahorses on the wall behind him. The second time she heard the story (she thought of it as being *subjected* to it) Ann laughed shortly and murmured, "How romantic!" Irene was blowing her nose; she stared. "That's what *you* think!" she said hoarsely. "I just hope nothing like that ever happens to us, that's all." "Of course not, Irene," Ann said. "I wouldn't *let* it happen."

How could an intellectual like Walker take his mother seriously?—a woman who called masonry masonerry, debris derbriss, and spoke of the prostrate gland; who awarded her vote to the handsomest political candidate, got her medical advice from pharmacists, and told you quite seriously that the best thing for an earache was a teaspoon of warm urine in the ear? Certainly her son should love and honor her, but how could he take her seriously? Walker did, though; he listened to the most absurd notions with a foolish patience, then some teasing criticism of himself, equally absurd, would make him flare up. But Ann didn't think about it often: Irene lived in Charlotte, a long way from Iowa, where Ann and Walker met and were married, and a long way from California, where they split up.

Six months after the divorce Irene wrote to Ann. She said she had cried when she heard the news; she seemed determined to share the blame. She hoped she hadn't brought Walker up to be selfish and inconsiderate; she had given him a lot of attention, of course, she had wanted him to follow his star—and she believed she'd been right, judging by the reviews of his new book. (Was she apologizing or bragging?) But she was sorry, especially on poor little Josh's account.

She enclosed a letter for Josh, and ten dollars. When Ann had read him the letter, they made a money belt from a cowboy belt and an old billfold, and he wore it for a week, keeping it on under his pajamas at night. The next day he said they ought to answer Irene's letter right away.

It was fall; they were living in Iowa City, Ann's hometown. She'd rented an old house, and enrolled Josh in first grade and herself in library school. At first she and Josh had stayed at her parents' on Summit Street, where Walker had courted her. She thought of him surprisingly often. How he was going to miss this street and this house! He'd admired the great arched windows that faced the side yard on two floors, had praised the lily-patterned stained glass in the front doors. When he'd first come to dinner (he'd been teaching in the writers' workshop; she'd been a graduate student) she'd taken him up to the attic to show him how far you could see. Perhaps if he'd known how many people in town were in love with Summit Street he'd have been less interested in it; but he was attracted to its old houses, hitching posts, and miraculously surviving elms—most of all to this house. Once he'd come up the walk while she and her mother were playing piano duets, and he had not rung the bell at all but sat on the steps half an hour, listening. (Once he'd thought he heard her playing Chopin as he approached but it had turned out to be her mother instead; this emotional turnabout had interested him, and he'd written it down in his notebook.) The next year, after they were married, they'd lived in her parents' garage apartment, the second floor of what had once been a carriage house.

The house she rented for herself and Josh had a sloping front porch, small, cramped rooms, and a mousy smell in the kitchen; still, it had touches of gingerbread, and an overgrown backyard that Josh said was full of good hiding places (wouldn't it stir a child's imagination more than their California ranchhouse?). There, in the breakfast nook of its sunny kitchen, Josh dictated his letter to Irene: he could print a little, but he wanted this letter to be in "cursive." He was a serious child whose laughter often came after a pause, as if it had taken a moment for him to come out of his thoughts; that morning he rose bouncily on the balls of his feet, pacing the scarred linoleum with what seemed to her a new authority. He was a nice-looking child, with a neat head of short brown hair and a little ice-pink color in his cheeks—more like her family, the Limoseths, than the Lashleys, who were a large, dark lot.

She took down his dictation in a large, neat, somewhat childlike hand, to show a good example of cursive, and to give Irene the feeling that the letter really was from Josh. Josh was telling Irene that he wished he still lived at his grandparents', near his friend Terry. This house was o.k., Terry came over sometimes, and they'd made a hideout under the back porch. But it wasn't as good as the house in South Laguna and the TV wasn't as good here either.

Waiting for him to go on, she stared out at the backyard. The bright leaves of October lay caught in the long, silky grass, grass that should have been cut again before the leaves fell, if she'd been able to afford it. The clumps of overgrown grass, the ancient garage and its sagging doors, the moldy lilac bush—everything in and around this lopsided house was worn-out and neglected. That afternoon she was a little ashamed of it, a little self-conscious, as if Irene had come in to take note of it all. Well, Irene didn't need to feel sorry for her!—she would tell Irene not to waste her tears, the divorce had been a move long overdue. She realized Josh was waiting for her to take down the next sentence: he was inviting Irene to come and see them next summer. Ann wrote it down in the large, careful hand: it was a long time till summer, and anyway, Irene had waited six months to write; surely she wouldn't take them up on it.

But Irene came the next summer. At the airport she began to cry, as if they had all suffered a common bereavement. She hugged them hard, shaking her head, her lips quivering.

She was a tall, thick-waisted woman with coarse black hair threaded with a little white; beneath her melancholy dark eyes there were chronic circles nearly as dark as bruises. She had traveled in dark pants and jacket; she wore a man's gold wristwatch, once her husband's, and had tied a strip of red net around her hair. In the car she unwound the net and put it in her vast purse, and she seemed to strip off her melancholy thoughts with it. "Josh, honey, I put all my quarters in the insurance machine for you; if the plane had gone down you'd've been a rich little boy." "I'm glad it didn't go down, Grandma," Josh said in his little tenor voice.

Ann and Josh were back at her parents'. "Josh is happier there, that's all," she said to Irene, unwilling, for some reason, to add that the crooked house had cost a fortune to heat, and that the student roomer-and-sitter she'd taken in hadn't hit it off with Josh. Irene said she didn't blame Josh, she loved Summit Street too; she'd visited Ann and Walker there once.

What a marvellous idea this had been after all, Ann thought, the first few days of the visit. She overheard Irene telling Josh family stories—about being roused from sleep to see Halley's Comet; about seeing her brother go off to the First World War; about Cousin Ouida Stoker, who at twenty had killed herself with Paris green, over nothing; about Great-grandpa Zack Hildreth, who jumped in the pond in his nightshirt to make the frogs stop hollering. (Did Walker tell Josh stories like that? Probably not: he was busy *using* them, and once he used them, he was through with them.)

Then, midway the week—midway her visit—Irene asked if she could see the apartment over the garage, where Ann and Walker had lived.

"Oh—I hate to bother the Appels, the people out there; they're both in law school and terribly busy," Ann said, not pleased at the request. Wasn't it slightly tactless to ask to revisit what had been Ann and Walker's honeymoon cottage? How could anyone who'd cried that much at the airport bear to see it? "Anyway, it looks quite different now."

"Oh—well. Sure. I see. Well, that's o.k.," Irene said. But the next evening, as Ann cleared the supper dishes from the table on the screened porch, she saw a figure in dark pants and flowered tunic on the far side of the backyard, by the phlox and daylilies, near the garbage cans: Irene, of course. How quietly she'd gone out, how carefully she'd observed at what hour Barbara Appel took out the garbage. While Ann watched, Barbara appeared; the two women talked for a moment, then disappeared around the corner of the garage.

"She's so stubborn!" Ann said to her mother in the kitchen. Hadn't they done enough for Irene? Hadn't the beef at dinner been well-done because she couldn't stand it bloody, the angel pie made in her honor? Hadn't Ann's father taken Irene and Josh to the little town of Rochester to show Irene the rare wild flowers in the cemetery there? But it hadn't been enough: what Irene wanted was to walk through the rooms where Walker had lived nearly a decade ago. "And all roads lead to Walker; he's never off her mind for long. Sometimes I thought she wanted to crawl into our skins and *be* us!"

Her mother was hurriedly rinsing plates; she was going to a meeting of the city zoning and planning commission and already had on her earrings and dress shoes; her expression said she would consider the Irene question impartially. "Well—she's getting on up there . . ." She was clearly not sorry to be the younger, slimmer, more civic-minded grandmother. "Why didn't you take her on out there—how could they have refused?"

"She hasn't come to see *me,* maybe not even Josh; she's come to see Walker's son and his son's mother—"

"And of course you invited her for the pleasure of her company," her mother said, dropping her voice as Irene came up the back steps.

Making her escape, she found her father in the living room, looking alert, the evening paper slack in his hands. Behind his steel-rimmed glasses his eyes looked gloomy and questioning. She sat down on the hassock by his feet and smiled, almost sincerely. "It's nothing important, Daddy. She wanted to see the apartment and I should've taken her out there, I should've known she'd see it or bust."

Her father shook his head. "She's nice but she's hard-headed." He chuckled rather maliciously. "Over at Rochester yesterday we got to talking about birds, and we got into evolution; Josh was telling her some things, and she said, 'I don't believe a word of it!' I tried to tell her I didn't think evolution was totally incompatible with Christianity, but I could tell she wasn't taking it in. She's quite *opinionated* . . ." He spoke softly but with an odd vehemence; was he really thinking of Walker? He'd insisted on talking books with Walker, and there'd been a time when she'd thought she'd better speak to each of them about it, in private. "Well, he can disagree with me all he wants to," her father had said, "but he ought to be polite about it. Maybe he doesn't *know* Ole Rolvaag or Hamlin Garland, they're another generation; but he ought not to smile like that." When she gave Walker a watered-down version of this, he said he didn't know he'd been smiling; but he shook his head. "I can't tailor my opinions to fit the occasion. You'd think he'd be interested in *my* opinion—I teach courses in fiction!—but he just wants me to agree with him."

"Really, it's nothing, Daddy," she said now. "And she's having a really good time—you and Mother have been really nice."

But that was talk meant for her father. The next day she woke up to find old grievances come to life overnight. "What an insane idea, to invite her!" she muttered to her mother. "You know what I woke up thinking about? The time she asked Walker which of us he'd save if we were in a boat that was sinking—" "Oh, isn't that some old joke?" her mother asked. "Why didn't he treat it like one then!" The night Irene asked that silly question—asked it twice, to rouse him from his newspaper—Walker had muttered, after a long pause, "I'd let you both go down!" Ann had stared at him indignantly; Irene laughed a guttural laugh, as if willing to be insulted as long as Ann was insulted too. And Ann had taken it up with Walker that night in their bedroom, in case there was something she hadn't understood; but Walker only groaned and said it was so awkward when she and his mother started fussing over him, couldn't she see that he was in the middle? "I wouldn't fuss over anyone!" she'd exclaimed, but Walker's voice got louder, threatening a quarrel—didn't he know his mother was the last person she wanted to overhear one? Oh, she was right to have divorced him, she was *glad* to have divorced him, and why hadn't she divorced his mother at the same time?

Those recollections put her in a bad humor, but Irene was in a wonderful mood the rest of the week, as if seeing the apartment had given her a deep satisfaction. Whenever she won a struggle she was likely to do some troublesome and unnecessary good turn for whomever she had bested; it was no surprise that she insisted on mending a nasty three-cornered tear in Ann's new silk blouse, and, for good measure, strained her eyes helping Josh put together his six-hundred piece model of an aircraft carrier. Then, at the end, there was a morning of presentations: Irene gave Josh her father's drawstring money bag and some silver dollars, and gave Ann her grandmother's sampler and garnet ring.

"Oh, Irene, it's sweet of you, but it's too much, really." When Josh was out of hearing she added, "You know, Walker may very well marry again, he might have more children and you might wish you'd saved some of these things." She was glad to have an occasion to show Irene that she thought of it all quite matter-of-factly.

Irene's face went gloomy. "I don't care! That's his business. I'd love any kids he had, but Josh was the first, nobody could ever take his place." After a pause she added, "And you were the first wife, too, that's something nobody can ever take away from you!"

"Goodness, who on earth would *want* to?" Ann said.

* * *

It was several years before she realized that Irene's visits had become irreversibly annual. By then they were nearly essential: Irene had become the go-between who delivered Josh to Walker for his summer visit. Usually she flew to California with Josh, with Walker footing the bill.

Walker could afford it; he was doing very well. His latest novel was reviewed everywhere and nominated for prizes; his face, darkened by an unfamiliar beard, smiled his familiar, uneasy smile at her from *Newsweek* and the book page of the Des Moines Sunday *Register*. Josh got picture postcards from New York and Arkansas and Arizona, where Walker was giving a reading or teaching at a writers' conference or serving as writer-in-residence. He'd had a Guggenheim, money from the National Endowment, awards she'd never heard of before. He'd married again—a girl named Bernadette, one of his former students; soon Josh came back from his visits with pictures of himself cheerfully holding the baby, who was named Dora.

"Bernie was raised a Catholic," Irene said impressively, as though that were unusual, "but she's not one now. I don't guess she's *anything* now . . . She's a pretty girl, but I liked to starved out there. Alfalfa sprouts and bean sprouts and all kind of sprouts; whenever I was out by myself I'd get me a hamburger. But she's crazy about Walker and I guess he is about her, too."

Was she trying to say that Walker had found the right person this time? Sometimes Ann felt the bright beam of Irene's curiosity playing over her, felt Irene wondering exactly how friendly Ann and Walker were. Ann believed they were friends, just barely. But the letters they wrote to arrange Josh's visits had grown a little longer; Walker sent news of friends in California, and she wrote him her own good news—about her trip to Spain with her parents and Josh, about the law professor she was about to marry, until she changed her mind, rather late. (Not the least of what she held against Walker was the fact that he'd spoiled a lot of people for her; listening to some of them, she'd think of the way his lips moved as he said "idée reçu." And how friendly, she wondered, did he feel? He'd put her name in *Who's Who,* and not all first wives made it, but perhaps that was on Josh's account. When he learned she was buying a house—her parents were moving to the Summit Apartments—he offered to help, but she declined the offer. It seemed to her slightly tactless, a reminder that he was in the money, while she was living on a high school librarian's salary—not that that was Walker's fault, exactly, but how could you calculate the cost of a ruined marriage, especially when there was a child involved? Of course the marriage had been an error in judgment on both sides. Walker had been somehow misled by her Chopin and her delicate blonde prettiness; he'd thought her softer and more malleable than she was. She too had been misled, charmed by his teaching and his first book; she'd got him and his book all mixed up together. There was a lot she hadn't noticed at first, including his haphazard manners (later she'd said, perhaps unfairly, that perfectly routine politeness sometimes seemed to Walker almost a sign of weakness). And how could she have guessed, dazzled by his book, that while he worked on the next ones she would be at pains to keep Josh quiet, taking him on long excursions almost daily, hoping always for good weather? "Can we go home now?" Josh asked plaintively, down on the beach one chilly afternoon. "Will Daddy care if we go home now?" Not that it was Walker's fault that he needed it quiet to work; and perhaps she'd paid too much attention to Josh's little murmurings. It had all seemed very complicated, though, and certainly there'd been too many quarrels. One Christmas Day an argument had almost flared, and Josh had murmured, with a soft groan, "Not fussing on Christmas!"; she had told herself it was silly to go on this way. That was a long time ago; now Walker was offering her money toward a house. Perhaps she ought to be grateful, even flattered (did Bernie know he was offering it?) but in the end she couldn't decide whether she was grateful or not. She wrote him a very polite thank-you, though, for that was how she believed in doing things.

Irene came in the spring, in Josh's thirteenth year: he was going to make his summer trip alone. It was during this visit that Keith Causey called.

"A man called—the nicest man!" Irene said, meeting Ann at the door when she came in from work. "Keith Causey!"

"Who?" Ann leaned around Irene to call hello to Josh, who was playing Panzer Blitz at a card table in the living room.

"He's a friend of Walker's, passing through; he called from somewhere out on the road, and he's going to come out tonight."

"He is!" Ann cried, stepping out of her damp boots. It had been a day of wild, restless weather, a wet spring morning followed by a windy afternoon that was rapidly turning colder. "Honestly, aren't people brassy, though, inviting themselves out—"

"Oh, no, honey, *I* invited him. He was so nice; he knew who I was, and he says he knows you too. He's been on his spring break, and he's going back to Colorado, he teaches out there somewhere."

"Keith Causey! I certainly don't place him. And I thought I might do some work tonight."

"Oh. Well, I didn't know what to say. I thought you knew him, a little bit, anyway. He's written a book about Walker—"

"A book about Walker? Really. Are you sure it's not just part of a book, a chapter or something?"

Josh got up and strolled around, listening. He'd grown taller in the past year and had a loose-kneed walk, as if he might suddenly leap to catch a fly ball; long lashes gave his small-featured face a slightly delicate quality. Walking around the room, he fingered the pencils and pens in the Keiller jam jar on the wicker desk, looked among the dried fronds in the vase on the bookcase, peered past the open wing of the piano into its depths, and silently touched one or two of its keys. "Maybe it's being published but hasn't come out yet," he said.

"Oh—that's certainly possible."

"Don't you think he'll have a whole book written about him sometime? He's had about every prize there is, and he's got things in a whole lot of *anthologies,*" Josh said in a tone of cheerful persuasion.

"Oh, of course; I just meant *now,* that's all."

Irene had been listening to Josh with a look of happiness; turning back to Ann, her face drooped. "You don't want to fool with it! I'm sorry, I didn't know you had something you had to do."

"Oh, it's not that urgent." It was a booklist for the newsletter at Josh's school, and it wasn't due for ten days, but hadn't Irene made rather free with her evening? A friend of Walker's! How close a friend could he be if he thought Walker's name gave him instant entree here? "It's all right; of *course* you want to meet him."

She'd met him before, after all. When the knocker banged and she saw him through the glass by the front door, carefully turned so as not to see in, she knew she'd expected someone that size and shape, someone rather like the bearded man in the duffel coat who stood there under the porch light, his high forehead exposed to the cold wind. She opened the door with a smile meant to hide all she couldn't remember, and Keith Causey came in with a gust of cold air, saying, in light-hearted apology, "I seem to have brought winter back."

He held her hand fondly, longer than necessary, and told her she hadn't changed at all, and that this was very kind of her; he declared that he'd have known Irene anywhere, she and Walker were so much alike. As he talked, she began to remember him: out in California he'd come to do an interview with Walker, pages and pages in a little magazine, which everyone had said was good. He hadn't changed much, though his dark, tightly-curled hair began farther back; hair and beard encircled his face, a face that looked younger than it probably was, with its open expanse of pale forehead, and his wide-eyed, taking-in gaze. But how on earth had she forgotten him? Maybe the name on that interview had been, not Keith, but his initials; anyway, he was stretching it a little, saying he knew her. When he'd come to tape the interview, she'd seen him only a few minutes before she and Josh left the house. It had been a year of quarrels; maybe she'd forgotten him because of all the other things she'd needed to forget.

Irene went to get coffee; Keith Causey turned to Ann. "I was going to call again after you got home and make sure this was all right—then I decided maybe I'd better let well enough alone."

They both laughed. "Oh, it's fine, really," Ann said. "Irene says you've done a book about Walker."

"It'll be out in the fall. Walker seems to think it's pretty good."

"He says the book about Walker is coming out next fall," Ann said as soon as Irene returned.

"That's wonderful! I'll bet it's a good book, and I hope I have the opportunity to see it sometime." Irene put down the tray; winking at Ann, she ran her finger down the sleeve of his jacket. "Let me touch you; maybe some of that *smart* will rub off on me."

"Oh, I've been working on Walker a long time; I staked out my claim some time ago."

Irene smiled warmly. "That's wonderful. I guess it helped for you to be out there near him—too bad you've left there."

"Where were you?" Ann asked. "San Diego? It's nice. Did you know the Lohrmanns?"

Irene leaned forward in her chair. "Mr. Causey—well, *Keith*—Ann has some work she has to do, I didn't know it when you called. I know you won't mind if she goes and does her work—"

In the end, she had to go; it was awkward to explain that most of the work had to be done at the library, and that he'd kept her from going out. "Well, half an hour then. And I'll call Josh, he wants to meet you."

"I know you've heard him mention Cheeke," Irene was saying downstairs in the living room.

"I know a great deal about Cheeke. The Goodnights and the Stoneys, and Mary Queen Somebody—"

"Mary Queen Johnson. Walker loved that town! We went there when he was four and everybody always made a big to-do over him. Alton, my husband, was principal there. You wouldn't believe how different it all was back then! The principal's house was right on the school grounds, and we had our chickens in a pen down in the woods . . ."

In the upstairs hall Ann stood listening: she'd heard the front door open and close. Keith Causey had gone out for a few minutes and returned, then he and Irene had gone on talking. It was still too soon to go back down.

"But my husband's health failed and we left there—he was in a sanitarium a while, and Walker and I went and stayed with Alton's father, he was a widower and needed somebody to keep house . . ."

Irene was prettying up the Lashleys' history, but who could blame her, Ann thought, tiptoeing back to her room. The sanitarium Walker's father had gone to had been a place for alcoholics. He'd been able to hide his drinking till one commencement day; handing out diplomas on the stage of the school auditorium, he'd begun to mix up the names. They came out funny, as funny as some of the remarks he made to the seniors who filed past. "What does a pretty girl like you want with this little piece o' paper? . . . Well, here's one I never expected to see up here, but you made it, didn't you, ol' buddy . . ." Whispers ran through the audience, and a few guffaws; Irene began to cry. She told the people around her that he had a terrible toothache and had taken some whiskey for it, which was *true,* she said when she told Walker about it years later. Walker had come to think it tolerably funny, and sometimes told the story of the last commencement; once when Ann had tried to get him to tell it, though, he'd clammed up.

When she went down to the living room, Keith Causey and Irene smiled up in silence: they were listening to a tape he'd just made. "He wanted to *record* me," Irene said, with self-conscious pleasure, when it was over.

"What a nice idea. I'll see where Josh has got to." He would be watching television in the basement rec room; when she appeared he sighed but got up. "I thought you were interested in this man," she murmured as they went up the stairs, Josh taking them three at a time. "Sure. But he was taping it all and I couldn't think of a whole lot to say." "Well, I think he's finished. Having preserved your grandma for posterity."

Keith Causey asked who played the piano. Then he asked Josh if he wanted to be a writer too. Josh, looking at Ann, said probably not; but maybe so. Ann said Josh was interested in science; his genetics project had won a first place in the school science fair. Josh frowned at her warningly. The talk turned to Walker, and to the trips Josh and Irene had taken to California. Josh excused himself; soon the refrigerator door slammed, then footsteps sounded on the basement stairs.

"Irene, I'm really indebted to you for this tape," Keith Causey said. "I don't want to wear you out, though, and I want to take a quick look around town. Maybe Ann will come with me—"

"You're not wearing me out," Irene cried. "Goodness, I don't go to bed this early! Stay as long as you like, you don't have to go!"

With disappointment, almost disapproval, she watched Keith hold Ann's coat. "I'm sure glad you came, you'll never know how much it's meant to me," she said. Keith kissed her cheek and said he might pass through Charlotte some day and would certainly call her. But her dark-circled eyes stayed melancholy, and she did not look at Ann as they said good night.

"Isn't she a sweetheart?" Keith Causey said, in the car. "You must get along pretty well, though I gather it's a grandmotherly visit. But I gather you and Walker get along well enough, as far as that goes."

"Well enough, yes."

"I'm aware that Walker wouldn't be the easiest person in the world to live with. Poor Bernie! I think he still amazes her sometimes. Every so often she and Dora go visit her folks in Tustin; it gives them a little relief from each other. But it's been touch and go a few times, mostly go."

Was this gossip meant as a little present for her? "She's been nice to Josh, that's really all I know." But she heard the excessive dignity in her voice, and relented. "Well, Walker fancies himself a father. He's good at reading them fairy tales. He and Josh get on fine now, of course."

"Before I forget it, did your folks live in this neighborhood? When you and Walker lived at their place?"

She directed him to her parents' old house; he turned into the driveway. Out in the garage apartment the lights were on and the blinds up; a hanging plant filled one window. He stared at it longer than she'd expected.

Downtown, he asked where Walker had lived before they were married. The building had been torn down during urban renewal, but she pointed out the vacant lot. "Well, well. Well, let's have a drink, if you can spare the time." In the bar, he asked if he might phone a couple he knew. "Former students of mine, here in the workshop—really very talented people; you might enjoy meeting them and they'd love to meet you."

The couple he phoned, the Dineens, arrived as rapidly as if they lived around the corner. They were nearly the same medium height and wore blue down jackets and hiking boots. They hurried in and told Keith it was wonderful to see him, and their eyes swept eagerly over her at the same time.

"This was your lucky day," Gary Dineen said. "Finding his mother here too, what luck!"

The Dineens began to tell Keith Causey about Iowa City. It was clear that they wanted to tell funny stories about the writers teaching here this year, but the stories seemed to her somewhat contrived. Keith had his own literary anecdotes; she felt obliged to correct the facts in one of them, and they all gazed at her respectfully. Later Gary and Lynn Dineen asked her polite questions: "How old is your son now?", as if they thought of Josh often. They were taking her in, memorizing her; they'd tell their friends that they'd met Lashley's first wife. Leaving, Gary Dineen made her a little bow and said, "I'm delighted to have met you; and it's a pleasure to meet the real Sara Moxley."

After the Dineens were gone, Keith Causey moved closer, his arm hooked over the back of her chair; he had looked at her a good deal this evening, a look partly admiring, partly the memorizing gaze of the Dineens. "I trust you know who Sara Moxley is?"

"Somebody in one of Walker's books, no doubt. And to save you the trouble: no, I haven't read them all. I did think Maggie, in the second one, was partly me. Sara Moxley! I must be a recurring character. I didn't read the last one because it didn't sound right for Josh, and I didn't want to read it in secret, so to speak. I read the one before that—I had to, Dad thought he was one of the characters in it, and I wanted to be able to tell him he wasn't. But I think he probably was."

"Did he and Walker get along? I can imagine that Walker might not be the easiest son-in-law in the world to have."

"Oh, they got along fine at first. Later on they rubbed each other the wrong way, but at first—it sounds silly, but I thought Dad might be some kind of substitute father; Walker's father's been dead quite a while, and he was gone a lot when Walker was growing up—you know, off getting dried out. They had kind of a rough time for a while, back there with Grandpa Lashley."

"Irene mentioned that. What town was that?"

"Medlin. About like Cheeke. Grandpa sat out on the porch all day and didn't say much, which was lucky for them; he was quarrelsome, he sued somebody over a property line and lost—money he couldn't afford to lose. But Irene and Walker moved in with him, and Irene got a job in the drugstore eventually, and when Walker's dad came back from the cure he got a job putting up signs on billboards. I'm not sure if his cure ever quite took—he went off on a spree a time or two, anyway. Whenever he started drinking Irene would hide the money, and one night they started fighting over it, and Walker got scared and waked Grandpa up. Grandpa would just threaten to put them out of the house whenever there was any trouble. Irene didn't care much for her in-laws, I don't know why she'd gone back there. Do you know the expression 'dirt-eater'? That's what Walker called some of his father's folks. One of them, somebody out in the country, had a liquor still; I've forgotten what kin he was. But Irene worried about Walker, some of the Lashleys had such a bad name; and the old man was a well-known eccentric, in this old run-down house. And Walker did say that when he met somebody new at school he wasn't in a big hurry to take them home with him."

"He'd have been ten or eleven?"

"Around that. Oh, he got along all right, but I wonder if it didn't help make him the way he is, give him that chip he's got on his shoulder. But Irene knew how to program him for success. He was supposed to make the world sit up and take notice! I'd like to know how she did it," she added, with a little laugh. A look that had crossed his face had given her an intuition, that though he was taking it all in and would remember every word, he might, later, smile over her having talked so much. "But I don't know how I got started on all this. But I thought you wanted to know all about him—"

"I do, I do. Go ahead."

"That's about all. Walker's father got a job in Charlotte, driving a laundry truck for Irene's cousin's laundry, and then through some miracle he got a job teaching high school and taught three or four years before he died . . . But it's amazing how well they came through all that, isn't it."

"It is, it is indeed."

She said she ought to be getting on home. Outside there were traces of light, granular snow on the ground, but the wind had whipped it off the sidewalks. On the way back neither of them mentioned Walker.

At her house a light showed in Irene's room. (She would be in bed, reading, probably *Downstairs at the White House;* her clothes, turned wrongside out, would be airing on a chair.) At the front door Ann and Keith Causey said good night. He thanked her; she wished him a good trip.

She waked up the next morning thinking of Walker. Last night, while Keith Causey and the Dineens had talked of books and writers, she'd thought of him: how careful, how informed his judgments were! How often she'd echoed them. And were these generous thoughts a kind of apology for all she'd said last night?

Well, if Walker turned out to be as important as everyone seemed to think, wouldn't everything that had ever happened to him come into the public domain? Surely there were still people in Cheeke and Medlin who remembered the Lashleys, whether Irene and Walker liked what they remembered or not; everything she'd said was true, and what difference did it make anyway, after all this time? Still, her thoughts of Keith Causey were cool. Good thing he wasn't recording *me,* she thought—but then it hadn't been her fault he was there asking questions; if it had been up to her, he'd never have come.

She found Irene eating breakfast at the kitchen table. Her smile came slowly; there was a reserve in her "Good morning." But the coolness was struggling with the wish to talk about last night, and in a moment she said, "Well!—how'd you like Mr. Causey—*Keith*?"

"Oh, I don't know. Not too well, in the end, I guess," Ann said, running some water into a pan. "He could certainly ask the questions, couldn't he?"

"Goodness, if he writes about Walker of course he's going to ask questions!" Irene said, almost indignantly. She came and stood by the stove, as if to put her self firmly in Ann's line of vision, though perhaps it was only in order to hear better. "I liked him fine, I'd have been glad to talk a lot more, you could've finished your work—and I bet I could've told him a lot more he'd have been interested in. Well, I thought you must've started liking him better, you stayed out so late; I had to get up to go to the bathroom, that's the only reason I noticed. And honey, you forgot to tell Josh good-bye and when you'd be back—"

"I know! I certainly should have; but you were here—"

Irene smiled knowingly. "You were in a hurry to get going; Mr. Causey was a good-looking fellow! But don't forget to tell Josh where you're going when I'm not here, and I'd tell him to lock up good."

"Don't worry, I've always been very careful with Josh, careful to a fault! Walker thought so, anyway: he'd put up with any old sitter as long as we got one, but if I couldn't find somebody good I'd stay home. Then he'd sulk; not that it took much to bring that on!"

Irene's big, dark-circled eyes stared at her defiantly. "I'm sorry, I can't help it! I raised him the best way I knew how, just like you're doing!" Her face crumpled as she began to cry. "And I did it alone a lot of the time!" She was talking through her sobs, a moaning sound, rather like the noises of the dumb. "I wish he wasn't the way he is, but I can't help it."

"Oh, Irene, I'm sorry—I'm not *awake*!" She patted Irene's shoulder; she was hoping Josh couldn't hear them upstairs. "But don't worry about Walker!—he's a big success."

Irene blew her nose. "I'm scared he'll break up with *her* sometime . . . I don't like Bernie as much as I did, but still—" She shook her head.

"He won't lack for companionship, believe me." She was thinking that, as Keith Causey had been a reminder of Walker's success, she herself was a reminder of his failures. Had some notion of making amends brought Irene here year after year? She would certainly have chosen for Walker another kind of life; she'd wanted him to do well, she'd wanted his picture to be in the paper, but she would have been very well satisfied with a secure local fame, back home, and an ordinary high-salaried prosperity. Maybe she'd pictured him as a county superintendent of schools, living not far from her—his children, dressed up from Sunday School, coming by for Sunday dinner. And, Irene might have cried out, wouldn't he have been happier? As well off, surely, as he was out in California, with his second family, living a life not unlike those of some of his unhappy characters. And his books had given Irene only a little incidental pleasure. "I skipped some," she'd said, reading one of them, "too many bad things happening." And wouldn't the rest of the world suspect that the bad things came out of Walker's life?

"My neighbor, Ada, says be glad he gets married, so many don't now. And she'll read his books or bust; soon as one comes out, she's got to run down to the library and get her name on the waiting list," Irene said resentfully. "I tell her my copy is too precious to lend." She laughed shortly. "Leila just reads the reviews, but sometimes she'll start talking about what-all he writes about."

"I wouldn't worry about it. Tell them he's *very highly* regarded."

But Irene's lower lip went petulant, as if Ann didn't take her friends seriously. She hadn't forgotten last night, when Ann had taken Keith Causey away. Had it stirred up memories of other departures, of Ann and Walker starting off to Iowa or California? And this morning Ann was uneasy before Irene's resentment: last night she'd told things that were Walker's and Irene's to tell or not, this morning she'd hurt Irene's feelings. "The coffee's done, Irene, don't you want some?"

Upstairs the bathroom door slammed; Josh was up. Josh, on whose account their friendship, such as it was, had endured, or that was what both of them would have said. Probably it was other unfinished business that had held them together, though. Maybe, if it hadn't been for last night and this morning, she might some day soon have settled it up, closed the books on Irene—was that possible?

"I was thinking last night, maybe Josh would like to come down and see *me* next year," Irene said. "It would save me making the trip—"

"Oh, Irene, you have to come, you love Iowa City, you know you like the change, and it does you good! Maybe he'd like to go back with you for a while, but you *have* to come. I'd feel terrible if you didn't." How true that was; truer than ever this morning.

Irene smiled shyly. "Well, I hear our boy up. I can fix his breakfast—I expect you want to get going pretty soon."

"That would be nice; I'd better get moving. Thanks a lot, Irene." Going upstairs to get ready for work she thought, with mingled relief and regret: till death us do part.

[1981]

Grace Schulman

"LET THERE BE TRANSLATORS!"

"And the Lord said, 'Behold, the people is one and they have all one language . . . Go to, let us go down, and there confuse their language, that they may not understand one another's speech."

Genesis xi: 6, 7.

When God confused our languages, he uttered,
in sapphire tones: "Let there be translators!"
And there were conjurors and necromancers
and alchemists, but they did not suffice:
they turned trees into emeralds, pools to seas.

God spoke again: "Let there be carpenters
who fasten edges, caulk the seams, splice timbers."
They were good.
God said: "Blessed the builder
who leaves his tower, turns from bricks and mortar
to marvel at the flames, the smith who fumbles
for prongs, wields andirons and prods live coals,
who stokes the hearths and welds two irons as one."

Praised was the man who wrote his name in other
handwriting, who spoke in other tones,
who, knowing elms, imagined ceiba trees
and cypresses as though they were his own,
finding new music in each limitation.

Holy the one who lost his speech to others,
subdued his pen, resigned his failing sight
to change through fire's change, until he saw
earth's own fire, the radiant rock of words.

[1982]

Stephen Spender

AFTER STEFAN GEORGE— MEIN KIND KAM HEIM

My boy came home
The seabreeze still curves through his hair.
His tread still rocks
Through fears withstood and his young love of faring.

The saltbrine spray
Still flares along the bronze bloom of his cheek.
Fruit quickly ripe
In foreign suns savage with haze and flame.

His gaze is weighted
Already with some secret from me
And softly veiled—
He stepped into our winter out of spring.

So open burst
His budding forth that almost shy I watched
And forbade mine
His mouth that chose another mouth to kiss.

My arm surrounds
Him who unmoved by me towards other worlds
Bloomed and grew—
My one my own endlessly far from me.

[1959]

Jean Stafford

WODEN'S DAY

A Note about "Woden's Day"

"Woden's Day" will apparently stand as Jean Stafford's last story. With her consent I extracted it and "An Influx of Poets," published in The New Yorker *last year, from her unfinished novel,* The Parliament of Women, *on which she had started work in June 1968, when the publishing firm in which I am a partner signed a contract for it. Despite her aphasia, the cruel illness with which she was stricken in her last years, Jean was able to go over both stories with me in the summer of 1978. On rereading the manuscript of her novel, I had realized that these two sections could, with minor emendations, stand alone as stories.*

"My roots remain in the semi-fictitious town of Adams, Colorado," Jean revealed in the preface to her Collected Stories, *and while Adams is not exactly the setting of "Woden's Day" it is in a sense the subject of the story, the destination towards which the Savage family is headed. Cora Savage, Jean's* persona *in her autobiographical fiction and the intended heroine of* The Parliament of Women, *is still a child in "Woden's Day," which is mainly about her parents and grandparents. It records, so to speak, the prehistory of Adams.*

From what she told me of him, I had always hoped that Jean would one day write a novel about her father. While he was still living, she sometimes read parts of his letters to me, and they were extraordinary. One sentence in particular I've never forgotten. It began, "The trouble with Lyndon Johnson and those people in Washington, Jean,—" and she laughed uproariously before completing it—"is that they have not read their Tacitus." As far as I know, there are only two pieces of writing about him. One is the preface to her Collected Stories, *from which we learn that he was a writer of Westerns, one of which was a novel entitled* When Cattle Kingdom Fell. *The other is "Woden's Day," with Jean's unforgettable portrait of the young Savage on the occasion of the acceptance of* his *first story by a magazine.*

—Robert Giroux

The Savages had come from Graymoor, Missouri, to Adams, Colorado, in 1925, when Cora was ten. Both parents had known the town at different times and in different ways: Maud, then Miss McKinnon, upon her graduation from Willowbrook Female Seminary—ten miles from Graymoor, where she boarded but at her father's command went home on Sundays lest she stray beyond the United Presbyterian pale and lie abed on the Sabbath or read Zola's brazen novels—had accepted the position of assistant mistress in a small private school in Adams named, remarkably, Summerlid. "What kind was it?" her children, doubled up with laughter, wanted to know. "A leghorn? A Panama? Was it a sunbonnet, Mama? Did it have a mosquito net on it to keep the horseflies off?" Mrs. Savage, who had taken her year-long academic career seriously, was vexed and wounded and tried to put them down by saying, "I have told you and told you that Mr. Summerlid of Grosse Pointe founded it for unfortunate tubercular children. Now stop fashing me." But the rotten children, especially Randall and Cora, helplessly seized with giggles, ran off howling, "Missy Maud McKinnon pounded fractions into the wallydrag noggins of head chiggers in a lousy limey sailor hat!" They'd one time heard Dan (as they called their father) say this as part of one of his long ridiculing, affectionate litanies. They did not know that it had made their mother cry and, if they had, probably would not have cared. Why Dan and Mama did not run away from each other and quit their endless insults, they could not imagine. (Once when they discussed the matter in a tentative and half-fearful way, they ended up by shrugging their shoulders and saying, "Ishkabibble. One of these sunshiny days we'll run away from them.") Miss McKinnon had loved her experience of being away from home out in the wilds that way, and while she was devoted to her family and her friends and sometimes was homesick enough to cry, it had been so nice to meet new people, to be taken into the Sororsis which had supper meetings at a different house each week (oh, those treats of Mexican chili con carne and of creamed sage-hen!). And riding burros! "We called them 'Rocky Mountain canaries,' you know. What pesky scamps they were! They'd find an appetizing bush and you couldn't budge them till they'd had their fill. We'd whip and kick and scold but it was *no ma'am* as far as they were concerned, and they were so comical about it we nearly fell off laughing. The big its!" She had loved to go on picnics beside waterfalls; they'd sing and gather wildflowers and sometimes pretend they were oreads and go prancing and weaving through the lodgepole pines. During the Easter holiday she had gone to Manitou Springs with some other young ladies from Summerlid and they had had a real lark, but, to tell the truth, they had found the mineral waters disagreeable beyond words: "Pew!" said Mama and held her nose.

Some years before Dan Savage's future wife had wended her slow way west on the Denver & Rio Grande with her trunk and her foulard parasol and her travelling tailormaid of grey De'Beige cloth, Dan had taken it into his quixotic head to go prospecting for gold in the Rockies. Throughout the summer of 1892, he had panned the rivers from the lower canyons to the tundra of the Wilson range and had found long tons of pyrites and his placer pan had brimmed with fool's gold. No, he hadn't made his fortune, but he had had a larruping good time; that had been far and away a summer better than all summers before when he and his older brother, Uncle Jonathan—a year ahead of him at college—had had to drive their father's herd up from the Panhandle to Dodge City through dust storms so bad that when you took a drink of water you had a mouthful of mud. He had graduated from Amity College that spring, *summa cum laude,* and this holiday had been his reward. Mind you, if he had wanted to go to sea or go to New York City to explore the music halls and free-lunch saloons and Turkish baths, his father wouldn't have put up a red cent for a fandango such as that; but while he was a cattle man and a crop man, he had an understanding of gold-fever and he staked his son to fare on the cars to Denver, the price of a horse to ride and a horse to pack with gear and grub. Dan had a companion, a college classmate, Thad McPherson, a fellow so brilliant at Hebrew that to the other students, all Methodist or Presbyterian, he was known as The Jew, and then, because he was so often lost in thought that, strolling by himself, he sometimes got lost in the woods by the river and missed classes and examinations, he came to be called The Wandering Jew. And to top it all off, he played a Jew's harp and played it like a professional, sometimes as rowdy-dowdy as a showboat skalawag, sometimes as sweet as a Muse. He was a pretty solemn man, and silent. Yet he had been a good friend to have along that summer to speculate on matters of geology, to wonder ("By the Lord Harry!") at the beaver's practicality and genius, to come, amazed, upon a solid acre of glacier lilies, to hack away with pick-axes (and find pyrites shining like pure gold), to pan in the ice-cold amber streams and, along with the fool's gold, get a mess of caddis worms. Often of an evening when they were full of trout, fresh-caught, and fried mush with bacon gravy, they would talk well past moonlight beside their camp fire about what they had learned at Amity of history and the literatures of ancient languages: they had learned little else—some mathematics, some chemistry and physics, some biology. Thad had a leaning toward The Almighty but Dan was an up-to-the-minute Darwinian and they had debated on this ticklish subject until the moon went pale, "I'd try my level best to rile him, but old Thad was as mild as mother's milk. *His* theology had no more brimstone in it than a daisy. I think that old Wandering Jew was a B.C. pagan, believed in the wee people, believed in Santy Claus." About once every two years, Dan got a letter from him, from a different state each time, for he had turned into a salesman for the Watkins Company that sold spices and condiments and soap and such like from door to door. One time he had turned up in Adams, a tall, gaunt awkward man, as red and yellow as a summer sunset. Mama saw his sample case and said, as she always said to peddlers, that the lady of the house was not at home; but he only asked, gently, to see Dan. The two of them with Oddfellow, the dog, a border collie, went off towards the mountains and Dan didn't come home until long after dark. "I declare," Mama was later and often to say to each child individually and in confidence as if she had never uttered this dread fear before, "that man looked like a *ghost* to me! I don't care about that carrot-top or that red face of his, he *felt* like a ghost, and when he went off with your father that way, I thought the pair of them would vanish. Just vanish."

The summer in Adams had been Dan's Wanderjahr, her nine months there at Summerlid had been Mama's debutante season, and when their life in Graymoor came crashing down upon them in disgrace, they picked this distant hiding place. Cora's last memory of Graymoor was of going to say goodbye to Albert and Heinie, the children of the chicken farmer next door. It was in the morning and Mrs. Himmel was busy with the wash so there was no Kinder Kaffeeklatsch (in the morning, of course, it would have been called Zweites Frühstück, which the Savage children pronounced "Fruit-stick"), but the little boys had taken them into the parlor and ritualistically had wound up the seven music boxes and when the nightingale, *Der Liebling Vogel,* sang to her for the very last time, huge golden globes of tears blinded Cora, but she managed not to let them burst and spill. They all shook hands then and, unsmiling, contrapuntally, the Scotch-Irish children said, "Auf Wiedersehen," and the German children said, "Ta-ta. See you in church."

* * *

Grandfather Brian Savage had died of dengue fever in Coffeyville, Kansas, when he and his youngest daughter were almost within hailing distance of home after having gone half way around the world to visit kinsmen in Australia. Aunt Caroline, her father's darling, his blooming emerald-eyed and raven-locked colleen, had been as quirky and as saucy as he and when she was seventeen the two of them took ship at San Francisco to go have a look at kangaroos and stranger, albeit technically human, beasts in the outback. And on the very day that they set sail for that outlandish continent, Granny and Aunt Elizabeth who was twenty, as spirited as the other two but brainier and more domesticated, embarked at New Orleans for a stylish and conventional tour of London and Paris, Vienna and Rome. They all went off at the end of June, the same June that Dan had gone to Colorado.

He would push his hat back, take off his glasses, close his eyes and, remembering, say, "Thad and I would have been about at Loveland when the tugs were toting their ships out to the bounding main, one east, one west; Loveland or a short piece beyond. We'd paid handsomely for those horses in Denver and we treated them like little Lords and Ladies Fauntleroy, not working them hard, keeping them in fettle. Besides, we weren't in any hurry and the weather was fine to mosey through." Then he would laugh his infernal laugh. "I'd lie there under the stars and think about Brother Jonathan with his mouth full of dust and his eyes full of the sweat of his brow, punching cows in Paris, Texas, while our sweet Sister Lizzie was buying kid gloves in Paris, France." But Jonathan had had his summer off the year before when he had gone to Crete to be Sir Arthur Evans' third water-boy's sixth water-boy. And then, almost to himself, with contempt, with pity, with disappointment, Dan mused, "If he wanted to be an archaeologist, why didn't he turn in and be one? Look at him now, tied to the Tammany lion's tail with all the rest of the rag-tag-bobtail tinhorns of New York City." Uncle Jonathan was a lawyer and Dan, despising the profession, looked on his success and his wealth as ill-got; moreover, Jonathan had political ambitions and Dan, schooled by his father and mother, had looked on politicians as scum.

The travellers had been gone for half a year. In the autumn, Uncle Jonathan had entered his second year of law school at the University of Missouri and Dan Savage was left alone in Kavanagh to study over what he wanted to do with the rest of his life. Should he be a scholar? Teach Greek at some high-falutin Eastern college? He read Herodotus, Thucydides, he read Xenophon and Arrian, Hesiod and Homer, Sophocles and Aeschylus. But then, languid in a hammock on an amber day, he'd be seduced by Vergil and he would meditate on vineyards and bees and growing melons under glass in a pastoral, green land like this thrice-blessed Missouri. He'd had his fill of Longhorn beeves and the crude company of drovers.

He had enjoyed being the boss of the Kavanagh house, being alone. Once in a while, he would invite Thad or some other of his Amity classmates to come and visit for a while and his mother's cook, accustomed to feeding a flock—for when the elder Savages were in residence they and their daughters had guests to dinner four or five times each week—was pleased to serve her Louisiana French specialities to these easy-going young men and to be praised by them. The trouble was that most of them weren't easy-going; they had found jobs and some of them had already married, or, like Jonathan, they had gone on to universities to prepare themselves for medicine or the law. "What's the hurry, boys?" he'd say to them. But their fathers were not rich as Brian Savage's was and their expectations, if there were any, were far in the future. For a few days they would ride and shoot, revel at table, play billiards after dinner ("Most of the poor coots had never seen a billiard table in a private house and, my! how they would carry on") and act the role of carefree young squires but then they would itch to be back in their harnesses: "For what? For *gain*! Aye, God, they were no better than my father's hands, shackled to the land. Pawns in the hands of nature. I recollect the way those bozos used to loaf around the kitchen stove before the sun was up and before the *women* were up to make their breakfast, just purely and simply waiting in their dumb animal way for the sunrise. Like apes. They'd been raised on the precept that a man must get up when the Lord gets up, and out of their abounding self-conceit, they reckoned to do the Lord one better, but it never got them anywhere. And then they took their pay and spent it all on Jamaica rum and the doxies who just *happened* to be ambling by the horse-troughs in town when they were watering their nags before they themselves went into the saloons to wallow. Yes sir, with the exception of Thad, that moon-struck old Wandering Jew, my college classmates were not different by a whit from Pa's help. The early bird catches the worm and it don't matter if the worm sticks in his craw."

One time Randall said to his father, "Sir, why do you get up before the sun?" and Dan replied, "I emulate Frederick the Great." His tone was final; the reminiscence and the metaphor were finished; he was through talking. Randall and Cora had looked up Frederick the Great in the Encyclopedia Britannica, but they could find no mention of his being an early riser. Just as on another occasion, when Dan had bragged for the seven hundred and nineteenth time that his pulse rate was 59, the same as Napoleon's, they had tried and failed to check this arresting detail. If they had persevered in their research and tried to pin Dan down, they would have got nowhere. Instead, they would have got rods and acres, *miles*, of the Seven Year's War and the French Revolution; once Dan started he would never stop. He knew too much for a child, for anybody, to bear.

It was along about Thanksgiving time when Dan had got his sister Caroline's telegram from Coffeyville, saying that his father was gravely ill. The ship bringing them back from Australia had docked at Galveston, and they had made their way up through Texas and Oklahoma, changing trains a dozen times and travelling often by stage from one depot town to the next. They had been headed for Wichita, whence they could get a through train to St. Louis, when the fever had laid the old man so low that they could not go on another mile. He was out of his head for a week before he died and he died in the evening of the day Dan got to his bedside in the one antigodlin hotel—the floors were so slanty that when a man walked through a door he thought he might pitch right through the window opposite. It was a hell of a note to meet your maker in that one-horse burg on the plains where the wind whipped along steady at a mile a minute and your handkerchief froze to your nose if you had to blow it. The irony, the almighty irony, of perishing of tropical breakbone fever in November in Coffeyville, Kansas! "Your mother's father's Father which art in Heaven every so often takes it into his cerebellum to play a practical joke and when he does, lo and behold and *mirabile dictu,* he does it up to a fare-thee-well. No holds barred when he wants to pull off a real dandy."

Granny Savage and Aunt Lizzie got to Kavanagh two days after Dan and Aunt Caroline came back with the coffin from Coffeyville. (Cora had made up a shameful rhyme, so shameful she never even told it to Randall: "When they brought the coffin from Coffeyville/I poured me coffee and drank my fill.") And so, instead of a grand family reunion with tales to tell of Europe's wonders and the marvels of the Antipodes, there was a funeral. "My mother and I mourned the man," said Dan. "The others . . ." he shooed off his sisters and his brothers with the back of his hand. Grandfather Savage's will was no surprise to Dan, his second son and second child: the burden of the estate was left to the widow and the rest was divided equally among the four children, but while Jonathan, Caroline and Elizabeth would receive their share in trust, Dan was given his in capital since he, according to the flowery testament, was the only one of the heirs who would know how to manage his money. The Texas holdings and the Missouri holdings (which Brian Savage had greatly extended after the War between the States by buying up bounty grants for next to nothing from veterans who wanted to join the westward push) and a ninety-thousand-acre tract in Arizona, not stocked or farmed but bought for speculation, were also parcelled out equally.

Dan, in those months alone in Kavanagh, pondering the route he wished to take, had concluded finally against school-mastering; he would be Vergil rather than Aristotle and when he was not upon his rural rides, overseeing his flocks and grain, his apiary and his vineyards, he would write: not idylls, not epic poetry but fiction and meditative essays. In time he would take a wife because he wanted sons, sons to teach, thereby combining all his talents, agrarian, literary, academic. But he was in no hurry.

Jonathan quit Missouri for New York City as soon as he had his law degree; Caroline went back to Australia to marry a sheep-rancher she had fallen in love with when her father had taken her to see the wallabies and kangaroos and her Irish uncles and cousins. You may be sure that one of the early kings of cattledom, Brian Savage, mightily shifted in his grave when this mésalliance took place. He couldn't have known what had been taking place behind his back: else he would have outwitted the Lord and risen from his bed in Coffeyville at least until he'd seen his darling girl-child wedded to a decent man. Sheep! And Lizzie, sap-sweet, sap-silly Lizzie took up with a sap-*sucker* she met during Mardi Gras in New Orleans and with him went off to California to grow oranges. With her money. He was a Lothario was Lizzie's pretty Cajun and after a year and a baby, he vanished, sank plumb out of sight. She married again and married this time sensibly: Uncle Frank Boatright was an engineer, a bridge-builder, a dull, good man and Lizzie had two more children by him. After the birth of the second, Cora's Cousin Lucian, poor headlong Lizzie, feeling her oats, was out riding by herself in wild country beyond the orange grove when her horse was spooked to frenzy by a sidewinder and threw her, breaking her leg so intricately and mangling it so grievously that it had to be amputated just above her knee. ("You recollect that your Dan was thrown from a horse when he was a chap," said Dan and reached for his blackthorn walking stick to illustrate. Usually the stick was not in the room and he would go to look for it; by the time he had come back, his audience had dispersed. They knew what came afterward: the children's mother's father's Lord had, for once in His life, been just–well, hardly just, but not as ornery as usual—it had been a cruelty to separate a woman from her leg but it would have been a sin crying to Heaven for vengeance if the victim had been a man.)

Dan stayed on in Missouri, lord of the manor, master of the hounds and the hinds, his mother's manager and playmate, her host when she was hostess. And, faithful to his promise to himself, he was a writer. There was a photograph of him sitting at his writing table beside an open and uncurtained window: some flowering tree is in bloom just outside and through its white, enclouded branches, the sun lies full upon a huge dictionary held closed by flanges on a stand; he has only to turn a little to the right to open the book which will lie flat, cleverly supported by the flexible brackets as he looks up a word. The table is square and its narrow aprons are carved with interlocking garlands and they are edged with egg-and-dart. The table is strewn with papers, on one of which Dan is writing with a long-stemmed pen; his other hand is relaxed, the fingers (how filled with ease they seem!) touching another sheet. He is in profile and because his sharply aquiline nose is in shadow, his face looks delicate and young. How young, unlined, how cleanly his high forehead reaches up to meet the dense curls of his dark hair. He has taken off his collar—you can see it lying on top of the bookcase just behind him—and the sleeves of his shirt look uncommonly full, they look as full as bishop sleeves, and the starched cuffs are closed with oval links; his galluses are wide. In the foreground, on the floor or perhaps on some low stool, there is a jardinière of branches bearing flowers. It is a portrait of youth in the youth of a year. You read his mortal vulnerability in his lowered eyes (he does not yet wear thick glasses) and in his bent, clean-shaven neck.

The photograph had been taken to commemorate the sale of his first short story to *Century* magazine and Granny Savage, who prided herself on her lack of pride, had had a man come over from Jefferson City to take it. Ostensibly he was there to photograph the new outbuildings, the new milkhouse and the new silo. At the same time, she and Dan had posed in the lounge where they sat playing war with their lead soldiers, smiling, both of them, Granny's white hair piled up in a pompadour with a coquettish bow above one ear. And there was another picture of them on their horses, Dan on his father's favorite, a strawberry roan named Jack, and Granny on her much smaller Betsy Ross: Dan wore a hard hat and an ascot and a jacket belted across the back, and Granny, in a broad-brimmed hat with an ostrich feather curling down against her cheek, wore a divided skirt and a pin-tucked shirtwaist beneath her tailored jacket with a perky peplum.

None of the children ever knew certainly how this loving son and mother had come to their violent and unconditional parting. It was not until they were grown that Cora and Randall understood how weak a man their father was for all his tempests and his brutality; and, seeing that, saw to their incredulity how strong their mother was, that often weepy, often quaking goose. They had been born in Graymoor, they deduced, in the shadow of the McKinnon house, rather than in Kavanagh near Granny Savage because Grandfather McKinnon had so willed. But why? They were only seven miles apart and if Mama had been dead set on being an obedient Sabbitarian daughter and bringing up her children in her own image, why could they not have made the weekly trip by buggy or, a year or so later by auto, to hear The Word and learn the topography of Hell? Had the McKinnon clan feared the snows of winter or summer thunderstorms? But, that aside, why had Dan knuckled under?

Kavanagh was not a town; it was a place, having two blocks of buildings that housed the barest essentials: a bank, a feed store, a general store for buttons and baking powder, the sheriff's office behind which was the jail and above which the doctor and the lawyer practiced (the doctor was also the dentist, and the lawyer was also the Justice of the Peace and the Notary Public and every second election or so, the Mayor), the saloon and over that the hotel; the post-office and the telegraph office were combined and so were the livery and the undertaking parlor. There was a single church, Methodist, and beside it stood the Manse. There was a barber chair in the pool-hall and the blacksmith and his sons were also the carpenters, the chimney-sweeps, the veterinarians and the well-diggers. On Saturday nights, the one-room schoolhouse was the grange hall. From this small, trim and modest hub narrow roads radiated out to a baker's dozen or so of large, rich homesteads like the Savage's.

But Graymoor was a town with a Main Street a quarter of a mile long and dozens of other streets named Front Street, Elm, Maple, Miller's Lane, Plainview, Bluff, First, Second, Third and (why on earth?) Lausanne. The McKinnons lived solitary on a hill that rose up from Aberdeen Avenue, and while the Savages were out of town a way so that their address was RFD, their road was known as The High Street. Dan, used to thinking of land in terms of miles, had a mere ten acres. And these adjoining a poultry farm run by a limberger who, never seeing the ring-tailed farce of it, had named one of his kids Heinie!

Graymoor was on the railroad, on a spur of the Missouri Pacific and Santa Fe, and at four o'clock each Monday morning, Grandfather McKinnon swung aboard and from then until late Friday evening he was a conductor, punching tickets and calling "All aboard!" from St. Louis to Los Angeles and back again. By his wife and his sister and his daughters and, until they learned the truth, his grandchildren, he was known as being "in railroads." At one time, thrilled, Cora thought he was the locomotive engineer; later, even more infatuated, she thought he travelled in a private car similar to Theodore Roosevelt's of which she had seen photographs in an old copy of the *National Geographic.*

Despite the fact that they no longer shared the same roof and nightly dined together, the devotion between Dan and Granny did not falter. And then, when Cora was nine years old, they quarreled and quarreled for keeps. Dan had gone to Jefferson City and had stayed there for two nights and when he got back to Graymoor, he came home in the jitney; this in itself had been unusual, for after a visit to the stock exchange, he liked to walk home in his important city clothes, his gray fur fedora at a rakish angle but maintaining its dignity the while, carrying his blackthorn in his suede-gloved hand, smoking a cigar. But on this day, he was in such a tearing rush that he got out of the snorting jitney and straight into the Franklin. Cora and Randall were playing mumblety-peg under the black walnut tree and they heard him call out, "To Kavanagh!" in answer, they supposed, to their mother who must have seen him from the kitchen door. It had been some time in the early spring, for Cora remembered that grape-hyacinths had come up in the lawn.

Afterward, they began to be poor. And never again, not once, did they see Granny Savage, although at Christmastime she always sent them presents, clothes, usually, from Marshall Field's, so grand they made the rest of their duds look like something the cat had dragged in. Their poorness showed itself gradually, so gradually, indeed, that they misconstrued it for something else: when their older sisters, Abigail and Evangeline, had to give up their fancy-dancing class, they thought Dan was only being cranky. For their friends, who were in their second year of ballet and were beginning round-dancing with boys, they invented a yarn that eventually they believed: they said they had no time for they were learning French because they were going to be sent to boarding school in Paris. (Who in all of Graymoor could say more than "Parlez-vous"?) Dan's bilious moods came oftener, his "spells" were terrifying: one time he went into Hubbard's Dry, where both Aunt Jane and Aunt Amy clerked, and inveighed against his father-in-law with such blood-curdling invective, such heart-splitting blasphemy that Mr. Hubbard himself ushered him out of the store like a hobo. And he looked a hobo: barefoot, his long underdrawers showing beneath his unlaced cavalry britches; his hair was as long as William Jennings Bryan's and he hadn't shaved in a week; tobacco juice oozed down his chin from the quid he held in his cheek. Mr. Hubbard sent the mortified McKinnon twin sisters home for the rest of the day, and they sent word to Mama by their hired girl to come right over. The town was appalled and off its head with delight; the school-children imitated Dan's limp and spat imaginary tobacco juice at the Savages' feet and made up tirades with nonsense words to scream at them until Abigail, with mysterious and quietly theatrical power, one day at recess stood on the top step of the stairs leading to the main door and commanded silence. "My father is a genius," she said. "My father is poetically licensed by President Wilson to do anything he likes. Hark to my words and from now on cease and desist this persiflage." It worked, as everything always worked for her when she let out those wondrous words and phrases, as harmless as fireflies but seeming, to her cowed audience, like red-hot buckshot. She must have been as shamed as the others but though she might be put on the rack or pinioned to the Catherine wheel, she was Dan's unflinching martyr.

When he was himself—that other self, the reader of Mommsen and Shakespeare and of Victor Hugo, the writer, the kindly spouse and papa—he would be barbered and shaved; he would whistle arias from *Madame Butterfly* and dance his little jig in front of Mama, sportively untie her apron strings and with it pretend to be a toreador and he would carol, "There's always the land, me bonny! There's always the star in the Lone Star State! The amber waves of grain wave o'er the Show-Me! And my ship, she is a-comin' in, lass o' the braes."

The children could not make head or tail of this impromptu spiel. Later on, they would learn that on those two days in Jefferson City, he had been wiped clean of all his capital and had, as well, made ducks and drakes of Granny's. Granny did not feel the pinch—the money he had hurled to the four winds had been her own, and Grandfather Savage's trust fund allowed her to go on being nearly as rich as she had always been. And he was far from destitute himself because he still shared the revenue from the productive Texas cattle ranches and the Missouri farms scattered all over the state. It was Granny's disgust at Dan's reckless, know-it-all prodigality that had made her send him packing. And there was something else: Granny, that smart, witty, well-read, sure-footed little woman had fallen hook, line and sinker for Mary Baker Eddy, led down the garden path by her daughter Lizzie who, in southern California, was prey to all diseases of the mind. And Granny, indignant over the encroachments of age (her hearing in one ear was much diminished, she had several times felt dizzy when she dismounted Betsy Ross after riding in the sun) was easily persuaded that she could handle her flesh with her mind. In the beginning, she had been skeptical when in the copy of *Science and Health* that Aunt Lizzie had sent her, she had read among the testimonials printed at the back the unequivocal claim of a man that while chopping wood, he had swung his hatchet too high and had deeply gashed his temple, an injury that would most certainly have been fatal had he not immediately requested his wife to read to him from Mrs. Eddy. Within half an hour the Mortal Error was corrected, and where the wound and rushing blood had been there was nothing but a white painless swelling. But while she knew this to be bosh and while some of Mrs. Eddy's God-talk affronted her, she was converted and believed that she could heal her servants and her livestock *in absentia.*

Sometimes, at winter dusk before the open fire in the living room, Dan, reflective as he peeled an apple with his Bowie ("I declare to goodness you're going to cut your fingers off with that desperado weapon!" cried Mama. "For land's sake, use your *pen*knife!" Dan went right on and finally let the whole unbroken dark red spiral skin fall into the kindling hod), would say to whoever was within earshot—Cora was sure that if there were no one in the room, he would address the stuffed golden pheasant on the mantel—"I mourned to see my Ma go daft. I lamented the degeneration of that fine intellect. It riddled her like ergot through a stand of oats. You see there yonder that fair crop shimmering? Now close your eyes and look again and what do you see? Black blight."

Then he would throw his naked apple into the fire and listen to its juices hiss. "But for all of that, it was a joke. A joke! A high larruping opera comique and not unlike the one the Great Lord put on for Job." His laughter strangled him; his eyes screwed up like a bawling baby's and the veins on his forehead swelled and pulsed, a dreadful blue.

Mama no longer had her chafing-dish suppers. Nobody came to call except the aunts. Now and then Aunt Rowena came with the first cousins, Fannie, Faith and Florence, with whom the Savages were instructed to play although the mothers knew that their children hated one another and even such a peaceable game as Statues could end in a nosebleed or a broken collar bone. Florence, the oldest and the biggest, had once clapped a pail on Evangeline's head, jamming it down so hard that it wouldn't come off and Dan had had to cut it with his tin-shears; there wasn't even enough room in there for Evangeline to scream but she hopped around like somebody with St. Vitus dance while Dan crooned softly to her, "Whoa, there, girl. Hold on there, girl. Your old Dan ain't going to cut your ear off." This reassurance sent her hurtling blindly into a cherry tree which she hugged for dear life and while she was thus occupied, Dan got the bucket off.

"It was all her fault," said Florence. "She double-dared me to."

"I never!" sobbed Evangeline, holding her ears. The tin-shears had cut clean through one of her pigtails and about an inch of it was gone. Abigail picked it up from the grass, its blue bow still tightly tied.

"You lie, Florence Sinclair," she said in her coldest, her most authoritative voice. "You lie like a rug. The Savages hate the Sinclairs and will forever and a day. Avaunt, you three witches! Graymalkin calls!" Evangeline was calmed. The Sinclair sisters gingerly backed away. But Dan broke the spell by clapping his hands and crying out, "Bravissima! It'll soon be time for your first buskins, Mamsell Bernhardt!"

Wholly baffled, the three sisters ran to the house. After that, when Aunt Rowena came, the children were put into the dining room to play Twenty Questions or I Spy, and the door to the small parlor was left open so that the mothers could hear if a ruckus broke out. It never did, for the seven children were as quiet as mice, trying to hear what the ladies were saying.

* * *

This life in Graymoor might have gone on for years and years, gone on until the last embattled tribesman was six feet under, if Grandfather McKinnon had not died. Or, as for some months afterward, Grandmother, Great Aunt Flora, Aunt Rowena and Mama were to say, been *murdered* by Jane and Amy, always known as "the girls." They ran away from home.

Who did they know in St. Louis high society to get them invitations to the Veiled Prophet's Ball? There were no kinsmen in St. Louis, no collaterals. A drummer come to Hubbard's Dry to sell a bill of goods and, by the way, to vamp those pretty twins with their mournful violet eyes and their perfect laughing lips? Of course not: drummers were not connected to high echelons. The store was closed on Wednesday afternoons as was every other place of business, a practice carried over from New England whence the founding fathers had come. One Wednesday, Jane telephoned home a little after eleven and there was no answer; Grandma and Great Aunt Flora were outside making sure that the men were transplanting that big old box elder to just the place they wanted it, and the hired girl was making soap and was at that tricky point of putting in the lye. But Central (Jessie Lovelady; after five o'clock Belle Bruce came on) said she'd keep on ringing and give the message which was, "Tell her we're going to have ourselves a picnic and won't be home for dinner." Well, Grandma was put out when Jessie Lovelady finally reached her, but she got over her pet—it *was* an awfully bonny autumn day, smelling of nuts. She always liked to have a little treat for dinner on the girls' day off and that day she had planned banana fritters, but never mind, she'd have them for supper instead. It didn't worry her until twilight came and they didn't come home and night came and they didn't come home. About nine o'clock she called Mama and Mama said she knew in her bones that something was *very* rotten in the state of Denmark. If they'd been abducted, they couldn't have telephoned. The picnic sounded to her like a fish-story, because from the year one the girls had been hemstitching linens and painting Haviland for their hope-chests on their free afternoons. (They couldn't let Grandfather know what they were doing so they couldn't sew their dreams on Saturday night. On Saturday night they hemmed didies for the Heathen Chinee.) Mama told Grandma that she'd better call the police and she did. She got the Marshal himself, Mr. Doff, who told her to look in their rooms and see if they had taken any clothes and then to call him back. I say! Their closets and their bureau drawers were as clean as a whistle! She looked in the attic and gone was the trunk Mama had taken to Colorado when she went to teach at Summerlid! Gone were both hat-boxes! And the only umbrellas left in the umbrella stand were Mama's and Aunt Flora's, and the spare one in case it rained as an afternoon caller was saying goodbye. As soon as Marshal Doff heard this, he called Frank Ferguson, the jitney driver. Frank Ferguson knew every bit of everybody's business because he eavesdropped while he drove his high maroon Hupmobile and at the same time spied on pedestrians: if you wanted to know who had stopped using the jakes and moved indoors, ask Frank Ferguson and he would tell you that he had seen Mrs. Cobbett come out of Hubbard's on

Tuesday at 11:22 a.m. carrying a sack that unmistakably contained a roll of bathroom paper.

Frank was asleep but he snapped to attention when the police chief called and he was overjoyed to say that why, yes, he had taken the McKinnon twins to the depot for the 1:45 inter-urban to Jeff City. Were they carrying any baggage? No, they weren't but one week ago that day, they had come up to him when he was parked in front of the P. O. and had asked him to come to their house at 7 p.m. to take a trunk and two hat-boxes and check them through to St. Louis. They gave him their tickets and he returned them the next day at Hubbard's Dry. All they had with them today was just their pocketbooks and umbrellas and a book apiece. They didn't do much talking; mainly they giggled, but they said enough to let him understand that they were going to the Veiled Prophet's Ball: he had wondered at the time, pardon him please, how they had managed to get their father's permission to go. Last Wednesday night at seven. The pieces were beginning to fit together. That was why those perfidious minxes, looking as if butter would not melt in their mouths, had said they were so absolutely, posi*tive*ly fagged out from unpacking a shipment of winter coats at the store that morning that they could *not,* absolutely, posi*tive*ly could *not* go to Prayer Meeting. Grandma and Aunt Flora and the girls always had supper with the Widow Bird on Wednesday night at her house (she came to them for "high tea" after Christian Endeavor on Saturday afternoon) at five o'clock and this gave them ample time to be leisurely at table and do the washing up and even crochet for a little while until they went to the church just across the road on the dot of seven. It was then that Frank Ferguson had come to pick up their traps. How did he manage that big trunk all by himself? He didn't. Chub Jackson, Judge McIntyre's yard man and strong as an ox, had brought it down the steep brick steps cut into the lawn and he and it and the hat-boxes and the girls were rowed up there right on Aberdeen Avenue. Chub was ready with a couple of ropes and he strapped the trunk on the running board and then rode in the back seat down to the depot and took it off and put it on the St. Louis through baggage wagon. One of the twins, it might have been Jane, it might have been Amy, you couldn't tell them apart, had given him what Frank was pretty certain was four bits. (And he himself only charged two bits for the run. Life is like that.)

Mama and Grandma and Great Aunt Flora were terrified out

of their wits. Aunt Rowena, basically a carnal woman, shrugged her shoulders and laughing meanly said, "I hope they get themselves some Good-time Charleys. I could put one to use myself." She despised Uncle Hugh who was despicable. And while she was mortified to be Dan's in-law (Catch Hugh Sinclair chewing: Never!), in her heart of hearts she admired his eccentricity. This was a fact known to the children because after school one day, Randall was lying under the bandstand in the Lincoln Park, thinking. All of a sudden he heard Aunt Rowena's voice coming, he thought, from a ringside bench on the northeast side. "My brother-in-law, you know who he is, Dan Savage?" she said to someone. "The writer. He got word yesterday that his novel has been accepted by Dodge and Company, the publishing concern in New York City." Her companion said, "Sakes! My, Maud must be proud." "She is," said Aunt Rowena. And she was. Only, at that time, the jealous sister's statement was not true because her sister had not told *her* the truth. The only one in Graymoor who knew the truth was Dan.

In those dreadful days (The Ordeal as it came to be known) between the twins' disappearance and Grandfather McKinnon's return for the Sabbath bonfire, so much simmered under so many kettle-lids that everybody walked on tippy-toe, including Dan, The Great.

That Sunday, the diminished McKinnon congregation sat in Grandfather's parlor, erect of spine and apparently alert, although a look of languid disease showed forth now and again in all the captives. It seemed to Cora that Grandfather had never read with so much righteous rage as he did this afternoon: his voice rocked the house, its walls were going to tumble down like Jericho. How had Grandma broken the news to him? Poor little tea-cosy of a woman, she must have been scared silly. The clock in the hall chimed four and, at the last sonorous boom, something happened.

Cora and Abigail were sitting side by side on an uncushioned ottoman. Cora was demented with discipline, distempered with swallowed screams and swallowed yawns. Silently she kicked her Mary Janes together; woefully, in the absence of anything else to do, she crossed her eyes. Suddenly, and she did not know why, she turned rogue and tried to tickle Abigail who wrenched away in surprise, almost toppling off the slippery seat. Although they were to one side of Grandfather's ken, he saw the quiet scuffle out of the corner of his eye and he wheeled on them like Wrath.

"Wantons!" and he would have impaled them on his pointing finger if they had not been across the room from him. "Is a man to be made a gowk of in his own castle by the blethering of females?"

Blethering! They had not made a sound.

Abigail hotly declared that Cora was solely to blame for this outrageous impudence, this dangerous breach of decorum on the Good Lord's day. But Grandfather ordered her to be silent and he gave a familiar lecture on the wages of sin, the high price of defiance of authority, the destiny of mockers who misconducted themselves on Sunday. He raved of the cauldrons and the griddles. Weeping, his sister, Great Aunt Flora, hysterically cried, "Don't faunch yourself into a lather! Duncan! Duncan!" and he gored her with a look.

By no means finished with his diatribe, he said, "Hark!" and flicking *The Book of Martyrs* to, he opened the Old Testament to Isaiah and read of the Fall of Babylon. Red in the face with rectitude, veins standing out, dark and vermicular in his neck and on his forehead, as Dan's did when he sneered, he read:

"Therefore the Lord will smite with a scab the crown of the head of the daughters of Zion, and the Lord will discover their secret parts. In that day the Lord will take away the bravery of their tinkling ornaments about their feet, and their cauls, and their round tires like the moon, the chains and the bracelets, and the mufflers, the bonnets and the ornaments of the legs, and the headbands, and the tablets, and the earrings, the rings, and nose jewels, the changeable suits of apparel and the mantles, and the wimples, and the crisping pins, the glasses, the fine linen, and the hoods and the veils. And it shall come to pass that instead of sweet smell, there shall be stink; and instead of a girdle, a tent; and instead of well-set hair, baldness; and instead of a stomacher, a girding of sackcloth; and burning instead of beauty. Thy men . . ."

It was probably the violent, accusing voice (which was really directed at his twins) more than the words that made Cora finally cry out with terror and she ran to hide her face in Mama's lap. She knelt there shuddering and hoarsely babbling, "I don't want to be bald! I don't! I don't!"

Her uproar was contagious and all the other Savage children and the Sinclairs, in their different ways, turned mutinous.

Abigail cried, "It isn't fair, Grandfather! It was all Cora's fault!"

Evangeline giggled and squeaked, "Oracay illway avehay otay

earway anay igway!" and Faith Sinclair, a precocious little snit, said, "Cora Savage is the Whore of Babylon."

"Grandfather McKinnon," said Randall solemnly, standing up as if he were in school, "is it true that we are descended from monkeys?"

"Children, children, that's enough!" said Grandma, shaking her head and clapping for order.

"Monkeys!" little Fannie Sinclair was fascinated. "How come, Randy? How come *monkeys*?"

The pandemonium lasted only a minute or two and then the children, realizing what they had done—had headed for the seething pits and locked themselves on the wrong side of the pearly gates—froze in their attitudes. But brief as the revolution had been, it had had a remarkable effect on their grandfather. He seemed to shrivel and his skin was as gray as the trunk of a tree. He pounded his craggy fists on the table. "What is the meaning of this sacrilege and insubordination?" he demanded, but he was so choked with passion that his voice lost its body and it came out thick and pallid. "Absconding and tricks and pranks and now *evolution*!"

Gasping for breath, coughing, alarmingly red again, he railed like a stark staring crazy man, called them all backsliders, apostates, iconoclasts, the gall and wormwood of his life. His storm was long but his thunder was a squawk and this thunderbolts were duds. He had lost his women and he had lost his only lad.

Holy cow! His face was bleeding. A fast red flood was coming from his beak; bewildered, he did nothing about it. His arms, too long for his coatsleeves so that his big wrists showed below the cuffs, hung slack at his sides and he relaxed his hands so that they were no longer fists. Everyone watched, astonished, as that red eruption continued to ride down his face. An age went by.

Then Grandma, galvanized at last, went to him, gently pushed him back into his chair and tried to stanch the nosebleed with a foolish little handkerchief.

"Send away the bairns," she said. "Maud, get me some ice." But Mama did not move. No one moved. They sat motionless, witless with astonishment and with a strange, inadmissable embarrassment; the crumbling of the tyrant made them shy.

Grandfather, accepting his wife's ministrations like a dog or a child, put his hand to his forehead. "Giddy," he said. His voice was as far away as if he were in another room. The forehead that he touched above his heavy, raven eyebrows glistened with a morbid sweat. Cora ran from the room, ran from the earthquake, and outdoors hurled herself into a pile of fresh raked maple leaves. But dreadful curiosity drove her back into the house and as she stood in the doorway, she saw Grandfather collapse, fall from the chair dragging the Bible with him. He lay there like a tree hewn down, his branches every whichway; his loud, jerky breathing was a funny wind and his nose kept copiously bleeding, spilling over his beard, staining the pages of the Bible where it had broken open.

"Maud!" said Grandma. "Will you let your father bleed to death for the want of a whang of ice?"

Mama got up then and seeing Cora said sharply, "Scat! You may have killed my father, you bad girl!"

He did not die that day. Dr. Grimes said that he had had a stroke and that he might live for long years yet, but on the other hand, he might go in a second apoplexy or a third, a fourth, a twenty-fifth. He wanted to know what had brought this on and when he heard about Jane and Amy, he, a sour elder of the U.P. church, was scandalized to bits.

The next Wednesday (three momentous Wednesdays in a row!) a postal came from the twins: they had had a tintype made of themselves, probably at an amusement park, posed in a cardboard Pierce Arrow and on the back of it they had written, "Having a wonderful time and never coming back to Graymoor. Love to all." There was a row of hugs and kisses and they had made a grinning face in the last hug.

And they never did come back to Graymoor, never in their lives. The next time they were heard from, more than a year later, they were both in New South Wales and both of them were married. No one ever knew whom they had gone to visit in St. Louis; they never were sure that the girls really had gone to the Veiled Prophet's Ball or had just said that to impress Frank Ferguson.

Grandfather had three more strokes within a month, and each one left him with a fresh derangement. He spent his time in the parlor in his black leather sermonizing chair, his great shoulders hunched together as he hugged Grandma's Paisley shawl to him, for he was always cold. His eyes were bloodshot; they looked sore. He seemed half asleep—his whole life was one long doze and when the grandchildren went to visit him, a different child each day, he paid no heed to them for the five minutes they stood before him. He said nothing but his stomach querulously growled. He withered and dried; sometimes his five wits were altogether lost to him and then he fought and sought tenaciously until he collected them.

He died in his sleep the night before Thanksgiving. Wednesday again. Woden's day. "Woden was the Norsemen's Jehovah," said Dan matter-of-factly. "His familiars were two black ravens named Hugin and Munin." And then, funereally he intoned, "There were twa corbies / Sat in a tree." And laughed his laugh.

Granny Savage had lost her mind; Grandfather McKinnon could no longer shackle Mama and, as soon as school was over in May, the Savages moved west.

[1979]

Howard Moss

Jean: Some Fragments

I met her by subletting an apartment in New York, hers and Robert Lowell's, in the early forties. The War was on; I had been hired by the Office of War Information on 57th Street and was looking for a place to stay. Cal was still in jail, serving out his term as a conscientious objector; Jean had finished *Boston Adventure* and was waiting for it to be published. She was going away somewhere for a few months—England, I think—but maybe it was Boston. I don't remember. The apartment, in a brownstone on 17th Street overlooking Stuyvesant Park, was graceful and old-fashioned and full of the things Jean loved: Victorian sofas, lamps with pleated shades, deep engulfing chairs, small objects on tables, and books, books, books. Those in the bedroom bookcase were mainly religious; she was a Catholic convert at the time, or at least receiving instruction. She had a weakness for mechanical toys: a bear that turned the pages of a book (named after a well-known critic), a fire truck that turned at sharp right angles and raced across the floor at great speed. When Jean returned from England (or Boston), she would visit me occasionally, always bringing a pint of whiskey in a brown paper bag—either as a matter of scrupulous courtesy or because she felt she couldn't count on my supply—and we would drink and talk. And laugh. A demure quality about her alternated with a kind of Western no-nonsense toughness, and she shed years every time she laughed, showing her gums like a child or an ancient. Funny and sharp about people, she loved gossip. We became friends.

We developed, over the years, a tendency to make elaborate plans that were never carried out. This was particularly true of travel, which we both dreaded. Europe eluded us at least six times. We *did* get to Boston once for a Thanksgiving weekend, but even then something went wrong. We were to meet on the train but never did. We found each other, finally, in South Station, exhausted and bewildered.

I remember seeing a life mask of Jean—Jean the way she looked before the car accident that changed her face forever. (I had known her only since the accident, which occurred while she was married to Lowell.) A handsome woman, she had once been beautiful in a more conventional way, or so the mask suggested. "The Interior Castle" describes the surgical procedure with chilling exactitude; its central conceit is of the brain as a castle probed and assaulted by alien forces. I often forgot that Jean had been through this traumatic ordeal, and the long adjustment that must have been necessary afterwards. That fact, when I remembered it, always made the killing of the girl (rather than the boy) in *The Mountain Lion* more poignant. It also cast a light on Jean's predilection for masks and disguises. She liked to dress up—but in the manner of a child at a Halloween party. Once she came to my house for drinks and emerged from the kitchen wearing a joke mask with a big red nose. Another time I visited her in East Hampton and she answered the door dressed as a cocktail waitress, or something very close.

On her back door, there was a warning sign forbidding entrance to anyone who used the word "hopefully" incorrectly.

A noted hypochondriac, she outdid everyone in real and imagined illnesses. I was waiting for her outside Longchamps at 48th and Madison (bygone days!) when I noticed her suddenly across the street on crutches. It was snowing, I think, a nice, light New York snow. Astonished, I walked over to help her—she was already in the middle of the street by the time I got to her. She was wearing a red plaid cape, very stylish, peculiarly suited to crutches—no sleeves got in the way. When we were safely back on the sidewalk, she said, "Look! Look at these!" and showed me her wrist. Little white blotches were appearing, a sort of albino rash. "What is it?" I asked. "I don't know." She hobbled into lunch. I hadn't even had time to ask about the crutches before she'd been stricken by something new. I never did get the story about the crutches straight. A hypochondriac myself, I was outclassed.

Jean enjoyed medical discussions, symptoms, diagnoses, horror stories, freak accidents, diseases, cures. She owned a Merck's Manual and a gruesome textbook we would sometimes pore over, looking at the more hideous skin diseases in color. She was an amateur authority on ailments, including her own.

Although she was easily influenced, she was the least imitative person I knew. Older women of distinction became her friends—at least twice—and she would bank her originality in a deference of a peculiar kind, as if a mother with standards—a woman of impeccable authority—had been in the back of her mind all the while. But in dress, manner, and ideas she was independent and crotchety, and about writers her opinions were her own and unshakable. She adored cats, old furniture—Biedermeier especially—books, bourbon, odd clothes. Like the dress she used to wear that looked like a man's tuxedo and seemed to have a watch pinned to the lapel. The plaid cape. Fawn slacks and sweaters. She was a special mixture of the outlandish and the decorous. She paid great respect to the civilized, but something ingrained and Western in her mocked it at the same time. Think of Henry James being brought up in Colorado. . . .

Her favorite cat, George Eliot, used to sit under a lamp, eyes closed, basking in the warmth. Jean was proud of that, as if it were some extraordinary feline accomplishment.

In Westport, before she married for the second time, she had her own apartment for a while. I noticed two typewriters, one big, one small. I asked her about them. "The big one's for the novel and the little one's for short stories."

We were going to a cocktail party for St. Jean-Perse. I called for her. We had a drink and then another. Then—and how many times this happened between us!—one of us asked the fatal question: "Do you *really* want to go?" We never got there.

The Met. An opera box. Jean and I turned to each other after the first act of *Andre Chenier.* This time, the fatal question remained unspoken. We got up and left.

Guilty dawdling became a kind of game between us, as well as a safety valve. If I secretly didn't want to go somewhere, I knew I could always stop off at Jean's and that would be a guarantee of never arriving at my original destination. In any case—or every—Jean was more interesting than anywhere I might be going.

A stitched sampler with the words "God Bless America" hung over her television screen.

She had a dream, a dream in which Arran Island (the one off Scotland, where her forebears came from, not the Aran Islands off Ireland) and the Greek island of Samothrace were historically connected. She paid a visit to Arran Island, and, eventually, she and A. J. Liebling, her third and last husband, went to Samothrace. She began to read seriously in anthropology and archeology, particularly Lehman on the digs in Samothrace. But I think the broad view of ancient history and mythology required to complete a project mainly intuitive and then oddly confirmed by fact became too complicated and technical for her. What she had started to write with so much enthusiasm couldn't be finished. I stopped asking her about it the way I later stopped asking her about the novel in which her father was the chief character. But one day she let me read what she had of the Samothrace piece—about forty pages—and it was some of the most extraordinary prose I'd ever read. After I'd finished it, I looked at her and said something like, "My God, Jean, if you don't go on with it, at least publish *this*. . . ." I don't know what happened to it. Although Joe Liebling did everything to encourage Jean to write, she was intimidated by his swiftness, versatility, and excellence as a reporter. She shot off in journalistic directions of her own—the book on Oswald's mother, for instance. One day, Joe and I were riding up together in the elevator at *The New Yorker*. I told Joe I'd read the Samothrace piece and how good I thought it was. "I know," he said, "I wish you'd tell her." "I *have,*" I said. And added, "I wish I could write prose like *that*. . . ." Joe, about to get off at his floor, turned to me and said, "I wish *I* could. . . ."

She was a born writer, and if certain mannerisms entered her prose later on, there was no question, in my mind at least, that she was one of the most naturally gifted writers I'd ever known. She simply couldn't write a bad sentence, excellence was a matter of personal integrity, the style was the woman. She couldn't stand the half-baked, the almost-good, the so-so. She made her views clear in a series of brilliant book reviews, still uncollected. They are all of a piece throughout, united by a single sensibility and an unwavering intelligence. And the annual round-up reviews of children's books she did for *The New Yorker* were scalpel-like attacks on mediocrity, commercial greed, stupidity, and cant.

One of her qualities hardest to get down on paper was the young girl always present in the civilized and cultivated woman. The balance was delicate and impossible to pin down. Like her conversation, it vanished into smoke. But what smoke!

A strangely momentous occasion: When she and Joe Liebling took an apartment on Fifth Avenue and 11th Street—an elegant, rambling apartment in a house built by Stanford White—before they moved in, Jean and Elizabeth Bowen and I walked about the rooms, talking about rugs, draperies, and so on. One of the rare times in New York City when people were dwarfed by space. Steve Goodyear gave Jean two plants. One, a rubber plant, had leaves that scraped the ceiling—eighteen, maybe twenty feet high.

Jean and I (at Fifth and 11th) sometimes would take out her ouija board when I came over early for a drink. (This must have been in the late fifties.) The person always summoned up by Jean was her brother Dick, killed in the Second World War. The board would begin to shake, she would become excited by the message she read. . . . But these sessions never lasted long. Joe Liebling didn't like Jean using the ouija board, and when we heard his key in the door, the board was hastily put away.

The farmhouse Joe Liebling bought in the thirties was first his, then theirs, then hers. It brought her enormous pleasure. She embarked on a long series of renovations, mostly of the interior; each change was a great source of satisfaction, perhaps too much so, for a writer discovers—especially a writer who lives alone—that a house can become a formidable enemy of work. Creative energy is drained off in redecorated guest rooms, expanded gardens, kitchens designed and redesigned to be more practical, new wallpaper, decking, house plants—the list is endless. In Jean's case, off the downstairs dining room she built a new bathroom in one direction and a new study-cum-guest room in another; a second new study appeared upstairs. The kitchen was revamped. The thirty or so acres surrounding the farmhouse boasted a particularly beautiful meadow some distance behind her house, a greensward worthy of a chateau. The shingled farmhouse was ample but modest. Its small living room had a fireplace set at an angle so that no one could ever quite face it. There was a larger dining room and a kitchen and pantry. Farmers didn't waste their money on unnecessary fuel, and, originally, the living room had been a concession to formality rather than a social center. The Liebling-Stafford house had been built for practicality (close to the road in case of a snowstorm), snugness and warmth. It was a comfortable house and Jean fell in love with it—slowly, I think. It became—in the end—her refuge and her garrison, the place she holed up in and from which she viewed the world. The literal view was pretty enough because, from the front window, across Fire Place Road, you could see the water of an inlet, often intensely blue. There was an apple tree in the backyard, seemingly dead. It developed a new twisted limb and became grotesquely lovely. Behind it, there were many yucca plants with their white desert flowers, and in front of the house a mimosa tree that bloomed each spring.

In spite of a certain reputation for waspishness, the result of a sharply honed and witty tongue, Jean was generous and courageous. When she was accused of being the leader of the supposedly quixotic NBA jury that chose Walker Percy's *The Moviegoer* as the best novel of the year (no one had ever heard of Walker Percy before), she stood up for herself, and for him. And the same thing was true when John Williams's Prix de Rome was withdrawn. She spoke up for anyone she admired. Her nervous but good-natured allure derived from a special combination of the tart and the sweet. She was a surprisingly fine cook, liked entertaining and being entertained (at least for the better part of her life), and, above all, enjoyed good conversation.

She could resist a good writer if she disliked his person, but she was far more open to affection and the giving of it than seems generally known. She put herself out for people she liked and did nothing at all for people she didn't.

Youthfulness of manner was belied by the satiric thrust of her language, the slightly breathless drawl of her speech, the odd sense that she was searching for the next installment of words, another piece of the story, some phrase that would precisely focus what she had in mind—habits of speech cruelly underlined by her stroke, when she became unsure—she, of all people!—of her words. It was unfair and particularly cruel to be stricken at the very center of her being: talk, words, speech. It was not unlike—in the meanness of the affliction undercutting the essential person—Beethoven's going deaf.

She was anecdotal in the extreme, turning everything into a story. This became, later on, and long before the stroke, somewhat edgy. A certain amount of complaining, of being the great-lady-offended had become habitual. Something on the order of "And do you know who had the *nerve* to invite me to dinner last Wednesday?" And so on. But then it would turn out that she had *gone* to dinner, so that the point of the complaint seemed muddled. Once she had taken a real distaste to someone, she refused any invitation, any offer of friendship. And she made enemies easily by being outspoken, opinionated, strict in her standards. Once she took a real scunner to someone, she rarely changed her mind.

She felt abandoned by her friends, sometimes, and they, sometimes, by her. She would forget you for a time and then be hurt and surprised that she had been temporarily forgotten. People I think she liked without qualification: Mrs. Rattray, Saul Steinberg, John Stonehill, Peter Taylor, Elizabeth Bowen, Peter DeVries.

We had dinner together for the last time on July 13, 1978, in East Hampton, at a restaurant called Michael's. I called for Jean. Not being able to drive had once united us; now I had a driver's license. Convenient as it was, I'm not sure Jean approved of it. We arrived—down dark paths to a restaurant on the water. Jean, who had been drinking at home, ordered another bourbon. The question of what to order loomed. No menu came to hand; a young waitress reeled off the available fish of the day. Jean deferring, I ordered striped bass. Then Jean said, "I cannot do striped bass." But she didn't seem to be able to do anything else, either, and, after some confusion, I asked the waitress to give us a few minutes. I went over what fish were available again. The waitress came back. Jean said, "Striped bass." I asked her if she was *sure*, considering that she'd said she couldn't do striped bass, and she said she was *absolutely* sure. But when her dish came, she said, "This isn't what I wanted." I wanted to send it back; Jean said not to. Then she added, "What I really wanted was the finnan haddie." There hadn't been any finnan haddie; it had never been mentioned. And I realized we were in some kind of trouble, though most of the conversation was rational, pleasant, at times funny. Suddenly she said, "What do you think of friends?" I was surprised, but babbled on about how they might be the most important people in one's life, not the same as lovers, of course, but desperately needed, a second family, essential. . . . Jean said, lighting a cigarette, "Yes, I must give them up. I'm going to give up smoking." And it became clear she meant the word "cigarettes" or "smokes" when she said "friends." And I suddenly remembered something: years ago, way back, a mutual friend had described cigarettes as "twenty little friends in a pack—twenty friends always available. . . ." I thought: Could there be a memory behind the choice of every mistaken word?

We talked on the phone twice while she was in New York Hospital. I called again on the afternoon of March 26th because I was going up to see my doctor on East 68th Street and thought I'd stop by and see her. The voice on the phone told me she was no longer there. They had no forwarding address, no information. I called East Hampton. No answer—odd, because there had always been a phone machine where you could leave a message. I couldn't figure out where she'd gone. To the Rusk Rehabilitation Center, it turned out later, a special outpost of the hospital. I found out the next day she had died that afternoon.

[1979]

A Commemorative Tribute
to
JEAN STAFFORD
Given by Peter Taylor, on November 13, 1979, at the National Academy and Institute of Arts and Letters, New York City

One of the great satisfactions derived from a life of reading fiction and poetry and looking at pictures and listening to music is the satisfaction of watching an individual artist grow and become a better and better artist through the years. Because some artists do that—grow and become better and better—especially those who were very good to begin with.

In one respect it was not pleasant to know Jean Stafford personally when she was twenty-two. Not, that is, if you were approximately two and twenty yourself and were one of those serious young persons of the thirties who aspired to become fiction writers. It was *not* pleasant because she was a damned excellent writer to begin with and didn't seem to have the hard work ahead of her that the rest of us did. Of course it turned out that we were wrong. Because always, through the years, Jean Stafford would work harder than any of the rest of us and she would keep getting better and better and better. It was not obvious to most of us that she was doing so. Perhaps it was not clear to Jean that she was, though I suspect in her heart of hearts she knew. Her knowledge of her own capacity for work and of her own worth as a writer was a knowledge she kept hidden from her friends, especially from those friends who also wrote fiction. Perhaps it was a knowledge she kept hidden from herself as well as she could.

Since her death last March, I have read through her work again. I did so because I thought that is what she would have liked best for her friends to do after she was dead. For if she seemed modest in her own opinion of her ultimate worth as a writer, she never tried to conceal her wish for attention and respect—for her work, that is—from her literary friends and from the most serious literary minds of the time. For the rest of it she didn't care a bit—for fame and glory, that is to say, as it is represented on the book page and in the book sections of newspapers and national magazines. She actually gave little thought to that sort of attention, only enough to say sometimes that the hacks, the authors of those pages, would at last follow the lead of the best literary minds in their judgment of her work.

Although it often may have seemed otherwise to those who didn't know her well, Jean set little store by the literary world. She had a puritanical loathing for it. The fame and glory that held an interest for her was of the larger sort. It's true she gossiped about literary people unceasingly. Even her letters were full of literary gossip. But in her letters and in her talk she gossiped also and just as happily about all other people at the center or on the periphery of her life. All breathing people interested her. The great world interested her. Especially any backwater of the world interested her. But it was only her work, not herself, that she wanted to deliver into the narrow ways of the literary world. She sent her work forth to have its own career there. But she was no careerist, herself. *She* remained a "private person" (her phrase). She was not, as she said, in "show-biz." She "abhorred" (her word) the idea of the culture hero or heroine. She "loathed" (her word) giving readings—considered it something for amateurs and careerists—and never read or spoke in public except when there was a desperate need for money. What she *seemed* to most of the world and what she actually was in that privacy she was forever trying to maintain were as unlike as the outward appearance and the inner life of some character in the novels of Marcel Proust.

Her students, one year at Barnard College, could see so plainly how she hated the role of "resident writer" that they—the most intelligent of them—begged her to give it up. She would have done so if she hadn't needed the money or imagined she needed it. She felt that teaching creative writing was the proper work for fools and charlatans. At Iowa, where she was teaching one year, she took permanent leave on a bus in the middle of the semester—in the middle of one winter night, in fact. The only way she could explain her unannounced departure, afterward, was to say that while reading her students' papers she discovered that in her class she had a Mr. Mahoney and a Mr. O'Mahoney. That made her understand once and for all, she said, how ridiculous the whole business was. She hated appearing "on the platform" alone or with other writers. Whenever she was dragged kicking and screaming—almost literally sometimes—into a public-forum or a panel-discussion she would cling to some friend who was a fellow member of the panel and try to turn the "discussion" into a private exchange between two private people, as though the audience were not out there and did not exist. She wrote numbers of book reviews and articles, of course, but frequently with tongue in cheek and always seemingly in a terrible rage, a rage against a life that had contrived to place her in such a ridiculous situation. She wrote those pieces always under pressure from some friend or from a real or imagined need for money. And the pieces themselves were memorable primarily for the remarkable vocabulary of the author, as indeed are some of her less serious works of fiction, as indeed are passages in some of her more serious works of fiction.

When one settles down to read Jean Stafford's novels and stories one advisedly has a dictionary—a big dictionary—close by. For she was a literary artist in the most literal sense. Her most profound and her wittiest effects alike are got through words, themselves. And her remarkable diction, her complicated syntax, her elaborate sentence structure all spilled over into her conversation (if it wasn't, as a matter of fact, the other way round) and were to some degree responsible for making her conversation the delight it was. In life—as a conversationalist, that is—she sometimes seemed at once the most articulate and the most inarticulate person one can imagine. She seemed to talk, as she sometimes seemed to write (in retrospect it is often difficult to distinguish between the two)—seemed to talk or write round and round a subject, dazzling you with her diction; but finally when she stopped (and it was hard to stop her) you realized that somewhere back there in her discourse she had penetrated the tough integument (as she might have put it) and touched the core of truth she had been probing for, had done so without your ever having realized that she had got to the heart of the matter. It was as though she wished always to conceal anything in her narrative so vulgar as mere purposefulness—her narrative spoken or written. Sometimes it was only in retrospect, and long after the conversation or the story was finished, that you saw what she had been saying. And somehow her statement was the more effective because of that.

In life Jean was, in a sense, always playing a role. She had many roles, roles like those in her written fiction—a grande dame, a plain spoken old maid, a country girl from the West, a spoiled rich woman, her diction always changing to fit the role. And sometimes she played the role of a writer, a woman writer. This surely entailed as much play-acting as the other roles. For it no more represented the real Jean than did those other roles, although many people—allegedly sophisticated people—mistook her play-pretend Manhattan bluestocking for the literary genius who wrote under the name of Jean Stafford. Actually, what she was like when she sat down to write her wondrous novels and stories may be something beyond the comprehension of any of us. In a sense, her literary personality remains her best kept secret. Perhaps it was in that role that she was the most private of private persons, and perhaps, in order to preserve that role, it was necessary for her to have the privacy she was always seeking. One thing is certain. With her close friends she always avoided the role of the professional writer, avoided any semblance of professionalism. Contrary to impressions she may often have given, Jean Stafford was *not ever* a professional writer—not in the bad sense of that phrase. (I am not sure there *is* a good sense of that phrase for literary artists.) Instead, she was first and last an inspired writer, a poet. She wrote because she had to, and not for professional advancement. She was keenly aware that it is but one easy step down from professionalism to commercialism and that therein lies inevitably the ruin of art of any kind.

One remembers Jean Stafford for her literary art, the art at which she labored during her entire adult lifetime, the art which she labored on for its own sake. One remembers her for her rages against stupidity and insensibility, for her expressions of passionate devotion to whatever of nobility and serenity can be salvaged from the ugliness of most lives, remembers her for her wit, for her humility, her modesty, and for her responsiveness to one's own ideas and feelings. Yes, how often one remembers her responding to something one has, one's self, said with: "Oh, yes! That's the way it is! Oh, God, yes, yes; yes!"

In the very private life which she insisted upon for herself she developed many domestic interests and accomplishments. During her last years she became so involved in the care of her house and acreage at East Hampton that she would sometimes go for weeks without leaving that neat little retreat of hers out there on Fire Place Road. During the past ten years of her life she had lived there alone, had lived there in privacy during what she sometimes termed her "final widowhood." For despite her concern for her privacy and for her work, she never forgot those she loved, certainly never forgot for a moment that she had been married three times. In 1940 she married Robert Lowell. They were divorced in 1949. She was married for less than a year to Oliver Jensen. This marriage also ended in divorce. In 1959 she married A. J. Liebling. Probably the years of that marriage were the happiest years Jean Stafford ever knew. And it is a satisfaction to her friends to remember that she and Joe Liebling are buried beside one another in the little graveyard at East Hampton and under the handsome gray tombstones that Jean caused to be designed five years before her death.

But finally, against Jean's rage for privacy, against all her great personal warmth, against this persistently unprofessional Jean Stafford, one must place the cold facts of the successful career of those books and stories that she sent out into the world to have their own career. And one must make whatever one will of the contrast. I think that's what she would have said to us about the contrast of the privacy of her life and the public life of her literary work. Her first novel, *Boston Adventure,* was published in 1944, when she was twenty-eight. With its publication her reputation was established. Her second novel was *The Mountain Lion,* published in 1947. Her third novel, *The Catherine Wheel,* appeared in 1952. From that time her literary genius was devoted almost entirely to writing her incomparable short stories. In 1970 her *Collected Stories* received general acclaim and was awarded the Pulitzer Prize for Fiction. When she died she was at work on a fourth novel, one chapter of which has since appeared in *The New Yorker.* Another portion of it will appear this winter in a Jean Stafford memorial issue of *Shenandoah* magazine.

Born at Covina, California, in 1916, Jean Stafford grew up, according to her own depictions, in Steamboat Springs, Colorado. She graduated from the University of Colorado, at Boulder, and attended the University of Heidelberg, in Germany. She lived at various times in New York City, in Boston, in Tennessee, in Louisiana and on Long Island. She died on March 26 of this year at White Plains, New York.

[1979]

Wallace Stevens

TWO POEMS

HOW NOW, O, BRIGHTENER . . .

Something of the trouble of the mind
Remains in the sight, and in sayings of the sight,
Of the spring of the year,

Trouble in the spillage and first sparkle of sun,
The green-edged yellow and yellow and blue and blue-
    edged green—
The trouble of the mind

Is a residue, a land, a rain, a warmth,
A time, an apparition and nourishing element
And simple love,

In which the spectra have dewy favor and live
And take from this restlessly unhappy happiness
Their stunted looks.

NOTE ON MOONLIGHT

The one moonlight, in the simple-colored night,
Like a plain poet revolving in his mind
The sameness of his various universe,
Shines on the mere objectiveness of things.

It is as if being was to be observed,
As if, among the possible purposes
Of what one sees, the purpose that comes first,
The surface, is the purpose to be seen,

The property of the moon, what it evokes.
It is to disclose the essential presence, say,
Of a mountain, expanded and elevated almost
Into a sense, an object the less; or else

To disclose in the figure waiting on the road
An object the more, an undetermined form
Between the slouchings of a gunman and a lover,
A gesture in the dark, a fear one feels

In the great vistas of night air, that takes this form,
In the arbors that are as if of Saturn-star.
So, then, this warm, wide, weatherless quietude
Is active with a power, an inherent life,

In spite of the mere objectiveness of things,
Like a cloud-cap in the corner of a looking-glass,
A change of color in the plain poet's mind,
Night and silence disturbed by an interior sound,

The one moonlight, the various universe, intended
So much just to be seen—a purpose, empty
Perhaps, absurd perhaps, but at least a purpose,
Certain and ever more fresh. Ah! Certain, for sure. .

[1952]

Dabney Stuart

VARIABLE SERVICE

All the worms are wet again.
My father hungers in his arm.
Needle, needle, keep him warm.

All the worms dance in a ring.
My father's thirsty in his veins.
Needle, needle, ease his pains.

I've been his cutting needle, knife.
What blood's between us he gave me.
I'd give it back to set him free.

But the worms are rending everywhere.
They tie his pajamas. They part his hair.
They wreck all needles.

Well, let them. Let them wind their ring
Into our fingers. That sharp trick
Marries us, father, to the quick.

[1965]

May Swenson

NIGHT VISITS WITH THE FAMILY

SHARON'S DREAM

We were rounding up cattle, riding trees instead of horses.
The way I turned the herd was let my tree limb grow.
Circling out around an obstinate heifer,
my horse stretched and whipped back, but too slow.

PAUL'S DREAM

Twelve white shirts and I had to iron them.
Some swirled away. They were bundles of cloud.
Hailstones fell and landed as buttons.
I should have picked them up before they melted to mud.

ROY'S DREAM

Down in the cellar a library of fruit:
berries, pears and apricots published long ago.
Two lids of wax covered my eyelids. A tart title
I couldn't read was pasted on my brow.

DAN'S DREAM

In the playhouse Dad made when I was six
I put my captive hawk. The chimney had a lid
that locked. The wallpaper of roses was faded and fouled.
I couldn't wake, and dirty feathers filled my little bed.

GRACE'S DREAM

Hindleg in the surf, my grand piano, groaning,
crawled ashore. I saw that most of the black keys
had been extracted, their roots were bleeding. It tried
to embrace me while falling forward on three knees.

MARGARET'S DREAM

There was an earthquake and Jordan's boot got caught
in a crack in the street. His bike had fallen through
and went on peddling underneath, came up the basement
stairs to warn me what had happened. That's how I knew.

BETTY'S DREAM

Aunt Etta was wearing a wig, of wilver. Its perfection
made you see how slack her chins were. Under the hair
in front was a new eye, hazel and laughing. It winked.
"You, too, will be 72," she said. It gave me a scare.

GEORGE'S DREAM

Old Glory rippling on a staff. No, it was a Maypole,
and the ribbons turned to rainbows. I saw a cat
climbing the iridescent bow. Then I was sliding down
a bannister. My uniform split in the crotch, I was so fat.

CORWIN'S DREAM

With my new camera I was taking a picture of my old
camera. The new one was guaranteed: it was the kind
that issues instant color prints. What came out
was an X-Ray of the tunnel in the roller of a window blind.

RUTH'S DREAM

Standing under the shower I was surprised
to see I wasn't naked. The streams had dressed
me in a gown of seed pearls, and gloves that my nails
poked through like needles. They pricked if I touched my breast.

STEVE'S DREAM

Two tiny harmonicas. I kept them in my mouth,
and sucked them. That made twin secret tunes.
Mother said, "What is it you are always humming?"
I told her they were only the stones of prunes.

DIANE'S DREAM

Grandmother wasn't dead. Only her ring finger.
Before we buried it, we must remove the ruby.
And the finger was jack-knifed. I offered to unclench it,
but couldn't do it. I was too much of a booby.

MAY'S DREAM

Cowpuncher on a tree-horse wears
a cloud-shirt with hailstone buttons.
He rides and, through wax eyelids, reads
a library of fruit. He passes a hawk
locked in a playhouse, a grand piano
with three broken knees. Nothing he can do
about any of these. When old, an Auntie
in a wilver wig, he goes. He's almost too fat
to slide down the rainbow's bannister that
ends in the gray X-Ray of a tunnel in the blind.
There he wears a water dress, tastes secret tunes.
Until I wake he cannot die. Until I wake,
the ruby lives on the dead finger.

[1978]

Eleanor Ross Taylor

RACHEL PLUMMER'S DREAM
WINTER 1836

You never shut your eyes.
You always looked.

At the grizzled scalp you somehow recognized
even without the blue eyes and mustache.
Through your blood that was Like to Strangle you
lying face down, tied,
        through the mass beating.

After five days without a Mouth of Food—
days of silence— slogging— stamina—
part of the skinclad band to the high timber,
you could not but Admire the Countrey
though short of breath from fasting, burdened with
your unborn baby, tentskins on your back.

You never turned your head
        from Little Pratt's
bruised face as it receded,   calling,
        drawn from you

When the unborn, born in captivity,
let live a week or so, was made their sport,
bounced on the frozen ground till lifeless,
you held your arms for it   and somehow
breathing new life in it, fired their new rage.
        You watched it   on a rope
whirled out by braves aponyback
till shredded on the cactus,
then thrown into your lap, a tattered mass,
and buried tearless with your hands and prayers
of thanks for its release.

You breathed the Purest Are you ever breathed
those snowy summits, Admired the Timber,
the Fine Springs, the Snow Rabbitt, undefiled—
(your fingers scarred with dressing hides, your feet
black-bitten) counted the advances of
the antelope, their turns, noting their
diminishing proximity, ghostly escape;
mused at the buffalo grazing in
the phantom sea— it was "a sort of gas."

Bound to see, you crashed the powwow, ignored
their cuffs— a dog that *would,* spoke Indian,
heard Indian— save one white curse
a fat-mouthed Beadie sought you out to give—
ate roots Stol'n from the Mouse's Holes,
refused the serving of roast enemy; it was a foot.

You burned to see— as for example,
the inside of those mountain caves
before decamping;
I see you all wrapped up
        dipping flax wicks
into some tallow got from buffalo—
with these your makeshift candles and firewood,
a flint— with your young mistress took the Pided Horse
on the uprising trail.
        Inside,
she took quick fright (she smelled the water)
but you would not go back.

Again, where it got dark, you struck the light,
and the splendor blinded—
she cried out, threatening you.
You slugged her with a piece of wood, wrestled,
ready to kill her for the sight
that was to come.

By some odd chance, your light knocked to the ground
burned on. You took it up, squinted—
the cave burst into light, imperative. But first
you led her, tamed, the miles back to the mouth;
at last made your long way in that unearthly
twinkling dark, beside the crystal river,
to sound of mighty falls ahead,
                                        plunging
how far?   into what unknown place?
        caught echoes of your dying baby's cries;
like tranced Ezekiel in Babylon
descried the noise of wings, of wings let down—
though briers and thorns be with thee, not afraid!

and a Human Being came   comforting
releasing   balming   transfusing . . . .

Your captors, waiting at the mouth, half gave you up.

How analyze
        this parapsychologic episode
        this spiritual hiatus where
you closed your eyes a whole day and a night,
again a second day?—
                        I discount sex.
So worn, half-starved, and suicidal—
        they say, consumptive, too.
The realist, you painted not at all.

I see him, see his gifts. He chose: to bathe
your wounds that never pained again,
that Resurrection flaring in the cave,
those stars in earth, time stopped
and you with eyes to see.

[1981]

Peter Taylor

THE HAND OF EMMAGENE

After highschool, she had come down from Hortonsburg
To find work in Nashville.
She stayed at our house.
And she began at once to take classes
In a secretarial school.
As a matter of fact, she wasn't *right* out of highschool
She had remained at home two years, I think it was,
To nurse her old grandmother
Who was dying of Bright's disease.
So she was not just some giddy young country girl
With her head full of nonsense
About running around to Nashville nightspots
Or even about getting married
And who knew nothing about what it was to work.

From the very beginning, we had in mind
– My wife and I did –
That she ought to know some boys
Her own age. That was one of our first thoughts.
She was a cousin of ours, you see – or of Nancy's.
And she was from Hortonsburg
Which is the little country place
Thirty miles north of Nashville
Where Nancy and I grew up.
That's why we felt responsible
For her social life
As much as for her general welfare.
We always do what we can of course
For our kin when they come to town –
Especially when they're living under our roof.
But instead of trying to entertain Emmagene
At the Club
Or by having people in to meet her
Nancy felt
We should first find out what the girl's interests were.
We would take our cue from that.

Well, what seemed to interest her most in the world
Was work. I've never seen anything quite like it.
In some ways, this seemed the oddest thing about her.
When she first arrived, she would be up at dawn,
Before her "Cousin Nan" or I had stirred,
Cleaning the house—We would smell floor wax
Before we opened our bedroom door some mornings—
Or doing little repair jobs
On the table linen or bed linen
Or on my shirts or even Nancy's underwear.
Often as not she would have finished
The polishing or cleaning she had taken upon herself to do
Before we came down. But she would be in the living room
Or sun parlor or den or dining room
Examining the objects of her exertions, admiring them,
Caressing them even—Nancy's glass collection
Or the Canton china on the sideboard.
One morning we found her with pencil and paper
Copying the little geometrical animals
From one of the oriental rugs.

Or some mornings she would be down in the kitchen cooking,
Before the servants arrived.
(And of course she'd have the dishes she'd dirtied
All washed and put away again before the cook
Came in to fix breakfast.) What she was making
Down there in the pre-dawn hours,
Would be a cake or a pie for Nancy and me.
(She didn't eat sweets, herself.)
Its aroma would reach us
Before we were out of bed or just as we started down the stairs.
But whether cleaning or cooking,
She was silent as a mouse those mornings.
We heard nothing. There were only the smells
Before we came down. And after we came down there'd be
Just the sense of her contentment.

It was different at night. The washing machine
Would be going in the basement till the wee hours,
Or sometimes the vacuum cleaner
Would be running upstairs before we came up

Or running downstairs after we thought
We'd put the house to bed.
(We used to ask each other and even ask her
What she thought the cook and houseman
Were meant to do. Sometimes now we ask ourselves
What did they do during the time that Emmagene was here.)
And when she learned how much we liked to have fires
In the living room and den, she would lay them
In the morning, after cleaning out the old ashes.
But at night we'd hear her out in the back yard
Splitting a fireplace log, trying to get lightwood
Or wielding the ax to make kindling
Out of old crates or odd pieces of lumber.
More than than once I saw her out there in the moonlight
Raising the ax high above her head
And coming down with perfect accuracy
Upon an up-ended log or a balanced two-by-four.

There would be those noises at night
And then we noticed sometimes the phone would ring.
One of us would answer it from bed,
And there would be no one there.
Or there would be a click
And then another click which we knew in all likelihood
Was on the downstairs extension.
One night I called her name into the phone—"Emmagene?"—
Before the second click came, just to see if she were there.
But Emmagene said nothing.
There simply came the second click.

There were other times, too, when the phone rang
And there would be dead silence when we answered.
"Who is it?" I would say. "Who are you calling?"
Or Nancy would say, "To whom do you wish to speak?"
Each of us, meanwhile, looking across the room at Emmagene.
For we already had ideas then, about it. We had already
Noticed cars that crept by the house
When we three sat on the porch in the late spring.
A car would mosey by, going so slow we thought surely it would
stop.

But if Nancy or I stood up
And looked out over the shrubbery toward the street,
Suddenly there would be a burst of speed.
The driver would even turn on a cut-out as he roared away.

More than once the phone rang while we were at the supper table
On Sunday night. Emmagene always prepared that meal
And did up the wishes afterward since the servants were off
On Sunday night. And ate with us too, of course.
I suppose it goes without saying
She always ate at the table with us.
She rather made a point of that from the start.
Though it never would have occurred to us
For it to be otherwise.
You see, up in Hortonsburg
Her family and my wife's had been kin of course
But quite different sorts of people really.
Her folks had belonged to a hard bitten, fundamentalist sect
And Nancy's tended to be Cumberland Presyterians
Or Congregationalists or Methodists, at worst
(Or Episcopalians, I suppose I might say "at best.")
The fact was, Nancy's family—like my own—
Went usually to the nearest church, whatever it was.
Whereas Emmagene's travelled thirteen miles each Sunday morning
To a church in the hilly north end of the County,
A church of a denomination that seemed always
To be *changing* its name by the addition of some qualifying adjective.
Either that or seceding from one synod or joining another.
Or deciding just to go it alone
Because of some disputed point of scripture.

Religion aside, however, there were differences of style.
And Emmagene—very clearly—had resolved
Or been instructed before leaving home
To brook no condescension on our part.
"We're putting you in the guest room," Nancy said
Upon her arrival. And quick as a flash Emmagene added:

"And we'll take meals together?"
"Why of course, why of course," Nancy said,
Placing an arm about Emmagene's shoulder.
"You'll have the place of honored guest at our table."

Well, on Sunday nights it was more like we
Were the honored guests,
With the servants off, of course,
And with Emmagene electing to prepare our favorite
Country dishes for us, and serving everything up
Out in the pantry, where we always take that meal.
It was as though we were all back home in Hortonsburg.
But if the phone rang,
Emmagene was up from the table in a split second,
(It might have been her own house we were in.)
And answered the call on the wall phone in the kitchen.
I can see her now, and hear her, too.
She would say "Hello," and then just stand there, listening,
The receiver pressed to her ear, and saying nothing more at all.
At first, we didn't even ask her who it was.
We would only look at each other
And go back to our food—
As I've said, we were more like guests at her house
On Sunday night. And so we'd wait till later
To speak about it to each other.
We both supposed from the start
It was some boy friend of hers she was too timid to talk with
Before us. You see, we kept worrying
About her not having any boy friends
Or any girl friends, either.
We asked ourselves again and again
Who in our acquaintance we could introduce her to,
What nice Nashville boy we knew who would not mind
Her plainness or her obvious puritanical nature—
She didn't wear make-up, not even lipstick or powder,
And didn't do anything with her hair.
She wore dresses that were like maids' uniforms except
Without any white collars and cuffs.
Nancy and I got so we hesitated to take a drink
Or even smoke a cigarette

When she was present.
I soon began watching my language.

I don't know how many times we saw her
Answer the phone like that or heard the clickings
On the phone upstairs. At last I told Nancy
She ought to tell the girl she was free
To invite whatever friends she had to come to the house.
Nancy said she would have to wait for the opportunity;
You didn't just come out with suggestions like that
To Emmagene.

One Sunday night the phone rang in the kitchen.
Emmagene answered it of course and stood listening for a time.
Finally, very deliberately, as always,
She returned the little wall phone to its hook.
I felt her looking at us very directly
As she always did when she put down the phone.
This time Nancy didn't pretend
To be busy with her food.
"Who *was* that, Emmagene?" she asked
In a very polite, indifferent tone.
"Well, I'll tell you," the girl began
As though she had been waiting forever to be asked.
"It's some boy or other I knew up home.
Or *didn't* know." She made an ugly mouth and shrugged.
"That's who it always is," she added, "in case you *care* to know."
There was a too obvious irony
In the way she said "*care* to know."
As though we ought to have asked her long before this.
"That's who it is in the cars, too," she informed us—
Again, as though she had been waiting only too long for us to ask.
"When they're off work and have nothing better to do
They ring up or drive by
Just to make a nuisance of themselves."
"How many of them are there?" Nancy asked.
"There's quite some few of them," Emmagene said with emphasis.
"Well, Emmagene," I suddenly joined in,
"You ought to make your choice
And maybe ask one or two of them to come to the house to see you."

She looked at me with something like rage.
"They are not a good sort," she said. "They're a bad lot.
You wouldn't want them to set foot on your front steps.
Much less your front porch or in your house."

I was glad it was all coming out in the open and said,
"They can't all be all bad. A girl has to be selective."
She stood looking at me for a moment
In a kind of silence only she could keep.
Then she went into the kitchen and came back
Offering us second helpings from the pot of greens.
And before I could say more,
She had changed the subject and was talking about the sermon
She had heard that morning, quoting with evangelistic fervor,
Quoting the preacher and quoting the Bible.
It was as if she were herself hearing all over again
All she had heard that very morning
At that church of hers somewhere way over on the far side
of East Nashville. It was while she was going on
About that sermon that I began to wonder for the first time
How long Emmagene was going to stay here with us.
I found myself reflecting:
She hasn't got a job yet and she hasn't got a beau.

It wasn't that I hadn't welcomed Emmagene as much as Nancy
And hadn't really liked having her in the house.
We're always having relatives from the country
Stay with us this way. If we had children
It might be different. This big house wouldn't
Seem so empty then. (I often think we keep the servants
We have, at a time when so few people have any servants at all,
Just because the servants help fill the house.)
Sometimes it's the old folks from Hortonsburg we have
When they're taking treatments
At the Hospital or at one of the clinics.
Or it may be a wife
Who has to leave some trifling husband for a while.
(Usually the couples in Hortonsburg go back together.)
More often than not it's one of the really close kin
Or a friend we were in school with or who was in our wedding.

We got Emmagene
Because Nancy heard she was all alone
Since her Grandma died
And because Emmagene's mother
Before *she* died
Had been a practical nurse and had looked after Nancy's mother
In her last days. It was that sort of thing.
And it was no more than that.
But we could see from the first how much she loved
Being here in this house and loved Nancy's nice things.
That's what they all love, of course.
That's what's so satisfying about having them here,
Seeing how they appreciate living for a while
In a house like ours. But I don't guess
Any of them ever liked it better than Emmagene
Or tried harder to please both Nancy and me
And the servants, too. Often we would notice her
Even after she had been here for months
Just wandering from room to room
Allowing her rather large but delicately made hands
To move lightly over every piece of furniture she passed.
One felt that in the houses she knew around Hortonsburg
—In her mother's and grandmother's houses—
There had not been pretty things—not things she loved to fondle.
It was heartbreaking to see her the day she broke
A pretty pink china vase that Nancy had set out in a new place
In the sun parlor. The girl hadn't seen it before.
She took it up in her strong right hand
To examine it. Something startled her—
A noise outside, I think. Maybe it was a car going by,
Maybe one of those boys.—Suddenly the vase crashed to the floor.
Emmagene looked down at the pieces, literally wringing her hands
As if she would wring them off, like chickens' necks, if she could.
I was not there. Nancy told me about it later.
She said that though there was not a sign of a tear in the girl's eyes,
She had never before seen such a look of regret and guilt
In a human face. And what the girl said
Was even stranger. Nancy and I
have mentioned it to each other many times since.

"I despise my hand for doing that," she wailed.
"I wish—I do wish I could punish it in some way.
I ought to see it don't do anything useful for a week."

One night on the porch
When one of those boys went by in his car
At a snail's pace
And kept tapping lightly on his horn,
I said to Emmagene, "Why don't you stand up and wave to him,
Just for fun, just to see what happens. I don't imagine
They mean any harm."
"Oh, you don't know!" she said.
"They're a mean lot.
They're not like some nice Nashville boy
That you and Cousin Nan might know."
Nancy and I sat quiet after that,
As if some home truth had been served up to us.
It wasn't just that she didn't want to know
Those Hortonsburg boys.
She *wanted* to know Nashville boys
Of a kind we might introduce her to and approve of.
I began to see—and so did Nancy, the same moment—
That Emmagene had got ideas about herself
Which it wouldn't be possible for her to realize.
She not only liked our things. She liked our life.
She meant somehow to stay. And of course
It would never do. The differences were too deep.
That is to say, she had no notion of changing herself.
She was just as sure now
About what one did and didn't do
As she had been when she came.
She still dressed herself without any ornamentation
Or any taste at all. And would have called it a sin to do so.
Levity of any kind seemed an offence to her.
There was only one Book anyone need read.
Dancing and drinking and all that
Was beyond even thinking about.
And yet the kind of luxury we had in our house
Had touched her. She felt perfectly safe, perfectly good
with it. It was a bad situation

And we felt ourselves somewhat to blame.
Yet what else could we do
But help her try to find a life of her own?
That had been our good intention from the outset.

I investigated those boys who did the ringing up
And the horn blowing. In Nashville you have ways
Of finding out who's in town from your home town.
It's about like being in Paris or Rome
And wanting to know who's there from the U.S.A.
You ask around among those who speak the home tongue.
And so I asked about those boys.
They were, I had to acknowledge, an untamed breed.
But, still, I said to Nancy, "Who's to tame 'em
If not someone like Emmagene. It's been going on
Up there in Horton County for, I'd say—Well,
For a good many generations anyway."

I don't know what got into us, Nancy and me.
We set about it more seriously, more in earnest
Trying to get her to see something of those boys.
I'm not sure what got into us. Maybe it was seeing Emmagene
Working her fingers to the bone
—For no reason at all. There was no necessity.—
And loving everything about it so.
Heading out to secretarial school each morning,
Beating the pavements in search of a job all afternoon,
Then coming home here and setting jobs for herself
That kept her up half the night.
Suddenly our house seemed crowded with her in it.
Not just to us, but to the servants, too.
I heard the cook talking to her one night in the kitchen.
"You ought to see some young folks your own age.
You ought to have yourself a nice fellow."
"What nice young fellow would I know?" Emmagene asked softly.
"I'm not sure there is such a fellow—not that I would know."
"Listen to her!" said the cook. "Do you think we don't see
Those fellows that go riding past here?"
"They're trash!" Emmagene said. "And not one of them
That knows what a decent girl is like!"

"Listen to her!" said the cook.
"I hear her," said the houseman, "and you hear her.
But she don't hear us. She don't hear nobody but herself."
"Ain't no body good enough for you?" the cook said.
"I'd like to meet some boy
Who lives around here," the poor girl said.
And to this the cook said indignantly,
"Don't git above your raisin', honey."
Emmagene said no more. It was the most
Any of us would ever hear her say on that subject.
Presently she left the kitchen
And went up the back stairs to her room.

Yet during this time she seemed happier than ever
To be with us. She even took to singing
While she dusted and cleaned. We'd hear
Familiar old hymns above the washer and the vacuum cleaner.
And such suppers as we got on Sunday night!
Why, she came up with country ham and hot sausage
That was simply not to be had in stores where Nancy traded.
And then she *did* find a job!
She finished her secretarial training
And she came up with a job
Nowhere else but in the very building
Where my own office is.
There was nothing for it
But for me to take her to work in my car in the morning
And bring her home at night.

But there was a stranger coincidence than where her job was.
One of those boys from Hortonsburg turned out to run the elevator
In our building. Another of them brought up my car each night
In the parking garage. I hadn't noticed before
Who those young fellows were that always called me by name.
But then I noticed them speaking to her too
And calling her "Emmagene." I teased her about them a little
But not too much, I think. I knew to take it easy
And not spoil everything.

Then one night the boy in the garage
When he was opening the car door for Emmagene, said,

"George over there wants you to let him carry you home."
This George was still another boy from Hortonsburg,
(Not one that worked in my building or in the garage)
And he saluted me across the ramp.
"Why don't you ride with him, Emmagene?" I said
I said it rather urgently, I suppose.
Then without another word, before Emmagene could climb in beside me,
The garage boy had slammed my car door.
And I pulled off, down the ramp—
With my tires screeching.

At home, Nancy said I ought to have been ashamed.
But she only said it after an hour had passed
And Emmagene had not come in.
At last she did arrive, though
Just as we were finishing dinner.
We heard a car door slam outside.
We looked at each other and waited.
Finally Emmagene appeared in the dining room doorway.
She looked at us questioningly,
First at Nancy's face, then at mine.
When she saw how pleased we were
She came right on in to her place at the table
And she sat down, said her blessing,
And proceeded to eat her supper as though nothing unusual had happened.

She never rode to or from work with me again.
There was always somebody out there
In the side driveway, blowing for her in the morning
And somebody letting her out in the driveway at night.
For some reason she always made them let her out
Near the back door, as though it would be wrong
For them to let her out at the front.
And then she would come on inside the house the back way.

She went out evenings sometimes, too,
Though always in answer to a horn's blowing in the driveway
And never, it seemed, by appointment.
She would come to the living room door

And say to us she was going out for a little ride.
When we answered with our smiling countenances
She would linger a moment, as if to be sure
About what she read in our eyes
Or perhaps to relish what she could so clearly read.
Then she would be off.
And she would be home again within an hour or two.

It actually seemed as if she were still happier with us now
Than before. And yet something was different too.
We both noticed it. The hymn singing stopped.
And—almost incredible as it seemed to us—
She developed a clumsiness, began tripping over things
About the house, doing a little damage here and there
In the kitchen. The cook complained
That she'd all but ruined the meat grinder
Dropping it twice when she was unfastening it from the table.
She sharpened the wood ax on the knife sharpener—or tried to,
And bent the thing so the houseman insisted
We'd have to have another.
What seemed more carelessness than clumsiness
Was that she accidentally threw away
One of Nancy's good spoons, which the cook retrieved
From the garbage can. Nancy got so she would glance at me
As if to ask, "What will it be next?—poor child."
We noticed how nervous she was at the table
How she would drop her fork on her plate—
As if she intended to smash the Haviland—
Or spill something on a clean place mat.
Her hands would tremble, and she would look at us
As though she thought we were going to reprimand her
Or as if she hoped we would.
One day when she broke off the head of a little figurine
While dusting, she came to Nancy with the head
In one hand and the body in the other.
Her two hands were held so tense,
Clasping so tightly the ceramic pieces,
That blue veins stood out where they were usually
All creamy whiteness. Nancy's heart went out to her.
She seized the two hands in her own

And commenced massaging them
As if they were a child's, in from the snow.
She told the girl that the broken shepherd
Didn't matter at all,
That there was nothing we owned
That mattered *that* much.

Meanwhile, the girl continued to get calls at night
On the telephone. She would speak a few syllables
Into the telephone now. Usually we couldn't make out what she was saying
And we tried not to hear. All I ever managed
To hear her say—despite my wish not to hear—
Were things like "Hush, George" or "Don't say such things."
Finally one night Nancy heard her say:
"I haven't got the kind of dress to wear to such a thing."

That was all Nancy needed. She got it out of the girl
What the event was to be. And next morning
Nancy was downtown by the time the stores opened,
Buying Emmagene a sleeveless, backless evening gown
It seemed for a time Nancy had wasted her money.
The girl said she wasn't going to go out anywhere
Dressed like that. "You don't think I'd put you in a dress
That wasn't proper to wear," said Nancy, giving it to her very straight.
"It isn't a matter of what you think
Is proper," Emmagene replied. "It's what he would think it meant—
George, and maybe some of the others, too."
They were in the guest room, where Emmagene was staying
And now Nancy sat down on the twin bed opposite
The one where Emmagene was sitting, and facing her.
"This boy George doesn't really misbehave with you
Does he, Emmagene?" Nancy asked her. "Because if he does,
Then you mustn't, after all, go out with him—
With him or with the others."
"You know I wouldn't let him do that, Cousin Nan," she said.
"Not really. Not the real thing, Cousin Nan."
"What do you mean?" Nancy asked in genuine bewilderment.

The girl looked down at her hands, which were folded in her lap.
"I mean, it's my hands he likes," she said.
And she quickly put both her hands behind her, out of sight.
"It's what they all like if they can't have it any other way."
And then she looked at Nancy the way she had looked
At both of us when we finally asked her who it was on the telephone,
As though she'd only been waiting for such questions.
And then, as before, she gave more
Than she had been asked for.
"Right from the start, it was the most disgusting kind of things
They all said to me on the telephone. And the language, the words.
You wouldn't have known the meaning, Cousin Nan."
When she had said this the girl stood up
As if to tell Nancy it was time she leave her alone.
And with hardly another word, Nancy came on to our room.
She was so stunned she was half the night
Putting it across to me just what the girl had told her
Or had tried to tell her.

Naturally, we thought we'd hear no more about the dress.
But, no, it was the very next night, after dinner,
That she came down to us in the living room
And showed herself to us in that dress Nancy had bought.
It can't properly be said she was wearing it,
But she had it on her like a night gown,
As if she didn't have anything on under it.
And her feet in a pair of black leather pumps—
No make-up of course, her hair pulled back as usual into a knot.
There was something about her, though, as she stood there
With her clean scrubbed face and her freshly washed hair
And in that attire so strange and unfamiliar to her
That made one see the kind of beauty she had,
For the first time. And somehow one knew what she was going to say.
"I'll be going out," she said, searching our faces
As she had got so she was always doing when she spoke to us.
Nancy rose and threw her needle work on the chair arm
And didn't try to stop it when it fell on to the floor.

Clearly, she too had perceived suddenly a certain beauty about
the girl.
She went over to her at once and said,
"Emmagene, don't go out with George again.
It isn't wise." They stepped into the hall
With Nancy's arm about the girl's waist.
"I've got to go," Emmagene said.
And as she spoke a horn sounded in the driveway.
"George is no worse than the rest," she said.
"He's *better*. I've come to like things about him now."
There was more tapping on the horn,
Not loud but insistent.
"He's not the kind of fellow I'd have liked to like.
But I can't stop now. And you've gone and bought this dress."

Nancy didn't seem to hear her. "You mustn't go," she said.
"I couldn't live through this evening.
I'd never forgive myself." The horn kept it up outside,
And the girl drew herself away from Nancy.
Planting herself in the middle of the hall,
She gave us the first line of preaching we'd ever heard from her:
"It is not for us to forgive ourselves. God forgives us."
Nancy turned and appealed to me. When I stood up
The girl said defiantly, "Oh, I'm going!"
She was speaking to both of us. "You can't stop me now!"
The car horn had begun a sort of rat-a-tat-tat.
"That's what he's like," she said, nodding her head
Toward the driveway where he was tapping the horn.
"You can't stop me now!
I'm free, white and twenty-one.
That's what *he* says about me."
Still the horn kept on,
And there was nothing we could think to say or do.
Nancy did say, "Well, you'll have to have a wrap.
You can't go out like that in this weather."
She called to the cook, who came running
(She must have been waiting just beyond the hall door to the
kitchen.)
And Nancy sent her to the closet on the landing
To fetch her velvet evening cape.

There was such a commotion
With the girl running out through the kitchen,
The cape about her shoulders and billowing out behind
Almost knocking over the brass umbrella stand,
I felt the best thing I could do was to sit down again.
Nancy and the cook were whispering to each other
In the hall. I could see their lips moving
And then suddenly I heard the groan or scream
That came from the kitchen and could be heard all over the house.

I went out though the dining room and the pantry
But the cook got there first by way of the back hall door.
The cook said she heard the back door slam.
I didn't hear it. Nancy said afterward she heard
The car door slam. We all heard the car roar down the driveway
In reverse gear. We heard the tires whining
As the car backed into the street and swung around
Into forward motion. None of that matters,
But that's the kind of thing you tend to recall later.
What we saw in the kitchen was the blood everywhere.
And the ax lying in the middle of the linoleum floor
With the smeary trail of blood it left
When she sent it flying. The houseman
Came up from the servants' bathroom in the basement
Just when the cook and I got there.
He came in through the back porch.
He saw what we saw of course
Except he saw more. I followed his eyes
As he looked down into that trash can at the end of the counter
And just inside the porch door. But he turned away
And ran out onto the back porch without lifting his eyes again.
And I could hear him being sick out there.

The cook and I looked at each other, to see who would go first.
I knew I had to do it, of course.
I said, "You keep Miss Nancy out of here."
And saw her go back into the hall.
I went over to the trash can,
Stepping over the ax and with no thought in my head
But that I must look. When I did look,

My first thought was, "Why, that's a human hand."
I suppose it was ten seconds or so before I was enough myself
To own it was Emmagene's hand
She had cut off with the wood ax.
I did just what you would expect.
I ran out into the driveway, seeing the blood every step,
And then back inside, past the houseman still retching over the bannister,
And telephoned the police on the kitchen telephone.
They were there in no time.

The boy who had been waiting for Emmagene
In the car, and making the racket with his horn
Used better judgment than a lot of people might have.
When she drew back the velvet cape and showed him
What she had done to herself
And then passed out on the seat,
He didn't hesitate, didn't think of bringing her back inside the house.
He lit out for the emergency room at the Hospital.
She was dead when he got her there, of course,
But everybody congratulated the boy—
The police, and the doctors as well—
The police arrested him in the emergency waiting room,
But I went down to the Station that night
And we had him free by nine o'clock next morning.
He was just a big country boy really
Without any notion of what he was into.
We looked after arrangements for Emmagene of course
And took the body up to Hortonsburg for burial.
The pastor from her church came to the town cemetery
And held a graveside service for her.
He and everybody else said a lot of consoling things to us.
They were kind in a way that only country people
Of their sort can be,
Reminding us of how hospitable we'd always been
To our kinfolks from up there
And saying Emmagene had always been
A queer sort of a girl, even before she left home.
Even that boy George's parents were at the service.

Nancy and I did our best to make them see
George wasn't to be blamed too much.
After all, you could tell from looking at his parents
He hadn't had many advantages.
He was a country boy who grew up kind of wild no doubt.
He had come down to Nashville looking for a job
And didn't have any responsible relatives here
To put restraints upon him
Or to give him the kind of advice he needed.
That might have made all the difference for such a boy,
Though of course it wasn't something you could say
To George's parents—
Not there at Emmagene's funeral, anyway.

[1975]

Robert Lowell

OUR AFTERLIFE

(For Peter Taylor)

1.

Southbound—
a couple in passage,
two Tennessee cardinals
in green December outside the window
dart and tag and mate—
young as they want to be.
We're not.
Since my second fatherhood
and stay in England,
I am a generation older.
We are dangerously happy—
our book-bled faces
streak like red birds,
dart unstably,
ears cocked to catch
the first shy whisper of deafness.
This year killed
Pound, Wilson, Auden . . .
promise has lost its bloom,
the inheritor reddens
like a false rose—
nodding, nodding, nodding.
Peter, in our boyish years,
30 to 40,
when Cupid was still the Christ of love's religion,
time stood on its hands.

Sleight of hand.

We drink in the central heat
to keep the cold wave out.
The stifled telephone that rings in my ear
doesn't exist.
After fifty,

the clock can't stop,
each saving breath
takes something. This is riches:
the eminence not to be envied,
the account
accumulating layer and angle,
face and profile,
50 years of snapshots,
the ladder of ripening likeness.

We are things thrown in the air
alive in flight . . .
our rust the color of the chameleon.

2.

Leaving a taxi at Victoria,
I saw my own face
in sharper focus and smaller
watching me from a puddle
or something I held—*your* face
on the cover of your *Collected Stories*
seamed with dread and smiling—
old short-haired poet
of the first Depression,
now back in currency.

My thinking is talking to you—
last night I fainted at dinner
and came nearer to your sickness,
nearer to the angels in nausea.
The room turned upside-down,
I was my interrupted sentence,
a misdirection tumbled back alive
on a low, cooling black table.

The doctors come more thickly,
they use exact language
even when they disagree on the mal-diagnosis
in the surgeon's feather-touch.

Were we ever weaned
from our reactionary young masters,

by the *schadenfreude* of new homes?

America once lay uncropped and golden,
it left no tarnish on our windshield . . .
In a generation born under Prohibition,
the Red Revolution, the Crash,
cholesterol and bootleg—
we were artisans
retained as if we were workers
by the charities of free enterprise.

Our loyalty to one another sticks like love . . .

This year for the first time,
even cows seem transitory—
1974
of the Common Market,
the dwarf Norman appletree
espaliered to a wall.
The old boys drop like wasps
from windowsill and pane.
In a church,
the Psalmist's glass mosaic Shepherd
and bright green pastures
seem to wait
with the modish faithlessness
and erotic daydream
of art nouveau for our funeral.

[1977]

Andrew Lytle

ON A BIRTHDAY

Peter Taylor is one of the best short story writers in English, and this is wherever English is written and at whatever time. I knew him long before he was born. Since he has been writing ghost stories recently, I think I may take this liberty, at least to assume certain essentials of composition. A Taylor married a Taylor, but I don't believe his father and mother were any kin. Geographically the two families were at the opposite ends of the state. On the distaff side the Taylors are from West Tennessee, and one of his best stories in his recent *In The Miro District and Other Stories* uses, I think, the west Tennessee grandfather. His father's people were East Tennesseans, that land of mixed loyalties and political prejudices. It was this side of the house which had the distinguished political reputation. His grandfather Bob, his great-uncle Alf, and his great great grandfather all ran for governor at the same time. Mrs. Taylor, the wife and mother, took to her bed.

This was after the Civil War (which that war was, certainly in the border states, in spite of the Daughters of the Confederacy's factitious definition: War Between the States) The race took place soon after the Bourbons had restored their political hegemony in the South, that is at home. The rest of the country tolerated but did not welcome the South back into the Union. This meant in politics a restrictive kind of attitude for Southerners. Tolerated in national affairs as a pro-consular province to be drained of its natural resources, first timber, then coal and iron, the South's state politics took on a special interest. And the Taylors were exemplars of this interest.

Tennesseans inherently understand history, even when it is mistaught. They referred to this family rivalry as *The War of Roses.* The voters saw nothing presumptuous in this. The English war of that name was a war of families, royal and noble by birth, most of whom were kin or had close connections by marriage, and most of whom were killed. (At the end of hostilities only eleven entered the House of Lords) The Tennessee Squirearchy held itself pretty high and in defeat was able to make a comparison to ancestral wars, differing only in that the English followers were generally spared their lives and livings.

When the father of the two brothers withdrew from the race, the state took it as a sensible act. The two brothers, Bob a Democrat, Alf a Republican, campaigned together, sleeping in the same inns and often in the same bed. The story goes that Bob got up early one morning, memorized his brother's speech and gave it with comments. The voters thought this the greatest of jests. At any rate it was Peter Taylor's grandfather who was elected and re-elected in these early years. Alf once, much later on.

The question can arise, and has arisen in my mind, as to what influence this political ancestry has to do with Peter Taylor the writer. I have never heard him mention politics or even say anything much about his family's prevailing occupation, that is directly. I was presumptuous enough at one time to think and maybe say that the flowery rhetoric of his grandfather's addresses and speeches was the corrective which is responsible for the purity of his style. But I forgot the fiddle and the bow. Bob Taylor often took that along on his campaigns for cheer and remembrance of things past, those eternal situations and truths which at that time, at least, informed each generation through ballads and songs. This was when Barbara Allen "lived on the other side of the mountain." The family was still pre-eminent; it dominated and was the society. Defeat and destruction of land and possessions still hurt. There were no real political issues. The issue was what Bob Taylor understood, that it was time for reprieve from sorrow, that the flowery language and the tributes to the old virtues of conduct, loyalty, honor, courage and domestic purity were powerfully reassuring to people who had had almost too much to bear. It was often said that "anybody less than kin is less than kind." All families understood this and for this instant of history such knowledge had turned all into one in feeling and sympathy. The sympathy grew enthusiastic when Bob Taylor rode through the country on a white horse, with out-riders and followers. This represented more than familial solidarity. To many he and his mount stood for a symbol of certain lasting aspirations Tennesseans still held. At Readyville, a village half-way between Woodbury and Murfreesboro, a lady and her servants stepped forth to serve them champagne.

The incident I take as the last gesture of a hope soon to be disappointed. The family would not survive as the norm of society. The restoration of conditions making for a human life, which Bob

Taylor seemed to hold out, was an illusion. The real Reconstruction, though already under way, withheld its lethal affliction until later. This subversion of the family becomes Peter Taylor's enveloping action. With his usual acumen and aversion for the threadbare, he avoided politics as a profession, now a secondary calling, but not his grandfather's concern, except that this time it could not be the family's restoration but its betrayal. Only a major art could explore the possibilities of this or use to the fullest Peter Taylor's great fictive gift.

The fall of the family follows the emigration from county to town, from town to the larger Tennessee city, itself largely an overgrown town, nothing like the modern industrial metropolis which it has become today. It is with this migration that Peter Taylor involves himself, but the migration is not his subject either. It is the medium through which the habits, conventions, institutions, manners and degrees of kin, sacraments (when there are any) undergo their changes. Coomaraswami, in *Christian and Oriental Philosophy of Art,* makes a profound observation, to the effect—new songs, yes; but a new music destroys a society. It is this knowledge which Peter Taylor knows and performs through the arts of fiction. His stories concern the various cacophonous intensities as the old songs are violated. The internal dissension between the traditional mores and disruptive influences are the discords of the new music.

His control and attitude is always ironic. This irony is very close to Jamesian irony. James has actors performing and representing two kinds of conventions; to oversimplify, European and American. But Taylor's actors rarely leave home. The changing conventions there, from outside pressure, precipitate the grounds for action. Or in a more deadly way the dissension can be within the individual's psyche itself. One of the terrifying uses appears in one of his ghost stories. A father uses a patriotic slogan to drive an unwilling son into a war he rejects. The mother urges a social fashion towards the same end. Instead of loving the boy and maybe learning from him, they substitute abstract public stances for love. They drive him into the army. He is reported missing in action, but he has merely deserted. His whistle out of the dark, where the family has cast him, brings him back into the house. He talks with each parent separately. In the end each parent agrees with the other that he is dead. He is very much alive. The substitute of a convention for a son describes their own situation, death in life. The usual human responses, particularly in a family, have been exchanged for an abstract idea. They are not aware that this has taken place. This is what gives terror to the irony, that people can be so damned, and not know it, not for Helen and all sensual delights and knowledge, but for a husk.

So the action of Peter Taylor's stories lies in the pit, the very sump of the pit, where the heart is embattled. He frequently takes the seemingly incidental, or the small ordinary actions, and from these indicates graver matters, such as a patronage which actually is a betrayal of kinship, household integrity, and finally the protagonists themselves. I am thinking of "The Hand of Emmagene." Betrayal involves almost all his stories, but they are never simple betrayals. His tone, when the narrator is the first person, is casual, as if all his readers were listeners by a neighborhood fire, shut in by the weather and in no hurry. But this seeming leisure is delusive and a quality of his irony, which I take to be Christian. The author's charity towards even his most heinous people has the quality of grace. This sympathy is pervasive but nowhere soft in judgment for actors or action. Many of his most convincing performers are monsters. (I take it that one definition of monstrosity assumes that an individual is consumed by one appetite or idea or passion.) Taylor's monsters are so urbane, so plausible in their self-righteousness or ignorance that we are tempted to accept their version of the action—until wonder asks the question: When they awaken in the night time, what do they think then? Again how can people be so aloof and yet so close and so involved with what is taking place? At this the dragon slaps his tail in the slime, and we all recognize the stench.

To continue the musical metaphor: so far there is no limit to his knowledge of the keyboard. For example, in "The Throughway" the need for place and fixity, both traditional attributes, becomes perverted by the protagonist's inadequacy before the world, or cowardice in its most unpleasing aspects, not only but especially when the throughway threatens to destroy his refuge, a rented house not even his own. He makes a masochistic fight which he must inevitably lose, until at the climax he retreats into a pathological fantasy rather than open his mind to the nature of things. At the end man and wife face each other with hostility, and this becomes the truth of seemingly peaceful years in which he avoided the responsibility of his role as man, as husband and father. Her failure is in putting up with him and not sending him forth to the fray. Why didn't she say once—Do you know what shampoo costs? Her punishment is their life together in his now narcissistic senility. This is a fresh view of self-love, where one does not act out of a tradition but uses its properties for the occasion to avoid a traditional life. The narcissim is of course universal.

One story troubles me: "The Captain's Son." The genesis of this action is a betrayal by a Spanish-American war hero of his patron, a governor who got him his captaincy and so made possible his reputation. When asked to support the governor in his race for the senate, the Captain refuses. This refusal was attached to the Governor's defeat. The action of the story concerns the Captain's son who arrives in Nashville and marries the Governor's grand-daughter. It turns out that the Captain's refusal to help his benefactor was due to the Captain's father-in-law, one of the richest planters in Mississippi, who disapproved of meddling in politics. Already here is the shift in power from politics to money, or the enemy's economy, since cotton at that time was a world commodity controlled by eastern finance. The quality in the Captain which had made him a hero was compromised. His disloyalty was due to a sell-out, riches for honor. Such a betrayal is always a self-betrayal. It makes the Captain impotent. He and his wife become habitual drunkards in an effort to overcome the sexual difficulty and get an heir.

The heir is the young man who marries the betrayed Governor's grand-daughter. And now comes the elaborate amplification of the act of betrayal. There is almost a conspiracy of understanding between the young groom and his father-in-law, who proposes, it seems in jest, that the young couple come live with them. The young husband had already discussed this seriously with his wife. So they sell the expensive house the young man had bought, which he does at a loss, and move in. The son of the betrayer now lives under the patronage of the son of the betrayed.

This is the situation in which Taylor likes to exercise his fine Eyetalian hand. It seems strange to the reader that a young couple with more than a plenty of money would move in with parents and in-laws when they didn't have to. The young wife, who has been in the habit of laughing at human complications, finds at last that she has something she can't laugh at. The marriage has not been consummated. She tells her mother that her husband is still a child, with a child's dependency. The impotency of the father has been passed on to the son, not by a violation of manhood but by the absence of the properties of manhood, virility, willingness to take responsibility for self and dependents. So it seems betrayal can be passed down, even to the Biblical third generation, which happens here. Out of fear or certainly his domestic discipline the boy has not been allowed to grow up. He wants a sister, not a wife.

The young wife, having met life with risibility, no doubt as a protest against the respectable attitudes of her parents, now is at a loss. With no better training, she lacks the knowledge to control the situation. We don't know who instigated it, or what mutual recriminations took place, but the wife let herself fall into the same desperate effort The Captain and his wife fell into. They become drunkards, locked in the soilure of their bedroom, which nobody is allowed to enter. The inlaws refuse to acknowledge that anything is wrong, at first that is, although the college age son indicates the excessive use of "booze" as he calls it. Finally the couple flees to Memphis and there continues, almost in stamped pattern, betrayal's inheritance. She writes back that they are having trouble with their son.

One wonders that she can write. The respectability which ignored the deepening trouble, sped the guests, but not until the daughter's secret life threatened to become a public scandal. Her mother discovered her one day, prepared to go to town. She was dressed in shoes and hat, but the rest of her was buck naked. The father probably had in mind a mild kind of vengeance by negating his son-in-law's use of his riches, as well as reducing him to a genteel dependency. But he had miscalculated the son-in-law's reason for acquiescence, and so brought about his daughter's ruin, with the mother's assistance. Once she was out of sight in Memphis, he did not even have to be aware of ruin's progress. What I found at first a little hard to accept is the exact reduplication of the occasion for a drunkard's solution to the spiritual cannibalism, which passes on impotency and dependency along with the family silver. I can accept this more easily now. I think I understand the wife-daughter's acceptance, but there is much behind the locked door which I ought to know. Since the mask was dropped between mother and daughter, if only for a short time, that would have been the time to ease a reader's skepticism.

The quality and tone of Peter Taylor's stories has the special quality of Tennessee manners and mores. This is a common restraint put upon the natural man in any good fiction. Action does not take place in a vacuum, and there is no longer any universal acceptance of those conventions which control behavior. What takes him beyond the border of Tennessee and the surrounding states is his subject, what human beings are capable of doing to one another. An ironic view of experience is the last look before the deluge. His irony suggests the deep tones of tragedy, but his world is no longer noble. It is Middle Class, therefore Satanic, because matter becomes the end and not the receptable for action. Being Tennessean and Southern, his characters are aware of manners even as they are being lost or perverted. They no longer keep the world at a distance but bring the desire of its gifts into the human spirit. Knowledge of this lies directly before Peter Taylor's post of observation.

[1977]

Barbara Thompson

TATTOO

The servant woman rolls back the sleeves of her kurta, throws off the flimsy scarf and pours a dollop of oil into her small fleshy palm. Julia is already naked on the cotton mat, her light hair held away from the massage oil by a child's plastic barrette. Her face in company is alert, sharp, foxy, but now in repose, unobserved by anyone, it slips back into the mild formlessness of the time before her marriage.

Kishwar transfers oil to the other hand, automatically invoking the blessing of Allah on her enterprise, falling back on her haunches to gain momentum for the next lunge at Julia's vertebral ridge. Julia tells her friends Kishwar grunts like a sumo wrestler.

Kishwar has been in the household for more than a year. She was hired as Sherezad's ayah, and when the little girl began school last September, she became Julia's part-time masseuse. She is short for a Punjabi, fat and dark, and she has a light merry laugh. Kishwar's husband works somewhere as a driver.

It is mid-May. The foreigners spend whatever time they can manage in swimming suits around the Punjab Club pool. Julia has her massage every day at eleven and goes off, oiled and sleek, to lunch there. Three or four times every month she meets a man. He is Pakistani like her husband, but younger than Julia and still unmarried. His family maintains a huge house on the Canal Bank, but when he can contrive an excuse to come to Lahore from his post in Peshawar, he stays in one of the old-fashioned suites the Club maintains for out-of-station members. This is the first day of such a visit; earlier, after her husband left, Julia spoke with him on the telephone. Smiling, she closes her eyes for what is meant to be a short nap. When she wakens it is well past the hour. Kishwar is still working over her, mindless of time as a water-wheel. Julia jumps up, fumbling for her terrycloth robe on the floor—and sees the tattoos. Kishwar has no time to cover them.

"They're all over her arms," Julia tells Nazir later at the Club. "Hearts and flowers, flying birds. All blue."

Julia lies in a pink bikini at the edge of the Club pool. The day is as hot and dry as if the country were a tandoor, one of the mounded earthen ovens that dot the city. Few people are out, even here: two English children and their doughy mother storing up sun for the summer of home-leave; a crew-cut American who swims ten measured laps and hurries away. Pakistanis are always rare. Only love or lust or cultural alienation would bring a Pakistani to a communal swimming pool at noon in May.

Nazir Ahmad, who possesses all these qualifications, lies next to Julia. He spent ten years in America on a student visa and has sloughed off his origins sufficiently to admire an even tan and be willing to strip to a bit of colored latex in the presence of strangers. He came back five years ago, summoned by a spate of cables warning of his mother's imminent demise. Once he returned her heart condition improved miraculously and his Berkeley Ph.D. in Political Science served to ease his way through the Civil Service Exam. He has become the Deputy Commissioner in Peshawar. And although he was sufficiently intimidated by his family not to bring back as wife the Jewish graduate student with whom he had been living, for the past ten months he has been seeing Julia. Today, as always, they will drink pink gins, lunch on kebabs and nan, and go up to his room. Julia will go separately, her arms full of brown shopping bags from the Mall, as though she is carrying parcels for some woman friend staying there. No one but the Club servants will know.

"She must have a past," Nazir says. "Your maidservant."

"Why?"

"Respectable 'desi' women don't go in for tattoos. But if one did, it wouldn't be the kind of design you see on British sailors."

"She has a perfectly respectable-looking husband," Julia says.

He is drowsy from the sun and gin and beginning to think of the cool dark room above. He calls the bearer and orders lunch. It is brought to them at the pool by two servants in starched white, their long coats cinched with cummerbunds, their pugris stiff and tall above their heads. Julia and Nazir eat with their fingers, their movements quick, expectant.

That night at dinner Julia tells her husband about the tattoos. It is one of her duties as his wife to be entertaining at dinner. She spends a fair amount of time preparing herself—collecting gossip at bridge parties, going to family weddings and funerals and circumcisions, reading the air mail magazines at the Club. *The New Statesman* is best for her purposes, though its politics are not her husband's. He owns a complex of textile mills.

After six years of marriage, her own politics are non-existent, which Julia herself in reflective moments knows to be an odd neutrality in a woman who came here as an officer, however junior, in the U.S. Foreign Service. Lahore was her first overseas post, and nothing in her training or the talk of others had prepared her for the emotions she would feel at the work assigned her, refusing visas to the legion of the hopeless who were trying to emigrate. In time it numbed her: her real life began at twilight on the race course grounds, urging a long-maned polo pony around the perimeter of the field while the men, Pakistanis and a few foreigners, played their games. The horse was lent her by the man who later became her husband, a stocky middle-aged Punjabi from an old family who was at least partially married: his wife lived in the village. The second summer Julia found herself pregnant, and in the lassitude of that state, intensified by the flower-rich monsoon heat, let go of her life of demanding autonomy. With something like relief she let herself be married to him under the polygamous dispensation of Islamic law.

They are dining alone tonight and so her husband summons Kishwar into the dining room. Julia has aroused his curiosity; he will inspect the tattoos himself. The servant woman toddles in raking at the dopatta over her hair, self-conscious at this notice by the Sahib. He is pleasant, hearty, almost flirtatious with her—his habitual manner with women who could not possibly misunderstand.

Because of this manner and its contrast to the strict formality with which he treats the wives of his friends and business associates, Julia believed in the beginning that he had no interest in other women. Then when Sherezad was three, she discovered that every Thursday night, before the ritual bath that purified him for his Friday prayers, he visited a singing woman in a brothel in the Hira Mundi.

When Julia told him she was leaving, he was courteous and calm and offered, with regret at her decision, to take care of the travel arrangements if she was sure that was what she wanted. Of course, she could not take her jewelry, the rubies set with pearls, the heavy kundan earrings with the emerald drops: Customs would search her for any gold illegally exported. And she could not take Sherezad, who was without a valid passport.

Julia, with the wisdom of the weak, gave in immediately and made no terms. She knew he would not relent or be subverted. He loved Sherezad as he loved his Rajput miniatures, rarely looking at them but always conscious that they hung in fine gold frames in an air conditioned room with black cloths over the glass to keep the colors from fading.

They went on as before, but imperceptibly, without any volition on her part, Julia changed. She continued her Urdu lessons with the old Kashmiri ustad who came three mornings a week, but her early proficiency left her; she was lapsing into the kitchen Urdu of the other foreign women who had not been scholars and government officers. And after a time she braved the company of other Americans, steeling herself against a continuation of the coolness they had shown her at the time of Sherezad's birth. But those days and that cadre of diplomats had passed. Julia's husband was rich and clubbable; they were welcomed everywhere.

Her husband rarely accompanied her; he did not want to be officially perceived as a client of the Americans. But he seemed glad that Julia was back with 'her own kind' as though he understood it to mean that she was abandoning the excessive expectations with which she had begun their marriage, and was accepting the compromises her circumstance required.

A summer ago at the Consul General's reception for the Fourth of July, Julia met Nazir Ahmad. If her husband knows about the affair, he has elected to be complaisant. Julia's virtue was never a commodity of great value; he knew there had been men before him. And he knows too, as Julia did only when it was too late, that if he should ever want to do so, he can use this indiscretion to send her back to her own country, cut her off forever from Sherezad.

But there is nothing of that menace in the air tonight as they dine together under the whirring fans while Sherezad sleeps in the adjacent garden in a cocoon of mosquito netting. Julia can see that he is enjoying his interrogation of the maidservant, the flutter into which he has cast her by his courtliness and the range of his questions: Has she sons? What is her village? How does she come to be in Lahore? Kishwar answers in monosyllables, smiling shyly, her eyes downcast. The sleeves of her cotton shirt are tight at the wrists.

He has not mentioned the tattoos, and after a while Julia realizes that he never will. That is not his way. He will lead her by indirection to tell him whatever he wants to know, either as an accidental self-betrayal or a free offering. His patience comes of knowing he has, at last resort, the power to command her. Julia feels a chill and goes out into the dark veranda to make sure that Sherezad has not thrown off her covers.

The next morning when she is again naked under Kishwar's kneading, Julia composes her questions in schoolbook Urdu, asking the woman where the markings came from, how she comes to have them. She cannot see Kishwar's face when she asks but she feels the woman's hands tighten. Then with a laugh, Kishwar's gives Julia's buttock an affectionate slap. "Meri jan bahaut passand—"

Julia cannot follow the language. "Your husband likes it?" she asks tentatively in English.

Kishwar laughs again, a lazy laugh laced with contempt for the little dark husband about whom Julia could have such an unlikely idea. "Not husband," she says in English. "Meri jan." My Beloved. She says it comfortably, companionably.

Julia tells Nazir at lunch: "You can't believe it! She's so ugly. She's fat and gap-toothed and black as the Ace of Spades. And she has a lover!"

As she says it she is sorry. Slurs against color are acceptable from him, not from her. She has heard the tales of British memsahibs who undressed in front of their servants as they would have their poodles because, being black, they were not quite men. She is never sure what Nazir feels; he himself is quite dark, a dull cafe-au-lait.

"Think of Cleopatra," he says. "Swarthy, short-legged and with a hooked nose." He congratulates himself on finding an image that is racially neutral.

"If it's her lover who likes it, I wonder what her husband thinks," Julia muses.

That is a line of speculation Nazir prefers not to follow.

In the evening as Julia and Kishwar return from the bazaar,

Kishwar's husband is waiting at the gate. Another man is with him, a tall lean Pathan with a sharp eye and the clothing of the Peshawar District. Julia hands over the parcels to the bearer, and Kishwar goes to her husband. There is a hasty exchange, monosyllabic and stacatto, and then Kishwar comes to ask Julia for leave. Julia gives her the night but tells her to be back by breakfast time. Tomorrow is Nazir's last day. She wants to go to him scented and oiled, a sun-flushed houri. She likes the image of herself as a gift, and she dresses in bright soft colors—saffron, peach, aquamarine—layers of cloth to be unwrapped and inside, the firm soft flesh that Kishwar has prepared.

It is noon when Kishwar turns up. Julia is late already, and still on the telephone negotiating with her sister-in-law that Sherezad will be delivered to her house after school. There have been nasty incidents involving little girls left alone with menservants even in the best regulated households. Her husband does not permit her to leave Sherezad without a woman. Julia has explained this more than once, a little frantically she knows. She has the uncomfortable feeling that the other woman knows exactly why she is in such a hurry.

Kishwar looks worn and dirty, and she makes no apology at all for her tardiness, not even the conventional lies about sudden illness or family crisis. Julia has girded herself against the falsehoods but now she finds herself resenting Kishwar's disregard of the forms; it is a little insulting.

Kishwar trails her to the car as though she has more to say. Another request. "Not now," Julia says firmly. Her good nature is being imposed on.

Kishwar goes into halting English. "Memsahib, you speak to Lat'-sahib for me," she says, using the word "lord" that is reserved for governors and high officials. "Nazir-sahib." Her manner is sullen for somebody, especially a Punjabi, asking a favor.

"I can't stop now. I'm late."

Kishwar looks around. The house servants are busy elsewhere. Only two male figures lounging at the gate would see her—if they turn around—as she throws herself at Julia's feet, pressing her little round belly against Julia's shins. She hangs onto them sobbing. The sobs seem real. With a sigh and a glance at her watch,

Julia urges Kishwar to her feet, and into the comparative privacy of the veranda.

Kishwar's husband has sent her. His honor is at stake. That much is clear; Julia can follow it even in the mix of Urdu, Punjabi and pidgin English. It is the usual story when some extraordinary request is about to be made. "Safarish," the favor that puts one eternally in somebody's debt, is a way of life here.

The details are difficult for Julia to follow. A Pathan tribesman—an Affridi from the hills outside Peshawar—came to Kishwar's husband yesterday morning. His only son is in jail in Peshawar, charged with murder. The boy is fifteen. He is accused of taking the gold earrings from a three-year-old girl of his village, and, when she said that she would tell her mother, of throwing her into the well. The earrings were knotted in the cord that fastened his baggy shelwar trousers. He said he had found them, but when the police beat him, he confessed. Now he will go to prison for life. The girl's family is willing to accept restitution—the blood-price: she was one of several daughters and the price includes not only gold but animals. But Government says the boy must go to trial. The Deputy Commissioner—Nazir Ahmad—has the power to release him.

"But he's guilty," Julia says. "Why should Nazir-sahib let him go free?" She is about to add, "and why do you plead for him?", when she understands. Of course, this Pathan, the sinewy man with the black moustache here yesterday in the courtyard is Kishwar's lover, the man for whom she had herself tattooed.

"If you want to, you can come with me to the Club. Nazir-sahib is likely to be there and you can speak with him yourself," she says. "I can't take any responsibility for it." She adds that for form; she has already taken on some responsibility just by listening.

The servant woman waits patiently at the edge of the Club lawn, a good distance from the swimming pool, where ayahs are permitted. She squats in the shade of the pink bougainvillea vine, every now and then getting up to look through the servants' gate at something or someone on the roadway. She has wrapped her sheer nylon dopatta over her head and neck, covering herself as much as possible. Near the pool the sahibs, in strength today because of the Friday holiday, lie glistening with sunoil on their bright terry towels. Occasionally a child dives off the board or paddles around the shallow end under the eye of his mother, but the real use of the blue water is to cool the tanning adults who float about on its surface in black truck inner-tubes, drinks in hand.

Nazir tries to ignore the maidservant. He doesn't like refusing favors and he doesn't want to grant this one. From Julia's report, the boy seems clearly guilty, and any official interference would be not only wrong but conspicuous. So he sucks on his drink, splashing pool water on his shoulders to cool himself. But whatever he does he feels Kishwar's black eyes on him. He may as well hear her out. He throws a towel over his bare torso and walks to the gate.

She stands up and squints over her shoulder as he approaches. He sees two men, one in Peshawari dress, at the end of the servants' walk. "Ji, Mai?" He addresses her in the familiar form of 'mother', glancing without meaning to at her arms. Only the faint blue edge of the tattoo is visible at the buttoned wrist of her shirt.

"I told Memsahib," she says. "I will be beaten if you do not do this thing."

"Why do you plead for this boy? What is the father to you?" Nazir says it in as kindly a manner as possible. He asks not because he doubts Julia's interpretation but out of curiosity, to hear what a traditional Punjabi woman would answer in such a case.

"He did my husband a service once," the woman replies.

Nazir tries not to smile at that way of speaking of it.

She looks him straight in the face as though she reads his thoughts. "This Pathan killed a man for him."

Nazir shouts to the bearer to bring him a chair, slumps into it. He should have known the story was not as simple as Julia said.

Kishwar does not speak again until the bearer is out of earshot. "My husband was in prison," she begins. "It was nothing." She makes a gesture with open palms to indicate the absence of any guilt. "He was innocent. There was a quarrel between families. Someone had to confess. He had no job so he was chosen. He came to prison here in Lahore."

Nazir's work is administering the law; he does not take easily to her assumption that while justice must be served, it need not be served with any precision. For nothing, for his family's convenience, a man will serve seven years Rigorous Imprisonment?

"We were married only a little time. I had no child. I was

prettier then. A man saw me. He would wait for me on the paths and give me sweets. He would come to the well and draw water for me. I was weak. I fell.

"When my husband's people came to know of it, they sent me away. I could not go back to my own people as I was, so I went to live with him. He was a good man, he never beat me. He kept me in the inner courtyard and never let me go anywhere, even to the shrine, but he bought me shiny cloth for clothes and pomegranates and wild honey so that I would conceive. Then at the end of the fourth year, he took me to Montgomery to the man who gives tattoos. He said it was so I could not run away. Where would I run to?"

She unfastens the buttons at the wrists of her shirt and rolls back the sleeves. Nazir sees that among the flowers and hearts, the birds in flight, are words in Urdu: a man's name, Asif Magid, and a date in the Islamic calendar. "Memsahib saw this."

"Memsahib can't read the Urdu," he says.

"It was the next year in the dry month before the rains. We were sleeping out on the roof, and on the night of the dark of the moon, someone came and killed him with a knife."

"Asif Magid?"

"Asif Magid, whom I loved. The man who killed him cut his throat so deeply that his head hung loose, and he cut the palms of his hands and his genitals. He must have done all that after he was dead because I did not wake until the flies began to buzz and the vultures circle over him. It was almost daybreak and he had been dead so long his blood was like river mud. I knew my husband had done it, or some of his kinfolk. When the constable came, I told him.

"But word came back that my husband was still in prison in Lahore, and that his kinfolk too had been locked up that night, taken in Lahore on suspicion of planning a burglary. So I went back to my husband's people and lived with them like a slave until my husband came out of prison. He beat me at first to take away the shame, but afterwards he brought me here to Lahore. He swore to me that he had no connection with the killing of Asif-sahib. I believed it because he swore on the heads of our unborn sons."

She smiles a queer smile. "I have no child to this day."

Nazir is impatient. "But what does all this have to do with that other business—the boy, the gold earrings?"

"Yesterday that Pathan came to my husband's quarters. He had shared my husband's prison cell those years ago. He knew—as everything, sahib, is known—that I have a place with Memsahib, and that you will not refuse Memsahib's safarish. He asked my husband to obtain his son's freedom."

Nazir is annoyed at the implication that his affair with Julia is generally known. They have been unfailingly discreet. Julia has never even been to Peshawar. "Why should your husband ask you to plead, even if I were able to grant it?"

"This man did my husband a killing once, out of friendship." Her tone is heavy, implying it is something he already knows. "He is the one who came at the dark of the moon and killed Asif-sahib as he lay next to me."

Nazir shouts for another gin. This is like everything else in his official life in this place. He longs for the orderliness of America, where appetites are simple and simply satisfied, where killings are done out of need and anger, not out of duty and friendship.

Kishwar sees his weariness and presses. "This Pathan lived with my husband in his cell. They shared everything, their grief at having no sons, my husband's shame at the dishonor I had brought him. They were closer than brothers.

"He was released from prison the year before my husband. His own village was in the Frontier, a thousand miles away. He had never been to our village, but he knew from my husband's telling that the house of Asif-sahib was the tallest of all, that it stood next to the ruin of the Sikh gurdwara and had wooden pillars carved with flowers.

"He sent a cable to my husband's kinfolk, calling them in the name of their jailed brother to meet him in the bazaar in Lahore. He met them at the tandoor, and while they were eating he went away on some pretext, leaving behind some pieces of luggage. They were filled with burglar's tools. He went to the police constable and told him that he had overheard those men from Montgomery planning a robbery and that their implements would be found with them. They were jailed for two days.

"That night this Pathan killed Asif-sahib as he lay next to me. No one suspected him. He was known to no one. Even my husband"—she spits on the grass—"knew nothing until yesterday."

Kishwar turns her back on Nazir without another word as though now that she has done what she was told to do it is no longer her concern whether Nazir honors her request. She walks slowly, heavily, down the cinder path to the road. Nazir sees that those two men are still there, waiting for her. For the first time he notices that the tall one is carrying a rifle.

"Half the population of Peshawar does," he mutters to himself, wondering why it seems menacing here. He goes back to the pool and lies down on the recliner next to Julia's and tries to unravel for her what the serving woman has said.

"But why on earth should she plead for him then?" Julia says.

He shrugs. Logic is irrelevant. "It's her husband's debt of honor." His tone is ironic: he knows that is what Julia expects of him. He has lost track of his own feelings except an overwhelming desire for tidiness, for a system of justice as clean of speculative mercy as the old Islamic code.

"But the debt he owes the Pathan is for killing the man she loved."

"It could have been worse, Julia. In the villages they don't take these things lightly. The old way was to kill them both and leave the bodies at the well as a warning to others." Nazir hears his own voice; it is so expressionless he cannot tell—so how can Julia?—whether he means to defend these barbarities or only explain them to her.

"You mean Kishwar should be grateful!"

"I didn't say that."

"It's what you meant." Her voice has a hard edge as though it is dammed against tears. Nazir raises himself to look over at her and sees that her face is pinched tight. He reaches across to stroke her arm, but not without first glancing over his shoulder to be sure they are alone.

Julia has seen that moment of carefulness; she is rigid and still.

"What I meant was that Kishwar sees these things differently than we do, Julia," he says gently.

She turns away from him, burrowing her face in the jumble of terrycloth. She knows she is waiting for something, but she perceives even less than Nazir does that she is waiting for a sign from him: some proof—an impolitic kiss here in the open, even an outburst of anger—that what he feels for her is deeper and more particular than what men customarily feel for women in this place.

He gives what he can: "I'll do whatever you want, Julia. Shall I let the boy go?"

"I wouldn't ask you that. You're not a 'jungly' to live by these insane rules."

"This isn't Berkeley, Julia. Maybe it *is* the jungle."

"Do you think that's *right*?"

"What does it matter what I think? Half the witnesses I hear are perjuring themselves and I know it and they know I know it. The bazaar rings with the real story and I make my ruling based on what is brought to my official attention. The British were lucky. They didn't know. And if that child's father will take some gold bangles and a mule or two for her life, why should Government involve itself?"

"You don't really mean that," Julia says.

He feels her relax, and takes his hand away. "Does it matter if he's guilty if no one cares?"

"You don't really know that he is, of course," Julia says.

"The child was dead. He had the earrings. He confessed."

"He said he found them. The police beat him."

"Julia!"

"If he was guilty there should have been witnesses. There are witnesses to everything in this country."

Her voice is tart. He can't help wondering if she means witness to them. Or if someone has whispered to her that his mother is pressing to arrange a marriage for him. "Julia, what do you want me to do?"

"Once you start weighing things, nothing makes any sense," she says. "Kishwar gets beaten again, and the boy goes to jail forever—"

"Not forever. And if he's pretty he'll have an easy enough time." He knows this will shock her, will make it even more difficult for her to think in terms of abstract justice. "What do you think these prisons are?" He has lost the thread of his argument, of hers. Which side has he taken?

"Do what you think is right," she says almost primly. She does not want to think about Kishwar's story any longer; it contains a source of pain that she does not want to identify. She stands up and stretches herself. The sun is directly overhead now; it reflects off everything, the enamelled white table-tops, the aluminum frames of the chairs, the river-mica in the concrete.

When Julia comes out of the changing room, Nazir has already gone up. Kishwar is back under the pink bougainvillea and Julia gives her the bag of wet things to put into the car. They do not speak but Julia knows that she is conveying to Kishwar that everything is within her control.

Julia believes it herself. It is a small thing, really, that has been asked of him. Nazir will find extenuating circumstances to justify his action; there are always extenuating circumstances when someone has the will to find them. She wonders fleetingly why it has become so important that Nazir do this for her—do it without her making a direct request. Is it out of sympathy with Kishwar, who tends her daughter and who knows as no one else does her body when it is loose and undefended? Or does she simply crave proof that he will do anything at all for love of her?

Whatever it is, she feels intensely the power she has over him, and borne along upon it, she walks up the wide main stairs to his room without making any attempt at all to conceal her destination. She feels immune from the world's judgment.

It is only afterwards, coming down the stairs in her limp summer dress, that she reflects that Kishwar too must have felt that power, lying on the flat mud roof under the stars with the lover who was so afraid of losing her that he had his name etched in blue arabesques on her skin. And that tiny girl too, angry over the rings torn from her earlobes, reminding the big boy what punishment she can bring down upon him. The moment of power is brief and the danger abiding. Julia knows that and something in her falters, but she can still perfectly remember the elegant tracery of Nazir's ribcage under the wiry hair as he sprawled beside her on the wide bed. She does not yet feel the danger she knows is everywhere.

In the morning, Julia's sister-in-law drops by for coffee. She is a cool woman with streaks of bright henna covering her grey hair. She wastes no love on Julia, but she is invariably correct. This morning, among things of no importance at all, she tells Julia that Nazir Ahmad is to marry Inayutallah's daughter Shams. Julia remains composed but she does not summon the bearer for the usual second cups of Nescafe. When her caller leaves, Julia awards herself a tumbler of gin before she calls Kishwar for her massage.

The strong hands rest her. And as the muscles relax, Julia's mind, too, lets go a little. Nazir will do whatever she wants except—now the perimeters are known—in matters that concern his family.

This wife will not matter. She is one of his own kind and will never understand that part of him that needs Julia. For Julia knows, has known all along, the source of her power over him, and for just a moment she permits herself to think about it, to give it a name.

It has nothing to do with her prettiness, the soft supple body, her cultivated passion. She can age and wither, it will make no difference. He cleaves to her whiteness, the foreign smell—a lifetime of other foods, different rituals of hygiene—and the unfalsifiable paleness of her secret hair. Julia is proof to him that he is not altogether one of these people, that he was changed irrevocably in those ten years away. Nazir never thought to marry her, or to stay free for her, but what she has of him she can keep as long as she wants.

Kishwar sighs as she pours the warm oil onto the soles of Julia's feet. She too moves in a liquid drifting manner as though her mind is far away. Julia wonders if she is thinking of Asif Magid. Did Kishwar love him? And how could she know what love was in a life like that, when she had nowhere else to go? But she must have felt something—pride or power if not love—when he took her to Montgomery to have his name put on her.

The sun has reached the dusty pane of the high window and falls on her back and Kishwar's head. She can smell the pine massage oil and the heavier oil that Kishwar braids into her black hair. Everything is still. Only Kishwar moves, her heavy rhythms a form of comforting.

Julia is half asleep when she hears her own rough sob like an infant's strangle, and wakes in time to bring back from sleep the image of a pale naked body engraved all over in an intricate calligraphy of fruits and flowers and the indelible names of men.

[1981]

Diane Vreuls

BEEBEE

When he was six weeks old his mother gave him back. The identity bracelet was still on his wrist: Baby Boy Brewster, known from the start as Beebee. The hospital sent him to the county orphanage. The following winter it burned to the ground. He was then placed in five foster homes in succession and only once adopted—by a couple killed in a plane crash two months after signing the papers. "I'm good at being orphaned," he likes to tell me. Sometimes he writes that in the blank that asks "Profession." Sometimes he prints "FOSTER SON."

His second decade was spent in reform school and homes of detention. He was your model juvenile delinquent back in the days boys earned the label for truancy, stealing cars, a little breaking and entering—nothing mean; you can tell Beebee's never been mean. More the kind of quiet that's taken for insolence, with a grace that combined with his small stature is felt by clumsy men—cops, judges, wardens—to be sly. When his juvenile years were numbered and the penalties grew stiff, he looked for another line of work. Having been trained to hand-tool leather, sweep shops, pick locks and beans, after lying his way quickly in and out of the army, he decided to be an actor. At twenty he landed a part in an off-Broadway show he won't forgive me for having missed, though he knows I was just a kid at the time and living in Simpson, Illinois, a place which didn't even get films to speak of. "Are you sure you didn't see me?" he asks. Most of his parts have been smaller since.

We met four summers ago when I started work at the nursery. As I marched twenty four-year-olds in pairs down the block to the park one Friday morning, he fell in with my step, walked me back to the school and then home to my apartment. He's been my partner since, more or less. More when he's waiting for work. Less when he's out on the road with second-string touring companies of last year's Broadway hits. It's an arrangement I try not to chafe at. I was attracted to him because he was so unlike the boys I grew up with, because he promised a future that cancelled my past in a way that wouldn't erase me in the process. It's what we all hope for, no? Truth is, he's been trying to get me to leave him from the first. His means are restricted. He will not argue, would never strike me, won't even contradict. But I know he's waiting for me to close the show. When he returns from a gig out of town he will not engage a cab until he's called from the Port Authority and checked with me first. He can't risk coming unasked. For God's sake, Beebee, I say. Prolonged courtesy is an insult; you can't help but wonder what rage it conceals. Look, I say, if you don't want to come back, don't. Then he always tells me he loves me—too easy, I think.

He has been in love only once. He was twelve and her name was Stella. Stella McNult. For her he learned every Stella poem in the western world lending library, or at least every branch he's been near. The Herrick Memorial Library in Wellington, Ohio, the Muhlenberg Branch of the NYPL, the dusty shelves of army bases in Alabama and Tennessee. He knows twenty-three poems to Stella, of which twelve are written by him. When he wants to tell me a love poem, I get one to Stella. He changes the name, but I know: the rhyme scheme is off.

She was his fourth foster mother, the only one he remembers aloud. She lived in the country with her husband, Bud, and the kids she took in to make ends meet: five or six day-boarders and Beebee full-time, on the state. He was proud of that, of being the only one of the lot truly residential. He had his own bed and chest in the glassed-in sunporch she used for sewing and though she sometimes napped the babies there when the cribs were full, she always referred to it as "Beebee's room" and asked his permission first. Being the oldest, he helped with the other kids, could do diapers and bottles and toss and tickle the bawlers and walk the toddlers and work the Busy Boxes on the cribs. He could run the washer and dryer and put on snowsuits, stuffing arms and legs in the proper casings as well as Stella did, and fix broken zippers and push their trikes and pull them in coaster wagons around the puddles out by the barn. On days she looked peaked, he stayed home from school and took over, while she baked and phoned and sometimes dozed on the sofa till Bud returned. The note she sent back to Beebee's teacher next day always said "He got sick in the night." When he missed so much school they refused to pass him in June, "night disease" he claims was the reason they gave on his report card, but the fact was he dropped seventh grade due to running a baby farm with Stella in Wakeman, Ohio.

She was younger than I am now, had married Bud out of high school. They were so dumb they thought they had to marry after Homecoming, but later she found out she wasn't pregnant at all.

"She told you that? At twelve?"

She told him everything, sipping her Mogen David with ice cubes in it, talking to him as if he were her mother, while she ironed, while she polished the silverplate coffee service she kept on the oak buffet, while she dusted Venetian blinds or shelled garden peas or poured hot jello into custard cups every day after lunch. The way he looks at me Sunday mornings when I'm making pancakes, I know he sees Stella, his first woman in a housecoat, hair uncombed, her broad flowered back to him as she stands at the stove, tending a life her husband and he can rise to, her cooking heat steaming the room. No matter how early I wake, she's there before me.

He asks me to tie up my hair as she must have worn hers. He buys me blue-flowered robes. He is still as she formed him, his hair cut short despite all changes of fashion, giving his long face an immaculate look of surprise. Cuts down your roles, I tell him, that hair, that demeanor of Fifties nostalgia which can't play forever, but he picks up a part in a commercial—the anti-hero, Brand X—just often enough to justify his looks. In fact, the residuals from his perennial performance as Vapor Lock are enough to land us in Darien, make burghers of us both. But Beebee won't buy that.

He comes into the kitchen fully dressed, wearing the lumber jacket she gave him for Christmas. He mumbles a soft good morning so she won't be startled and burn herself, but she always jumps, regardless, scattering grease. "You're up early, Beebee," she says more sharply than he deserves, and he hurries to help her wipe up the floor with paper towels from the sink.

He has tried to delay. He has pulled on his clothes slow motion, dallied making the bed, tucking the army blankets in one by one. Then, already trained not to sit on beds, he'd hunched at the sewing machine, snapping the catch on the cover, pulling out drawers in the stand. Or he'd peered through the blinds to check on the progress of dawn, found the yard dark, the street lamp down where the road met the county highway the only thing lit for miles. He'd listened for animals, then, knew they were out there in the yard, feeding not far from his windows—he'd see their small tracks later in the snow—but all he could hear was the scrape of breakfast plates pulled from shelves in the kitchen, the chime of cups set into saucers, the clang of something metal dropped in the sink. He'd feared, then, that he had been dreaming, that he had lost all track of time, that he would run into the kitchen and find the food cold on his plate, Bud gone to work, Stella doing the dishes, and the cars that brought the babies already turning into the drive. This has never happened, but he is terrified it might.

"Did you wash?" Stella asks.

He nods. The daily lie. Bud is in the bathroom, how could he have washed? It's something he's never been able to figure out through four foster homes: how to get a turn in the john. He was too shy to share the room as they did in some families; if he managed to enter alone, he worried he might be forcing someone to wait. The one other place he'd slept on a porch, he'd simply used the yard, but here the door was nailed shut year round and stuffed with weatherstripping. So he'd trained himself to wake late at night and feel his way down the hall, hoping his hands would push the right door, while floor-plans of earlier houses whirled in his brain. He was less afraid of the dark than of his own noises: of stumbling into furniture, brushing objects off a hall table, releasing a doorknob too quickly and waking the sleepers with the sudden recoil of its spring. By the time he stayed with Stella, he'd become expert at prowling at night. It can't have been good for his growth, this chronic lack of sleep. I see it in some of the kids I work with—a fatigue that thins the skin, shrinks the frame, gives them a fitful precocity; one moment they're wired, the next the fuse has blown. Beebee's sallow still.

"Sleep well?" Stella asks, as she does every morning. He always says yes.

He sits at the table and waits for Bud. She won't serve till he comes, stacks the pancakes upright in an old metal dishrack she's set in an oven, where they'll keep crisp. Beebee is fascinated by this trick, by all her kitchen skills, the twist of the wrist that dollops out batter exactly into pancakes that spread to identical size on the grill, the body rhythm that measures how long something's broiled or perked or simmered so that she never need glance at a clock or lift a lid to tell if it's done. He watches her intently. She doesn't notice or doesn't mind if she does, chatters brightly at him as she moves around the room. But she is tense this morning, tight-lipped. She doesn't even acknowledge his sitting there until she leans to an old roller tray by the stove and turns on the T.V. She never has it on when she's alone.

Bud enters without a greeting, face raw from the razor, his

movements stiff and painful as if he were injured in his sleep. He's a small man and so thin you wouldn't think he could put away the stacks of pancakes she puts at his place. Beebee inches his chair from the table to give the man space. In the seven months he's been there, they've barely spoken, he and Bud. It wasn't a matter of resentment or suspicion, he knew even then, but only a simple shyness on both sides. Beebee eats with his eyes to his plate but monitors Bud's presence so acutely that he can describe to this day the way his hair, sculptured high in a wave, parts and falls onto his forehead whenever he bends to his food, how the wet wool of his collar and cuffs (he must dress before he washes and not bother to roll up his sleeves) emits a smell which, mixed with that of coffee, seems as male to Beebee as musk. That morning he senses in Bud something acrid as well, metallic. He thinks back on the previous evening. The babies were gone by five thirty, Bud came home at six. At dinner Stella talked about her day. After Beebee'd washed up the plates, he retired to the porch to do homework. If they'd argued, he hadn't heard them. Yet what Bud says next sounds like the clincher.

"You can shove it. I'm not going back."

Stella, leaning against the counter, answers directly to the T.V.: "Suit yourself."

"Fat chance," he says.

"What's that supposed to mean?"

"This wasn't *my* idea. Things are bad enough as it is."

"Well, we have to start sometime, don't we?"

"Not now."

"Then when?"

He doesn't answer. She watches an ad, switches channels, turns to the sink. Bud balls up his napkin and stuffs it into his juice glass. He sets the glass inside his coffee cup, then slow as a child building blocks he centers his cup in his saucer, sets the saucer on his plate and crosses knife and fork along the rim. He regards his construction a moment, then with a nod of satisfaction, he pushes back his chair and leaves the room. Minutes later the front door clicks. The truck door slams. Stella doesn't let on she's been listening to gears shift, the truck break the ice in the drive, then turn down the road and out of hearing until she says "He forgot his lunch."

The first baby arrives. It's Beebee's signal to leave, to strike out for the highway where he'll wait half an hour for the bus. He'd rather wait out there today, sets off without asking for milk money, afraid that in the time it will take her to remember where she left her purse, he might decide to stay behind and help.

On the road he's passed by women driving babies. He loathes them. The way they fuss when they hand the kids to Stella, butts propping open the storm door to let in the icy cold. The way they whine out needless instructions and complaints of the jobs they'll run off to. Worst of all the lingering mamas who step inside to undress their children. You know at once the kid's got strep and they'll all take sick within the week.

"Not fair," I interrupted.

"What's not?"

"About the mothers. Why blame them?"

"Come to think of it," he shrugged, "I didn't catch things, from the babies or anyone else." When he was a recruit at Fort Rucker, the entire camp came down with dysentery; it was his luck to stay hale, to man the bedpans and buckets. When he was a busboy in the Berkshires, a fish fry poisoned the hotel. One of the few remaining upright, he had to dash from room to room with burned toast. His resistance, he claimed, is total and dates from an early orphanage where a fever got you slapped in isolation—a sickbay the size of a gym where you lay in a sea of white beds, forgotten till the next state inspection. I doubt his stories, of course, but it's true he's never ill. And is good at tending those who are. He's nursed me through the usual flus, as caring as any mother.

"Get on with the story," I said.

"Where was I?"

Jones Road and Route 80. He studies white letters on green signposts he's sure no one's noticed but him: locals know the roads too well to look for markers and who else would ever drive by? Six other children use this bus stop, all from a family called Welling who live a quarter mile up Jones Road. Appalachians, says Stella, and too dumb to count their own kids. They treated Beebee with the scorn that any pack reserves for a stray. To dodge them, he chooses not to wait. Besides, he can't take the wind. It comes from Canada, he explained. Down three states every morning, looking just for him. He walks the two miles to the junior high backwards, counting his steps in the drifts. He arrives at school exhausted; the heat puts him instantly to sleep. He wakes for roll call, for lunch, for a film. In between he's so perfectly propped (chin on palms, face towards book) his teachers' reports on his conduct commend his as "well behaved."

He was never caught sleeping, he says. I think he was the one child in ten that studies show teachers overlook. I understand why the tenth was Beebee. Say we've made plans to meet at a drugstore or gallery or entrance to a park; even when the place is deserted Beebee isn't easily seen. Once I pick him out of the landscape like the face hidden in a print, I wonder why I didn't spot him sooner. Must be a psychic form of coloration, which would also explain why at auditions producers don't often select him—they can't single him out of the crowd. Let me stay with this a moment; it seems to explain other things. His attraction, for one. It is not as my former roommate supposes, that he appeals to my suppressed maternal instinct. (*How* suppressed? I work at a nursery, she seems to forget.) No, it's his habit of eluding definition, of inviting you to see him as you will and then—and this trait is even rarer—of conforming absolutely to your needs. How can you ditch someone like that? To reject him is to abandon your own invention. At times it's eerie, though, his camouflage. There are days when I've come home from work and haven't known he's in the apartment until I'm about to flop on the sofa and there he is, sprawled with a book.

When Beebee returned from school, he could hear the wail of babies from the drive. One step inside, he was hit by a wall of noise, the smell of urine and worse. The living room was an aural fever ward: babies shaking the rails of their playpens, toddlers buried beneath sofa pillows, sobbing as remorselessly as they breathed. At his entrance they stopped for a moment, then resumed in more desperate pitch. Stella was nowhere in sight. He attended them one by one, changing diapers, gagging their screams with cookies and bottles of juice. When their mothers came to collect them, they were sleeping in front of the tv. It wasn't till seven that Stella emerged from the bedroom. "How'd it go?" she asked. Then: "Oh, I thought you were Bud."

He made them toasted cheese sandwiches with mustard, and undiluted tomato soup.

"You're a good cook, you know that? I mean, when you think how most men can't take care of themselves at all, you're way ahead, Beebee, you really are."

She didn't eat a bit of what he'd made.

"They called. Twice. Bud never went to work."

Bud worked in a local sandstone quarry; had to, Stella once explained, since they'd sold off the land from the farm and sunk all their cash into a garage. The garage had failed. Not Bud's fault—he was a good mechanic, she said, but so were half the men in the county. From time to time, he'd look for other jobs, would be gone two days, come back drunk as a loon. This had not happened since Beebee moved in. "You can't blame him," she said. "He hates the quarry but there's no one else hiring now."

"When will he be back?" Beebee asked.

"When he's out of cash. He can't have much on him. Maybe tonight."

But it wasn't that night, though they thought they could hear the truck a dozen times over. Whenever a car passed the house, Stella would jump up from the couch, part the drapes of the picture window to watch the taillights burn down the road. Then she'd return to the tv set and lower the volume a twist—as if hearing the next car sooner would cause it to turn up the drive. By the time Beebee went to bed, she was watching a silent screen.

Next morning she woke him stirring buttons. A soft clatter, pause, then a long spill. He reached for his bed light; she was kneeling at the sewing table across the room. In one hand she held a man's shirt, from the other buttons poured into the drawer like coins into a chest.

It was the first of her Saturday projects. While Beebee did the regular cleaning she shampooed the living room rug. She emptied shelves, put down new paper, sponged fingerprints off of door frames. He tried to stay out of her way, but she filled the house with a heat lightning he knew wasn't aimed at him but seemed dangerous anyway. When she baked, she was better, calmer. Watching butter on a slow melt, she began to relax, even hum in her tuneless way. He curled up in a chair to wait for pans to lick. But she had other ideas.

"Bud might not be back for a while, maybe not for days. We'd better get in food." So he was sent with a list and a sled to the nearest grocery, a crossroads affair with a gaspump a mile away. It was a nasty trip—wind and a stinging snow blowing into his face and, coming back, grocery sacks bumping off the sled. If Bud's such a good mechanic, he thought, they should have a car as well as a truck. From all the wrecks Bud towed into their fields, couldn't he have built a single working car? Suppose Bud stayed away for a long time? They could eat from the freezer for months but milk was required almost daily. He made a plan. He would board the school bus next Monday and with Bud's old rifle from the barn, force the driver to stop at the town IGA, raid the shelves, and return to Stella with a busful of cola and steaks. The thought warmed him all the way back to the farm.

"Well, we just can't sit around waiting," she said. "It's Saturday night." She combed out her curlers, put on lipstick, fried up popcorn and laid out Scrabble.

Games depressed Beebee. Once over an orphanage Christmas he'd played Monopoly for four days, caught in a marathon the older boys wouldn't let him quit. Down $550,000, he shook the dice, paused, picked up the board by the corners and proceeded to fold it in half, scattering money, hotels, houses onto the floor of the rec room. The others were so stunned, Beebee almost made the door before they attacked him. But Scrabble was different, Stella maintained. As Bud didn't like it, she hadn't played much lately, which was a shame. It increased your word power, helped you read books. Stella was strong on anything literary. She had a glass bookcase in the frontroom ("She always said *frontroom* for *living room,*" Beebee noted) filled with Readers Digest Condensed Books. "Perfect," I said, but he wouldn't hear the put-down. She was the first person he'd met who bought hardbound books.

The game lasted five hours. Stella took twenty minutes a turn. She made *nadir. Beautify. Empathy. Poleax* with the x on a triple. "The most important *acquisition* you can have," she said, "is a first-rate vocabulary. Crossword puzzles are *utile,* but you can't beat Scrabble for words." He didn't stand a chance. It didn't matter. He liked watching her squint at her letters, busily rearrange her tiles, then triumphantly slap down a seven-letter creation. "Never mind, it's just a game," she said with a delight that showed they both knew different. They celebrated her victory by toasting marshmallows over the stove. She stared into the gas ring, her eyes glowing. "You know what I always wanted to be?" she confided. "A stewardess. It's corny, I know. Just a waitress, really. But think of the places you visit."

"Where would you go?"

"St. Louis, for starters. That's where my sister lives." Beebee wasn't impressed. "How 'bout a singer?" he suggested. He thought she looked, at that moment, exactly the way Patsy Cline sounded late at night on the truck radio.

"Beebee," she laughed, "you've heard me sing! Once I tried out for choir in high school because my best friend was in it. I wanted to be a soprano so I could stand next to Marge. You know what they made me? Utility alto—you ever heard of that?"

Beebee shook his head.

"Me neither," she said. "So I quit. But you know, I bet there's lots of things I could do, things I haven't thought of yet." She was doing a kind of dance on the kitchen floor, marshmallow dangling from the end of her fork. "One thing—I'm smart. I really think I am."

She was happy all of Sunday. For breakfast she made them Humpty-Dumpty eggs—fried bread with a hole cut out for the eggs—and squeezed oranges for juice. "You call it today," she commanded as they ate. He knew what she usually had in mind for Sunday—the Mall that had opened twenty minutes away. He and Bud hated the place, always found something that needed attention back in the barn just when she said they should go, left her to sit in the cab of the truck, honking the horn till they came. It was her weekend spa. "It's like this place I once saw in a museum," she explained to Beebee, trying to get him to see it her way. "The Main Street of Yesterday. A whole street of stores and things, only all indoors, you know? And people walking around, like villages in Europe. People out strolling, meeting their friends." The fact that she never saw a familiar face didn't daunt her; she loved watching families marching down the concourse (to Beebee they all looked fat); liked seeing what women wore (garbardine slacks and bowling jackets, says Beebee) and the special exhibits of high school art hung on beaverboard screens she made him study (fifty sailboats, Beebee remembers, twelve ballerinas, and dogs.) "Can't go to Westgate," he said in a voice he hoped sounded stricken. "No truck."

"I was thinking of something here," she said. "Looks almost warm out."

"We could build an igloo," he suggested, then felt like a fool. He never was sure just how old Stella was; when he tried to act his most adult to impress her, he felt she was bored; on the other hand, his rare lapses into childishness annoyed her. "Cut it, Beebee," she'd say, "I can't take one more baby today." But she considered the igloo with a gravity that surprised him, made sketches, calculating the size of the blocks, how many they'd neeed to cover them when they stood, how wide the fire pit should be. It suddenly seemed like a lot of work, another whole house to attend to. He thought that would be the end of it, that she'd bury herself in some sewing or maybe a book—she was an indoor person at heart and hated the cold. Still he risked suggesting a walk, hoping the novelty would intrigue her: she knew only the geography of the truck. "Sure thing," she said. "On with the wraps." He loved that word, *wraps.* Only grade school teachers used it ("put on your wraps boys and girls")—and Stella.

"That's another thing you could do," he said as they headed across the pasture, stepping light on the icy crust that coated the snow. "You'd be a good teacher." "You think so?" She stopped, surprised and clearly flattered. Then, in a teasing voice: "And what would you say I could teach?" Her tone, not the question, abashed him. She laughed, gave him a jab. He lost his balance, fell backwards, broke through the crust of ice. In a moment he found himself sitting, mired shoulder-deep in the snow. Once the shock of falling was past, he discovered he liked it there. It was an oddly pleasant place, like a lake that you've sat down in when you're tired of keeping afloat and won't leave because it's warmer than the wind. Or a bed, vast as the pasture, muffled in down. "Come on," he heard her shout across the glare of the sun-struck snow. Through squinted eyes he could just make out her red scarf flying, mittens rowing the air as she plunged deeper and deeper into the snow until at last she gave up and dove in too. He lay back and closed his eyes.

He hears doors slamming and voices. He turns over, is roused again, falls back into nightmare. At the sound of his name he bolts up, fully awake.

The man and the woman stand at the living room drapes. He remembers the curtains as lighted from behind so that the figures appear in silhouette, but it must have been pitch black out, so that can't have been the case. What he's sure of is that the man was striking the woman over and over across the side of her face, across the chest, then back up to the face with something that looked like a bottle but bent on impact, something that would not break. What seemed odd was not the man's steady and unimpassioned violence but the way the woman simply stood there, arms at her sides, while the man continued to hit her with such force that she was knocked off balance, had to steady herself against the drapes, against the back of the sofa; not once did she even try to move from his reach.

Neither one saw—or acknowledged—his presence. If she had cried out to him for help, she gave no sign now of wanting assistance. Yet it must have been she who had called into his sleep. He ran into the kitchen and phoned the police.

For what seemed like hours, he crouched by the phone, straining for sounds from the other room, the blood in his ears pounding with such a roar he only saw but did not hear the men who entered. "You called?" He led them into the front room.

The two were standing exactly where they had been before but were now turned awkwardly to face the intruders.

For a moment no one spoke. Beebee studied Stella. Her face was beginning to swell. When she held her sleeve to her nose he thought he saw blood.

"What the hell are you doing here, Cochrane?" Bud walked towards the men, careful—Beebee could tell—not to sway, not to lurch. His voice held more command than Beebee had ever heard him summon. His hands, Beebee noticed, were empty.

"We received a call . . ." the man named Cochrane began. He stopped. Jammed his hands into his pockets, shifted uncomfortably. The other had pulled out a pad, was clicking a ballpoint pen in and out with his thumb.

"What you writing, Beeler?"

Beeler looked over at Bud, shrugged, and gazed around the room. It was in perfect order, still smelled of ammonia and wax from yesterday's cleaning. He cast his eyes to his boots and noticed the puddle of melting snow that was staining the rug.

"Nobody called you," said Bud.

Cochrane and Beeler both looked at Stella, the first time since they'd entered. "That so?"

She nodded. "Beebee might've." Her voice was muffled behind her sleeve.

"How's that?"

She withdrew her arm; there was no sign of blood.

"Beebee. He sometimes has nightmares."

Beeler put away his pad. Cochrane said they had to check out every call but they wouldn't file a report unless someone might want to press charges. This last was addressed to no one, least of all

Stella. Bud said there was no chance of that. He was sorry they'd had to come out on such a bad night and wouldn't they like a shot before hitting the road? They said no.

While Bud saw the men to the door, Stella made her way around to the front of the sofa and gripping the armrest, lowered herself to the cushions. Her face was enormous now; her eyes had almost disappeared, but the look she gave Beebee was clear: pure contempt.

"Cute," she told him. "That was real cute."

Beebee's going away again, I found out last night. I'd heard him banging around the apartment, dropping things. He often quits the bed to pace in the dark, his way lit only by the small glow of clocks or the quick shaft of icebox light as he reaches for food. He's usually so quiet I don't hear him till he returns, carefully folding himself back between the sheets. I'll stir then, roused when another's breathing alters my own. Last night, however, he switched on the overhead light and asked if I knew where he'd put his rubber boots.

"Is it raining?" I said with the narrow logic of one who is wakened from sleep.

"I'll need them; I'm taking that job on the coast."

"What job?"

"Oh, didn't I tell you?" He's joining a rep group in Seattle, leaves in two days.

"For how long?"

"Three months."

"And then?"

"And then?" He looks blank.

He'll be back, of course. We'll go on as we always have. He's got to engineer things so that I finally send him away. Or take leave myself. I'm not ready to do that yet. On the other hand, once I'm awake I almost never go back to sleep.

"I've been thinking," I began. "It's four years since we met. And though I'm leery of long-term commitments, it might be good to settle some things."

"Like what?"

"Like my employment. I'm sick of Head Start. I'm sick of raising other people's kids."

"Wait a minute, you lost me," he said.

"Figure it out."

He was concerned. "Jesus, not now."

"Then when? Come on, Beebee. Orphans want big families, didn't you know? Besides, think of all that practice you had with Stella."

That's when he filled me in on that weekend and other details of his life in Wakeman, Ohio, most of which he'd mentioned at one time or another but never in sequence. It was a long account and took us to dawn.

"And what happened then? I asked.

"I'll tell you in the morning."

"It's morning now."

The first thing he stole from her was a silver charm bracelet. Then the tongs to the coffee service on the buffet. He took them with him to school, found no place to stash them, finally tossed them into a culvert down their road. He still stayed home several days a week to help with the babies, but Stella remained withdrawn: she wasn't unfriendly, exactly; more preoccupied. Since she didn't seem to need him as much as before, he kept to the yard, isolated in an extended recess he soon wearied of. Bud went back to work at the quarry and seemed to settle. He was around more, helped Stella, even warmed up to Beebee, teaching him to bowl on the weekends and shoot rabbit. Beebee went through a padded blue box Stella kept on her dresser. He stole what he thought was a genuine diamond brooch. A week later, the earrings to match. After a storm in late June, the farmer who owned their fields was repairing fences down by the creek and found the tongs and brooch caught on weeds. His wife thought they might just belong to Stella McNult. "It isn't that you stole, Beebee, you know that," she said as they drove him back to the county home. Well, it could have been lots of things. His flunking seventh grade. The caseworker's obvious disapproval during her frequent visits that spring. Stella's pregnancy, which he'd only noticed when she suddenly changed her style of clothes. Or physical changes of his own which—he'd read in the pamphlets they'd passed out in health class—signified he was becoming a man, a condition he supposed disqualified him once and for all from adoption. Whatever it was, he didn't ask and she didn't explain. But she did hug him and tell him to come out to see them and added she was sorry he couldn't stay.

[1982]

Eudora Welty

A NOTE ON JANE AUSTEN

Jane Austen will soon be closer in calendar time to Shakespeare than to us. Within the reading life of the next generation, that constellation of six bright stars will have swung that many years deeper into the one sky, vast and crowded, of English Literature. Will these future readers be in danger of letting the novels elude them because of distance, so that their pleasure will not be anything like ours? The future of fiction is a mystery, it is like the future of ourselves. But, we exclaim, how could it be possible for these novels to seem remote?

For one thing, the noise! What a commotion comes out of their pages! Jane Austen loved high spirits, she had them herself, and she always rejoiced in the young. The exuberance of her youthful characters is one of the unageing delights of her work. Through all the mufflings of time we can feel the charge of their vitality, their happiness in doing, dancing, laughing, in being alive. There is always a lot of jumping, and that seems to vibrate through time. Motion is constant—indeed it is necessary for communication in the country. It takes days to go some of the tiny distances, but how the wheels spin! The sheer velocity of the novels, scene to scene, conversation to conversation, concert to picnic to dance, is something equivalent to a pulsebeat. The clamorous griefs and joys are all giving voice to the tireless relish of life. Surely all this cannot fade away, letting the future wonder, two hundred years from now, what our devotion to Jane Austen was all about.

For nearly this long already the gaiety of the novels has pervaded them, the irony has kept its bite, the reasoning is still sweet, the sparkle undiminished. Their high spirits, their wit, their celerity and harmony of motion, their symmetry of design, are still unrivalled in the English novel. Jane Austen's work at its best seems as nearly flawless as any fiction could be.

The felicity the novels have for us must partly lie in the confidence they take for granted between the author and her readers. We remember that the young Jane read her chapters aloud to her own lively, vocative family, upon whose shrewd intuition, practiced and eager estimation of conduct, and general rejoicing in character she relied almost as well as she could rely on her own.

The novels still have the bloom of shared pleasure. The young author enjoyed from the first a warm confidence in an understanding reception. As all her work testifies, her time, her place, her location in society, are no more matters to be taken in question than the fact that she was a woman. She wrote from a perfectly solid and firm foundation, and her work is wholly affirmative.

Is there not some good connection between this confidence and the flow of comedy? Comedy is sociable and positive, and exacting; its methods, its boundaries, its *point,* all belong to the familiar.

Jane Austen needed only the familiar. Given: one household in the country; add its valuable neighbor—and there, under her hand, is the full presence of the world. Life, as if coming in response to a call for good sense, is instantaneously in the room, astir and in strong vocal power. Communication is convenient and constant; the day, the week, the season, fill to the brim with news and arrivals, tumult and crises, and the succeeding invitations. Everybody doing everything together—what mastery she has over the scene, the family scene! The dinner parties, the walking parties, the dances, picnics, concerts, excursions to Lyme Regis and sojourns at Bath, all give their testimony to Jane Austen's ardent belief that the unit of everything worth knowing in life is in the family, that family relationships are the natural basis of every other relationship and the source of understanding all the others.

Perennial objectors like to ask how Jane Austen, a spinster who lived all her life in her father's rectory and in later family homes in Bath, Southampton, and Chawton, whose notion of going elsewhere was an excursion to Lyme Regis, could have had any way of knowing very much about life. But who among novelists ever more instantly recognized the absurd when she saw it in human behavior, and then polished it off to more devastating effect, than this young daughter of a Hampshire rectory? Jane Austen was born knowing a great deal—for one thing, that the interesting situations of life can, and notably do, take place at home. In country parsonages the dangerous confrontations and the decisive skirmishes can very conveniently be arranged.

Her world, small in size but drawn exactly to scale, may of course be regarded as a larger world seen at a judicious distance—

it would be the exact distance at which all haze evaporates, full clarity prevails, and true perspective appears. But it is more to the point to suppose that her stage was small because such were her circumstances and that, in fact, she was perfectly equipped to recognize in its very dimensions the first virtue and principle of her art. The focus she uses is for the same end: it is central. A clear ray of light strikes full upon the scene, and the result is the prism of comedy.

And of her given world she sees and defines both sides—sensibility as well as sense, for instance—and presents them in their turns, in a continuous attainment of balance: moral, esthetic, and dramatic balance. This angelic ingenuity in the way of narrative and this generous apportioning of the understanding could be seen in their own brilliant way as still other manifestations of her comic genius. The action of her novels is in itself a form of wit, a kind of repartee; some of it is the argument of souls.

It cannot be allowed that there is any less emotional feeling contained in the novels of Jane Austen because they are not tragedies. Great comic masterpieces that they are, their roots are nourished at the primary sources. Far from denying the emotions their power, she employs them to excellent advantage. Nothing of human feeling has been diminished; its intensity is all at her command. But the effect of the whole is still that of proportions kept, symmetry maintained, and the classical form honored—indeed celebrated. And we are still within the balustrades of comedy.

If the life Jane Austen wrote about was different from ours, how more different still was the frame through which she saw it. Her frame was that of *belonging to her world*. She could step through it, in and out of it as easily and unselfconsciously as she stepped through the doorway of the rectory and into the garden to pick strawberries. She was perfectly at home in what she knew, and what she knew has remained what all of us want to know.

Pride and Prejudice, Sense and Sensibility, Persuasion, looked at not only as titles but as the themes they are, are lustrous with long and uninterrupted use. Though at first glance they might not be recognized, it is possible to see most of them today in their own incarnations. They withstand time, and Jane Austen's comedies withstand time, for the same reason: they pertain not to the everchanging outside world but to what goes on perpetually in the mind and heart.

We have our own fiction about the mind and heart today, but these are still the same dangerous territories that Jane Austen knew as well as the shrubbery walks at Steventon. The fact of their unchangeableness brings its own pleasure and amusement when we read her today and to her it would likely have brought not a trace of surprise. How familiar and how inevitable is the motivation of man—whose deeds by now may be numberless, whose flight to the moon may come at any moment, but whose motives can still be counted on his fingers.

What is the real secret of the novels' already long life except life itself? The brightness of Jane Austen's eye simply does not grow dim, as have grown the outlines and colors of the scene she herself saw while she wrote—its actualities, like its customs and clothes, have receded from us forever. But she wrote, and her page is dazzlingly alive. Her world seems not only accessible but near, for under her authority and in her charge all its animation is disclosure. She has directed upon it a point of view that is not quite like that of any other novelist at any time on earth. We cannot mistake it; it is her own; it must be the most personal expression of her own original mind. It is inimitable, forever so.

Then will her novels not always reach out to her readers as the generations fly? We wonder if into the farthest future some of the characters might not always travel. We think especially of some of the great secondary characters: the eccentrics, like Mr. Woodhouse—but he is already feeling the draft; or the steady talkers, like Miss Bates, who has just recollected what she was talking *about,* her mother's spectacles. But it is already clear what Jane Austen's characters are made of: they are made of the novel they are in, and never can they come away from their context. Miss Bates, though always so ready to go anywhere, is not moveable; she is part of *Emma.*

It might even be the case that the more original the work of imagination, the greater the danger of its succumbing to the violence of transportation. Insomuch as it is alive, it must remain fixed in its own time and place, whole and intact, inviolable as a diamond. It abides in its own element, and this of course is the mind.

Jane Austen cannot follow readers into any other time. She cannot go into the far future, and she never came to us. She is there forever where she wrote, immovable to the very degree of her magnitude. The readers of the future will have to do the same as we ourselves have done; using the best equipment they can manage, they must make the move themselves. The reader is the only traveller. It is not her world or her time, but her art, that is approachable. The novels in their radiance are a destination.

[1969]

FIVE TRIBUTES TO EUDORA WELTY

Martha Graham

"Out of Chicago, suddenly here in New Orleans, Laurel Hand sat inside the windowless room . . ." How lovely: it is Eudora Welty speaking. You know it at once. Of all the millions of voices, this is hers alone and cannot possibly be mistaken for any other. And that is what I respect most, admire most and cherish most: the pure distilled individual singing away better than any nightingale.

Years ago my Company and I performed in Jackson. We were very nervous because we heard that Eudora Welty was in the audience. It puts you on edge knowing an eye, let alone a heart, like that is out front. Then she came backstage and the Company went off with her and had a wonderful time; I was taken in the other direction and missed all the delight. But I have had it since, having been privileged to be in her company, and it is the same delight one takes from her writing.

These dark days it is all the clearer that her novels and stories are a national treasure. We must guard it most zealously for such a glory as Eudora does not often come to look at us, study us and sing about us.

Walker Percy

EUDORA WELTY IN JACKSON

What is most valuable about Eudora Welty is not that she is one of the best living short story writers. (It was startling that when I tried to think of anybody else as good, two women and one man came to mind, all three Southerners: Katherine Anne Porter, Caroline Gordon and Peter Taylor.) Nor is it that she is a woman of letters in the old sense, versatile and many-voiced in her fiction and as distinguished in criticism. No, what is valuable is that she has done it in a place. That is to say, she has lived all her life in a place and written there and the writing bears more than an accidental relation to the place. Being a writer in a place is not the same as being a banker in a place. But it is not as different as it is generally put forward as being. It is of more than passing interest that Eudora Welty has always lived in Jackson and that the experience has been better than endurable. This must be the case, because if it hadn't been, she'd have left. Although I do not know Eudora Welty, I like to imagine that she lives very tolerably in Jackson. At least she said once that she was to be found "underfoot in Jackson." What does such an association between a writer and a town portend? It portends more, I would hope, than such and such a trend or characteristic of "Southern literature." For Eudora Welty to be alive and well in Jackson should be a matter of considerable interest to other American writers. The interest derives from the coming need of the fiction writer, the self-professed alien, to come to some terms with a community, to send out emissaries, to strike an entente. The question is: how can a writer live in a place without either succumbing to angelism and haunting it like a ghost or being "on," playing himself or somebody else and watching to see how it comes out? The answer is that it is at least theoretically possible to live as one imagines Eudora Welty lives in Jackson, practice letters—differently from a banker banking but not altogether differently—and sustain a relation with one's town and fellow townsmen which is as complex as you please, even ambivalent, but in the end life-giving. It is a secret relationship but not necessarily exploitative. One thinks of Kierkegaard living in Copenhagen and taking great pride in making an appearance on the street every hour so that he would be thought an idler. But it is impossible to imagine Kierkegaard without Copenhagen. Town and writer sustain each other in secret ways. Deceits may be practiced. But one is in a bad way without the other.

The time is coming when the American novelist will tire of his angelism—of which obsessive genital sexuality is the most urgent symptom, the reaching out for the flesh which has been shucked—will wonder how to get back into a body, live in a place, at a street address. Eudora Welty will be a valuable clue.

Allen Tate

I deeply regret that I have not been able to write a considered, retrospective appreciation of Miss Welty's work. One cannot imagine what Southern literature in the past thirty years would be without her: she is unique—an "original" who has never strained her language for the sake of innovation, and whose originality is in her unstudied observation of people and places, so that we see human nature as it had not been seen before. She is a great craftsman, and thus a perfect case of art added to genius.

Malcolm Cowley

Others having spoken of the work, I should like to pay a brief tribute to the personal qualities of Eudora Welty. Gentle, unruffled, unassuming, kind, she is an unusual figure in a profession that is marked too often by the dry clash of unsheathed vanities. "Isn't she nice!" other writers always say of her. Her writing is nice, too, but in the older sense of the word, that is, fastidious, scrupulous, marked by delicate discrimination, but never weak or paltering. Let us salute her achievements in literary style and personal style, in prose and life.

Robert Penn Warren

OUT OF THE STRONG

It is easy to praise Eudora Welty, but it is not easy to analyze the elements in her work that make it so easy—and such a deep pleasure—to praise. To say that may, indeed, be the highest praise, for it implies that the work, at its best, is so fully created, so deeply realized, and formed with such apparent innocence that it offers only itself, in shining unity.

But some nagging curiosity about the *why* of things may persist, and if it does, that, too, may be a kind of tribute, a tribute to the implicatory power of the work, to its depth. This curiosity persists for me, and when I puzzle the question, I come up with something like this. Eudora Welty's vision of—her feeling for—the world is multiple. She never, even when she nods, sinks into what Blake called "the single vision and Newton's sleep." There is a strain of merciless mirth, as in "The Petrified Man" or "Why I Live at the P.O." There is a strain of tenderness and pathos, a sense of what life is like for all the lost and rejected ones in the world. There is a strain of violence, muted but compelling, an awareness of the potential terror in experience. There is a strain of fantasy which may eventuate in tales not so different in dimension from those of Hawthorne, sometimes giving us the teasing charm of work like "The Wide Net." But her imagination gives us, too, a tough and beautiful poetry of the thing-ness of things, of the "real."

I am not saying that she writes many different kinds of stories—though there is considerable variety in her work. I am saying that in her work these various impulses work themselves out in differing combinations and with different emphases.

What makes her work hang together? What keeps it from appearing as a kind of anarchy of talent, an irresponsible glitter, like a slowly turning kaleidoscope? I am about to answer "temperament"—though aware that the word may seem to beg the question. So I want to elaborate a little and say that it is a temperament so strongly and significantly itself that it can face the multiplicity of the world. Art is the appropriate expression of such a temperament—art not as an escape from the incoherence of the world, but as a celebration of its richness—secure in an instinctive trust of self and in the knowledge that only out of the strong shall come forth sweetness. [1969]

Edmund White

A MAN OF THE WORLD

My father wanted me to work every summer in high school so that I might learn the value of a dollar. I did work; I did learn, and what I learned was that my dollars could buy me hustlers. I bought my first when I was fourteen.

The downtown of that city of half a million was small, no larger than a few dozen blocks. Every morning my stepmother drove me into town from our house, a fake Norman castle that stood high and white on a hill above the steaming river valley; we'd go down into town—a rapid descent of several steep plunges into the creeping traffic, dream dissolves of black faces, the smell of hot franks filtered through the car's air-conditioned interior, the muted cries of newspaper vendors speaking their own incomprehensible language, the somber look of sooted facades edging forward to squeeze out the light. Downtown excited me: so many people, some of them just possibly an invitation to adventure, escape or salvation.

As a little boy I'd thought of our house as the place God had meant us to own, but now I knew in a vague way that its seclusion and ease were artificial and that it strenuously excluded the city at the same time it depended on it for food, money, comfort, help, even pleasure. The black maids were the representatives of the city I'd grown up among. I'd never wanted anything from them—nothing except their love. To win it, or at least to ward off their silent, sighing resentment, I'd learned how to make my own bed and cook my own breakfast. But nothing I could do seemed to make up to them for the terrible loss they'd endured.

In my father's office I worked an Addressograph machine (then something of a novelty) with a woman of forty who, like a restless sleeper tangled in sheets, tossed about all day in her fantasies. She was a chubby but pert woman who wore pearls to cover the pale line across her neck, the scar from some sort of surgical intervention. It was a very thin line but she could never trust her disguise and ran to the mirror in the ladies' room six or seven times a day to re-evaluate the effect.

The rest of her energy went into elaborating her fantasies. There was a man on the bus every morning who always stationed himself opposite her and arrogantly undressed her with his dark eyes. Upstairs from her apartment another man lurked, growling with desire, his ear pressed to the floor as he listened through an inverted glass for the glissando of a silk slip she might be stepping out of. "Should I put another lock on my door?" she'd ask. Later she'd ask with wide-eyed sweetness, "Should I invite him down for a cup of coffee?" I advised her not to; he might be dangerous. The voraciousness of her need for men made me act younger than usual; around her I wanted to be a boy, not a man. Her speculations would cause her to sigh, drink water and return to the mirror. My stepmother said she considered this woman to be a "ninny." Once, years ago, my stepmother had been my father's secretary—perhaps her past made her unduly critical of the woman who had succeeded her. My family and their friends almost never characterized people we actually knew, certainly not dismissively. I felt a gleeful shame in thinking of my colleague as a "ninny"—sometimes I'd laugh out loud when the word popped into my head. I found it both exciting and alarming to feel superior to a grown-up.

Something about our work stimulated thoughts of sex in us. Our tasks (feeding envelopes into a trough, stamping them with addresses, stuffing them with brochures, later sealing them and running them through the postage meter) required just enough attention to prevent connected conversation but not so much as to absorb us. We were left with amoeboid desires that split or merged as we stacked and folded, as we tossed and turned. "When he looks at me," she said, "I know he wants to hurt me." As she said that, her sweet, chubby face looked as though it were emerging out of a cloud.

Once I read about a woman patient in psychoanalysis who referred to her essential identity as her "prettiness"; my companion—gray-eyed, her wrists braceleted in firm, healthy fat, hair swept up into a brioche pierced by the fork of a comb, her expression confused and sweet as she floated free of the cloud—she surrounded and kept safe her own "prettiness" as though it were a passive, intelligent child and she the mother, dazed by the sweeping lights of the world.

She was both fearful and serene—afraid of being noticed and more afraid of being ignored, thrillingly afraid of the sounds outside her bedroom window, but also serene in her conviction that this whole bewildering opera was being staged in order to penetrate the fire and get at her "prettiness." She really was pretty—perhaps I haven't made that clear: a sad blur of a smile, soft gray eyes, a defenseless availability. She was also crafty, or maybe willfully blind, in the way she concealed from herself her own sexual ambitions.

Becoming my father's employee clarified my relationship with him. It placed him at an exact distance from me that could be measured by money. The divorce agreement had spelled out what he owed my mother, my sister and me, but even so whenever my mother put us kids on the train to go visit him (one weekend out of every month and all summer every summer), she invariably told us, "Be nice to your father or he'll cut us off." And when my sister was graduated from college, he presented her with a "life bill," the itemized expenses he'd incurred in raising her over 21 years, a huge sum that was intended to discourage her from thoughtlessly spawning children of her own.

Dad slept all day. He seldom put in an appearance at the office before closing time, when he'd arrive fresh and rested, smelling of witch hazel, and scatter reluctant smiles and nods to the assembly as he made his way through us and stepped up to his own desk in a large room walled off from us by soundproof glass. "My, what a fine man your father is, a real gentleman," my colleague would sigh. "And to think your stepmother met him when she was his secretary—some women have all the luck." We sat in rows with our backs to him; he played the role of the conscience, above and behind us, a force that troubled us as we filed out soon after his arrival at the end of the work day. Had we stayed late enough? Done enough?

My stepmother usually kept my father company until midnight. Then she and I would drive back to the country and go to bed. Sometimes my father followed us in his own car and continued his desk work at home. Or sometimes he'd stay downtown till dawn. "That's when he goes out to meet other women," my real mother told me at the end of the summer, when I reported back to her what went on in Daddy's life. "He was never faithful. There was always another woman, the whole 22 years we were married. He takes them to those little flea-bag hotels downtown. I know." This hint of mystery about a man so cold and methodical fascinated me—as though he, the rounded brown stone, if only cracked open, would nip at the sky with interlocking crystal teeth, the quartz teeth of passion.

Before the midnight drive back home I was sometimes permitted to go out to dinner by myself. Sometimes I also took in a movie (I remember going to one that promised to be actual views of the "orgies at Berchtesgarten," but it turned out to be just Eva Braun's home movies, the Führer conferring warm smiles on pets and children). A man who smelled of Vitalis sat beside me and squeezed my thigh with his hand. I had my own spending money and my own free time.

I had little else. No one I could meet for lunch and confide in. No one who liked me. No one who wanted to talk with me about books or opera. Not even the impulse to ask for love or the belief that such things could be discussed. Had I known in any vivid or personal way of the disease, starvation and war that afflicted so much of humanity, I might have taken comfort at least in my physical well-being, but in my loneliness I worried about sickness, hunger and violence befalling me, as though precisely these fears had been visited on me by the jealous world in revenge against so much joyless plenty.

I hypothesized a lover who'd take me away. He'd climb the fir tree outside my window, step into my room and gather me into his arms. What he said or looked like remained indistinct, just a cherishing wraith enveloping me, whose face glowed more and more brightly. His delay in coming went on so long that soon I'd passed from anticipation to nostalgia. One night I sat at my window and stared at the moon, toasting it with a champagne glass filled with grape juice. I knew the moon's cold, immense light was falling on him as well, far away and just as lonely in a distant room. I expected him to be able to divine my existence and my need, to intuit that in this darkened room in this country house a fourteen-year-old was waiting for him.

Sometimes now when I pass dozing suburban houses I wonder behind which window a boy waits for me.

After a while I realized I wouldn't meet him till years later; I wrote him a sonnet that began, "Because I loved you before I knew you." The idea, I think, was that I'd never quarrel with him nor ever rate his devotion cheap; I had had to wait too long.

Our house was a somber place. The styleless polished furniture was piled high and the pantry supplies were laid in; in the empty fullness of breakfront drawers gold flatware and silver tea things remained for six months at a time in mauve flannel bags that could not ward off a tarnish bred out of the very air. No one talked much. There was little laughter, except when my stepmother was on the phone with one of her social friends. Although my father hated most people, he had wanted my stepmother to take her place—that is, my mother's place—in society, and she had. He'd taught her how to dress and speak and entertain and by now she'd long since surpassed his instructions; she'd become at once proper and frivolous, innocent and amusing, high-spirited and reserved—the combination of wacky girl and prim matron that world so admired.

I learned my part less well. I feared the sons of her friends and made shadows among the debs. I played the piano without ever improving; to practice would have meant an acceptance of more delay, whereas I wanted instant success, the throb of plumed fans in the dark audience, the pulse off diamonds from the curve of loges. What I had instead was the ache of waiting and the fear I wasn't worthy. When I'd dress I'd stand naked before the closet mirror and wonder if my body was worthy. I can still picture that pale skin stretched over ribs, the thin, hairless arms and sturdier legs, the puzzled, searching face and the slow lapping of disgust and longing, disgust and longing. The disgust was hot, penetrating—nobody would want me because I was a sissy and had a mole between my shoulder blades. The longing was cooler, less substantial, more the spray off a wave than the wave itself. Perhaps the eyes were engaging, there was something about the smile. If not lovable as a boy, then maybe as a girl; I wrapped the towel into a turban on my head. Or perhaps need itself was charming or could be. Maybe my need could make me as appealing as the woman who worked the Addressograph machine with me.

I was always reading and often writing but both were passionately abstract activities. Early on I had recognized that books pictured another life, one quite foreign to mine, in which people circled one another warily and with exquisite courtesy until an individual or a couple erupted and flew out of the salon, spangling the night with fire. I had somehow stumbled on Ibsen and that's how he struck me: oblique social chatter followed by a heroic death in a snowslide or on the steeple of a church (I wondered how these scenes could be staged). Oddly enough, the "realism" of the last century seemed tinglingly far-fetched: vows, betrayals, flights, fights, sacrifices, suicides. I saw literature as a fantasy, no less absorbing for all its irrelevance—a parallel life, as dreams shadow waking but never intersect it.

I thought to write of my own experiences required a translation out of the crude patois of actual slow suffering, mean, scattered thoughts and transfusion-slow boredom into the tidy couplets of brisk, beautiful sentiment, a way of at once elevating and lending momentum to what I felt. At the same time I was drawn to . . . What if I could write about my life exactly as it was? What if I could show it in all its density and tedium and its concealed passion, never divined or expressed, the dull brown geode that eats at itself with quartz teeth?

I read books with this passion, as one might beat back pages of pictures, looking for someone he could love. The library downtown had been built as an opera house in the last century. Even in grade school I had haunted the library, which was in the same block as my father's office. The library looked up like a rheumy eye at a pitched skylight over which pigeons whirled, their bodies a shuddering gray haze until one settled and its pacing black feet became as precise as cuneiform. The light seeped down through the stacks that were arranged in a horseshoe of tiers: the former family balcony, the dress circle, the boxes, on down to the orchestra, still gently raked but now cleared of stalls and furnished with massive oak card files and oak reading tables where unshaved old men read newspapers under gooseneck lamps and rearranged rags in paper sacks. The original stage had been demolished but cleats on the wall showed where ropes had once been secured.

The railings around the various balconies still described crude arabesques in bronze gone green, but the old floors of the balconies had been replaced by rectangular slabs of smoked glass that emitted pale emerald gleams along polished, bevelled edges. Walking on this glass gave me vertigo, but once I started reading I'd slump to the cold, translucent blocks and drift on ice floes into dense clouds. The smell of yellowing paper engulfed me. An unglued page slid out of a volume and a corner broke off, shattered—I was destroying public property! Downstairs someone harangued the librarian. Shadowy throngs of invisible operagoers coalesced and sat forward in their see-through finery to look and listen. I was reading the libretto of *La Bohême.* The alternating columns of incomprehensible Italian, which I could skip, made the pages speed by, as did the couple's farewell in the snow, the ecstatic reconciliation, poor little Mimi's prolonged dying. I glanced up and saw a pair of shoes cross the glass above, silently accompanied by the paling and darkening circle of the rubber end of a cane. The great eye of the library was blurred by tears.

Across the street the father of a friend of mine ran a bookstore. As I entered it, I was almost knocked down by two men coming out. One of them touched my shoulder and drew me aside. He had a three-day's growth of beard on his cheeks, shiny wet canines, a rumpled raincoat of a fashionable cut that clung to his hips and he was saying, "Don't just rush by without saying hello."

Here he was at last but now I knew for sure I wasn't worthy—I was ugly with my glasses and my scalp white under my shorn hair. "Do I know you?" I asked. I felt I did, as if we'd traveled for a month in a train compartment knee to knee night after night via the thirty installments of a serial but plotless though highly emotional dream. I smiled, embarrassed by the way I looked.

"Sure you know me." He laughed and his friend, I think, smiled. "No, honestly, what's your name?"

I told him.

He repeated it, smile suppressed, as I'd seen men on the make condescend to women they were sizing up. "We just blew into town," he said. "I hope you can make us feel at home." He put an arm around my waist and I shrank back; the sidewalks were crowded with people staring at us curiously. His fingers fit neatly into the space between my pelvis and the lowest rib, a space that welcomed him, that had been cast from the mold of his hand. I kept thinking these two guys want my money, but how they planned to get it remained vague. And I was alarmed they'd been able to tell at a glance that I would respond to their advances so readily. I was so pleased he'd chosen me; because he was from out of town he had higher, different standards. He thought I was like him, and perhaps I was or soon would be. Now that a raffish stranger—younger and more handsome than I'd imagined, but also dirtier and more condescending—had materialized before me, I wasn't at all sure what I should do: my reveries hadn't been that detailed. Nor had I anticipated meeting someone so cross-hatched with ambiguity, a dandy who hadn't bathed, a penniless seducer, someone upon whose face passion and cruelty had cast a grille of shadows. I was alarmed; I ended up by keeping my address secret (midnight robbery) but agreeing to meet him at the pool in the amusement park tomorrow at noon (an appointment I didn't keep, though I felt the hour come and go like a king in disguise turned away at the peasant's door).

The books in the bookstore shimmered before my eyes as I worked through a pile of them with their brightly colored paper jackets bearing photographs of pensive, well-coiffed women or middle-aged men in Irish knit sweaters with pipes and profiles. Because I knew these books were by living writers I looked down on them; my head was still ringing with the full bravura performance of history in the library-opera house. Those old books either had never owned or had lost their wrappers; the likeness of their unpictured authors had been recreated within the brown, brittle pages. But these living writers—ah! life struck me as an enfeeblement, a proof of dimmed vitality when compared to the energetic composure of the dead whose busts, all carved beards and sightless, protuberant eyes I imagined filling the empty niches in the opera lobby, a shallow antechamber, now a home to sleeping bums and stray cats but once the splendid approach across diamonds of black-and-white marble pavement to black-and-gilt doors opening on the brilliant assembly, the fans and diamonds and the raised ebony lid of the spotlit piano.

At home I heard the muted strains of discordant music. One night my stepmother, hard and purposeful, drove back downtown unexpectedly to my father's office after midnight. Still later I could hear my stepmother shouting in her wing of the house; I hid behind a door and heard my father's patient, explaining drone. The next morning the woman who worked the Addressograph machine with me broke down, wept, locked herself in the ladies' room. When she came out her eyes, usually so lovely and unfocused, narrowed with spite and pain as she muttered a stream of filth about my stepmother and my father, who'd tried to lure her to one of those flea-bag hotels. On the following morning I learned she'd been let go, though by that time I knew how to get the endless mailings out on my own. She'd been let go—into what?

That man's embrace around the waist set me spinning like a dancer across the darkened stage of the city; my turns led me to Fountain Square, the center. After nightfall the downtown was nearly empty. A cab might cruise by. One high office window might glow. The restaurants had closed by eight, but a bar door could swing open to impose on me the silhouette of a man or to expel the sound of a juke box, the smell of beer and pretzels. Shabby city of black stone whitened by starlings, poor earthly progeny of that mystic metal dove poised on the outstretched wrist of the verdigris'd lady, sad goddess of the fountain. Men from across the river sat around the low granite rim of the basin—at least I guessed they were hillbillies from their accents, a missing tooth, greased-back hair, their way of spitting, of holding a Camel cupped between the thumb and third finger, of walking with a hard, loud, stiff-legged tread across the paved park as though they hoped to ring sparks off stone. Others sat singly along the metal fence that enclosed the park, an island around which traffic flowed. They perched on the steel rail, legs wide apart, bodies licked by headlights, and looked down, into the slowly circling cars. At last a driver would pause before a young man who'd hop down and lean into the open window, listen—and then the young man would either shake his head and spit or, if a deal had been struck, swagger around to the other side and get in. Look at them: the curving windshield whispers down the reflection of a blinking neon sign on two faces, a bald man behind the wheel whose glasses are crazed by streaks of green light from the dashboard below, whose ears are fleshy, whose small mouth is pinched smaller by anxiety or anticipation. Beside him the young man, head thrown back on the seat so that we can see only the strong white parabola of his jaw and the working Adam's apple. He's slumped far down and he's already thinking his way into his job. Or maybe he's embarrassed by so much downtime between fantasy and act. They drive off, only the high notes from the car radio reaching me.

A charged space where all eyes take in every event—I'd never known anything like that till now. Maybe in the lobby of Symphony Hall, where as a child I'd gone every Friday afternoon for the kiddie matinee, but there little feudal hordes of children, attached to a mother or nurse, eyed each other across acres of marble unless ordered to greet one another, the curtest formality between hostile vassals who might as well have spoken different languages. But here, in Fountain Square, though two or three men might cluster together and drink from a paper bag and argue sports or women, each group was meant to attract attention, every gesture was meant to be observed and transgressed, and the conversation was a pretense at conversation, the typical behavior of desirable types.

That night, however, I had no comfortable assumptions about who these men were and what they were willing to do. I crossed the street to the island, ascended the two steps onto the stone platform—and sat down on a bench. No one could tell me to leave this bench. No one would even notice me. There were policemen nearby. I had a white shirt on, a tie at half-mast, seersucker pants from a suit, polished lace-up shoes, clean nails and short hair, money in my wallet. I was a polite, well-spoken teen, not a vagrant or a criminal—the law would favor me. My father was nearby, working in his office; I was hanging around, waiting for him. Years of traveling alone on trains across the country to see my father had made me fearless before strangers and had led me to assume the unknown is safe, at least reasonably safe if encountered in public places. I set great store by my tie and raised the knot to cover the still unbuttoned collar opening.

It was hot and dark. The circling cars were unnerving—so many unseen viewers looking at me. Although this was the town I'd grown up in, I'd never explored it on my own. The library, the bookstore, Symphony Hall, the office, the dry cleaners, the state liquor commission, the ball park, my school, the department stores, that glass ball of a restaurant perched high up there—these I'd been to hundreds of times with my father and stepmother, but I'd always been escorted by them, like a prisoner, through the shadowy, dangerous city.

And yet I'd known all along it was something mysterious and anguished beyond my experience if not my comprehension. We had a maid, Blanche, who inserted bits of straw into her pierced ears to keep the holes from growing shut, sneezed her snuff in a fine spray of brown dots over the sheets when she was ironing and slouched around the kitchen in her worn-down, backless slippers, once purple but now the color and sheen of a bare oak branch in the rain. She was always uncorseted under her blue cotton uniform; I pictured her rolling, black and fragrant, under that fabric and wondered what her mammoth breasts looked like.

Although she had a daughter five years older than I (illegitimate, or so my stepmother whispered significantly), Blanche hummed to a black station only she seemed able to tune in, and she seemed like a girl. When she moved from one room to the next, she unplugged the little bakelite radio with the cream-colored grille over the brown speaker cloth and took it with her. That music excited me, but I thought I shouldn't listen to it too closely. It was "Negro music" and therefore forbidden—part of another culture more violent and vibrant than mine but somehow inferior yet no less exclusive.

Charles, the handyman, would emerge from the basement sweaty and pungent and, standing three steps below me, lecture me about the Bible, the Second Coming and Booker T. Washington and Marcus Garvey and Langston Hughes. Whenever I said something he'd laugh in a steady, stylized way to shut me up and then start burrowing back into his obsessions. He seemed to know everything, chapter and verse—Egyptians, Abyssinians, the Lost Tribe, Russian plots, Fair Deal and New Deal—but when I'd repeat one of his remarks at dinner, my father would laugh (this, too, was a stylized laugh) and say, "You've been listening to Charles again. That nigger just talks nonsense. Now don't you bother him, let him get on with his work." I never doubted that my father was right, but I kept wondering how Dad could *tell* it was nonsense. What mysterious ignorance leaked out of Charles's words to poison them and render them worthless, inedible? For Charles, like me, haunted the library; I watched his shelf of books in the basement rotate. And Charles was a high deacon of his church, the wizard of his tribe; when he died his splendid robes overflowed his casket. That his nonsense made perfect sense to me alarmed me—was I, like Charles, eating the tripe and lights of knowledge while Dad sat down to the steak?

I suppose I never wondered where Blanche or Charles went at night; when it was convenient to do so I still thought of the world as a well-arranged place where people did work that suited them and lived in houses appropriate to their tastes and needs. But once Blanche called us in the middle of an August night and my father, stepmother and I rushed to her aid. In the big Cadillac we breasted our way into unknown streets through the crowds of naked children playing in the tumult of water liberated from a fire plug ("Stop that!" I shouted silently at them, outraged and frightened. "That's illegal!"). Past the stoops crowded with grown-ups playing cards and drinking wine. In one glaring doorway a woman stood, holding her diapered baby against her, a look of stoic indignation on her young face, a face one could imagine squeezing out tears without ever changing expression or softening the wide, fierce eyes, set jaw, everted lower lip. The smell of something delicious—

charred meat, maybe, and maybe burning honey—filled the air. "Roll up your windows, for Chrissake, and lock the doors," my father shouted at us. "Dammit, use your heads—don't you know this place is dangerous as hell!"

A bright miner's lamp, glass globe containing a white fire devoid of blues and yellows, dangled from the roof of a vendor's cart; he was selling food of some sort to children. Even through the closed windows I could hear the babble of festive, delirious radios. A seven-foot skinny man in spats, shades, an electric green shantung suit and a flat-brimmed white beaver hat with a matching green band strolled in front of our car and patted our fender with elaborate mockery. "I'll kill the bastard," Dad shouted. "I swear I'll kill that goddamn ape if he scratches my fender."

"Oh-h-h . . .," my stepmother sang on a high note I'd never heard before. "You'll get us all killed. Honey, my heart." She grabbed her heart; she was a natural actress, who instinctively translated feelings into gestures. The man, who my father told us was a "pimp" (whatever that might be), bowed to unheard applause, pulled his hat down over one eye like Chevalier and ambled on, letting us pass.

We hurried up five flights of dirty, broken stairs, littered with empty pint bottles, bags of garbage and two dolls (both white, I noticed, and blond and mutilated), past landings and open doors, which gave me glimpses of men playing cards and, across the hall, a grandmother alone and asleep in an armchair with antimacassars. Her radio was playing that Negro music. Her brown cotton stockings had been rolled down below her black knees.

Blanche we found wailing and shouting, "My baby, my baby!" as she hopped and danced in circles of pain around her daughter, whose hand, half lopped off, was spouting blood. My father gathered the girl up in his arms and we all rushed off to the emergency room of a hospital.

She lived. Her hand was even sewn back on, though the incident (jealous lover with an axe) had broken her mind. Afterwards, the girl didn't go back to her job and feared even leaving the building. My stepmother thought the loss of blood had somehow left her feeble-minded. My father fussed over the blood on his suit and on the strangely similar Cadillac upholstery, though I wondered if his pettiness weren't merely a way of silencing Blanche, who kept kissing his whole hand in gratitude. Or perhaps he'd found a way of re-introducing the ordinary into a night that had dipped disturbingly below the normal temperature of tedium he worked so hard to maintain. Years later, when Charles died, my father was the only white man to attend the funeral. He wasn't welcome, but he went anyway and sat in the front row. After Charles's death my father became more scattered and apprehensive. He would sit up all night with a stop-watch, counting his pulse.

That had been another city—Blanche's two rooms, scrupulously clean in contrast to the squalor of the halls, her parrot squawking under the tea towel draped over the cage, the chromo of a sad Jesus pointing to his exposed, juicy heart as though he were a free-clinic patient with a troubling symptom, the filched wedding photo of my father and stepmother in a nest of crepe-paper flowers, the bloody sheet torn into strips that had been wildly clawed off and hurled onto the flowered congoleum floor. Through a half-open door I saw the foot of a double bed draped like a veteran's grave with the flag of a tossed-back sheet.

In my naivete I imagined all poor people, black and white, liked each other and that here, through Fountain Square, I would feel my way back to that street, that smell of burning honey, that blood as red as mine and that steady, colorless flare in the glass chimney. . . . These hillbillies on the square with their drawling and spitting, their thin arms and big raw hands, nails ragged, tattoos a fresher blue than their eyes set in long sallow Norman faces, each eye a pale blue ringed by nearly invisible lashes—I wove these men freely into the cloth of the powerful poor, a long bolt lost in the dark that I was now pulling through a line of light.

I opened a book and pretended to read under the weak street lamps, though my attention wandered away from sight to sound. "Tommy, bring back a beer!" someone shouted. Some other men laughed. No one I knew kept his nickname beyond twelve, at least not with his contemporaries, but I could hear these guys calling each other Tommy and Freddy and Bobby and I found that heartening, as though they wanted to stay, if only among themselves, as chummy as a gang of boys. While they worked to become as brutal as soon enough they would be, I tried to find them softer than they'd ever been.

Boots approached me. I heard them before I saw them. They stopped, every tan scar on the orange hide in focus beyond the page I held that was running with streaks of print. "Curiosity killed the damn pussy, you know," a man said. I looked up at a face sprouting brunette side-burns that swerved inwards like cheese knives toward his mouth and stopped just below his ginger mustaches. The eyes, small and black, had been moistened genially by the beers he'd drunk and the pleasure he was taking in his own joke.

"*Mighty* curious, ain't you?" he asked. "Ain't you!" he insisted, making a great show of the leisurely, avuncular way he settled close beside me, sighing, and wrapped a bare arm—a pale, cool, sweaty, late-night August arm—around my thin shoulders. "Shit," he hissed. Then he slowly drew a breath like ornamental cigarette smoke up his nose, and chuckled again. "I'd say you got Sabbath eyes, son."

"I do?" I squeaked in a pinched soprano. "I don't know what you mean," I added, only to demonstrate my newly acquired baritone, as penetrating as an oboe, though the effect on the man seemed the right one: sociable.

"Yessir, Sabbath eyes," he said with a downshift into a rural languor and rhetorical fanciness I associated with my storytelling paternal grandfather in Texas. "I say Sabbath 'cause you done worked all week and now you's resting them eyeballs on what you done made—or might could make. The good things of the earth." Suddenly he grew stern. "Why you here, boy? I seed you here cocking your hade and spying up like a biddy hen. Why you watching, boy? *What* you watching? Tell me, what you watching?"

He had frightened me, which he could see—it made him laugh. I smiled to show him I knew how foolish I was being. "I'm just here to—"

"Read?" he demanded, taking my book away and shutting it. "Shi-i-i . . ." he hissed again, steam running out before the *t*. "You here to meet someone, boy?" He'd disengaged himself and turned to stare at me. Although his eyes were serious, militantly serious, the creasing of the wrinkles beside them suggested imminent comedy.

"No," I said, quite audibly.

He handed the book back to me.

"I'm here because I want to run away from home," I said. "I

thought I might find someone to go with me."

"Whar you planning to run to?"

"New York."

There was something so cold and firm and well-spoken about me—the clipped tones of a businessman defeating the farmer's hoaxing yarn—that the man sobered, dropped his chin into his palm and thought. "What's today?" he asked at last.

"Saturday."

"I myself taking the Greyhound to New Yawk Tuesday mawning," he said. "Wanna go?"

"Sure."

He told me that if I'd bring him forty dollars on Monday evening he'd buy me my ticket. He asked me where I lived and I told him; his willingness to help me made me trust him. Without ever explicitly being taught such things, I'd learned by studying my father that at certain crucial moments—an emergency, an opportunity—one must act first and think later. One must suppress minor inner objections and put off feelings of cowardice or confusion and turn into a simple instrument of action. I'd seen my father become calm in a crisis or feel his way blindly with nods, smiles and monosyllables toward the shadowy opening of a hugely promising but still vague business deal. And with women he was ever alert to adventure: the gauzy transit of a laugh across his path, a minor whirlpool in the sluggish flow of talk, the faintest whiff of seduction . . .

I, too, wanted to be a man of the world and dared not question my new friend too closely. For instance, I knew a train ticket could be bought at the last moment, even on board, but I was willing to assume either that a bus ticket had to be secured in advance or that at least my friend thought it did. We arranged a time to meet on Monday when I could hand over the money (I had it at home squirreled away in the secret compartment of a wood tray I'd made last year in shop). Then on Tuesday morning at six a.m. he'd meet me on the corner near but not in sight of my house. He'd have his brother's car and we'd proceed quickly to the 6:45 bus bound East—a long haul to New Yawk, he said, oh, say twenty hours, no, make that twenty-one.

"And in New York?" I asked timidly, not wanting to seem helpless and scare him off but worried about my future. Would I be able to find work? I was only sixteen, I said, adding two years to my age. Could a sixteen-year-old work legally in New York? If so, doing what?

"Waiter," he said. "A whole hog heaven of resty-runts in New Yawk City."

Sunday it rained a hot drizzle all day and in the west the sky lit up a bright yellow that seemed more the smell of sulfur than a color. I played the piano with the silencer on lest I awaken my father. I was bidding the instrument farewell. If only I'd practiced I might have supported myself as a cocktail pianist; I improvised my impression of sophisticated tinkling—with disappointing results.

As I took an hour-long bath, periodically emptying an inch of cold water and replacing it with warm, I thought my way again through the routine: greeting the guests, taking their orders, serving pats of butter, beverages, calling out my requests to the chef . . . my long, flat feet under the water twitched sympathetically as I raced about the restaurant. If only I'd observed waiters all those times. Well, I'd coast on charm.

As for love that, too, I'd win through charm. Although I knew I hadn't charmed anyone since I was six or seven, I consoled myself by deciding people out here were not susceptible to the larceny (which I thought grand, they petty) of a beguiling manner. They responded only to character, accomplishments, the slow accumulations of will rather than the sudden millinery devisings of fancy. In New York I'd be the darling boy again. In that Balzac novel a penniless young man had made his fortune on luck, looks, winning ways (since I hadn't finished the book, I didn't yet know where those ways led). New Yorkers, like Parisians, I hoped and feared, would know what to make of me. I carried the plots and atmosphere of fiction about with me and tried to cram random events into those ready molds. But no, truthfully, the relationship was more reciprocal, less rigorous—art taking the noise life gave and picking it out as a tune (the cocktail pianist obliging the humming drunk).

Before it closed I walked down to a neighborhood pharmacy and bought a bottle of peroxide. I had decided to bleach my hair late Monday night; on Tuesday I'd no longer answer the description my father would put out in his frantic search for me. Perhaps I'd affect an English accent as well; I'd coached my stepmother in the part of Lady Bracknell before she performed the role with the Queen City Players and I could now say *cucumber sandwich* with scarcely a vowel after the initial fluty *u*. As an English blond I'd evade not only my family but also myself and emerge as the energetic and lovable boy I longed to be. Not exactly a boy, more a girl, or rather a sturdy, canny, lavishly devout tomboy like Joan of Arc, tough in battle if yielding before her visionary Father. I wouldn't pack winter clothes; surely by October I'd be able to buy something warm.

A new spurt of hot water as I retraced my steps to the kitchen, clipped the order to the cook's wire or flew out the swinging doors, smiling, acted courteously and won the miraculously large tip. And there, seated at a corner table by himself, is the English lord, silver-haired, recently bereaved; my hand trembles as I give him the frosted glass. In my mind I'd already betrayed the hillbilly with the sideburns who sobbed with dignity as I delivered my long farewell speech. He wasn't intelligent or rich enough to suit me.

When I met him on Monday at six beside the fountain and presented him with the four ten-dollar bills, he struck me as ominously indifferent to the details of tomorrow's adventures which I'd elaborated with such fanaticism. He reassured me about the waiter's job and my ability to pull it off, told me again where he'd pick me up in the morning—but, smiling, dissuaded me from peroxiding my hair tonight. "Just pack it—we'll bleach you white win we git whar we gohn."

We had a hamburger together at the Grasshopper, a restaurant of two rooms, one brightly lit and filled with booths and families and waitresses wearing German peasant costumes and white lace hats, the other murky that smelled of beer and smoke—a man's world, the bar. I went through the bar to the toilet. When I came out I saw the woman I'd worked with in a low-cut dress, skirt hiked high to expose her knee, a hand over her pearl necklace. Her hair had been restyled. She pushed one lock back and let it fall again over her eye, the veronica a cape might pass before an outraged bull: the man beside her, who now placed a grimy hand on her knee. She let out a shriek—a coquette's shriek, I suppose, but edged with terror. (I was glad she didn't see me, since I felt ashamed at the way our family had used her.)

I'd planned not to sleep at all but had set the alarm should I doze off. For hours I lay in the dark and listened to the dogs barking down in the valley. Now that I was leaving this house forever, I was tiptoeing through it mentally and prizing its luxuries—the shelves lined with blocks of identical cans (my father ordered everything by the gross), the linen cupboard stacked high with ironed if snuff-specked sheets, my own bathroom with its cupboard full of soap, tissue, towels, hand towels, wash cloths, the elegant helix of the front staircase descending to the living room with its deep carpets, shaded lamps and the pretty mirror bordered by tiles on which someone with a nervous touch had painted the various breeds of lapdog. This house where I'd never felt I belonged no longer belonged to me and the future so clearly charted for me—college, career, wife and white house wavering behind green trees—was being exchanged for that eternal circulating through the restaurant, my path as clear to me as chalk marks on the floor, instructions for each foot in the tango, lines that flowed together, branched and joined, branched and joined . . . In my dream my father had died but I refused to kiss him though next he was pulling me onto his lap, an ungainly teen smeared with Vicks Vaporub whom everyone inexplicably treated as a sick child.

When I silenced the alarm, fear overtook me. I'd go hungry! The boarding house room with the toilet down the hall, blood on the linoleum, crepe-paper flowers—I dressed and packed my gym bag with the bottle of peroxide and two changes of clothes. Had my father gone to bed yet? Would the dog bark when I tried to slip past him? And would that man be on the corner? The boarding house room, yes, Negro music on the radio next door, the coquette's shriek. As I walked down the drive I felt conspicuous under the blank windows of my father's house and half-expected him to open the never-used front door to call me back.

I stood on the appointed corner. It began to drizzle but a water truck crept past anyway, spraying the street a darker, slicker gray. No birds were in sight but I could hear them testing the day. A dog without a collar or master trotted past. Two fat maids were climbing the hill, stopping every few steps to catch their breath. One, a shiny, blue-black fat woman wearing a flowered turban and holding a purple umbrella with a white plastic handle, was scowling and talking fast but obviously to humorous effect, for her companion couldn't stop laughing.

The bells of the Catholic school behind the dripping trees across the street marked the quarter hour, the half hour. More and more cars were passing me. I studied every driver—had he overslept? The milk man. The bread truck. Damn hillbilly. A bus went by, carrying just one passenger. A quarter to seven. He wasn't coming.

When I saw him the next evening on the square he waved at me and came over to talk. From his relaxed manner I instantaneously saw—puzzle pieces sliding then locking to fill in the pattern—that he'd duped me and I was powerless. To whom could I report him? Like a heroin addict or a Communist, I was outside the law—outside it but with him, this man. He didn't attract me but I liked him well enough.

We sat side by side on the same bench. A bad muffler exploded in a volley and the cooing starlings perched on the fountain figure's arm flew up and away leaving behind only the metal dove. I took off my tie, rolled it up and slipped it inside my pocket. Because I didn't complain about being betrayed, my friend said, "See those men yonder?"

"Yes."

"I could git you one for eight bucks." He let that sink in; yes, I thought, I could take someone to one of those little flea-bag hotels. "Which one do you want?" he asked.

I handed him the money and said, "The blond."

[1981]

Reed Whittemore

SUMMER CONCERT

We could get the whole town out on a Tuesday night,
With katydids in the trees and bikes in the gutters,
Could get the whole town out, and horns would tootle,
And kids would surge in the grass, and the maestro wiggle,
And we'd all twitter like sparrows in creaky hangars,
As culture rustled the aspen back of the high school.

But when we woke to the sizzle the next a.m.,
It was dead, dead, dead under the shingles,
And Sousa was gone, and Bach, and the Army and Navy,
And all we could do to be doing would be to be Wednesday.

[1963]

Richard Wilbur

POETRY AND HAPPINESS

I am not perfectly certain what our forefathers understood by "the pursuit of happiness." Of the friends whom I've asked for an opinion, the majority have taken that phrase to mean the pursuit of self-realization, or of a full humane life. Some darker-minded people, however, have translated "happiness" as material well-being, or as the freedom to do as you damn please. I can't adjudicate the matter, but even if the darker-minded people are right, we are entitled to ennoble the phrase and adapt it to the present purpose. I'm going to say a few things about the ways in which poetry might be seen as pursuing happiness.

There are two main ways of understanding the word "poetry." We may think of poetry as a self-shaping activity of the whole society, a collective activity by means of which a society creates a vision of itself, arranges its values, or adopts or adapts a culture. It is this sense of "poetry" which we have in Wallace Stevens's poem, "Men Made Out of Words," where he says

> The whole race is a poet that writes down
> The eccentric propositions of its fate.

But "poetry" may also mean what we more usually mean by it; it may mean verses written by poets, imaginative compositions which employ a condensed, rhythmic, resonant, and persuasive language. This second kind of poetry is not unconnected with the first; a poem written by a poet is a specific, expert, and tributary form of the general imaginative activity. Nevertheless, I should like to begin by considering poetry in the second and restricted sense only, as referring to verse productions written by individuals whose pleasure it is to write them.

Back in the days of white saddle shoes and the gentleman's grade of C, college undergraduates often found that they had an afternoon to kill. I can remember killing part of one afternoon, with a literary roommate, in composing what we called *A Complete List of Everything*. We thought of ourselves, I suppose, as continuators of *Dada,* and our list, as we set it down on the typewriter, amounted to an intentionally crazy and disrelated sequence of nouns. A section of our list might have read like this: Beauty,

---

Mr. Wilbur delivered this lecture at the invitation of the Glasgow Endowment Committee on Feb. 20, 1969, at Washington and Lee University.

carburetor, sheepshank, pagoda, absence, chalk, vector, Amarillo, garters, dromedary, Tartarus, tupelo, omelet, caboose, ferrocyanide and so on. As you can imagine, we did not complete our list; we got tired of it. As in random compositions of all kinds—musical, pictorial, or verbal—it was possible to sustain interest for only so long, in the absence of deliberate human meaning. Nevertheless, there had been a genuine impulse underlying our afternoon's diversion, and I think that it stemmed from a primitive desire that is radical to poetry—the desire to lay claim to as much of the world as possible through uttering the names of things.

This fundamental urge turns up in all reaches of literature heavy or light. We have it, for example, in the eighteenth chapter of Hugh Lofting's *Story of Doctor Dolittle,* a chapter in which all children take particular joy. As you will remember, Doctor Dolittle and his animal friends, on their way back from Africa, come by chance into possession of a pirate ship, and find aboard her a little boy who has become separated from his red-haired, snuff-taking uncle. The Doctor promises to find the little boy's lost uncle, wherever he may be, and Jip the dog goes to the bow of the ship to see if he can smell any snuff on the North wind. Jip, it should be said, is a talking dog, and here is what he mutters to himself as he savors the air:

> Tar; spanish onions; kerosene oil; wet raincoats; crushed laurel-leaves; rubber burning; lace-curtains being washed—No, my mistake, lace-curtains hanging out to dry; and foxes——hundreds of 'em . . .

These are the easy smells, Jip says; the strong ones. When he closes his eyes and concentrates on the more delicate odors which the wind is bringing, he has this to report:

> Brick,—old yellow bricks, crumbling with age in a garden-wall; the sweet breath of young cows standing in a mountain-stream; the lead roof of a dove-cote—or perhaps a granary—with the mid-day sun on it; black kid gloves lying in a bureau-drawer of walnut-wood; a dusty road with a horses' drinking-trough beneath the sycamores; little mushrooms bursting through the rotting leaves . . .

A catalogue of that sort pleases us in a number of ways. In the first place, it stimulates that dim and nostalgic thing the olfactory memory, and provokes us to recall the ghosts of various stinks and fragrances. In the second place, such a catalogue makes us feel vicariously alert; we participate in the extraordinary responsiveness of Doctor Dolittle's dog, and so feel the more alive to things. In the third place, we exult in Jip's power of instant designation, his ability to pin things down with names as fast as they come. The effect of the passage, in short, is to let us share in an articulate relishing and mastery of phenomena in general.

That is what the cataloguing impulse almost always expresses—a longing to possess the whole world, and to praise it, or at least to feel it. We see this most plainly and perfectly in the Latin canticle *Benedicite, omnia opera domini.* The first verses of that familiar canticle are:

O all ye Works of the Lord, bless ye the Lord:
praise him, and magnify him for ever.
O ye Angels of the Lord, bless ye the Lord:
praise him, and magnify him for ever.
O ye Heavens, bless ye the Lord:
praise him and magnify him for ever.
O ye Waters that be above the firmament, bless
ye the Lord: praise him and magnify him forever.

I needn't go on to the close, because I am sure that you all know the logic of what follows. All the works of the Lord are called upon in turn—the sun, moon, and stars, the winds and several weathers of the sky, the creatures of earth and sea, and lastly mankind. There is nothing left out. The canticle may not speak of crushed laurel leaves and sycamores, but it does say more comprehensively, "O all ye Green Things upon the Earth, bless ye the Lord"; it may not speak of foxes and of young cows in a mountain stream, but it does say "O all ye Beasts and Cattle, bless ye the Lord." What we have in the *Benedicite* is an exhaustive poetic progress from heaven, down through the spheres of the old cosmology, to earth and man at the center of things—a progress during which the whole hierarchy of creatures is cited in terms which, though general, do not seem abstract. It is a poem or song in which heaven and earth are surrounded and captured by words, and embraced by joyous feeling.

It is interesting to compare the strategy of the *Benedicite* to that of another and more personal poem of catalogue and praise, Gerard Manley Hopkins's "curtal sonnet" "Pied Beauty."

Glory be to God for dappled things—
For skies of couple-colour as a brindled cow;

For rose-moles all in stipple upon trout that swim;
Fresh-firecoal chestnut-falls; finches' wings;
Landscape plotted and pieced—fold, fallow, and plough;
And all trades, their gear and tackle and trim.
All things counter, original, spare, strange;
Whatever is fickle, freckled (who knows how?)
With swift, slow; sweet, sour; adazzle, dim;
He fathers-forth whose beauty is past change: Praise him.

As in the old canticle, God is praised first and last; but what lies between is very different. Hopkins does not give us an inventory of the creation; rather he sets out to celebrate one kind of beauty—pied beauty, the beauty of things which are patchy, particolored, variegated. And in his tally of variegated things there is no hierarchy or other logic: his mind jumps, seemingly at random, from sky to trout to chestnuts to finches, and finally, by way of landscape, to the gear and tackle of the various trades. The poem *sets out,* then, to give scattered examples of a single class of things; and yet in its final effect this is a poem of universal praise. Why does it work out that way?

It works that way, for one thing, because of the randomness which I have just pointed out; when a catalogue has a random air, when it seems to have been assembled by chance, it implies a vast reservoir of other things which might just as well have been mentioned. In the second place, Hopkins's poem may begin with dappled things, but when we come to "gear and tackle and trim," the idea of variegation is far less clear, and seems to be yielding to that of *character*. When, in the next line, Hopkins thanks God for "All things counter, original, spare, strange," we feel the poem opening out toward the celebration of the rich and quirky particularity of all things whatever.

The great tug-of-war in Hopkins's poetry is between his joy in the intense selfhood and *whatness* of earthly things, and his feeling that all delights must be referred and sacrificed to God. For Whitman, with whom Hopkins felt an uncomfortable affinity, there was no such tension. It is true that Whitman said, "I hear and behold God in every object," yet the locus of divinity in his poetry is not Heaven but the mystic soul of the poet, which names all things, draws all things to unity in itself, and hallows all things without distinction. The divinely indiscriminate cataloguing consciousness of Whitman's poems can consume phenomena in any order and with any emphasis; it acknowledges no protocol; it operates, as Richard Lewis has said, "n a world . . . devoid of rank or hierarchy." In Section V of the "Song of Myself," Whitman describes an experience of mystic illumination, and then gives us these eight remarkable lines:

> Swiftly arose and spread around me the peace and knowledge
> that pass all the argument of the earth,
> And I know that the hand of God is the promise of my own,
> And I know that the spirit of God is the brother of my own,
> And that all of the men ever born are also my brothers,
> and the women my sisters and lovers,
> And that a kelson of the creation is love.
> And limitless are leaves stiff or drooping in the fields,
> And brown ants in the little wells beneath them.
> And mossy scabs of the worm fence, heap'd stones,
> elder, mullein and pokeweed.

That passage happens to proceed from God to man to nature, but there is nothing hierarchical in its spirit. Quite the contrary. This is the Whitman who said, "I do not call one greater and one smaller . . . The Insignificant is as big to me as any." He speaks in the same rapt voice of men and women and moss and pokeweed, and it is clear that he might have spoken to the same purpose of ducks or pebbles or angels. For Whitman, as for the Zen Buddhist, one thing is as good as another, a mouse is sufficient "to stagger sextillions of infidels," and any part, however small, includes by synecdoche the wonder of the whole.

I could go on to speak of still more list-making poets. I could quote the Rilke of the *Duino Elegies,* who asks

> Are we perhaps here merely to say, House, Bridge,
> Fountain, Gate, Jug, Fruit-tree, Window,
> Or Column, or Tower . . . .

In our own immediate day there would be David Jones, Theodore Roethke, and Ruthven Todd in their later work; and indeed, there have been poets in all lands and ages who have sought to resume the universe in ordered categories, or to suggest its totality by the casual piling-up of particulars.

But I've given enough examples already, and my aim here is not to make a catalogue of poetic catalogues, but to suggest by a few illustrations that the itch to call the roll of things is a major motive in the writing of poetry. Whether or not he composes actual catalogues like Whitman or Hopkins, every poet is driven by a compulsion to designate, and in respect of that drive the poet is not unlike people in general. We all want to be told, for no immediate practical reason, whether a certain column is Ionic or Corinthian, whether that cloud is stratus or cumulus, and what the Spanish word for "grocer" is. If we forget the name of a supporting actor in some film, or the roster of our Supreme Court bench, we are vexed and distracted until we remember, or look it up in some book of reference. If we travel to the tropics for the first time, and find ourselves surrounded not with oaks and maples but with a bristling wall of nameless flora, we hasten to arm ourselves with nature-books and regain our control over the landscape.

The poet is like that, only more so. He is born, it appears, with a stronger-than-usual need for verbal adequacy, and so he is always mustering and reviewing his vocabulary, and forearming himself with terms which he may need in the future. I recall the excitement of a poet friend when he discovered in a mushroom guide the word *duff,* which signifies "decaying vegetable matter on the forest floor."

He was right to be excited, I think. *Duff* is a short, precise word which somehow sounds like what it means, and it is a word which poets must often have groped after in vain. My own recent discovery of that kind is the term for the depression in the centre of one's upper lip. It had annoyed me, on and off, for many years that I had no word for something that was literally under my nose; and then at long last I had the sense to enquire of a dentist. He told me that the word is *philtrum,* deriving from the Greek word for "love-potion," and implying, I should think, that the upper lip is an erogenous zone.

That sort of word-hunting and word-cherishing may sound frivolous to some, and it must be admitted that the poet's fascination with words can degenerate into fetishism and the pursuit of the exotic. More often, however, such researches are the necessary, playful groundwork for that serious business of naming which I have been discussing. Not all poets, especially in the present age, can articulate the universe with a *Benedicite,* or possess it by haphazard mysticism, but every poet is impelled to utter the whole of that world which is real to him, to respond to that world in some spirit, and to draw all its parts toward some coherence. The job is an endless one, because there are always aspects of life which we acknowledge to be real, but have not yet truly accepted.

For an obvious example, one has only to think of those machines which science has bestowed on us, and which Hart Crane said it was the great task of modern poetry to absorb. The iron horse has been with us for a century and a half, and the horseless carriage for eighty-odd years, but it is only in recent decades that *train* and *car* have consorted easily, in our verse, with *hill* and *ship* and *hawk* and *wagon* and *flower*. And indeed there are still readers who think it unpoetic to bring a pick-up truck into the landscape of a poem. The aeroplane has the aesthetic and moral advantage of resembling a bird and of seeming to aspire, but it took some hard writing in the thirties to install such words as *pylon* and *aerodrome* in the lexicon of modern verse. And for all our hard writing since, we have still not arrived at the point where, in Hart Crane's words, machinery can form "as spontaneous a terminology of poetic reference as the bucolic world of pasture, plow, and barn."

The urge of poetry is not, of course, to whoop it up for the automobile, the plane, the computer, and the space-ship, but only to bring them and their like into the felt world, where they may be variously taken, and to establish their names in the vocabulary of imagination. One perpetual task of the poet is to produce models of inclusive reaction and to let no word or thing be blackballed by sensibility. That is why I took a large pleasure, some years ago, in bringing off a line which convincingly employed the words "reinforced concrete." And that is why William Carlos Williams, with his insistence on noting and naming the bitterest details of the American urban scene, was such a hero of the modern spirit; he would not wear blinders in Rutherford and Paterson, but instead wrote beautifully of peeling billboards, wind-blown paper bags, and broken bottles in the gravel, claiming for poetry a territory which is part of our reality, and needs to be seen and said. For poetry, there is no such thing as no-man's-land.

The drive to get everything said is not merely a matter of acknowledging and absorbing the physical environment. The poet is also moved to designate human life in all its fullness, and it may be argued, for an extreme example, that the best of Henry Miller arises from a pure poetic compulsion to refer to certain realities by their real names. Mr. Miller's best is not very good, actually, and Aretino did it far better some centuries back; but there are passages in the *Tropics* which are clearly attempting, by means of an exuberant lyricism, to prove that the basic four-letter words are capable of augmenting our literary language without blowing it to pieces. I expressed this view not long ago, when testifying for Mr. Miller at an obscenity trial, and the judge replied only with a slow, sad shaking of the head. But I remain unshaken. I don't think that Mr. Miller succeeds very often in his aim, partly because the words he champions are what the theater calls bad ensemble players. But as for his aim, I recognize it as genuine and would call it essentially poetic.

Thus far I have been speaking of poetry as an inventory of external reality; now let me speak of poetry as discovery and projection of the self. The notion that art is self-expression, the expression of one's uniqueness, has provoked and excused a great deal of bad, solipsistic work in this century; nevertheless, the work of every good poet may be seen in one way or another as an exploration and declaration of the self.

In Emily Dickinson, for instance, we have a poet whose most electrifying work is the result of a keen and dogged self-scrutiny. Having spied for a long time on her own psyche, she can report that "Wonder is not precisely knowing, And not precisely knowing not." Or she can produce a little poem like this, about how anguish engrosses the sense of time:

> Pain has an element of blank;
> It cannot recollect
> When it began, or if there were
> A day when it was not.
> It has no future but itself,
> Its infinite realms contain
> Its past, enlightened to perceive
> New periods of pain.

Those lines are a pure trophy of introspection; they are not the re-phrasing of something known, but the articulation of one person's intense inward observation. Yet because they are so articulate and so true, they light up both the poet's psychology and everyone else's.

Another version of self-discovery is implied in Edwin Muir's statement that "the task of a poet is to make his imaginative world clear to himself." What Muir meant was that every poet, owing to his character and early life, has a predisposition to project his sense of things by telling this or that story, by using this or that image or symbol. It may take a poet years to stumble on his destined story or symbol and set it forth, but for Muir they are always vaguely and archetypally there, at the back of the poet's mind.

When we say of a poet that he has found his subject, or found his voice, we are likely to be thinking about poetry in Muir's way, as a long struggle to objectify the soul. Marianne Moore sketching her first emblematic animal, Vachel Lindsay first attempting to catch the camp-meeting cadence, Frost first perceiving the symbolic possibilities of a stone wall—at such moments the poet is suddenly in possession of the formula of his feelings, the means of knowing himself and of making that self known. It was at such a moment that Rilke wrote in a letter, "I am a stamp which is about to make its impression."

As I have said, these moments of self-possession can be a long time in coming. Looking back at his early poems, and finding them cloudy and abortive, Yeats sadly wrote in his *Autobiography*, "It is so many years before one can believe enough in what one feels even to know what the feeling is." It was late in his life that a Scots poet whom I knew, while buckling his belt one morning, heard himself saying the Lord's Prayer, and concluded that he must be a Christian after all. Or to speak of a deconversion, there were eight years of silence between the clangorous, prophetic early books of Robert Lowell and the publication of *Life Studies*, in which a flexible worldly voice suddenly speaks, with a whole personality behind it. What had happened to Lowell was, in Yeats' phrase, a "withering into the truth," and some such process must occur, I think, in the life of every poet.

It is Yeats above all, in the present age, who has preached and embodied the notion that poetry is self-projection; that the poet creates his world "lock, stock and barrel out of his bitter soul." "Revelation is from the self," he said; and though his way of putting it altered, he never ceased to think as he had done in 1893, when he wrote in his book *The Celtic Twilight*,

> What is literature but the expression of moods by the vehicle of symbol and incident? And are there not moods which need heaven, hell, purgatory and faeryland for their expression, no less than this dilapidated earth?

What's fundamental in poetry, according to that definition, is moods—that is, the poet's repertory of emotions, his spectrum of attitudes. All else is instrumental; persons, things, actions, and ideas are only means to externalizing the states of the poet's heart. Before Yeats was through, he had as you know constructed a visionary system full of cycles and interpenetrating gyres which embraced all possible experience, all human types, all ages of man, all ages of history, this world and the next. It was a vision as inclusive as that of the *Benedicite,* but whereas the latter was for its poet an objective poem, Yeats' vision is all a deliberate ramification of his subjective life. The phases of the moon, the gong-tormented sea, the peacock's cry, hunchback and saint, Cuchulain—the ground of their reality is the various and conflicting spirit of the poet. When the young Yeats says

> Before us lies eternity; our souls
> Are love, and a continual farewell,

and when he later proclaims that "men dance on deathless feet," he is not expounding the doctrine of reincarnation, but exploiting that idea as a means of expressing his own heart's insatiable desire for life. The spirits who brought Yeats the substance of his system did not bring him an epitome of external truth; rather they said, "We have come to give you metaphors for poetry." And when Yeats felt that certain of his expressive fictions were exhausted, he turned for a new start not to the world but to what he called, in a famous line, "the foul rag and bone shop of the heart."

I have said something now about two impulses of poetry—the impulse to name the world, and the impulse to clarify and embody the self. All poets are moved by both, but every poet inclines more to one than to the other, and a way of measuring any poet's inclination is to search his lines for moments of descriptive power. Description is, of course, an elaborate and enchanted form of naming, and among the great describers of the modern period are Hopkins, or Williams, or Lawrence in his animal-poems, or Marianne Moore, who once described a butterfly as "bobbing away like wreckage on the sea." And then there is that thunderstorm in a poem of Elizabeth Bishop's, which moves away, as she tells it,

> in a series
> Of small, badly-lit battle scenes,
> Each in 'Another part of the field.'

Or there is the beautifully realized little sandpiper, in her latest book, who runs "in a state of controlled panic" along a beach which "hisses like fat."

Now, Yeats had his sea-birds too, and in his youthful novel *John Sherman* there were some puffins very accurately observed; but soon he became concerned, as he said, with "passions that had nothing to do with observation," and the many birds of his subsequent work are a symbolic aviary of no descriptive interest. Yeats rarely gives us any pictorial pleasure, in birds or in anything else, being little concerned in his naming of things to possess them in their otherness and actuality. Nevertheless he, like all poets, is a namer; and Miss Bishop, for all her descriptive genius, is like all poets a scholar of the heart. It is a matter of proportion only, a matter of one's imaginative balance.

And having said the word "balance," I want to offer a last quotation from Yeats, which speaks directly to the question of art and happiness. In a letter to Dorothy Wellesley, written sometime in the 30's, Yeats said,

> We are happy when for everything inside us there is a corresponding something outside us.

That is an observation about life in general, but above all it applies to poetry. We are happy as poets, Yeats says, when our thoughts and feelings have originals or counterparts in the world around us—when there is a perfect conversancy or congruence between self and world. In Yeats' poetry, the chief symbol for such happiness is the marriage-bed, and his artful lovers Solomon and Sheba, each striving to incarnate the other's dream, represent the mutual attunement of imagination and reality. Keat's lovers Madeline and Porphyro, in "The Eve of St. Agnes," accomplish the same miracle and symbolize the same thing; each, without loss of reality, becomes the other's vision, and the poem is one solution to Keats's continuing enquiry into the right balance between vision and everyday experience. Elsewhere he employs or espouses other formulae, as in the poem "To Autumn," where imagination does not transmute and salvage the world, but rather accepts it in all its transient richness, and celebrates it as it is.

There is a similar quality of acceptance in Robert Frost's poems about imaginative happiness, and I am going to read you one called "Hyla Brook."

By June our brook's run out of song and speed.
Sought for much after that, it will be found
Either to have gone groping underground
(And taken with it all the Hyla Breed
That shouted in the mist a month ago,
Like ghost of sleigh-bells in a ghost of snow)—
Or flourished and come up in jewelweed,
Weak foliage that is blown upon and bent
Even against the way its waters went.
Its bed is left a faded paper sheet
Of dead leaves stuck together by the heat—
A brook to none but who remember long.
This as it will be seen is other far
Than with brooks taken otherwhere in song.
We love the things we love for what they are.

It doesn't trouble him, Frost says, that the brook on his farm runs dry by June, and becomes a gulley full of dead leaves and jewelweed; it may not be Arethusa or smooth-sliding Mincius; it may not, like Tennyson's brook, go on forever; but it has real and memorable beauties that meet his desire. Loving it for what it is, the poet does not try to elevate his subject, or metamorphose it, or turn it into pure symbol; it is sufficient that his words be lovingly adequate to the plain truth. In another and comparable poem called "Mowing," Frost builds towards a similar moral: "The fact is the sweetest dream that labor knows." One doesn't think of Wallace Stevens, who so stressed the transforming power of imagination, as having much in common with Frost, and yet Stevens would agree that the best and happiest dreams of the poet are those which involve no denial of the fact. In his poem "Crude Foyer," Stevens acknowledges that poets are tempted to turn inward and conceive an interior paradise; but that is a false happiness; we can only, he says, be "content, At last, there, when it turns out to be here." We cannot be content, we cannot enjoy poetic happiness, until the inner paradise is brought to terms with the world before us, and our vision fuses with the view from the window.

Regardless, then, of subjective bias or of a reverence for fact, poets of all kinds agree that it is the pleasure of the healthy imagination to achieve what Stevens called "ecstatic identities with the weather." When the sensibility is sufficient to the expression of the world, and when the world, in turn, in answerable to the poet's mind and heart, then the poet is happy, and can make his reader so.

Now, if I were satisfied with my use of the word *world,* which I have been saying over and over in an almost liturgical fashion, I might feel that I had come near to the end of my argument. But *world,* in contemporary usage, is a particularly sneaky and ambiguous term. I see that I must try to use it more precisely, and that once I have done so there will be more to say. What might I mean by *world*? I might mean what Milton meant when he spoke of "this pendant world"; that is, I might mean the universe. Or I might mean the planet Earth; or I might mean the human societies of Earth, taken together. Or if I defined *world* by reference to the soul or self, I might mean what a German philosopher called the "Non-Ego," or what Andrew Wyeth meant when he called one of his paintings "Christian's World." I am sure that you have all seen that touching painting of Wyeth's: it shows us a crippled girl sitting in a field of long grass, and looking off toward a house and barn; her "world" consists of what she can see, and the desolate mood in which she sees it.

Literary critics, nowadays, make continual use of the word *world* in this last sense.They write of Dylan Thomas's world of natural process, Conrad Aiken's world of psychic flux, John Ransom's gallant and ironic world of the South, or the boyish, amorous, and springtime world of E. E. Cummings. Any of us could assign a "world," in this sense, to any poet whose work we know; and in doing so, we would not necessarily be blaming him for any narrowness of scope. Robinson Jeffers on his mountaintop by the Pacific, writing forever of hawks and rocks and of the violent beauty of nature, was not prevented from speaking, through his own symbols and from his own vantage, of God and history and cities and the passions of men and women. Like any good poet of this American century, he found images and symbols which could manifest the moods of his heart, and elected a world of his own through which the greater world could someway be seen and accounted for.

And yet if one thinks back to the Italian fourteenth century, if one thinks of the "world" of Dante's imagination, how peripheral and cranky Jeffers seems! Dante's poetry is the work of one man, who even at this distance remains intensely individual in temper and in style; and yet the world of his great poem was, for his first readers, quite simply the world. This was possible because he was a poet of genius writing from the heart of a full and living culture. He lived and wrote, in Stevens' phrase, "at the center of a diamond."

I bring up Dante not merely to belabor the present with him, but because there is something which needs to be explained. We are talking of poetry as a mode of pursuing happiness; we live in a century during which America has possessed many poets of great ability; nevertheless, it is no secret that the personal histories of our poets, particularly in the last thirty years, are full of alcoholism, aberration, emotional breakdowns, the drying-up of talent, and suicide. There is no need to learn this from gossip or biography; it is plainly enough set down in the poetry of our day. And it seems to me that the key to all this unhappiness may lie in the obligatory eccentricity, nowadays, of each poet's world, in the fact that our society has no cultural heart from which to write.

Alberto Moravia, in a recent article on a great American writer and suicide, Ernest Hemingway, describes our country as "a minor, degraded and anti-humanistic culture," and observes that our typical beginning novelist, lacking any faith in the resources of culture, "confines himself to recounting the story of his youth." Having done so once successfully, the novelist proceeds for lack of any other subject to do it again and again, and, as Moravia puts it, "mirrors increasingly, in the mechanization of his own work, the mechanization of the society for which he is writing." I am sorry to say that I cannot brush aside Signor Moravia's general judgment upon us. I wish that I could.

One can protest that not all of our novelists are the prisoners of their own early lives, and that most of our poets are cultured in the sense of being well schooled in the literary and artistic tradition. But one cannot deny that in the full sense of the word *culture*—the sense that has to do with the humane unity of a whole people—our nation is impoverished. We are not an articulate organism, and what most characterizes our life is a disjunction and incoherence aggravated by an intolerable rate of change. It is easy to prophesy against us. Our center of political power, Washington, is a literary and intellectual vacuum, or nearly so; the church, in our country, is broken into hundreds of sorry and provincial sects; colleges of Christian foundation hold classes as usual on Good Friday; our cities bristle like quartz clusters with faceless new buildings of aluminum and glass, bare of symbolic ornament because they have nothing to say; our painters and sculptors despair of achieving any human significance, and descend into the world of fashion to market their Coke-bottles and optical toys; in the name of the public interest, highways are rammed through old townships and wildlife sanctuaries; all other public expenditure is begrudged, while the bulk of the people withdraw from community into an affluent privacy.

I could go on with such sweeping assertions, and soon, no doubt, I would go too far, and would have to admit that anarchy is not confined to America, and that here or there we have the promise of cultural coherence. But I would reluct at making too much of the present boom in education, or the growth of regional theatres and symphony orchestras. Such things may be good in themselves, but they are not the kind of culture I am talking about. Houston has an admirable symphony orchestra, but the nexus of human relations in that city is the credit card, and where art does not arise from and nourish a vital sense of community, it is little more than an incitement to schizophrenia.

The main fact about the American artist, as a good poet said to me the other day, is his feeling of isolation. To Dante, at the other extreme, the world appeared as one vast society, or as a number of intelligibly related societies, actual and spiritual; his *Commedia* was the embodiment and criticism of a comprehensive notion of things that he shared with his age. Or think, if you will, of the sure sense of social relevance with which Milton embarked on the writing of an epic poem which was to be "exemplary to a nation." Or think of that certainty of the moral consensus which lies behind the satires of Alexander Pope, and makes possible a wealth of assured nuance. How often, I wonder, has an American poet spoken so confidently from within the culture?

I began by distinguishing two ways of understanding the word *poetry*: first, as verse compositions written by individuals, and second, as that ensemble of articulate values by means of which a society shapes and affirms itself. It is the natural business of the first kind of poetry to contribute to the second, clarifying, enriching and refreshing it; and where the poet is unable to realize himself as the spokesman and loyal critic of an adequate culture, I think that his art and life are in some measure deprived of satisfaction and meaning.

To be sure, every poet is a citizen of the Republic of Letters, that imaginary society whose members come from every age and literature, and it is part of his happiness to converse, as it were, with the whole of tradition; but it is also his desire to put his gift at the service of the people of his own time and place. And that, as I have been saying, is a happiness not easily come by in contemporary America. It is possible, however isolated one may feel, to write out of one's private experiences of nature or God or love; but one's poetry will reflect, in one way or another, the frustration of one's desire to participate in a corporate myth. In some of our poets, the atomism of American life has led to a poetry without people, or an art of nostalgia for childhood. Elsewhere, we find a confessional poetry in which the disorder and distress of the poet's life mirrors that cultural disunity to which he, because of his calling, is peculiarly sensitive. When the poet addresses himself directly to our society, these days, it is commonly in a spirit of reproach or even secession, and seldom indeed in a spirit of celebration. I do not hold the poet responsible for that fact.

At the close of one of his eloquent poems, Archibald MacLeish exhorts the modern poets to "Invent the age! Invent the metaphor!" But it is simply not the business of poets to invent ages, and to fashion cultures single-handed. It may be that Yeats's Ireland was in good part Yeat's own invention, and he may have made some of it stick; but America is too huge a muddle to be arbitrarily envisioned. The two modern poets who tried to put a high-sounding interpretation on our country—Lindsay, whose Michigan Avenue was a street in Heaven, and Crane, whose Brooklyn Bridge leapt toward our spiritual destiny—ended by taking their own lives.

Now, all I wanted to say was that the poet hankers to write in and for a culture, countering its centrifugal development by continually fabricating a common and inclusive language in which all things are connected. But I got carried away by the present difficulty of attaining that happy utility.

Of course I have overstated the matter, and of course there are fortunate exceptions to be pointed out. Robert Frost was strongly aware of the danger that accelerating change might sweep our country bare of all custom and traditional continuity; some of his best poems, like "The Mountain," are about that threat, and it is significant that he defined the poem as "a momentary stay against confusion." Frost staved off confusion by taking his stand inside a New England rural culture which, during the height of his career, still possessed a certain vitality, and remains intelligible (if less vital) today. In general I should say that Frost *assumed,* rather than expounded, the governing ideas and ideals of that culture; but that, after all, is the way of poetry with ideas. It does not think them up; it does not argue them abstractly; what it does is to realize them within that model of felt experience which is a poem, and so reveal their emotional resonance and their capacity for convincing embodiments.

I was looking the other day at what is doubtless the best-loved American poem of this century, Robert Frost's "Birches," and it occurred to me that it might be both pertinent and a little unexpected if I finished by quoting it and saying one or two things about it.

When I see birches bend to left and right
Across the lines of straighter darker trees,
I like to think some boy's been swinging them.
But swinging doesn't bend them down to stay.
Ice-storms do that. Often you must have seen them
Loaded with ice a sunny winter morning
After a rain. They click upon themselves
As the breeze rises, and turn many-colored
As the stir cracks and crazes their enamel.
Soon the sun's warmth makes them shed crystal shells
Shattering and avalanching on the snow-crust—
Such heaps of broken glass to sweep away
You'd think the inner dome of heaven had fallen.
They are dragged to the withered bracken by the load,
And they seem not to break; though once
they are bowed
So low for long, they never right themselves:
You may see their trunks arching in the woods
Years afterwards, trailing their leaves on the ground
Like girls on hands and knees that throw their hair
Before them over their heads to dry in the sun.
But I was going to say when Truth broke in
With all her matter-of-fact about the ice-storm
I should prefer to have some boy bend them
As he went out and in to fetch the cows—
Some boy too far from town to learn baseball,
Whose only play was what he found himself,
Summer or winter, and could play alone.
One by one he subdued his father's trees

By riding them down over and over again
Until he took the stiffness out of them,
And not one but hung limp, not one was left
For him to conquer. He learned all there was
To learn about not launching out too soon
And so not carrying the tree away
Clear to the ground. He always kept his poise
To the top branches, climbing carefully
With the same pains you use to fill a cup
Up to the brim, and even above the brim.
Then he flung outward, feet first, with a swish,
Kicking his way down through the air to the ground.
So was I once myself a swinger of birches.
And so I dream of going back to be.
It's when I'm weary of considerations,
And life is too much like a pathless wood
Where your face burns and tickles with the cobwebs
Broken across it, and one eye is weeping
From a twig's having lashed across it open.
I'd like to get away from earth awhile
And then come back to it and begin over.
May no fate willfully misunderstand me
And half grant what I wish and snatch me away
Not to return. Earth's the right place for love:
I don't know where it's likely to go better.
I'd like to go by climbing a birch tree,
And climb black branches up a snowwhite trunk
Toward heaven, till the tree could bear no more,
But dipped its top and set me down again.
That would be good both going and coming back.
One could do worse than be a swinger of birches.

To begin with, this poem comes out of the farm and woodland country of northern New England, and everything in it is named in the right language. Moreover, there are moments of brilliant physical realization, as when the breeze "cracks and crazes" the "enamel" of ice-laden birches, or the birch-swinging boy flings out and falls in a perfect kinetic line, "Kicking his way down through the air to the ground." The poem presents a vivid regional milieu, and then subtly expands its range; naturally, and almost insensibly, the ground and sky of New England are magnified into Heaven and Earth.

Considered as self-projection, "Birches" is an example of how the pentameter can be so counter-pointed as to force the reader to hear a sectional and personal accent. Frost's talking voice is in the poem, and so too is his manner: the drift of the argument is ostensibly casual or even whimsical, but behind the apparent rambling is a strict intelligence; the language lifts into rhetoric or a diffident lyricism, but promptly returns to the colloquial, sometimes by way of humor. The humor of Frost's poem is part of its meaning, because humor arises from a sense of human limitations, and that is what Frost is talking about. His poem is a recommendation of limited aspiration, or high-minded earthliness, and the birch incarnates that idea perfectly, being a tree which lets you climb a while toward heaven but then "dips its top and sets you down again." This is a case in which thought and thing, inside and outside, self and world, admirably correspond.

Because of his colloquialism and his rustic settings, Frost has often been thought of as a non-literary poet. That is a serious error. Frost was lovingly acquainted with poetic literature all the way back to Theocritus, and he was a conscious continuator and modifier of the tradition. Formally, he adapted the traditional meters and conventions to the natural cadence and tenor of New England speech. Then as for content, while he did not echo the poetry of the past so promiscuously as T. S. Eliot, he was always aware of what else had been written on any subject, and often implied as much. In "Hyla Brook," which I read to you a few minutes ago, Frost makes a parenthetical acknowledgement that other poets—Tennyson, Milton, Theocritus perhaps—have dealt more flatteringly with brooks or streams than he feels the need to do.

In "Birches," Frost's reference is more specific, and I am going to re-read a few lines now, in which I ask you to listen for the voice of Shelley:

> Often you must have seen them
> Loaded with ice a sunny winter morning
> After a rain. They click upon themselves
> As the breeze rises, and turn many-colored
> As the stir cracks and crazes their enamel.
> Soon the sun's warmth makes them shed
> crystal shells
> Shattering and avalanching on the snow-crust—
> Such heaps of broken glass to sweep away
> You'd think the inner dome of heaven had fallen.

Many-colored. Glass. The inner dome of heaven. It would not have been possible for Frost to pack so many echoes of Shelley into six lines and not be aware of it. He is slyly recalling the two most celebrated lines of Shelley's *Adonais*:

> Life, like a dome of many-colored glass,
> Stains the white radiance of eternity.

Such a reminiscence is at the very least a courtesy, a tribute to the beauty of Shelley's lines. But there is more to it than that. Anyone who lets himself be guided by Frost's reference, and reads over the latter stanzas of Shelley's lament for Keats, will find that "Birches," taken as a whole, is in fact an answer to Shelley's kind of boundless neo-Platonic aspiration. It would be laborious, here and now, to point out all the pertinent lines in *Adonais*; suffice it to say that by the close of the poem Keat's soul has been translated to Eternity, to the eternal fountain of beauty, light, and love, and that Shelley, spurning the Earth, is embarking on a one-way upward voyage to the Absolute. The closing stanza goes like this:

> The breath whose might I have invoked in song
> Descends on me; my spirit's bark is driven
> Far from the shore, far from the trembling throng
> Whose sails were never to the tempest given;
> The massy earth and sphered skies are riven!
> I am borne darkly, fearfully, afar;
> Whilst, burning through the inmost veil of Heaven,
> The soul of Adonais, like a star,
> Beacons from the abode where the Eternal are.

Frost's answer to that is, "Earth's the right place for love." In his dealings with Shelley's poem, Frost is doing a number of things. He is for one thing conversing timelessly with a great poem out of the English tradition; he is, for another thing, contending with that poem in favor of another version of spirituality. And in his quarrel with Shelley, Frost is speaking not only for his own temper but for the practical idealism of the New England spirit. Frost's poem does justice to world, to self, to literary tradition, and to a culture; it is happy in all the ways in which a poem can be happy; and I leave it with you as the best possible kind of answer to the question I have been addressing.

[1969]

William Carlos Williams

TWO POEMS

JUNE 9

That profound cleft
at whose bottom
is the surface
          where we would hide

Clap! clap! claps
at us
not merrily
but as a catbird calls

—not of Athens
not out of Athens but
from a privet hedge

here!

drenched with that tone
of dread we feel
          (bred of the newspapers
          What bread!)

generally

How can we love
hearing that cry always
in our ears
          half drowned out by

roars of trucks
and motor cars? Our bottoms
          ache from the heat

STILL LIFE

Astride the boney jointed ridge
that lifts and falls
to which

in pain and ecstasy the hand
is lifted for assurance
ride

the tender pointed breasts
and there in women when
they are young

they ride twin fountains to
the whole dry world's gaping
misery

[1951]

Charles Wright

PORTRAIT OF MARY

(After Montale)

Mary, your twenty-odd years now threaten you,
A widening fog which, little by little, you enter;
Once in, we'll see you in its cloud-shapes and mist-shapes
Which wind, from time to time, will open or thicken.

Then from its swell, in passing, you will come
More white than ever, more multiple and new;
Clear, re-awakened, and turning toward other things.
The winds of autumn rise; past springs still hold you.

Stretched out, face down, glistening with salt in the sun,
For you tomorrow's raw estate is welcome;
You call to mind the lizard motionless
On stone—youth traps you, her the child's grass snare.

The ocean is the force that tempers you;
We think of you as alga, a pebble, a creature
Which sea-wash and sea-salt can't lessen or corrode,
But return to the beach more perfect than before.

You shrug your shoulders; vast walls and castles crumble
Holding your future, loosing whatever will come.
You rise, walk out the small wood pier over
The creaking rise and fall, the suck of the sea;

You hesitate at the end of the trembling board,
Then laugh, and, as though knocked off by a wind,
You cut down to the water, which gathers you in.
We watch you, we who must remain ashore.

[1966]

Marguerite Yourcenar

A CRITICAL INTRODUCTION TO CAVAFY

translated from the French by Richard Howard

Constantine Cavafy is one of the most famous poets of modern Greece; he is also one of the greatest, certainly the subtlest, perhaps the most modern, though sustained more than any other by the inexhaustible substance of the past. The poet was born, of Greek parents from Constantinople, in 1863 in Alexandria, where he worked for thirty years in the Ministry of Irrigation and where he died in 1933. Cavafy soon discovered his vocation, but preserved only a small number of all the poems written before he was fifty, few of which figure among his masterpieces; even these early poems, moreover, show signs of subsequent retouching. During his lifetime Cavafy permitted only a few poems to be published in periodicals; his fame, which was to be gradual, depended on fugitive pamphlets distributed parsimoniously to friends or disciples; thus a body of work which at first glance seems astonishingly detached, almost impersonal, remained "secret" to the end, subject to constant revision, profiting from the poet's experience until his death. And only in his last years did Cavafy express more or less openly his most personal obsessions, emotions and memories which had inspired and sustained his work all his life, but more vaguely, in a more veiled fashion.

A few lines account for Cavafy's external biography; his poems tell us more about this existence apparently limited to the routine of office and café, library and low tavern, confined in space to a monotonous itinerary through one city, yet extraordinarily free in time. We might attempt more—to decipher what the poet's art consists precisely in encoding, to extract from this or that poem a plausible if not a verifiable personal memory. For example, "Apollonius of Tyana in Rhodes" echoes, we are told, Cavafy's distaste for the copious and often declamatory works of his contemporary Palamas; again, two or three profiles of noble Byzantine or Spartan mothers ("In Sparta", "Come, O King of the Lacedaemonians", "Anna Dalassané"), the only feminine figures in an *oeuvre* decidedly alien to woman[1], appear to be inspired by the memory of his own mother, widowed when Constantine was seven, and left to raise him and his six older brothers. Clearly autobiographical, "Dangers" records that brief moment when the young man wavered, like so many others, between pleasure and asceticism. "Satrapy" translates the bitterness of a man who to succeed in the material world must renounce high literary ambitions: Cavafy the functionary must have suffered such misgivings. "Sculptor of Tyana" and "For the Shop" are suggestive, with their allusions to works of art apart from what is shown and offered to the public, objects created exclusively for the artist. With the help not only of the few erotic poems in which Cavafy speaks in his own name ("Gray", "Far Away", "Afternoon Sun," "On the Deck of the Ship", "The Next Table"), but also of the many more numerous ones in which the lover is designated by an impersonal "he", we might establish the habitual catalogue of pursuits and encounters, of pleasures and partings. Finally, his almost obsessive insistence on specifying ages ("Two Young Men 23 to 24 Years Old", "Portrait of a 23-year-old Youth", "For Ammonis, Dead at 29", "Cimon, Son of Learchos, a 22-year-old student"), along with a few descriptions of faces and bodies would suffice to delimit what for Cavafy were the beloved's ideal age and type. But to use the poems in the hunt for biographical details contradicts the poetic goal itself: the most clear-sighted poet often hesitates to retrace the route which has led him from the more or less chaotic emotion, the more or less insignificant incident, to the poem's precision and its calm duration. A commentator is therefore all the more likely to go astray. Cavafy said many times that his work originated in his life; henceforth his life abides entirely in his work.

Accounts by the poet's disciples and admirers afford at most a characteristic or colorful touch; however, the most enthusiastic see little and describe badly, not from a failure of attention or of eloqu-

[1]To complete the list: Demeter and Metaneira ("Interruption"), Thetis ("Infidelity"), an old servant woman ("Kleitos' Illness"), the sailor's mother ("Prayer") and Aristoboulos' ("Aristoboulos") are also personifications of maternity. We may note three or four allusions to the political role of Byzantine women: Irene Doukaina ("A Byzantine Nobleman in Exile"), "Anna Komnina", Irene Assan ("Of Colored Glass"), Anne of Savoy ("John Kantakuzinos Triumphs"); a few names of Jewish princesses ("Aristoboulos", "Alexander Jannaios"), a reference to Cleopatra as Caesarion's mother ("Alexandrian Kings"). Never has a female cast been more reduced. Erotic concerns aside, Cavafy's poems resemble those Near Eastern cafés frequented only by men.

ence, but for reasons which relate, perhaps, to the very secret of life and of poetry. I have questioned Greek friends who saw something of the sick and dying poet, already famous at the time of his last stay in Athens, around 1930; he lived, they told me, in a seedy hotel on Omonia Square, a new and noisy business neighborhood; this supposedly solitary man seemed to be surrounded by devoted friends whose praise he welcomed politely, merely smiling when it seemed excessive; he corrected the manuscripts of young admirers with gentle severity. His anglomania surprised them; they found he spoke Greek with a faint Oxford accent.[2] As often happens, these young people were disappointed that the great man's literary tastes were less advanced than their own; the singularity, novelty and boldness of this poetry they so admired seemed to be nourished, by an incomprehensible osmosis, on works they regarded as superannuated. Cavafy enjoyed Anatole France and had no use for Gide; he prized Browning above T. S. Eliot; he scandalized them by quoting Musset. I inquired as to his physical appearance and was assured he looked quite ordinary—like a Levantine broker. A photograph of him at about forty shows a face with heavy-lidded eyes, a sensual judicious mouth; the reserved, pensive, almost melancholy expression may have more to do with milieu and race than with the man. But let us turn to E. M. Forster, who knew Cavafy in Alexandria a few years before this photograph was taken:

> Modern Alexandria is scarcely a city of the soul. Founded upon cotton with the concurrence of onions and eggs, ill built, ill planned, ill drained—many hard things can be said against it, and most are said by its inhabitants. Yet to some of them, as they traverse the streets, a delightful experience can occur. They hear their own name proclaimed in firm yet meditative accents—accents that seem not so much to expect an answer as to pay homage to the fact of individuality. They turn and see a Greek gentleman in a straw hat, standing absolutely motionless at a slight angle to the universe . . . He may be prevailed upon to begin a sentence—an immense complicated shapely sentence, full of parentheses that never get mixed and of reservations that really do reserve; a

[2]This same anglomania dictated, I am told, the poet's use of the double initial C.P. instead of his given name Constantine, as is customary in Greek. The surname itself, traditionally written Kavafis, can be transcribed in various ways, but the poet's heirs have chosen Cavafy, eliminating the final *s*, which is no longer pronounced in modern Greek.

> sentence that moves with logic to its foreseen end, yet to an end that is always more vivid and thrilling than one foresaw. Sometimes the sentence is finished in the street, sometimes the traffic murders it, sometimes it lasts into the flat. It deals with the tricky behavior of the Emperor Alexius Comnenus in 1096, or with olives, their possibilities and price, or with the fortunes of friends, or George Eliot, or with the dialects of the interior of Asia Minor. It is delivered with equal ease in Greek, English, or French. And despite its intellectual richness and human outlook, despite the matured charity of its judgments, one feels that it too stands at a slight angle to the universe: it is the sentence of a poet . . .

We might contrast Forster's irreverent sketch with a few sober lines by Ungaretti which evoke, in a milk-bar in the Ramleh district of Alexandria, at the table of the young editors of the review *Grammata* (one of the first to present his work to the public), a sententious, measured but affable Cavafy, occasionally uttering a remark not to be forgotten. To which may also be added the account I once heard from a young woman who, as a child, had known the poet in Alexandria, at the end of his life. The little girl would hide in order to spy on this mild, courteous old gentleman who occasionally visited her parents and who inspired her with a passionate curiosity, along with a certain terror, because of his way "of looking like no one else", his pallor, his bandage-swathed neck (Cavafy was to die of throat cancer a few months later), his dark clothes and his habit, when he thought he was alone, of pensively murmuring something. An indistinct murmur, the young woman told me, for the sick man was already almost voiceless, but one which suggested all the more the incantation of a sorceror . . . We may allow such fragmentary testimonies to complete each other and turn instead to the poems themselves, a distinct murmur, insistent, unforgettable.

*

What strikes us first is the almost complete absence of any Oriental or even Levantine "picturesque". That this Alexandrian Greek should have given no room to the Arab or Moslem world can surprise no one even slightly familiar with the Near East, its juxtaposition of races and their separation rather than their mixtures.[3] Cavafy's Orientalism, that Orientalism perpetually in

[3]The abstract yet ardent tone of certain erotic poems irresistibly recalls some Arabic, or rather Persian, poetry, but Cavafy would surely have rejected any such comparison.

suspension in all Greek thought, is located elsewhere. The fact that nature, that landscape explicitly, is passed over in silence relates chiefly to his personal sensibility. The one poem which explicitly considers natural objects yields the secret of this soul voluptuously immured in the human.

> I'll stand here and look at nature a while.
> The brilliant blues of the morning sea, the cloudless sky,
> and the yellow shore: all lovely,
> all bathed in light.
>
> I'll stand here and make myself believe I really see it
> (I did, for a moment, when I first stopped)
> and not just my illusions, my memories,
> my images of sensuality.

We may not call this indifference to landscape Greek or Oriental without having to limit, define, explain. Greek poetry abounds in natural images; even the later epigrammatists who lived for the most part in that "resolutely modern" world of ancient Antioch or Alexandria constantly invoke the shade of a plane-tree, the waters of a spring. And the Oriental poets ecstatically apostrophize fountains and gardens. In this realm, Cavafy's dryness is a distinctive feature; quite his own are those perspectives deliberately limited to the streets and suburbs of the great city, and almost always to the decor, to the stage-set of love:

> The room was squalid and mean,
> hidden above the dubious tavern.
> From the window you could look down
> into the dirty narrow alley. From below
> came the voices of some workmen
> playing cards and having a good time.
>
> And there, on the filthy sheets of that bed,
> I possessed the body of love, possessed the lips,
> the swollen dark lips of intoxication—
> so swollen and with such intoxication that even now
> as I write, after so many years,
> in my lonely house, I am drunk again.

Workmen's cafés, avenues darkening at nightfall, sinister establishments frequented by young and suspect figures, are presented only in terms of the human adventure, of encounter and parting, and it is these terms which lend such an accurate beauty to the slightest sketches, street scenes or interiors. The poet could be speaking of Piraeus, of Marseilles, of Algiers, of Barcelona—of any great Mediterranean city just as well as of Alexandria. Except for the color of the sky, we are not so far from Utrillo's Paris; certain bedrooms suggests those of Van Gogh with their rattan chairs, their yellow pots, their bare, sun-drenched walls. But a wholly Greek light touches everything here: vitality of air, clarity of atmosphere, the sun on human skin and that incorruptible salt which also saves from total dissolution the characters of the *Satyricon,* that Greek masterpiece in Latin. And indeed the Alexandrian plebs often suggest Petronius; the casual realism of a poem like "Two Young Men 23 to 24 Years Old" irresistibly evokes the fortunes of Ascyltus and Encolpius:

> . . . His friend brings unexpected news:
> he has won sixty pounds playing cards . . .
>
> And filled with excitement and longing
> they go off—not to their respectable families
> (where they are no longer wanted anyway)
> but to a very special house, one they know well,
> they ask for a room and they order
> expensive drinks, they drink again . . .

Perhaps not everyone will appreciate these singular realistic sketches in Cavafy's final manner, almost banal in their exactitude. Yet nothing deserves our interest more than these dry, delicate poems ("The Tobacco-shop Window", "He Asked about the Quality", "In the Monotonous Village", "Lovely White Flowers that Became Him": I deliberately select those most likely to try the reader's indulgence), where not only the erotic or sometimes picaresque element but even the stalest situations and settings, the occasions dearest to sentimental ballads, scoured here by a kind of pure prosaicism, regain their true resonance, their values and, so to speak, their standing:

> But now there is no need of suits of clothes
> or silk handkerchiefs or twenty pounds
> or twenty piasters, for that matter.

On Sunday they buried him, at ten in the morning.
On Sunday they buried him, almost a week ago.

On the cheap coffin he put flowers,
lovely white flowers that became him,
that became his beauty and his 22 years.

In the evening when a job came his way—
he had to live on something—and he went to the café
where they used to go together, it was a knife in his heart,
that dreary café where they used to go together.

But I was speaking of the setting, the decor of these poems: by a transition inevitable in Cavafy, any mention of the decor leads us back to the passions of the characters.

*

"Most poets are exclusively poets. Not Palamas, he writes stories too. I am a poet-historian. I cannot write novels or plays, but inner voices tell me that the historian's calling is within my reach. But there is no time left . . ."[4] Perhaps there was never time: Cavafy deliberately scorns the broad perspectives, the great movements of history; he makes no attempt to grasp a human being in his deepest experience, his changes, his duration. He does not paint Caesar; he does not revive that mass of matter and passions which was Mark Antony; he shows a moment in Caesar's life, he meditates on a turning-point in Mark Antony's fate. His historical method is related to Montaigne's: he extracts certain examples, certain counsels, sometimes very specific erotic stimulants from Herodotus, from Plutarch, from Polybius, from the obscure chronicles of the late Empire or of Byzantium.[5] He is an essayist, often a moralist, supremely a humanist. Intentionally or not, he confines himself to the swift glimpse, to the naked, sharply-etched feature. Yet the narrowly-limited field of vision is almost always of

---

[4]Quoted by Theodore Griva in his preface to a translation of Cavafy's poems, Lausanne, 1944.

[5]A man of letters rather than a professional scholar, Cavafy did not necessarily read so widely in every instance. Most of the poems in his Ptolemies-Seleucids-Greek Defeats cycle were apparently inspired by E. R. Bevan's splendid book *The House of Seleucus*, London, 1902, where Cavafy could also have found the detail he borrows from Malalas ("Greek since Ancient Times") and the photograph of the young king's profile "that seems to smile" ("Orophernes"). The poems of the Byzantine cycle, on the other hand, appear to be documented from the chronicles rather than, as has been said, by a reading of Gibbon.

the strictest accuracy.[6] This realist never burdens himself with theories, ancient or modern, thereby discarding that stew of generalizations, clumsy contrasts and clotted scholarly commonplaces which give so many minds indigestion at the feast of history. This precisionist breaks, for example, with a long romantic tradition when he shows us Julian the apostate as a young fanatic marked despite himself by Christian influence, unwittingly distorting the Hellenism he claims to defend, a butt for the mockery of the pagans of Antioch:

> "I find you very indifferent toward the gods,"
> he says solemnly. Indifferent! What did he expect?
> He could reform the priesthood to his heart's content,
> write every day to the high priest of Galatia
> or to other pontiffs of the kind, exhorting . . .
> His friends were not Christians, granted . . .
> But they couldn't get involved, as he did
> (brought up a Christian as he was) in that whole
> system of religious reorganization,
> as ridiculous in theory as in practice.
> After all, they were Greeks . . . Nothing in excess,
> Augustus.

We may indicate further points of detail, such as noting that the Homeric period has inspired only some fine early poems, the sombre "Infidelity" or the subtle "Ithaca"[7]. Fifth-century Greece, the traditional Hellas of Attica and the Peloponnesus and the islands, is virtually absent from this alexandrian poetry, or approached obliquely by an interpretation dating from six or eight centuries later ("Dimaratos", "Young Men of Sidon"). It is the exile and death of King Cleomenes in Alexandria which appear to have drawn Cavafy's attention to the drama of Sparta's decline ("In Sparta", "Come, O King of the Lacedaemonians"); Athens is mentioned only once, apropos of one of the great sophists of the imperial epoch ("Herodes Atticus"); the Roman world is seen

[6]Yet we must distinguish, in Cavafy, between the supurb poems of an authentic Hellenism and those in which he yields to a period taste for a knick-knack Greece. I wanted to indicate at once this mixture of the exquisite and the mediocre so that ultimately I could indicate only the exquisite.

[7]"Infidelity", inspired by a fragment, quoted in Plato, from Aeschylus' *Tragic Iliad*, and the three or four poems more or less directly inspired by Homer, represent Cavafy's only borrowings from the poets of Antiquity. Elsewhere he draws almost exclusively on the historians and the sophists, *i.e.*, on the Greek prose-writers.

from Greek perspectives. The poet prefers to deal with a period of Antiquity known chiefly to specialists, the two or three centuries of cosmopolitan life which followed the death of Alexander in the Greek Orient. Cavafy's humanism is not ours: from Rome, from the Renaissance, from the academicism of the eighteenth century, we inherit an heroic and classical image of Greece, a white marble Hellenism: the center of our Greek history is the Acropolis of Athens. Cavafy's humanism passes through Alexandria, through Asia Minor, to a lesser degree through Byzantium, through a palimpsest Greece increasingly remote from what seems to us the golden age, but in which a living continuity persists. Moreover we must not forget that by an age-old mistake we have regarded "Alexandrianism" as a synonym for decadence: it was during the rule of Alexander's successors, it was at Alexandria and at Antioch, that an extra-mural Greek civilization was elaborated, one which assimilated foreign contributions and in which patriotism of culture prevailed over a patriotism of race. "We call Greeks," Isocrates said, "not only those who are of our blood, but also those who follow our ways." In every fiber of his being Cavafy belongs to this civilization of the *koine*, the common tongue—to that immense outer Greece resulting from diffusion rather than from conquest, a Greece patiently formed over and over again down through the centuries, a Greece whose influence lingers still in the modern Levant of merchants and ship-owners.[8] The array of compromises, participations, exchanges, the image of the young Oriental more seduced than defeated gives a touch of pathos to that admirable historical narrative "Orophernes":

> The figure on this tetradrachma
> who seems to be smiling, the face
> with the pure outline, beautiful, delicate,
> is Orophernes, son of Ariarathis . . .

It is a destiny to be Greek, or to desire to be, and we find in this Cavafian poetry the whole range of the mind's reactions to this destiny, from pride ("Epitaph of Antiochus, King of Kommagini" to irony ("Philhellene"). These short poems, overinscribed like palimpsests but haunted by no more than two or three problems of sen-

[8]Neither here nor elsewhere, moreover, is Cavafy representative of the tendencies of his neo-Greek milieu. Modern Greek poets are usually more Romaic, more Italianizing, or more vehemently westernized. Even their humanism (if it exists) has an Occidental stamp.

suality, politics or art, frequented by a type of beauty always the same, vague yet very specifically characterized, like those burning-eyed Fayum portraits that stare out at you with a kind of dizzying insistence, are unified by climate even more than they are diversified by time. For a French reader, despite obvious differences, this authentically levantine climate of Cavafy's suggests that Greco-Syrian Orient so miraculously divined by Racine: Oreste, Hippolyte, Xipharès, Antiochus, Bajazet himself have already made us familiar with this atmosphere of refinement and passion, this complex world which dates back to the Diadochi if not to the Atrides, and which does not end with the Osmanli Turks. Whether Cavafy speaks of the young prince "adorned in Greek silks, with turquoise jewelry" from pre-Christian Ionia, or of the young vagabond in a cinnamon-colored suit ("Days of 1908"), we always catch the same accent, the same just-perceptible pathos, the same reserve, I was about to say the same mystery. Voluptuaries, too, have their sense of the eternal.

*

Suppose we group in cycles these historical poems Cavafy has distributed, like all the others, according to their order of composition; we shall then see the poet's preferences, his rejections, even his lacunae more clearly focussed. First, the *Ptolemies-Seleucids* cycle, which we might also call the *Fall of the Hellenistic Monarchies-Triumph of Rome,* the largest since it includes at least two dozen poems and the one most charged with pathos and irony; the four *études de moeurs* in the *Hellenized Jews* cycle; seven poems in the fine Alexandrian *Caesar-Caesarion-Antony cycle;* ten poems in the *Sophists- Poets-Ancient Universities* cycle, which constitutes the equivalent of Cavafy's *ars poetica;* two poems on *Nero,* one still decked with the futile ornaments Cavafy was later to discard, the other among the subtlest and surest in the canon; some twenty poems in the *Pagans-Christians* cycle, as we may call it, making little of the banal contrast between Christian austerity and ancient license, showing life persisting beneath all formulas; two poems about *Apollonius of Tyana;* seven poems on, or rather against, *Julian the Apostate;* seven in the *Orthodoxy-Byzantine Chronicles* cycle, jumbling together an encomium of Orthodox ceremonies ("In Church"), an erotic notation ("Imenos"), glosses on the poet's reading such as the exquisite "Of Colored Glass", filled with a tender piety for the past of the race but also including "Aimilianus Monai," one of the purest of all Cavafy's threnodies. It is again to

Alexandrianism that we must attach most of the *Illnesses-Deaths-Funerals* cycle, which cuts across the others; this group, which contains some of the most famous of Cavafy's poems ("In the Month of Athyr", "Myris", and the modern, very picturesque "Lovely White Flowers" which, curiously, is in this same vein), also includes some highly literary poems of a rather flaccid charm, more or less related to the traditional genre of the erotic elegy or the fictive funerary epigram. Putting matters in the best possible light, "Cimon, Son of Learchos", "Kleitos' Illness" and "The Tomb of Lanes" afford Cavafy masculine equivalents of the young Clyties and the Tarentines of that other poet—half-Greek by parentage—André Chénier.

Instead of this quite external classification of the historical poems, let us now take deeper soundings: *poems of fate,* in which disaster befalls man from without, the consequence of unexplained forces which seem to take a conscious pleasure in leading us into error—more or less the ancient view of man's relation to fatality, to the huge mass of causes and effects inaccessible to our calculations, indifferent to our prayers and our efforts. Cavafy, haunted from the outset by this problem of fate, has inventoried the recipes of defiance, of acceptance, or prudent audacity: "Prayer", "Nero's Respite", "Interruption", "On the March to Sinope", "The Ides of March", and above all "Infidelity", that harsh acknowledgment of what seems to man the incomprehensible perfidy of his god or his gods:

> At the wedding feast of Peleus and Thetis,
> Apollo stood up to salute the bride and groom.
> They would be fortunate, he said, in the son
> who would be born of their union. Never
> could sickness harm him, and his existence
> would be long . . . And as Achilles grew up,
> the admiration of all Thessaly,
> Thetis remembered the god's promises . . .
> But one day, old men came bearing news,
> and they told how Achilles had been slain at Troy.
> And Thetis tore off her purple robes, tore off
> and cast upon the ground her bracelets and rings . . .
> Where was he, the poet-god who had spoken
> such fair words at the feast? Where was he,
> the prophet-god, when they had murdered Achilles

in the flower of his youth? And the old men answered
that Apollo himself had come down before Troy
and that with the Trojans he had slain Achilles.

The tragi-comic predominates in the *poems of character,* outlines sure as an Ingres drawing, exact tracings of weaknesses, follies, failings of a lively, frivolous and yet lovable humanity, inventive in trifles, almost always baffled by the tremendous, swept by misfortune to extreme solutions, by misery or indolence to timid or base ones, though not without a certain quick wisdom: "From the School of the Renowned Philosopher", "Alexander Valas' Favorite", "The Gods Should Have Bothered." A perspective without illusions, but not desolate even so: we should hesitate to call it bitter, yet it is certainly bitterness and rigor that we discover under the imperceptible curve of a smile. Consider, for example, "The Gods Should Have Bothered":

I am virtually a pauper now, a vagrant:
Antioch, this fatal city
has swallowed all my money—
this fatal city with its extravagant life.

But I'm young and in good health.
My Greek is extremely good . . .
I have some notion of military matters . . .
So I regard myself as quite qualified
to serve this country, my own
beloved Syria . . .

I'll apply to Zabinas first
and if that dolt doesn't appreciate me
I'll go to his rival, Grypos,
and if that fool doesn't hire me either
I'll go straight to Hyrkanos . . .

As for my conscience, it's clear:
why should I worry which one I choose,
all three are equally bad for Syria!

But what can a poor devil like me do?
I'm only trying to make ends meet.
The almighty gods should have bothered
to create a fourth, an honest man.
I'd gladly have gone over to him.

The *poem of character* almost always coincides with the *political poem:* Cavafy devotes to Ptolemaic or Byzantine intrigues that chess-player's sagacity, that passionate interest in the fine art of public life, or what is called public life, which almost no Greek is without. Further, like many of his compatriots, Cavafy seems bitterly sensitive to the spectacle of perfidy, disorder, futile heroism or base inertia which so often characterizes Greek history (though scarcely more than any other, ancient or modern): his absence of moralism, his disdain for the sensational and the grandiloquent, afford such themes, compromised by so much pompous oratory, a striking immediacy. It is hard to believe these poems of humiliation and defeat were not inspired by the events of our own day, rather than having been written over thirty years ago on themes dating back twenty centuries. Neither the cunning opportunist nor the myopic patriot who sacrifices his country to his grievances nor the adventurer who openly profits from the miseries of the moment is denounced with vehemence: each is accurately judged. They continue to belong—though at their own level, an extremely low one—to that civilization which they are helping to destroy and to which they owe the remains of that elegance in which they drape their selfishness or their cowardice. Similarly, the heroes are surrounded by no applause which might distract us from the spectacle of their serenity: the symbolic soldiers of Thermopylae or a noble mother like Cratesicleia move silently toward "that which is willed for them". A slightly intensified conviction, an almost imperceptibly deepened pathos in the monologue's movement is enough to turn the cynicism of "The Gods Should Have Bothered" into the heroic sadness of "Demetrius Soter" with its undertone of indignation and scorn:

> . . . He used to dream he would achieve great things,
> ending the humiliation that had oppressed his country
> ever since the battle of Magnesia. He was convinced
> Syria would be a powerful nation again, with her fleets,
> her armies, her great fortresses, her wealth.
>
> He suffered bitterly in Rome when he realized,
> listening to his friends, young men of prominent
> families,
> that for all the delicacy and politeness they showed him,
> the son after all of King Seleucus Philopator—

when he realized that nonetheless there was always
a secret contempt for the fallen Hellenized dynasties:
their time was past, they weren't fit for serious things,
for governing people—quite unfit.
Left to himself he would grow angry, and swore
it would not turn out the way they thought . . .
He would struggle, would do what had to be done,
awaken his country . . .

If only he could get back to Syria!
He had been so young when he left, he hardly
remembered what it looked like. But in his mind
he had always seen it as something sacred,
to be approached reverently, a vision
of a lovely land, with Greek cities, Greek harbors.

And now?
Now despair and desolation.
The young men in Rome were right.
The dynasties created by the Macedonian Conquest
could not survive any longer.

Still, he had made the effort, struggled all he could.
And in his black disillusion, there is one thing
he is still proud of: even in disaster
he stills shows the world the same indomitable courage.

The rest was dreams and wasted energy.
This Syria almost seems not to be his country any
more,—
This Syria is the land of Balas and Heracleides.

In a sense, the political poems are still poems of fate, but in them fate is created by man. From the Theophrastian technique of the *Character,* in which an individual's qualities and defects are supremely important, there is a gradual shift to those astonishing poems where the interplay of expedients, fears and political calculations acquires the dry clarity of a blueprint. Here emotion is deliberately suppressed; if there irony, it is honed so exquisitely that its wounds are imperceptible. The allegorical (and almost too famous) "Waiting for the Barbarians" is a demonstration *ad absurdum* of the politics of defeat; "In Alexandria, 31 B.C.", "Alexander Jannaios," "In a Large Greek Colony", "In a Township of Asia Minor" epitomize—in street scenes, in the gossip of bureaucrats—the eternal comedy of State; poems like "Displeasure of the Seleucid" or "Envoys from Alexandria" bring political realism to the level of pure poetry, a very rare success shared by Racine's historical plays. Their beauty consists in a complete absence of vagueness and inaccuracy:

> For centuries, no one had seen gifts at Delphi
> so fine as those sent by the two brothers,
> the rival Ptolemies. But now that they have them
> the priests are uneasy about the oracle expected of them:
> they will need all their wits to determine which one
> of two such brothers will have to be offended.
> And so they meet secretly, at night,
> to discuss the family affairs of the Lagides.
>
> But now the envoys are back, to take their leave.
> They are returning to Alexandria, they say, and want
> no oracle whatever. The priests are delighted
> (it is understood they are to keep the marvelous gifts)
> but also totally bewildered, not understanding
> what this sudden indifference means.
> For they don't know that yesterday serious news
> reached the envoys. The oracle was pronounced
> in Rome; the dispute was settled there.

Setting aside the historical poems of erotic inspiration, which overlap the personal poems and should be studied with them, I come at last to those splendid half-gnomic, half-lyric poems I prefer to call *poems of passionate reflection*. Here the concepts of politics, of character and of fate seem to melt into an ampler, looser concept of destiny, of a necessity at once external and internal, associated with a freedom implicitly divine. "Theodotos", which suggests a Mantegna drawing, is such a poem, as is the one entitled "The Gods Abandon Antony," accompanied by that "defunctive music" of the tutelary gods abandoning their former favorite on the eve of battle—a fanfare out of Plutarch which has also passed through Shakespeare:

> At midnight, when suddenly you hear
> an invisible procession passing
> with exquisite music, with voices calling,

don't mourn your Fortune that's deserting you,
your work that has failed, your plans
that have all turned out to be illusions—
don't mourn them uselessly:
as if long prepared for this, and bravely,
bid her farewell, the Alexandria that is leaving.
Above all, don't make this mistake, don't say
it was a dream, that your ears deceived you;
don't stoop to empty hopes like those.
As if long prepared, and bravely
as becomes you, who are worthy of such a city,
with emotion but not with regret
or a coward's whining, listen to the voices,
to the exquisite music of that mysterious procession
and bid her farewell, the Alexandria you are losing.

*

Alexandria . . . Alexandria . . . In the poem just quoted, Antony seems to see not his tutelary gods leaving him, as in Plutarch, but the city which he may have loved more than Cleopatra. For Cavafy, in any case, Alexandria is a beloved being. The Parisian's voluptuous enjoyment of Paris, savored, possessed from its outer boulevards to the memories of its Louvre, might be for us the closest equivalent of such a passion. But one difference subsists: despite her upheavals, despite the rage to destroy and the craving to renew, Paris has kept very visible testimonies to her history; Alexandria has retained, of all her remote splendors, no more than a name and a site. Cavafy may have been well served by the luck which granted him a city thus bereft of glamor and the melancholy of ruins. For him the past lives *new,* conjured up from the texts with none of those lovely intermediaries which baroque painting and romantic poetry have accustomed us to put between Antiquity and ourselves. The very fact that the break caused by Islam occurred eight centuries earlier in Alexandria than in Athens or Byzantium forces the poet to relate directly to an older, culturally richer Hellenic world anterior to the Orthodox middle ages, and thereby saves him from that Byzantine turn of mind which often, and to excess, marks neo-Greek thought. Alexandria in the most cosmopolitan sense, but also in the most provincial, of this misunderstood word: Cavafy passionately loves his great city, noisy and restless, rich and poor, too busy with its commerce and its diversions to brood over a past fallen into dust. Here this exemplary bourgeois has savored his pleasures, known his victories and his failures, run his risks. He steps out onto his balcony to get a breath of air, "watching for a moment the movement of the street and the shops"; merely by living in it he has "impregnated with meaning" the city he adores. Here he has had, in his own fashion, his *inimitable life.* It is himself he admonishes through Mark Antony.

Now let us turn to the domain of the strictly personal poems; more particularly, that of the love poems. We may regret, in passing, that the phrase "erotic poetry" bears such an unfortunate connotation; rinsed of what is worst about it but not entirely scoured of its ordinary acceptation, the expression precisely defines these poems at once so marked by sensual experience and so remote from the excesses of amorous lyricism. The incredible control of expression Cavafy nearly always manifests[9] derives perhaps, and in part, from their exclusively pederastic inspiration—from the fact that the poet, born a Christian and a nineteenth-century man, deals with forbidden or disapproved feelings and actions. Incontrovertible *I*'s, associated with grammatical specifications leaving no doubt as to the gender of the beloved, appear quite rarely in his work and only after 1917, which is however *before* the period when such audacities of expression were to become relatively common in western poetry and prose. The rest of the time, it is the historical poems, the gnomic and impersonal ones which complete for us (and supplemented for him) the more infrequent and almost always more veiled personal avowals. But the interest of these half-silences would be slight if they did not ultimately confer upon these deliberately specialized poems something abstract which enhances their beauty, and which, as with certain rubaiyats of Omar Khayyam in Fitzgerald's translation or with Shakespeare's sonnets, makes them, even more than poems to the beloved, poems about love. So much so that poems like "Afternoon Sun" or "On the Deck of a Ship", in which

[9]I except some ten poems of a slack and self-satisfied sentimentality, while wondering if the modern reader's (and my own) irritation in the presence of such effusion does not constitute a form of prudery as dangerous as any other. It is a perverse constraint upon passion, our recognition of its right to violence and not to a languishing or tender reverie. Nonetheless, and from a purely literary point of view, a few of Cavafy's poems seem to me of a flat sentimentality which it is hard not to find "indecent".

the poet-lover speaks in his own name, seem tainted by weakness, or let us say by self-consciousness, compared to those distinct, limpid poems in which the author's presence, recessed from his work, is revealed at most by the shadow it casts. The "I" may burst forth upon an unpremeditated impulse, but the use of "he" presupposes a stage of reflection which reduces the share of the fortuitous and diminishes the risk of exaggeration or of error. Further, the "I" in certain carefully delimited confidences—for example, "Far Off"—ends by acquiring in Cavafy a meaning as naked, as detached, as the "he" of the impersonal poems, and a kind of admirable extraterritoriality:

> I should like to tell this memory . . .
> but it has faded now . . . almost nothing is left,
> it was so far off, in my first years of manhood.
>
> A skin that seemed made of jasmine . . .
> August, that night . . . Was it August? I hardly remember
> the eyes. I think they were blue.
> Oh yes, blue—sapphire blue.

An essay on Cavafy's love poetry would take into consideration his Greek predecessors, the *Anthology* in particular, of which his own works are after all the latest segment, as well as the fashions in erotic expression prevailing in Europe early in the twentieth century: the latter, ultimately, count much more than the former. Greek poetry, however intellectualized its expression, is always direct: cry, sigh, sensual appeal, spontaneous affirmation born on a man's lips in the presence of his beloved. Such poetry rarely mixes either pathos or realistic elaboration with its almost pure lyricism or obscenity. A Callimachus would never have dreamed of describing the young workman's hands grimy with rust and oil in "Days of 1909, 1910, 1911". A Strato would have seen them at most as no more than an erotic stimulant. Neither, surely, would have made out of such a subject this short, dense meditation on poverty and wear, in which desire is accompanied by muted pity. On the other hand, the sense of a moral constraint, the rigor or hypocrisy of propriety did not burden those ancient poets as they did the modern one, or rather (for the problem is complex and even in Antiquity was framed differently from country to country, from century to century) did not burden them in the same way, nor above all with the same weight; they did not have to transcend the inevitable first phase of the struggle with oneself:

Quite often he promises himself he will reform.
But when night comes with its promptings
and its promises and prospects,
when night comes with its own power
of the body's longings and demands,
he returns, bewildered, to the same fatal pleasure.

Any concept of sin is distinctly alien to Cavafy's work; on the other hand, and on the social level entirely, it is clear that the risk of scandal and censure mattered to him, and that in a sense he was obsessed by them. At first glance, it is true, all signs of anxiety seem to have been quite rapidly eliminated from this orderly writing: this is because anxiety, in sensual matters, is almost always a phenomenon of youth; either it destroys its victim, or it gradually diminishes with experience, with a more accurate knowledge of the world, and more simply with habit. Cavafy's poetry is that of an old man whose serenity has had time to ripen. But the very slowness of his development proves that such equilibrium was not easily achieved: the interplay of concealment and confidence, of literary masks and avowals mentioned earlier, the curious mixture of rigor and excess at the very heart of this style, and above all the secret bitterness permeating certain poems, testifies to the fact. "The Twenty-fifth Year of his Life", "On the Street", "Days of 1896", "A Young Poet in his Twenty-fourth Year" are so many high-water marks in a field once flooded and allowed to drain. In "Their Beginning", the shame and fear inseparable from any clandestine experience give the poem the beauty of an etching made with the most corrosive acid:

Their forbidden pleasure has been taken.
They get up from the bed and hurriedly
put on their clothes without speaking.
They leave the house furtively, and out
on the street they walk somewhat uneasily,
as if they suspect that something about them
betrays what kind of pleasure they have just taken.
But how much the artist has gained from it!
Tomorrow, the next day, years later, he will write
the powerful poems that had their beginning here.

Like any reflective man, Cavafy varied not in his degree of adherence to his own actions, but also in his moral judgment as to their legitimacy, and his vocabulary preserves the traces of the hesitations he passed through. He seems to have started from what we may call the romantic view of homosexuality, from the idea of an abnormal, morbid experience outside the limits of the usual and the licit, but thereby rewarding in joys and in secret knowledge—an experience that would be the prerogative of natures sufficiently passionate or free to venture beyond what is known and permitted ("Imenus", "In an Old Book"). From this attitude, one conditioned precisely by social repression, he moved on to a more "classical", certainly a less conventional view of the problem. Notions of happiness, fulfillment, and the validity of pleasure gain ascendancy; he ends by making his sensuality the mainspring of his work ("He Asked about the Quality", "In the Monotonous Village", "He Came to Read", "Passage", "Very Seldom"). Some poems, dated near the end, are even calmly licentious, though without our being able to determine if the artist has here achieved a total liberation, has reached, so to speak, the comedy of his own drama, or if they simply testify to the gradual weakening of the old man's controls. Whatever the case, and even in the erotic realm, Cavafy's development differs very distinctly from that of the western writers of his time with whom it first seemed possible to compare him. His exquisite lack of imposture keeps him from yielding, as Proust did, to a grotesque or falsified image of his own inclinations, from seeking a kind of shameful alibi in caricature, or a glamorous one in disguise. On the other hand, the Gidean element of protest, the need to put personal experience in the immediate service of rational reform or of what (it is hoped) will constitute social progress, is incompatible with Cavafy's dry resignation that takes the world as it is and people's ways as they are. Without much concern for being approved or not, the old Greek openly returns to the hedonism of Antiquity. This poignant yet light view, totally free from the delirious pursuit of "interpretation", to which we are accustomed since Freud, ultimately leads him to a kind of pure and simple assertion of all sensual freedom, whatever its form:

> Joy and fragrance of my life, those moments
> when I found pleasure as I desired it.
> Joy and fragrance of my life: that distance
> from all habitual loves, from all routine pleasures.

Erotic poems, gnomic poems on erotic themes, as we see, rather than love poems. At first glance, we may even wonder if love for anyone in particular appears in these poems: either Cavafy experienced it very little or he has been discreetly silent in its regard. On a closer look, however, almost nothing is missing: encounter and parting, desire slaked or unappeased, tenderness or satiety—is this not what remains of every erotic life once it has passed into the crucible of memory? Yet it is evident, too, that clarity of vision, refusal to overestimate, hence wisdom, but no less perhaps the differences in condition and age, and probably the venality of certain experiences, afford the lover a kind of retrospective detachment in the course of the hottest pursuits or the most ardent carnal joys.[10] Doubtless, too, the poem's slow crystalization, in Cavafy's case, tends to distance him from the immediate shock, to confirm presence only in the form of memory, at a distance where the voice, so to speak, no longer carries, for in this poetry where "I" and "he" contend for primacy, "you", the *beloved addressed,* is singularly absent. We are at the antipodes of ardor, of passion, in the realm of the most egocentric concentration and the most avaricious hoarding. Consequently the gesture of the poet and of the lover handling his memories is not so different from that of the collector of precious or fragile objects, shells or gems, or even of the numismatist bending over his handful of pure profiles accompanied by a number or a date, those numbers and dates for which Cavafy's art shows an almost superstitious predilection. Beloved objects.

*

"Body, remember . . ." This preference for life possessed in the form of memory corresponds, in Cavafy, to a half-expressed mystique. And certainly the problem of memory was "in the air" during the first quarter of the twentieth century; the best minds, in the four corners of Europe, strove to multiply its equations. Proust and Pirandello, Rilke (the Rilke of the *Duino Elegies,* and even more of *Malte Brigge*: "To write good poems, you must have

[10]We may also wonder if Cavafy's sensual life was not intermittent or impoverished, especially during just the period when his poetic sensibility was being formed, and is the constant rumination upon past pleasures is not primarily, in his case, the mania of a solitary man. Certain poems sustain this hypothesis, others dispute it. Such secrets are almost always well kept.

memories . . . And you must forget them . . . And you must have the great patience to wait for them to come back") and Gide himself, who in *The Immoralist* adopts the extreme solution of instantaneousness and of subsequent oblivion. To these versions of memory, subconscious or quintessentialized, deliberate or involuntary, the Greek poet adds another, born, it would seem, of the mythologies of his country, a Memory-as-Image, a quasi-Parmenidean Memory-as-Idea, incorruptible center of his universe of flesh. We have reached the point where we can say that all of Cavafy's poems are historical poems, and the emotion which re-creates a young face glimpsed on a street corner in no way differs from the emotion which "recreates" Caesarion from a collection of Ptolemaic inscriptions:

> . . . Ah, there you are with your indefinable charm!
> In history, you rate only a few lines,
> so I was free to picture you in my mind.
> I made you handsome and sensitive.
> My art gives your face
> a dreamy, appealing beauty,
> and so completely did I imagine you
> that late last night,
> as my lamp went out—I let it go out on purpose—
> I thought you came into my room;
> you seemed to stand there in front of me
> as you would have stood in conquered Alexandria,
> pale and weary, ideal in your grief,
> still hoping they would pity you,
> those traitors who whispered: "Too many Caesars."

Now let us compare this son of Cleopatra with a less celebrated youth, an anonymous figure in the dark streets of modern Alexandria:

> Looking at an opal with grayish lights in it
> I remembered two beautiful gray eyes
> I had seen—it must have been twenty years ago . . .
>
> For a month we had loved each other.
> Then he went away—to Smyrna, I think,
> where he had a job, and we never saw each other
> again.

The gray eyes—if he's still alive—will have lost
their lustre; the handsome face grown ugly.

Memory, show them to me tonight as they once were.
Memory, bring me back tonight all that you can
of this love, all that you can.

If a modern poet at grips with the past (his own or that of history) almost always ends by rejecting or altogether negating memory, it is because he confronts a Heraclitean image of time, that of the river eating away its own banks, drowning both contemplator and the object contemplated. Proust struggled with this image throughout his work, and only partially escaped it by mooring to the Platonist shores of *Time Regained*. Cavafian time belongs, rather, to the space-time of Eleatic philosophy, "the arrow, flying, that does not fly", identical segments, firm, solid, but infinitely divisible, motionless points constituting a line that seems to us to be moving. Once gone by, each moment of such time is surer, more definite, more accessible to the poet's contemplation and even to his delight than the unstable present, always likely to be still in the future or already in the past. It is fixed, as the present is not. Seen from this perspective, the poet's effort to return to the past is no longer located in the realm of the absurd, though still pathetically situated on the confines of the impossible. In "According to the Formulas of the Ancient Greco-Syrian Magi", the unrealizeable demands of memory filter out the sediment of a facile sentimentality:

"What magic philtre," wondered the lover of perfection,
"what herbs distilled according to the formulas
of the ancient Greco-Syrian magi could give me back
for a day or even for a few hours (if its power
can last no longer) my twenty-third year, or
could give me back my friend when he was twenty-two—
his beauty, his love?
"What herbs distilled according to the formulas
of the ancient Greco-Syrian magi, turning time
backward, would give us back as well
that same little room?"

This poem is the only one in which Cavafy records a partial failure of memory, due in part to time's irreversibility, in part to the extraordinary complexity of the nature of things. Ordinarily it is not so much the resurrection of the past that he seeks as it is an image of the past, an Idea, perhaps an Essence. His sensuality leads to a mystical sifting of reality, as spirituality would have done in another case. The gaps in history, and consequently the absence of details which for him are superfluous,[11] help the amorous necromancer evoke Caesarion more effectively; it is because of a twenty-year separation which isolates and definitively seals the memory that the poet conjures up out of the depths of his recollection the image of the young man with gray eyes. In "Days of 1908", the figure of the swimmer standing on the beach, fastidiously scoured of anything incongruous and mediocre, is silhouetted forever against a splendid background of oblivion:

> . . . Summer days of 1908! that cinnamon-colored suit
> has fortunately faded from your image.
> All that remains is the moment when he removed,
> when he flung from him the worthless clothes,
> the mended underwear, and stood there
> entirely naked, flawlessly beautiful,
> a marvel. His uncombed hair pushed back,
> his body slightly tanned by the sun, by going
> naked, mornings, to the beach.

On the other hand, in "To Remain", it seems as if the wish formulated in "According to the Formulas of the Ancient Greco-Syrian Magi" has been granted; the sensual reminiscence brings with it a fringe of banal external references which serve to authenticate it; the work of art receives *as is* the wretched, scandalous and yet almost sacred memory:

> It could have been at one in the morning,
> or one-thirty.
> In a corner of the tavern,
> behind the wooden partition . . .
> There were only the two of us in the empty room,
> dim by the light of one kerosene lamp.
> The waiter was dozing on his feet in the doorway.

---

[11]It is hardly necessary to remark that Cavafy, "poet-historian", here puts himself at the antipodes of history proper. No serious historian has ever rejoiced at knowing too little.

No one could have seen us. But already
passion had robbed us of all precautions.

Our clothes were unbuttoned—we weren't wearing much,
it was scorching hot that divine July.

Delight of the flesh between the gaping clothes!
Sudden baring of the flesh! That image
has passed over twenty-six years, and now has come
to remain in this poem.

Carnal reminiscence has made the artist master of time; his loyalty to sensual experience leads to a theory of immortality.

*

Each poem by Cavafy is a memorial poem; historical or personal, each poem is at the same time a gnomic poem; such didacticism, unexpected in a modern poet, constitutes perhaps the boldest aspect of his work. We are so accustomed to regard wisdom as a residue of extinguished passions that it is hard for us to recognize it as the toughest and most condensed form of ardor, the gold dust born of fire and not the ashes. We resist such chilly, entirely allegorical or exemplary poems as "Apollonius of Tyana in Rhodes", a lesson in perfection, "Thermopylae", a lesson in constancy, "The First Step", a lesson in modesty; we accept with difficulty the abrupt transition from didacticism to lyricism, or *vice versa,* in splendid poems like "The City," a lesson in resignation but even more a lament for the human incapacity to escape oneself, or "Ithaca," poem of the exoticism and of the quest, but above all plea in favor of experience, a warning against what I should call the illusions of disillusionment:

When you set out for Ithaca,
pray that your road is a long one,
full of adventure, full of discovery.
Lestrygonians, Cyclops, angry Poseidon,
don't be afraid of them:
you won't find things like that on your way
as long as your thoughts are exalted,
as long as a high emotion
stirs your spirit and your body.

Lestrygonians, Cyclops, angry Poseidon,
you won't find them

unless you bring them along inside you,
unless your soul raises them up before you.

Pray that your road is a long one.
May there be many a summer morning when—
full of gratitude, full of joy—
you come into harbors seen for the first time;
may you stop at Phoenician trading centers
and buy fine things, mother-of-pearl and coral,
amber and ebony, voluptuous perfumes of every kind,
as many voluptuous perfumes as you can;
may you visit numerous Egyptian cities
to fill yourself with learning from the wise.

Always keep Ithaca in mind.
Getting there is your goal.
But don't hurry the journey at all.
Better if it lasts for years,
so that you're old when you reach the island,
rich with all you've gained on the way,
not expecting Ithaca to make you rich.

Ithaca gave you the wonderful journey.
Without her you would never have set out.
She hasn't anything else to give.

And if you find her poor, Ithaca has not deceived you.
Wise as you have become, with so much experience,
you'll have understood by then what an Ithaca means.

It is eminently worth our while to watch this wisdom ripen, to see the emotions of anxiety, solitude, separation, still very apparent in the early poems, give way to a tranquility deep enough to seem facile. It is always important to know whether a poet's writings ultimately side with rebellion or acceptance; in Cavafy's case, a surprising absence of recrimination and reproach characterizes the work. Along with the importance assigned to memory, it is undoubtedly this lucid serenity which gives him his very Greek aspect of the poet-as-old-man, at the antipodes of the romantic ideal of the poet-as-child, the poet-as-adolescent; and this precisely though old age occupies, in his universe, the place almost everywhere reserved for death or else counts as the one irreparable disaster:

> The ageing of my body and my face:
> wounds from a terrible knife.
> I am anything but resigned.
> I take refuge in you, Art of Poetry,
> who know something about remedies . . .
> who try to numb suffering by imagination, by words.
>
> Wounds from a terrible knife . . .
> Bring your remedies, Art of Poetry,
> that keep us (for a while) from feeling the wound.

We may say without paradox that here rebellion is located within acquiescence, becoming an inevitable part of the human condition which the poet acknowledges as his own. In the same way, the splendid lines inspired by a passage in Dante, *"Che fece . . il gran rifiuto"*, a poem of revolt and denial, nonetheless remain at the very heart of acceptance, formulating the extreme and personal case in which there is a rebellion in not rebelling. This is because a completely accepting perspective can only be based on the very powerful sense of what is unique, irreducible, and finally valid in each temperament and each destiny:

> For some people there comes a day
> when they must come out with the great Yes
> or the great No. It's clear at once
> who has the Yes ready in him; and saying it,
>
> he goes on to find honor, strong in his conviction.
> He who refuses never repents. Asked again,
> he'd say No again. Yet that No—the right No—
> defeats him the whole of his life.

Finally, with even more finality than for Mark Antony as cited earlier, everything comes down to a divestment too readily consented to not to be secretly desired:

> When the Macedonians abandoned him
> and showed they preferred Pyrrhus,
> King Demetrius (he had a great soul)
> didn't behave—so they said—
> at all like a king.

He took off his golden robes,
discarded his purple buskins,
and quickly dressing himself
in simple clothes, he slipped out—
just like an actor who,
when the play is over,
removes his costume and goes away.

The same absence of rebellion allows Cavafy to move easily within his Orthodox heredity, and makes him, ultimately, a Christian. A Christian as remote as possible from torment, outpourings of the heart, or ascetic rigor, but a Christian nonetheless, for *Religio,* in the ancient sense of the word, as well as *Mystica,* belong to the universe of Christianity. The "good death" following—for the Cleon of "The Tomb of Ignatius", for Myris, for Manuel Komninos—upon a sensual existence is another kind of submission to the nature of things; this monastic divestment extends in its own fashion the themes of stoical wisdom, secretly satisfies that Oriental nihilism often infused into Greek thought, which at first appears so contrary to it in every regard. But the Orthodox tradition chiefly remains, in Cavafy, a form of attachment to milieu and atmosphere; it takes, all told, only a secondary role in his poetry. The strictly mystical elements are rather to be found in the pagan part of the poems, in the scrupulous concern not to hamper the demonic or divine endeavor ("it is we who interrupt the task of the gods, we impatient, inexperienced mortals"), and still more in the perpetual equation poem-memory-immortality, *i.e.,* in the intimation of the divine in man. Morality scarcely departs from what a contemporary of Hadrian or Marcus Aurelius might have practiced. Like the flesh bearing within itself an armature of bones and tendons, these poems conceal at their core the vigor necessary to any sensual soul. Everywhere, even in the most deliciously softened forms, we find the hard vertebrae of Stoicism.

*

This quasi-Goethean mystique is linked, in Cavafy, with the elements of a poetics which at first glance seems to derive from Mallarmé. An aesthetic of secrecy, silence, and transposition:

He wrapped them carefully, methodically
in costly green silk.

Roses of ruby, and lilies of pearl, and violets
of amethyst, beautiful, perfect, the way

he wants them to look, not as he saw them
in nature, or studied them. He leaves them

in the safe, a proof of his bold and cunning art,
and if a customer walks into the shop

he takes from their cases other wares, splendid
jewels, bracelets, chains, necklaces and rings.

But secrecy does not lead to a linguistic or literary hermeticism[12]; the poet's position remains what it was in the great periods, that of an exquisite artisan; his function is limited to bestowing upon the most ardent and chaotic substances the clearest and smoothest forms. Nowhere is art considered more real or noble than reality, or even transcendentally opposed to notions of sensuality, of fame, even of common sense with which it remains, on the contrary, prudently linked. Art and life assist each other: everything becomes an asset to the writer, sometimes love ("The Silversmith"), sometimes humiliation ("Their beginning"). Conversely, art enriches life in its turn ("Very Seldom"); it has remedies which, "for a while", heal our wounds ("Melancholy of Jason"); it collects, in the manner of a precious vessel, the distillation of memory ("One Night", "To Remain"). Further—an avowal made almost accidentally by this poet of the past-as-present—art has means of "combining the days" ("I Brought to Art"). But it achieves its ends only by the most dedicated study. A series of historical or fictive portraits illustrates this art of writing which is also a strict art of living: Aeschylus was wrong to have his tombstone report his heroism at Marathon, whereby he was a Greek like any other, and not his works, whereby he was irreplaceable ("Young Men of Sidon"); Eumenes will learn to be content with his rank, already a high one, as a secondary poet ("The First Step"); the disasters of war, *i.e.*, reality endured, will not keep Phernazis from concerning himself with his task, which is reality transcribed:

[12]This is what gives the poetry its strange quality of authentic, i.e., well hidden, esotericism. Thus in "Evocation" and in "Caesarion", the real or allegorical darkness, the image of the candle and of the extinguished lamp, seem to forsake the realm of literary ornament, or even of erotic fantasy, for that of occultist reference; we are inevitably reminded of the magician's formula: *extinctis luminibus*. The same is true of that enigmatic poem "Chandelier". A subtle light.

The poet Phernazis is composing
the important part of his epic:
How Darius, the son of Hystaspes,
assumed the kingdom of the Persians.
(From him is descended our glorious king
Mithridates, hailed as Dionysus and Eupator.)
But this calls for serious thought; he has to analyze
the feelings Darius must have had:
arrogance, perhaps, and intoxication? No—more likely
a certain insight into the vanities of greatness.
The poet ponders the matter deeply.

But his servant interrupts, running in
to announce very important news:
the war with the Romans has begun.
Most of our army has crossed the borders.

The poet is dumbfounded. What a disaster!
How can our glorious king,
Mithdridates, Dionysus Eupator,
bother about Greek poems now?
In the middle of a war—just think, Greek poems!

. . . But are we really safe in Amisos?
The town isn't very well fortified . . .
Great gods, protectors of Asia, help us.

. . . But through all his distress and agigation
the poetic idea keeps fermenting in him:
arrogance and intoxication—that's most likely, of course:
arrogance and intoxication are what Darius must have felt.

This apparently banal poetics is based on literary methods which are insidiously, perhaps dangerously simple. The author early renounced the impulse to oratorical amplification, to lyrical reduplication (of which a poem like "Ithaca" still affords examples), in favor of the unadorned idea, a kind of pure prosaism. The dry, flexible style makes no commitments, not even to concision; admirers of ancient Greek will recognize this smooth surface, without highlights, almost without accents, which like certain modeling in Hellenistic statues reveals itself, when seen at close range, to be of an infinite subtlety and, one may say, mobility. In the best poems, at least; for there are some in which Cavafy affects a lyrical or erotic effusiveness ("In the Evening", "In an Old Book", "In Despair") flavored on occasion with a rosewater Hellenism ("Tomb of Iases", "Sophist Leaving Syria", "Cimon, Son of Learchos", "Kleitos' Illness"), and even elaborates an occasional scholarly and futile pastiche ("Greek since Ancient Times", "Before the Statue of Endymion").[13] The number of these suspect poems increases or diminishes, of course, with each reader's severity or good will; however few, they mar this poetry in which nothing has been left to chance, and Cavafy's exegete ends by wondering if these poems tainted with self-indulgence do not represent, somehow, the paradoxical result of the Cavafian *ars poetica,* or if on the contrary they should be regarded as the vestiges of bad taste often latent in almost any work of extremely refined sensibility and against which the poet has tried to defend himself by using such means of expression so deliberately discreet, so deliberately chary. As in the *Greek Anthology,* in any case, as in certain productions of Alexandrian or Greco-Roman statuary which also obey esthetic canons of the same order, a scarcely perceptible demarcation-line separates what is exquisite from what is trifling, factitious, or flat.[14]

---

[13]Critics often dispute the definition of the *scholarly pastiche.* I use the term to refer to a work, in the category of an exercise or a game, in which the author confines himself to imitating, in its every detail, a form of archaic art, without determining a new content and without attempting to revive its old content. At least ten of Cavafy's poems, chiefly in the genre of the funerary elegy, tend toward such pastiche in their lack of convincing emotion. Other poems, especially those which present, for all their Grecian drapery, street scenes or low-life studies which might be (and perhaps are) modern, actually belong to the realm of disguise and concealment.

[14]I should add that frequently what first struck me as a defect has, on rereading, seemed an essential characteristic, a bold stroke, perhaps an ultimate strategy. I have come to find in this disconcerting mixture of dryness on one hand, of pliancy on the other, the equivalent of the two styles of Greek popular music, the facile grace of Ionian island songs, the harsh pathos of those of the Aegean islands. The undeniable monotony of erotic expression now seems to me a warrant of authenticity in a domain where secret routines almost always prevail. The obvious cluminess of certain poems prevents one's thinking of Cavafy as a mere virtuoso. What once seemed insipid now seems limpid, what once figured as poverty is now an economy of words. The same is true of the deliberately banal, almost conventional adjectives Cavafy uses in his erotic evocations of youth and beauty. Stendhal, Racine and the Greeks before them were also content to say "delicate limbs", "fine eyes", or a "charming head".

Subtlety and clumsiness are not mutually exclusive, quite the contrary. Remoteness from major literary movements, from clans and sects, may account for something dated and yet extraordinarily fresh in Cavafy, something both elaborate and ingenuous which is often the mark of an artist who works "out of the way". One

But perhaps we should consider, should study Cavafy's poetry as a whole not so much from a stylistic as from a compositional point of view. The typically Alexandrian juxtaposition of erudite poem, popular sketch and erotic epigram allows the poet to avoid the appearance of striving for effect: such disparity and such continuity are those of life itself. The Alexandrian preference for the minor work, an art which can be controlled down to the last detail, becomes in Cavafy an exclusive system: his longest poems are no more than two pages, his shortest, four or five lines. The passion to elaborate on the one hand, and to simplify, to shorten on the other, produces at the end an extremely curious method for lack of a better term I should call that of the memorandum or the marginal gloss. A good number of these fastidiously reworked masterpieces are scarcely more than a line of script, at once cursive and cryptic, a slender paraph traced by the pen beneath a known and beloved text, the torn-off leaf from a solitary's engagement-book, the code of a secret expenditure, perhaps a riddle. With all their lyricism, they retain the naked beauty of a note jotted down for oneself. His loveliest lines give us only the point of departure or the conclusion of their author's ideas or experiences; they leave aside everything which, even in the most discriminating writers, is evidently addressed to the reader, everything which belongs to the realm of eloquence or explanation. His most moving poems are sometimes confined to a barely annotated quotation. Rarely has so much solicitude been put in the service of so little literature.

Another specifically Cavafian characteristic, the extraordinary elaboration of monologue, seems to have affinites with both Hellenistic comedy or mime and, more particularly, the old exercises of Greek rhetoric. "The Gods Should Have Bothered" or "From the School of the Renowned Philosopher" suggest the techniques of Herondas' *Mimes*: brief pieces without action in which, for our greater diversion, a character describes himself. "The Battle of Magnesia", "John Kantakuzinos Triumphs", "Demetrius Soter", "In a Large Greek Colony, 200 B.C.", and especially "Dimaratos", a masterpiece of the genre, have for their prototypes the schemas of orations, the models of epistles, or the summaries of famous trials dear to the ancient Sophistic, whose

might take the liberty of saying that "Portrait of a 23-year-old Youth Painted by his Friend of the Same Age, an Amateur" irresistibly suggests a Douanier Rousseau; Cavafy himself has his Sunday-painter aspects.

tradition survives so pathetically in our *lycée* assignments. These clear and complex poems sometimes suggest Browning's intricate monologues, but a Browning in whom drawing has replaced all the painter's colors and impasto; they permit Cavafy the potential dramatic poet to internalize the emotions of others and to externalize his own; they offer this mind so closed and at certain points so fixed upon itself the possibilities of *acting* in every sense of the word. In "The Battle of Magnesia", the indirect presentation and the use of the present tense recapture the past in its weltering actuality; in "In a Large Greek Colony, 200 B.C.", the murmur of Greek voices commenting on an inscription of Alexander's at over a century's remove achieves an effect of choral poetry, helping us by comparison to measure the time which has accumulated between Philip's son and ourselves. In "Dimaratos", a dissertation-topic sketched by a young sophist of the late Empire summarizes in twenty lines an episode in the Median wars, and with it the eternal drama of the deserter torn between two causes and two camps: the very dryness of the academic exercise safeguards this story of an insulted man from all false pathos.[15] This technique of intermediaries sometimes corresponds to Cavafy's concern for discretion, but more often to his desire to have his own emotions confirmed by another mouth: in "Imenos", for instance, two passionate lines, which might have found a place in any love poem, are given as citations from a letter written by an imaginary or forgotten Byzantine. In the tragic "Aimilianos Monai", Cavafy manages to make the monologue express precisely *what is kept silent,* the shyness, the pathos, the melancholy gaze under the discreetly lowered visor:

> Out of my talk, appearance, and manners
> I shall make an excellent suit of armor;
> and in this way I shall face evil men
> without fear or weakness.

[15]Not without an obscurity which is one of Cavafy's defects and which derives less from his subjects than from stylistic mannerisms. The shift from direct to indirect discourse within the same short poem often presents the reader (and the translator) with extraordinary obstacles. Of the same order are those breaks within certain gnomic poems at which the poet addresses in turn the reader, himself, and an allegorical character who is only half himself; also in this category is Cavafy's preference for what I should call the indirect title, *i.e.*, one taken from a secondary figure or incident and not from the poem's main theme or its central character. This is an obliquity to be studied on its own.

They will try to harm me. But of all
who approach me, none will know
where to find my wounds, my vulnerable places,
under the lies that will cover me . . .

So boasted Aimilianos Monai.
Did he ever make that suit of armor?
At all events, he did not wear it long.
At the age of 27, he died in Sicily.

Thus the study of technique has brought us back to what matters, which is to say, to the human. Whatever we do, we always return to this secret cell of self-knowledge, at once narrow and deep, sealed and translucent, which is often that of the pure sensualist, or of the pure intellectual. The extraordinary multiplicity of intentions and of means ultimately constitutes, in Cavafy, a kind of closed circuit, a labyrinth in which silence and avowal, text and commentary, emotion and irony, voice and echo inextricably mingle, and in which disguise becomes an aspect of nakedness. At last this complex series of mediating personae releases a new entity, the *self,* a kind of imperishable person. We said earlier that all of Cavafy's poems are historical poems; "Temethos of Antioch" warrants the assertion that in the last analysis all of them are personal poems:

Verses by young Temethos, the lovelorn poet,
and entitled "Emonides." This Emonides, a very
handsome young man from Samosata, was the beloved
companion of Antiochus Epiphanes. But if
these verses are impassioned, it is because Emonides
(he lived in a very early period, around the year 137
of that Hellenic dynasty, perhaps even a little earlier)
is only a made-up name, though a well-chosen one.
The poem expresses the love felt by Temethos himself,
a beautiful love, and worthy of him. We his friends,
we know for whom these verses were written.
The Antiochians, who do not know, say "Emonides".

Translator's note: Though I have consulted and combined the Keeley-Sherrard, Dalven and Mavrogordato versions of Cavafy, I have relied heavily on Marguerite Yourcenar's own versions to which this study originally served as a preface in 1958.

[1981]

CONTRIBUTORS

Many of the contributors to this anniversary anthology hardly need an identifying note, but for the sake of consistency I have included everyone, if only to mention his or her publisher.

ALICE ADAMS' most recent novel is *Superior Women* (Knopf, 1984) ★ Norton published A. R. AMMONS' *Selected Longer Poems* in 1980 ★ Random House is W. H. AUDEN's publisher ★ Auden's *The Age of Anxiety* was the inspiration for LEONARD BERNSTEIN's "The Age of Anxiety (Symphony No. 2 for Piano and Orchestra)" ★ JOHN BERRYMAN's books include *Homage to Mistress Bradstreet* (1956) and *The Dream Songs* (1969) ★ JOHN BETJEMAN was Poet Laureate of Great Britain and the author of the verse autobiography *Summoned by Bells* (1960) ★ LOUISE BOGAN was for many years poetry editor of *The New Yorker;* her books include *The Blue Estuaries: Poems 1923-1968* ★ GEORGE BRADLEY's *Where the Blue Begins* is forthcoming from Seacliff Press ★ MICHAEL BRONDOLI's story is included in *Showdown and Other Stories* (North Point Press, 1984) ★ KENNETH BURKE is the author of *Language As Symbolic Action* and *Towards a Better Life* ★ALFRED CORN's most recent volume is *Notes from a Child of Paradise* (Penguin, 1984) ★ MALCOLM COWLEY is the author of *A Second Flowering* and *The View from Eighty* (Viking, 1980) ★HARRY CREWS is the author of *A Childhood: The Biography of a Place* ★ Harcourt, Brace is E. E. CUMMINGS' publisher ★ Swallow published J. V. CUNNINGHAM's *Collected Essays* and *Collected Poems and Epigrams* ★ DONALD DAVIE's *Collected Poems: 1970-1983* was published by University of Notre Dame Press (1984) ★ JAMES DICKEY's many books include *Deliverance,* a novel; *Babel to Byzantium,* critical essays; and *The Strength of Fields,* poems ★ RICHARD EBERHART's *The Long Reach: New and Collected Poems 1948-1984* was published by New Directions last year ★ Random House is WILLIAM FAULKNER's publisher ★ IRVING FELDMAN's most recent collections are *Teach Me, Dear Sister* and *New and Selected Poems,* both from Viking/Penguin ★ DONALD FINKEL's most recent book is *The Detachable Man* (Atheneum, 1984) ★ M. F. K. FISHER's most recent books are *As They Were* (1982) and *Among Friends* (1983) ★ FORD MADOX FORD's novels include *No More Parades* and *The Good Soldier* ★ University of Missouri Press published EUGENE

GARBER's *Metaphysical Tales* (1981) ★ CAROLINE GORDON's stories were gathered in *The Collected Stories* (Farrar, Straus and Giroux, 1981) ★ MARTHA GRAHAM is the great American choreographer and dancer ★ Knopf is publisher of MARILYN HACKER's new book, *Assumptions* ★ DONALD HALL's most recent book is *Fathers Playing Catch with Sons: Essays on Sport (Mostly Baseball)* (North Point Press) ★ GEOFFREY HILL is the author of *King Log* ★ DARYL HINE's latest book, *Q. E. D.*, will be published by Atheneum ★ DANIEL HOFFMAN is the author of *Brotherly Love* (Random House, 1981) ★ JOHN HOLLANDER is a recent winner of the Bollingen Prize and the author of *Powers of Thirteen* (Atheneum, 1983) ★ RICHARD HOWARD's most recent book of poems is *Lining Up* (Atheneum, 1984) ★ Norton published RICHARD HUGO's *Making Certain It Goes On: The Collected Poems* in 1984 ★ HUGH KENNER is the author of *The Pound Era* and *A Colder Eye: The Modern Irish Writers* (Knopf, 1983) ★ THOMAS KINSELLA is the author of *Peppercanister—Poems 1972-1978* (Wake Forest, 1979) ★ LINCOLN KIRSTEIN was founder of the New York City Ballet and is the author of *Rhymes of a Pfc.* (Godine) ★ CAROLYN KIZER won this year's Pulitzer Prize in poetry for *Yin: New Poems* (BOA Editions) ★ ROBERT LOWELL's books include *For the Union Dead, Near the Ocean,* and *Day by Day* ★ ANDREW LYTLE's novels include *The Velvet Horn* ★ ROBIE MACAULEY is an editor at Houghton Mifflin and is the author of *The Disguises of Love* ★ CYNTHIA MACDONALD's volumes of poetry include *Transplants* (Braziller) and *(W)holes* (Knopf) ★ J. D. MCCLATCHY is the author of *Scenes from Another Life* (Braziller) ★ WILLIAM MEREDITH is the author of *Earth Walk: New and Selected Poems* and *The Cheer* ★ JAMES MERRILL's newest book is *Late Settings* (Atheneum) ★ CHRISTOPHER MIDDLETON is the author of *Woden Dog* and *Anasphere,* both published by Burning Deck ★ JOSEPHINE MILES' *Collected Poems, 1930-1983* was published by University of Illinois Press ★ PAUL MONETTE is the author of *The Gold Diggers* ★ MARIANNE MOORE's *Complete Poems* is available from Penguin ★ HERBERT MORRIS' *Peru* was published by Harper and Row (1983) ★ JOHN N. MORRIS is the author of *The Life Beside This One* and *Glass Houses,* both published by Atheneum ★ HOWARD MOSS is poetry editor of *The New Yorker;*

his *New Selected Poems* is being published by Atheneum ★ University of Chicago Press published *The Collected Poems* of HOWARD NEMEROV in 1981 ★ JOYCE CAROL OATES' most recent novel is *Solstice* (Dutton, 1985) ★ Farrar, Straus and Giroux is the publisher of FLANNERY O'CONNOR's *The Complete Stories* ★ WALKER PERCY is the author of *The Last Gentleman, The Second Coming,* and *Love in the Ruins,* all from Farrar, Straus and Giroux ★ ROBERT PINSKY is the author of *Sadness and Happiness: Poems* and *An Explanation of America,* both from Princeton University Press ★ KATHA POLLITT's *Antarctic Traveller* was published by Knopf (1982) ★ KATHERINE ANNE PORTER's *Collected Stories* is published by Harcourt Brace Jovanovich ★ New Directions is EZRA POUND's publisher ★ REYNOLDS PRICE's more recent titles include *The Surface of Earth* and *Mustian: Two Novels and a Story,* both from Atheneum ★ LIAM RECTOR's poems have appeared in *Partisan Review, Kayak,* and other magazines ★ JEAN ROSS has published stories in *The Missouri Review* and *Esquire* ★ GRACE SCHULMAN's books include *Burn Down the Icons* (Princeton University Press, 1976) and *Hemispheres* (Sheep Meadow, 1984) ★ Random House is publisher of STEPHEN SPENDER's *Collected Poems* and *The 30's and After* ★ Farrar, Straus and Giroux published JEAN STAFFORD's *Collected Stories* ★ Knopf is the publisher of WALLACE STEVENS' *The Palm at the End of the Mind* and *Opus Posthumous* ★ DABNEY STUART is the author of *Round and Round: Poems* and *Common Ground,* both from LSU Press; for ten years he was poetry editor of *Shenandoah* ★ MAY SWENSON is the author of *New and Selected Things Taking Place* (Atlantic/Little, Brown, 1978) ★ ALLEN TATE is the author of *Collected Poems 1919-1976* (Farrar, Straus and Giroux, 1977) and *Essays of Four Decades* (Swallow, 1968) ★ ELEANOR ROSS TAYLOR's *New and Selected Poems* was published by Stuart Wright in 1983 ★ PETER TAYLOR's newest book is *The Old Forest and Other Stories,* published this year by Doubleday ★ BARBARA THOMPSON's "Tattoo" was reprinted in *The Pushcart Prize VII: Best of the Small Presses* (1982-3) ★ J. R. R. TOLKIEN's reading of Anglo-Saxon poetry at Oxford strongly influenced Auden's work, as the poet attested in his Inaugural Lecture as Professor of Poetry at Oxford ★ DIANE VREULS has published a novel, stories, and poems; she teaches creative writing at Oberlin ★ ROBERT PENN WARREN celebrates his eightieth birthday this year; *New and Selected Poems: 1912-1985* has just been published by Random House ★ EUDORA WELTY is the author of *Losing Battles* and *The Optimist's Daughter* ★ EDMUND WHITE's novels include *Nocturnes for the King of Naples* and *A Boy's Own Story* ★ Poetry Consultant at the Library of Congress, REED WHITTEMORE is the author of *The Feel of Rock: Poems of Three Decades* (Dryad Press, 1982) and a biography of William Carlos Williams ★ RICHARD WILBUR is the author of *Walking to Sleep: New Poems and Translations* and the translator of Moliere and Racine ★ New Directions is WILLIAM CARLOS WILLIAMS' publisher ★ EDMUND WILSON's critical and historical studies include *Axel's Castle* and *Patriotic Gore* ★ CHARLES WRIGHT is the author of *The Other Side of the River* (Random House, 1984) ★ MARGUERITE YOURCENAR, the first woman to be elected to the French Academy, is the author of *Memoirs of Hadrian, The Abyss,* and most recently translated, the collection of essays *The Dark Brain of Piranesi* (Farrar, Straus and Giroux)

Cover: Design by Barbara Crawford

(Acknowledgments cont'd. from pg. 3)

"Night Visits with the Family" by May Swenson from *New and Selected Things,* ©1978 by May Swenson, reprinted by permission of Little, Brown and Co.

Allen Tate's Tribute to Eudora Welty reprinted by permission of Helen H. Tate.

"For W. H. A." by J. R. R. Tolkien reprinted by permission of The Executors of the late J. R. R. Tolkien.

"Beebee" by Diane Vreuls, ©by Diane Vreuls, reprinted by permission of the author.

"A Note on Jane Austen" by Eudora Welty from *Brief Lives: A Biographical Guide to the Arts,* edited by Louis Kronenberger, ©1971 by Little, Brown and Co., reprinted by permission of Little, Brown and Co.

"A Man of the World" by Edmund White appeared in a different version in Chapter Two of *A Boy's Own Story,* Dutton 1982, reprinted by permission of the author.

"Summer Concert" by Reed Whittemore, ©1967 by Reed Whittemore, reprinted by permission of the author.

"Poetry and Happiness" by Richard Wilbur from *Responses* (Harcourt, Brace Jovanovich, 1976), reprinted by permission of the author.

"June 9" and "Still Life" by William Carlos Williams, ©1951 by William Carlos Williams, reprinted by permission of New Directions Publishing Corp.

"A Critical Introduction to Cavafy" by Marguerite Yourcenar, translated by Richard Howard, reprinted by permission of Farrar, Straus & Giroux.